D0929713

COLUMBUS
AND CAONABÓ

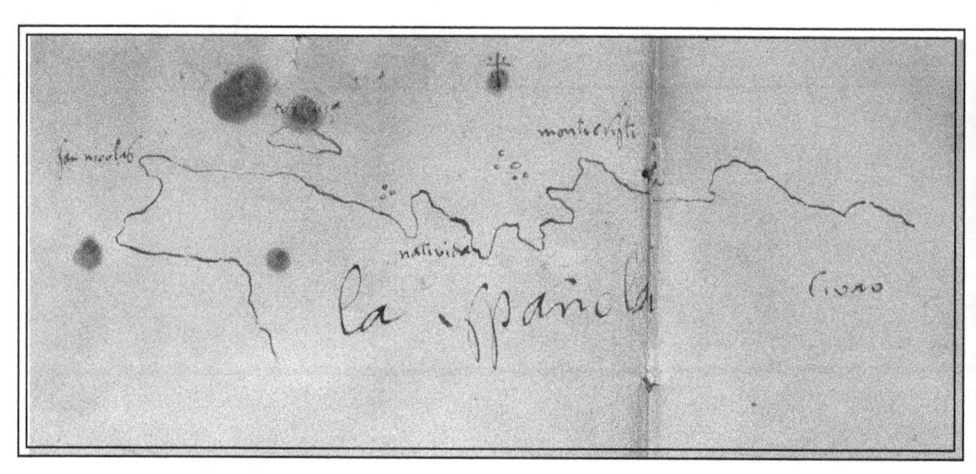

Columbus's map of the northwest coast of the island he named Española, sketched in January 1493 as he explored the coastline eastward en route home to Spain on his first voyage. It marks the site of Navidad, the temporary settlement that he'd established within Guacanagarí's chiefdom of Marien, leaving almost forty men there after the *Santa María* sank on December 25, 1492

COLUMBUS AND CAONABÓ

1493–1498 Retold

Andrew Rowen

ALL PERSONS PRESS
New York, New York

All Persons Press
New York, New York
First published in 2021 by All Persons Press

Columbus and Caonabó: 1493–1498 Retold

Permissions and Credits on pages ix–xi and 440.

Library of Congress Control Number: 2021911690
ISBN13: 978-0-9991961-3-7

Cover and Book Design by Glen Edelstein, Hudson Valley Book Design
Cover Illustration by Robert Hunt
Interior Maps by David Atkinson
Interior Illustrations by Boris De Los Santos

For Mary Anne
lover, wife, mother, mate

CONTENTS

LIST OF MAPS AND ILLUSTRATIONS

Stories are told from the perspective of the participants' probable knowledge of geography at the time of the story, and maps presented herein are from the fifteenth or sixteenth centuries, except those designated by an asterisk, which have been drawn by David Atkinson. The sketches of the Taíno owl and Yúcahu, Caonabó, and Anacaona are by Boris De Los Santos.

HISTORICAL NOTE

This novel dramatizes the European usurpation of much of the island Columbus named Española and the resistance fought by its Native peoples during the period and aftermath of his second voyage, from 1493 to 1498. The history is presented through the eyes and intimate relationships of the conflict's principal Taíno chieftains—Caonabó, his wife Anacaona, Guacanagarí, and Guarionex—and Columbus himself, his principal slaves, and Queen Isabella and King Ferdinand. Today, we understand the outcome as one of history's darkest conquests, but in 1493 neither the chieftains nor Columbus perceived that outcome as inevitable or its contours.

The narrative depicts what Columbus and his men did or attempted, Queen Isabella and King Ferdinand's oversight and participation therein, and the responses and countervailing strategies of the chieftains, including hostilities. The focus extends to the evolution of the European justification for enslavement of "New World" indigenous peoples, the first "treaties" imposed and then broken, the chieftains' reactions to the initial Christian missionary efforts, and the ravage of epidemic disease transmission. Throughout, I have sought to portray the Taíno and European protagonists with commensurate stature and gravitas and to avoid the traditional Columbus- and European-centric focus of most accounts of the events, including those critical of Columbus and colonialism.

While readable independently, the novel is the sequel to *Encounters Unforeseen: 1492 Retold*, which dramatizes the lives of the same protagonists from youth through their first encounters in 1492 and 1493. Following *Encounters Unforeseen*, I continue to present the protagonists' actions and thoughts as I believe they would have lived them day to day, in the immediacy and chaos of their present moment, without imposing historical conclusions drawn in hindsight or inventing an overarching literary story plot, seeking foremost historical validity. To that end, I have considered first the primary accounts written by the conquering Europeans who witnessed the events, knew the participants, or lived in the sixteenth century (to the extent credible) and, as they had no written history, studies of the Taínos by modern anthropologists, archaeologists, and other experts. Each participant's actions and thoughts are presented consistent with my interpretation of the historical record to the extent one exists and—to the extent not—as I speculate likely could have occurred, fictionalizing detail in novel form. *Encounters Unforeseen* described the Taíno and European societies and cultures in which the protagonists lived, including the respective political hierarchies, social castes, marriage customs, and religious practices, and these frameworks apply to the protagonists' thoughts from 1493 to 1498 but are not repeated herein. I have resisted—undoubtedly imperfectly—embellishing hero or villain in my interpretation of the record. Moral and historical judgments are left for the reader.

The European accounts considered include the correspondence, orders, proclamations, and other preserved communications by or among Columbus, Isabella and Ferdinand, and crown officials in Spain and Española; the commentaries of Isabella and Ferdinand's court chroniclers; and the letters and reports of doctors, missionaries, and others who traveled to Española from 1493 to 1498. These sources often are conflicted and quite partisan, as Columbus's reports increasingly include exaggeration and concealment to prove accomplishment and counter criticisms, and other accounts typically are colored—sometimes overtly—by the source's own stake in the events and/or pro- or anti-Columbus sentiment. Modern historians generally agree on much of what happened, but there is no uniform understanding regarding the specific events that occurred, in which order, how, where, or why, and fundamental disagreements remain, as noted below. The novel's stories portray only my own interpretation of the events, and, for readers interested, the Sources section at the end indicates the primary and secondary sources considered for each story and sometimes explains my reasoning and that of contrary interpretations.

The novel's depiction of Taíno actions and thoughts considers these European sources, which reflect a conqueror's perspective and bias and often lack credibility and knowledge, and the analyses of the anthropologists and other experts seeking a more complete and bias-free understanding. Much is unknown, and I have speculated as to many of the chieftains' reactions to European incursions and demands, particularly regarding military strategy and the terms of truces and surrenders, as the European sources often focus simply on European military superiority and objectives. The chieftains did not have the experience of the five centuries following to draw upon. In instances, when I have found portions of primary accounts not credible, I have contradicted them by presenting what I suspect more likely occurred, noting such in the Sources section.

More fundamentally, historians and others continue to debate the basic magnitude and causes of Taíno death. Substantial disagreements remain over the size of Española's indigenous population at the conquest's inception (estimates generally range from one hundred thousand to eight million) and the relative extent that its rapid decline should be attributed to Spanish brutality (warfare and the harsh conditions of servitude and slavery), the collapse of the indigenous social system occasioned thereby (famine, flight to remote areas, and suicide), or the ravage of European diseases. Epidemiologists offer varied analyses of the diseases transmitted. I do not attempt to answer these questions, but the novel presents my interpretations or speculations of the protagonists' perceptions of the underlying answers, sometimes together with a summary of the modern debate in the Sources section.

The novel also seeks to place Isabella and Ferdinand's decisions regarding the Indies in the larger framework of their European and Christian perspective, both politically and intellectually. During the period presented, they and their counselors were unaware of the vast

American landmasses that lay close beyond Española, and domestic and European matters usually dominated their attention. The narrative integrates depictions of the European war and alliances that preoccupied them and affected their relationship with Pope Alexander VI, influencing papal bulls in their favor, and their continued subjugation and Christianization of their other overseas conquest, the Canary Islands.

As in *Encounters Unforeseen*, almost all persons identified with proper names herein are historical, although Taínos known to history by their baptized Christian names are given fictitious birth names—such as Bakako. The stories include a few fictitious relatives or intimates who are given proper names to facilitate the narrative's continuity, and these persons are identified as fictitious in the Participants or Sources sections. Conversations are fictionalized when possible based on primary sources either recounting the conversation or indicating the views of the participants. Stories occasionally quote or paraphrase words from primary sources to best capture the participants' intent and fifteenth-century perspective; to preserve the novel style, these incorporations are not designated by quotation marks, but the Sources section indicates the chapter, section, paragraph, and/or date of the source relied on. Taíno words (other than proper names) are italicized and translated when first introduced and then compiled at the end in the Glossary.

When promoting his second voyage, Columbus assured Isabella and Ferdinand that the Taíno people were too timid and possessed too inferior weaponry to mount armed resistance to subjugation. While Taíno weaponry was inferior, I think the assurance of timidity has persisted over centuries to taint understanding of events in various epochs and by certain audiences—in spite of contemporary observations to the contrary. I hope to rectify that herein.

August 20, 2021 ANDREW ROWEN

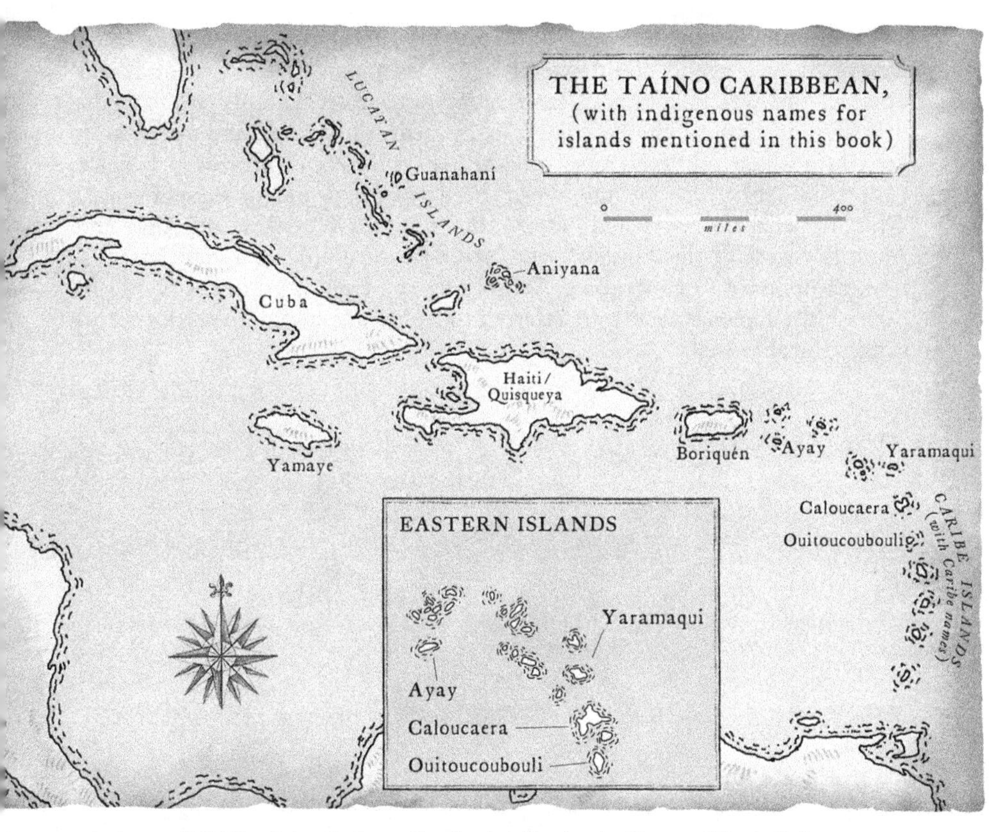

Aniyana (Middle Caicos); Ayay (St. Croix); Boriquén (Puerto Rico); Caloucaera (Guadeloupe); Cuba (Cuba); Guanahaní (San Salvador); Haiti or Quisqueya (Haiti and Dominican Republic); Lucayan Islands (the Bahamas and Turks & Caicos); Ouitoucoubouli (Dominica); Yamaye (Jamaica); Yaramaqui (Antigua).

TAÍNO, CARIBE, LUCAYAN, INDIAN

It is doubtful the peoples now known as the Taínos (whose civilization spread across modern eastern Cuba, Haiti, the Dominican Republic, Puerto Rico, and the Bahamas) conceived of themselves as one people or nation or used the word *Taíno* to refer to themselves collectively, other than to distinguish themselves from the peoples known as the Caribes (who lived in the Lesser Antilles, i.e., Guadeloupe, Dominica, and nearby islands). Instead, they probably referred to themselves in relation to their tribe or the region of their tribe, much as Europeans referred to themselves in relation to their principality. For simplicity, persons herein sometimes are referred to as Taínos to distinguish them from Europeans or Caribes. Bahamian Taínos are sometimes referred to as Lucayans (from the Taíno word meaning "island people").

Fifteenth-century European geographic usage of the word *Indies* was not uniform and could stretch as far as Japan to the east and Ethiopia to the west. Columbus and most Europeans initially believed his first voyage had reached a place in or near the Indies and referred to the Taínos encountered as Indians (*Encounters Unforeseen* depicts Columbus's first use of the word in his journal of the first voyage). That appellation persisted after the European realization that the Americas weren't the "Indies" and assumed an ethnic or racial connotation, as opposed to geographic. When a story herein is from the European perspective, Taínos typically are referred to as Indians in the fifteenth-century geographical sense.

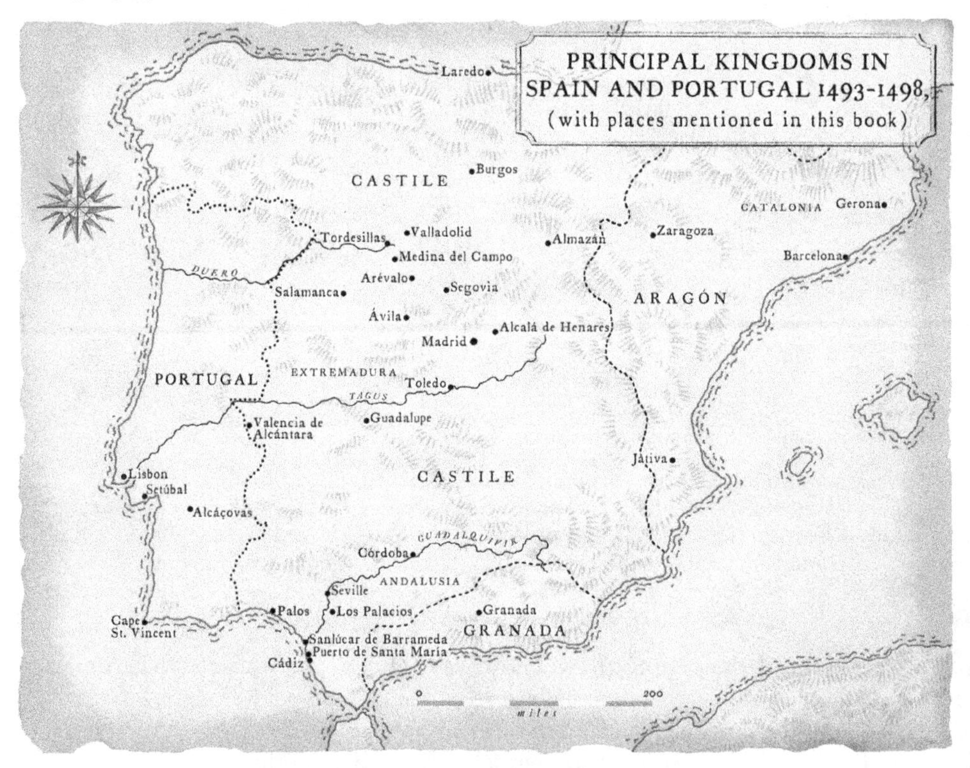

NAMES OF PEOPLE AND PLACES

Names of Spaniards and Portuguese are in Spanish and Portuguese, respectively. Columbus and his family's names are in Spanish, rather than Ligurian. Names of other Europeans sometimes are in English translation. Names of Taíno chieftains have the spellings currently used by anthropologists, historians, and others writing in English. Names of places typically are the English or Spanish version of the names that would have been used by the persons in the passage, usually with the modern spelling.

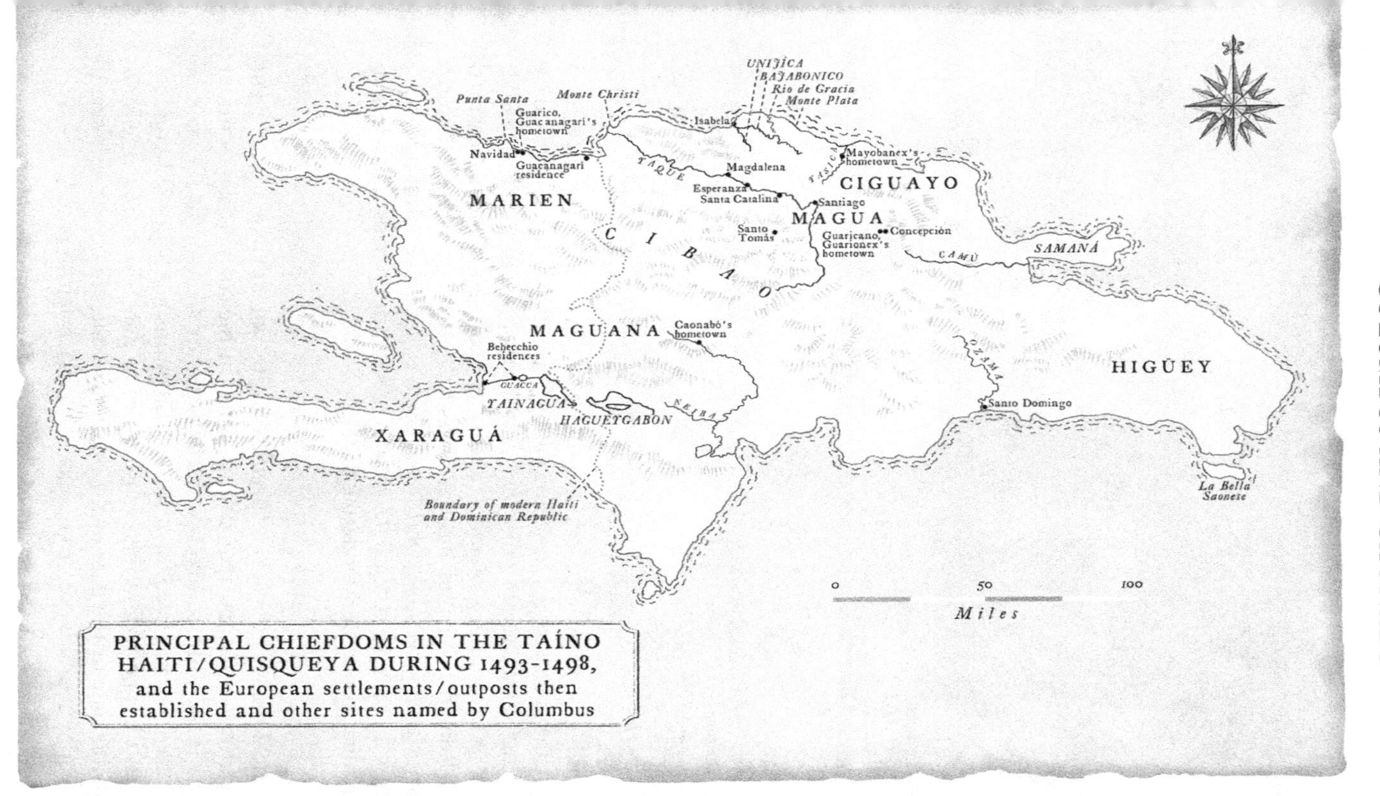

PRINCIPAL CHIEFDOMS IN THE TAÍNO HAITI/QUISQUEYA DURING 1493-1498, and the European settlements/outposts then established and other sites named by Columbus

Locations of the chiefdoms are consistent with those proposed by Irving Rouse. Sites of some of the hometowns, residences, and European forts are unknown and reflect the author's speculation based on primary sources. There were at least three indigenous names for the island of the modern Haiti and Dominican Republic—Haiti, Quisqueya, and Bohío—and Haiti (phonetically, *Ayiti*) is mostly used herein. The map shows the boundary between modern Haiti and the Dominican Republic so readers can see that places identified as being in the indigenous Haiti often are within the modern Dominican Republic.

TIME AND DISTANCE

While Taínos had their own measures of time and distance, for simplicity and uniformity, time and dates are based on Julius Caesar's calendar then used by Europeans, and distances are presented in modern US statutory miles, with one significant exception. Columbus and other Europeans often measured distance in Roman miles and "leagues," and the text uses these measures when appropriate to the story, with one league equal to four Roman miles, one Roman mile equal to about 0.92 modern US statutory miles, and a league thereby equaling about 3.68 modern US statutory miles.

DATING OF STORIES

If the historical record indicates a specific or approximate date for an event or events central to a story, that date is noted in the story's title—without parentheses. If the historical record is conflicted or silent as to the date of the central events dramatized, or if the central events are fictional but a historical context has been described as of a specific date, the story's title indicates a possible date or the date of the historical context—in parentheses. If history provides no guidance or context, the story is left undated.

FOOTNOTES

...are for historians and those inclined but need not be read to follow the story.

I
AUTUMN 1493

CAONABÓ,
Maguana, Haiti (September 1493)

A harbinger of death soared silently across the heavens, silhouetted momentarily by the moon, and abruptly swooped down to alight on a tree rising from the plaza of the small village nestled in the valley below. Its wings and crown shimmered with a silver hue. Caonabó was startled, and he studied the reactions of his lieutenants, huddled naked beside him on an overlooking promontory. They understood owls as guardians of the dead, and they confidently perceived one's arrival as heralding their attack as a resolution of prior wrongs and portending victory. Caonabó also was confident of victory, but he grimly reflected that none of the other supreme Haitian *caciques* (chiefs)—or even Anacaona—condoned the attack.

He peered down to survey the village layout with a general's acumen, seeking to determine where the pale men slept. In his midforties, Caonabó had achieved renown decades before as Haiti's greatest warrior by vanquishing Caribe raiders, ascending to rule his chiefdom of Maguana by virtue of his valor. Weeks earlier, he'd received a runner dispatched by Guacanagarí, the supreme cacique of Marien to the northwest, warning that eleven pale men were wandering south to befriend him, bent on trading for gold, and that Guacanagarí had refused to escort them, knowing Caonabó would be hostile. Caonabó's scouts had tracked the band to this village, reporting that the pale men straggled through his chiefdom with an unruly malevolence—seizing food from his subjects, disparaging the nobility of his local caciques, rudely displacing everyone from their *bohíos* (homes, houses), and luridly entreating women and girls.

The village cacique had been a loyal friend for years. Caonabó surmised that the pale men had expelled him from his *caney* (a chieftain's home), the band's leaders usurping it to sleep inside, with the remainder commandeering the adjacent bohíos circling the plaza. He ordered his lieutenants to execute the pale men summarily, without torture, and deployed them to lead his warriors in stealth left and right on the valley's hillside rims to surround the village. They'd strike when the moon dipped to the hill line and the village slipped into darkness, just before dawn's twilight.

The jagged streaks oiled in red and black on his men's olive-brown skin occasionally flickered through the underbrush as they advanced, and Caonabó observed the owl rotating its head nearly a full turn to scrutinize their movement. Victory in battle rarely was inevitable, and, for an instant, he contemplated whether the owl foretold his own men's death. The intruders below were hopelessly outnumbered, but their weapons were reputed to be fearsome, and it was possible that they—or their spirits—would prove formidable opponents.

Caonabó took final stock of the grave command that now was upon him. The pale men had first arrived off Haiti's northern coast less than a year before, venturing in an enormous vessel of unknown construction. Many of his subjects believed them to be spirits rather than men. Caonabó's *nitaínos* (noblemen) had traded gold with them profitably for a week, obtaining marvelous objects previously unseen, as had other supreme Haitian caciques. Pale men borne in two other vessels had visited Guacanagarí's chiefdom to trade for gold, as well. But one of those vessels had sunk, and Guacanagarí had befriended the pale men's leader and permitted him to establish a settlement near Guacanagarí's town. More than three dozen pale men had lived there since their leader departed to his homeland.

Caonabó grimaced, vexed by a pang of scorn directed at Guacanagarí, as the settlement had proved a disaster, the pale men growing uncivil, lawless, and contemptuous of Taíno customs and spirits.

They had slid to indolence, too lazy to grow, hunt, or fish for their own food, stealing it instead. They craved gold insatiably, and many had grown too impatient to trade for it, resorting to looting jewelry and ripping gold inlays from venerated face masks. Their lust for Taíno women had surged unrestrained—regardless of countless warnings to desist—and rape now constantly threatened. They had even murdered two of their own.

A soft light glowed dimly on the opposite hillside, a lieutenant fluttering a cotton satchel of *cocuyos* (large fireflies), signaling encirclement was complete. Caonabó shook his own sack of cocuyos in return, and a lone warrior began to descend to the village, deftly avoiding the rustle of leaves and trample of stalks that would alert his presence. His mission, to the extent stealth permitted, was to alert villagers sleeping in bohíos near the plaza to depart for the forest perimeter just before the attack began.

Caonabó's scorn for Guacanagarí surged fleetingly to anger at Haiti's other supreme caciques, whom he'd met in council over the summer. He'd admonished the council that the pale men could be a powerful invader intent on establishing a foothold on the island and implored Guacanagarí to execute them all. Guacanagarí had defended his visitors, assuring their conduct would be restored when their leader returned. Guarionex, cacique of Magua to the northeast, had insisted that Guacanagarí simply discipline miscreants, as if dispensing ordinary justice to his own subjects. Behecchio, cacique of Xaraguá to the west, had scoffed that killing them would forsake trading when their leader returned. Spurned, Caonabó had vowed that he would execute any pale man who entered his own chiefdom.

But Caonabó now felt neither pride nor conceit in fulfilling that vow. As his custom before battle, he simply paused to protect his warriors and seek victory by invoking the alliance of the most important spirit in daily life—Yúcahu, the spirit of *yuca* (yucca, manioc) and male fertility, and master of the sea. He withdrew a small stone *cemí* (an object representing or being a spirit) carved with the spirit's image from a pouch strung at his waist. As always, Yúcahu's omnipotent presence comforted, the wide eyes glaring imperiously forward, the enormous mouth poised to devour earth and all opposed, the legs folded as a frog set to pounce, and the forehead prescient with infinite vision and wisdom.

In the village below, Rodrigo de Escobedo, the royal secretary for Admiral Cristóbal Colón's small fleet, stirred inside the local ruler's hut, awoken by the hoot of an owl. He overheard sailors snoring nearby and observed that Pedro Gutiérrez, the fleet's royal observer and leader of their small band, had shifted to lie beside the hut's stone fire ring, embers glowing dimly within. Rodrigo judged by the moonlight and coolness of the hut that dawn was an hour off, and he wondered how many more days' march they would suffer until they met the lord the Indians called Caonabó. Several weeks before, their band had quit the settlement Admiral Colón had named Navidad, disgusted with the meager gold jewelry obtained trading with Guacanagarí, seeking the gold mines Caonabó reputedly controlled. The Admiral had expressly prohibited such an expedition without Guacanagarí's escort, warning that men dispersed about the island would be vulnerable to ambush by the Indians. But most sailors had believed—as the Admiral himself had observed repeatedly—that the Indians were too timid and cowardly, and their spears, bludgeons, and arrow slings too backward, to brave a fight.

Rodrigo brooded—half conscious, half nightmare—whether that assessment was correct, and he was tormented by the specter of the moonlit evacuation of the *Santa María* when it foundered on Christmas Eve past and his decision to join the many gold seekers then volunteering to remain in Navidad. He reproached his motives—both a naive call to duty and a base craving for gold. Rodrigo proudly had recited the formal proclamations whereby the territories discovered during the voyage were possessed for Queen Isabel and King Fernando, and the Admiral had entrusted him as diplomat to meet with the Indian kings encountered. In their final conversation—on the beach at Navidad, when the Admiral sailed for Spain January past—the Admiral had charged him to see that gold was collected for the king and assured rewards for so doing. But that charge had been doomed from the outset! The men had deteriorated to a faithless rabble on the Admiral's departure, heedless of God's commandments, laws, and royal authority in the absence of churches, priests, and the sovereigns' soldiers to remind them. The gold collected lined their pockets rather than the king's chests! Improvidently, the Admiral had selected his lover's cousin, Diego de Arana, to command the garrison, and the men had splintered menacingly into three hostile factions. A third had chosen loyalty to royal authority, following Pedro and himself, a third remained in Navidad to follow Arana, obeying the Admiral's wish, and the remainder, a gang of the worst misfits, mostly Basques and Galicians, cavorted under the spell of the *Santa María*'s boatswain.

Footsteps outside the hut abruptly wrenched Rodrigo from slumber to vigilance. The patter seemed distant, removed from the hut, possibly at the village edge. Rodrigo sat up, scanned the prone bodies of his fellow Christians, and strained to discern more. Fires had to be stoked to avoid the labor of rekindling them. Perhaps lovers had crept away for a tryst. Pedro and he had borne along a silver washbasin to present to Caonabó as an offering of friendship and alliance, and the basin lay with their provisions and other trading truck in the plaza—admirers could have tiptoed to study it. After moments of silence, Rodrigo reclined to sleep, satisfied nothing was amiss.

Caonabó watched his warrior slipping in and out of bohíos and flushed with pride as his subjects emerged—fathers, mothers, and grandparents, hauling children and cradling infants, retreating silently into the forest perimeter. They trusted and adored that he would reciprocate their obedience by rescuing them and their village. According to ancestral wisdom, the Taíno had first emerged to populate the world from a cave within Haiti, which lay at the center of their civilization and the universe.* Caonabó's pride leapt to a vision that—someday—these villagers also would understand he'd rescued the very island.

At last, the moon slipped into the hillside, the entire village darkened but for starlight, and Caonabó waved his satchel of cocuyos, commanding his men to descend to the plaza. Tall, lean, and hardened, he dropped from his perch to accompany them and nodded to the owl, thanking it for serving as sentry.

Rodrigo woke again, quit trying to sleep, and rose to stretch and wait in starlight for dawn in the plaza. He relieved himself there, callous that it was the Indians' central meeting place, and heard the

*The Cacibajagua (Jagua Cave).

solitary flap of a bird's wings as it took flight. Otherwise, the village was quiet. No one was stirring—not even a servant tending a fire, a wife preparing breakfast, or an infant crying. Rodrigo sensed the unnaturalness of the silence and crossed himself. He grasped the wooden crucifix strung to his necklace, revered the image of Christ's final suffering carved upon it, and prayed for Christ and the Virgin to bring him home to Castile. He was startled as a dim glow suddenly fell in the forest before him, as if a lantern had dropped.

Caonabó's warriors shrieked a cry that resounded off the hills and stormed the caney from all directions. Rodrigo beheld the onslaught in terror, stepping backward in retreat, screaming to warn the others. But he was ravaged by blistering pain and the horror of his death as a spear impaled his backside and emerged at his chest beside Christ's image. He stumbled, aghast he'd belittled the Indians' weaponry and fortitude, agonized that he'd never see Spain again, tortured by the oblivion of his demise. Wife, daughter, and queen would never learn of his service and accomplishment! The warriors swept past him as he crumpled to the ground and burst into the caney and neighboring bohíos, bludgeoning *macanas* (wooden clubs) and thrusting spears tipped with the stingray's jagged, poisonous spine.

Petrified by the war cry, Pedro and his band struggled urgently to confront the attack, staggering to their feet, clutching their daggers and swords, and flailing wildly to strike their assailants in the dark. Pedro shouted for them to regroup outside the huts, but the doorways swarmed with Indians rampaging inward, sealing escape and the band's fate. Half a dozen were trampled before they could stand, their skulls and bones crushed by the swipe of macanas. Others were hurled against the huts' walls, their chests pierced by spears, and they writhed in agony as poison radiated through their limbs. Some had lain with women, who weren't harmed but wailed in fright. Gore draped the huts' walls and pooled on the earthen floors. As he gasped his last breath, blood gushing through his teeth, Pedro was tormented by a vision of the comfortable courtier's life he'd forsaken to accompany Colón and hatred for the lies Colón boasted. The grave impending was the impoverished dirt of naked heathens, not a temple in the stately court of Cathay's Grand Khan!

Caonabó strode from the forest barking that the enemy dead and dying be dragged to the plaza to lie beside the corpse of the man slain there, all facing skyward. He inspected his warriors' own casualties, observing a few slashed and bleeding—none mortally—and, as villagers emerged cautiously from the forest, he beckoned them to attend the wounded. He recognized and summoned the village cacique to his side. Graven by the pale men's invasion and their massacre, the elderly man praised Caonabó, reaffirmed undying loyalty, and asked how to help.

Caonabó augustly raised the palm of his hand to indicate that he'd answer shortly, after victory was complete. As the astonished villagers gathered round, he commanded his lieutenants to execute those pale men yet alive by impaling their hearts and to bludgeon each man's eyes and testicles to ensure the man's spirit could never return. Silence replaced the din of battle as the villagers contemplated Caonabó's domination, spellbound. Caonabó then broke it, comforting the cacique that his only responsibility was to clean the village and heal the angst of his subjects. Caonabó would dispose of the corpses.

As twilight emerged, the cacique's wives and *naborias* (servants) served *cazabi* (cassava, a toasted bread made from yucca) and pineapple juice to all and offered bohíos for rest. But Caonabó was keen to fulfill his entire design, and, after thankful parting salutations, he ascended into the hillside. The warriors followed, clutching the corpses' hands and feet to lift and transport them while bearing the washbasin and other strange objects, which would be taken to Caonabó's hometown. Near the summit, the entourage came upon a barren gulley carved into the hillside—void of herbs or other nourishment—where Caonabó brought his men to halt and rest. The corpses, he ordered, would be laid there.

He sat briefly alone, considering the thoughts he'd communicate to the other supreme caciques, arrested by the parting warnings from the two of his dozen wives with whom he shared his most guarded thoughts.

On the eve of his departure, Anacaona—his premier wife, born of the Xaraguán caciqual family, acclaimed as Haiti's most beautiful woman—had wrapped her arms about his waist and drawn them together at the hip, an embrace inviting affection before sleep but prompting discussion first. In her midtwenties, she'd supported Caonabó dutifully at the summer's caciqual council, but privately she opposed executing pale men, believing as Guarionex that Taíno spirits favored a more harmonious solution until the pale men were determined to have hostile intentions.

"Caonabó, Guarionex and my brother will think poorly of this action," she'd counseled softly, referring to her older brother, Behecchio.

"It's my chiefdom. Their approval isn't required," he'd replied. But her frown had condemned the answer's shallowness, so he'd added, "I'll dispatch messengers to them as soon as the attack's done, explaining my decision again. Their concern won't jeopardize relationships."

"That's essential. Decisions regarding these few pale men shouldn't disturb the harmony among the island's rulers," she'd advised, maintaining the frown. "What will you tell Guacanagarí?"

"I'll tell him what I told him before—that he should execute the remaining pale men he's harboring. I'll warn him that I'll kill those men myself if he fails to."

"That's his chiefdom—his decision to make," she'd opposed, shaking her head vigorously and slackening her grip.

"We share one island, homeland to us all. He had no right to invite pale men to remain, jeopardizing everyone."

Onaney—Caonabó's first wife, a childhood girlfriend, younger by a few years—had also cautioned him as they sat together the following morning, watching the sun rise. Decades ago, he'd brought her to Haiti from their birthplace on Aniyana (Middle Caicos, Turks and Caicos), a Maguanan settlement, and she'd always appreciated their Lucayan heritage and the challenges of his initial acceptance by Haitian caciqual society.

"What will the other supreme caciques do when they learn of your attack?" she'd asked, placing her head on his shoulder.

"They'll talk about it, nothing more."

"I suppose so—assuming the pale men's leader never returns," she'd conceded. Yet she'd shifted to kneel directly before him, eye to eye, drawing his shoulders to bring him close. "But what if their leader does return and learns that you've killed his men? Guacanagarí won't defend your attack then. Will Behecchio, Guarionex, and the others?"

"I doubt they would," he'd admitted. "Particularly if the pale men become advantageous trading partners."

"What if even more pale men come to invade?" she'd pressed. When he'd failed to respond, she'd sternly exclaimed, "Don't fight the pale men alone."

Caonabó's heart pounded and he exhaled deeply, somberly acknowledging his wives' concerns, as well as those expressed at the caciqual council. But the general within him remained undaunted—no pale man could be permitted to live on Haiti.

He summoned his runners. The one bound for Guacanagarí would relate that he'd executed the pale men in Magauna because they posed a threat to all Haitians, fulfilling his word, and demand that Guacanagarí promptly execute all the remaining pale men. Otherwise, Caonabó's warriors would enter Marien and do it. The runners bound for the other supreme caciques would inform similarly. Caonabó wasn't seeking their approval but inviting their participation in the massacre if Guacanagarí refused.

The runners departed at dawn, and Caonabó set his warriors on their homeward march through mountains, leaving him behind for a few moments alone among the dead, save for the buzzards that now hovered above. As the warriors' voices faded into the distance, he studied the corpses, observing that twisted about most of the necks were necklaces that strung a small cemí shaped as crossed sticks. The cemí of the pale man first executed gruesomely depicted a pale man dying upon such a cross, undoubtedly the so-called Christ-spirit the pale men were known to worship. Caonabó recalled Anacaona's last entreaties.

"We don't understand the pale men's spirits," she'd warned, herself renowned for wisdom in composing *areítos* (songs, dances) about life's meaning and Taíno spirits. "Their weapons are daunting, and their spirits might be, too. A powerful people may have powerful spirits." She'd paused for emphasis, setting her arms about his neck, concerned that he rarely respected that spirits influenced destiny, as opposed to men—such as himself. "A brutal people may have brutal spirits."

"I've considered this," he'd replied. "Our spirits are unwavering. Yúcahu will protect our men from harm." He'd tightened their embrace, moved by her concern, but she'd resisted a kiss. "Attabeira will heal our wounds," he'd retreated partially, referring to Yúcahu's mother, the spirit of fertility and nurturer of crops.

"Your scouts' reports are ominous, indicating the pale men believe their so-called Christ-spirit is paramount to all others. The pale men denigrate our spirits, as if the Christ-spirit were the only spirit worthy of veneration."

"I've heard that, and it isn't surprising. Their belief is consistent with their arrogance. That doesn't make it true." He'd shrugged his shoulders. "We'll discover the Christ-spirit's potency when the attack's engaged."

Taíno owl and Yúcahu.

Caonabó squatted to touch the cemí of the Christ-spirit, which was spattered with the dead man's blood, and realized it was carved of a tree, just as many Taíno cemís. He grasped that the morning's victory had been easily attained, regardless of this spirit's presence. *Had Yúcahu prevailed over it?* he pondered. *Would the pale men have prevailed had their leader commanded?* Caonabó surmised that the band's failure of vigilance was due to the leader's absence, and he was unsettled to know nothing of this person's courage or skill to seek vengeance.

Caonabó removed the necklace from the corpse and stuffed it and the cemí into the pouch tied at his waist, intending to show them to Anacaona. The rising sun cast his shadow long and inimitable as he rose to depart, and he invoked Yúcahu's wrath to deny the pale men and their leader from ever so strutting on the island.

Isabel and Fernando,
Gerona, Catalonia, September 8, 1493

On September 8, Castile's Queen Isabel woke in the predawn twilight to the clop of horses gathering to feed in a stable beyond her window in a nobleman's mansion, close inside the high walls of the city of Gerona's centuries-old stone fortress. The day before, she, her husband, and an elite nucleus of their court had ridden north from Barcelona on the ancient road built over a millennium before—still hailed as the Via Augusta—to arrive in Gerona for a day of ceremony and homage before continuing north to reclaim two Catalonian provinces from the French.* As she sat on the bedside, Isabel marveled that the road endured and still led to Rome, and she contemplated whether her achievements would so endure.

Two ladies assisted her into a robe and slippers, and a once-Mohammedan girl enslaved during the Reconquista—the war to reclaim Granada from the infidel—attended her chamber pot.† Isabel stood to gaze through the window and recalled that, at but ten, Fernando had been besieged for weeks with his mother in the fortress tower by Catalans rebelling against Aragón's rule. She studied

*Rosellón and Cerdaña.

†The girl likely was enslaved at Málaga (1487).

the tower's arrow slits and parapets, puzzling where her husband and mother-in-law had taken final refuge from the artillery's bombardment, reflecting proudly on him.* He was as wily and cunning in statecraft as on the battlefield, and, within a week, he would retake the two provinces without firing a shot. She savored that she'd now participate in his victories as king of Aragón—as his queen, at his side. For over two decades, he had stood at hers, marrying as teenagers while her succession to the Castilian throne was in doubt, scheming and warring so that she seize and defend it, and steadfastly pursuing the greatest campaigns to restore and purify her realms—the Reconquista's fulfillment, the Inquisition's establishment, and the Jews' expulsion. They'd labored together to subjugate and Christianize Castile's first overseas conquest, the island of Gran Canaria, and, over the summer, to organize Cristóbal Colón's mission that would depart to establish Castile's dominion over Colón's astounding discoveries in the Indies. If Colón's promises bore true, thousands of simple heathens would welcome her and Fernando's sovereignty and Christianity without a fight, and Castile's coffers would overflow with gold.

Isabel's butler served her bread, ham, and honey, and she then withdrew to the mansion's small chapel, where Cardinal Pedro González de Mendoza, a statesman, cleric, and her most senior advisor for decades, was waiting.

"Any word on Colón's departure?" she asked, their intimacy forgiving a salutation.

"None, Your Highness." Isabel repeatedly had dispatched letters to Colón and others over the summer urging prompt departure, including but three days prior, and Mendoza sought to calm her impatience with the delay. "The logistics for provisioning your settlement dwarf those required for Mina, no less your initial Canarian garrisons. Fonseca's efficiency has been remarkable." The sovereigns had appointed a veteran administrator of the Reconquista, the archdeacon of Seville Juan Rodríguez de Fonseca (b. 1451), to organize, recruit, and administer the Indies expedition jointly with Colón.

"It rarely hurts to push one's ministers," Isabel responded curtly, reminding that she needed no lecture on how to rule, as she had well proven. But she admitted to herself that Mendoza was correct.

*Isabel's mother-in-law was Queen Juana Enríquez of Aragón.

Colón's proposed settlement was unprecedented. Its incredible overseas distance from Spain posed logistical hurdles dwarfing those that Portugal's King João II had surmounted a decade prior when establishing his trading post at Mina in Guinea (southern Africa), now famously rich for gold and slaves.* Fonseca had provisioned Colón's large fleet in but months, more rapidly than typical for far lesser missions.

"Any more spats between Colón and the treasury officials?" she asked.

"None that have been brought to my attention," Mendoza replied.

"I'll join you soon," she pronounced, indicating she sought solitude in the chapel. The immediacy of sovereign decisions rarely impeded Isabel's communication with the Lord and Virgin, a dialogue fundamental to her deliberations and comfort that decisions were righteous. She prayed briefly, adoring the Virgin's beneficence and absence of sin. Her thoughts also flickered affectionately to her children, who'd remained in the protection of the court in Barcelona, proudly and sadly aware that her daughters—when old enough for wedding nights—would depart for other kingdoms to bear her dynasty. Her temperamental Juana, thirteen, had been offered to the son of the Austrian Maximilian I, the Holy Roman emperor, and her pensive redhead Catalina, seven, to the first son of England's King Henry VII, unions designed to counter French aggression. Princess Isabel, the oldest at twenty-two, had been married to King João's son and already widowed, robbed of joy, and both she and good-natured Maria, eleven, had been offered for another Portuguese union to preserve peace on the Hispanic peninsula. Isabel beseeched the Virgin to bless their marriages and fertility, as well as the delicate health of their brother, Prince Juan, who would inherit Castile and Aragón.

With devotion concluded, Isabel's chambermaids dressed her in an elegant jewel-studded gown befit for meeting local nobility, and she strode at a measured pace to greet the mansion's patriarch, her closest counselors, and the king in the mansion's grand room. At forty-two, plumper than before and her auburn hair paling, she entered regally, not as guest, wife, or mother, but as the most powerful and renowned woman in Christendom.

*São Jorge da Mina, established in 1482 at modern Elmina, Ghana.

Save Fernando, all bowed, and she bid them rise and continue their conversation, an exposition on bargain and betrayal and France's King Charles VIII.

"In days, we reclaim what my father hungered to recover for decades," Fernando exclaimed, addressing the patriarch. "Charles returns our provinces in exchange for our promises of mutual defense and that we won't oppose *just* claims he asserts for my cousin's throne in Naples. Tonight, we celebrate!"

"Your Highness, a tremendous victory!" the nobleman acclaimed in response.

But Fernando hushed and raised a finger. "Yet we must remain wary," he cautioned. Decades before, Fernando's uncle had conquered Naples and, on death, passed its throne to an illegitimate son, to whom Fernando's sister had been wed.* "Last month, Charles cajoled the pope to invest him as the rightful ruler of Naples—based on some obscure ancestral claim."

"Peace with France has been one of our paramount objectives," Cardinal Mendoza interjected. "The treaty with Charles advances it, and Charles now expects we won't oppose his ambitions in Naples."

"Perhaps, but we've always supported my uncle's lineage and my sister, and we have our own *just* claims to Naples's throne to consider defending," replied Fernando, puckering his lips wryly. "To date, the pope has braved rebuffing Charles's request, and our interest is that the pope holds firm—without our involvement." Fernando crossed his arms upon his chest, recollecting his long relationship with the pope—Alexander VI, the Aragonese Rodrigo Borja—including the pending marriage of another cousin to the pope's son.† "But a king must stand ready to favor and defend the pope's wishes."

Isabel flinched, pregnant with baseness, admitting complicity with her husband. He grasped how to prevail, including bucking for the pope, whose life and rule had been characterized by nepotism and promiscuity, vices she tolerated in her own court but loathed in the Lord's. She turned to Mendoza. "Any fresh word regarding His Holiness's discussions with Charles?"

---

*Fernando's father was King Juan II of Aragón; his uncle, King Alfonso V of Aragón; and his sister, Juana of Aragón. The treaty is the Treaty of Barcelona, January 18 and 19, 1493, as supplemented August 25, 1493, and Alfonso's son was King Ferrante I of Naples.

†The marriage of Fernando's cousin, María Enriquez, to the pope's son, Juan Borja.

"No news, Your Highness."

Isabel raised her chin, signaling she would redirect the discussion to the other substantial matter then involving the pope—and her kingdom. "Any word whether His Holiness has agreed to adjust his proclamations on the Indies?"

Over the summer, the pope had issued bulls recognizing Castile's right to the islands and mainlands Colón had discovered, establishing a longitudinal line one hundred leagues west of the Azores and Cape Verde islands and granting Castile all islands and mainlands found from that line west or south in the direction of India.* While the bulls had delighted Isabel and Fernando, Portugal's King João II had been enraged, decrying that Aragonese back-scratching had cheated him of the Antillia of Portuguese lore and a continent he expected to exist in the southern hemisphere off Guinea. João insisted that the papal bulls he and his predecessors had obtained decades prior already awarded lands Colón discovered west and south of the Canary Islands to Portugal.† He also exhorted that—regardless of papal pronouncements—Isabel and Fernando had agreed as much in the Treaty of Alcáçovas (1479), when recognizing Portugal's exclusive right to circumnavigate Guinea to reach the Indies. Isabel and Fernando had belittled these claims with matching vehemence but grown anxious their grant didn't definitively entitle Castile to the Indies themselves in the absence of possession and that, if João were prescient that such a continent existed, it was theirs, not his. Over the past months, both kingdoms had urgently dispatched special envoys to the pope, pleading a restatement of his proclamations, and to each other, seeking a territorial compromise to avert hostilities.

"Your Highness, our last report was that the pope is preparing a pronouncement in our favor," added Mendoza. "The absence of a fresh dispatch bodes well."

"What news of João's navy?" she asked.

"Our spies warn that it's ready to sail, either to usurp Colón's discoveries or sink his ships," responded Mendoza.

"Our own is now poised to defend?"

---

* *Inter Caetera* (May 3, 1493), *Eximiae Devotionis* (May 3, 1493), and *Inter Caetera* (May 4, 1493).

† *Aeterni Regis* (June 21, 1481), clarifying the bulls obtained by Prince Henrique (Henry the Navigator), *Romanus Pontifex* (January 8, 1455), and *Inter Caetera* (March 13, 1456).

"It is standing ready, Your Highness," Mendoza assured. Over the summer, the sovereigns had commandeered ships to confront those João threatened to dispatch.

"Shouldn't Your Highness resolve the quarrel with João before battle?" the patriarch asked.

"We've no intention of resolving anything with João at this time," Fernando replied. "Colón will sail as soon as ready, and our navy will defend him in the improbable event João seeks war over this." He looked through the mansion's windows to the high parapets above, where he'd walked as a boy, confident he yet retained a soldier's vigor. "We'll negotiate with João only after Colón finishes reconnoitering the territory he's found—so we know what's important to possess. If the pope grants our pleas—the Lord willing—we'll then have a stronger hand to play. Our envoys to João have been instructed to bumble and dither, but nothing more."

Fernando glanced to Isabel to confirm her consent and then drew the discussion from the Indies back to planning their triumphal march into Perpiñan, the Catalonian provinces' capital. She was content that he dictate the pageantry's symbolisms and drifted to muse silently on the discord brewing between Colón and their key administrators.

In August, she and Fernando had learned that the chief accountant for Indies matters had openly disregarded Colón's provisioning instructions, perhaps with Archdeacon Fonseca's knowledge, and they'd dispatched reprimands to the accountant twice, commanding that he honor and obey the Admiral with the respect due the title or face punishment. They'd also dispatched a politer letter to Fonseca, reminding that he, too, should do as the Admiral wished, without arguments over points of honor, pronouncing that the Admiral's opinions had to be followed in everything, since all of the Indies was his responsibility. She herself had intervened to permit Colón to enlist a household staff of thirty despite Fonseca's refusal to approve that number.

Isabel ruminated that the problem ran deeper than two courtiers—most of her court resented the nobility she'd granted Colón, his foreign and common lineage, and his lack of their experience in conquest, government, and administration. But she esteemed that

Colón had surmounted seven years of naysaying and ridicule by all experts—geographers, cosmographers, mariners, and clerics—to deliver on his promises, just as she'd overcome years of dismissive hostility to a queen's rule. Regardless of her courtiers' jealousies, she and Fernando did trust Colón's judgments above all others as to what needed to be done to achieve their objectives in the Indies, and they'd empowered him like an overlord there and were resolute that all obey him.

These objectives were to establish a trading settlement like Mina, a crown base to explore the Indies and obtain gold, from which they would rule as emperors over all the kings and princes of the Indies they subjugated. All merchandise bartered and obtained would be the Castilian crown's property, except Colón would share one-tenth of the profits and an additional one-eighth to the extent he underwrote ships. Unlike their Canarian and Granadan conquests, she and Fernando wouldn't share the land or vassals subjugated with the nobility or other men who assisted the conquest—except Colón—and private enterprise would be prohibited. They had named Colón and his heirs admiral, viceroy, and governor of the islands and mainland possessed in perpetuity, awarding him the executive, administrative, military, and judicial power therein—including to choose government officials, other than those of the royal treasury, and to impose the death penalty. His actions were subject only to his paramount oath of fealty to them, to obey their express orders, and to submit merchant activities to the treasury officials' accounting. They had required that every other person departing to the Indies swear two oaths—of fealty to them and to render obedience to Colón, both at sea and on land.

"My lady, it's time for mass," Fernando announced, smiling to Isabel, rousing her from her concerns, appreciating that, while they ruled as one, she deferred to him on Aragón's singular matters.

"Splendid." Isabel waited for those assembled to arrange a procession to Gerona's immense cathedral, whose highest facades rose as tall as the fortress walls. Cardinal Mendoza led, closely followed by Fernando and herself at his side. A thunderous applause of Gerona's prelates, noblemen, royal officials, and common subjects welcomed them as they stepped into the street and paraded uphill to the church for Mendoza's performance of the service. Then commenced a day of gracious salutations, private audiences, and a grand luncheon for the sovereigns and local nobility, hosted by Gerona's bishop in the canopied gardens of his residence.

Word buzzed of the mercantile opportunities and new royal offices occasioned by the integration of the Catalonian provinces into the realm. But the Indies whetted fascination and greater attention. All present had read Colón's letter, published by the sovereigns in Barcelona that April, heralding his astonishing discoveries.* The lands found beckoned extraordinary rewards—gold, spice, mastic, and as many slaves as the sovereigns ordered—and an exotic heathen population, naked and timid, as well as a ferocious people who ate human flesh. Isabel and Fernando were delighted to answer their vassals' eager inquiries.

"Is there time for loyal Catalans to enlist?" the second son of a gentleman asked.

"Unfortunately not. The Admiral will sail in days," Isabel replied. "The Lord willing." She politely refrained from reminding that general enlistment had been limited to Castilians.

"Thousands sought to enlist, well beyond the fleet's capacity and payroll," Fernando added. "Many had to be turned away. The ships are pressed with livestock, as well, to seed our presence permanently. But there'll be future opportunities."

"Does the crown seek additional financing?" a pawnbroker for landed gentry inquired.

"Not at this time," responded Isabel, gratified by the unsolicited interest, having spent much of two decades laboring to finance their great endeavors. "But we might soon."

"There're no more participations to award on this voyage," Fernando noted. Conveying the imprimatur of renowned financiers, he added, "The Duke of Medina Sidonia has kindly lent a large share, and Juanoto Berardi assisted as well."†

The duke, one of Andalusia's preeminent noblemen and seaborne merchants, had lent five million maravedís, secured by gold and jewels confiscated from conversos by the Inquisition and Jews on their

*The "Letter to Santángel," published in Barcelona on April 1, 1493.

†The duke was Juan de Guzmán, son of Enrique de Guzmán.

expulsion from Spain.* Berardi—the leading Florentine slave-trader resident in Seville, well known at court as a financier—had funded the acquisition of Colón's flagship and provisioned the fleet's biscuits, for which Isabel and Fernando had dispatched him a gracious thank-you note. Additional financing had been secured from other sources, including the Castilian Hermandad, a militia.

After luncheon, Isabel rested on a sofa in the bishop's private quarters, alone but for servants, and she revisited her concern whether Colón was receiving the necessary support and obedience, and her prior consternation dissipated. She and Fernando had selected Colón's key expedition leadership themselves, usually subject to Colón's confirmation, with the goal of filling the gaps in his experience with compatible men.

Most critically, they'd placed three accomplished men at his side, a cleric, a gentleman, and a commander, and early indications suggested harmony and obedience would be achieved. The Catalan friar Bernardo Buil would assist Colón in the heathens' conversion, and it had been Buil who alerted them to the frictions between Colón and the chief accountant. Older than the sovereigns, Buil had been both a devout monk and an accomplished royal envoy for Fernando, most recently having traveled to France in 1492 to discuss the Catalonian provinces' return, and Pope Alexander had confirmed his selection as papal nuncio to the Indies in June. His faith was as genuine as Colón's and their own, and he grasped their objective of sovereign dominion. For civilian leadership, Isabel had selected Antonio de Torres, a prominent courtier with whom Colón had been friendly for years and would feel comfortable delegating governance of the settlement and managing the fleets that would resupply it. A brother to Prince Juan's governess, Torres fully appreciated both the sovereigns' objectives and Colón's desires—cravings, Isabel admitted, for wealth, nobility, and acclaim—and he might serve amicably as a linchpin to reconcile the two. For military expertise, the sovereigns had selected a distinguished nobleman Fernando esteemed, Pedro Margarite, born of the illustrious family of a bishop of Gerona and whose great-uncle had sheltered Fernando and his mother within the fortress tower decades prior. Margarite had served Fernando for some doz-

*The maravedí was then an accounting unit fixed to gold, not a coin, and a gold ducat or castellano was said to represent 375 maravedís.

en years, including administering the Inquisition in Zaragoza and participating in Granada's conquest, and Fernando trusted his generalship to assist Colón in leading the thousand men now under his command—another experience Colón lacked.

At sunset, Isabel's chambermaids arrived with a more splendid gown and more opulent jewelry and shoes. After redressing, she and Fernando attended an intimate banquet in the bishop's reception hall, recognizing those with greater stature and affording the opportunity for more prying questions. Candelabras flickered resplendent, butlers attended each guest's every want, and the bishop blessed all for their contributions to the sovereigns' kingdoms.

"Does Colón expect the Indies' gold and spice will repay the financiers?" a nobleman asked.

"Absolutely," Fernando replied with assurance. "He's promised that, and vastly more. It remains to be seen, but he expects the gold alone will recover the costs in short order. It may take some months to establish the settlement—perhaps longer—and the ongoing costs are uncertain. But we expect profitability soon."

"Is Colón really in the Indies?" a knight inquired.

"Certainly," Fernando exclaimed. "We think he's offshore terra firma's eastern tip and urged him to find it promptly."

"We've beaten João there, no doubt," Isabel relished pronouncing.

"Will Colón take slaves?" a seaborne merchant probed.

There was silence, and, for an instant, Isabel and Fernando each wondered how the other would answer. "No, the inhabitants will be brought to the faith, as our vassals," Isabel responded.

"The Admiral believes they're ready to embrace the Lord, in peace," Fernando explained.

When the evening grew long, Fernando rose to conclude with rousing toasts to the crown of Aragón and raucous applause exalting that he and Isabel would ride at dawn for Perpiñan. The royal party departed for their lodging, and Isabel said good night to all at the cathedral, bidding that her new confessor be escorted there to take her confession. In solitude but for guardsmen bearing torches, she dutifully mounted a steep stone staircase to enter the edifice and sit in its cavernous nave at the first pew, waiting his arrival and pondering the seaborne merchant's question, which she'd heard before and irritated her. Colón had assured that the Indians would be subjugated easily and embrace the faith, obviating reason or justification for enslaving them. His fleet bore soldiers and arms to quash any who resisted, Portuguese trespassers, and, if necessary, the flesh eaters. But she and Fernando had contemplated broad acquiescence in vassalage on the island he'd named Española, not slavery.

Isabel and her husband had always honored the doctrine that enslavement of heathens on the path to Christianity was forbidden. Their Canarian conquests hadn't required a fresh papal award of sovereignty, and, when the Canarians resisted subjugation, they'd obtained interpretations of this doctrine from local prelates that resisters weren't so protected and could be enslaved, permitting the sale of those taken on the battlefield. Slave trading of Canarian resisters had since been incorporated as key elements of the conquests' financing arrangements. Earlier that year, their Canarian conquistador, Alonso de Lugo, had completed the subjugation of the island of Las Palmas, welcoming the inhabitants who had agreed to peaceful alliances as the sovereigns' free vassals and conducting a military conquest of the others. Those captured had been sold into slavery to fund the conquest after deducting one-fifth of the proceeds as Alonso's share. Juanoto Berardi had provided Alfonso financing and conducted the slave trading in partnership.

But Pope Alexander's bulls awarding sovereignty over Colón's discoveries hadn't addressed enslavement of the inhabitants—resisters or otherwise—and were resoundingly clear on two points. The Lord was pleased that barbarous nations be overthrown and led to the faith, and she and Fernando had a duty to so lead the peoples in the lands the pope awarded them. Their written instructions of May 29 to Colón had acknowledged this duty, pronouncing that their principal concern was the increase of the faith and directing Colón to convert the inhabitants by all ways and means. They'd admonished that the objective of conversion might be better attained if Colón compelled all who voyaged there to treat the Indians very well and lovingly and abstain from doing them any injury, arranging that both peoples hold much conversation and intimacy, each serving the other to the best of their ability. He was to give the Indians gifts and punish severely those who maltreated them.

In the dim flicker of torchlight, Isabel eyed about the cathedral, studying the celebratory royal bunting darkly draped about the chapels, emblazoned with her and her husband's royal marks, proudly heralding their rule and ever-expanding empire. As she reverted to the high altar cross, she invoked the Lord to guide her thoughts.

Is enslavement of Indians consistent with the bulls' duty to convert? she asked him. In the absence of hostilities or other excuse, it seemed not, and the notion of relying on the ongoing sale of resisters to fund conquest seemed beyond the bulls' spirit. Isabel recalled the enslavement of Indians heralded in Colón's letter, published prior to the pope's pronouncements, and surmised that many of her subjects assumed she and Fernando would permit it. She well understood that Colón, Berardi, and other financiers earnestly so favored.

Footsteps then echoed faintly through the darkness, and Isabel cut the dialogue and qualms short, placated that neither Indian resistance nor enslavement were then issues. She missed the compassionate mercy of her prior confessor, Hernando de Talavera, whom she'd appointed to serve as archbishop of Granada, so he might persuade the infidel there to convert. Yet the intense, uncompromising, and uncorruptible faith of his replacement had brought her extraordinary contentment, and she harkened to his arrival.

An elder man in a simple monk's habit, with a wasted frame, pallid complexion, and eyes shimmering ecstatic in the torchlight—as if an ancient biblical prophet—placed a bench and sat gravely before her. Ximénez de Cisneros, born (ca. 1436) near Madrid into a family of modest means, had studied law and been unjustly incarcerated for six years in a dispute regarding his first ecclesiastic appointment. After release, he'd sought the most austere of the austere Franciscan postings, retiring to isolated rural communities to live alone as a hermit. For years, he'd sought to achieve an ongoing communication with Christ, subsisting on bread, herbs, and water, donning but sackcloth, sleeping on straw, and scourging himself regularly. He'd rebuffed Isabel's first entreaty that he serve as confessor, relenting only when she agreed he could return to a monastery and cell when not needed (1492). While welcome, he had avoided this day's celebrations as pernicious allurements and delights. But he could be worldly when the situation required.

As the moon rose high, Isabel chose to confess the imperfection of her impatience—with the time diverted to reclaiming her husband's provinces and the delay in Colón's departure for the Indies.

Ximénez's intensity left little concern for patience, either as one of his own failings or that of others, and he readily absolved her. He'd gleaned enough information on her day to offer, instead, what he perceived as greater solace—and direction.

"As for the Indies, Your Highness, your greatest glory will be the heathens' conversion to the faith—regardless of whether gold abounds."

CRISTÓBAL,
Cádiz, Castile, Mid-September 1493

The ancient port of Cádiz had been settled by Phoenicians (ca. 1,100 BC) on the first defensible peninsula sheltering a good harbor in the Sea of Darkness (Atlantic Ocean) west of the Pillars of Hercules (Strait of Gibraltar).* It had been claimed thereafter by Romans, who extended the Via Augusta to it, and Mohammedan and Christian princes. In recent decades, the great merchant trading families of Genoa, Venice, and Florence—including Centuriones, Spinolas, Di Negros, and Dorias—had established a small community there to service their maritime operations. In 1492, after the death of Rodrigo Ponce de León, the Marquis of Cádiz and the most celebrated general of the Reconquista, Isabel had claimed the port as crown property to regulate Castile's African trade and, upon learning of Colón's discoveries, its Indies trade.

Admiral Cristóbal Colón stood at dawn on the harbor's main quay, gauging the preparedness and utility of some two dozen ships at anchor, placidly undulating in tidal swells. The ships bustled with commotion as scores of sailors tended to their readiness and stowed provisions ferried by launches departing from the quay. About him, merchants with laborers and an occasional black-skinned African or olive-skinned Canarian slave were arriving from towns throughout Andalusia to deposit even more provisions.

*The pillars being the Rock of Gibraltar and Jebel Musa, Morocco.

Cristóbal was confident that his fleet—seventeen of the ships—would sail within a week, and, at forty-two, he was outright doubtless of his ability to lead them, undaunted that he'd never commanded so many. His king and queen wished he'd already departed, fearing both winter weather and King João's dispatch of a competing or hostile squadron. But Cristóbal understood, as well as any man alive, that the fleet couldn't embark until each ship was fit to cross the ocean, which the Lord had made sovereign to all mariners. He wasn't concerned with the onset of winter, as his route would be southern, although he did hope to replicate the mild weather experienced on the first voyage, which had departed Gomera (Canary Islands) in September. It seemed unlikely King João would risk war by intercepting the fleet, and, if hostilities came, a half dozen of the ships before him would defend, sailing under the command of the sovereigns' naval commander.*

Yet Cristóbal also felt departure urgent, harboring a grim premonition that the men he'd left on Española had flaunted the Lord's teachings and succumbed to base instincts, displeasing the Lord Guacanagarí and abusing his naked subjects, particularly the womenfolk. His stern orders to the garrison had been to deal respectfully with Guacanagarí and the island's peoples, trading civilly for gold and locating a site for the permanent settlement he'd establish on his return, retaining by all means Guacanagarí's goodwill and generous disposition to assist and protect them. Española's conquest, subjugation, and gold mining would be tangled if the heathens' welcome had soured due to distrust or dislike. Worse, if hostilities arose, conquest itself could be costly and difficult, perhaps even jeopardized, as the heathen population was enormous and vastly outnumbered his recruits, albeit lacking effective weaponry.

After tireless effort, Cristóbal at last was satisfied that the fleet's composition would meet the varied demands of conquest, settlement, and exploration. Berthed at the quay, the fleet's largest vessel was his flagship, a square-rigged nao capable of loading almost two hundred tuns of wine—nearly twice the capacity of the lost *Santa María* of the first voyage—with a large captain's quarters in the stern castle

*Admiral Iñigo de Artieta.

for himself and the staff administering the fleet and settlement.* Although he'd renamed it the *Santa María*, as its predecessor, the crew still preferred its nickname, the *María Galante*, as it was a good sailor. There were four other naos, responsible for bearing substantial provisions, and twelve smaller, more nimble caravels, mostly square-rigged, a few lateen. Cristóbal's command was as the fleet's captain general, with ships to be captained by the sovereigns' ranking representatives and a few mariners. Antonio de Torres would captain the *María Galante*, Pedro Margarite a caravel.

One of the larger caravels was the *Niña*, refit and repaired from the storms of the homeward voyage last February, with a load capacity of fifty-three tuns, approximately seventy feet long on deck bow to stern, and six feet of draft. The sovereigns had instructed Cristóbal promptly to discover and possess new territories to preempt João and, most immediately, to explore the land the inhabitants called Cuba to ascertain whether it was the Indies mainland. He intended to use the *Niña* as his flagship for that exploration, confident in its seaworthiness and maneuverability. The fleet's lighter caravels would assist reconnoitering shorelines, with the shallower drafts of Cantabrian barques.

As the sun rose, Cristóbal strode up the *María Galante*'s gangplank—now a nobleman, his tall sturdy frame and gray hair buttressing that eminence. He waved magnanimously from the deck to a line of artisans and peasants that already had formed on the quay to enlist and then assumed his chair in the captain's quarters, where he was greeted by several of his staff. He intended to limit fleet enlistment to just over twelve hundred men, including the necessary sailors, averaging about seventy men per ship and thereby permitting stowage of food, wine, and other supplies to last six months. Far more had applied than could be accommodated, and most enrollments had been arranged in Seville during the summer. The majority would be artisans and peasants from Andalusia and Extremadura, selected to build the settlement, farm land, tend livestock, dig for gold, and otherwise do whatever ordered—all on the crown payroll. Those skilled were entitled to a thousand maravedís a month, the unskilled about six hundred, and payment would accrue in Spain.

*About 250 gallons per tun.

Space was reserved for some two hundred unpaid volunteers, gentlemen, and a few noblemen, mostly from Andalusia. Rodrigo Ponce de León's cousin Juan and Seville's Diego Velázquez de Cuéllar had taken berths. The sovereigns' May 29 instructions had required that every voyage participant appear before himself, Fonseca, and the sovereigns' chief accountant, or subordinates, to swear oaths of fealty and obedience—one to the sovereigns and one to himself.

As the morning's first applicant was ushered aboard, Cristóbal mused upon the dreams that had urged such crowds to apply and their loyalties. He'd promised recruits the same as the sovereigns—that Española abounded with gold and its natives were timorous, servile, and disposed to embrace Christians and their faith and customs. The gold undoubtedly had lured all of them, pining fortunes. The peasants also contemplated a new beginning might raise their lot in rank and status—just as he'd ascended from the alleyways of Genoa and fate as a weaver to become their admiral. They couldn't expect that elevation, but they would relish any modest rise from their rustic poverty and feudal vassalage. The gentlemen were drawn by fame, adventure, and appointments he would award to offices and territories in the Indies. The Reconquista had been won, and the Indies settlement might now become their outlet for glory. Cristóbal suspected the oaths taken—at least to king and queen—were mostly honest, as nearly every recruit did honor the sovereigns with devotion. He well appreciated most everyone would secretly hoard a stash of gold rightfully the king and queen's and that none would esteem him if their dreams weren't realized.

The first applicant entered and bowed, a young, swarthy peasant farmer subsisting in a small hamlet remote in Extremadura.

"What's your skill?" Cristóbal asked.

"Your Lordship Admiral, I farm wheat, barley, and vegetables, as well as cows for milk and cheese."

"All that?" Cristóbal replied, suspecting a single cow and patch of wheat to serve the man's family. "What works best?"

"Mostly the vegetables. But I can grow or tend anything. I can do whatever you want. I could help with the spices trade."

"Good. I expect you to work hard—the spices won't come tied in bundles at the seashore. You'll seed wheat and vegetables smartly after we land. Now take your oaths." Cristóbal motioned for a scribe to assist, and the farmer set his palms upon a crucifix and missal and solemnly—and jubilantly—pledged the obedience the scribe recited.

A carpenter with a family of six from Córdoba entered next.

"How many houses have you built?"

"Many, your excellent Admiral. I've been doing it all my life."

"I trust you're bringing your tools and equipment."

"I have them—a hammer, saw, files, an ax and chisels for log splitting, and some shovels. I can use the shovels to assist with the gold mining."

"We'll need a church, a royal warehouse for the gold, and my command house built right away. The mines may require lots of shovels, lots of labor. Take your oaths."

A well-dressed middle-aged gentleman volunteer from the outskirts of Seville entered third, bowing properly.

"How do you intend to help?" Cristóbal asked.

"Your Admiralship, I led men at Granada's siege last year, and I'd be proud to assist you in the leadership of the men on Española."

"Understand that I'm going to conquer and won't return right away," Cristóbal counseled. "Men suffer deprivations and disease when settling foreign lands." For an instant, he recalled his voyage to Mina a decade earlier and the diseases that beset its garrison and fed its graveyard. "Most who sail to Mina never return, and the mosquitoes plague those who survive."

"I embrace these challenges and the glory of overcoming them for the king and queen."

"Española's gold will be theirs, and its natives their vassals. Your duty is to that end."

"It's my honor to serve. I trust I may take servants among the natives? I'm not bringing my own."

"In due course," Cristóbal affirmed. "We must establish the settlement and the queen's dominion first." He had received this question often—not only from the gentlemen aspiring lordship over naked heathens but from peasants and artisans keen on alleviating their daily hardship. He perceived the inquiry as reflecting the just, instinctive desire of all men who conquered, since Creation. "The Indians are intelligent but docile and will make good servants when the time comes. You'll find them easy to boss about."

As the morning waned, a short, wiry young man with wide eyes confidently ignored the applicant line and strutted onto the gangplank, impudently vaunting that the Admiral awaited him. He was an old acquaintance of Cristóbal's with a rare confluence of credentials—Cristóbal respected him, Fonseca recommended him, and the queen knew of him.

Alonso de Hojeda (b. ca. 1470) had met Cristóbal four years earlier when they both served the Duke of Medinaceli, the seaborne merchant of Puerto de Santa María (near Cádiz) who had intended to sponsor Colón's first voyage before the sovereigns so committed.* Cristóbal welcomed his enlistment, as well as a more intimate and sophisticated conversation.

"I trust the Indies' gold entices you," Cristóbal posed with a wry smile. "Or is it adventure you seek? Or danger?" Alonso was renowned in Seville for having caught the queen's attention by walking deftly before her on a beam high atop Seville's cathedral, risking a plunge to certain death.

"The gold and the marvels of the Indies," Alonso replied cautiously. "I can do whatever you need done, on land or at sea." Years earlier, he'd afforded Colón the respect due age but nothing more, judging Colón an impoverished washout. He winced whether Colón had perceived the scorn. "I come to express my loyalty to the king, queen, and yourself, now my admiral."

"I'm glad for that," Cristóbal affirmed, noting the circumspection but reminded of his friend's slyness. "As you can see, the king and queen have rewarded me well for the success I've brought them. In turn, I'll well reward those loyal to me."

"You can count on me for that, my lord," Alonso assured. A memory of Colón railing against detractors shot through his thoughts, and he cowered to imagine the punishment Colón might inflict on a critic aboard the voyage. But Alonso maintained an impassive visage. "I applaud your singular vision and appreciate the challenges looming. I will stand at your side, throughout."

They discussed Alonso's impressions of the fleet and recruits for some moments, and Cristóbal inquired what he had done with

*Luis de la Cerda.

himself recently. Alonso's youth had been strewn with quarrels and scrapes, Alonso always drawing first blood, and Cristóbal probed to confirm that the impetuousness could be harnessed. Recognizing energetic competence and brazen ambition, Cristóbal bid the oath be taken and awarded responsibility.

"You'll captain one of the ships," Cristóbal pronounced, observing Alonso's immediate grin of satisfaction. "The crews are local, and you're bound to know some. I'll hand you and the other captains my sailing orders when we depart the Canaries. Until then, we need absolute secrecy, as the port abounds with João's informants."

Most of the fleet's sailors had been recruited in Palos and the neighboring Andalusian ports, as on the first voyage, and more than twenty of the fifty-some crewmen who'd returned to Spain on the first voyage had enlisted again, confident in trusting their fortunes to their admiral. A few Niños would sail—including Juan, the *Nina*'s owner, and Pero Alonso, the lost *Santa María*'s pilot—as well as Juan de la Cosa, the lost *Santa María*'s owner and master. There were some Basques, Galicians, and a few Genoese. But Pinzóns hadn't sought enlistment, nor would Cristóbal have accepted them, never forgiving Martín Alonso Pinzón's and the *Pinta*'s desertion off Cuba during the first voyage.

After the final interview, Cristóbal commenced his daily inspection of the fleet's provisions and trading truck. The dockside now teemed with stevedores hustling through myriad stacks of cargo as ships berthed one by one at the quay to load barrels of water and wine, jugs of oil and vinegar, and the bulk foodstuffs—crates of biscuits, cheese, and salted bacon; casks of cured beef carcass; sacks of wheat, flour, barley, rice, chickpeas, lentils, and garlic; and boxes of nuts and raisins. It wasn't practical to examine each item—which the accountants might do when approving payment—but Cristóbal and his staff pried open or untied an occasional crate or sack to permit a peek, sniff, or taste of the contents. They also glanced inside the chests containing the trading truck, consisting largely of the trifles the Indians had favored receiving on the first voyage, including hawks' bells, skullcaps, bead necklaces, and gloves. The sovereigns' May 29 instructions required that all trade in the Indies be conducted by bartering these or other goods on behalf of the sovereigns, with every transaction concluded in Cristóbal's or a subordinate's presence, together with the voyage's accounting staff—to keep Cristóbal and everyone else honest. The sovereigns had appointed Bernal de Pisa as the chief accountant sailing, responsible for reporting to the chief accountant in Seville, and they'd expressly warned Pisa not to exceed his responsibilities in any way.

Tasting a biscuit, Cristóbal mused that what he saw this day was acceptable, and he grudgingly admitted to himself that Archdeacon Fonseca was providing what was required. But he stewed that Fonseca had second-guessed or delayed responding to his requests too many times to be trusted, and he rankled that the biscuit's provisioner—his own financier, Juanoto Berardi—was easier to work with and better incented as financier to promote Cristóbal's success than a crown minister. For an instant, Cristóbal chafed that Berardi also was far more experienced than Fonseca in overseas conquest, well proven in trading most goods anywhere ships sailed. Berardi had built his reputation on trading slaves from distant and heathen Guinea, and it had been Berardi who had taken responsibility for lodging the Indian interpreters brought to Spain on the first voyage when in Seville. The biscuit was hard and fresh—hardtack at its best, baked to endure moisture and heat to provide nourishment for months—just as Cristóbal had expected.

In the afternoon, when others rested, Cristóbal dismissed his staff and boarded a launch to review the ships last commissioned, berthing first alongside one of the smaller caravels. Those on deck respectfully stood at attention, and Cristóbal inquired of the ranking officer what of the caravel was fit, what wasn't, and what was being done. Cristóbal gaited about the deck, scrutinizing the ship as he listened to the response, and then added his own commands.

"Reset the boom port of the mast," he ordered, pointing to a small lateen sail. "You'll take tailwind mostly to starboard as we cross." The insight impressed the caravel's pilot, who nodded gratefully.

"Replace the rudder, less draft, more extension astern," he barked. "You'll course shallows more safely when we explore Cathay's coastline." The caravel's tillerman recognized the improvement and saluted to indicate concurrence.

"After the Canaries, add seawater to the ballast as the wine and water are spent," he instructed. "The crossing's so long you'll float too high otherwise." The caravel's boatswain bowed to register assent, humbled to obey.

Cristóbal sensed the crews' kinship and trust, as they appreciated he'd braved the sea, just as they. They adulated him—not as the captain general of the fleet, nor as the sovereigns' admiral, but as the greatest mariner alive. He ordered some adjustments to the rigging, which, as his previous commands, they received as truths, and then departed for other ships.

As the sun dipped west, Cristóbal returned ashore to coordinate the embarkation of the professional soldiers, who had established makeshift barracks about a plaza nearby the sailors' pubs and brothels. There were two contingents, one that he perceived respected his authority and another not. A gentleman from the queen's household commanded the first, a troop of foot soldiers, bowmen, and gunmen with light body armor.* Their weaponry included swords, crossbows, and artillery, including *harquebuses* (handheld muskets), *falconets* (small swivel cannons), and *lombards* (larger cannons), as well as a vicious supplement of two dozen attack dogs. The second was a squad of twenty mounted horsemen with heavier body armor and lances, selected at the sovereigns' direction from a proud brotherhood—the Lanzas Jinetas (horseback lancers)—of the Hermandad, some knighted. Cristóbal gleaned the horses and hounds would strike terror in the Indians, as they knew neither, possessing but small, barkless dogs.

As Cristóbal approached, the gentleman brought his men to stand at attention, and the Lanzas' commander also rose, although he left his men as they were, some tending their horses, others lounging. Cristóbal advised both that their units be prepared to sail before month's end and identified the ships onto which they and their animals should embark the afternoon prior to departure.

"Confirm the sufficiency of the corrals, both above and below deck," Cristóbal ordered the Lanzas' commander.

"We won't sail unless they're adequate," the commander responded. He lingered, sipping from a flask, and added, "We've brought five mares to replenish the twenty mounts, and they'll have to be corralled separately."

*The gentleman was Bartolomé de Las Casas's uncle, Francisco de Peñalosa.

Cristóbal nodded. "Confirm the sufficiency of the hay, oats, and water to be stowed."

"Obviously. We're always prepared when we serve the queen."

The men parted professionally, but Cristóbal's resentment surged that the commander dismissed the sea's conquest as a glory inferior to routing an enemy. The commander's disdain for the Genoese commoner swelled likewise.

Unsatisfied but tiring, Cristóbal strode south from the port toward the accommodations he'd arranged for his family in Cádiz's old town, with the same Genoese trading families who had sheltered him almost two decades prior—after the sinking of a merchant ship on which he'd served (1476). He passed through the gates of the ancient city wall and merchant bazaars to arrive at a small mansion just down the street from Cádiz's principal church, the Cathedral of the Holy Cross, in whose garden the seven surviving Indians he'd brought from the Indies were encamped.

Cristóbal's sons, thirteen-year-old Diego and five-year-old Fernando, sidled affably beside him as he entered the vestibule, and their banter briefly cheered him. Cristóbal's wife and Diego's mother, Filipa, had died a decade prior, and Cristóbal had discarded Fernando's mother, Beatriz, after a relationship of seven years.* Thoughtfully, Queen Isabel had arranged for the boys' care after he departed, providing a house in Seville confiscated by the Inquisition for Cristóbal's sister-in-law, Violante Moniz, with whom the boys would live until the following year. Isabel then would receive them at court to serve as pages to Prince Juan.

After sunset, Violante called all to supper, where they were joined at the table by her husband, who would sail on the voyage.† Over the summer, Cristóbal had dispatched letters to his two younger surviving brothers, recounting the triumph of his first voyage and ascent to nobility, imploring them to join the second and conquer and rule the Indies with him. Diego (b. ca. 1466) eagerly had departed Genoa and fate as a wool weaver to reunite with Cristóbal in Seville and now sat at the dinner table, but Bartolomé (b. ca. 1461) hadn't responded, his whereabouts and receipt of the letter uncertain. Cristóbal had

*Filipa Moniz Perestrelo and Beatriz Enríquez de Arana.
†Miguel Muliarte.

lost hope Bartolomé would arrive to sail, and he'd entrusted Violante with a letter instructing Bartolomé to contact Berardi and escort the boys to court when he showed up.

After dinner, when others lay to sleep, Cristóbal slipped from the mansion to worship at the church's Genoese chapel. As he approached, he scanned the church garden where his Indian interpreters slept, all naked according to their custom, regardless of having spent months in Spain. The two most dependable were seated together in the moonlight, teenagers seized on the island he'd named San Salvador, apparently healthy enough to be conversing—which was precisely why they were critical to conquest, perhaps even more so than the fleet's weaponry. The sovereigns had no objection to the youths' enslavement as interpreters, practiced by the Portuguese for decades and conquerors of foreign lands since Creation, and justified by that utility alone. Cristóbal waved, and he was pleased they waved back, albeit wanly. He wondered whether they were reminiscing of San Salvador, which they called Guanahaní.

Cristóbal knelt before the chapel's altar to pray. The pope's pronouncements had applauded him as Christianity's beloved son for discovering new peoples to be brought to the faith, as well as King Fernando and Queen Isabel for their inflamed devotion for so sponsoring. He'd asked Fernando and Isabel to dispatch friars to convert the Indians, and they'd responded in their May 29 instructions that conversion was their first charge to him. Cristóbal venerated the altar cross and realized that he hadn't reviewed the arrangements for the missionaries sailing that day.

For an instant, he felt Christ gazing skeptically back, not for this failure—which readily could be cured in the morning—but for one as to which time had run out, just as it had for Bartolomé's arrival. Regardless of pronouncements, inflammations, and instructions, of the twelve hundred recruits enlisted—and after hundreds more had been rejected—the sovereigns and Fray Buil had recruited but a mere dozen priests and friars to sail.

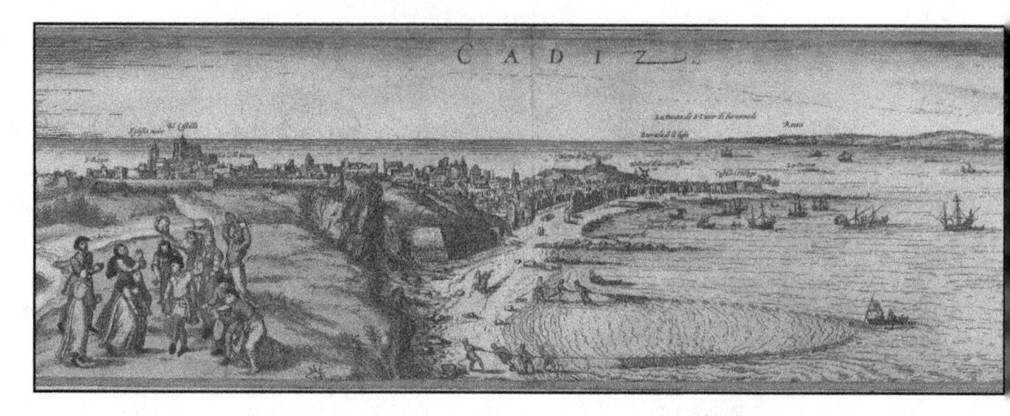

Cádiz in the sixteenth century. Civitates Orbis Terrarum.

Bakako and Yutowa,
Cádiz (Mid-September 1493)

The two Taíno youths sat beside the pale men's church in the semidarkness of moonlit heavens, staring despondently into the small garden of flowers and fruit trees about them. In their people's tradition, their black hair remained cut short above the ears, with a few strands dangling untouched at the back. After Admiral departed, they continued their conversation.

"They must have two kinds of *behiques* [shamans]," Yutowa rasped hoarsely.

"Most speak to their spirits," replied fourteen-year-old Bakako, the younger and shorter of the two, nodding. "But the first who came yesterday focused only on the body." Bakako considered the latter practice mysterious, and he was gratified that Yutowa's observation confirmed his own.

"None have healed us."

"But we'll make it home," Bakako responded quickly, concerned that his friend not plummet into the despair that frequently gripped him and their five companions. "Admiral said we'll depart in days. You should rest."

Yutowa obliged and lay back on the grass, the ground still warm from the day's bright sun. The others apparently were sleeping, and

Bakako glanced to confirm they weren't simply suffering mutely. Seven of the ten Taínos who'd crossed the ocean remained to cross back, five—including Bakako—who'd traveled over the summer to the city the pale men called Barcelona and two—including Yutowa—who'd remained in Seville, too sick to travel. Their leader, Xamabo, a nitaíno related to Guacanagarí, slumbered close by, and his breath was the most belabored. The others were scattered among the tree trunks and flowerbeds, captives abducted with Bakako and Yutowa on Guanahaní or on Haiti's eastern peninsula, Samaná. Of the three missing, two had died in Seville, their emaciated bodies laced with reddish welts and scabs of white puss, a pestilence more horrific than Bakako had ever witnessed.* Yutowa and another had been similarly stricken yet survived, their skin grotesquely disfigured by pocks, as if they'd been born ugly as iguanas. The last of the ten—Abasu, seized by Admiral on Cuba—would remain in Spain forever, captive to Admiral's caciques, Fernando and Isabel.

All in the garden were feverous and nauseous, coughing and racked by chills and pains from head to foot, those not pocked dreading that pocks would scourge them, too.† The day before, Admiral and a behique named Chanca had visited the garden to examine their bodies and offer remedies. Chanca would accompany the voyage home, Admiral had explained, as he possessed superior knowledge, having served as behique for Fernando and Isabel's eldest daughter, Princess Isabel. Chanca had ordered them to use the pale men's blankets to stay warm, and he'd served them a potion of honey, herbs, and horseradish. Admiral also had brought traditional behiques to the garden, including one named Pané, who'd invoked the Christ and Virgin spirits for their recovery.

"They're trying very hard to save us," Yutowa observed bitterly, refusing to sleep. "Because Admiral needs us. As his tongue and ears."

Bakako sighed, aware his friend was correct. But he chose to not answer, sapped by his own affliction and resigned that his friend lament.

"Shouldn't the Christ-spirit have healed you by now?" Yutowa persisted. "You've honored him."

*Either chicken pox or smallpox?

†Pneumonia?

Bakako faltered uneasily before responding. The assertion, rather than the question, had gnawed him from the moment of his so-called baptism ceremony that summer, when he, Xamabo, and the others in Barcelona had submitted to the pale caciques' instruction to honor the Christ-spirit. At the time, he'd known the pale men believed their spirits were the only spirits and that a person's baptism acknowledged that. But he and the others had never forsaken Yúcahu, Attabeira, or any other Taíno spirit, and he'd acquiesced in the pale men's ceremony as a matter of necessity, not conviction. The insincerity unnerved him, and he quailed Admiral's men would disapprove if they knew and that the Christ-spirit could be jealous and vengeful.

"I've prayed to him, but I've chosen to honor Yúcahu and our spirits in preference to him. So have Xamabo, Abasu, and the rest of us who were 'baptized.' I can invoke the Christ-spirit whenever I wish and seek his healing—for myself, you, and all of us—and I've done so. But I'm not sure he hears or cares. He's the pale men's spirit."

"Do you mind when Admiral calls you Diego?" Yutowa asked, referring to the name designated for Bakako during the baptism ceremony.

"All the pale men call me Diego, Diego Colón. They think I've been born a second time—as a 'Christian'—to be devoted to their Christ-spirit forever, and that Diego is now my name, replacing Bakako. It's the same name as Admiral's brother and son. Xamabo received the name of their cacique, Fernando. Abasu, the name of Fernando's son. The concept is primitive."

"It's arrogant. But do you mind?"

"I don't like it. They intend it as an honor. But it's demeaning—replacing my true name with a pale man's name, as if I were our captor's beloved son and image, as opposed to his slave." Bakako's anguish hardened to anger and resolution, and he raised his voice. "Regardless, I will stomach it—and whatever else necessary to survive and return to Guanahaní." He was silent for a moment and then reached to caress Yutowa's shoulder. "Call me Bakako."

"I'd have been baptized, just as you, if they hadn't left me behind," Yutowa solaced. "This morning, while you were gone, the friendly behique Pané returned to teach about the Christ-spirit. He asked whether I thought there was a spirit who made all things and created the heaven and the earth."

"Admiral's always telling people we believe that—when he's imagining we're eager to worship the Christ-spirit."

"It's possible—the heavens and the earth could have been made by a spirit." Curiosity brought a slight vigor, and Yutowa rose to sit again.

"When I was baptized, they told me their own spirit did it—the Lord-spirit," Bakako observed. "That's what Pané told you?"

"Yes, but he didn't push it. He simply asked if I thought it made sense."

"It just as well could have been one of our own spirits." Bakako reflected on his boyhood learning about Yaya, the spirit to whom all other spirits answered, present at the sea's creation and resident in the heavens, while Yúcahu and other spirits worked on earth. "Yutowa, the pale behiques will urge their spirits and baptism to you. Remember that you've survived your life—and this horror—by honoring our own spirits and with their protection. I'd avoid baptism—so long as you have the choice. You may continue to worship our spirits—and theirs, if you wish—without it."

Yutowa didn't respond. As the silence extended, Bakako's distrust of the behiques drew him inward to reflect more broadly—and tortuously—on the ordeal that now imprisoned him. He'd spent the last six months in Spain trailing Admiral, and he and his companions had studied the pale men's world carefully. They were awed and humbled by the pale men's exceptional know-how and tremendous industry. The inventiveness of their devices was extraordinary. "Wheels" affixed to wood platforms or bins for portage of most anything! "Paper," "quills," and "dyes" for communicating speech silently! Metals bent in fire into cooking pans, tools, and incredibly powerful weaponry! The beasts they ate and mastered in farming and other labor were astonishing.

But Bakako and the others also had perceived a shocking lack of civility and brutality among the pale men themselves, pervasive throughout their lands. There was an ever-present construction of walls about ports, villages, and homes for protection—from other pale men. They maintained a selfish precept that food wasn't common property and those without could be left to hunger! They burned to death those not believing in the Christ-spirit! They used slaves in their households and daily work, and most slaves weren't pale but either astonishingly black-skinned or, ominously, olive-skinned, as Taínos.

Bakako gazed at the moon and shuddered indignantly that the pale men appeared utterly unconcerned that he and his companions now understood Admiral's intentions—or, more contemptuously, held their wit too dim for understanding. The cacique Fernando had responded to Xamabo's request for an exclusive trading relationship with but platitudes, and Admiral professed the weapons provisioned were for use against Caribes and any Portuguese. Yet he and Yutowa had become proficient in the pale men's tongue, and Admiral's intent to possess, rule, and trade throughout the Taíno homeland had been expressed in his daily conversations for months. Since arriving in Cádiz, they'd wandered about the quays to advise Xamabo of the provisions arriving and other clues—a reconnaissance that hadn't been precarious, as voyagers perceived they were following Admiral's instructions. They and Xamabo had long since discerned that Admiral sought to subjugate the entirety of Haiti and to compel Guacanagarí's submission to Fernando and Isabel. The presence of so many soldiers, farmers, beasts, and artisans incontrovertibly manifested a plan to construct a permanent establishment on Haiti the likes of which Guacanagarí had never remotely imagined.

Xamabo stirred and requested water, propping himself on his elbows. Bakako rose to attend and gently held a jug to his lips.

"What more did we learn today?" he asked. Bakako had departed the garden as informant that morning, Yutowa that afternoon. Bakako had even ambled aboard the flagship, welcome as Admiral's favorite interpreter.

"'Cows,' 'sheep,' and a few 'mules' were corralled in pens today," Bakako replied.

"They're bringing seed for their 'wheat' and 'barley,' as well as saplings for their fruit trees and vines," added Yutowa.

"The cacique Isabel has sent cloth for a 'church' they intend to build and a large 'bell' for it," Bakako noted. "I overheard that a house will be built for Admiral, as well as a house to store the gold."

"Are they bringing their womenfolk?" inquired Xamabo.

"Only Admiral's naboria, perhaps a few others," Bakako replied, shrugging his shoulders.

Xamabo beheld the heavens. The absence of women voyagers was striking, foreboding that the pale men would take Taíno women as their own. "Who will do their household work?" he asked. "Are they bringing slaves?"

Bakako and Yutowa shook their heads, and Xamabo cursed, jarred by the threat looming. Coughing, he released his elbows to lie again and soon slumbered.

The two teenagers contemplated the stars, and memories of their youths fondly and sadly flickered through their thoughts. Bakako remembered his girl on Guanahaní, Kamana. He missed her, and a vision of her dancing naked before him at Guanahaní's southern tip now soothed him, expunging other thoughts. She had recited verses from a wedding areíto she was practicing, giggling that her part was mostly to coo as a bird, although at the very end she got to sing as a human being. The innocence of Kamana's face when she said those words charmed him for some moments. But then beyond consciousness, obscured from precise articulation, a pang of revulsion shot through Bakako's body, his heart missed a beat, and his image of Kamana abruptly vanished. Slowly, he grasped that being perceived as human now was at stake.

Somewhere above, perhaps in a tree or the church steeple, an owl hooted. The two teenagers stared warily into each other's eyes and then lay to sleep.

GUACANAGARÍ,
Guarico, Marien

Guacanagarí sat with his brother in the central plaza of Guarico, the village from which he governed (now Bord de Mer de Limonade, Haiti), seething as a messenger delivered Caonabó's contemptuous warning. He wasn't surprised that Caonabó had executed the pale men trespassing in Maguana. Nor with Caonabó's demand that he execute those dozen remaining in Guarico. But the threat Caonabó would invade Marien to assassinate those dozen violated

Guacanagarí's sovereignty and brandished the scorn that Caonabó and other supreme caciques had directed toward him, his caciqual family, and their rule of Marien for decades. Almost forty, Guacanagarí acridly recalled the rude dismissal he'd received a decade earlier—from another messenger—that Caonabó had won Anacaona's hand in marriage.

"Tell your master that I view his decisions in Maguana as rightfully his own folly," Guacanagarí admonished the messenger. "But caution him not to lead a single warrior into my chiefdom, as I will massacre any and all of them."

As the messenger was shunted away, Guacanagarí reflected that Gutiérrez, Escobedo, and their gang had deserved their fate. Their execution was appropriate justice for their vile conduct, and, while Guacanagarí hadn't wished it, he realized that it gave him satisfaction. He'd warned them repeatedly against quitting his chiefdom and even admonished that Caonabó would slay them. But they, too, had disdained him, rejecting the relationship he'd initiated to trade gold in favor of a relationship with Caonabó.

"Let's talk privately," his brother, Matuma, suggested.

Guacanagarí surmised Matuma's concern, and the two ambled to Guarico's great beach on Haiti's northern shore. Matuma had faithfully assisted Guacanagarí's rule for over a dozen years, attending Caonabó and Anacaona's marriage when Guacanagarí shirked it and participating in Admiral's rescue when his vessel sank.

"Why risk confrontation with Caonabó over the remaining pale men?" Matuma asked deferentially. "We despise their presence among us, and they deserve death anyway."

"We must let them survive through Admiral's return, so he favors trading exclusively with us. If he never returns, they'll perish soon enough—some of scabs [syphilis], since they dismiss the cure we've shown them." Three pale men had died of it over the summer.

"Admiral might accept your innocence if your subjects simply avenged themselves, without your participation," Matuma observed. "Just as you're blameless for the deaths of the pale men who departed east."

Guacanagarí didn't respond. After Gutiérrez and Escobedo's departure, the worst band of Admiral's men—pillagers, lechers, and spirit defilers led by the *Santa María*'s boatswain, the brazen Chachu—had straggled east to the Yaque River.* Guacanagarí hadn't interfered or even condemned when his vassal caciques had dispensed their own justice, massacring the entire band and torturing some, including binding one's hands to a wooden cross in mockery of the pale men's Christ-spirit.

"Your vassal caciques urge the pale men's elimination," Matuma persisted. "Permit them to do it, instead of yourself. If you don't, they may welcome Caonabó's trespass. Mayreni might have invited that already."

Guacanagarí pondered silently, gazing west along the beach toward the mountainous cape (Point Picolet, at Cape Haitien, Haiti) that majestically towered over the intervening farmland, proud of his realm. He recalled he was standing at the very spot where he and Admiral had first discussed their peoples' friendship. Beholden for Guacanagarí's rescue, Admiral had promised a trading relationship, protection from the Caribes, and to take Xamabo to meet the caciques Fernando and Isabel.

"I won't permit our subjects to harm the remaining pale men," Guacanagarí finally judged, recalling the promise he'd made in return. "I gave Admiral my word that I'd protect his men. I'll honor that—as far as the men who've relied on my protection."

Guacanagarí pivoted to the sea, seeking solitude. "Inform my nitaínos that I've warned Caonabó to back off. We await Xamabo's return to recount how he struck friendship with Admiral's caciques." Anticipating Matuma's discontent, he added, "We must always proclaim our sovereignty, regardless of whether we intervene to protect the pale men."

As waves broke on the barrier reef before him, Guacanagarí jealously rued that the respect and courtesy Admiral had shown for him in but a few weeks—even complimenting his civility and grace—exceeded that displayed by other supreme caciques over a lifetime.

*The river retains its Taíno name today.

Guarico and Navidad. Panel from cover page of Herrera's *Historia General*, vol. 2, 1601.

Pope Alexander VI, Dudum Siquidem (Bull of Extension),

Vatican, Rome (September 25, 1493)

Seated in a private residence of the Papal Palace, His Holiness Alexander VI—born in Játiva, Aragón (near Valencia)—reflected on the risks to his reign and papal authority posed by the ever-changing ambitions and alliances of Italian and foreign princes, shrewdly weighing the utility of satisfying Fernando and Isabel's plea for yet another proclamation relating to the Indies. He'd already issued them four that summer. That morning, the curia's staff had brought for his approval the parchment setting forth yet a proposed fifth, reflecting the past month's discussions with the Spanish ambassadors. At sixty-two, Alexander's expertise in crafting policies and blessings to augment both the church's and his family's power and wealth were renowned—infamous, to his steeled critics—and he considered for the last time whether this new grant was the right action, at the right time, to those ends.

Alexander was well versed in the bulls awarded Portugal's Prince Henrique and King João. He'd examined them not only that summer—when granting Fernando and Isabel dominion over Colón's discoveries—but upon their very issuance to Henrique decades prior (1456), when Alexander had begun his Vatican training, and then to João (1481), after he had risen to prominent papal authority. Alexander had first come to Rome to assist his uncle upon the latter's ascension to the papacy as Pope Calixtus III in 1455, just before issuance of Prince Henrique's bull, and his uncle had soon appointed him a cardinal and vice chancellor of the papal government. Unambiguously, these bulls had granted Portugal exclusive jurisdiction to traffic along Guinea south of the Canaries all the way east to the Indies.

The parchment before him baldly undid this grant, extending Isabel and Fernando's exclusive territory to include all islands or mainland discovered west, east, or south of the Canaries or in the Indies themselves if not actually then possessed by the Portuguese, wholly revoking all earlier inconsistent papal grants to lands discovered but not possessed. The text was short and to the point, dispensing with the customary accolades for the Hispanic sovereigns' efforts to bring infidels and heathens to the faith.

Alexander was pleased the proposed bull offered a hand to Fernando without a slap to France's King Charles, offending only João, who ruled a smaller kingdom. With experience of three decades, Alexander well understood papal authority was served when the powers of Italian princes were balanced, diffused, and free of foreign influence and that the friendship of the possessor of the Neapolitan throne—whoever it might be—was critical to papal security. Charles's rude insistence on taking it, and the formidable army he could muster, threatened to destroy that balance and friendship. Alexander had no doubt that Fernando—his countryman, steadfast supporter, and vested with an interest in that throne—was the most likely powerful counterweight and friend, making it prudent to extend him yet another assistance and victory, while not harming or inciting Charles.

More darkly, Alexander also desperately reflected that his very papacy now was at risk, not just the Neapolitan throne. King Charles had secured the loyalty of Alexander's implacable long-time rival, Cardinal Giuliano della Rovere, who'd also risen to Vatican prominence through nepotistic appointment years earlier by a papal uncle, Sixtus IV. Alexander had prevailed to take the papacy upon Pope Innocent VIII's death in 1492, triumphing by doling out benefices, land, and gold to the cardinals voting to a degree exceeding prior practice, thwarting Giuliano's opposition, which Charles had supported. A pope's authority might be challenged, and his reign deposed, if a general council of the church so chose, and rumors now abounded that—with Charles's support—Rovere would seek Alexander's removal on the grounds of the electoral simony. Rovere and his supporters—particularly those cardinals who hadn't received Alexander's payments—had escalated an outcry over Alexander's simony, as well as his nepotism, promiscuity, and extravagant lifestyle, which mostly did exceed their own. Rodrigo had flouted chastity and zealously womanized since youth, his potent presence and virility a magnet drawing beautiful women to lie with him within but moments, and he'd fathered at least seven children. His current lover was a delight of twenty-some years.*

Alexander rose to stroll and ordered that the bull be issued the following morning. His entitlement to call upon Fernando with respect to Naples would be enhanced without openly opposing Charles's ambition for it. As he ambled through the Sistine Chapel, Alexander was moved to reflect that God and the church were strengthened by the division of the world just accomplished and the attendant reaffirmation that the papacy was supreme in awarding the dominions of Christian princes. He also grimly observed that he much preferred an unambitious local ruler at his doorstep on the Neapolitan throne to either the king of France or Spain.

*Giulia Farnese.

II
SECOND CROSSING

CRISTÓBAL, CÁDIZ TO SAN SEBASTIAN,
Gomera (Canary Islands), September 25–October 13, 1493

Admiral Cristóbal Colón's fleet of seventeen ships, together with its naval escort, weighed anchor in Cádiz's harbor at dawn on September 25, triumphantly flying the sovereigns' standards beneath fireworks pluming the sky. Trumpets and horns blared ashore, flutists and lyrists jigged aboard, and cannons ashore and aboard roared back and forth. Days before, those aboard had confessed their sins and parted optimistically and tearfully from their loved ones, enthralled to seize the opportunity of a lifetime. Pride burst of the Spanish kingdoms' ascension in the world, the correctness of Spanish custom and tradition, and the trueness and supremacy of Christianity.

Cristóbal's sons and noblemen waved goodbye from the high parapets of the town's castle, the youths entranced their father would found their legacy on a distant land, the courtiers confident their sovereigns' rule would be imposed upon it.* Aboard ship, Bakako, Yutowa, and Xamabo beheld the exaltation with foreboding, perceiving the hubris and avarice of a war dance, dreading how the civilization they'd witnessed would descend upon that of their heritage. Their own destinies remained frightfully indiscernible,

*The castle, Castillo de la Villa de Cádiz, no longer exists.

subject to Admiral's whim and command and the outcome of the looming collision of peoples they knew to be at hand.

The fleet departed smartly in favorable wind, and Cristóbal set the course southwest for Gran Canaria, ill and fatigued. But the departure's pomp gratified him immensely, and he was invigorated to be at sea, the home he knew best, liberated from the haggle and compromise with Fonseca to become fully Admiral—his dictate promptly obeyed. Brother Diego's presence aboard the *María Galante* comforted him. He was cheered by the camaraderie of a childhood friend, Michele da Cuneo (b. 1450), a genial, well-educated Ligurian from Savona (near Genoa) of means and purported ancestral nobility, who'd enlisted game for sharing a new adventure. He also was fortified that two of his personal servants on the first voyage, the steward Pedro de Terreros and page Pedro de Salcedo, continued at his side, true beyond doubt and well experienced in spying the moods and frights—and loyalties—of men under duress. His trusted Guinean manservant, Juan Portugués, had been left behind to serve his sons, but a chambermaid, María Fernández, would attend instead, one of merely a handful of women aboard the fleet. He focused more on his Indians' persistent illnesses than his own discomfort, and he'd berthed the most important of them on the *María Galante* under the physician Diego Alvarez Chanca's watch—Xamabo, Bakako and Yutowa, and the best interpreter seized on Española's eastern Samaná peninsula.

Each ship carried a few cats to reduce its rat infestation and protect the foodstuffs, and by nightfall, the customary frugal rationing of food, water, and a mug of wine per day was imposed throughout the fleet. At that moment, Cristóbal was satisfied with the fleet's provisions and livestock, and, as far he knew, so was the voyage's chief accountant, Bernal de Pisa. Cristóbal intended to purchase pigs, goats, and more chickens when they laid over at Gomera, the final Canarian landfall before the crossing. The cows and sheep already aboard were important to the settlement's food and clothing supply, but they were less adaptable, requiring grassland. Pigs could be seeded most anywhere but dry savannah or desert and would eat most anything growing or habiting grassland, forest, or jungle, and the sows routinely produced litters of up to ten, ensuring rapid growth of the supply. Goats and chickens had similar adaptability and fecundity.

In Cádiz, Cristóbal had reviewed the geography of the Indies with Bakako, Yutowa, and the Samanán captive briefly, seeking to determine the Indian islands farthest east—to which the route from Gomera across the ocean would be the shortest. That evening, he bid his page Pedro to summon the three of them to his private quarters to decide the matter, seated at his feet in the glow of candlelight.

"Last January, we departed Española—which you call Bohío or Haiti—to search for islands you call Matininó and Carib," Cristóbal reminded, enunciating slowly in Spanish, believing the latter two to be islands identified by Marco Polo in the Indian seas, one where women lived alone, the other only men.* "But we didn't find them. You've said they're east of Española—and that there're many other islands east and south of Española. How many days' journey by canoe from Española to these islands?"

"I no know day's journey canoe," Bakako responded in Spanish, accustomed to Admiral's penchant for reconsidering geographical questions.

"No many days," Yutowa replied.

"Some no many days. Some many days," the Samanán added, repeating what he'd told Admiral before.

"How do you know that?" Cristóbal asked, gazing at the Samanán. "Have you ever been there?"

"No. Never. I slaved. I eaten," the Samanán responded. Bakako and Yutowa had explained to Admiral many times that the Caribes who lived in Carib and neighboring islands were an enemy people, who would kill, enslave, or eat them.

Cristóbal nodded. "Then how do you know some islands are many days from Española?"

The Samanán searched for words in Admiral's tongue. "We capture Caribe. Before kill, talk. Caribe say many days."

"East? Southeast?"

The Samanán nodded.

---

*Islands of Males and Females.

"Will we find islands in the ocean ten days' journey by canoe east of Española?" Cristóbal lifted his hands, spreading his fingers and thumbs.

"I think yes," the Samanán replied. "Two hands' days' journey."*

"Will we find a great shoreline?" Cristóbal probed. He'd understood from Bakako and Yutowa that a great coastline lay south of Española, perhaps a very large island.

"No," Bakako exclaimed. "Much, much far south."

Cristóbal bid Pedro serve each captive a biscuit with honey and water. "Diego, how do you feel today?"

"Still sick," Bakako replied.

Cristóbal glanced to the others, and they nodded, also affirming illness.

"When we arrive on the islands ten days' east, will we find Caribes—like on the island Carib?" he resumed, completing his inquiry. "Are there Caribes on all the islands east of Española?"

"I taught all Caribes, all islands," Bakako responded.

"Some yes. Some no," replied the Samanán.

Cristóbal patiently waited for his captives to finish their biscuits and then dismissed them. As the moon rose, he ascended to the flagship's poop deck to observe the fleet surging forward across a large swath of undulating, windblown ocean, pondering how many days he could risk searching for and exploring islands east of Española. Prompt return to Navidad was critical, not only to curtail the garrison's likely misconduct but to debark the vast number of landsmen and livestock onto Española. Confining them shipbound during a seaborne exploration would wear their patience and consume provisions while delaying the settlement's establishment and planting of crops. Cristóbal scanned the enormity of the heavens and beseeched the Lord that the men at Navidad had done their duty, identifying a site for a town near the island's gold mines and amassing a chest or two of gold for the sovereigns. If so, most of the fleet's ships could quickly return to Spain to reduce the sovereigns' expeditionary costs and prove to them he'd found the wealth of the Indies.

---

*Taínos may have used a vigesimal number system, i.e., based on twenty, where one "hand" was five, "two hands" ten, a "man" twenty, etc.

Though lookouts were vigilant, João's navy never appeared on the horizon that night or during the journey to the Canaries. Cristóbal had arranged a private room aboard the *María Galante* for Fray Buil, and the two men became acquainted over the passage. Cristóbal was a harsh judge of whether a friar's faith was as true as his own—rather than a veneer to achieve a comfortable post—and he found Fray Buil exemplary. Buil had entered the monastery at Monserrat (near Barcelona) in his youth to mature as a hermit priest in the neighboring mountains, his devoutness intensifying with age. While serving as Fernando's envoy in France, he'd joined the austere, hermetic Order of Minims, founded by Saint Francis of Paola and dedicated to a vow of Lenten abstinence, as well as those of poverty, chastity, and obedience. Fernando had even nominated him to establish his own hermitage before requesting that he sail to the Indies. As they chatted, Cristóbal appreciated Buil's sincerity and his selection by the sovereigns, but he puzzled whether Buil's inward focus and purity were temperaments suited to inspiring the naked heathens' conversion. They hadn't procured cleric enlistments on the voyage.

One evening, Cristóbal sat alone with Michele da Cuneo on the poop deck, reminiscing of their youth, marveling at Cristóbal's nobility and fame and the parting celebrations at Cádiz. Strong winds whistled through the rigging about them, muffling their voices from others, and, as the conversation grew intimate, Michele softly probed his friend's anxiety over the grand expectations burdening this acclaim.

"What's most important to please the Spanish king and queen?" he asked.

"Gold," Cristóbal flatly replied. Proclamations of faith aside, his fundamental assurance—and their fundamental expectation—was simply that.

"Converts to the faith?" Michele pressed. "Spices?"

"Gold alone will quash the need to satisfy any other expectations," Cristóbal responded. "It'll satisfy not only king and queen, but the financiers and all those sailing with us." He frowned. "The entire enterprise may rest on it."

"What about slaves? Genoa's noble families have amassed fortunes selling them, just as spices."

"The king and queen won't permit it yet." Cristóbal brooded—as he had time and again since the landfall at San Salvador—that enslaving and selling Indians could provide the wealth necessary to delight the sovereigns and everyone else, in lieu of gold. He chafed that João's Guinean slave trading had been blessed by popes, no less, and that Isabel and Fernando permitted Lugo and Berardi to finance the Canarian conquests by enslaving the Canarians.

"The conquered are the conquered, wherever they're from," Michele observed. "Why should the weak of the Indies be treated differently than those of Guinea, the Balkans, or the Holy Land? No Genoese or Venetian merchant would see the distinction."

"Nor Florentine nor Andalusian," Cristóbal responded. "Conquest has its entitlements. But the queen has spoken." He ruminated whether Isabel could accept enslaving Caribes—as enemies to her vassals on Española. The horrific evil of eating human flesh seemed reason enough to permit it, and he hoped his route would discover a great supply of them.

The fleet harbored in Gran Canaria on October 2, where sugar was stocked and a leaking ship repaired, and anchored in the tiny harbor at San Sebastian on Gomera on October 5. Cristóbal saluted his former lover, Beatriz de Peraza, governess of the island for her son, with cannon shot and fireworks, which she reciprocated with great festivities, but nothing more. Cristóbal was grateful for the pageantry and not otherwise disappointed, for he no longer held passions for women. He'd achieved nobility without one, and his zeal had narrowed to but his Indian enterprise and faith.

Fresh water and wood were brought aboard, and Cristóbal arranged the purchase of eight pigs for seventy maravedís each, as well as the goats and chickens, a few yearling calves and sheep, and other supplies. The naval escort sailed back for Cádiz, responsible for transporting Granada's former Mohammedan leadership to exile in Africa. Cristóbal entrusted sealed sailing instructions to the captains of his fleet's other ships, to be opened only if lost from the *María Galante* at sea, preserving—to the utmost—the route's secrecy from those João could bribe to reveal it.

Cristóbal also took the opportunity to better acquaint himself with these captains' loyalties. In addition to Pedro Margarite and

Alonso de Hojeda, they included important courtiers appointed to serve in Española, including—undoubtedly—as the eyes and ears of others in Spain. One was a supply provisioner who'd worked in Isabel's household, Juan Aguado, and another a gentleman who'd fought in the Reconquista and served Fonseca, Ginés de Gorvalán. There was a city councilman who'd served on Isabel's staff during the Reconquista and helped provision the fleet, Alonso Sánchez de Carvajal. There was a crown overseer appointed to work with the voyage's treasurer and accountant, the gentleman Diego Marquez.

By October 13—a year and a day after Cristóbal's landing on San Salvador—the twelve hundred voyagers, crowded with baying livestock, sailed beyond Hierro, the westernmost of the Canaries, to make the landless crossing to the Indies he had shown possible. Save seven, almost all placed their trust in their Lord for a safe passage.

Though the voyagers weren't conscious of it, there also were unidentified riders sailing with, or within, them. They and their animals bore latent viruses that might cause disease to persons previously unexposed, such as pneumonia and influenza strains borne by humans or pigs. The voyagers and the rats also likely carried lice, which themselves transported typhus from host to unexposed host. The afflictions with which the seven captives suffered on departing Gomera likely wouldn't remain contagious by the time they arrived at Española, but diseases they succumbed to en route might. The crowding of men and beasts together risked bacterial infections.

CAONABÓ AND GUACANAGARÍ, *Marien (Late October 1493)*

At dusk, Caonabó strode to sit in council with vassal caciques on *duhos* (ceremonial seats) set in a circle at the midfield of the enormous *batey* (ballcourt) that lay before his caney.* The caciques had arrived from their villages throughout Maguana's great valley and,

*The ballcourt is preserved as Corral de los Indios, San Juan de la Maguana, Dominican Republic, and *Encounters Unforeseen*, chapter 3, depicts a game of *batey* and a *cohaba* ceremony.

over the past days, sought purification prelude to a *cohaba* ceremony, abstaining from food, *chicha* (corn beer), and women. They'd grown weaker and unharnessed from the constraints of ordinary perception so as to better commune with Yúcahu and other spirits. The prior afternoon, they'd induced vomiting by placing a ceremonial stick down the throat, the final cleansing for the cohaba to consider Caonabó's unprecedented intrusion into Marien.

"Guacanagarí never should have lodged and fed the pale men, and he's failed his caciqual duty to eliminate them, even after warnings to do so," Caonabó pronounced. "It falls on me to fulfill that duty. We meet to seek Yúcahu's concurrence." He turned about the circle, inviting each man to express concerns or recommendations.

"Take care not to harm Guacanagarí or his subjects," cautioned one of the elders. "We aren't seeking to depose him or shed his people's blood."

"We won't attack them, and we'll fight them only if necessary to accomplish the objective," Caonabó assured, nodding. "Guacanagarí won't be touched. I'll lead an overwhelming number of warriors—far more than necessary—which should deter them from defending the pale men. Guacanagarí's vassal Mayreni has encouraged this trespass, and Mayreni will provide scouts to identify the pale men's bohíos. There won't be confrontations elsewhere."

"Will you punish Guacanagarí?"

"Severe punishment is due!" Caonabó proclaimed, raising his voice. "Yúcahu may summon it." He motioned for his elderly behique to commence the ceremony.

The behique placed a cemí of Yúcahu and a seashell filled with a powerful narcotic—the cohaba powder—on a ceremonial stand set at the circle's center and, beholding the sky, invoked Yúcahu's presence. He passed Caonabó a hollowed stick shaped like a Y, which Caonabó used to inhale the powder through his nostrils, and then offered the stick around the circle to each man. Within moments, all hallucinated presciently as bubbles and contortions seemingly cascaded before their eyes and through their limbs.

Caonabó and the caciques conversed aloud with Yúcahu into the night, affirming the wisdom of the massacre. Yúcahu had embraced

Caonabó's execution of the pale men violating Maguana. Yúcahu exhorted final elimination of all remaining on the island.

In the morning, Caonabó quenched his hunger. Within days, he and a thousand warriors were hiking north through the mountainous Cibao region into Marien.

▫ ▫ ▫

When scouts reported that Caonabó's army had encamped south of Guarico, Guacanagarí grasped that defending the remaining pale men would accomplish nothing but the loss of his own subjects' lives and inestimable erosion of his stature. Brother Matuma consoled him, arguing that this was the best of bad outcomes—they'd rid themselves of the pale men, and, if Admiral did return, the guilt was Caonabó's. Guacanagarí directed Matuma to station their warriors to defend Guarico if necessary but not to interfere with the destruction of Admiral's Navidad, which lay at the riverbank on Guarico's western perimeter.

Guacanagarí wandered alone for hours through his subjects' yuca fields, mulling the explanation he'd give Admiral, quivering that Admiral would conclude he'd broken his promise. At sunset, when returning home, Guacanagarí skirted the river and chose to visit the garrison a last time, somberly drawn to behold the pale men's unwitting arrogance as their demise loomed. He entered the clearing surrounding a lone bohío and their defensive structure, a fort built from the wood of the sunken vessel, and spied a half dozen pale men lounging about. Their gardens had long since decayed to weed, their bodies sullied to grime from failure to bathe, and their daily routine reduced to loitering in wait of Guacanagarí's food allotments, hoarding gold, and lusting for women.

As Guacanagarí approached, Diego de Arana, Admiral's chosen leader for the garrison, sat before the tiny fort with his two concubines as they cooked dinner in a fireplace. Diego hadn't forced himself upon either of them. They cared for and slept with him of their own volition because they perceived him a powerful cacique. Occasionally, he now admitted to himself that he held much affection for them. Both were pregnant, and he'd begun to reflect on what would become of them and his children when he returned to Castile.

Diego rose to greet Guacanagarí, affecting a nobility that—as a wine presser's son—he'd never known. Guacanagarí saw through it but afforded Diego a gracious salutation in Taíno nonetheless. The two men communicated by gestures and the Spanish words Guacanagarí now understood.

"Escobedo? Gutiérrez?" Diego asked, shrugging his shoulders.

Guacanagarí pointed south, as if they were in Maguana meeting Caonabó.

"Chachu?"

Guacanagarí pointed east, as if he survived.

Diego pointed to the baskets, sitting empty beside the fireplace, in which Guacanagarí's subjects brought the garrison its weekly food allotment. "Need more food."

Guacanagarí smiled and nodded in reply. He glinted at the women and spoke casually, as if saying hello or goodbye. "You will always be my subjects." He saw their bewilderment, hoping they soon would understand.

As Guacanagarí parted from Arana, Caonabó and his renowned general, Uxmatex, brought their warriors down from the foothills to the great plain that extended north to Guarico. Their substantial presence ignited urgent rumors, barked from village to village north. When the moon rose, they advanced toward Navidad, stalking through field, marsh, and mangrove swamp, driving terrified villagers to retreat within their bohíos. They arrived in the forest immediately south of Navidad when the moon was cresting, and Caonabó transferred command to Uxmatex, instructing him to delay some moments and then launch an assault that would trap the pale men against the river and sea. Guacanagarí's warriors weren't present, although Caonabó's scouts had discovered them stationed in the plaza to the east, prepared to defend Guarico itself.

Uxmatex studied the pale men's defensive structure and the adjacent bohío, surprised no sentry stood guard and that his warriors' presence remained undetected. The pale men's weaponry was ferocious, but they weren't soldiers. He waited patiently and, whispering, then ordered his lieutenants to slay the pale men as they fled and to torch both structures, flushing out any who remained hidden within. Confident in victory, he strode into the clearing's perimeter, beseeched Yúcahu's alliance, and raised his arm in the moonlight. A thunderous cry pierced the night, and his warriors swarmed past him.

The cry itself brought Diego close to death, but he leapt to his feet, aware there wasn't time to arm a crossbow, no less a harquebus. Even if there had been, his band of men weren't prepared or disciplined to fight as a unit—and there wasn't a real commander to lead them, since he hadn't been trained for that. Diego clutched his sword, stepped from the fort, and shouted for his band to rise and defend themselves. Others desperately exited behind him, and some from the bohío, and all quickly grasped that a battle was hopeless and bolted toward the sea. Uxmatex bellowed that the women present wouldn't be harmed if they fled immediately, and the structures were set ablaze. Three of Arana's band emerged from the smoke, to be bludgeoned by macanas.

Wretched, beholding death nigh certain, Diego and seven others crashed through underbrush and forest to Guarico's beach, their flight for naught save sprinting into the sea. Diego plunged into the surf, wailing for the tragedy that he'd never see his wife and daughter again. As arrows and spears whooshed close about, he chose to dive, and, as his lungs burned for air, his final thought was a parched loathing that Colón hadn't returned. The Genoese had deserted him among savages, achieving nobility over his dead body! The others were speared, bludgeoned, or drowned close by.

Guacanagarí, Matuma, and their warriors were anxiously waiting out Caonabó's advance when the cry resounded from Navidad, and they sprinted from the plaza to behold the incursion. Shadows darted among the bohíos, trees, and gardens, alarming Guacanagarí as he ran, and, when they arrived at Navidad's clearing, he was aghast to hear cries to his rear that fires were spreading in Guarico itself. He turned behind to sight flames rising from several bohíos scattered throughout the village—including at the plaza! Outrage consumed him—Caonabó's transgression had stepped beyond the cause of their disagreement to violate his own home! Guacanagarí shrieked for his warriors to reverse course, to charge back to the plaza to defend their bohíos and the caciqual family.

Lurking in the darkness of a hillside garden, Caonabó envisioned his scouts fanning the blazes that now threatened the town. He whispered urgently to his small escort of warriors to prepare to flee as soon as the prisoner was taken and to treat her gently, as she was nobility. Caonabó had an unobstructed view into but a portion of the plaza, and he riveted to it, straining to discern any clue how the capture progressed.

Chaos engulfed the plaza—women screaming, children wailing, men scrambling to douse fires, warriors furiously barging every which way to confront the unseen enemy. The most tormented cries came from Guacanagarí's caney, then billowing smoke, as his nitaínos discovered its sentries strangled to death. Household naborias howled that many of Guacanagarí's wives remained petrified inside, likely mauled, trampled, and suffocating, perhaps violated or worse, others possibly abducted, and they dove within, braving the blaze.

Guacanagarí staggered breathless into the plaza to be advised immediately of these affronts, and he commanded his warriors to disperse throughout Guarico to annihilate the enemy, his naborias to account for his wives. The naborias dragged over two dozen wives, gasping, blinded, and scorched, from the smoldering caney and hauled them to the plaza, where nitaínos soon confirmed an abduction. Caonabó's men had seized one of the youngest, one of Guacanagarí's favorites—constituting the gravest insult to a Taíno cacique imaginable.

Hatred supplanted outrage as Guacanagarí grasped the calculated, barefaced deprecation of his honor. He struggled to maintain his caciqual demeanor, incredulous that his decision to harbor a few unknown beings whose vessel had sunk less than a year before had led to such an irrevocable insult! Caonabó's execution of the pale men could be forgiven and forgotten, as might the trespass into Guarico for that purpose. But not the trespass into his caney! Not the violation of a wife! Guacanagarí shrieked that she be recaptured before Caonabó escaped, and he rued his humiliation if she wasn't.

Atop the hillside, Caonabó observed his warriors bind and gag the young woman seized and hoist her on a litter as they began to flee south. Her beauty was outshone only by her terror and, for an instant, Caonabó contemplated that he'd gladly take her as another wife. But that wasn't his message to Guacanagarí. The invitation to harbor the pale men on Haiti had been wrong and would never be forgiven.

Caonabó's destruction of Navidad.
Panel from cover page of Herrera, 1601.

HIERRO (CANARY ISLANDS) TO CALOUCAERA (GUADALUPE, CARIBBEAN ISLANDS), *October 13–November 9, 1493*

As Colón sailed southwest, the Italian humanist serving as tutor to educate Prince Juan—Pedro Mártir de Anglería (b. ca. 1457)—began describing Colón's discoveries in letters he dispatched to his former benefactors in Italy and others to inform about the goings-on at Isabel and Fernando's court. In correspondence that September, he explained that Colón was exploring the half of the world then untraveled—from the Golden Chersonese (the Malay Peninsula) known by Ptolemy (ca. AD 100–170) east to Cádiz, journeying in a new hemisphere. In October, he wrote that Colón believed he'd sailed west up to the Indian coasts. In November, without ascribing geographic specificity or particular significance to the words then first chosen, he praised Colón in a passing reference as the discoverer of a *New World*.

As Mártir's letters of September and October, Cristóbal, the voyagers, and their sovereigns' peoples then understood—based on Aristotle's (384–322 BC) and Ptolemy's teachings—that the fleet was traversing the ocean that separated the western and eastern ends of the globe earth's principal landmass, terra firma, crossing westerly to that landmass's eastern tip. The fleet's mariners appreciated the Admiral's astonishing discovery—that strong northeasterly winds and ocean currents pushed their ships on their course across the ocean without the need for tacking. The landsmen marveled at the immensity of the Lord's creation as the swells of the sea marched infinitely all about them between landless horizons, day after day, illuminated by the sun the Lord had furnished and—when it set to orbit the earth—the moon and starry heavens. At sunset, all sang a hymn to the Virgin to protect their ships through the night, and at dawn the friars led a prayer for her protection that day. The landsmen quickly wearied to the tight quarters and grumbled over the meagerness of their daily ration and its crude plainness, but their prayers were met, and the fleet sailed for almost two weeks without a storm, breezeless calm, or even contrary wind.

Yet the foreboding Bakako and the other Taínos sensed when Hierro slipped from the horizon turned inward and more desperate as each grew increasingly feverish and nauseated. Most suffered from diarrhea and vomiting.* Dreadfully, some blistered with the reddish welts and scabs that foreshadowed death or disfiguring pocks, and they were quarantined to lie alone before the bowsprits so the air about them drew off to sea.† Xamabo grew too weak to stand without assistance, and Chanca warned Cristóbal that survival was in doubt. Day and night, Bakako and Yutowa honored Yúcahu and Attabeira for survival.

Late one evening, as a waning half moon cast a silver sheen across the ocean, Xamabo summoned Bakako and Yutowa to hear his thoughts, as if they were his last. "You must understand what to warn Guacanagarí—if I can't," he whispered.

*Typhus or dysentery?
†Chicken pox or smallpox?

Bakako glanced at Yutowa, frightened by the responsibility, uncertain how to respond.

"You'll talk to him yourself, Xamabo," Yutowa replied. "But we're ready to do so. What must we say?"

"Tell Guacanagarí that he's been betrayed," Xamabo instructed. "Admiral's betrayal is monumental, reciprocating rescue and support with invasion."

"We understand, and we'll relay that," Bakako assured.

"Warn Guacanagarí that Admiral covets the entirety of Haiti. He intends that Guacanagarí bow servant to the pale caciques. He'll set the weapons and beasts upon our people if Guacanagarí resists."

Xamabo coughed and shuddered, and Bakako put a jug of water to his lips, from which he sipped.

"Explain that Fernando and Isabel proclaim they seek warm friendship between peoples and that this is Admiral's constant refrain," Xamabo directed. "But admonish Guacanagarí that these are either crafty lies, or Admiral and his caciques are simply arrogant and deluded. I suspect arrogance—they're convinced of their superiority." He vacillated. "They believe Guacanagarí and other caciques will simply forsake their sovereignty in panic and awe, acknowledging our people may be *improved* to be like them! Just as they thought we'd welcome their 'baptism' ceremony because it 'saved' us. But it could be lies, and the distinction doesn't matter anyway."

Xamabo rested for a few moments to muster his waning strength. "Warn Guacanagarí not to trust Admiral's assurances of kindness. Tell him that the pale men use slaves to do their work, particularly those of our color, and that they haven't brought these slaves along, likely intending to use Guacanagarí's subjects instead. They also haven't brought their own women to farm or cook, and, undoubtedly, they intend to master and violate our own."

Bakako and Yutowa nodded obediently, in trepidation.

"When you let him know all this, he'll ask what Xamabo thought he should do." Xamabo peered into the teenagers' eyes, and they realized they didn't know the answer and winced to learn it.

"The choices are telling the pale men to be gone, fighting to repel them, acquiescing until they leave, or submitting forever. Warn him

I'm certain they won't go away peacefully—demanding them to isn't an option. For me, neither is submitting forever."

"And what of the other two?" Bakako whispered.

Xamabo's fragile frame shook as he coughed sharply, and Bakako cringed that his passion was sapping remaining strength. But Xamabo concluded, reflecting thoughts like those of threatened rulers in all worlds. "Tell Guacanagarí I died not knowing. Without women, they may intend to remain only briefly. If we acquiesce, we might be spared bondage for a temporary or kinder subservience. If we resist, we may suffer countless casualties for naught, only to be enslaved."

◘ ◘ ◘

The weather grew hot and muggy as the journey continued through the third week from Hierro. One by one, the captives aboard the other ships died, sorrowing Bakako and Yutowa, disheartening Cristóbal. Xamabo lost consciousness, and Cristóbal asked Fray Buil to administer his last rites as Fernando, the name conferred in Barcelona. After Xamabo expired, a brief funeral was held and his body dumped to the sea. Bakako and Yutowa despaired as it vanished into the deep, dreading the expression on Guacanagarí's face when they fulfilled Xamabo's instructions. Cristóbal retained Xamabo's belt and headdress to return to Guacanagarí, fretting that only three interpreters survived but heartened that their health appeared on the mend.

At sundown on November 2, Cristóbal determined that flocks of birds and cloud masses signaled islands close beyond, and he ordered the fleet's sails reefed to avoid overshooting landfall during the night. At 5:00 a.m. the next twilight, a lookout on the *María Galante* sighted a distant volcano topping the sea mist, illuminated by the sliver of moon then descending. He shouted out and the sailors on watch erupted into celebration, quickly joined by everyone else, all but three pressed to the rails to behold the Indies and praise their Lord. The mariners marveled that the Admiral had dead reckoned a constant compass bearing from Hierro to landfall on islands he had never visited, reducing the landless distance across the ocean—in the Admiral's estimation—to merely 820 leagues and the sailing time to three weeks, almost two weeks shorter than his first voyage.*

At dawn, a half dozen islands came into sight, and the voyagers were astounded by the archipelago's beauty, as if they were in a new world. Soon, the scent of earth, forest, and flowers wafted through the rigging, and the beasts aboard clamored that they were coming home. Lush green mountains rose majestically from a sublime turquoise sea, often ringed by surf breaking on encircling reefs and rimmed by sand beaches curling at the shoreline. In rough seas, Cristóbal directed the fleet to the largest island off the bow, which he named Dominica, as it was Sunday.† He found neither a good harbor nor anchorage and took the fleet north to harbor for the night at the next large island, where he and a small party debarked before sunset.

At Cristóbal's side, with the sovereigns' banners fluttering in the breeze, the fleet's secretary loudly recited in Spanish a proclamation that Queen Isabel and King Fernando would take the island's possession and sovereignty unless someone objected—which none of the island's inhabitants did, since none were present. The fleet's notary recorded the nonobjection, fulfilling the prerequisites for dominion, and Cristóbal named the island María Galante, after the flagship.‡ His men planted a cross and took on water and wood, and Fray Buil presided over the first mass ashore in Cristóbal's Indies.

The next morning, the fleet coursed west to the largest island sighted, whose mountainous grandeur outshone the rest, including a waterfall cascading from a terrific height, visible from miles at sea. Upon arriving off its southern shore, Cristóbal dispatched a light caravel to explore closer, and its captain debarked by launch near a river abutting a small village of bohíos, whose naked inhabitants fled, other than a toddler left behind. The captain and his men entered the bohíos briefly and looted some trophies, including a few human arm and leg bones. In search of a harbor, Cristóbal skirted the island's coastline southwest, and naked peoples ashore vigilantly tracked his reconnaissance by running alongside, themselves intently scrutinized by the voyagers. The fleet anchored in coves near the island's southern tip by late afternoon, and, fulfilling a promise he'd made

*Equivalent to 3,018 statutory miles, an overstatement of roughly 4 percent from the modern scientific measurement.

†As so named today. The indigenous name was Ouitoucoubouli, meaning "tall is her body."

‡So named today (Marie-Galante in French).

that June to the monks in Guadalupe's Monastery of Santa María de Guadalupe, Cristóbal named the island for the monastery.* He saw a village of a few bohíos close to a black-sand beach and dispatched a launch to meet its inhabitants, but they fled. A few children remained wandering about, and Cristóbal's men gave them hawks' bells to reassure their parents that Christians came with peaceful intentions. That evening, word of the bones reverberated through the fleet, and voyagers ranted they'd arrived at the islands where men ate human flesh—proving Cristóbal's accounts of the Caribe peoples bore true.

On November 5, Cristóbal summoned Bakako to the captain's quarters before dawn, and he entered anxiously, recognizing Admiral now would compel his services for conquest.

"Is this a Caribe island?" Admiral asked. He expected as much but had reserved judgment, recalling that his first impression on the prior voyage was that the Indians possessed skulls and bones to venerate ancestors.

"I believe yes," Bakako replied. "Men hair long," he added, having learned that from sailors returning from the beach. "Not Taíno."

"You must go ashore and find a cacique willing to discuss our intentions and point the direction to Española."

Bakako nodded gravely, appreciating Admiral meant to protect him from Caribes, yet frightened by their legendary bloodthirst and cruelty to Taíno peoples.

"You'll be accompanied by soldiers, as before," Admiral assured. "If possible, bring me Caribes by persuasion, but by force if necessary. We must complete a chart for the queen depicting Española, España, and the islands in between."

Bakako nodded obediently, certain that wasn't the only intent.

By dawn, he departed ashore in the *María Galante*'s launch, seated in the bow, as on the first voyage, with soldiers rowing. A throng had gathered on the beach to observe the fleet, including warriors armed with spear and bow and arrow, and most retreated to the forest perimeter when the launch neared. Bakako shouted, "*Taíno*, *Taíno*"

*Spelled Guadeloupe in French. Guadeloupe consists of two proximate islands, Basse-Terre and Grande-Terre. The caravel likely landed near Capesterre-Belle-Eau, Basse-Terre, and the fleet likely anchored at coves west of Trois-Rivières, Basse-Terre, debarking on the beach at Grande Anse.

to indicate *good people* or *friendly people* approached. Grimly, he lied to lure the villagers back from the forest, exclaiming, "I bring men who are good and harm no one."

Bakako shivered that the warriors were ferocious—their hair flailing with a deliberate rabidity, as long as the women's, their bows more powerful than he'd ever seen. Many of the women wore tight cotton bands around their ankles and calves, causing the girded flesh to bulge, perhaps signaling nobility but threatening brawn.

Raising his arms to signal he was weaponless, Bakako walked tentatively onto the beach, and the crowd at the perimeter retreated backward into the forest, concealing most but their eyes and spear tips. Yet, to Bakako's surprise, two youths stepped a few paces toward the sea, their arms raised in response, also weaponless. Bakako bid the soldiers to debark slowly and remain at the water's edge, and he cautiously ambled to the beach's midpoint, repeating "Taíno" again and again, and then halted.

"Taíno," one replied. "Who are you and what brings you here?"

Although the Taíno dialect was strange, Bakako understood the words spoken and was astonished that conversation would be possible without gestures. "I'm Bakako, from Guanahaní. These pale men are with me, and they come in friendship. They just want information. They won't harm you or your people."

The two youths approached closer, and Bakako smiled amiably. Yet inwardly, he palled with revulsion, recognizing that both youths had been dismembered, their penises cut off.

"What floats in the sea?" one of the youths blurted, astounded by the extraordinary appearance and size of the fleet's ships. "Who are these beings and where do they come from?"

"Those are vessels, made of wood. They harness the wind and won't harm you any more than a canoe would." Bakako sensed a longing for kinship, not fear. "These are men, traveling from across the ocean." He pointed to the villagers huddled in the forest and asked, "Are those your family?"

The youths hesitated before responding, glancing back and forth to each other and the forest, spooked. After a long silence, they drew paces closer to Bakako, and one responded, speaking softly.

"None are, except our mothers are among them. We aren't

Canibas [Caribe persons]. They are, and this is their homeland, Caloucaera.* The warriors call themselves Kalinago."

"We're the sons of men they slaughtered on Boriquén [Puerto Rico] years ago, when they seized our mothers to serve as slaves and concubines," the other explained. "We were captured then, too, and have been slaves ever since."

Bakako was stunned by the admission—and by the bitter irony that three slaves were conversing under the scrutiny of their respective captors. For an instant, he was the one speechless, glancing back and forth between Admiral's fleet and his footprints on the sand, marking his subservience to Admiral. He overcame his incredulity and shrugged. "I am sorry for you." He also recovered his bearings and, pointing to his soldiers, added, "They aren't Caniba, and they bear you gifts."

The youths stepped yet closer, and Bakako bid a soldier with a sack to come forward and withdraw a skullcap. "This is to wear, just as a headdress."

The soldiers charged as the youths studied the trifle and subdued them. For an instant, Bakako pondered whether the two had even attempted flight or merely dissembled that.

"You won't be harmed," Bakako reassured. "You'll meet my cacique."

Aboard the *María Galante*, Cristóbal offered the youths biscuits and honey and then probed their situation and the geography of the Indies. But the interrogation was interrupted when a launch returned from the beach bearing six women—without leg bands—who had requested coming aboard, as well as a few women—with bands—captured by force.

Bakako greeted them and could understand the speech of the six but not the others, whom he surmised were Caribe. He brought the six unbanded to stand before Admiral, together with the youths.

"Why have you come aboard?" Bakako asked the women.

"We want your protection!" the eldest exclaimed. "The Caribes have slain our husbands and enslaved us to serve as wives or worse."

"They treat us cruelly and crop our sons' manhood," another wailed, pointing to the youths.

---

*Basse-Terre, Caloucaera being the Kalinago name. The Taíno name for the island was Turuqueria.

"Every year, they raid for more women and husbands to sacrifice," a third exhorted. "They tear our husbands' bodies apart and gnaw their flesh to boast victory and domination."

"We beg that you take us back to our home!" the eldest implored. "We can guide you there through the islands."

Cristóbal and Bakako were stunned. Cristóbal pondered a moment. Bakako brooded, recalling the dread Guanahaniáns had felt when they first beheld pale men, cowed that the women's plight could be so dire to compel them to overcome that.

"I don't believe the women," Cristóbal concluded, turning to Bakako. "They may be lying to escape their lawful husbands or masters. We must befriend these people to establish a relationship and locate our position. We must speak with a cacique."

Cristóbal instructed soldiers to mete gifts of necklaces and other trifles to the six women and ferry them home. But, within moments ashore, armed villagers stripped the women of their gifts, and they begged to return aboard, together with children. Cristóbal relented, and a substantial interview then transpired. He surmised the women did understand the geography of neighboring islands, such as an Ayay (Saint Croix) and a Yaramaqui (Antigua), as well as Boriquén and others extending all the way to Española, and he decided to retain them and the youths aboard, as well as the women with leg bands seized.

As the afternoon waned, Cristóbal was outraged to learn that, without his authorization, one of the ship's captains—Diego Marquez, the crown overseer—had led men ashore to plunder gold and trophies and failed to return. Cristóbal had intended to depart for Española the next day, and he dispatched a search party to scour the neighboring area, but it returned empty-handed by nightfall. Four squads resumed the search the next day and also failed. Furious, Cristóbal postponed sailing and appointed Hojeda to reconnoiter the island comprehensively, identifying its treasures while finding Marquez. To alleviate the voyagers' confinement, he permitted many to go ashore, warning that those who failed to return promptly would be abandoned when he sailed on Hojeda's return, whether Marquez's band was found or not.

Cristóbal and others used the delay to enter and examine bohíos in nearby villages, discovering for themselves human skulls hanging from the rafters and gourds filled with men's bones. Chanca surmised that the women were truthful in claiming the Caribes ate flesh. So did Michele da Cuneo, and he and others railed that Marquez's band had been eaten. A fleet surgeon, Guillermo Coma, concluded that the dismembered boys were being fattened to eat, like capons, rather than permanently enslaved, and that the Caribes ate their sons born to their women captives. Pedro Margarite claimed he saw Indians fixed on spits, roasting over coals, in advance of the Caribes' meals. Some judged—without Cristóbal's prompting—that, unless these people learned to abstain from flesh, they deserved to be reduced to bondage and taken to Spain in chains.

As for Cristóbal, he perceived he'd obtained adequate proof and justification for the enslavement of Caribes. They ate human flesh and endangered the peoples on Española and elsewhere destined to become the sovereigns' vassals—the Indians. He envisioned sending Isabel and Fernando a few of those captured as evidence on the very first ships dispatched home.

On November 8, the avaricious Marquez was found, and Cristóbal had him thrown in chains for delaying seventeen ships and twelve hundred voyagers five days, setting an example to the fleet's courtiers that no one—including their own—was beyond punishment for exceeding his authorization, no less disobeying orders. Cristóbal also cut Marquez's rations and those of the men who had accompanied him, demonstrating to all that following the mistaken command of a crown official also wouldn't escape justice.

Cristóbal directed that the fleet sail at dawn on November 10. A few more enslaved women and dismembered boys—Indians—had accompanied the search parties back to the ships to request asylum, and Cristóbal received them, augmenting the total number of Indians and few Caribes taken to about twenty. He also ordered soldiers to burn the Caribes' canoes so they couldn't raid other islands, fulfilling the promise he'd made to Guacanagári to defend his people from Caribe attack. But he instructed that the Caribes' bohíos be left untouched, reasoning that the Caribes could help resupply Christian convoys returning to Castile via their islands. He learned that the lone toddler sighted at the first landfall days earlier remained wasting alone, and he instructed that the boy be taken for care by his chambermaid and other women voyagers.

One night, Bakako lay beside the two youths he'd deceived to offer comfort that they'd be fed yet warn they weren't free. When their shock subsided, he asked, "Do the Caribes really eat men?"

"Yes, but it's a warrior's rite," the oldest responded. "They grow plenty of food to eat, and their seas and sky abound with fish and fowl. It's part of their war cry when they raid for women—a warning they're heinous and invincible, that an opponent's death will be horrific and his body desecrated."

"They gnaw a chew or two of slain opponents to celebrate victory on the battlefield," the other interjected. "They also capture a husband or two every year, whom they sacrifice to share the flesh within their villages, exulting their people's bravery. But the rite is to celebrate domination and terrify future opponents, not quench hunger."

Bakako drew inward, appalled and embittered by the recognition that his people's terror of the Caribes was just as the Caribes intended.

"Do the pale men eat other men?" the oldest questioned.

"No. I've never seen it. They pretend to eat their Christ-spirit—but it's also only a ceremony." Bakako reflected. "They prefer their enemies as slaves."

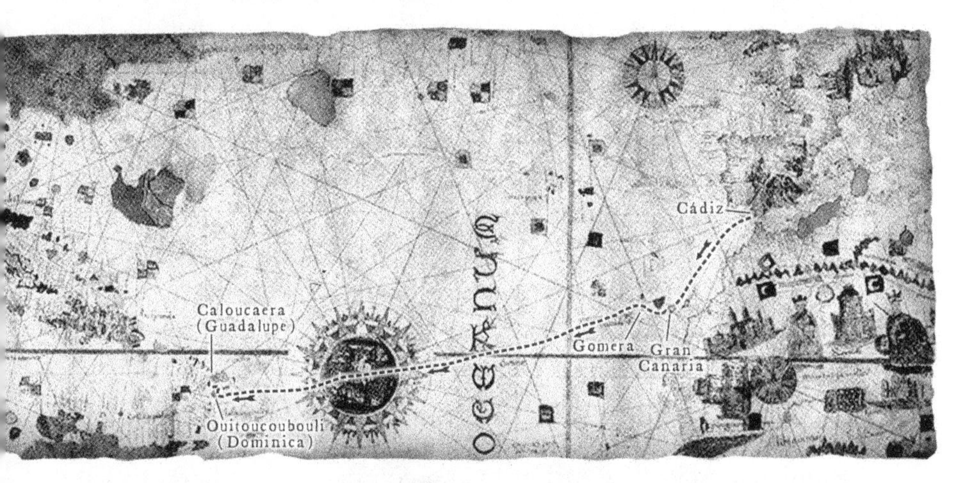

Portion of Juan de la Cosa's World Map, 1500, marked for route from Spain to Canary Islands to Guadalupe.

Hostilities and Violations,

Ayay (Saint Croix) and Boriquén (Puerto Rico), November 10–19, 1493

The fleet weighed anchor before dawn to explore the archipelago north of Guadalupe for a few days. Cristóbal named the first island sighted for Fray Buil's former monastery, Monserrat, due to the similarity of its mountainous terrain. But he didn't debark men ashore, as the women boarded at Guadalupe indicated it was deserted—Caribes had slaughtered or eaten all its inhabitants, they explained. He named another island for the Virgin icon who worked miracles in Seville's cathedral, Saint Antigua, and a third—as the day of anchorage was the saint's feast—for Saint Martin of Tours (now Nevis). Before midday on November 14, in strong winds the fleet approached an estuary (Salt River Bay) on the northern coast of an island the women referred to as Ayay, which he named for the holy cross, Santa Cruz (Saint Croix).

Smoke signals rose ashore, warning of the fleet's arrival, and the Caribe residents of a once Taíno village—conquered generations prior—fled to the surrounding hills. Cristóbal dispatched the *María Galante*'s launch to the village beach with some two dozen armed sailors and his friend Michele da Cuneo, instructed to haul or entice some inhabitants back to the ship to explain the fleet's location. After plundering trophies from bohíos surrounding a withering Taíno ballcourt, the sailors rounded up a half dozen women and dismembered boys—some forcibly corralled, others surrendering for asylum. When returning to the flagship, the sailors spotted a few men, women, and dismembered boys in a canoe, drifting west with the wind at the estuary's mouth, gawking at the fleet in awe.

The launch's captain hailed the canoeists to invite a meeting and pursued when they paddled furiously away. Trapped fatefully between launch and fleet, the men and women rose to fire a barrage of arrows, and, while shields deflected most, two sailors in the launch were gravely wounded. The captain surged his craft forward to ram the canoe, capsizing it upon a shallow reef. But the canoeists didn't succumb—arrows flew furiously and combat ensued hand to hand, shoulder-deep in the sea.

The fleet's voyagers gaped warily as the skirmish unfolded. Christians outnumbered heathens three to one, but the heathens weren't peaceful, timid, or cowardly—as Cristóbal had assured—and their arrows were just as deadly as the Christians' weapons. One of the wounded heathens fiercely endured to discharge his bow after his guts had spilled to the sea, surrendering only when impaled on a lance. Cuneo wrestled one of the women into the launch, but it took three sailors to pin her to the floorboards. The sailors did prevail, and the heathens were dragged onto the flagship, brawling and howling, including the man mortally lanced. The two wounded sailors wailed and bled as horrifically. The voyagers' wariness grew to alarm.

Cristóbal also was startled by the islanders' ferocity, although he'd experienced a similar skirmish at Samaná on the first voyage. Steadfast in resolution and demeanor, he reciprocated the ferocity, seeking to demonstrate to the native peoples ashore and aboard that he would crush all resistance summarily—and to assure his voyagers the same. He ordered the execution of the lanced canoeist. With Bakako and Yutowa's assistance, he interrogated the rest and pronounced the hostile natives were Caribes, not the peaceful Indians with whom the voyagers would live. He'd never intended to release any taken aboard who were fit to serve as samples for the sovereigns. Those surviving were retained captive as the fleet departed west, so the total cargo of islanders then approached thirty, predominantly—Cristóbal surmised—Indians enslaved by Caribes. He awarded Cuneo the defiant Caribe woman.

That evening, Michele had no doubt what the Admiral's award permitted him to do. He lusted for his young captive, and he took her to a cabin to have sex. When she refused, he forced himself upon her, and when she fought back, shrieking and scratching his face, he whipped her with a rope and then raped her. Her cries and torment resounded through the ship. Bakako and Yutowa shuddered to acknowledge their role in facilitating Admiral's conquest. Many of the naked women aboard relived the nightmares of their own rapes, reviling the eternal, brutal misogyny of enemy men. Some of the voyagers were pleasantly titillated, anticipating their own fulfillment when they arrived in Española. Fray Buil was astonished and speechless, bewildered by the crude violence of the earthly situation over which he was to preside.

Cristóbal's ships coursed east over the next few days to arrive at the island many of the Indian women and boys aboard called home, Boriquén, on the morning of November 19. The fleet traversed its northern coast, entering a bay on its western shore for two days.* The voyagers—including Juan Ponce de León—were astonished by the island's size, beauty, and fertility.† The inhabitants fled when voyagers went ashore, and the Indian women aboard related that the inhabitants lived in constant alarm of Caribe raid. Cristóbal was impressed by the inhabitants' building structures, including watchtowers to guard against raid, but disappointed by the failure of encounters. He named the island San Juan Bautista (Saint John the Baptist).

Attack on Caribes, taken from Honorius Philoponus, 1621. John Carter Brown Library, portion of rec. no. 04056-10.

*Bahía de Aguadilla or Bahía de Añasco?
†Juan would serve as the island's Spanish governor over a decade later.

The women and boys from Boriquén were devastated that Admiral wouldn't liberate them, and, during the night, three jumped ship to swim to home. Cristóbal had never contemplated their liberation either—the women and boys had been enslaved by barbaric, heathen conquerors before his arrival, their continued servitude would introduce them to Christianity, and they'd never been the sovereigns' vassals on Española. On the eve of returning to Española, he rankled whether the sovereigns would find merit in permitting enslavement once they saw the cargo of specimens.

GUARIONEX,
Magua

Renowned for spiritual wisdom, Guarionex rose from his duho set in council in Guaricano's central plaza and announced to his nitaínos assembled that they should resolve his chiefdom's ordinary affairs that afternoon without him, as he intended to seclude himself at his ceremonial bohío on the village outskirts. Some asked what troubled him. He replied disingenuously nothing—he sought merely the ongoing spiritual communication for which he was responsible as Magua's supreme cacique, reconciling the spirits of fertility and destruction for the benefit of his subjects. Departing the plaza, he gazed from hillside to the enormous fertile central valley of Haiti below, farmland blessed by the waters of the river Camú and its tributaries and that had nourished Haiti's peoples since their ancestral emergence from the cave, and he reflected that little should concern him.* The spirits had blessed beneficent rains in recent months and forborne storm. But he anguished that he'd put off a private communication for too long, a procrastination born of discomfort rather than neglect.

Guarionex let his vexation surge, not to direct his thoughts, but to purge it, so he could confer with spirits free of self. He recalled with disgust that both Guacanagarí and Caonabó had ignored the advice he'd imparted at the summer's caciqual council—to treat the pale men just as if they had been their own subjects, dispensing stern justice to those deserving and preserving civility with the rest, as well as the

*The tributaries include the Río Verde, which flowed through Guaricano, its indigenous name unknown.

potential of a fruitful relationship. Guacanagarí had simply tolerated the pale men's conduct, coveting a material relationship with them, likely too cowardly to do otherwise. Caonabó had crudely annihilated the lot of them, arrogantly dismissing the primacy of achieving harmony favored by Taíno spirits.

When Guarionex arrived at the bohío, his elderly behique set a duho, cohaba table, and gourd of pineapple juice in the bohío's shade. Guarionex thanked his old friend warmly, sipped briefly from the gourd, and studied the bohío, where his father, Cacibaquel, had taught him to honor the spirits decades before. The shade, the behique's enduring loyalty, the soothing juice, and the solitude dissipated his consternation.

"Retrieve my cemís of Yúcahu and Guabancex, and bring my father," Guarionex directed softly, noting the behique's surprise at the latter request. In his midforties, short and slender, Guarionex shut his eyes and welcomed father Cacibaquel's presence, expressing gratitude for Cacibaquel's decades of tutelage but signaling that today's reunion would probe an experience once gravely troubling to both—although long since forgotten by others. As the behique returned, Guarionex glanced into the bohío, graven that within it, decades before, he and his father's principal caciques had participated in a cohaba ceremony at which father had received the direst communication from Yúcahu ever revealed.

The behique placed the cemís of Yúcahu and Guabancex and a small reed basket on the table. Reflexively, Guarionex dutifully honored Yúcahu for favoring Magua's crops and Guabancex—the spirit of hurricanes—for her forbearance in the hurricane season just ended. He respectfully implored Yúcahu to guide his fellow caciques to remain at peace.

"I wish to consult my father, alone," Guarionex instructed. Nodding, the behique gently withdrew Cacibaquel's skull from the basket, set him on the table facing Guarionex, and withdrew to sit in the forest nearby. The skull had been severed from its corpse prior to burial decades before, the skin and flesh then burned away.

"Father, I come to revisit Yúcahu's terrible prophecy," Guarionex advised, addressing the skull in thought alone. "There's no present danger of its fulfillment, but I need greater understanding, to be prepared." He assisted Cacibaquel's memory, articulating the communication precisely. "Yúcahu revealed to you that those who remain after your death would rule for a brief time before a clothed people arrived to overcome and kill them, and they will die of hunger."

Guarionex traced the prophecy's initial fulfillment. "I've ruled for almost two decades since your death. A clothed people has arrived. They've also been destroyed—but may return." He recounted his warning at the caciqual council that any decision allowing pale men to remain on Haiti must be that of a unified council, not any cacique alone.

"Father, together let's remember the evening of the ceremony—at this very bohío. Those present felt the prophecy ambiguous, confused, or even misunderstood—they puzzled whether it applied to Magua's peoples alone, all of Haiti's peoples, or all Taíno peoples everywhere, and whether some of our peoples would survive to resist." He touched his chest. "I shared their bewilderment, and I confronted you that no such risk then existed, either from Caribes—who don't wear clothes—or from those of the southern and western shores."

Guarionex peered directly into his father's eye sockets. "You remained convinced that the prophecy wasn't a warning, as to which I might take preventative measures, but a prediction. Yet you were equally steadfast that our response to such a clothed people could be to annihilate them or to compromise with them, but that merely succumbing to them was unthinkable. Those were your very words to me."

Guarionex's heart pounded, anxious the deads' spirits weren't accustomed to challenge and that affronting his father was inappropriate. "I agreed then, and remain in agreement with you today," he assured his father.

Guarionex felt Cacibaquel's stern glare and recalled being scolded for vanity in his youth. "Father, I acknowledge Caonabó's destruction of the pale men has concluded the matter, if the pale men never return. Then we must have misunderstood Yúcahu's communication. But, if these men do return, I'll have to decide what to do, what to recommend the other caciques should do."

As the afternoon waned, Guarionex let Cacibaquel accompany his thoughts, and together they coursed openly through the perceptions, conversations, and arguments about the pale men that he'd shared with the other caciques and his nitaínos over the past year. By sunset, he gradually understood—with Cacibaquel's concurrence—that it was premature to make any decision, regardless of Caonabó's impetuous actions. The threshold question remained as it always had been since the pale men's first arrival—were they friend or enemy?

Guarionex rose at sunset and bid his behique to shelter Cacibaquel and the cemís back inside the bohío, meditating that friendship defeated the prophecy, just as annihilation.

III
BETRAYAL

SAMANÁ AND MONTE CHRISTI,
November 22–26, 1493

At dawn on November 22, Cristóbal's fleet departed west for Española, and by dusk the ships lay anchored off a flat landmass that lacked the mountains he recalled of the island. But he recognized the climate—hot in daylight, temperate or cool at night—and the Indian women aboard confirmed it was Haiti. The ocean-weary voyagers delighted they would disembark soon, but their optimism was tamped when last rites were given the sailor most seriously wounded at Santa Cruz.

That dusk, Cristóbal summoned his three surviving interpreters to sit at his knees, alone in the captain's quarters, wanly lit by a setting sun. He turned to the Samanán, instructing slowly in Spanish.

"Tomorrow, I hope to return you to your village." Cristóbal studied the astonishment beaming from the Samanán's eyes, as well as Bakako and Yutowa's. "You'll wear clothing and bear gifts to your family and cacique. Tell your cacique Christians have returned in peace. Understand?"

The Samanán nodded gravely. Bakako and Yutowa quivered, pining to learn whether they, too, would be released.

"Inform your cacique that you've always been treated well and that your three friends died of pestilence, not blows. Describe the marvelous possessions and know-how of Christians and our customs and clothing. Reveal that you love Christ." The Samanán had been baptized in Barcelona, and Cristóbal studied his reaction, searching for doubt or insincerity. "Win your cacique's heart to love and serve King Fernando and Queen Isabel. Assure that he'll remain cacique of your people, all will prosper, and everyone's soul will be saved."

"I tell cacique all," the Samanán responded, trembling that his true thoughts not wrinkle his brow or curl his lips.

"Diego and Yutowa will accompany me to reunite with the cacique Guacanagarí and locate the Cibao's gold." Cristóbal glowered sternly. "After your cacique understands everything, then you must travel west to join me in the Cibao." Cristóbal lifted a small crucifix from his desk and held it inches from the Samanán's face. "Promise before Christ that you will do so—or suffer Christ's wrath, if you lie."

"I promise. No lie," the Samanán replied plainly, concealing his dread of the Christ-spirit's vengeance.

Cristóbal bid his page Pedro to serve the interpreters nuts and raisins and then dismissed them. While the Samanán's faith might be false and the promise broken, Cristóbal was content that the magnanimity of the gesture—returning him unharmed to his very home—was the strongest demonstration of peaceful intent that could be made.

Bakako, Yutowa, and the Samanán slunk to the *María Galante*'s bowsprit to confer, heedful of appearing witless, unassuming, and docile. They knew the promise false, never to be honored. The two Guanahaníans applauded the Samanán on his liberation, yet the three were daunted.

"You must warn your cacique, just as Xamabo instructed that we warn Guacanagarí," Bakako somberly reminded.

"He'll embrace war," the Samanán exclaimed in Taíno.* "Admiral's expectation of submission will be shattered."

"You must shed your clothes immediately—as soon as Admiral can't see you—or else your own people may slay you," Yutowa cautioned.

*The Samanán's first language would have been a Macorís dialect, not Taíno, although he (and other Samanáns) would have communicated with Bakako and Yutowa in Taíno, which served as a lingua franca in the Taíno Caribbean. For information on the indigenous languages spoken, see Sources, chapter II, in the discussion relating to Guadalupe.

"Hide yourself well!" Bakako urged. "Admiral rarely forgives."

"I shudder to think what he'd do to me—if he ever finds me."

In the morning, Cristóbal coursed the fleet north and was gratified to find the great bay at Samaná, and, by noon, the ships hove to abreast the mountainous peninsula at the beachhead where the *Niña* and *Pinta* had anchored the previous January. Cristóbal uneasily recalled the menacing appearance of the local peoples—nakedness darkened by charcoal and curls of black dye—and the bloody skirmish that had transpired with the *Niña*'s sailors. He had accepted the reigning cacique's truce offer after the altercation, but the cacique had broken a promise to meet again. A repetition of hostilities would daunt the voyagers further.

The Samanán captive was escorted to the beach, clothed and gift-laden, and Cristóbal studied as the youth vanished into the forest, without a wave goodbye. The wounded sailor had died that morning, and he was given a Christian burial ashore. Cristóbal directed that caravels stand closely off the beach to warn inhabitants from approaching, wishing to limit encounters during the funeral and promptly depart for Navidad. The local Samanáns also recollected the truce and sought to trade, and, at Cristóbal's instruction, the sailors ashore refused the locals' entreaties to be taken aboard the fleet.

Regardless, two Samanáns wouldn't be denied, and they canoed to the ships to wring Cristóbal's reluctant invitation to board the *María Galante*. Bakako and Yutowa translated as Cristóbal gifted shirts and skullcaps. They then promptly ushered the canoeists to depart, but not before a brief conversation, alone.

"Pale men whom your leader left on Haiti have died," one of the canoeists remarked.

Bakako and Yutowa froze but for the dart of their eyes, which met riveted in alarm. Yutowa steeled his composure and probed, "How do you know that?"

"Those are the rumors from the west."

"Just a few or many?" Bakako interjected.

"Most all, but I'm not sure."

"How did they die?" Bakako pumped.

The canoeists glanced skittishly at each other, shrugged, and descended overboard into their canoe.

Bakako and Yutowa anxiously debated how to inform Admiral, and they approached him on the poop deck after the ships weighed anchor.

"Admiral, Samanáns give news men Navidad," Bakako related.

It was then Cristóbal who froze. His heart missed a beat, and a premonition that his worst fears were to be realized crept through him. He dismissed the sailors on the poop deck, and, with the wind muffling their voices, he drew the Guanahaníans close. "Tell me."

"Say men dead. Many."

Cristóbal winced. "They died of pestilence or were slain?"

"No know."

"The peoples here want to trade, as if we're friends! Doesn't that signal friendship has prevailed at Navidad?"

Bakako and Yutowa shrugged.

"Don't tell others," Cristóbal scowled. *It's premature, and all will know the truth soon*, he acknowledged to himself grittily.

⊡ ⊡ ⊡

On Haiti's northern coast, word soon reached the Ciguayans' supreme cacique that vessels of pale men were approaching from the east along his chiefdom and had restored one of his subjects abducted in January. Astonished, Mayobanex—a contemporary of Guarionex—recalled his prior truce with the pale men and his warning to the other supreme caciques that the pale leader comported himself as a conqueror. Mayobanex had been unequivocal at the summer's caciqual council—if the leader ever returned, he should be admonished to depart. Mayobanex summoned for the youth and, accompanied by nitaínos, departed his highland village to trek to a seaside promontory, where he would encamp the night and await the vessels' passage.*

At dawn, oblivious to a fierce thunderstorm, he stood to behold an armada, aghast at its enormity, gruffly surmising that such an admonishment would be rejected, with evil intent and force. The youth was ushered before him, apparently weakened by pestilence but in stable condition. Mayobanex received the pale men's gifts and set them aside with disdain.

---

*The village likely was at the Río Yasica, Dominican Republic.

"What's the pale men's intent?" he asked.

"They come to make a home," replied Cristóbal's former captive.

"And if Guacanagarí says no to that?"

"I expect they'll insist and attack. There are thousands of them. Their weapons are powerful, including beasts."

"Is their leader the same one I met?"

The youth nodded.

Mayobanex inquired as to the pale men's civilization and their homeland for some hours, marveled at the weaving, glimmer, or construction of the gifts, and then dismissed the youth. He dispatched runners to warn the other supreme caciques that the pale men's leader had returned with an army in at least seventeen ships. Cautious and unnerved, he refrained from offering any advice, respectfully omitting a reminder that he'd told them so.

◘ ◘ ◘

On the afternoon of November 25, the fleet arrived at the mountain promontory Cristóbal had named Monte Christi on the first voyage (Cabo del Morro, Dominican Republic) and anchored to its west in the large sheltered cove into which the Yaque River flowed, which he'd named the Río de Oro (River of Gold). He directed a search party to examine whether the area had a site appropriate for the settlement, having concluded on the first voyage that Guacanagarí's village was too damp and too far west of the gold mines he envisioned finding in Española's Cibao.

The search party found the area waterlogged and unsuitable but returned excitedly in the evening to report that two corpses had been discovered near the river, both men. Cristóbal questioned the party's captain.

"Were the corpses Indian or European?"

"They've been dead too long to tell. They were naked." Shaken, the captain rasped his voice. "One had a grass rope strung about his neck—the same as the strand we use for cargo. His arms had been laid out on a wood piece, his hands bound to it. As if hoisted on a cross. The other's feet were bound."

Cristóbal shuddered, not to the information imparted, but to the gasps of those witnessing the conversation, including crown officials and Fray Buil. Some murmured it appeared an evil deed, others an evil omen. Cristóbal writhed that it was evidence of disaster, but he maintained an impassive visage, instructing that the reconnaissance for an appropriate settlement site continue the next day, alert for conclusive signs of a European corpse and insight into the cause of death. He took heart that numerous Indians continued to paddle to the ships to trade for trifles, apparently unconcerned there was cause for retribution. Yet privately, he instructed Bakako and Yutowa to ascertain if these Indians knew whether the Navidad garrison had survived.

The search party ventured farther from the river the next day, discovering two more naked male corpses, aghast that one of them was heavily bearded—establishing he wasn't Indian. The captain delivered his report to Cristóbal, and cries of astonishment and fright passed throughout the fleet. Shouts of indignation, contempt, and vengeance for Indian betrayal quickly followed, as well as whispers criticizing the Admiral's assurances that the Indians were timid and passive. Cristóbal pronounced that he'd warned his men not to leave Navidad and those who had disobeyed may have met a fate they well could have avoided. Outwardly, he displayed confidence that all was well.

That evening, he huddled alone with Bakako and Yutowa to ascertain what they had gleaned from the Indians trading. The two Guanahanians infrequently felt they shared a common bond or interest with their master, perhaps only when their survival depended on his own, such as during the storms at sea on their voyage to Spain. But the impending confrontation of peoples forebode risks to their safety just as the storms, and they were cowed by what they had heard that day and drawn to communicate that to him.

"What did you learn?" Cristóbal asked.

"It doesn't sound good," Bakako began.

Guarico and Navidad,
November 26–December 3, 1493

After Guarico's torching, Guacanagarí had relocated to an eastern village on a protected inlet with his wives and nitaínos (near Baie de Fort-Liberté, Haiti). He received Mayobanex's messenger in his caney there and jolted, wrought the reckoning long looming was at hand. He summoned brother Matuma and a cousin, a nitaíno who'd participated in discussions with Admiral the prior year.

"If Admiral blames you, he'll punish you," the cousin admonished. "He might take vengeance on our people."

"But Caonabó did most of the killing," Matuma urged. "You yourself murdered none." Matuma stared into Guacanagarí's eyes. "Not one."

Guacanagarí shrugged contritely. "I gave my word to protect his men."

"You'll explain that you tried to, and Admiral should believe you," Matuma pressed. "He'll see that your own caney and village were scorched because you defended them."

Guacanagarí groped desperately for an honest strategy. "Shouldn't I tell Admiral the truth about his men's conduct?" he sounded. "That they deserved their fate, regardless of my promise."

"Chieftains rarely blame their warriors for their own murders," Matuma pronounced.

"The rabble left with us weren't soldiers, and we weren't at war with Admiral then—or yet." Guacanagarí shook his head, judging that Admiral did have the temperament to evaluate his own men's conduct. "Their conduct points to the injustice of punishing me or our people."

"We retain few friends—if any—on Haiti who'd come to our defense from the pale men, if we need it," Matuma responded. "War looms if you tell Admiral to depart, as other caciques would have you do. Averting vengeance is just as critical. You must maintain absolute innocence."

Guacanagarí agonized that the prize of an exclusive trading alliance with Admiral, and the stature it would have boasted to other supreme caciques, were utterly lost. The outcome was even worse—his very sovereignty was imperiled—and he burned to defend it. "If I convince him that we didn't kill his men, what relationship should I pursue instead?"

"He's always sought an alliance to trade the gold they covet," Matuma proffered wanly.

"Alliance or obedience?" Guacanagarí barked hoarsely, indicating a reply unnecessary. "Admiral doesn't need seventeen ships to trade for gold."

Silence deafened, and Matuma and the cousin waited instruction.

"Matuma, you and I shall remain here while Admiral's vessels pass by to Guarico. My cousin, canoe to intercept him and accompany him to his so-called Navidad. Before he's outraged, apprise him that some of his men died of disease and some deserted and that Caonabó invaded, destroying the fort and massacring those remaining." Guacanagarí scoured for proof of his exoneration. "Tell Admiral I was wounded in the thigh while defending them. Confer discreetly with Xamabo to ascertain his understanding of Admiral's intent and how he advises that we respond."

⊡ ⊡ ⊡

The fleet departed Monte Christi at dawn on November 27 and sailed smartly west in brisk winds toward Navidad. Cristóbal fought to disguise his surging apprehension that his garrison's conduct and Indian retaliation had imperiled his conquest, his nightmare of almost a year.

After midday, a canoe approached from a cove ashore to intercept the fleet, its paddlers shouting for Admiral, but Cristóbal brushed them off, resolved to avoid even the slightest delay trading with local Indians. Regardless, the canoeists pursued the fleet through the afternoon, past dusk, and into the night, and Cristóbal marveled that the speed of Indian canoes nearly matched that of caravels with a gale for tailwind.

As night fell, Cristóbal flushed with the haunting sensation of a ship pivoting upon a reef, a reminiscence of the *Santa María*'s foundering in moonlight west of Navidad. Similar moonlight now revealed the same landmarks observed that fateful night, including the great cape he'd named Punta Santa (Point Picolet). As he came upon Navidad from the east, Cristóbal ordered sails trimmed and sounding lines hurled. By 10:00 p.m., the fleet hove to offshore a line of barrier reefs stretching west, peril burned indelibly in his memory.

Portion of Juan de la Cosa's World Map, 1500, marked for route from Guadalupe to Monte Christi to Navidad.

The voyagers pressed to the ships' rails, scanning the dark silhouette of their admiral's Española as it rose and fell beneath starry heavens east and west to the horizon, searching for signs of Spanish life. No fires were visible. Cristóbal bid the discharge of two lombards, yet the failure of flares or other response ashore grew long and eerie. For an instant, Cristóbal rued that his men's conduct must have so displeased the Lord that he had doomed them all.

The canoeists trailing the fleet soon caught up, shouting for Admiral while searching from ship to ship, declining to come aboard unless they beheld him. Startled, Cristóbal recognized one of the canoeists as Guacanagarí's cousin and beckoned him aboard, whereupon the cousin presented two gold-inlaid face masks as intimate gifts on Guacanagarí's behalf.

After sharing biscuits and water, Cristóbal interrogated him in the moonlight with Bakako and Yutowa's assistance, learning that some of Navidad's men had died of disease, quarrels among themselves, and an attack by another cacique. Guacanagarí himself had been wounded defending the men and now lived elsewhere. The cousin was distraught to learn that Xamabo had perished, and, before departing, he promised that Guacanagarí would come to greet Admiral himself. Cristóbal then lay to rest, churning as the garrison's likely demise was decried by hoot and shout from ship to ship. The voyagers' bewilderment and distrust surged to horror and indignation.

In the morning, he awoke to find that not a single Indian canoe approached to trade—although hundreds had swarmed his ships on the prior voyage. He dispatched teams of sailors and soldiers to scour Navidad for signs of life and to entreat Guacanagarí's cousin to return to the *María Galante*. Pining for more revelations, Cristóbal served the cousin not only Spanish food but wine.

"Ask him forthrightly if any of my men survive," Cristóbal directed Bakako.

Guacanagarí's cousin woefully shook his head to Bakako's translation. "The cacique Caonabó massacred all those who didn't die of sickness or at each other's hands. He is Guacanagarí's enemy."

"Guacanagarí bears no responsibility?" Cristóbal pressed.

"No. He is heartbroken he couldn't protect your men from the attack." Guacanagarí's cousin described the garrison's conduct, criticizing the men's abuse of women, recounting that Escobedo, Gutiérrez, and many others had ignored Guacanagarí's pleas to remain in his protection and died wandering about the island.

"I give you gifts for my friend Guacanagarí," Cristóbal pronounced when he felt further interrogation unproductive, pointing to satchels of tin bells, scissors and knives, and glass beads. "I also command that he come to this ship to tell me what happened himself."

After Guacanagarí's cousin departed, the search party returned to report that Navidad's fort had been burned to the ground, as well as portions of Guacanagarí's own village, but that no bodies or graves had been discovered. Accusations that Guacanagarí's absence proved his own treachery flew from ship to ship, as did snarls for stern justice.

⊡ ⊡ ⊡

Canoeists. Benzoni's *History of the New World*, 1565.

Guacanagarí's cousin took his canoe east after slipping from the *María Galante*, returning to Guacanagarí, his crew laboring mightily through the night against wind and current. Some aboard the *María Galante* believed he'd drunk too much wine to navigate directly ashore. The next day, he briefed Guacanagarí and Matuma.

"Will there be reprisals?" Guacanagarí asked.

"I didn't see that in Admiral's eyes. But your absence makes him think you are hiding and guilty."

"Did you reunite with Xamabo?"

"Admiral said he died of pestilence."

Guacanagarí was stunned, and his heart thumped to a sorrowful recollection of Xamabo's steadfast friendship and loyalty. But a sharper pang of devastation engulfed him as he grasped he'd lost the very informant he'd intended to rely on, not only to decipher Admiral's immediate plan, but to report on the relationship he'd sought with Fernando and Isabel, and—more desperately now—the pale men's customs of conquest, warfare, and enslavement. Despondent that the answer could hardly be informed, he yet asked, "Admiral's intent?"

The cousin shrugged. "You can't risk ordering him to leave the island. It's best to be friends. Perhaps he could settle outside our territory."

□ □ □

On November 29, Cristóbal reconnoitered Navidad himself and directed soldiers to excavate for the chests of gold that the garrison was to bury near the fort. He and his search party observed clothing strewn about the site and that charred weapons remained within the fort's skeleton. When the excavations found nothing, he barked for the diggers to redouble their efforts. That also proved for naught.

Cristóbal finally admitted to himself that all were dead and any gold they'd gathered would never be found. The evidence of a massacre was overwhelming, and Cristóbal steeled himself to maintain the peace between his Christians and Española's Indians that he saw essential to the latter's subjugation. It also urgently fell to him to locate the permanent settlement site where the voyagers and animals could debark.

To the latter end, he surveyed an area some miles west of Navidad. Villagers constantly fled as he approached, avoiding all contact, perturbing him. The reconnaissance was unsuccessful and further troubling, discovering yet more Spanish clothing and one of the *Santa María*'s anchors.

When they returned to Navidad, Bakako whispered to Cristóbal that he'd ferreted out where the bodies lay, and the search party soon unearthed eight corpses lightly buried between Navidad and the sea and three in fields adjacent the fort. Voyagers were shocked that the bodies' eyes were missing, and rumblings reverberated that the Indians had eaten them. Cristóbal commanded that the corpses be given Christian burials.

That evening, Cristóbal listened patiently as Fray Buil and the sovereigns' senior appointments admonished that Guacanagarí be incarcerated to demonstrate to the island's heathens that injury to Christians would be punished. Cristóbal responded that more evidence was necessary before justice was dealt.

On November 30, Cristóbal's own suspicions of Guacanagarí's guilt grew as Guacanagarí failed to appear. Yet Cristóbal maintained a demeanor of unruffled dispassion, pronouncing he would muster the facts before judgment. In the meantime, he and the voyagers would obey their sovereigns' order to establish a town forthwith. He arranged for two caravels to search for an appropriate site, captaining one himself westward toward the cove sheltered by the great cape. The other sailed east, under the command of a minor diplomat the sovereigns had prevailed to enlist, Melchior Maldonado, and piloted by Pero Alonso Niño, Cristóbal's former pilot on the *Santa María* and *Niña*.*

As Maldonado's caravel explored the protected inlet to the east, a canoe approached, and Pero Alonso recognized that it bore Matuma, whom he'd met on the prior voyage. The two men hailed each other, and through hand motions and a few Spanish words, Matuma invited the pale men's delegation ashore to meet Guacanagarí.

Guacanagarí's naborias had dressed his thigh with a cotton bandage, and he lay anxiously in his hammock. Never rising, and never revealing his consternation, he cordially received Maldonado and the delegation, conferred gifts of gold for Admiral and others present, and invited Admiral to visit as soon as possible.

Guacanagarí echoed his cousin's account of the garrison's fate and expressed that, with Xamabo's passing, he was eager to talk directly with the two young Guanahaníans to learn of Admiral's homeland. He desperately hoped to learn much more.

⧈ ⧈ ⧈

Apprised of Guacanagarí's invitation, Cristóbal brought his fleet to the inlet the next day. With Matuma's escort, he and a hundred of the most distinguished voyagers, finely attired, marched inland to the tune of lutes and drums to meet Guacanagarí, accompanied by heavily armed breast-plated soldiers, heralding the consequentiality of a state visit—and forewarning more. Bakako and Yutowa scurried close at their master's side, breathless whether peace or vengeance followed, cowed by the responsibility Admiral would place on them to achieve whatever purposes he revealed, and haunted by their promise to Xamabo to deliver his last words to Guacanagarí.

Guacanagarí's subjects reciprocated the pageantry, lining the village streets with armed warriors in an orderly fashion to usher

*Maldonado had served as an emissary at the Holy See.

the entourage to Guacanagarí's caney, which Cristóbal, together with Bakako, Yutowa, Torres, and Maldonado, solemnly entered.

Cristóbal saluted Guacanagarí, who invited him to the hammock where he continued to lie, and the two men embraced to the cheers of those assembled, including some twenty of Guacanagarí's wives, his cousin, and important nitaínos. A ceremonial duho was brought for Cristóbal, and Guacanagarí recognized Bakako and Yutowa, summoning them to sit on the ground between Cristóbal and himself. The remainder of Cristóbal's entourage and soldiers waited outside, surrounded by a multitude of Guacanagarí's subjects and warriors.

"Sometime, you must tell me everything," Guacanagarí remarked to Bakako and Yutowa, smiling with apparent cheer but punctuating the words to suggest they not be interpreted—which the youths obliged. Turning to Cristóbal, he pronounced, "I'm delighted you have returned. How fare your Fernando and Isabel?"

Cristóbal barely waited for the translation. "My Lordship, Fernando and Isabel send their love. My joy at returning to you is as great as your own. It grieves me to see you injured. It also saddens me to report that your ambassador, Xamabo, died of pestilence on the voyage home. He met Fernando and Isabel in royal audience, and Fernando embraced him. Xamabo received Christ's baptismal waters, taking none other than Fernando as his own name, and his soul is in Heaven. I have brought his crown to return to you."

Guacanagarí hid his incredulity that Xamabo had embraced the Christ-spirit or abandoned his birth name, merely nodding in appreciation. "It heartens me that Xamabo and Fernando became friends." For the moment, he chose not to ask what Xamabo and Fernando had agreed.

Cristóbal conspicuously studied Guacanagarí's bandage and engaged the issue that loomed forefront in the thoughts of everyone present—naked or clothed, bearing spear or sword.

"My Lord, how were you injured, and what became of the men I left in your protection?"

From his hammock, Guacanagarí chronicled what had happened since Admiral's departure the prior January, describing the garrison's descent into incivility and lawlessness over the spring and summer, including their neglect of gardens, stealing of food, and fighting among themselves, culminating in murders. In a graver tone, he recounted the looting of gold jewelry, denigration of Taíno spirits, and prurient relations with women and girls, including abuse and rape, and his attempts to curb these failings and crimes, the pleas he'd made to Arana, Escobedo, and Gutiérrez. He lamented Escobedo and Gutiérrez's desertion to meet Caonabó—who'd slain their band—and the Chachu band's desertion east toward the river Yaque.

Guacanagarí paused frequently as Bakako and Yutowa translated, studying whether Cristóbal's expressions revealed understanding and acceptance. Tears came to Guacanagarí's eyes when he described the abuses to his women. Cristóbal interrupted with questions infrequently. Confident the framework had been laid, Guacanagarí recounted that he and his warriors had defended Arana's band and Guarico from Caonabó's onslaught unsuccessfully, but in honor of his promise, when he was wounded and Guarico set ablaze. He finished somberly, "You find me here, in this inferior village, as my caney and Guarico were scorched."

Without waiting for a response or question, Guacanagarí limply rose from the hammock to stand before Cristóbal, transferring a coronet embedded with a *guanín* emblem heralding caciqual authority (gold alloyed with copper and silver) from his forehead to Cristóbal's. He directed nitaínos to present gold jewelry, cotton belts inlaid with gold and bone, and carved stone amulets as gifts for Cristóbal and the gentlemen present. Cristóbal reciprocated, his gentlemen tendering a silk robe, brass washbasin, and tin rings, and he bestowed—with a more solemn flourish and design—a necklace bearing the Virgin's image. Bakako and Yutowa sighed tentatively that violence had been averted.

But then Cristóbal pronounced, "I've brought my fleet's doctors. Let's step outside so they may examine your ailment in the sunlight and offer a remedy." He stared sternly into Guacanagarí's eyes to impart the severity of the request and that much rode on Guacanagarí's credibility.

Guacanagarí's eyes honed to Bakako's, begging any indication what Admiral intended, but Bakako looked away in fright.

"I'd be delighted for your behiques to cure me," Guacanagarí replied with a gracious smile.

Slowly, with Matuma's assistance, he hobbled from the caney to sit upon a duho outside it, and the multitude parted to make space for them, Cristóbal, and the doctor Chanca and surgeon Coma.

"It was blow to the thigh, inflicted by a stone," Guacanagarí explained as Coma assisted unwrapping the bandage. "It's painful but will heal."

The multitude grew silent, observing that no wound was visible. Tenderly, Chanca poked to probe Guacanagarí's thigh, and Guacanagarí groaned.

Cristóbal's instincts cried that most of Guacanagarí's story bore true—it was consistent with the other information he'd gathered, including the bodies discovered, and Guacanagarí wouldn't have burned his own village. But the wound was a lie! For an instant, Cristóbal faltered, gauging whether the deception was born of treachery or timidity, and he studied the chieftain—trapped, humbled, and ignominious before him—to discern which. While his judgments of men's faults were harsh, Cristóbal appreciated fear as well as anyone alive—of the sea, failure, or the Lord's justice—and his own fear that violence jeopardized his settlement crept through him. Decisively—for himself—he chose to forgive the lie as rooted in fright, insufficient to prove guilt.

"I'm sorry for your pain. We shall pray to the Virgin for your recovery," Cristóbal proclaimed loudly, placing his hand on Guacanagarí's shoulder so those beyond earshot would understand a friendship survived, signaling to Chanca and Coma that they were dismissed. "Let's continue our discussion here."

Guacanagarí flushed with relief and, as Matuma and nitaínos reapplied the bandage, he ordered duhos fetched for Cristóbal and his noblemen.

"I look forward to a close relationship," Cristóbal remarked, sensing advantage, an opportunity to follow charity with intrusion, dissembling that he was entirely satisfied with Guacanagarí's innocence. "Fernando and Isabel have dispatched me and many men to live with you, so we may introduce you and your peoples to our customs and our true faith. We will barter with you, trading our goods for your gold and spices, and you will remain the king of your people, treated as Fernando and Isabel's friend—and, of course, my own."

Guacanagarí remained silent and impassive, signaling he sought more explanation. Fleetingly, Cristóbal recalled the offers of alliance and submission that Alonso de Lugo and other Canarian conquistadors made to heathens at a conquest's outset and the stark threat for refusing—a requirement to choose the sovereigns' rule and Christianity or death. Spears and bludgeons vastly outnumbered swords and crossbows in the multitude about him, and Cristóbal cautiously advanced a softer approach.

"We seek to live in peace with all living on the island," he explained. "Rulers throughout who permit us to establish our settlements in Fernando and Isabel's name will prosper trading with and serving them. You will be Fernando and Isabel's most important ally, above all others, and they shall protect you from your enemies, the Caribes." Cristóbal puckered his lips. "My soldiers will deal with the island's rulers—if any—who oppose this."

Bakako's voice wilted to a whisper as he translated the warning. Yutowa mustered a nod to Guacanagarí, indicating that Cristóbal intended as he spoke. Cristóbal gleaned the Guanahaníans' sympathies but was pleased their expressions augmented the threat he intended.

Guacanagarí shuddered, aghast at the betrayal of rescue with invasion, mortified that other supreme caciques had warned him of just this moment, shamed by his foolish ignorance. Suffering months of the garrison's ungrateful, repulsive, and criminal conduct had proven naive folly. For an instant, he was tormented by visions of Caonabó's contemptuous smirk, brazen trespass and abduction, and impudent dismissal of his thoughts and stature. He trembled despondent that his choices were all terrible, as if caught by a relentless current, eventually to drown at sea regardless of which direction he swam. Distraught, he sought to avoid a subservient vassalage while protecting himself and his people from retribution.

"If you wish, I invite you and your men to settle here."

"It is too damp for us. I will take my men east." Cristóbal paused, resolute to achieve closure, but cautious. "You do welcome Fernando and Isabel's sovereignty and protection?"

"An arrangement where I remain cacique of my people, and we remain free as before, is acceptable," Guacanagarí replied circumspectly. He studied the satisfaction in Cristóbal's face and probed the promise of an ascendant alliance. "As for my enemies, would you help me punish Caonabó and abscond with his wives?"

Cristóbal was startled, recalling his impression on the prior voyage that Guacanagarí was as deft and crafty as a European prince. "I'd be pleased to, but not now," he replied. "I must establish a township first. Once settled, I'll bring Caonabó and those guilty of murdering my men to stern justice." Cristóbal studied Guacanagarí's apparent contentment and was pleased to have identified a common interest—and one that divided Española's Indians.

Guacanagarí remained devastated that Admiral's betrayal portended further betrayals and by his own ignorance of the customs and faith Admiral sought to impose. Xamabo's death precluded critical insight. "I wish to learn of your customs and homeland," he remarked. "I invite Bakako and Yutowa to spend the night with me here and tell me all they saw."

"Tonight, we all will return to my ships," Cristóbal replied, broaching no risk of the Guanahaníans' disloyalty.

"May I then visit with you upon your vessels?"

"That would be my greatest pleasure," Cristóbal replied, observing that the injury now apparently didn't impede that. "We shall celebrate our friendship and alliance tonight aboard my flagship."

Guacanagarí instructed Matuma to present Bakako and Yutowa each with a gift of a venerated stone amulet. "This is for facilitating our peoples' friendship," Guacanagarí pronounced warmly, addressing Cristóbal, but then staring to the youths. Bakako gaped fearfully to the ground.

At dusk, Guacanagarí and Cristóbal's peoples arrived at the shoreline, Guacanagarí borne by litter, his hobble mending after dismounting. Impassively, he concealed his foreboding while studying the massive vessels spread throughout the inlet, brimming menacingly with soldiers and beasts.

The two men toured the fleet in a launch, first boarding a nao bearing horses, and Guacanagarí was astonished by their height, girth, and brawn. "The pale soldiers mount atop these," Bakako explained. "Joined, they attack at terrific speed, as if evil spirits."

Drums beat, cymbals clashed, and cannons discharged aboard the *María Galante*, inviting Guacanagarí to a royal reception. Cristóbal escorted him onto and about the ship, presenting the captain's cabin, chickens and pigs, and the larger cannons of the fleet. As they ambled about midship, the two men encountered the naked women and boys taken from the islands east, huddled beside the forecastle wall. Their presence surprised Guacanagarí.

"Who are you, and why are you here?" he asked one of the women, hoping she would understand his Taíno dialect.

"We are Boriquén," she replied, in her own. "Once enslaved by Caribe, now captive to these pale men."

Guacanagarí quivered warily, recalling that Admiral had seized Cubans on his first voyage. Turning to the Guanahaníans, he inquired, "Why doesn't your master free these people?"

"We harbored on Boriquén," Bakako replied, understanding not to translate for Admiral's benefit. "He didn't release them."

"We don't know how they will be used," Yutowa observed. "But consider them enslaved—as both of us."

Cristóbal hosted Guacanagarí to a formal banquet that evening, and the two men conversed at length, each intending to strengthen their personal relationship. Guacanagarí forlornly perceived he'd already conceded too much to choose otherwise, that the current which transported him couldn't be fought, only navigated. He consented that the gift of the Virgin be strung about his neck. As the evening waned, Cristóbal introduced Guacanagarí and Fray Buil, who was ill and cabin bound.

"My lord, meet Fray Buil, who is Fernando and Isabel's supreme representative charged for bringing Christ and salvation to you and your people. Father, I introduce the Lord Guacanagarí, king of many of the island's peoples."

Buil stared at Guacanagarí's nakedness in the candlelight, startled that Cristóbal referred to him as a lord, irritated that Bakako and Yutowa were necessary to translate the simplest greeting, righteous for the justice due three dozen slain Christians, and at a loss to explain how he would implement Christ's teachings. Guacanagarí stared at the silver cross about the behique's neck and the cap atop his skull, immediately sensing the presence of the Christ-spirit.

"It's a pleasure to meet," Buil mustered. "I hope to bring you and your people to Christ and proper custom—clothing and the Spanish language."

"It'll be my pleasure to understand what you believe," Guacanagarí replied.

Cristóbal and Guacanagarí concluded the evening with goodbyes at the *María Galante*'s rail, and Guacanagarí vowed to himself never to return.

⊡ ⊡ ⊡

At the break of dawn, Cristóbal summoned Torres, Margarite, Maldonado, and Fray Buil to the captain's cabin to review the response to the garrison's massacre.

"Guacanagarí's a liar," Maldonado charged immediately. "He has no wound, and he's concocted this Caonabó attack to save his skin. He must be thrown in chains, if not worse. We must teach the naked heathens a lesson they'll remember."

"I agree Guacanagarí's guilty—at least of failing to protect our men—and likely of many of their murders, if not all," Margarite pressed. "His flight from his hometown establishes guilt, as does feigning the wound. The savages in his hometown lurked about, as if complicit." He paused, reflecting as a military commander. "I'm not sure this is the moment to punish him beyond incarceration. But we must establish at the outset that the sovereigns will tolerate no opposition to their rule."

"I said I thought he was guilty before I met him, and nothing has changed my opinion," Buil pronounced. "Whether this Caonabó did some of these deeds I don't know, but Guacanagarí's lie exposes that he participated. The Lord will deny him Heaven." He glowered at Cristóbal. "You're responsible for serving Christ's justice upon him. No heathen can escape the consequence of murdering Christians."

"I don't disagree about the wound," Cristóbal rejoined. "But I doubt he set fire to his own village." Cristóbal glared back into the eyes of each man. "We must be mindful that we are few and the inhabitants of the island many. There likely are other lords on the island friendly to Guacanagarí who would take offense if we punish him. As in our kingdoms, there may be family ties that bind them to

Guacanagarí. Punishing a lord isn't the first impression we want to impart on the others. We want their permissions to settle, not their armies to dislodge us."

"Christ's justice is blind to expediency," Buil retorted.

"So is Castilian justice," Maldonado insisted.

Cristóbal scowled to display that he scorned the last statement as ridiculous. "War with the Indians would jeopardize our execution of the sovereigns' orders—a settlement and advancement of the faith. Christ's justice demands that the truth be known first, and I doubt we know the full truth yet. If we punish him unjustly, there'll be widespread hatred of Christians. This isn't the time to irritate the islanders."

"I agree with the Admiral," Torres intoned.

"There'll be no punishment at this time," Cristóbal concluded, abruptly adjourning the meeting without further discussion. Buil, Maldonado, and Margarite departed insulted, perceiving an aloofness and condescension inappropriate for a foreigner, particularly one of newfound rank, and a disrespect for their own office and relationship with the sovereigns.

Ashore, Guacanagarí, Matuma, and their cousin held a similar council, more distraught, alone at the inlet's beach, watching the sun's first rays illuminate the masts of Admiral's vessels.

"Admiral has come to conquer," cousin lamented.

"The other caciques so perceived this," Guacanagarí responded desolately. His thoughts cascaded through visions of his interactions with Admiral, Arana, Escobedo, Gutiérriez, and other pale men over the past year, as well as with Caonabó, Guarionex, and the other supreme caciques. He rued that—of all of them—the person he'd perceived most respectful was Admiral.

"Admiral has acknowledged that I remain cacique of our people, and I expect he'll take his men to settle elsewhere, east of here," Guacanagarí pondered out loud. "Others may face his weapons, beasts, and spirits, but we can be spared." Guacanagarí pointed to the fleet. "We can't risk opposing that at this moment—all three of us would perish, along with countless of my subjects. Our only path is to accept Admiral and his army as our ally—so long as he takes no action against us."

"I'm not sure that he won't punish us," Matuma observed.

"Nor I," Guacanagarí agreed. "You must return to his vessel this morning to ascertain what he intends, including when he'll depart and to where. Trade gold for their goods. No more gifts." He addressed the sky, consulting Yúcahu.

Matuma and cousin waited patiently, observing the eerie placidity of the scene before them. Gulls, herons, sandpipers, and a few flamingos fished gracefully in the early sunrise as ever before, regardless of the alien menace intruding among them.

Guacanagarí reverted, issuing an order. "Matuma, when you're aboard Admiral's vessel, promise the Taíno women and boys he imprisons that we will harbor and protect them if they bolt ashore."

Matuma and cousin were stunned. Matuma protested, "That'll trigger vengeance."

"I understand the risk. If these Taínos bolt, we'll depart this village before vengeance can be taken. We're now Admiral's ally, and, when he asks, we'll support his settlement. But we won't support this enslavement. I hope Admiral will understand the distinction I draw."

⊡ ⊡ ⊡

That afternoon, naborias canoed Matuma to the *María Galante*, and he traded for the pale men's goods in return for gold jewelry. He spoke at length with Admiral, who intended to depart east the next day, and he surmised that punishment of Guacanagarí wasn't envisioned.

Admiral and he strolled on deck, accompanied by Bakako and Yutowa, and Matuma halted when passing the Boriquén women and boys, then squatting near the bowsprit. As if complimenting the women's beauty, he casually remarked, "If you swim ashore, the cacique Guacanagarí will protect you." Matuma shot a glance to Bakako and Yutowa, a plea to ignore the remark, which they did. Some of Admiral's men perceived Matuma flirting, prelude to intercourse, and Admiral permitted Matuma and the women to converse briefly.

That evening, as the moon approached its zenith, Bakako lay midship beside Yutowa, with only a skeletal crew alert on duty, as Admiral slept. The two Guanahanians observed the Boriquén feigning slumber, and each youth knew the other's thoughts and angst.

"Guacanagarí is our friend, as his gifts to us attest," Bakako whispered.

"Bakako, the offer of protection was made to the Boriquén, not us," Yutowa replied.

"Matuma couldn't openly speak to us," Bakako implored. "Why wouldn't Guacanagarí protect us if we swim with the women?"

"We're not ordinary slaves. We're Admiral's ears and tongue. Guacanagarí understands Admiral will pursue us, if we flee, and punish those who harbor us—far more vigorously than for these Boriquén." Yutowa despaired. "We're also Guacanagarí's ears and tongue with Admiral."

Bakako peered into Yutowa's eyes, as if to plead another conclusion.

"For days, there have been opportunities for Guacanagarí's people to encourage us to flee, and they haven't done so," Yutowa answered. "Flight's not safe—at this time."

"Will it ever be?"

As the moon descended, ten of the Taíno women and boys quietly slipped over the rail to swim a lengthy distance to shore. Their absence was discovered, Cristóbal awoken, and launches dispatched to seize them. Four were captured clambering onto the beach, but the remainder escaped into the forest.

In the morning, Cristóbal dispatched Maldonado ashore to demand that Guacanagarí hand the six over. But Maldonado returned to report that Guacanagarí's village had been deserted and that the lord and his noblemen had fled. Cries multiplied that Guacanagarí's guilt now was proven, and Maldonado, Margarite, and Fray Buil pointedly reminded Cristóbal that they'd disapproved his leniency.

Contemptuous and resolute, Cristóbal ignored them and commanded that the fleet prepare to sail east, concluding there were no practical means for seizing Guacanagarí and that doing so stupidly risked war with the Indians. He writhed that it was urgent to locate the site for a settlement where the voyagers could debark and to collect a stash of gold for prompt dispatch to the sovereigns, and he released the avaricious overseer Marquez from chains to circumnavigate Española to find some.

IV

SETTLEMENT AT ISABELA, CONQUEST PROCLAIMED

Voyage East and Establishment of Isabela, *December 4, 1493–January 6, 1494*

Cristóbal had scanned Española's northern coast on the first voyage, and, while the cove at Punta Santa west of Navidad suited a settlement, he was keen to investigate two natural harbors he'd sighted farther east, both much closer to the gold mines he envisioned in the island's interior region the Indians called the Cibao. He continued to suspect the mountainous Cibao was none other than or neighbored the Cipangu (Japan) told of by Marco Polo, vouched by the amassing of over nine hundred pesos of gold by the *Pinta*'s captain, Martín Alonso Pinzón, when trading in its foothills. Martín then had sheltered the *Pinta* in a perfectly encircled inlet with a small river, which Cristóbal had renamed Río de Gracia (River of Grace, Luperon, Dominican Republic), regardless that Martín had named it for himself. Farther east, Cristóbal also had admired a likely superior choice, a small bay at the base of a dominant coastal peak he'd named Monte Plata (Puerto Plata, Dominican Republic).

In addition to all-weather anchorage, Cristóbal sought a harbor with a beach for unloading the livestock and a natural quay, from which a pier could be extended. Ashore, it was essential that the site be dry and habitable, supplied by a river that could support twelve hundred men and the animals, proximate to fields and grassland that could be farmed and set for pasture, and blessed with earth, stone, and wood appropriate for construction. He brooded that the fate of the Navidad garrison compelled that the site be uninhabited—or at least relatively so—to avoid any immediate territorial dispute with local Indians, as well as defensible from attack.

Winter rains and adverse winds delayed departure from Guacanagarí's chiefdom until December 7, when the fleet sailed briskly east to the bay at Monte Christi. But relentless easterly winds and storms then halted the ships' progress for almost a week. The fleet braved advancing against the headwinds in daylight, but progress was so meager it retreated to Monte Christi repeatedly at night. The voyagers appreciated Cristóbal's objective, but the landsmen were unaccustomed to the pervasive drenching by storms in turbulent seas, and they trembled as the fleet floundered. Many retched, seasick. Food dampened and rotted, livestock whined and teetered or collapsed as the ships lurched, and visions of riches and glory spoiled bittersweet. All invoked the Virgin for temperate weather, for naught.

Cristóbal shifted his quarters to one of the nimble caravels and departed with a few smaller escorts into the gales, braving the storms at night, the naos and the bulk of the fleet languishing at Monte Christi. His caravels tacked arduously back and forth offshore for days, and Cristóbal barely slept while plotting and gauging their advance. Mercifully, they hove to one night in a river-mouth cove sheltered from wind and current by a western-facing promontory where the coastline jutted north, not even forty miles' sail east of Monte Christi. Days later, barely ten miles farther, they gratefully attained the haven of Río de Gracia, which Cristóbal explored. While blessed with defensible promontories and beaches to unload animals, he concluded its stream was too meager and distant from the promontories to support his settlement.

The towering Monte Plata was visible from Río de Gracia, and the caravels wanly reentered the tempestuous sea, coursing farther east. But they never arrived at the peak's harbor. Miles from Río de Gracia, a violent storm terrified even Cristóbal, and he abandoned the attempt, downhearted. When the deluge abated, he brought the caravels about to speed west with a blistering tailwind, eventually anchoring at the river-mouth cove and promontory where they'd previously sheltered. There was no harbor, but the promontory and a line of reefs extending west provided an adequate break from easterly winds and current, not nearly as protective as at Monte Christi, but ample for the entire fleet. Cristóbal debarked to explore.

The promontory was on dry, higher, defensible ground situated within fifteen minutes' walk of the river, bordered by a beach and tidal lagoon at its northern end, the sea to the west, and the river's ravine to the south. Its long eastern flank was pregnable to attack but forested, and Indians weren't resident, although fishermen occasionally appeared, likely residing inland. Although unfortunately distanced, the river was impressive, gushing fulsome through a second beach to the sea, far more water than necessary and so forceful that its waters remained sweet close upriver at low tide. A lengthy wall of stone—astonishingly perfect for a quarry—flanked the riverbed close to the promontory, and a verdant floodplain extended southwest for miles. Year-end approached, the voyagers and livestock had been at sea far longer than anticipated, and the remaining food stores were no longer adequate to last through the harvesting of crops. All clamored for their settlement—and Cristóbal chose to make it there.

The caravels returned to Monte Christi and, reunited, the entire fleet once again bore the headwinds, resolutely tacking miles from side to side to advance paltry distance ashore, beating from headland to headland, day and night, rain and storm. Early on New Year's Day, the spriest ships arrived to anchor in the cove, their wet and exhausted voyagers jubilant finally to debark, engulfed by the warmth and tranquility of firm earth. As the day grew long, ship after ship made the site, until all seventeen ships lay in calm water, fourteen weeks from departing Cádiz, having lost not a single ship and only five of twelve hundred men—four of them Indian—the entire journey. The perilous sail short of forty miles east from Monte Christi had endured as long as the entire ocean crossing from the Canaries—a ghastly three weeks, challenging and wasting the voyagers' grit, patience, and faith in their admiral. But they'd enlisted with the expectation of some hardship, particularly at sea, and their hopes and dreams were rekindled and the curse of the past weeks momentarily forgiven.

Cristóbal's plan was to construct a Spanish town just as at home, with a church, crown, and military buildings at its core, and an imposing, fortified residence for himself and his staff, all to be constructed with stone, packed earth, and tiles. The voyagers' homes would emanate from the core, ordered by social rank and built with wood and thatch. The next day, he selected the southernmost site on the promontory's seaside for his residence, overlooking his ships at anchor and the river, and a nearby spot for the church and the town's main plaza. He chose the promontory's northern bluff, abutting the beach, for the crown's custom and powder houses, which would store most everything—food and wine, gold and spice, trading truck, and weapons and munitions. A watchtower would be erected beside them, and an earthen wall would protect at least the eastern flank. He commanded his staff to line out streets and awarded small lots to voyagers on which to build their homes as soon as possible—yet consistent with their duty to construct his residence, the crown buildings, the wall, and, first and foremost, a temporary church. Plots would be designated along the riverbank for gardens, kilns would be built to bake tile and brick, and a pier would be constructed at the promontory's beach. Given the river's distance, he envisioned dikes and trenches constructed from it to channel water into the town.

Most urgently, Cristóbal directed that the fleet's provisions be brought ashore at the promontory's beach and protected from rainfall to prevent further spoilage and that corrals be roped for the livestock. The horses and other animals required prompt debarkation to curtail further losses. Rather than relaxing the shipboard daily ration, he commanded that it be tightened, most strictly for the meat. Anticipating pilfering ashore, he ordered all food and wine placed under armed guard, day and night.

During the day, Indians resident nearby cautiously approached, and Cristóbal greeted them warmly with Bakako and Yutowa's assistance, conferring gifts and receiving cazabi. The locals spoke Taíno and called the bountiful river the Bajabonico and its main floodplain tributary the Unijíca. The encounters were wary but peaceful, and many voyagers boldly encamped ashore that night. Others stuck with security aboard ship. All were cool and wet in intermittent rain yet still eager and thankful.

Shortly, the weary livestock were shoved overboard into the surf near the Bajabonico and clambered meekly onto its beach. Lanzas summarily seized the best floodplain scrub for their mounts, pigs were let to roam freely, and animal excrement dropped all about. Thatched sheds were erected hastily to store, dry, and preserve the foodstuffs, but the humidity onshore was barely less than afloat and the temperature hotter as the sun rose—so rot continued unabated. Voyagers fished the cove for the local seafood in the absence of an ample meat ration. All drank the waters of the Bajabonico for the first time, most defecated where they were—as latrine areas hadn't been designated—and few bathed, not perceiving that healthful. Some of the fleet's rats debarked.

As the settlement's construction began, the enormity and urgency of the tasks to accomplish became glaringly obvious, the sense of duty or obligation uneven, the site chaotic and increasingly unclean. Carpenters, masons, and other artisans understood their responsibility to build structures for the crown, the Admiral, and the clergy, as well as their own, and they banded together to share the construction of huts, each accommodating half a dozen or more of themselves. But the gentlemen volunteers were offended that Cristóbal demanded that they labor to build anything, even their own accommodations. As unpaid notables loyal to the crown, they envisioned supervising commoners who labored instead, or perhaps the local heathens. Gentlemen and commoners alike were affronted that Cristóbal expected all work to proceed immediately, without respite, impervious to the privations they'd already suffered.

Within four days of arrival, a third of the voyagers—some four hundred men—succumbed to grave fevers, headaches, vomiting, and diarrhea, suffering such debilitation that construction of the settlement was dramatically impeded, and those not stricken panicked that the immediacy and pervasiveness of the onslaught meant inevitably they would be.* Doctor Chanca diagnosed the illness's causes as the labor and privations of the voyage and the change of climate. Some speculated that the native fish were unhealthy. Others gloomed that the Lord was punishing a prior sin

*Modern epidemiologists speculate the causes likely included dysentery from exposure to Caribbean and European bacteria and/or parasites and influenza borne by the pigs.

or condemning the voyage. Cristóbal concluded it was the change of air, water, rain, and seafood.

He, too, grew painfully sick, but he continued to work indefatigably and insisted that those ill still work. This angered many, including crown appointments and Fray Buil, who was appalled by the absence of Christian charity, dismissive of the argument that all would be better off the sooner the settlement became functional. The gentlemen who grew sick felt doubly insulted, not only by the demand to work but for failure of excuse of illness. Cristóbal ordered that a hospital be constructed. The voyagers' morale again swooned.

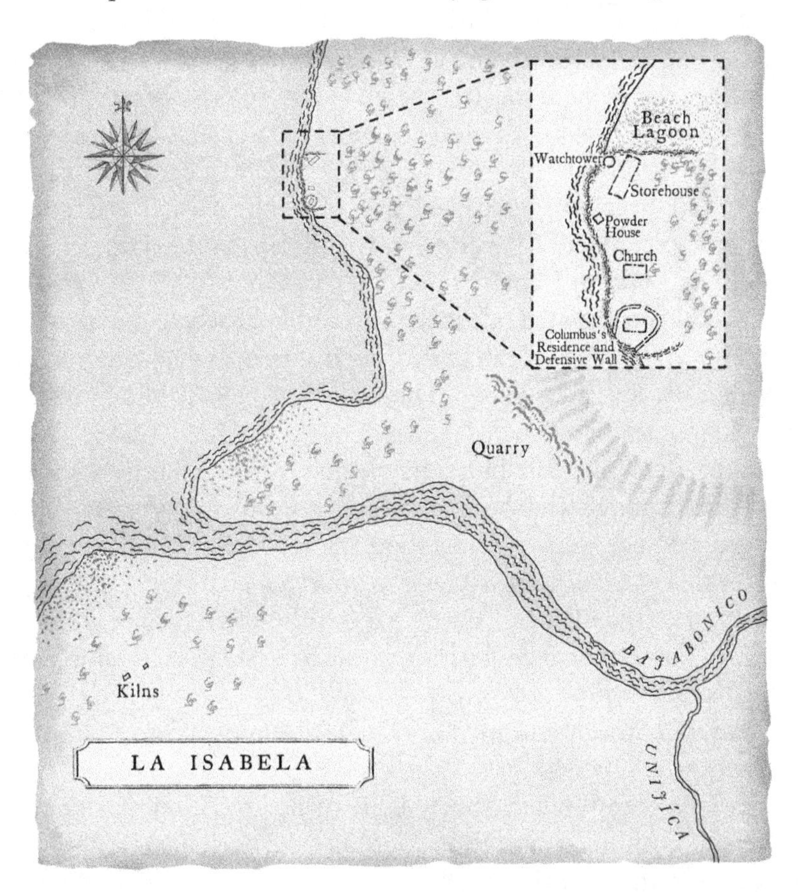

The illustration of La Isabela and the Bajabonico floodplain considers the illustrations in Kathleen Deagan and José María Cruxent's *Columbus's Outpost among the Taínos: Spain and America at La Isabela, 1493–1498* (New Haven, CT: Yale University Press, 2002) and reflects the author's evaluation of the site.

There were Indian villages nearby, and Cristóbal promptly strove to establish peaceful relations with their caciques, as the fate of the Navidad garrison continued to haunt him. Concord came readily, as the caciques feared provoking any dispute with the pale men, and they approached to introduce themselves. Cristóbal traded with them for both gold and the food the expedition now required, bartering in accordance with the sovereigns' instructions in the presence of Bernal de Pisa or a subordinate.

◘ ◘ ◘

A middle-aged cacique of hillside territory upstream the Bajabonico halted his band's approach and charily raised his arms as a gesture of friendship. "We come in peace," he hailed in Taíno, dispatching two women forward toward Cristóbal, one with a basket of cazabi, the other with a gourd of pineapple juice.

Cristóbal graciously received the offering, sniffed the gourd, sipped, and exclaimed, "We come in friendship, in the name of King Fernando and Queen Isabel."

As Bakako translated, Cristóbal waved for the cacique to stand beside him and bestowed a skullcap and mirror, which the cacique admired. Cristóbal instructed, "Diego, award bells to the noblemen and necklaces to the women."

Bakako dutifully distributed hawk's bells to the nitaínos accompanying the cacique and bead necklaces to the two women. There were four teenage girls bearing food baskets, and Bakako handed them necklaces, too. The last was a younger girl perhaps his age, slightly shorter than he, entirely naked—without a *nagua* (a woman's loincloth), so unmarried—bearing a turtle's shell brimming with turtle stew. She smiled at him.

"I can wear this about my neck?" she asked pleasantly, although the answer was obvious.

"Yes," Bakako replied, diverted. He turned to Admiral, signaling readiness to continue translation. But his gaze darted back upon the girl to discern the charm of her face—as her eyes shone directly back into his—and the firmness of her breasts.

"I seek Cipangu and the island's gold mines," Cristóbal explained, addressing the cacique. "Can you lead me to them?"

Bakako interpreted, repeating *Cipangu* precisely as Admiral had pronounced it, aware that neither he, Yutowa, nor any Taíno Admiral yet had met had ever heard of it.

"The island's peoples conduct an annual gold homage in our mountain streams," the cacique responded, ignoring the odd reference. "The regions that possess the most gold are the Cibao, to the south, and Niti, in the cacique Caonabó's chiefdom, even farther south." As Bakako translated, the cacique scrutinized Cristóbal's reaction to the mention of Caonabó, but none was revealed. "Does your cacique understand our gold homage?" he asked Bakako, whispering to indicate translation wasn't necessary.

"A bit," Bakako replied summarily, reflecting that Admiral did know of it and appeared to admire it, but conscious Admiral had no desire to discuss it then. During the rainy season, men made an annual homage—fasting and celibate—to mountain streams to honor their spirits and dig for gold the spirits revealed.

"How far are these places?" Cristóbal asked.

"The Cibao is five- or six-days' walk, depending which stream you wish to dig. Niti is twice as far. The paths to both are mountainous. You'd need Caonabó's permission to visit Niti."

"I'd be obliged if your men led mine to both places," Cristóbal replied, eyeing whether the chieftain flinched to the request to enter Caonabó's territory.

"I'd be delighted to provide guides," the cacique responded impassively. "I trust we may trade in the future?"

"We shall trade and be friends," Cristóbal replied heartily, concealing his relief that the cacique hadn't challenged the settlement's establishment. For an instant, he pondered whether to discuss Fernando and Isabel's sovereignty, as he had with Guacanagarí, but he perceived the cacique less politic, and he chose to leave discussion of subjugation conveniently to follow construction of the settlement's wall. "I'll advise you when my men are ready to depart," he added. "My interpreters—including this boy, Diego—will accompany the expedition so all can communicate."

The cacique raised a forefinger and sharpened his tone. "I trust you and your men will always treat my people lovingly."

"We shall," Cristóbal pronounced forthrightly, disguising his startle that he'd underestimated the naked man before him.

The cacique ushered the four teenage girls forward. "We've brought more food to celebrate our understanding." Pointing to the basket borne by the first girl, he said, "*mahisi*" (corn); to the second, "*boniata*" (sweet potato); to the third, "*aji*" (hot pepper); and to the fourth, "*hicotea*" (turtle). Bakako stared as the youngest girl held the turtle shell for Admiral to inspect. She was graceful, self-possessed, and beautiful.

Cristóbal expressed his gratitude once again, instructing his men to confer gloves and shirts in return and indicating the audience's conclusion. The girl pivoted slightly toward Bakako, and he instinctively stepped forward, opening his arms to receive the shell, and, for a moment, they both held it, standing close together.

"Are you a nitaíno?" she asked, her lips slightly curled to a grin, as if the answer was of interest but not concern.

"No."

She was confident his eyes wandered beyond the shell, down between her breasts to the tender skin and hair of her thighs and crotch. "But you must be very important."

Bakako was stunned, and a cry rose within that he barely restrained, *Yes, the most important slave!* But he felt a rush of bravado, an instinct to demonstrate power and authority, an urge to impress and possess. After a moment, he nodded. "I serve an important role."

"There are hundreds of pale men. How many are like you—with them?"

"Just two, myself and another."

"And you are—*Diego*?" she asked, attempting to replicate the pale cacique's pronunciation. "Such a strange and beautiful name."

"No, I'm not," Bakako firmly exclaimed. "That's what they call me. But my name is Bakako—call me Bakako."

"I think I understand. My name is Niana," the girl replied. She peeked into his eyes invitingly, pondering whether he was smitten. "You must be lonely, Bakako." She released the shell and looked to the cacique, who was departing with his entourage. "My father is leaving, I must go. I hope you enjoy the stew."

Bakako flushed with a confidence long forgotten. "I'll let you know."

◻ ◻ ◻

Within days, Cristóbal ordered Alonso de Hojeda and Ginés de Gorvalán, the gentleman captain with combat experience in the Reconquista, to organize an expedition of over thirty lightly armed soldiers to explore for gold in the Cibao and, if prudent, toward Niti, to be accompanied by the local guides arranged. Cristóbal impressed the two with the urgency of gold's discovery in the absence of a hoard stowed by the Navidad garrison, imperative for satisfying the sovereigns when ships soon returned to Spain. Gold's shimmer also would bolster the voyagers' plummeting morale, as it was uppermost in their minds and their reason for suffering the voyage's privations and dangers. Cristóbal warned Hojeda and Gorvalán to restrain the soldiers from bartering meanly with the Indians, looting their trophies, or disparaging or molesting them—as peaceful relations were essential. To reduce nighttime contact with women, Cristóbal forbade the expedition from sleeping in Indian villages whenever possible. Gorvalán was to withdraw if advancing into Caonabó's territory appeared to engender hostilities.

Hojeda and Gorvalán embraced their appointments and appreciated Cristóbal's concerns. They had little difficulty recruiting men, as many volunteered, and word of the pending reconnaissance swept through the encampment to cheer even those ill.

By January 6, wood and thatch huts dotted the site, including makeshift structures for the church and Cristóbal's residence, and the promontory had been trodden to mud by the daily toil and rain. The church was sanctified by an altar cross and adorned with cloth tapestry furnished by the queen, and Cristóbal summoned the entire expedition to celebrate the Feast of Epiphany, standing in the muck surrounding it. Isabel had bestowed a church bell, too, which graced their midst on a bed of branches, awaiting its berth's construction with stone.

Still ill, Fray Buil presided over the settlement's first mass. He heralded his mission and led a prayer for a voyager who'd died of fever, as well as for a few others whose death loomed, as the daytime heat prevented cooling them. The voyagers sang hymns invoking the

Virgin's protection, which murmured through the humidity to the settlement's environs, where neighboring Taínos gathered to observe in fascination. Cristóbal named the town and the Bajabonico for the queen, Isabela and Río Isabela.

One of the religious enlisted, the Catalan Ramón Pané, a young Hieronymite friar, proudly embraced Fray Buil's sermon and glowed that Christ's word had crossed the Ocean Sea for the benefit of the Indians watching. He was ennobled by his duty to spread that word yet uncertain how he and his colleagues would accomplish the task. Ramón studied the congregation's suffering and appreciated that Christ's work would occupy him with it, too—a task he hadn't appreciated but welcomed. The men about him were rougher than the peasant farmers who neighbored the countryside monastery he'd served in near Barcelona, and Ramón mused whether they would assist in bringing the Indians to Christ.*

After the service, Cristóbal summoned Bakako and Yutowa to account, standing alone on the bluff where his residence would be built.

"What happened to my Samanán?" Cristóbal brusquely pried. "He tempts the Lord's punishment."

The two teenagers shrugged anxiously, staring to the ground.

"When he's found, I'll punish him severely," Cristóbal pronounced sternly. He let the sea's rumble preside a moment and then, as a Genoese merchant, pivoted from fear to want.

"Remember King João? The Guineans his men seize to become interpreters are freed after four voyages—if they've served obediently."

The teenagers raised their sights but not their hopes.

"I haven't decided whether that's appropriate for you," Cristóbal lied, staring back at them. "But I do know this—as long as you serve me, you'll talk and dine with the kings of your people. You'll never want for your women, and you may marry a princess. That's far more than your wildest dreams when I took you from Guanahaní."

In silence, Bakako trembled, Yutowa writhed.

"I'm dispatching you with Hojeda and Gorvalán," Cristóbal ordered, glaring at Yutowa. "Help them find the Cibao's gold and keep peace. Return with them to me." Turning to Bakako, he warned,

*The Monastery of Sant Jeroni de la Murtra, Badalona.

"You'll remain with me—but times will come when I dispatch you, too, with others." Cristóbal raised a forefinger to each. "The consequence will be severe if you dare desert me. Understand?"

Cristóbal's arrival. Honorius Philoponus, 1621.
John Carter Brown Library, rec. no. 04056-9.

Cristóbal studied them as they nodded. "Now, swear that loyalty before the Lord."

◘ ◘ ◘

Caonabó and the other supreme caciques had received frequent reports from informants about the pale men's audiences with Guacanagarí and his relatives, and scouts now daily spied upon the settlement at the Bajabonico and drew information from caciques who traded with it. Caciques throughout the island came to acknowledge Caonabó's foresight—that the pale men intended to usurp territory—yet the purpose and extent of incursion were unknown, the danger uncertain.

Caonabó remained resolute that ceding any territory to the pale men risked the entire island, and he grew impatient that caciques, nitaínos, and wives counseled restraint, observation, and even friendly communication with the pale men. He summoned his general, Uxmatex, to stroll alone by his village's river to consider the threshold question (the San Juan River, Dominican Republic).

"The caciques at the Bajabonico have no alternative but to befriend the pale men," Caonabó observed. "I don't begrudge that. Mayobanex might lead warriors to oust them. I doubt Guarionex or Behecchio will, and Guacanagarí obviously won't."

"You must seek as broad an alliance as possible, given their weaponry," Uxmatex cautioned.

"We'll seek that alliance, but that will take words and time. My question is immediate, simply of combat. Shouldn't we attack right now, alone? Aren't the pale men at their most vulnerable before they construct defenses?"

"Taínos would never build a village so close to the sea, so openly exposed to Carib raid and *huricáns* [hurricanes]. They've built there to guard against an inland attack—precisely from us, no doubt, blaming us for their men's execution, expecting we'll try again. The site is well protected by the sea, the Bajabonico, tidal marsh, and forest. Warriors could charge through the forest and on the narrow beach, but our advantage is our overwhelming number, and the forest and other barriers impede that advantage."

"But their eastern flank will never be weaker than it is today. Why delay?"

Each man racked that victory was doubtful. The pale men's beasts were reputed to be terrifying and their weapons already known to be powerful. While their number was insignificant, their site was well chosen and defensible and their confidence brazen and foreboding.

Caonabó grimly answered himself. "We must find more advantage before attempting to drive them out. I expect they'll enter the interior, diffusing and exposing themselves band by band, just as before. Perhaps other caciques will wake to the threat and deny them food." He faced the sky. "Perhaps Guabancex will unleash her wrath upon them." He admonished his general. "An attack must vanquish them entirely, or they'll regroup for vengeance."

Cristóbal, His Officers, and Slaves, *January 7–March 11, 1494*

Alonso de Hojeda, Ginés de Gorvalán as his lieutenant, and their squadron departed after Isabela's first mass to garner the gold their admiral had promised their king and queen. At Cristóbal's request, Michele da Cuneo accompanied them. Their local guides and Yutowa led them along a footpath tracing the Unijíca, meandering through a verdant plain to rise southwest into foothills and mountains. They passed villages occasionally, encountering friendly locals offering cazabi and water. Heavy rain muddied the narrow trail and, as they transported rations for two weeks, the ascent grew arduous. They camped the second night at a high pass with views peeking south through heavy foliage and mist into a great valley, extending east and west to the horizon. Alonso understood that the *Pinta*'s captain had surmounted a pass en route to the Cibao's gold on the first voyage, and Yutowa confirmed that the locals assured this was the same.

In the morning, Alonso's men tramped the slippery path down the mountainside to emerge from forest onto an enormous expanse of villages, gardens, and fields lining the river Yaque with a tremendous population. The vista reminded them of the Guadalquivir's floodplain at Córdoba and Seville. Word of their expedition preceded them, and local caciques greeted Alonso warily and courteously, seeking to trade gold jewelry for the unknown cloth, glass, and metal items for which the pale men now were associated.

Yutowa quickly recognized that the caciques spoke a different tongue, that of their fellow Samanán captive (Macorís), although he was able to converse with them in Taíno to accomplish Alonso's barter and arrange the expedition's journey. The local caciques appreciated the pale men sought to trade for gold, assured that the Cibao's streams overflowed with it, and offered to guide them there, leading them first east along the Yaque.

As they strode through villages, Alonso's men quickly recognized that the opportunity beckoning enlistment now was at hand and that the Admiral wasn't. On the sly, barely, each man began to trade personal items for his own stash of jewelry and trophies—a spare button for a gold earring, a worn sock for a gold-inlaid face mask, a soiled handkerchief for a guanin-studded amulet. Villagers eagerly accommodated.

Alonso quickly chose to look away. He understood his oath that the gold collected was for the king and queen, as well as Cristóbal's instruction that the men not swindle the Indians for trophies. But he dismissed that strict adherence to these rules was expected of Christians in the field among heathens. Obedience would require stern discipline and quash the men's enthusiasm and vigor—and deny their keenest aspiration for enlisting. Nor would the squad tolerate of him the same discipline paid the Admiral.

As the afternoon waned, Alonso's expedition and escort arrived at a switchback where the Yaque broadened and shallowed, and they forded and continued south. At dusk, all arrived at a village on the plain, and a local cacique offered bohíos for the night. Ignoring Cristóbal's instruction, Alonso permitted his men to shelter within to avoid the rain. The daily ration of Spanish food was insufficient for the expedition's exertion, and, although the taste displeased them, many men reluctantly ate the food their host offered, and all drank from the Yaque's tributaries.

That night, Alonso did seek to enforce Cristóbal's sternest command that the men not mingle with or abuse the Indian women, and his men resented him for that, coolly observing that was a dream of enlistment, too. At dawn, Yutowa and the guides helped themselves to minor portions of their host's cazabi, considering food common property to be shared gratefully in moderation. Alonso and his men beheld the custom yet took the liberty of serving themselves the much larger portions they hungered, as well as sweet potato and peppers. Although he would have served them freely, the host was affronted, both for failure of an expression of thanks and by the immoderacy of the amount taken.

The expedition trekked south in intermittent storms for two days, ascending the foothills of the Cibao, and all grew keen that their exertion and hardship would be rewarded with the discovery of streambeds glistening with gold nuggets. Most also grew ill with fever. They came to a river torrent, heavily swollen by downpours, and Alonso chose not to risk fording but to encamp in a nearby village until the waters subsided.*

They remained there some nights, and, with Yutowa's assistance, Alonso bartered with the local cacique for three large uncut gold nuggets and more jewelry. Cristóbal maintained that Ptolemy and the ancients had predicted that gold deposits abounded in the earth's torrid zones, close to the heat of the equator, and, in the swelter of Española's day, Cuneo considered that the three pieces so confirmed. Alonso interrogated the cacique whether the Cibao's streambeds bore similar nuggets and concluded that fifty streambeds did. The cacique demonstrated how his people searched for gold, boring his arm into the silt of a streambed to retrieve a handful of muck from which kernels or dust might be separated. Alonso surmised that the picks, shovels, and superior know-how of Christians could dramatically increase the streambeds' yield.

The cacique offered to ferry the expedition by canoe across the river, but the stifling humidity had spoiled the remaining Spanish foodstuffs, and Alonso doubted most men were fit to hike into mountains. He ordered Gorvalán to cross the river with a reduced contingent, while he returned to Isabela with the confirmation Cristóbal sought—although without more gold. Alonso bid the cacique provide naborias to port the expedition's gear back to Isabela, which was obliged.

Gorvalán and men ascended for another day into the Cibao's mountains, where they met an artisan tamping gold ornaments and picked grains of gold and silver from river sand beds. At night, some sought to entice village women to lie with them.

Haggard, Alonso and his squad returned to Isabela on January 21, and Gorvalán's contingent a day later. Rumor of their discoveries spread as windblown wildfire, with judgments scattered just as wildly. Many brimmed with optimism—even merriment—including

*Likely the Río Amina, which retains its Taíno name.

Cuneo and the doctors Chanca and Coma. Chanca expressed that the sovereigns henceforth could regard themselves as the richest princes in the world. Others were more measured, concluding that samples had been found indicating large gold deposits might be dug. Some were openly dismissive, including Bernal de Pisa and his subordinates, deriding that the nuggets and jewelry were meager and motley. The sovereigns had enlisted a goldsmith on the voyage, Fermín Zedo, and he scoffed at the pieces, observing that almost all were jewelry amassed over generations.

Cristóbal proclaimed triumph, Alonso echoing him. Yet privately Cristóbal vexed that he possessed merely samples of gold to dispatch to his sovereigns, not a barrel. The overseer Marquez had returned from encircling Española without collecting more—at least for the sovereigns' account. Cristóbal despaired Isabel and Fernando's impatience for ready success—which he'd whetted—and he was enraged by a rumor that Pisa charged he'd lied about gold's abundance.

⊡ ⊡ ⊡

Regardless of gold's urgency, the settlement's health remained a graver calamity. During Hojeda's reconnaissance, the voyagers fever-stricken had swollen to surpass six hundred men—a majority of the entire expedition—debilitating or incapacitating their construction of the crown structures, living huts, and protective wall. Doctors Chanca and Coma labored to discover and offer cures, and the fleet's supply of medicines soon exhausted, save stores reserved for Cristóbal and his senior command. While most voyagers gradually recovered over weeks, some dozens succumbed, and the church's graveyard filled faster than the erection of its walls.

The supplies of Spanish food were nearly depleted, the meat entirely consumed when voyagers shunned the local fish for fright of pestilence. The settlement's gardens had been sown, and germination was encouraging, with sprouts rising, including wheat, chickpeas, and beans. But the yield was unknown and weeks or months away, and Cristóbal grittily reduced the men's daily ration even further. The lure of provisioning a sovereign-sponsored fleet always attracted cheaters, and Cristóbal was quick to observe that defects in supplies exacerbated the crisis. He deemed wine the singular essential strengthening provision that fortified crews over the privations of long voyages, and he angrily concluded the leakage in the fleet's wine casks had far exceeded his prior experience and that coopers supplying the casks had cut corners in their construction to reduce their cost. He also suspected some foodstuffs and equipment inventoried had never been loaded.

The pace of Isabela's construction slowed beyond his worst expectation. Of the men healthy, many attended the ships and guarded the settlement's perimeter—day and night—and weren't available for building work. He'd forced the volunteers to contribute, but he cursed that their efforts were half-hearted, often disingenuous. Infuriating him, the Lanzas refused to permit their mounts to be used for labor, or to do any labor themselves other than for their and the mounts direct benefit, regardless that the sovereigns had compensated them to serve him. He'd been shocked by the poor health of the horses when they debarked at Isabela, and rumors abounded that Lanzas had sold their battle-ready mounts dearly in Cádiz before sailing and replaced them with nags bought on the cheap, pocketing the difference.

Every voyager—every waking moment—now desperately hungered for Spanish food, starved by the rationing, the sickness, and the exertion. Cristóbal reinforced the guard duty at the food stores, but tampering and pilfering grew frequent. When men were caught, he applied justice severely, imprisoning those who traded personal items for rations with the guards, as well as the guards. Those who stole provisions lost their hands or feet to the sword. All violators forfeited future rations.

Cristóbal met frequently with Torres, Fray Buil, and Margarite to discuss the settlement's trials and the scalding discontentment then surging.

"Admiral, your punishments are too harsh," Fray Buil admonished.

"Father, harsh they are," Cristóbal acknowledged. "But not unknown at home for similar offenses."

"Perhaps, but not in practice," Buil responded. "The motive of those guilty was hunger, not evil. Mercy is due."

"If not mercy, restraint," Margarite cautioned. "Punishments due often don't help in the field. Avoid the men's contempt. Be clement and politic. Incarcerating is essential for deterrence, but more unwise."

"I'll risk contempt before disobedience," Cristóbal replied. "Our provisions must hold until crops are fit for harvest or the sovereigns resupply us." He turned to Buil. "I'm admiral ashore, as well as at sea. I understand the men's hunger, but all enlisted with some expectation of hardship, and mercy for this disobedience isn't due."

Buil shook his head. "Withholding rations is un-Christian, even from the sinful—if these men be that. Forgive men their trespasses."

Cristóbal was shocked by the charge's gravity and the speaker's high authority. He shook his head in denial but withheld a scornful response. "The Lord appreciates the punishments have curtailed the trespasses—to everyone's benefit."

There was silence, but Torres alertly saw to break it. "Gentlemen, the situation is dire, and dire measures justified. The king and queen wouldn't take issue with the punishments to date—I certainly don't." He clenched his lips to indicate finality and then addressed Cristóbal. "But your governance must retain the men's support. The sovereigns expect that."

Cristóbal fought again to restraint an outburst, outraged that Torres, Buil, and Margarite had witnessed the volunteers' and Lanzas' brazen disobedience. *The support due is to obey me!* he barked to himself. But he gathered his wits and chose to probe—or challenge—the loyalty of those present.

"I do understand my command," he retorted, casting a glance into each man's eyes. "All of us must support the queen's mission! I've heard the queen's own accountant criticizes it behind my back—and hers." Cristóbal glared to Buil and squinted to Margarite. "Did you know that? Pisa's insubordination hardly rouses the men's support."

Buil glared in return, but Torres preempted a response. "Pisa is but an accountant. He may express an opinion. We have ignored it, and so will others."

Eschewing conflict, Torres steered the remainder of their council to the arrangements for returning most of the fleet's ships to Spain, as always contemplated, and the potential for transporting home a substantial proportion of the voyagers ill and disaffected. None could disagree—their removal would reduce the drain on the settlement's resources and the sovereigns' ongoing costs.

Cristóbal also huddled often with his trusted servants—the steward Pedro de Terreros, page Pedro Salcedo, and Bakako—ensconced alone at his residence's ledge overlooking the cove, where their voices were drowned by the sea's wash.

"What are my detractors scheming—Pisa and the Lanzas' commander?" Cristóbal queried Terreros.

"Pisa calls you a cheat daily, both to his assistants and those from the queen's household. He derides the men's rations, claiming it evidence of your incompetence and cruelty."

"A courtier," Salcedo interjected. "Unaccustomed to the mariner's regimen."

Cristóbal shook his head. "Accustomed to favor, privilege, and immunity."

"He charges that you've lied about the gold—there's hardly any," Terreros recounted. "You've deceived everyone that the Indians are friendly—they're murderers. Your fantasy that this is the Indies is absurd—it's a forsaken bog of savages, poor and brutish, undeserving even a ducat of the sovereigns' purse." Terreros looked to the ground. "The Lanzas refer to you as the conniving Genoese."

"Does Pisa plot or merely bloat? Does he have henchmen?"

"He'll report criticisms to the sovereigns when Torres sails, undoubtedly. His assistants chime in unison."

"I've seen him confer with Fray Buil often," Salcedo charged.

"Spy on them closely, root out evidence," Cristóbal directed. He turned to Bakako. "What of the local Indians? Do they remain content with us?"

Since the settlement's establishment, Cristóbal had posted Bakako, an accounting officer, and soldiers at the promontory's perimeter to barter with visiting Indians for food baskets, often dispatching them on trading forays to neighboring villages. Bakako had established relationships with several caciques, visiting a few of them repeatedly, including Niana's father. He'd even lingered to flirt with Niana but always returned to Isabela with the soldiers.

"Admiral, still friends."

"A single torch could raise the entire encampment," Cristóbal observed, studying the myriad of wood huts under construction. "Is any cacique dissatisfied?"

For an instant, Bakako reflected that all were dissatisfied, affronted, and distrustful, deploring the pale men's presence. But he recognized Admiral didn't care about that and sought only to know if the settlement risked attack—which it didn't, since the local peoples appeared too cowed to seriously contemplate that. "None anger. None attack."

"Any word of Caonabó?"

Bakako shook his head.

"Be alert. You needn't always be in the company of soldiers—so long as you return to me. Mingle with the caciques, accept their invitations to dine, and get to know them and they you. Be my eyes and ears. Discover their sentiments and intentions, and keep me informed."

Cristóbal concluded the audience. After the three departed, he knelt to pray, beseeching the Lord to continue shepherding him through the mounting woes—over enemies both within and without.

⊡ ⊡ ⊡

As January waned, Cristóbal set the arrangements for Torres's return to Spain with twelve ships bearing short of three hundred men, voyagers too sick or disgruntled to remain and the necessary crews, reducing those at Isabela to nine hundred. Cristóbal would retain indefinitely two naos—the *María Galante* and *Gallega*—and three caravels, including the *Niña*, for protection from Indian danger and terra firma's discovery. He concluded a private letter to Isabel and Fernando that chronicled the voyage unfolding and presented the unexpected news that would capture their immediate attention. He also crafted a memorandum instructing Torres what to request of the sovereigns for remedying needs and setbacks, prepared so it could be shared with courtiers as Torres lobbied for fulfillment. The posts pronounced the Indies would be most prosperous and affirmed that Cristóbal hadn't found less than he'd promised—although setbacks had prevented more from being dispatched home. Neither revealed the number of voyagers dead or disillusioned after residing barely a month at the settlement.

To the sovereigns, Cristóbal's letter divulged that the entire garrison at Navidad had perished, mostly massacred by the Indians, assessing that the garrison had disobeyed his orders to remain vigilant and at the fort and, through their own misbehavior, brought vengeance upon themselves, particularly for excessively frequenting the Indian women. But it reaffirmed the Indians' timidity and disposition to follow orders without resistance, claiming these traits so obvious that the voyagers wondered at the carelessness by which the garrison had died. Cristóbal well understood his sovereigns' penchant for stern justice, and the letter excused Guacanagarí, blaming Caonabó instead but advising that destroying Caonabó would have to follow the settlement's establishment. It also apprised that voyagers had grown gravely ill with fever but reassured that the illness typically ran its course in but four to five days.

Cristóbal did wax unequivocal of the settlement and gold. A town had been founded in the queen's name, and he begged the sovereigns to make it a city, for which it possessed ample anchorage, water, and farmland. Hojeda had located rich mines in proximate riverbeds and secured samples from each river, although Cristóbal had ordered him not to gather more to avoid angering the locals. Gorvalán's expedition had similar success in a different area, and captured Caribes had revealed that their islands east of Española possessed infinite gold.

The memorandum's most urgent request was for ships to arrive in Española by May with fresh supplies, particularly medicines, wine, and meat, with two ships sailing forthwith. While the soil and climate were fertile, Cristóbal admitted farming had been tested only recently, owing to the delay in siting the settlement. Wine and food shipments would be required indefinitely, until the agriculture was established. He feared Fonseca and the sovereigns' chief accountant, Juan de Soria, would delay, and he authorized Torres to engage a Sevillian merchant—leaving Berardi unnamed—to finance the first two ships' immediate dispatch, repayment secured by a pledge of the gold samples Torres brought home. Cristóbal also elaborated practical reasons why Torres brought but specimens of gold rather than barrels, citing lack of roads and beasts for portage, and he requested the dispatch of knowledgeable miners. He characterized

Caonabó as evil and daring and forthrightly warned that the settlers risked Indian attack if they failed to openly display their watchfulness and military superiority, and he requested the prompt dispatch of more weapons and ammunition.

"What should I tell the sovereigns about your senior command?" Torres asked when Cristóbal summoned him to review the memorandum aboard the *María Galante*.

"Praise Margarite, Hojeda, and Chanca," Cristóbal responded. "The memorandum specifies the persons you'll recommend for recognition or extra compensation or emoluments—particularly yourself, on whom I've steadfastly relied." He smiled to affirm his and Torres's friendship and then puckered his lips to reveal disgust. "I assume there are volunteers who've done good service, but you'll request that the lot of them be salaried so they become accountable and obedient." He pointed a finger, marking an accusation. "You'll also expose that Soria substituted men I never met for Lanzas and that the Lanzas substituted lame mounts. My letter demands punishment of the wine-cask coopers and those who stole provisions prior to our departure from Cádiz. Be sure the sovereigns understand Fonseca was responsible for these provisions and that some officials here care more for their personal interests than their duties."

Torres nodded somberly, indicating agreement yet shy of the intrigues and perils inherent in accusing other sovereign appointments, no less ranking administrators. "And Pisa?"

"I want him removed to Spain, and I beg you seek the sovereigns' approval."

"The papal legatee?"

Cristóbal looked bitterly away, chafing that any derogation of Fray Buil would echo to discredit himself, merely shaking his head.

Cristóbal's posts observed that if Isabel and Fernando so permitted, an infinite number of Caribes—flesh eaters hostile to their Indian subjects—might be enslaved each year, and each Caribe possessed strength and intelligence superior to three Guinean slaves. He invited the sovereigns to examine the Caribes Torres was transporting, keen that they evaluate the wealth obtainable through slave trading these people, and suggested that these Caribes be trained as interpreters to assist the Indians' conversion, which was hampered by the language barrier. Española's Indians—Cristóbal argued—would credit enslavement of their enemy and be brought to obedience as the sovereigns' vassals when they saw the punishments inflicted on evildoers. Inspired by Berardi's financing of Canarian conquests, he ventured even further to propose that the sovereigns license merchants every year to bring desired livestock to Española to be bartered for enslaved Caribes, on which the sovereigns would impose an import duty when hauled to Spain for resale.

Torres's fleet sailed for Spain on February 2. The key cargo was thirty thousand ducats' worth of gold—almost entirely jewelry or pieces removed from face masks or other ornaments—obtained in trade with Guacanagarí, at Isabela, or in the Cibao. There were samples of novel spice plants and cotton, spears and other trophies, sixty parrots, and the then remaining twenty-six heathens from Guadalupe and Santa Crux. While Cristóbal understood these heathens included many previously enslaved by Caribes, neither his letter nor the memorandum differentiated their treatment in the sovereigns' hands from that contemplated for the few Caribes among them—as slaves. The only heathen not bound for Spain was the toddler, whom Cristóbal felt too young to travel—although he promised to send the boy when the sovereigns so ordered. Torres also bore the ocean map that Cristóbal had completed with the assistance of the Boriquén women, depicting Spain and all the islands yet found on both voyages, plotted on quadrants of latitude and longitude Cristóbal believed consistent with Ptolemy's geographic teachings.

Cristóbal was sorry to lose Torres's hand in corralling Fray Buil and Margarite's cooperation, but Torres's imprimatur before the sovereigns was critical. Cristóbal anguished that Torres also conveyed the sovereigns' sealed letters from Fray Buil and others of their household.

⧈ ⧈ ⧈

As the settlement slept, Pedro de Terreros and Pedro de Salcedo reported in the predawn twilight to their admiral the dirt they had gathered surreptitiously about Pisa and his assistants, who worked aboard the *Gallega*. They spoke softly, seated on benches within the walls rising to become Cristóbal's fortified residence, now waist-high in a rectangular plot, some forty by eighteen feet.

"Loyal crew on the *Gallega* have spied for us," Terreros related. "They say Pisa and henchmen have drawn written charges against you—for delivery to the king and queen. The guilty include Gaspar de Salinas and at least three others."

"Reward those revealing this scandal extra rations and bid they remain alert," Cristóbal ordered. "Is Fray Buil involved or aware?"

"The crew wouldn't necessarily know, and that's not alleged. But there's more," Terreros replied, rasping hoarsely. "Pisa implored sailors that sovereign duty called all to deliver these charges to the king forthwith—by commandeering the *Gallega* and caravels homeward while you sleep! He's conspiring mutiny!"

Cristóbal was stunned, and a vision of Soria and Pisa scheming together to sabotage the voyage and denounce him before the sovereigns overwhelmed him, their abiding hatred for his nobility and Genoese origin enraging him. Yet he steadied, surmising that the plan's conception was too outlandish, its execution too improbable, to be realistic. "That's treason on land, mutiny at sea, and a violation of Pisa's oath to remain but an accountant. Perhaps the crew misunderstood. Wasn't Pisa just bemoaning jealousies, exhorting whims not seriously contemplated?"

"Your sailors thought Pisa resolute, cajoling them to sail under his command, usurping yours."

"How did my sailors respond?"

"Admiral, everyone hungers, most are sick, some have lost companions, and few—if any—have yet found what brought them here. I expect many relish returning to Spain with him. But they're sailors, and they understand their paramount duty to you—regardless of the privations. They haven't any affection for royal courtiers, and they won't participate in his mutiny."

Cristóbal pondered. "Has anyone seen the written charges? What's the evidence of conspiracy—but testimony of sailors? Are any officers or educated?"

"No one's found a document. The sailors are simple men, but honorable."

"Should I arrest Pisa and the cohorts now—or wait until the crime's hatched?"

Cristóbal ruminated over the question for days, reluctant to shatter the superficial accord yet observed between himself and the sovereigns' appointments. But the reports of impending mutiny multiplied, and he soon ordered Pisa and four assistants seized and incarcerated—to the shock of the entire settlement. Pisa's written charges were found stuffed in a buoy aboard the *Gallega*, and the accomplices soon confessed under whiplash.

Cristóbal forthrightly manifested his authority to decide criminal cases and brandished the severity of his justice. He found Gaspar de Salinas, Pisa's assistant and scribe of the charges, as guilty as Pisa and—since Gaspar was but a commoner—sentenced him to a prompt public hanging. Cristóbal felt he lacked the authority to so sentence a royal official, and Pisa was chained and hauled to the *María Galante*'s brig, to be held for surrender to the sovereigns when ships next sailed. Pisa's rations, and those of the remaining conspirators, were severely curtailed, and the remaining conspirators were punished with an additional whipping and indefinite incarceration.

After the execution, Cristóbal, Fray Buil, and Margarite had words at the church site, where walls on a plot fifty by twenty feet now were shoulder height.

"As the pope's representative, I condemn these punishments as too severe," Buil admonished. "The men are under stress. The Lord disapproves withholding food from those hungry, even the guilty."

"What crime is as severe as treason to one's sovereigns?" Cristóbal responded brusquely.

"These men conceived their actions as loyal to the king and queen—who remain unaware of the deprivations to which you've brought everyone."

"Father, these men weren't loyal, by any stretch," Margarite sternly interjected. Turning to Cristóbal, he warned, "But many sympathize with them. Be less harsh. Don't fuel the charge that you're cruel." Gazing at them both, he implored, "The men's leadership must be united."

The three parted acrimoniously. Cristóbal directed that the fleet's firearms and munitions be removed from the site for the powder house, under guard of soldiers, to aboard the *María Galante*, under guard of sailors.

◻ ◻ ◻

"The pale men are dying and departing home," Uxmatex reported to Caonabó. "Over a thousand arrived, yet hundreds fewer remain. Many are ill. It's incredible—although fish, fowl, yuca, and fruit abound, many appear to be starving."

"Yúcahu may intend to rid them by pestilence, hunger, and misfortune rather than arrows," Caonabó replied. "Or perhaps Yúcahu reveals that is how we should fight them."

"We must now enlist or force the local caciques to withhold food," Uxmatex urged.

"We could, but that would put them in jeopardy. We can inflict misfortune ourselves."

Uxmatex's eyes glimmered, and Caonabó was pleased his general was quick to anticipate his thoughts.

"We must scorch their village, just as Guacanagarí's," Caonabó commanded. "It must appear as the spirits' condemnation, not attributable to us or the local caciques. It'll demoralize the pale men to behold their shelters destroyed, and even more may depart."

"I'll dispatch stealthy warriors, instructed to wait the moon's wane and strong winds."

◻ ◻ ◻

At dusk, upstream the Bajabonico, the cacique of hillside territory summoned his daughter, Niana, to kneel before him in the seclusion of a verdant gorge descending to the river. The pale men had visited his village repeatedly to barter for food, and he expected they would return soon.

"You've spoken to the pale cacique's interpreter a number of times," he observed. "The boy enjoys your company."

Niana nodded, uncertain what followed, anxious that her flirtations with Bakako had irritated her father.

"Befriend him," he continued, outstretching his hand tenderly to lift Niana's chin so their eyes met. "Of necessity, we've acquiesced in the pale men's occupation of neighboring land, but I haven't decided whether we should indefinitely. I need to understand their intent for us, and you must help me find out."

Niana nodded again, frightened by the responsibility. "Father, I do expect they intend to rule us."

"Child, I expect the same. But they wouldn't be the first, or the last, to so intend, and I don't know whether their rule would be kindly or terrible. We provide tribute to the cacique Guacanagarí every season, dispatching him a portion of our food production. We do the same for Mayobanex. I must determine the best outcome for our villagers, whether to oppose the pale men's presence or not."

"Father, we could never oppose them. They're too powerful."

"Not alone. But Caonabó or others may choose to do so and seek our assistance, in secret." The cacique pondered uneasily, sobered by his daughter's youth yet proud of her cleverness. "I might offer you in marriage to the boy to cement friendship with his masters. I might ask you to betray his confidences to identify and exploit their vulnerabilities."

Niana flushed, unsure exactly how he expected her to proceed.

"Befriend him, body and soul. Report to me what you learn of his cacique's intent for us."

Days later, Bakako assembled with a lieutenant, accountant, and foot soldiers outside the custom and storehouse under construction, a plot 160 by 40 feet, temporarily surrounded by storage huts filled with trading truck but mostly barren of foodstuffs. While feigning respect, Bakako had grown contemptuous of accompanying voyagers without Admiral, as their want for looting trophies, denigrating villagers' nakedness or spirits, and lusting women burgeoned unrestrained. The lieutenant informed Bakako—*Diego*, he said—that cazabi was the day's essential need, and Bakako led the band from Isabela's perimeter on a trail curling southwest along the hillside rising above the Bajabonico to arrive at the village he thought of as Niana's.

The lieutenant offered Niana's father a shirt and glove and beads for his wives, and Niana and her sisters and cousins presented baskets of cazabi to the soldiers. Bakako winced, ashamed, as the lieutenant bantered derisively with his soldiers that Niana's father resembled a beast more than a prince. Bakako turned away, embarrassed and disgusted, when soldiers cockily propositioned the wives and girls, including Niana. The womenfolk all demurred, with a politeness that Bakako despised as unwarranted.

When the trade was done, Bakako informed the soldiers he'd remain to confer with the cacique alone, and, as they departed for Isabela, he sought to converse with Niana's father. But the cacique retired to his caney with his wives, leaving Bakako with the girls.

"You're on your own today?" Niana cheerfully remarked. "Would you like to see our papaya grove? Some are ripening."

"Sure. I can speak with your father another time," Bakako replied, relieved of the anxiety of shepherding the pale men, content that information from Niana might be less guarded than from her father, and keen for whatever she intended.

"I'll take you." Niana winked for him to follow, and they strode through forest on a narrow trail to arrive at an expansive field where, in the distance, a band of women were hoeing yuca mounds. The path widened, and Niana slowed so they ambled side by side, passing a lean-to where more women were baking yuca pulp to cazabi. She pointed to papaya trees in the distance.

"Bakako, the pale men are gone. So tell me—how did they take you from Guanahaní?"

"By trickery. Admiral invited me and others to visit his vessel and then abruptly sailed away. His men restrained us from diving to the sea."

"Were you beaten?" she wondered. Recalling her duty, she added, "Do the pale men seize villagers often?"

"I was kicked a few times, not injured. Yes, they take captives almost everywhere they stop."

"What do they make you do?" she asked and, after further reflection, added, "What do they use captives for?"

"My task is to introduce them wherever they go and translate," Bakako replied, too ashamed to admit he also lied repeatedly that the pale men were safe to meet. "They hauled me to their homeland to meet Admiral's caciques and to teach me to worship their spirits."

"Do you?" Niana whispered, shocked.

"I don't," Bakako replied, shying from acknowledging or explaining his baptism. But an urge to confess to her overcame him. "But I pretend to when I'm with the pale men."

Niana was saddened and she touched Bakako's shoulder, slackening their pace to a dawdle. "I'm sorry." She felt her heart pound and realized she'd touched him for herself, not her father. He was handsome, clever, and possessed of a strange power and advantage, straddling two peoples. But she caught herself. "Do they want my father's subjects to worship their spirits, too?"

"Yes, it's important to them that everyone worship their spirits. I can't explain why. They denigrate the spirits we know." Bakako's heart also thumped with the touch of her hand, and he asked, "What do you think of the pale men?" Steeling himself, he added, "What does your father and other caciques think of them?"

"You know the pale men. You tell me how we should think of them."

Bakako struggled to formulate a response loyal to Admiral yet true to this new friend, smitten that Niana's coquetry veiled wit and mettle. "They're very powerful. You'd best not cross them." Slowly, he returned her touch, extending his hand to squeeze hers lightly. There was no resistance, and the young teenagers' fingers parted and clutched together, hand in hand, their shoulders rubbing as they minced. "But what does your father think of them?"

"I'm not sure. I think he's confused—I think we're all confused by them."

Bakako recognized the lie, and he drew breathless. Niana was decent in spirit, regardless of what she intended to accomplish at the papaya grove. He stopped abruptly and turned to face her, grasping her waist and pulling her close, letting his eyes fall upon her breasts and navel. "Is your father angry that the pale men sit upon his land?"

"Do the pale men want more land than they've seized so far?" she replied, pining that he would kiss her. "Do they take slaves, like the Caribes?"

Bakako felt arousal, which aroused Niana, and he sensed a tearing and desire in her eyes as she peered invitingly into his own. Each had been smitten prior to their instructions to inform—and each suspected that true of the other. Bakako whispered, "Let's not answer these questions now. Neither my cacique nor yours is here." He kissed her passionately, embraced lustfully, and caressed her body, seeking that she part her legs.

Niana hesitated, both hungry and instructed to do so, but suddenly discomforted, offended by an impurity and deceit both unnecessary and inappropriate. While resolute to honor her father's wish—be it marriage or betrayal—intimacy and love to those ends were hers alone, beyond her father's authority and review.

"Father is here, Bakako," she said, gently restraining him, pointing to the women baking cazabi. "Not here. Not now. Come to me at night, when we can be alone."

Bakako glanced at the women, detesting his imprisonment in a larger encounter and contrite that he'd enveloped Niana therein. But he panted, eagerly, "We'll lie beneath the papaya trees."

Taíno women baking cazabi. Benzoni's *History of the New World,* 1565.

⌑ ⌑ ⌑

By March 1493, Isabela's church had been roofed with wood, the first structure completed. Together, the church, the rising walls of the storehouse and the Admiral's residence, the two hundred wooden hovels, and the quarry and vegetable gardens by the Bajabonico proclaimed a permanent Christian and Spanish presence. The reduction in the settlement's population, and the departure of those most ill, made it easier to feed a more productive, fit workforce. Chickpeas, cucumbers, and melons had vegetated.

But hunger, illness, and death remained ever present. Voyagers distrusted the Indians' food and diet, often disgusted that the latter included insects, spiders, and worms. While most tolerated the cazabi to survive, some simply didn't and starved. Their demises were desolate, lacking servants or friends even to bring them water as they lay to die, aghast they had thrown their lives away for an illusion or lie. Voyagers had lain with women in the neighboring villages, and many winced in pain from an illness Cristóbal believed borne from excessive sex. Red sores stung the penis, with rash often nettling the palms and soles of feet, followed by scabbing, burning, headache, fever, and even debilitation (syphilis). Margarite suffered from it, as did many soldiers and volunteers who had shirked work. Local caciques recommended an herbal cure, but voyagers trusted that even less than the Indian food. Men also were afflicted with chiggers, mites that burrowed in the feet to nest, itch, and infect, rendering it painful to walk and work. The only remedy was to pick away or amputate the affected area or toes.

As for leadership, Cristóbal and Fray Buil still hadn't discovered how to work together. They met and argued often, sometimes without Margarite's mediation. Cristóbal visited the church regularly to receive the sacraments until that, too, ruptured.

"Father, take my confession," Cristóbal requested, slipping from a bench to kneel alone before the papal legatee.

"Hear me, my Admiral. I've warned you repeatedly—the punishments you administer are too severe. They're cruel, unconscionable. Desperate Christians lose their limbs for stealing but morsels of food they hunger, yet the heathen Guacanagarí remains free after murdering almost forty of them. I've implored you not to withhold rations from those you find guilty—and I'll no longer absolve you if you persist."

"Father, you must absolve that which I do loyally in the sovereigns' name and benefit—because that is in my authority—and outside your own."

"I won't absolve that which the Lord condemns. Your exercise of authority must conform to the Lord's word. Reinstate the rations of those you're punishing."

Silence followed, and Cristóbal rose from his knees to sit back upon the bench. "You withhold my absolution?"

"Your absolution is within your own power to achieve—simply conform to the Lord's word."

"Father, you best attend your heavenly duty rather than interfere with my temporal one," Cristóbal warned. He whispered hoarsely, "We've been here two months, but not a single Indian has received baptism. That must be your focus, not my justice—as to which the sovereigns awarded me plenary authority."

"Instruction precedes baptism, and you've failed to provide interpreters," Buil snapped in return.

Cristóbal's anger welled, incredulous that anyone would impugn his fidelity to the Lord's word. His tolerance for Buil's company and criticisms were spent, and he knelt again. "You shall receive my confession in fulfillment of your duty to our king and queen."

Buil shook his head.

"Then, until you do, I shall curtail your and your household's rations."

Cristóbal abruptly rose, the two men glowered at each other with implacable hatred, and Cristóbal departed. The church and his residence were but a shout distant, yet the gulf between them now was extraordinary.

⊡ ⊡ ⊡

Soon, on a gusty night when the moon was a sliver and shrouded in cloud, a fire caught hold on the exposed eastern perimeter and spread rapidly across the promontory to destroy more than two-thirds of the voyagers' huts. Some deemed it a portent that the Lord disfavored the settlement and doomed it to failure. Cristóbal suspected another explanation that he kept to himself, indisposed to advise either the sovereigns or voyagers that it could have been an Indian attack. In the morning, he simply ordered the voyagers to rebuild, steadfastly refusing any further delay in his conquest of Española.

CONQUEST PROCLAIMED,
Fort Santo Tomás, March 12–29, 1494

On March 12, with Isabela's construction and repair underway, Admiral Cristóbal Colón heralded that conquest, marching with five hundred men into the interior to build a fort in the Cibao to maintain a garrison of soldiers who would protect Christians prospecting for gold, resolved to instill fear and demonstrate he could quash any resistance. Every fit voyager participated, save those necessary to guard the settlement and ships. Caciques at the Bajabonico provided naborias to haul the fort's building materials and provisions. An advance party bearing axes departed Isabela first, widening the Indian footpath along the Unijíca to accommodate the supplies, weaponry, and horses. Soldiers, Lanzas, artisans, and workmen followed, two by two in battle formation, beneath crosses and banners hoisted, with body armor glistening, horns and trumpets blaring, and harquebuses discharging.

The invasion followed the same route to the Yaque taken by Hojeda weeks earlier, with Hojeda, Bakako, and Yutowa at Cristóbal's side. The two Guanahaníans and guides from the Bajabonico introduced Admiral to local caciques, pronouncing that he came to establish a permanent fort to trade for gold and—regardless of his failure to seek permission for the trespass—in peace. The brazen confidence and ostentation of the intruders terrified villagers, who hid in their bohíos. Dread abounded that the mounted Lanzas were man-eaters or hostile spirits.

The weather was as dismal as Hojeda had experienced, with frequent downpours. Cristóbal named the high pass on the mountain range bordering the sea Puerto de los Hidalgos—for the gentlemen in the advance party who cleared the trail to it (Pass of the Gentlemen). He christened the great fertile interior valley the Vega Real (the Royal Plain) and the river Yaque the Río de las Cañas (River of Canes) for its cane thickets, not aware he'd already named it the Río de Oro (River of Gold) farther west. Bakako learned that the territory south of the mountains was ruled by a proud intermediate cacique, Guatiguaná. The Yaque was flooded, and a village cacique cautiously welcomed Cristóbal and assisted fording, whereupon the procession paraded south through the valley toward the Cibao, surmounting more river crossings assisted by local caciques. Bakako discovered the peoples there were subordinate to the renowned Guarionex.

The marchers ascended into the Cibao's foothills and, by March 15, arrived at a high pass, likely farther south than Gorvalán had ventured. Cristóbal named it Puerto de Cibao (Pass of the Cibao), and, anticipating a site's selection soon, he dispatched a contingent of men and horses back to Isabela to fetch the intended garrison's food and wine supply. Bakako gleaned that the Cibao lay beyond, and, gingerly, he informed Cristóbal that *cibao* was the Indian word for rock and stone, suitably chosen as the name for the rocky mountain range to the south. Cristóbal surveyed the rugged mountains and ruefully admitted to himself that the *Cibao* wasn't *Cipangu* and the two words bore no relation. But he and his men relished they'd arrived at last at the rivers of gold that he'd promised and Hojeda had confirmed.

The next day, Cristóbal surmounted the pass. When the trail grew too hazardous for horses, he selected a hilltop for the fort's site, surrounded on three sides for protection by an ample river (the Jánico, near Jánico, Dominican Republic). The builders and artisans promptly commenced the fort's construction with wood and earth, excavating the dirt to form an encircling defensive ditch. Cristóbal named the fort for the apostle who initially doubted Christ's resurrection, Santo Tomás, a retort to those who doubted Española's gold until they saw it. He chose Margarite as its captain, stationing a command of almost sixty men.

The Indians at the site weren't hostile but warned Cristóbal that Caonabó—who lived abutting the Cibao's southern flank—was, and they confirmed that Caonabó had massacred the men at Navidad. Regardless, Cristóbal dispatched the courtier Juan de Luján south with a small party of men to explore for gold.

Cristóbal departed for Isabela on March 21, leaving Margarite to complete the fort's construction. Storms closed in, the rivers swelled, and he and some four hundred men encamped by the Yaque in the Vega Real—Guarionex's Magua—for a few days. Mud overtook glory, and he resorted to trading daily for Indian food, as well as gold jewelry.

◻ ◻ ◻

While Fort Santo Tomás was perched on a hilltop, just across the river gorge a ridge rose higher, affording Caonabó's scouts a view onto the fort and surrounding terrain. The scouts studied the defenses and men and beasts posted and, after the pale cacique departed, swiftly trekked south to report to Caonabó and Uxmatex, traversing fifty miles of rugged mountain in just a full day and night. After hearing the scouts, the two men spoke alone after dinner, seated at the firepit before Caonabó's caney at the edge of his ballcourt.

"He's brazen and resolute," Uxmatex observed of the pale men's cacique. "He never asks permission to visit, no less possess, any cacique's territory. Nothing intimidates him—fire, storm, hunger, sickness, or death."

"Nothing yet," Caonabó agreed. "His incursion was martial, not diplomatic, struck to intimidate rather than befriend, testing our resolve to repel him."

"We should respond with greater resolution. There're only a few dozen men at the hilltop. We could besiege and annihilate them, bludgeoning them one by one if necessary when they descend to the river for water."

Caonabó shook his head. "Preliminary steps are prudent, without arrows, to whittle their strength further before war." He was impatient to counter the pale cacique's advance promptly and indisposed to consult others. "Dispatch the scouts back to convey my order that local caciques depart the territory surrounding the site and withhold food or other assistance to the pale men. Threaten I'll punish any cacique who disobeys. I doubt the pale cacique can supply his men stationed at the site—the path from the coast is sixty miles. So, his men in the Cibao will starve or straggle back to him, frustrating his incursion and sapping his men's stamina."

Caonabó dismissed Uxmatex and summoned Anacaona and Onaney as night approached.

"Shouldn't you consult Guarionex before threatening his subordinate caciques?" Anacaona softly asked.

"He'd deny permission, there's no point in asking." Caonabó responded, frowning. "It's essential to force the pale cacique to abandon conquest."

"If not Guarionex, shouldn't you consult other supreme caciques—as a first step toward an alliance?" Onaney pleaded. "So you don't battle the pale men alone."

Caonabó fought to contain his frustration, but his voice hardened. "The enemy's already in battle formation! The enemy's already seized land! Guarionex and the others have simply watched and wilted." He caught his breath and sighed. "Words will fail. Guarionex and the others need an example to follow."

Anacaona nodded deferentially, but her discomfort compelled a final prod. "The pale cacique hasn't invaded Maguana. Might you contact him to reach an understanding that he stays away?"

"No, we can't tolerate an enemy entrenched on the island!" Caonabó replied angrily, exasperated. "The longer we delay, the harder to expel them."

He waved his arm to conclude the conversation. He would sleep alone that night.

⧈ ⧈ ⧈

Guarionex sat in solitude inside his ceremonial bohío, chastened by the wind and rain swirling about it, a din in which he often sought the spirits' blessing. Yet he was too honest to seek blessing when he reproached his own conduct for falling short.

The pale men had invaded his Cibao. They'd built and manned a fort simply by brandishing weapons, flouting his dominion by ignoring even a discussion of their intent, no less his permission. He'd let it happen, merely standing aside, too meek to encounter them, too cowardly to proclaim his sovereignty. He'd hid confused and noncommittal while his vassal caciques were forced to harbor the pale men's trespasses, directionless.

Guarionex recalled berating Guacanagarí for excusing far lesser transgressions by the pale men, and a pang of guilt and recrimination overwhelmed him. His supremacy demanded confronting the pale cacique to resolve the terms of the pale men's presence. He shuddered with remorse that he'd forsaken the opportunity to do that prior to their advance from the Bajabonico.

Guarionex steeled himself and departed the bohío to return to his caney, resolved to dispatch nitaínos with gifts to greet the pale cacique at the encampment by the Yaque and request that the two men parley. Rain drenched him, reminding that destruction was ever present, and the trees about him bent wildly to accommodate the wind, illustrating that compromise was a recourse and permitted survival. His civilization had always understood compromise as virtue—as a path to an ideal harmony among men, nature, and spirits. He vexed what bending might require with the pale men.

◻ ◻ ◻

Historians and anthropologists differ on Cristóbal's route from Isabela to Fort Santo Tomás. The above is generally consistent with that presented in Carl Ortwin Sauer's *The Early Spanish Main* (London: Cambridge University Press, 1966) and also reflects the author's exploration along the Yaque River and at Santo Tomás.

Cristóbal's expedition ran out of Spanish food encamped in the thunderstorms at the swelling Yaque, and they subsisted thereafter on cazabi and sweet potato. He received Guarionex's nitaínos and agreed to meet Guarionex soon, although he wouldn't wait at the Yaque to do so. He marched to Isabela when the rain subsided, arriving March 29, his men wet, hungry, and exhausted.

During the invasion, Cristóbal had traded for some two thousand castellanos worth of gold jewelry, a yield for the sovereigns falling short of that he'd envisioned. Cuneo observed that the expedition had failed to find any significant gold specks or nuggets in the many rivers encountered. While not surprised, Cristóbal was furious that some of his men had hoarded their own stashes of gold, diminishing that collected for king and queen. He ordered stern, exemplary punishment for those found guilty—public floggings, most with ears or noses slit, resulting in permanent mutilations ever visible in daily life that continuously warned the consequence of transgression. For Cristóbal, harmony was secondary to conquest, and many perceived uncommon cruelties.

Isabel and Fernando's First Impressions, *February–April 1494*

After reclaiming the Catalonian provinces, Isabel and Fernando took their court west from Barcelona to winter in December in Zaragoza, the ancestral seat of Aragón's crown, and, by mid-January, Valladolid, which would become the new seat of Castile's crown. They waited eagerly for Colón's first dispatches from their Indian possessions, but the threat of French aggression in Naples preoccupied their attention.

The Neapolitan king Ferrante I—Fernando's brother-in-law and successor to Fernando's uncle—had died in January, and young Charles VIII had demanded that Pope Alexander VI invest Charles himself, rather than Ferrante's son Alfonso, as the successor to the Neapolitan throne. The pope had equivocated on succession, receiving homages from both Charles and Alfonso, but admonished Charles against using force.

Ever cautious, Fernando judged that remaining on the sidelines wouldn't suffice to retain his lineage's dominion, and he instructed his ambassadors to beseech Alexander to maintain peace with France, suggesting he would provide arms if war came, and to warn Charles to arbitrate claims with Alexander, without soldiers. He and Isabel loathed committing their treasuries to a new war. Together with Alexander, they loudly criticized Charles's threat as selfish, diverting Christian resources from the holy war to reconquer Constantinople and Jerusalem from the infidel, to which all Christian princes were duty bound. Ever sly, Fernando mused that, while his own usurpation of the Neapolitan throne from Alfonso could be similarly criticized, reclaiming it as his own after French usurpation might not.

By February, the flurry of diplomatic correspondence relating to the situation was interrupted by the sovereigns' receipt of a request for an audience by the Admiral's brother, Bartolomé Colón, who had arrived in Seville at last and sought to escort the Admiral's sons to court.

⌑ ⌑ ⌑

Bartolomé had been Cristóbal's partner in seeking royal sponsorship for a voyage from the earliest moments Cristóbal conceived of it, assisting in his brother's first presentations to Portugal's King João (1484) and Isabel and Fernando (1486). After the sovereigns' initial rejection, Bartolomé had traveled to England to entreat its king Henry VII for sponsorship and, when that failed (1488), to Charles's court in France, where Charles also declined. But when news of Cristóbal's triumphant return from the first voyage reached Charles, he chivalrously paid Bartolomé's travel expenses to join his brother.

Bartolomé received the sovereigns' invitation to Valladolid while lounging in the garden of Violante Moniz's mansion in Seville, where he was kindling affections with his nephews Diego, whom he'd last seen in 1487, and Fernando, whom he'd never known. Although slighter in height, Bartolomé's sturdy, tall frame resembled Cristóbal's, and his wit was as keen and his rigor sterner, with a harshness that rarely melted to reveal the courteousness and generosity Cristóbal often displayed at court. Bartolomé's singular warmth was for family kinship, and he reminded his nephews of their Genoese heritage, cradling Fernando on his knee, Diego nestled at his side.

"Your grandfather Domenico still survives in Genoa," he told them. "So do your Aunt Bianchinetta and cousins."

"Were you ever a weaver?" Diego asked.

"No. Grandfather wanted that once, but I went to paint maps with your father in Lisbon before you were born. Grandfather was pleased, as we two banded together."

"You'll help Papa and Uncle Diego in the Indies?" Fernando asked.

"I expect to. I must obtain the king and queen's permission first," Bartolomé responded. "Then I'll leave you two at court, where you'll serve the prince with utmost obedience." He gazed to Diego. "You'll also pay close attention. When your father returns, you'll inform him of the court's opinions about his islands—which shall be yours one day."

"Father says critics abound," Diego replied, nodding.

"The king and queen's opinion is what counts," Bartolomé comforted. "But it's important to observe which courtiers are friends to our family or foe."

Following Cristóbal's instruction, Bartolomé contacted Juanoto Berardi in Seville prior to departing for the audience, whiling hours fascinated as Juanoto recounted how Cristóbal's two voyages had been launched. Juanoto waxed how he'd financed Cristóbal's contribution to the first voyage and provisioned the second. Slightly older than Cristóbal and Fonseca (b. 1447), he proudly vouched readiness to finance the family in the future—be it on the security of gold, spice, slaves, or whatever made the Indies profitable. He'd nimbly assist Bartolomé in his arrangements with the sovereigns for passage to the Indies.

Bartolomé entered the audience room in Valladolid's Pimentel Palace with his nephews at his side, poised and confident, already accomplished at presenting himself before kings without Cristóbal. Isabel and Fernando appreciated the credential and, after welcoming the boys to Prince Juan's service, searched for insight.

"Why did my friends King Henry and King Charles decline the voyage?" Isabel asked.

"Your Highness, they possessed neither your understanding of the geography nor fervor to increase the faith," Bartolomé replied, studying each sovereign's visage. Addressing the king, he added, "Nor did they perceive the potential rewards sufficient to justify the risks inherent in exploration."

"Now that we've succeeded, what will they do?" Isabel responded.

"I was never their confidant. But Charles seems preoccupied with Naples, as you know."

"And Henry?" Fernando pressed.

"Your Highness, I have no concrete insight. But my brother has established that the Ocean Sea is navigable, and one may expect that other princes will launch their own explorations. You must seize your advantage and expand your possessions, without delay. My brother needs my assistance in serving you to that end."

"In insight's absence, what do you surmise brother João intends?" Fernando drove further, scrutinizing Bartolomé's eyes.

"His mariners will continue the circumvention of Guinea, undoubtedly. But he'll never stomach that Antillia be yours, wherever found."

The discussion continued for some hours, the sovereigns probing Bartolomé's experience at sea and capacity for leadership. Prince Juan eventually joined to greet his new pages and receive their oaths of loyalty. Isabel invited Bartolomé to remain at court as they waited word from Cristóbal, and the prince led the boys to introduce them to his own staff.

"Would you like to meet my Indian?" the prince asked. Though often riding at Fernando's side and participating in crown pageantry, Prince Juan had been frail since childhood, and Isabel and Fernando cautiously had controlled his upbringing and diet to avoid illness. "Your father gave him to me last year in Barcelona, and he was baptized in my name. He's taken sick but can see visitors at a distance."

The boys nodded, and Prince Juan led them through servants' quarters to a small alcove where Abasu slumbered ill on a bench, covered by a blanket, fitfully dreaming of his family in Cuba.

"Juan, these are the Admiral's sons," Prince Juan exclaimed, rousing his namesake. "They, too, will serve me."

Diego and Fernando waved graciously and said hello, recognizing that the slumbering Juan's complexion was similar to that of the Indian youth Diego, who served their father.

Astonished, Abasu squinted back and managed a nod in return before shutting his eyes. As death approached, he found it increasingly difficult to distinguish whether the nightmare was real or dream.

⌑ ⌑ ⌑

On departing Isabela, Torres's fleet replicated the Admiral's northern route home on the first voyage. It tacked arduously east into headwinds along Española's northern coast for a week, beat smoothly on a starboard tack northeast by north into the same winds to attain Spain's latitude, and coursed east with tailwinds to arrive in Cádiz on March 7—twenty-five days after Española had fallen from the horizon. The gold, cotton, and trophies were deposited with treasury officials, and the naked captives from Guadalupe and Santa Cruz were transferred to Berardi's associates, who had the know-how for holding and transporting slaves. Torres promptly dispatched a horseman to announce his arrival to the sovereigns but retained the written correspondence from Cristóbal and others that he was carrying, intent on explaining the voyage's accomplishments in person before delivering them.

The sailors and settlers returning from Española dispersed to their homes in Andalusia, Galicia, and elsewhere in Castile, bearing gold pieces taken on the sly and ribald stories of their ordeal in the Indies. Some who'd slept with or raped Indians also bore strains of venereal disease then unknown in Europe, to be transmitted to their wives, lovers, prostitutes, and others with whom these women thereafter slept, and so on. The captives now had lived among the voyagers and their livestock for four months, and most had grown severely ill, just as the captives seized on the first voyage. Of the twenty-six that departed Española, ten died by the time Berardi transported them to Seville, where those surviving would reside pending their display to the sovereigns.

Isabel and Fernando promptly summoned Torres to court, which, by mid-February, had moved to reside the spring in Medina del Campo, a vibrant mercantile city south of Valladolid set in rolling farmland. The threat of French aggression was escalating gravely and demanded close attention. On March 16, the pope recognized the Aragonese claim to the Neapolitan throne. Charles pronounced the next day that he would invade Italy to take the throne by force, and the pope then beseeched Fernando and Isabel to defend papal territory. But the threat of João's aggression in the Indies lurked darkly, as well, and decisions regarding the Indies weren't delayed by much.

Isabel and Fernando, Cardinal Mendoza, and other courtiers received Torres in the royal palace overlooking the town's central plaza by late March, together with Cristóbal's loyal pilot, Pero Alonso Niño, who had returned to explain the map and assist with the Portuguese territorial dispute.* Melchior Maldonado, the diplomat, and Gines de Gorvalán, who could attest to the riverbed gold, also attended. After kissing the sovereigns' hands and feet on the Admiral's behalf, Torres proclaimed that the Admiral was overcoming many obstacles to deliver on his promises and recounted the story of Navidad's demise, Isabela's founding, and the rich gold deposits nearby. A hush enveloped the room as he related the garrison's massacre and the voyagers' illnesses and deaths, and silence followed.

Fernando broke it, asking, "If the Indians attacked Navidad, why haven't they attacked Isabela? Can't we expect that?"

"The Admiral believes most Indians will submit peacefully to your rule—so long as we remain watchful and respectful," Torres responded. "Isabela is being built to withstand attack and therefore never will be. The Indians are cowards and their weaponry is backward."

"Did they murder our men because they're Christians?" Isabel inquired. "Do they oppose the faith?"

"Your Majesty, I doubt that. The Indians are ignorant of Christianity, but those who visit Isabela are wondrous of it. The men at Navidad were killed not because they were Christian but for abusing the Indians—particularly the women."

"Nevertheless, will my subjects' murderers be brought to Christian justice?" Isabel probed.

"The Admiral believes one of Española's kings—a warlike overlord named Caonabó—was mainly responsible, and he'll be brought to justice. But the settlement's defenses must be built and the

*The palace is the house where Isabel would die, now called the Palacio Real Testamentario.

gold mining operations established first."

"You should alert the Admiral that making this prince an ally may serve conquest more effectively than justice," Fernando observed, recalling lessons learned during the Reconquista and the Canarian subjugations. He scrutinized Torres and the others present. "How many voyagers have died in the field? How many have returned home with you?"

"Your Majesty, I expect scores have succumbed to pestilence, but the vast majority recover promptly," Torres responded. "Many hunger because the provisions are depleted and the Indians' food isn't healthy, and it'll take time for the wheat and other crops to root. Shy of three hundred returned with me, including sailors. Some of those are sick, some unproductive or lazy, others unsuited to or frightened by the rigors of strange lands."

Isabel and Fernando glanced warily at each other, startled that the conquest's hurdles were larger than they'd anticipated, stunned that so many had returned so quickly. Fernando folded his arms, keen to root out whether the dreams that had enflamed enlistment remained grand. "Tell us about Española's gold—how much, how far from Isabela, how easy the access?"

Torres bid a servant set a silver bucket containing the finest gold pieces brought home at the sovereigns' feet. "These are but samples, the bulk held by Fonseca. The Admiral has identified over fifty rivers bearing gold, some two dozen leagues from Isabela. Knowledgeable miners are required to dig it and beasts of burden to load upon." Torres paused to address accessibility. "The Indians don't have horses or roads, only footpaths."

"So you'll need to build roads, and possibly defend the men from attack, over a considerable distance?"

Torres nodded. "That's a reason we haven't brought more gold back."

"When the mining's established, will the gold surpass Mina's?" Isabel interrupted.

"Admiral and I certainly believe so."

The audience ran on, focused on Isabela's immediate needs. In the afternoon, Isabel and Fernando conferred privately with Torres at length, and then Maldonado and Gorvalán, to glean different perspectives on the gold and whether the exodus home revealed disillusionment with its abundance. They also read Cristóbal and Fray Buil's letters for the first time.

That night, alone, they surmised that the obstacles to establishing the settlement appeared substantial but surmountable and that the gold obtainable could be spectacular, dwarfing the increased expenses required, even assuming undue optimism. The years of war over Isabel's ascension, the Reconquista, and Canarian conquests had seared their appreciation of the hardships of men in the field, and of misfortunes that upset the most earnest planning, and they saw both at hand, rather than incompetence or misjudgment. They were loath to throttle the expedition or criticize their commander after but one report, confident in the Lord's continuing assistance in overcoming the trials he set to test them. Fray Buil's criticisms of Cristóbal's command were noted, but neither sovereign sympathized the slightest with their subjects' disobedience to that command—which was theirs.

In the morning, Torres reviewed the memorandum's specific requests, and the sovereigns signaled their approval of most of them, including for miners, arms, and livestock for food and transport. Most critically, they endorsed the immediate dispatch of ships with food, wine, and medicine. They were favorably disposed to make rewards, appointments, or entitlements for those Cristóbal praised and to pay worthy volunteers wages no longer due those who had died or otherwise failed. Angered, they ordered Fonseca to investigate the Lanzas' horse trading and Soria's complicity.

In a private moment, Torres bluntly revealed that Pisa openly criticized the Admiral and sought to undermine his authority. More gently, he noted Cristóbal's fractious relations with Fray Buil—readily apparent in the friar's letter—and even Margarite. Disappointed, Isabel and Fernando concluded that Colón wasn't receiving the support necessary and contemplated bolstering it, reflecting positively on appointing Bartolomé as an officer to assist him. They also mused on the apparent uneasy relationship between the two men entrusted with the entire Indies business, Colón and Archdeacon Fonseca. Colón plainly preferred dealing with Berardi, and they considered greater utilization of Berardi for voyage outfitting.

That afternoon, Torres presented Cristóbal's proposals for the Caribes, pronouncing that the sovereigns soon would meet specimens of these people then waiting in Seville.

"These are the ferocious peoples the Admiral previously warned of—the Caribes—who plunder Indians' villages, enslave their women, and eat human flesh," he recounted. "The Admiral believes they'll make excellent slaves. He proposes that those brought here be trained to serve as interpreters to assist the Indians' conversion."

Isabel and Fernando nodded their approval, and Isabel replied, "That is very well and should be done. But the Admiral must endeavor to convert these peoples, as well as the Indians."

"The Admiral also proposes to finance Española's ongoing resupply by enslaving Caribes and bartering them to licensed merchants for horses, cattle, and other supplies," Torres broached. "Your Highnesses could levy duties when the slaves are resold in Spain."

Isabel and Fernando grew uncomfortable, perturbed by Cristóbal's promotion of this in his letter, suspicious why it was necessary, and anxious that the pope's pronouncements hadn't touched on it. After a moment of silence, Fernando inquired, "Won't the gold alone surpass our expenses? The Caribes' enslavement as interpreters is sensible—and consistent with our zeal to spread the faith—but why is this broader plan necessary?"

"Enslaving the Indians' enemy should compel the Indians' love and fear, and thus their obedience," Torres responded.

"But we ask whether it's necessary—for the Indies' prosperity?" Isabel pressed, raising her voice.

Torres shrugged. "Whether necessary or not, it would assist the settlement and reduce expenses. Similar to financing the Canarian conquests. João's Mina has a slave trade, as well as gold."

"We will study it," Isabel replied. Sternly, she added, "We don't approve this idea at this time."

◻ ◻ ◻

At the sovereigns' request, Juanoto Berardi now presented himself at the royal palace for multiple reasons—to display the so-called Caribes, resolve matters relating to his financing of Alonso de Lugo's Canarian conquests, and offer assistance in the immediate dispatch of the two resupply ships that Cristóbal had hoped Berardi would organize instead of Fonseca.

The naked peoples presented were not as robust or fit for slavery as Cristóbal had promised. All were sick, and a few more had succumbed since arriving at Seville. Berardi paraded a dozen of them before the sovereigns, mostly women, including three dismembered boys. In the absence of a translator, Isabel and Fernando welcomed them kindly, with food and refreshment, and exhorted that they learn of Christ and Spanish in advance of their baptism and renunciation of flesh eating. Isabel directed Berardi to treat them well and provide their Christian instruction, which he promised to do. When the parade was done, he dispatched them back to his business associate in Seville, another Florentine, one Amerigo Vespucci.

⊡ ⊡ ⊡

By mid-April, the sovereigns set the arrangements responsive to their admiral's requests.

On April 13, they wrote Cristóbal to commend his great service, praising that he'd accomplished much with such good order and planning that it could not have been done better. They assured they were hastily requisitioning ships with items he requested urgently and that Torres would supply the remainder, as well as answers to unresolved questions, when Torres sailed later with more supplies. They confirmed their anger that things had been done against Cristóbal's wishes, which they were correcting and punishing. Cristóbal was to send Pisa back on the next ships departing Isabela and, with Fray Buil, select Pisa's replacement.

On April 14, they appointed Bartolomé captain of the immediate resupply fleet, directing he assist Cristóbal in the Indies thereafter, having burnished his stature with recognition as a *caballero* (gentleman). Fonseca remained responsible for requisitioning Bartolomé's ships, which would depart Cádiz in May. But the sovereigns afforded Berardi a role in their provisioning and in arranging the larger fleet that Torres would sail thereafter.

As for the Neapolitan situation, the papacy itself was engulfed in turmoil—which jeopardized the many advantages of Fernando's relationship with its leader. Charles had pronounced he'd withdrawn his obedience to Alexander and would withhold French benefices from cardinals remaining obedient. Worse, Alexander's rival, Cardinal Rovere, had fled from Rome to Charles's side, exhorting that a general council of the church be convened to strip Alexander of the papacy owing to the simony of Alexander's election.

Isabel retired to worship often, including for the Lord's guidance on her Indies decisions. One particularly concerned her, and, as she knelt before her confessor one evening, she shared her angst.

"Colón and those about him wish that I approve enslavement of the heathens he's encountered—at least those who eat human flesh. Can that be permitted? Should I ask the pope or our clergy?"

"Your Majesty, you might ask, if you wish to permit their enslavement," Cisneros replied, concealing his disgust that a ruler so pious as his queen would need to consult so corrupt an authority as Alexander. "But if you wish to prohibit it, that is within your temporal authority, without asking—simply a sovereign, mercantile prohibition applicable to your Indies."

Isabel thanked and dismissed Cisneros, remaining to worship at the altarpiece. She intended to supplant this analysis with more learned authority when time permitted, but her conscience would never forget it.

Punishments,
March 29–Mid-April 1494

On returning from the Cibao, Cristóbal was pleased to find that a defensive wall had been erected about his residence, encircling an ample inner courtyard, and that artisans were constructing a watch-tower rising from the building's northeast corner. Isabela's other principal structures were advancing, and a kiln near the Bajabonico now produced tiles to roof the residence and storehouse. But he was rudely shocked to learn that those who'd guarded the settlement suffered pestilences anew, with fevers, chills, aches, and grotesque red skin blisters, debilitating them to a doleful stupor. Those who'd marched trembled they would share the same horror, and many promptly did.*

*Perhaps the first round of typhus transmitted by the rats' and other animals' lice, new strains of bacterial dysentery, and a resurgence of influenza borne by the pigs.

Just as dire, the last remaining Spanish foodstuffs—biscuits and wine—were nearly spent. Fresh melons and cucumbers provided some relief, but gardens had been neglected, chickpeas and wheat sown had wilted, and sacks of wheat grain remained unplanted—the men too ill or despondent to hoe or mulch, most so bent on returning to Spain that investment in a garden seemed pointless. Cristóbal ordered the construction of a gristmill to grind the remaining wheat to flour, but his threats to punish those who shirked the substantial task—healthy or ill—quickly yielded widespread opprobrium rather than bread. He prayed that Torres had arrived in Spain safely and convinced the sovereigns to dispatch supplies, but the men's hunger didn't permit waiting on that.

Gravely, Cristóbal concluded that every voyager simply had to accept subsisting daily on Indian food and that far too many of the town's population—largely soldiers and gentlemen volunteers—contributed disproportionately little to its completion. He resolved to dispatch hundreds of these men into Española's interior to complete discovery of the island's territory and potential, living off food from Indians encountered and establishing the sovereigns' dominion throughout. He resented Margarite's criticisms of his leadership and would draw relief transferring direct oversight of these men—the most disloyal and unruly—to Margarite himself. He also pined for fresh victories to offset the disappointments. He'd told the sovereigns that exploration would follow gold mining's establishment, but he now decided to sail for new discoveries—prior even to the settlement's completion, no less gold mining—taking crews of almost sixty men. The combined head count drawn for both conquests—of Española's interior and mainland and islands yet discovered—would reduce the town's population to some three hundred men, a number more appropriately supportable by the food supplied by the Indians at the Bajabonico.

Yet that plan, too, loomed imperiled. Ominously, on April 1, just three days after his return, Cristóbal received an urgent dispatch from Margarite requesting reinforcements. The local Indians had abandoned the territory surrounding the fort abruptly, and Margarite surmised Caonabó plotted to attack and massacre the garrison. Frictions also had risen along the fort's supply route, as men returning sick to Isabela reported that Indians at the Yaque had stolen their clothing as they forded the river.

Cristóbal remained resolute that his soldiers and weaponry would prevail over Indian resistance, but his alarm surged, and he turned to the man most suited to brave the precarious, summoning Hojeda to instruct him on the next steps to Española's conquest.

"Margarite fears Caonabó will attack the fort. Reinforcements are required urgently, and I'll dispatch them tomorrow," Cristóbal related, studying Hojeda's demeanor. "You must now serve as Santo Tomás's warden, relieving Margarite—if you're well enough."

"I'm honored, and I'm fully recovered," Hojeda declared robustly, having suffered severe intestinal illness following his first march into the Cibao. The pluck and vigor of the response attested a craving for battle, and Cristóbal was pleased.

"I also plan to conscript four hundred men to serve under Margarite's command so he can survey the island, uncover its riches, and cow the Indians to obedience." Cristóbal raised the palm of his hand. "Heed my instructions—to both Margarite and yourself. They're essential for Española's peaceful subjugation while I'm away. I'll depart within the month to explore terra firma."

Hojeda hearkened.

"Your men at the fort, and his in the field, must learn to live on the Indians' food alone, bartering for it fairly as the sovereigns require. Take care that the men don't harm or steal from the Indians, who must be treated with respect so they don't rebel. The king and queen care more for the Indians' conversion than their gold."

Hojeda nodded respectfully, although he understood the last remark perfunctory, but a hollow platitude, and that the Admiral's rectitude belied a desperation that the sovereigns expected him to procure gold before all else.

"If your men mistreat Indians, punish them severely. Likewise, if Indians steal or resist, punish them severely. Indians friendly will see that those hostile are harmed while they're treated well—and the friendly will obey us."

"Slicing off noses and ears is always an effective deterrent," Hojeda replied with conviction.

Cristóbal nodded. "Margarite will be responsible for Caonabó. I'm ordering him to feign friendly relations by dispatching embassies to shower Caonabó with gifts and assure that friendship will be valued and rewarded. When he takes the bait, Margarite's men will seize him." Cristóbal raised a finger, pointing to Hojeda. "When you march to Santo Tomás, you're responsible for investigating reports that Indians at the river crossing have stolen Christians' clothing. Identify the guilty, discipline them, and dispatch their leaders back to me for sterner justice."

The next day, advance reinforcements of seventy men departed for Santo Tomás, including laborers tasked with improving the pathway there from Isabela. On April 9, Hojeda departed with the squadron of almost four hundred men—including sixteen Lanzas, over three hundred soldiers bearing crossbows and firearms, and Yutowa. He also bore Cristóbal's written instructions to Margarite, which formally conceded to Margarite Cristóbal's authority as viceroy and captain general of the Indies in implementing the mission to reconnoiter Española, including power to improvise and impose such punishments as Margarite deemed necessary. The instructions directed the establishment of a separate squadron of well-led men that alone would barter with the Indians for food or, to the extent necessary, procure it as respectfully as practical, thereby minimizing abuses of the Indians.

Dear to his faith, Cristóbal also instructed Margarite that tall crosses be erected throughout the island to mark it as now Christian. That was dear to most settlers, too, as many drew comfort from cross plantings, believing Christ would drive away the infernal spirits who'd long mastered the Indians, including Satan himself.

◻ ◻ ◻

At dawn, Yutowa waited anxiously at Hojeda's side as the pale nitaíno barked orders for the squadron to ford the Yaque with Indian assistance and set crosses on the facing riverbanks. With mounting apprehension, Yutowa followed as Hojeda then led ten soldiers, armed with harquebuses fully cocked and porting stakes, farther east along the riverbank toward a nearby village, where two of the soldiers—whose clothing and a sword had been stolen—suspected the transgressors would be caught.

The village women were cooking, with children and toddlers wandering about, their husbands preparing to hunt fowl or fish the rivers, most loosely congregated at or near the village plaza. The pale men's approach alarmed everyone, the women dashing to the plaza's perimeter with their infants and children, the men clutching their spears and rushing to defend—all in a calamitous pandemonium that assembled the entire village and left smoking fires unattended. Hundreds huddled in consternation as the pale men's leader strutted brazenly to the center of their plaza, accompanied by an accomplice or servant born of their civilization.

"Demand that their cacique present himself," Hojeda commanded Yutowa, believing the guilty would have offered the items stolen to their ruler.

Yutowa obeyed, speaking slowly, aware that the local peoples, subjects of the cacique Guatiguaná, could understand his dialect only partially.

"I am the cacique of these people," an elderly man replied, stepping forward solemnly, with two nitaínos trailing close behind. "What business do you have here?"

"I believe your subjects have stolen clothes and weapons from Christians," Hojeda charged. "If you have them, return them."

The cacique pondered a moment, gazing first to his people surrounded about, and then back to Hojeda. "I have them and will do so." He waved to naborias, who retrieved clothes and a sword from the cacique's caney and fearfully placed them at Hojeda's feet.

"Did you punish your subjects who did this?" Hojeda interrogated, glaring into the cacique's eyes.

"No. I did not think to," the cacique replied, reflecting that he would have if they'd stolen from his own villagers. "My subjects have assisted yours to ford the river a few times now, and we've observed that your people frequently take possessions without asking permission or giving thanks—isn't that your people's custom?"

"No. The Lord's commandments prohibit stealing," Hojeda replied. A foreboding silence enveloped those congregated, pale- and olive-skinned, clothed and naked, bearing firearms and spears. "You've failed to respect our rule—identify those guilty."

Before the cacique could respond, one of the soldiers looted pointed to two teenage boys hovering within the crowd. "It's them!"

he shouted, purporting to recall his river crossing two weeks prior.

Hojeda raised his arm, silently invoking the Virgin for her protection. His men aimed the harquebuses at the rising sun, and Hojeda shouted, "Fire!"

The discharge's crack terrified the villagers, auguring the wrath of evils spirits. Pandemonium resumed as women fled into the forest with the children. Their husbands trembled, petrified as Hojeda's soldiers rushed to bind the cacique, the two nitaínos, and the two teenagers in rope, at the ankles and wrists.

"Stake these two," Hojeda ordered, pointing to the teenagers. He confronted the cacique, hovering but inches face-to-face. "They'll receive Christian justice. You'll submit to the Admiral."

Yutowa trembled as stakes were planted at the plaza's center and the youths lashed on, reviling his participation in the pale men's cruelty yet again. He shuddered as Hojeda barked that the youths' ears be cut off, shattered by remorse that he'd saved Admiral's life in a hostile encounter on Cuba on the first voyage.* For an instant, he implored that the villagers grasp they could spear the pale men to death, forlornly resigned that he also might be slain.

The youths shrieked in pain, and the villagers gasped in horror, as the pale men slashed off the youths' ears. As blood gushed to their shoulders, Hojeda loudly addressed his final remark to everyone present. "Understand this—those who harm Christians will be harmed, those who help Christians will prosper."

Hojeda and soldiers towed the bound cacique and nitaínos back to the river crossing and dispatched them to Isabela. The soldiers looted trophies while departing the village—a face mask inlaid with gold, a gold earring fallen in the pandemonium, a gold-studded cotton belt stripped from among the crowd. Hojeda well appreciated that the reward for soldiers in battle—during the Reconquista and likely since Creation—was such booty. He looked the other way, considering the booty due regardless of the Admiral's instructions and the Lord's commandments, conceiving the latter never graven to apply to relations with naked heathens.

---

*December 3, 1492, near Baracoa, as depicted in *Encounters Unforeseen*, chapter IX.

Punishment of a villager, taken from Theodor de Bry, 1598. John Carter Brown Library, portion of rec. no. 0683-18.

Word of the cacique's abduction and the mutilations reverberated from village to village throughout Haiti. The cacique who'd welcomed Cristóbal at the river crossing but weeks before was so distraught by his peer's abduction that he trailed the captors and peer back to Isabela. The villagers' horror turned to rage, and, with swelling confidence, warriors seeking vengeance surrounded a half dozen pale men who were returning to Isabela. But Hojeda had anticipated retaliation, and, before departing for Santo Tomás, he'd stationed Lanzas to linger behind, who routed the warriors, inflicting severe wounds.

⌑ ⌑ ⌑

Bakako stood at Admiral's side in the plaza beside Isabela's church as Admiral rendered justice to the cacique and nitaínos for their subjects' clothes looting, in open audience before the pale men, including the supreme behique and Admiral's nitaínos. All pale gaped to learn how Admiral would protect them from Indians. The cacique who'd welcomed Admiral at the Yaque was permitted to observe.

"We have come in peace to bring your people salvation and Christian custom," Admiral pronounced. "Those who do good deeds will be honored, those who do evil will be punished."

As he translated, Bakako spied Admiral from the corner of his eye, unnerved that Admiral would dispense mutilations similar to those inflicted on pale men for stealing food or hoarding gold. His eyes darted to Admiral's critics, the supreme behique and voyagers who denounced Admiral's cruelty, and he bitterly surmised they wouldn't be critical of these punishments when dealt to Haiti's caciques and nitaínos.

"Your deeds are evil," Admiral judged. "You've permitted your subjects who harmed Christians to go unpunished. I will never tolerate that, so let your sentence inform your fellow princes throughout the island." Admiral paused for Bakako's interpretation and to whet the voyagers. He then proclaimed, "I sentence you to die at the sword, beheaded here and now."

Bakako struggled to translate as he quivered. He beheld the prisoners shudder in disbelief. He was frightened by scattered cheers and clapping among the voyagers. He despised that the supreme behique and nitaínos appeared surprised but content.

"*Guamiquina*, no!" a voice from the crowd suddenly exclaimed in Taíno, the appellation referring to Admiral as the leader of his people, comparable to *Admiral* or *Your Highness*. "Please no. These men don't deserve that." The cacique voluntarily present outstretched his arms to identify himself. For an instant, Bakako puzzled whether Admiral disfavored a translation, but a contempt for the proceeding surged within him, and he spoke loudly, so all present would understand.

"My friend, why do they deserve mercy?" Admiral replied.

"Guamiquina, our peoples must understand each other better—before coming to harsh judgments. These men have helped you and yours, providing food when yours were hungry—including to yourself." The cacique removed a face mask embedded with gold from a pouch and raised it for all to see. "I offer this in friendship and for their release."

Cristóbal pondered briefly and was satisfied that his stern dominion and rule had been established by the punishment's pronouncement, regardless of its application. Warning of his severity would travel regardless of mercy, and a singular mercy might also induce obedience.

"I'll reward your friendship and service by granting your request, and I expect to enjoy your continued friendship. You may take these prisoners home. Keep your gift—justice can't be bought with gold."

⧈ ⧈ ⧈

Shaken, Bakako was unable to sleep that night, longing for friendship and solace, and he resolved to visit Niana, whom he'd dreamed of loving for weeks. He arranged to accompany soldiers departing for food the next day and led them through hillsides above the Bajabonico on a route that concluded at her father's village near dusk.

As they hiked, Bakako anxiously scrutinized the greetings of passersby, gleaning that suspicion and chill had supplanted courteous deference. His salutations often were met without response, his grin and cheer ignored or avoided. He anguished whether venom was directed to the soldiers alone or to both him and them or—worst of all—especially to him. He ached that Niana wouldn't even meet, no less love, him. But when the troop arrived at Niana's village, the trade commenced routinely in the plaza before her father, who hailed Bakako warmly before a crowd of onlookers. To Bakako's relief, Niana stood at her father's side.

"Thank the Guamiquina on my behalf for the mercy bestowed yesterday," the cacique pronounced. "Friendship blossoms with such understanding and forgiveness."

Bakako faltered in a ready reply, doubtful of the cacique's sincerity but reluctant to disavow that Admiral was merciful or forgiving. He glanced to Niana, who smiled wanly and looked to the ground, wishing to obscure her own thoughts, perhaps also startled by her father's posture.

"I'll pass that on, which will please the Guamiquina," Bakako promised. "The Guamiquina sends his love for the food you share."

Niana pondered Bakako's candor and goodness and kept her eyes averted, but his aplomb, wit, and stature to converse directly with her father warmed her. The trade ensued, baskets of cazabi, corn, and sweet potato bartered for iron utensils and pots. As her father negotiated with the soldiers' captain, Niana quietly minced to stand at Bakako's side as he interpreted, which warmed him, as well.

"How are you?" Bakako whispered.

"I'm fine. I worried you'd never come," she whispered back. The shuffle of goods passing between villagers and soldiers provided cover for her to finish. "Depart with the pale men into the forest, and then wait for me beyond the papaya grove."

Bakako nodded, his elation betrayed by a grimace suppressing a grin.

Niana's father, the captain, and Bakako concluded the trade with perfunctory farewells, and Bakako accompanied the pale men back toward Isabela, quitting them at the village outskirts. He mused how much of the cazabi would be eaten before the soldiers deposited the remainder at the storehouse, and he wondered how long he'd wait on Niana.

As he ambled toward the papaya trees, Bakako's longing and lust for Niana simmered, but he churned with disquieting emotions and thoughts. Admiral's command to spy on the villagers filled him with shame. His desire to escape Admiral's enslavement still burned, yet Niana sought his love simply because he served Admiral. She was daughter to a Haitian cacique, and—without Admiral—he was but a Guanahanían fisherman.

He arrived at the papaya grove as the sun set, and, as Niana had instructed, he ventured beyond it to discover a narrow grassland ridge facing the sea, with a breeze to dispel mosquitoes. There were palm trees nearby, and he plucked their leaves to lay a mat on the grass where he would invite her to lie. He waited as the moon and stars rose, certain she would come to love him, uncertain whether she did.

As she passed the papaya trees, Niana brimmed with confidence that she'd entice Bakako to the intimacy of which she'd daydreamed for weeks, but admonishments tormented her thoughts. A vision of the two youths' mutilation at the Yaque begged an answer whether Bakako possessed the cruelty to approve and participate. Her father's instruction that she befriend him warned that true intimacy was forbidden and that it'd be treacherous for her to desire marriage before betrayal—which remained father's decision alone.

Birds took flight from the palms, signaling Niana's approach, and, as he scanned the ridge for her, Bakako felt the warmth of her palm upon his shoulder. He gently pulled her to sit beside him, wrapping his arm about her shoulder, as she laid hers upon his thigh.

"Why did it take you so long to return?" Niana quietly asked cheerfully.

"The Guamiquina invaded the Cibao, and I had to assist. I longed to be with you." He gazed into her eyes, twinkling in the moonlight, and kissed her softly. "Very much."

"I missed you, Bakako."

Bakako lay back upon the mat, bringing Niana to his side, and they embraced fully. Smiles and blushes surpassed words, they hugged ever more passionately, and their teenage arousal sparked quickly. He felt the firmness of her nipples upon his breast and the wet invitation between her legs as she wrapped her arms about his shoulders to induce his mount. They joined in heat, thrusted and received in harmony, and climaxed in a rush that banished every unpleasant thought from their minds, leaving but a delight that their courtship had been consummated. The breeze grew cool, and they snuggled tightly for warmth and talked into the night.

"Were you married on Guanahaní?" Niana asked.

"No."

"Were you ever betrothed?"

"No." For an instant, a vision of Kamana flickered through

Bakako's thoughts, and he recalled that he'd dreamed of marrying her before his seizure. But he released the memory from his thoughts as Kamana was lost forever, invigorated by the love achieved. "Why haven't you been married?" he asked with a smile. "You're a prize."

Niana laughed. "Father's always scheming an alliance, since I was born, but he's never agreed to one, always suspecting something better would come along." She averted her eyes, shying from a topic so proximate to father's plan, yet puzzling whether the Guamiquina or Bakako would decide Bakako's marriage. She diverted the conversation, curious of her lover's voyage with the pale men. "What was it like when you visited the Guamiquina's homeland?"

Bakako unburdened his perceptions with relief—both admirations and criticisms—but he avoided revealing Admiral's intentions for Haiti. He recounted that the pale men's possessions and know-how—be it homes, vessels, weapons, foods, beasts, or whatever else—were astonishing, so advanced as to be almost indescribable. But their brutality and sense of superiority were commensurate, as they warred among themselves, enslaved those they conquered, and burned to death those denying their spirits. He somberly recalled the fate of the first voyage's captives.

"Ten of us were taken there. We all became deathly sick, and most of us died of a spell that pocks the skin grotesquely."

"The pale men's spirits directed that evil?" Niana asked, caressing Bakako's shoulders.

"I think so. Or it's their food or drink. Or simply being around them."

Niana was startled. "Bakako, word has it that people suffer unknown ailments in the villages closest to the pale men's settlement, as well as nearby their crossing sites at the Yaque. Is that also their spirits' evil?"

Bakako shrugged, then little interested in this information. He restrained from further criticism of the pale men but sought to warn his lover. "It's best to have little contact with them—they abuse women often." He kissed her tenderly. "Let's not talk more of them tonight." He caressed her gratefully, cherishing that she—alone with Yutowa—now understood him for what he had been and now become.

They embraced and, more slowly and softly than before, came to make love again, completely discarding anxieties over shame or treachery, skin color, spirits, and all peoples about them in favor of the warmth and excitement of their singular union—until dawn.

V
EXPLORATIONS, PILLAGES, AND ALLIANCES

TERRA FIRMA, CUBA, AND YAMAYE (JAMAICA), *Mid-April–July 7, 1494*

After entrusting Margarite and Hojeda with Española's interior, Cristóbal established a five-member ruling council to govern the settlement with his full authority while he went exploring for terra firma, appointing his brother Diego, as president, and Fray Buil. The three others were men whose leadership, loyalty, and practicality Cristóbal felt proven since departing Cádiz—a gentleman whom he'd appointed the fleet's chief constable, Pedro Fernández Coronel, the sovereigns' courtier whom he'd dispatched with soldiers south of Santo Tomás, Juan de Luján, and a voyage provisioner, city councilman, and now friend, Alonso Sánchez de Carvajal. Gentlemen volunteers and crown officials roundly disparaged Diego's inexperience and common and Genoese heritages, but commoners weren't so jealous and largely recognized his nepotistic appointment as the natural exercise of Cristóbal's hereditary entitlement, typical of Spanish nobility. Cristóbal viewed Fray Buil's appointment as an odious burden, and he prayed that the three worldly men would assist Diego to build Isabela, maintain discipline, and avoid Indian hostility in his absence in accordance with written instructions he left them.

For the expedition, Cristóbal enlisted crews of almost thirty for the trusted *Niña*, his flagship, and fifteen each for the two smaller caravels remaining at Isabela, the *San Juan* and *Cardera*. Soldiers and scribes were enrolled, but most were salted sailors—a few from the first voyage, including Juan de la Cosa—and ship artisans, who could caulk and repair. His friend Michele da Cuneo, steward Pedro Terreros, and page Pedro Salcedo also accompanied, and an attack dog was included with the weaponry. Bakako would sail as interpreter on the *Niña*, and youths resident at the Bajabonico now under his tutelage would serve on the other two.

On the eve of departure, Cristóbal huddled alone with Bakako in his residence's courtyard.

"You've always said Cuba was an island, and sometimes I've believed you," Cristóbal noted.

"Admiral, everyone live here know Cuba island—not me only," Bakako replied courteously, comfortable that Admiral wouldn't begrudge a slave's contrary geographic understanding, if privately expressed.

"Diego, that can't be true." Cristóbal shook his head firmly. "The map you helped chart accurately depicts the Ocean Sea from España to Española, and all the islands to the east and north—including your Guanahaní. What it doesn't show is the remainder of the earth, the globe." Cristóbal studied Bakako, confident he now understood the earth's roundness.

Bakako obliged with a nod, although his boyhood learning was that earth was flat, tucked between heavens and the sea's depths.

"The prophet Esdras foretold the world is one part water and six parts land, and the distance west we've traveled from Spain approximates my calculation of one seventh of the distance around the world."* For an instant, Cristóbal appreciated that the annoyance of establishing the calculation's Ptolemaic consistency was unnecessary—as typically required by Isabel's geographers. "So, terra firma must lie nearby, possibly north or south, but inevitably west—and Cuba must be part of it."

"So that's where the 'Grand Khan' lives, in 'Cathay,'" Bakako responded, vouching he'd learned Admiral's entire theory.

Cristóbal shrugged. "What you Indians call Cuba may be the territory the Grand Khan's subjects call Mangi [south China],

*The calculations are depicted in *Encounters Unforeseen*, chapter V.

or perhaps the land farther south Ptolemy knew as the Golden Chersonese [Malay Peninsula]."

"Admiral, I know great land west south north—but no know where 'terra firma.' I know Cuba island."

On April 24, Cristóbal's three ships departed west to explore the Indies mainland, assert the sovereigns' possession of newly found territories, and confront any Portuguese intruders. Cristóbal left behind a letter to the sovereigns—for dispatch with the next ships departing for Cádiz—summarizing his Cibao march and delegations of authority on Española, assuring the Cibao might have more gold than the rest of the world and that the voyagers held great desire to please him to serve the sovereigns.

Guacanagarí soon learned that Admiral's ships would course by, and he grimly mulled extending an invitation to meet, having been exonerated for the garrison's massacre. But his liberation of the Boriquén women hadn't been judged, and the mutilations of Guatiguaná's subjects along the Yaque reflected a maliciousness in Admiral's heart that portended a change in their relationship, or at least caution. Guacanagarí chose to retreat inland with his household, and he instructed nitaínos to advise Admiral simply that he was away, which they did when Admiral passed on April 25. Cristóbal didn't linger for Guacanagarí's return, but he left a sailor ill for care with Guacanagarí's household.

At sunset on April 29, Cristóbal departed Haiti for Cuba and, by dawn, anchored off Cuba's easternmost tip (Point Maisí), where he debarked to plant a cross and the sovereigns' emblems and reaffirm the sovereigns' possession of Cuba as Juana, in recognition of the prince. He'd named the point Cabo Alpha y Omega when exploring the northern coast on the first voyage, signifying that was where the east ended when the sun set and the west began when the sun rose.

After a council of those of rank, Cristóbal chose to reconnoiter Cuba's southern coast, more likely to possess gold and gems according to Aristotle's teachings, and the ships coursed southwest to anchor for a night in a splendid natural harbor (Guantanamo Bay), where Bakako coaxed the locals to trade. The encounter was friendly, but the local cacique advised that his people hadn't any gold and recommended that the pale men sail to Yamaye (Jamaica), where it was plentiful. Bakako had grown accustomed to this refrain on the prior voyage—*we have no gold but leave us, and you'll find it at the next island.* He was dumfounded that Admiral and the pale men still trusted in it. The fleet traced the shoreline west for two days of peaceful but goldless encounters, and, when the coast turned northeast at a promontory he named Cabo Cruz (Cape Cross), Cristóbal impatiently veered the ships south for a two-day sail—in a blistering gale and pounding seas—to search for Yamaye's gold.

When they arrived on May 5, the Yamayans at the first landfall (Saint Ann's Bay) were vigorously hostile, charging in seventy war canoes, shrieking and brandishing spears to drive the fleet away. Soldiers made a blank discharge of their harquebuses and the canoes scattered, although Bakako soon was successful in entreating a few to trade. The ships had sprung leaks in the rough waters, and Cristóbal withdrew west along the coast to locate a better shore to careen and caulk them. When he found one (Puerto Bueno), the locals there were even more belligerent.

Cristóbal wouldn't tolerate a second precedent of resistance from those to be subjugated, and he dispatched the ships' launches ashore with soldiers, armed with crossbow, harquebus, and the dog. The Yamayans fought vigorously at the outset, but the crossbow and harquebus quickly decimated their ranks—over a dozen slain within moments—and the large unknown dog petrified them, and they fled. Cristóbal harbored for a few days of repair, possessing the island for the sovereigns and naming it Santiago, and Yamayans took the initiative to propose a truce and trade peacefully. To everyone's astonishment, a youth even requested being taken to Castile, overwhelmed by the pale men's superior know-how—and unaware of the servitude to be imposed. Cristóbal obliged, handing him over to Bakako to initiate training as an interpreter. But the locals had no gold to trade—as Bakako expected—nor did other Yamayans at sites the fleet then visited. On May 13, Cristóbal departed frustrated back to Cabo Cruz on Cuba.

The ships anchored that evening within the shelter of a long coral reef tracing the cape, nurturing a mangrove swamp teeming with fish and fowl and a few Indian villages. A nitaíno canoed aside bearing delicacies to eat and invited Cristóbal ashore to meet the local cacique of a chiefdom called Macaca, declaring that the cacique knew of Cristóbal's prior visit to the northern coast (near Río e Bahía de Gibara) and was friend to Abasu's father. Astonished, Cristóbal took the launch with Bakako and soldiers to befriend the cacique and his wives in his village, reciprocating the refreshments with hawks' bells and other truck. Frightened, Bakako brooded whether Abasu yet survived his captivity in Spain and if his abduction would be revenged.

"How's my friend's son," the cacique inquired.

"He has the honor of being a gentleman to my prince," Cristóbal responded. "He's received the holy waters and Christ to be born again in Prince Juan's name, ensuring his soul's salvation."

Bakako struggled to translate, regardless that he understood Admiral's words, aware Abasu detested his captivity and false name. "Abasu lives with Admiral's supreme caciques," Bakako mustered. "Abasu sends his love."

An elderly woman gasped with relief. "Is he healthy and well fed?" she implored.

A vision of his own mother arrested Bakako's thoughts, and he winced for the pain she must have felt on his abduction. The woman before him obviously knew Abasu's mother, and there was no point in aggravating another mother's misery.

"You may assure his mother that Abasu eats the best food the pale men have, and he's content," Bakako lied, saddened that retribution for Abasu's abduction appeared beyond contemplation.

Unmoved by concern for Abasu, Cristóbal focused on his objective, prodding the cacique, "Is Cuba an island?"

"Yes," the cacique affirmed with assurance.

"Have you ever visited its western tip?"

"No," the cacique responded, perceiving the question but incidental.

The expedition sailed on the next day, soon finding itself mired in an extended labyrinth of tiny coral islands and shoals, mangrove swamps, sandbars, and muddy shallows that rendered progress difficult and hazardous for over a week. The sea bottom undulated mere fathoms below, requiring the constant identification of channels forward through which the caravels could float. Frequently, there were none, and the crews labored to kedge the ships over impeding sandbars or mud—using a launch to lodge an anchor forward, and then winching the rope to yank the hull across—straining as the sand and muck clamped tightly.

Severe weather harshened the ordeal, with mist and storm clouds massing during the afternoon to burst into fierce rains and gales at night, exhausting the crews. Hardtack and other supplies dampened and molded and everyone hungered. Cristóbal slept barely an hour or two at night, constantly attending navigation of the shoals and furling of sails when gusts imperiled the course.

But the labyrinth possessed an eerie majesty, and Cristóbal named it El Jardíne de la Reina (the Queen's Garden). In the calmer morning air, sweet scents of flowers wafted from the islands as if in a rose garden, hordes of large turtles nested all about, and enormous flocks of exotic birds abounded and often darkened the sky. The crews were captivated by thousands of bright pink flamingos that ran in fright atop the water when approached, their long necks extending gracefully forward but inches above the sea as their wings flapped furiously to attain flight. The local fishermen were friendly and their method startlingly clever. They corralled sucking fishes they called *guaicáns*—remoras or shark suckers—to the hulls of their canoes, bound the remoras' tails with rope, and, when prey was sighted, such as a large fish, released a remora to attack and attach to it. The fishermen then yanked both remora and prey aboard, whereupon the fright of air caused the remora to yield the prey.

Bakako had never witnessed such fishing. He drew breathless as a fisherman hauled a large turtle into his canoe, placed the gasping remora back into the sea—stationed for duty again—and then beheaded the turtle as it lunged to snap. Devastated, utterly shamed, Bakako admitted to himself that he now served as the pale men's remora.

Cristóbal was relieved the caravels found deep water on May 24, and they coursed smartly west for two days along beautiful coastal mountains the Indians called the Guamuhaya. He had a cross planted on a crusty promontory at a river mouth and traded with friendly inhabitants, albeit goldless, in a nearby village (likely the San Juan River, west of Trinidad). He delighted to learn from a cacique that the territory west was known as Magón—which rhymed portentously with Mangi—and that Magón's peoples had tails that, due to the embarrassment of it, they hid by wearing clothes. Bakako delighted at the cacique's insinuation that the pale men's clothes served the same purpose.

But on May 26, the fleet again mired in shallows, even more treacherous than before, the white bottom glowing softly as milk through crystalline waters, beautifying the treachery. For days, the caravels grounded frequently, abruptly grating the hulls against coral and wrenching the rigging and equipment, torturing everyone's patience, draining their stamina (Banco de los Jardines and Cayera las Cayamas). Cristóbal debarked with soldiers to commandeer a local cacique to navigate the ships through the nightmare, on promise of release after that service.

Eeriness burgeoned pervasive. A crossbowman dispatched ashore to hunt fowl claimed sighting lighter-skinned men wearing white tunics (near Batabanó), and locals confirmed that a cacique so dressed. Cristóbal eagerly sped more men ashore to confirm a nobler civilization but was dejected when they found naught, save apparent lion and griffin tracks. Encounters were hampered when Bakako no longer understood the local dialect.* The coastline soon relentlessly curled southwest into the distance, but the commandeered cacique steadfastly maintained Cuba was an island, regardless of never having visited its tip.

Grittily, Cristóbal reduced the daily ration as the stores dwindled and rotted. The crews' famine and grumbling mounted, and all dreaded a single mishap or moment of neglect could sink them. But their loyalty to their admiral held on, rooted in admiration for his extraordinary endurance and care for their ships' safety.

Regardless, on June 12, Cristóbal scanned a coastline of verdant embankments and beaches—yet barren of bustling ports—stretching southwest to the horizon, and he concluded that the risks of sailing on were no longer tolerable. The ships were dangerously worn—the sails torn, rigging frayed, and hulls sieving—and the crews' trust in his seamanship couldn't be pushed further, as terror mounted

*The ships had passed west into the territory of Taíno peoples often referred to as the Ciboney Taíno or Cuban Ciboney.

whether the hulls could survive the return voyage. The paltry provisions remaining were waterlogged, most of the hardtack having been thrown overboard for rot. He brought his ships to rest in tranquil waters off a beach by a river mouth (in the Bahía de Cortés, north of the Lagoon of Cortés) to load fresh water and terminate the exploration, six weeks after passing Cabo Alpha y Omega, reckoning they had coursed 335 leagues therefrom.* Neither gold, golden temples, or stately cities of the Grand Khan had been found, but neither had a western tip for Cuba. He somberly recalled that Bartolomeu Dias's crewmen had denied his advancing to the Indies after Dias became the first to round Guinea's southern cape (1488) and that Dias had required them to swear to his triumph.

After erecting a cross on the beach, celebrating mass, and christening the area for Saint John the Evangelist, Cristóbal addressed his crews aboard the ships, loosely tethered broadside at anchor.

"Since Cabo Alpha y Omega, we've been sailing along the Indies mainland, past the province of Mangi, to arrive here, approaching the Golden Chersonese. The Indians believe Juana an island—regardless that none we've met have actually beheld a western tip to it. Our sovereigns' charge has been to discover the mainland, and we've gone far enough—and you've suffered long enough—to consider it proven that we've done that. It'd be pointless and endless to follow terra firma farther—taking us past the Ganges, the Arabian Gulf, and Ethiopia. So we'll turn back for Española."

Rousing applause followed, and some men slumped to their knees in elation and others cried. Cristóbal warmly commended them for their courage, fortitude, and loyalty. But before their cheer subsided, he commanded, "All will swear that the mainland has been discovered, in accordance with an oath drawn by the fleet's notary on my instruction. Never deny it hereafter."

The crews didn't question whether they were in the Indies. But Cuneo doubted many agreed that Juana had been proven to be the mainland, and he knew Cristóbal intimately enough to surmise that Cristóbal certainly understood such hadn't been proven and the oath disingenuous.

*Or thirteen hundred miles, a gross exaggeration. The actual overwater distance, without giving effect to the exploration's contorted route and avoidance of shoals, is shy of seven hundred miles.

Yet none objected to the oath, all awash in solace, awe, or fright of the Admiral. Nor did they begrudge him for their misery and hunger, as they'd seen him bear the same. The fleet notary visited each caravel to take the oath of each man—save Cuneo, Bakako, and the other interpreters—that Juana was the mainland, expressing the logic that he'd never seen an island 335 leagues long. Each man forswore remarking to the contrary, consenting to a penalty of ten thousand maravedís for violation, as well as excision of the tongue or a hundred lashes.

The next day, the ships departed east on a homeward voyage that loomed yet more daunting, coursing the same obstacles but wounded and bucking the wind and storm. Cristóbal sought to evade the labyrinths and avoid revisiting the same goldless coastline by coursing south to complete Yamaye's exploration, from where he could return to Española and survey its southern coast himself. But when the fleet sailed south, a maze of reefs entrapped it, forcing a grisly backtracking and reversion to Cuba's coastline. On June 30, the *Niña* sustained considerable damage while impaled on a shoal. The last rations were spent, and the men subsisted on fish, oysters, crayfish, and turtle alone. Cristóbal barely slept at all over long stretches of the ordeal, as he directed most every tack, kedge, and trim of the rigging. When he did rest, he mulled that Dias's oath had done nothing for Dias's career in the absence of sighting Indian temples roofed with gold.

On July 7, Cristóbal's fleet anchored along the mountainous coast at the crusty river-mouth promontory where he'd planted a cross in late May. It was a Sunday, and he named the river Río de las Misas after celebrating mass aboard ship, whereupon he sought to conclude worship at the cross and barter for food in the nearby Indian village. The local cacique and an elderly behique met Cristóbal and Bakako as they debarked and accompanied them to the cross, observing patiently as Cristóbal recited prayers. The behique then approached to stand close before him, offering a basket of fruit, as Bakako and the cacique listened at their sides.

"I understand you've visited throughout my people's islands," the behique remarked sternly, pointing a finger to the sky and fixing eye contact with Cristóbal. "You've inspired great fear."

Bakako grew wary, cautiously translating with precision, and he glanced to ascertain whether Admiral perceived a reprimand, which Admiral's alert visage confirmed.

"Let me warn you something you should know," the behique admonished. "When the soul quits the body, it follows one of two courses. The first is dark and dreadful, reserved for the enemies and tyrants of the human race. The second is joyous and delectable, reserved for those who during their lives have promoted the peace and tranquility of others." The behique waited Bakako's translation and then threatened, "If you are mortal and believe each one meets the fate he deserves, you will harm no one."

There was silence. Bakako anxiously studied the cacique, puzzling whether the behique's remarks had surprised him or were his own, delivered cautiously through another. The cacique urgently scrutinized Admiral, alarmed he was affronted, searching for whether the pale men held similar beliefs, or at least perceived the difference between good and evil. Cristóbal took stock of the behique, perceiving him over eighty and solemnly distinguished by a marble necklace, and judged that the remarks—while accusatory—did emanate from a faith Cristóbal appreciated as genuine, as sincere as his own.

"I have knowledge of the two courses and destinies of our souls, but until now I'd thought them unknown to you and your countrymen," Cristóbal replied calmly, signaling he took no offense. "Your understanding delights me. Let me inform you whom I serve and why I've been sent here." He peered intently into the behique's eyes. "I have done no evil except to bad people."

The behique slumped breathless, startled that Admiral recognized his evil but esteemed it justified and that he owed obedience to another. The cacique trembled to learn Admiral's mission.

"I have come on behalf of my supreme princes, King Fernando and Queen Isabel of Castile, to possess these lands in their name. I extend their friendship to your peoples who are innocent and welcoming. I'll make war on your people's enemies, the Caribes, and those guilty of crimes." Cristóbal prolonged his stare, steeling eye contact. "Those who accept my sovereigns' friendship will be protected and honored. They need not be afraid."

The behique stared back, comprehending, and then responded courteously, shying further challenge. "I'd be honored to meet these caciques and visit your homeland, but my family wouldn't permit that. Tell me of them."

"Fernando and Isabel are the most virtuous Christian princes in the world, and their kingdoms possess unsurpassed wealth and might." Cristóbal turned to catch Bakako's eye, enlisting his participation. "My servant Diego has accompanied me to Castile, and he can tell of it."

Bakako hesitated, sensing the suspicion of all three men, and responded in Taíno cautiously, even though Admiral wouldn't understand a word.

"The peoples in Admiral's homeland are like those you see here—pale, energetic, willful, and intrepid. They possess astonishing know-how and weaponry, just as the vessels you see. His caciques Fernando and Isabel are the most powerful rulers known to men." Bakako glimpsed to the cross, lamenting that he never intended to serve as a remora fish, and continued seamlessly, with the same tenor. "The pale men seek to impose their rule and beliefs on others, and they make slaves of those who oppose." He welled with contempt that Admiral would condone the last remark's intimidating thrust. He raged that Admiral and his men considered a bad Indian simply one who opposed them.

There again was silence as the behique and cacique searched how to respond, warily observing Admiral's ongoing contentment. Cristóbal waited patiently.

"What's your role in the pale men's mission?" the cacique asked Bakako.

"I was seized on Guanahaní over a year ago to participate in greetings like this."

"Just like those abducted on Cuba's northern shore?"

"Yes."

The behique concealed his angst and knelt at Admiral's feet, mumbling and crying. Bakako couldn't decipher the words or even the sentiment, bewildered whether the behique pled for mercy, submitted woefully, or cast a spell of destruction. Bakako's gut gauged the last, but his eyes met Admiral's, and he lied. "He asks if Castile is Heaven."

"Tell him no," Cristóbal responded. "But assure we'll teach his people how to attain it."

Soon, the four men ambled back to the launch, and the cacique imparted a final thought to Bakako. "Admiral should understand that, if threatened, the good aren't made bad by fighting back."

Bakako nodded but didn't translate. He grasped neither Admiral nor his men saw it that way.

Rape of the Vega Real,
Mid-April–July 1494

In mid-April, as Cristóbal prepared to depart for terra firma, Caonabó bristled on receiving Uxmatex's report of the ear slashings by the Yaque. He sobered as Uxmatex recounted that hundreds of pale men had marched to reinforce their fortress in the Cibao.

"They're advancing on us to avenge the deaths of their men," Uxmatex admonished.

"The Guamiquina's design is revealed," Caonabó mused, gazing at the moonlight's illumination of his ballcourt, where the two men sat alone. "He intends to invade and subjugate the island, not slaughter. The mutilations and threatened beheadings weren't massacres but a warning for all to submit." He grimaced and nodded. "He does seek my head, and yours."

"We must prevent him from violating our territory."

"Station our warriors at the Cibao's passes," Caonabó ordered, reproaching himself for the exposure of fighting alone. "But we fight only if the pale men invade Maguana, in defense. An alliance with Behecchio and Guarionex must be secured before we attack their settlements. The Cibao affords substantial defense until then."

"Even their beasts labor to advance in the mountains," Uxmatex agreed.

"Were we successful starving them at their fort prior to this reinforcement?" Caonabó probed.

"The local caciques obeyed, fleeing and withholding food, and the enemy hungered. Perhaps half succumbed to starvation or illness."

"That serves us as well as arrows. Order the local caciques to stick with it. Direct those in Maguana to do the same if pale men trespass. The Guamiquina's reinforcements must famish, wherever they go."

"That's all?" Uxmatex challenged, disappointed.

Caonabó shut his eyes, bidding Uxmatex's patience, and invoked Yúcahu to guide the soundness of his deliberation—to balance boldness and caution, confidence and wariness, desire and calculation. After some moments, he replied, "Command our most prudent lieutenants to ambush and execute pale men who wander alone or in small bands outside their fort in the Cibao. The attacks must be covert, without warning, and our warriors must vanish quickly, leaving no target for reprisal."

Uxmatex warmed but pressed further. "Only the Cibao?"

"I'll encourage other caciques to do the same in their territories." Caonabó frowned. "Be patient. We'll have the Guamiquina's head before he has ours."

⌑ ⌑ ⌑

Shortly after arriving at Santo Tomás, Yutowa squatted dutifully outside the fort's small command house, a wood hut set within the fort's earthen walls, overhearing Hojeda and Margarite review Admiral's instructions. The murmur, shuffle, and clank of hundreds of soldiers raising camp on the surrounding hillside reverberated forbiddingly inward over the walls, foreshadowing that the hostilities he and Bakako had foreseen were at hand. Yutowa spied above the walls and realized warriors likely were staring back at him from behind trees on the high ridge across the river. He strained to identify his next duty and for which pale man.

"I requested men to defend the fort from attack, expecting provisions to feed them!" Margarite stammered, hurling Cristóbal's letter of instructions on a heap of empty sacks. "This says we're to procure our food only from the heathen while we subjugate them, marching about!"

"Don Pedro, it'll be your honor to conquer the entire island and report its riches to the king and queen—a glory Colón reserved for you," Hojeda counseled. "You and the men will live off the people you subjugate, as in the final years of the Reconquista, and the sovereigns will reward you handsomely. Digesting the Indians' food is a small sacrifice compared to seizing their land and gold." Hojeda studied the older man scowl. "I've recovered from sickness and can tolerate the cazabi and sweet potato."

Margarite glared incredulous at the younger man, perceiving banality and ignorance in his lesser stature, welling with contempt. "This squalid conquest is but a travesty of the Reconquista, holding none of its glory! The heathens' huts and roots are rubbish to the farmhouses and vineyards of Andalusia. They're savages—primitive, naked, illiterate, bestial in their diet and habits, worshipping false idols. The land's impoverished, humid, and mosquito infested, hardly worthy of being called Española."

There was silence as Margarite regained composure and sought to articulate a commander's concerns. "So Colón expects me to feed four hundred. For the past month, I've struggled to feed sixty, and half of them have perished."

"Starvation or pestilence?"

"Both. The locals have vanished, so it's impossible to barter for food. Some of my men succumbed in agony—from a scourge borne of the naked wenches." Margarite sighed to emphasize he commiserated but shied from admitting that he, too, now writhed from the disease. Hojeda suspected as much anyway, as Margarite had delighted in mounting the women as much as anyone, although more discreetly, perceiving it the conquest's only reward.

"Colón expects me to defend the fort from Caonabó's attack—so it falls to me to feed the garrison remaining here," Hojeda consoled. "But, as you explore, you may pass through territory where the savages' food supplies are plentiful. It should be easier to feed your men."

"Perhaps," Margarite acknowledged. "But it'll be impossible to enforce the men's discipline as Colón envisages." For an instant, he contemptuously recalled chiding Colón for excessive severity, perceiving an abysmal failure to comprehend leadership. "I simply won't. Soldiers in the field are accustomed to seizing food to quench hunger, and gold and women as their reward. The king understood as much when reclaiming Granada from the infidel." He raised his eyebrows. "Must soldiers be punished for that?" he asked, gazing away to indicate he expected no response.

"The savages are cowardly, and these rewards may be taken easily," Hojeda replied. "The king and queen expect us to subjugate, and they understand how soldiers conquer."

Yutowa shuddered, discerning his and Bakako's worst suspicions bore true—Admiral's lieutenants shared Admiral's intent to instill fear but none of the pretense to instill love. He surmised that either of the pale men he'd now serve would expect him to assist plunder rather than trade.

Margarite glowered, infuriated by the five-man council appointed to govern when Colón departed. "Colón breaches his authority!" he assailed. "This is the king and queen's settlement, not his family's! If I'd known, I'd have thwarted his brother's appointment to the council. The sovereigns would annul it—if they only knew."

Hojeda fawned affirmation, gleaning the venom for failure of Margarite's own appointment. "An unworthy delegation, augmenting the swell of discontent." He sought to soothe commander's vanity. "But your task is more glorious—the conquest of the entire island and submission of its greatest lord. Caonabó's capture requires a diplomat's persuasion and a general's cunning. Will you march the men south to that end?"

For an instant, Margarite did savor the honor of the assignment, but the logistics of feeding men while hiking through the mountains loomed daunting. "I'll have to consider where I march carefully," he faltered. "I'll need to take the boy with me to deceive Caonabó."

◘ ◘ ◘

Margarite soon chose to retreat his four hundred men back to the fertile Vega Real near the Yaque crossing sites along the trail to Isabela now cut, certain of the valley's ample food supply. He caustically dismissed that Española possessed the booty essential for motivating ordinary soldiers in disciplined military conquest, and he foresaw never obeying the instructions to march his men through the island. He shared none of these intentions with Cristóbal and, to avoid confrontation, departed from Santo Tomás in late April, only after Cristóbal had sailed for Cuba.

Yutowa assisted Margarite and aides in commandeering a large village by the Yaque for their headquarters, meeting the local cacique to demand bohíos for residences and fields for horses, warning that the pale men expected to barter for large quantities of food. He also remorsefully excused why the pale men erected a cross midfield in the village ballcourt without asking permission—to introduce their Christ-spirit. The cacique was responsive, but Yutowa recognized that the cacique's trepidation served as his singular motivation to accommodate and that none of the villagers approached to be friendly, the mutilations of their neighbors having darkened their thoughts. No one offered the traditional greeting of cazabi, none of the womenfolk came to flirt, and many villagers even departed, fleeing to reside in the mountains.

Over the following days, Yutowa accompanied Margarite's lieutenants to establish similar encampments in other villages, receiving similar receptions. Margarite expected that no single village could provide sufficient food for the entire squadron, and his men were dispersed widely through the Yaque's floodplain, miles east and west of his headquarters.

As May came and passed, peaceful relations frayed. Yutowa beheld as Margarite's men began to demand food rather than barter for it and, when denied, to threaten punishment and loot it, often followed by beatings or whippings. Soldiers exacted that caciques provide manservants and maids and, when unsatisfied, seized boys and girls, threating mutilations if they failed to serve. The pale men's lust found fewer and fewer willing partners, and they began to seize wives and daughters from their husbands and fathers for use as concubines at night. Brawls ensued, with husbands and fathers lanced or hacked by sword, wives and daughters raped in broad daylight.

More crosses were erected throughout the floodplain, comforting Margarite's men that Christ protected them from both the Indians and their evil spirits. Many surmised that the devil spoke through the Indians' cemís, and Yutowa witnessed as disparagement of the villagers' spirits and rites darkened to include the seizure and burning of cemís, sometimes throughout entire villages. Villagers were horrified by the sacrilege and desperately hid their cemís and face masks whenever bands of pale men approached.

The peace was kept by arms and the villagers' horror of horses. Margarite cautioned his men against excesses, but the only discipline applied was to Indians, never to his men. He commiserated with his soldiers for their hardship, doubted their loyalty and support if reprimanded, and felt the Indians undeserving of Christian treatment.

Isabela's council soon understood Margarite's disobedience, and Diego Colón dispatched a letter reprimanding him and ordering that he fulfill the Admiral's instructions. Margarite replied that Diego and the council had no authority to tell him to do anything, the Admiral's delegation having conferred plenary authority for Margarite's mission, including to improvise, and that he now served the king and queen directly in that appointment, in the Admiral's stead.

Missionaries toppling an idol in Hispaniola, taken from Philoponus, 1621. John Carter Brown Library, portion of rec. no. 04056-11.

To everyone's rapture, a resupply fleet rose from the horizon and anchored off Isabela on June 24, and the men at Isabela erupted in celebration for fresh Spanish food and wine. When the fleet's captain was identified as the Admiral's brother Bartolomé, his brother Diego and the Admiral's loyalists swooned with delight. But the crown officers, the Lanzas, and other critics fumed, scalded that the sovereigns had placed confidence in yet another Colón—and even proclaimed him a gentleman. Bartolomé soon replaced Diego as president of the council and energetically took up Cristóbal's feud with Fray Buil and Margarite's failure to execute Cristóbal's instructions.

Margarite's rage on learning of the sovereigns' trust in Bartolomé exceeded his other rancors. He berated that Isabel and Fernando did conceive of their Indian conquest as a family affair, relegating him to an inappropriate subservience to foreign commoners. He decried that the fresh provisions were withheld from his troops, regardless of his disobedience. Scratching his burning crotch with one hand, swatting mosquitoes with the other, he deplored the soiled, sweaty hut now his headquarters, ruing the day he'd promised Fernando to serve.

◻ ◻ ◻

In early July, Yutowa stood patiently before the local cacique in the village ballcourt at sunset, summoned to discuss the village's descent to lawlessness and violence, the cross's long shadow branding the court to its perimeter.

"They erect this to invite worship or instill fear?" the cacique asked acridly, directing a penetrating glance into Yutowa's eyes.

Yutowa shrugged. "Both. Many think their Christ-spirit will drive our spirits away."

"Their Christ-spirit helps them loot, trample, and rape my people and desecrate our spirits?"

"They believe their Christ-spirit teaches goodness and proper conduct," Yutowa replied, shaking his head to show his commiseration, his contempt for his masters.

"They've been taught nothing of good or evil—that it's sinful to steal, covet another's wife, dishonor one's neighbor, or even that it's wicked to kill." The cacique glared at the cross, abhorrent. "When I plead to your master that his men behave as men should, he apologizes, recognizing their wrongs. Yet he does nothing but threaten that I continue to provide food and obedience."

Yutowa waited for the cacique to calm and indicate what he wished. There was silence.

"I've given up appealing to him," the cacique reproached. "But I need to understand the Christ-spirit's role in their invasion and whether it's he who brings illness and death."

"What do you mean?"

"Pestilence abounds in most of the villages uprooted by the pale men. It's horrid and unknown, and the behiques don't know how to cure it, either by invocation or balm." The cacique studied the pocks that wrought Yutowa's skin. "How did you come to have those pocks?"

"The pale men abducted me and others to their homeland. We all were stricken there." Yutowa summarized the symptoms and pain. "Most of us died."

The cacique drew pensive, astonished. "Follow me. You must tell me what you know about what you see."

The cacique led Yutowa on a trail tracing the Yaque for almost a mile to reach the outskirts of a neighboring village where pale men were idling in its plaza, watching a lone naboria roast them fish. There was an eerie stillness, an absence of the bustle of women preparing dinner, children playing, and men returning from hunting or fishing. The cacique pointed to the doorway of a nearby bohío. "Look inside," he directed.

Yutowa scanned within, and, as his eyes adjusted to the inner darkness, he recognized the contours of bodies of dozens of adults and children lain strewn on matted palm leaf. Eyes glimmered in the faint light staring back, and he heard the murmur of labored breathing and coughing. An infant cried and a mother wept. The air was moist and tepid, seemingly pregnant with the affliction, and the lethargy of the bodies portended the rigidity of corpses. Yutowa strained to study the torso of a man closest the doorway and shuddered to discover the skin inflamed with grotesque red skin blisters, reminding him of those suffered by the pale men at Isabela.* In revulsion, he stepped abruptly backward.

*Perhaps a round of typhus borne by lice carried by the soldiers and rats.

"Look inside the next bohío," the cacique ordered. As Yutowa complied, he added, "You could also visit the bohío after that and the lean-tos by the yuca fields. It's the same in each, and it's the same in other bohíos and lean-tos in the villages east and west. Hundreds of my subjects have succumbed, and most not ravaged have fled in terror. Few remain to attend the sick or even bring them water, and now hundreds more will perish without care."

"This is the pale men's pestilence," Yutowa confirmed.

The cacique shook his head vehemently, raising his voice accusatorily. "You know as well as I—this is the design and work of spirits, who walk unseen among us to penetrate our bodies and destroy us. The pestilence extends far beyond the pale men's grasp, the reach of their weapons or beasts, or even their presence." The cacique thrust his arm toward the cross. "Only a powerful spirit could cause this devastation." He cursed and lowered his voice. "They plant him everywhere, to harm us, and they destroy our own spirits, who would defend us."

"When I was ill, the pale men invoked the Christ-spirit to heal me," Yutowa responded, shaken.

"Because you serve them! But for those who don't—or don't wish to—they invoke this spirit to afflict misery and death."

Yutowa shrugged. "Whether true or not, I've survived because I've honored Yúcahu, and he's protected me. You must do the same."

The cacique spat in contempt at Yutowa's feet.

As daylight faded, the cacique led Yutowa back to his village and pondered whether mercy was appropriate. "Why do you remain with the pale men? Hasn't there been a moment when you could have fled?"

Yutowa's shame boiled within, his gait wobbled, and he trembled to respond.

But before he could, the cacique admonished, "Whatever the answer, don't try to now. Stick close to the pale men, or you'll soon be dead."

◘ ◘ ◘

In late July, as the moon rose high, Caonabó sat close beside Anacaona within his sanctum, the innermost space of his caney, quietly reviewing how best to form the alliance to drive the pale men from Haiti. Naborias fanned them, and a small fire smoldered before them, flickering wanly, darting upon her long black hair, which parted on her shoulders, falling to her back and chest and shrouding a finely carved azure shell necklace.

Husband and wife appreciated that Haiti's important caciques would make their own judgments on warring against the pale men. The support of some of those in territory yet unaffected could be counted on, including that of Anacaona's brother, Xaraguá's Behecchio, and Caonabó's friend, Cayacoa of Higüey, at the island's southeastern tip. Yet many caciques in unoccupied territory shunned involvement, hoping or praying they'd be left alone, forever.

Closer to the pale men's invasion, war jeopardized not only caciques and warriors but their women, children, villages, and farms. Over years, Caonabó had brought his younger brothers born on Aniyana to Maguana to assist his rule, and Manicoatex, the eldest, shy of forty, now governed Maguanan villages in the mountains bordering Guarionex's chiefdom, and Manicoatex's participation was assured. But the pale men hadn't encroached on Mayobanex, whose chiefdom lay east of the coastal settlement, and he might prefer to sit aside, regardless that he'd always opposed the pale men's presence. Guarionex and his vassal Guatiguaná had borne the brunt of the pale men's incursion, and their enlistment would be essential.

"Neither Guarionex nor Guatiguaná has sought our assistance against the pale men," Caonabó observed.

"Guarionex is the essence of Taíno," Anacaona responded. "He believes in resolving discord peacefully, with reciprocity and compromise, achieving harmony after discussion, and he won't favor war lightly." She softened her voice, seeking to avoid any hint of criticism. "He likely distrusts you. You threatened his subordinate caciques without consulting him. He might suspect you'd fight to remove the pale men only to possess the territory reclaimed yourself."

"The pale men's conquest is more terrible than any Haitian cacique's would be," Caonabó replied emphatically but without indignation.

"Perhaps, but Guarionex may not perceive that proven yet. The informants say the Guamiquina offers caciques that they may remain rulers of their people, and Guacanagarí apparently has that understanding. Why not Guarionex?" She drew his eyes to hers. "He might prefer that to vassalage to you."

"It's imperative we convince him to fight." Caonabó waved his hand to brush aside further speculation. "We must act promptly. We must call another caciqual council, inviting everyone except Guacanagarí, and I'll assure everyone that I harbor no territorial ambition. The alliance's singular objective is the pale men's expulsion." He reflected coldly. "In their hearts, all hold expulsion necessary for our people's survival. The issue is whose blood is spent to win it. Those participating in council will have to stand brave or sit coward."

Anacaona rose to kneel behind him to massage his shoulders, and he grew silent, solaced. But her agenda wasn't yet concluded. "Remember, you yourself said we'll discover the Christ-spirit's power when war comes."

"I haven't forgotten."

She reached to a reed basket lying at the sanctum's wall, withdrew the cemí Caonabó had stripped from the corpse of the first pale man he'd slain, and shifted back to huddle against her husband's shoulders. She stretched her arm forward to hold the cemí close before him so they beheld it together.

"Scouts report the pale men set tall crosses everywhere they intrude, demanding all worship their Christ-spirit," she observed. "Those crosses are the same as the one you see on this cemí, with the Christ-spirit dying."

"I understand this—they mark the territory they seize and subjugate," Caonabó replied. "When we vanquish Caribes, we invoke Yúcahu's alliance and presence on the battlefield, just as they invoke their spirit."

"It's more than that, Caonabó. You don't plant cemís of Yúcahu with every vassal cacique who submits to you. You slay Caribes because they steal our women, but you don't seek that they worship our spirits and deny their own."

"What's the point?" Caonabó puzzled. "The pale men are brutish, not spiritual. They've come to subjugate us and steal gold."

"The essence is that I sense their Christ-spirit does more than assist their conquest. He may stand sentry and conquer alone, wherever they plant him, wherever they instruct he be worshipped. We're not accustomed to this manner of conquest and rule. But to vanquish the pale men, you'd best invoke Yúcahu's alliance in defeating both—the pale men and this spirit."

LUGO AND BENITOMO,
Tenerife (Canary Islands), May 1494

In early May 1494—as Cristóbal commenced exploring Cuba and Yamaye—Alonso de Lugo landed at a beach on the southeastern coast of mountainous Tenerife to subjugate the island with 1,500 soldiers and 150 cavalry. He also brought as allies and diplomats a few indigenous noblemen of Gran Canaria, who had accepted vassalage to Isabel and Fernando and Christianity as resolution of the sovereigns' conquest of that island (1483). Fernando Guanarteme, the Canarian ruler Fernando had embraced and baptized in his name, led the diplomats. It was the Festival of the Holy Cross, and Alonso named the site Santa Cruz.

Isabel and Fernando had supplied the transporting fleet of some thirty ships but otherwise provided less funding than for their conquests of Gran Canaria and Las Palmas (1493). Alonso was entitled to hereditary governorship upon Tenerife's conquest, with the right to apportion territory among his commanders and financiers, yet he had to obtain most of the financing himself, for which he'd turned principally to Juanoto Berardi and associates. The inhabitants submitting peacefully to the sovereigns' rule would become the sovereigns' vassals, and Alonso was entitled to enslave those resisting and take their property, livestock, and the proceeds of their sale as slaves in Spain.

The Guanches of Tenerife lived like the peoples on other Canary Islands—residing in stone huts and caves, dressed in loincloth or naked, herding sheep, goats, and pigs—and their weaponry consisted of spears, clubs, and rocks. With the assistance of Gran Canaria's nobility, Alonso dispatched lieutenants to meet the *menceys* (chiefs) of the island's nine tribes, including the most powerful one, Benitomo of the Taoros.

"My Lord Alonso has come to court your friendship and that of your brethren rulers," the lieutenant pronounced to Benitomo. "He invites you to embrace Christianity and requests that you accept vassalage to Castile's King Fernando and Queen Isabel, just as rulers on neighboring islands have done."

"I'm happy to accept Lord Alonso's friendship, as I wouldn't reject it of any man," Benitomo replied. "I don't understand Christianity, so I can't respond to that." Benitomo shook his head. "I also don't know either King Fernando or Queen Isabel."

"Your people may continue to live in their homes, and you to rule them, as Lord Fernando Guanarteme can vouch."

"I was born a freeman and intend to die such." Benitomo glowered back. "The island's rulers have never submitted to foreigners."

"Well then, Lord Alonso requires that you make a choice. You may either submit to Fernando and Isabel's rule and accept Christianity or you and your people will be slain. My Lord gives you some time to think it over."

Soon, brandishing the threat of attack, Alonso extracted peace and vassalage treaties with four of the island's tribes—the Abona, Adeje, Anaga, and Güimar. They surmised their arms were outmatched by the pale men's harquebuses, crossbows, and mounted soldiers. They also occasionally warred with other tribes, including Benitomo's, and reflected bleakly that alliance with the pale men might cure that.

Benitomo never wavered, and, within days, Alonso marched toward the northern coast to compel submission. Benitomo was prepared, and, with substantially fewer warriors, he ambushed Alonso's squadron as they traversed the gulley of a narrow ravine (at Acentejo). The assault's viciousness terrified Alonso's troops and they fled. A hurtled stone smashed Alonso's face and knocked him from his horse, but the loyalty of brave lieutenants spared him from a spear's impalement. He regrouped those surviving for a second attack, only to be routed again, losing eight hundred men in one day, nearly all survivors wounded. Benitomo could have slaughtered more pale men but was content with repelling them from the island.

Shocked, Alonso and the decimated troop retreated to Gran Canaria. Mortified, he turned delicately to advise the sovereigns that backward heathens had rebuffed Spanish soldiers and expansion of their realms. Perhaps more unpleasantly, he alerted his financiers, including Berardi, that there weren't any slaves to sell to pay off their loans.

Treaty at Tordesillas and Isabel's Gentle Instructions,
May–August 1494

On May 8—as Cristóbal reconnoitered Yamaye and Benitomo prepared his ambush—Isabel and Fernando rode from Medina del Campo to the nearby village of Tordesillas, where they and advisors met King João's envoys to resolve the dispute over dominion to Colón's territories. The sovereigns would reside for a month in a lovely palace once dear to Isabel's father as the advisors and envoys negotiated in another palace some feet away, both manors with commanding views of the Duero River flowing through rolling farmland and vineyards.*

The untimely death of João's son Afonso in 1491 had sundered the marriage bond uniting the Hispanic kingdoms, leaving Princess Isabel a widow and succession to the Portuguese crown in doubt. Isabel and Fernando had coaxed the princess toward another Portuguese union but the princess yet had rejected marriage in favor of a reclusive Christian devotion. Neither Isabel and Fernando nor João felt comfortable letting relations with their closest neighbor and kindred civilization deteriorate further, feuding over unknown lands no less. The sovereigns deemed credible João's threat to seize territories at will with his expert mariners. João carped on that he'd been robbed of a southern landmass west of his Guinean possessions. He smoldered the sovereigns were due a stern reminder that—regardless of the pope's whorish bull of September 1493—the Treaty of Alcáçovas remained their guarantee they wouldn't circumvent

*Isabel's father was Juan II of Castile, and the palace for negotiations is now the Museo del Tratado de Tordesillas.

Guinea to reach the Indies. Past dynastic rivalries simmered darkly in their hearts, particularly Isabel's. But peace on the Hispanic peninsula was essential for both kingdoms given the uncertainties elsewhere in the world, foremost French aggression.

João chose not to attend in person, remaining in Setúbal with Queen Leonor, his wife of twenty-three years and cousin, both ill, both forever dispirited by the loss of Afonso, their only child, and now often gravely distraught with each other. João desperately had sought Pope Alexander's legitimization of João's remaining natural son, Jorge, born of a Portuguese noblewoman João long since had discarded, prelude to selecting Jorge as successor to the throne instead of the lawful heir—Leonor's younger brother, Manoel.* Leonor had permitted Jorge to live at court with Afonso, and a decade prior she had stomached João's assassination of her brother Diogo to protect Afonso's succession, but with Afonso gone she refused to countenance the crowning of another woman's bastard in place of Manoel. Regardless of this intimate quarrel, they remained a couple, perhaps appreciative of their long journey together, having wed at their earliest fertility—he fifteen, she twelve—although many whispered that she was poisoning him.

Isabel felt no loss in João's absence at Tordesillas. She'd never forgiven his support for his cousin Juana's rival claim to the Castilian throne two decades before, and she raged that—in violation of the Treaty of Alcáçovas—he permitted Juana to flaunt the life-long monastic seclusion imposed on her to mince coquettish at his court, styling herself as the queen of Castile.† As did Leonor, Isabel and Fernando favored Manoel's succession to the Portuguese throne, as well as Manoel's marriage to Princess Isabel, and Fernando had pressed Alexander to deny Jorge's legitimization. But the princess yet refused any remarriage at all.

Inimitable, João kept abreast of the negotiations through messengers dispatched by horseback nightly, who transported not only Isabel and Fernando's proposals but the strategy and fallback alternatives behind them, revealed by informants within the sovereigns' own court, whom João well compensated. João's negotiators

*Jorge was born of Ana de Mendoça, 1481.

†"La Beltraneja," born in 1462 of Queen Juana, wife of Castile's King Enrique IV.

also had a far greater understanding of Ptolemy's geographic principles and the likely circumference of the globe. But the sovereigns' advisors came armed with Cristóbal's map, depicting the direct route from Hispania to Cathay and all the islands in between.

On June 7, the Treaty of Tordesillas was executed, superseding between the kingdoms Alexander's bulls issued in 1493. For the first time, João accepted the concept of a longitudinal, rather than latitudinal, division of the world, as previously introduced in the bull *Inter Caetera* of May 4, 1493. But the treaty moved the line delimited by the bull—100 leagues west of the Cape Verde islands—to 370 leagues west. Discoveries to the west of that new line were Castile's, to the east Portugal's, regardless of how far north or south. No one knew where Colón then was, so an accommodation was stipulated that any lands he discovered by June 20, 1494, lying within the band 250 to 370 leagues west would also be Castile's. Isabel and Fernando reaffirmed the Treaty of Alcáçovas, recognizing Portugal's exclusive right to circumnavigate Guinea to the Indies. They and João mutually pledged to map the actual line within ten months, with each party together dispatching an equal number of ships, pilots, astrologers, and sailors west from the Cape Verde islands to jointly determine the precise spot of the world's division, and then north and south, marking the line on the lands encountered with towers so that the subjects of one kingdom would not enter the other's dominion. Both parties entreated the pope to approve the agreement and render appropriate consistent bulls if requested.

All were satisfied and relished the other duped. Isabel and Fernando delighted their man Colón was already in the Indies and that they would claim most of it—if not all—before João's mariners slogged through from the other direction. João delighted that, wherever he was, Colón wasn't in the Indies and that João's mariners would claim all of it before Isabel and Fernando realized they weren't close.

Isabel and Fernando departed Tordesillas for Medina del Campo and took their court briefly to Isabel's childhood home, Arévalo, and then to Segovia for most of the summer. They soon dispatched letters to learned men seeking astrologers and cosmographers to participate in the mapping and marking. On August 16, they wrote Cristóbal from Segovia, forwarding a copy of the treaty and requesting that he return from Española to do so himself, or in his stead, Bartolomé.

By then, the sovereigns had reflected more fully on the correspondence and information received from Torres and others in March, including Cristóbal's accusations and Fray Buil's criticisms. Their hearts had hardened that their admiral—albeit imperfect—deserved more support and obedience. Lugo's defeat on Tenerife reminded that conquest was never assured and required steadfast prosecution. They had instructed Fonseca that Berardi was to be involved and heeded—as the Admiral's own representative—in arranging the resupply ships remaining to be dispatched. On August 16, as they wrote Cristóbal, they issued orders to all in the Indies warning that disobedience to the Admiral displeased them and would be punished, reminding that the Admiral's commands and penalties were to be obeyed as if their own. Their letter to Cristóbal promised that no one else in Spain could give valid orders regarding his settlement and assured they would take his advice and opinion about it, delegating all to him.

But their letter also kindly suggested how Cristóbal might do better and that the sovereigns wished to supervise him far more closely. Isabel's softer, more intimate touch graced the words chosen, as if they were talking face-to-face, reminding of their special bond, disguising any lack of confidence.

"All that you said could be achieved has turned out to be true," she commended. "For the most part."

"It's a great joy to read your letters," she exclaimed. "But write us more." She wanted to learn how many islands had been found, both their Indian names and his own, the distances between them, and discoveries made on each or as reported by the Indians, as well as fulsome information about the weather and seasons. "Tell us what has been harvested from that sown, because time has passed for harvesting."

"We're ordering resupply of everything you requested," she assured. "In order to know how you and all the people there are doing, and for ongoing resupply, we'd like—if you agree—that one carvel should be dispatched each way every month, peace with Portugal now permitting that."

"We approve of the relations you've established with your men up to now," she noted. "That's how you should continue, giving them the most satisfaction possible but not any license to exceed the things they're supposed to do."

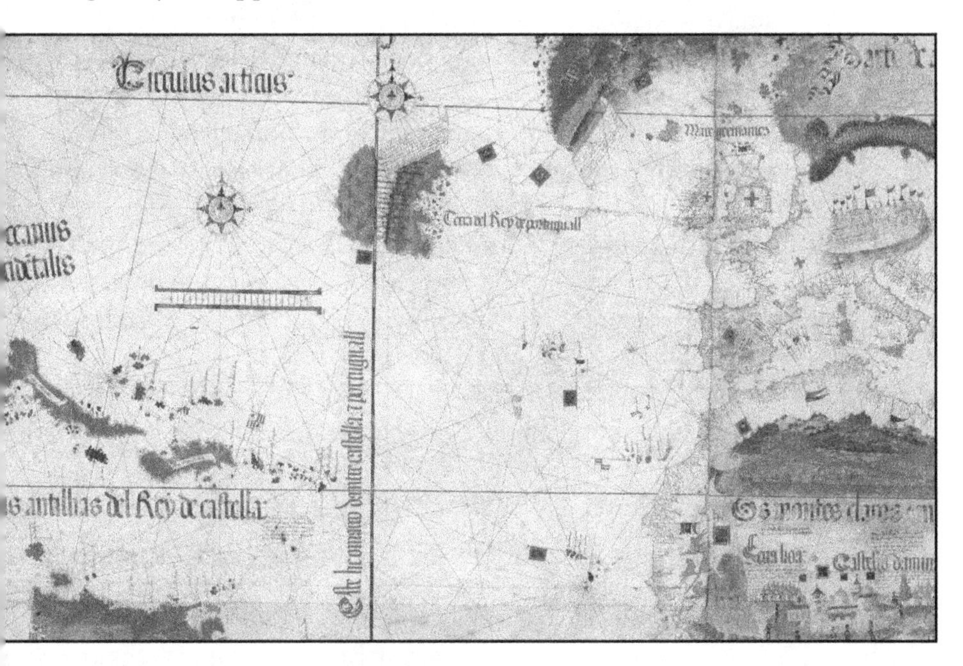

Demarcation of Tordesillas Treaty, on a portion of the Cantino World Map of 1502.

Return to Haiti, Desertions, Delirium, *July 8–September 28, 1494*

On July 8, Cristóbal's fleet weighed anchor offshore the promontory where he'd defended his soul's destiny and tacked into the easterly gale, seeking to course but two hundred miles to attain Cabo Cruz, which he'd last visited two months before. Squalls buffeted the ships frequently, and a violent thunderstorm unleashed such a deluge that, regardless of the crews' feverish pumping, water rising in the holds drove the decks to submerge. Spanish foodstuffs didn't survive, the crews beheld death by drowning or starvation, and the journey wore on over ten days. But disaster was skirted, and the villagers at Cabo Cruz welcomed Cristóbal's return and shared cazabi, fruit, and fish.

After days of recovering, Cristóbal again designed a southerly route to Isabela, praying for better weather and desperate to reconnoiter Yamaye's southern coast. It remained the solitary unexplored hope for amassing gold or sighting majestic temples before returning to Isabela empty-handed.

The ships arrived off Yamaye in a day and commenced a counterclockwise circumnavigation, still suffering frequent squalls but trading daily for food in friendly encounters with Yamayans. By August 17, they anchored in a large bay on the southern shore (Portland Bight), where Cristóbal had an amiable audience with a cacique of considerable veneration. The cacique asked why he'd come, and Cristóbal answered to honor the good and destroy the bad.

The next morning, when the fleet departed east, the cacique and his staff followed in canoes and clambered aboard to make an entreaty, including musicians, gift-bearing nitaínos, and a wife and lovely teenage daughter—all naked but for jewelry, cotton bands, and the wife's nagua. Astonished, Bakako learned that the cacique and his family wished to travel to Castile. Cristóbal instructed an officer to provide the two women clothing, to hide their privates from his crew, but the mother refused because nakedness was their custom.

"Why have you come, my friend?" Cristóbal probed.

"To meet the greatest rulers in the world—your cacique and his wife—as they've conquered so many here," the cacique replied. "My people tremble before you. Those who don't have been slain. I wish to submit to your caciques—before you take my dominion."

Bakako translated, recognizing that the cacique's submission was the most forthright he'd yet heard, exceeding even Guacanagarí's.

Cristóbal, too, was shocked. For a moment, he relished that the cacique and his family possessed the regal demeanor, urbanity, and civility that would impress the sovereigns and vouch for the Indians' timidity. Yet he doubted the practicality of taking them to Spain, as it could be months before they were shipped there, as well as risks of disease and mistreatment of the lovely girl, and he hesitated before responding.

Bakako scrutinized his master's indecision and perceived that Admiral did respect the well-being of a cacique and family who submitted unequivocally. A remembrance of the pale lieutenant mocking Niana's father flickered through his thoughts, and he cursed that other pale men failed even that.

"I'd be delighted to introduce you to my king and queen, but I've much to discover before I return home," Cristóbal replied. "You'll have opportunities to visit them later." He appreciated the cacique's dejection and bestowed additional gifts to the family but then ferried the entire delegation back ashore.

The fleet coursed on, departing Yamaye, and Michele da Cuneo observed that they hadn't found a single thing better there than in the other islands. The ships reached Haiti's southwestern tip on August 20, where Cristóbal named a cape for Michele in recognition of sighting it first. The weather improved, although the absence of gold persisted. In early September, Cristóbal brought the ships to anchor in a large river mouth on a fertile plain (Río Jaina, near Santo Domingo) and, with Bakako's assistance, determined from villagers that men could hike overland from there to Santo Tomás and Isabela. He dispatched nine armed men to do so and herald his return.

⊡ ⊡ ⊡

As Cristóbal encircled Yamaye, the missives passing between Bartolomé and Pedro Margarite were vitriolic, and Bartolomé and Fray Buil ceased conversing. Margarite strode with lieutenants to Isabela, quitting his troops in the Vega Real, and the three men met icily in a fractious audience in the courtyard of Cristóbal's residence.

"I shall bring my men back to Isabela," Margarite blustered. "We'll remain here until the sovereigns are fully informed and decide what becomes of this forsaken business."

"Your orders—your service to king and queen—are to discover Española's treasures," Bartolomé retorted brusquely. "Depart and do your duty."

"I don't answer to younger brothers!" Margarite thundered, glaring into Bartolomé's eyes. "This is a crown mission, not a rubes' cabal."

"You answer to the Admiral's command, and you've failed him miserably—sitting on your rump, fornicating like a whore!"

Bartolomé replied, neither cowed nor respectful of rank. He glanced to Buil. "Both of you have failed your king and queen. I understand not a single Indian has been baptized under your watch."

"I'd have you flogged for that insult, if this were Aragón," Margarite warned, gritting his teeth. "You're common dirt, not even Spanish nor the king and queen's subject. You've no authority to invoke my king and queen to tell me to do anything, and may the Lord smite you for impugning the pope's representative."

Malice surged, and Margarite and Bartolomé prepared to grip their daggers and pounce. But each appreciated that the sovereigns expected their unity, and, barely renitent, they retreated from the precipice.

Margarite lowered his voice to reason, seeking to cast observations as dispassionate. "The truth is there's nothing of value to find on Española. Your brother's mistaken. There're no gold mines here. There's no civilization to trade goods with. No Spaniard wants to settle here. This is a waste of the sovereigns' effort and expense."

"Interpreters are necessary and the natives bestial," Buil pronounced. "Their conversion requires an expenditure not supported by the settlement itself. The sovereigns never contemplated that."

"I've pledged my loyalty to the king and queen in this business, just as you," Bartolomé responded tartly to Margarite. "They've authorized me to assist the Admiral." But he lowered his voice, as well, seeking to avert final rupture. "The sovereigns never expected Española's gold could be plucked from its beaches, nor should you. They grasp that the samples found auger great returns."

"That's your brother's lies," Margarite scowled.

"That's your opinion. But the king and queen are more optimistic. They've also directed Española's subjugation, and they'd consider your refusal to lead that grave disobedience. Your failure to discipline your men incites the savages' revolt."

Exasperated, Margarite exclaimed, "So, you reject that I return my men here?"

"Yes. Survey the island, subjugate the savages."

The audience terminated abruptly, with glowers rather than handshakes, and Margarite angrily returned to his bohío in the Vega Real.

Over the summer, Bartolomé's sway over the men stationed at Isabela withered as the community splintered into factions favoring or opposing the Colón brothers. With Alonso de Carvajal's assistance, Bartolomé rewarded those loyal to Cristóbal with better food rations than those opposed. But that didn't retard the swell in the ranks of men disloyal.

Margarite and Fray Buil soon conspired to commandeer the three ships Bartolomé had brought to Isabela to take themselves and others disgruntled to Spain. When sailors appeared from Española's southern coast to herald Cristóbal's return, Margarite deserted his post and troops and sped to Isabela. By mid-September, before Cristóbal's arrival, he, Fray Buil, and some hundred disaffected—including half of the friars serving Fray Buil—seized the ships to depart. Bartolomé and Colón loyalists demanded the deserters desist but were overpowered.

The four hundred soldiers in the Vega Real took their commander's desertion as further license to ignore Spanish law, military discipline, and the Ten Commandments to loot, rape, and indenture Indians, beating or killing those who resisted. Cemís were burned in jest or scorn. The soldiers split into small bands—each dedicated to its own survival—and diffused throughout the great valley as food in the villages initially populated grew scarce. In turn, local caciques—particularly those subordinate to Gautiguaná in affected areas along the Yaque—began to extract revenge, ambushing and executing lone bands when unvigilant. Blood of both peoples bled often into the Yaque.

⌑ ⌑ ⌑

Unaware of the commotion at Isabela, by mid-September Cristóbal brought his ships to rest at Española's southeastern tip in a tranquil strait formed by an offshore island, which he named La Bella Saonese (Saona), a reference in Cuneo's honor to his hometown (Savona). The sighting of a huge unknown fish at the sea's surface, together with ominous clouds and winds, had led Cristóbal to predict a dangerous storm and seek shelter. When the onslaught hit, Bakako reported that a hurricán was distant. Cristóbal ordered the weary crews to rest and mend equipment as they waited out the tempest, wet and hungry. The sea was too rough to sail for over a week.

Four months of sleepless nighttime navigation, scant diet, and constant exposure to ocean storms had rendered Cristóbal exhausted and prone to illness, and he turned despondently to composing his next report to the sovereigns. His utter failure over these months to fulfill the promise of discovering a rich trading civilization racked him, and he despaired the sovereigns wouldn't long support an unprofitable enterprise. He wrote to relate the triumph of attaining the Golden Chersonese and reaffirm gold's abundance in Española's Cibao. He waxed of Cuba and Yamaye's productive lands and large populations as more valuable than gold. He proclaimed that Española was superior to them, as well as to all other islands of the world.

Cristóbal frequently rose from his desk to monitor the storm and the ships' anchorage, bitterly begrudging the obstacles the Lord relentlessly imposed yet grateful most had been overcome. At dawn, beneath dark storm clouds, he thanked the Lord for Isabela's establishment despite adverse weather, sickness, indolence, disrespect, and betrayal. At noon, as the gale smacked his back, he begged the Lord to grant Española's peaceful conquest. At dusk, as rain drenched him, he implored the Lord to reveal Española's gold or otherwise permit it to become profitable. In the deathly glow of a clouded moon, he sank to his knees and cried jealously to the Lord that elsewhere—João's Guinea, Lugo's Canaries, the Caribes' homeland, and the courts of Christian and infidel princes throughout terra firma, including the sovereigns' very own—peoples who could be enslaved were enslaved.

The sea became navigable on September 24. Cristóbal well understood that every mariner's judgment loudly forewarned him, as admiral, to return to Isabela—his ships were leaking and damaged, he and his crews even more worn, his provisions gone, and the route to Isabela was known, previously traversed, and mostly downwind. Every judgment as viceroy and governor dictated the same—he'd been absent from Isabela far too long given its unfinished business and discord, and there wasn't any justification for diverting to islands previously discovered—save one, which the sovereigns hadn't approved. But Cristóbal now perceived enslavement essential. Entreating the Lord's blessing, he commanded the fleet to sail east into the wind to slave raid on Boriquén.

The ships never made landfall there. Cristóbal collapsed feverous and unconscious en route, after harboring on an island in the waters between Española and Boriquén (Mona), perhaps a reaction to food eaten there. Frightened death was imminent, the fleet's officers took control and ordered the ships to come about and return to Isabela. Some said he suffered from gout, others from overwork or food poisoning, and still others from preconditions unknown.*

Cristóbal regained consciousness at sea but remained delirious. He understood the Lord had chosen to redirect the ships, and, from the haze of his delirium, he exhorted the Lord to reveal Española's gold.

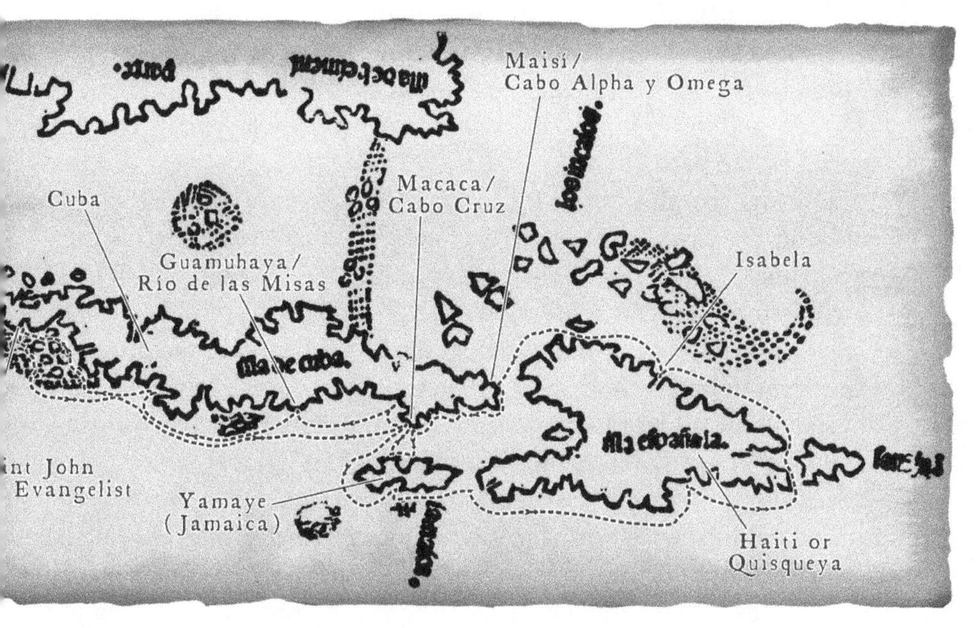

Portion of Peter Martyr d'Anghera's map of New World, 1511, marked for the Cuban exploration. John Carter Brown Library, rec. no. 0232-1.

Caonabó's Council and the Alliance against Pale Men,

Maguana, (Autumn 1494)

At sunrise, Caonabó sat with Anacaona in her garden, a lovely sanctuary nestled beside the village river, nursery to trees, shrubs,

*Modern epidemiologists' speculations include typhus or typhoid fever.

flowers, and cacti transplanted from throughout Haiti, blooming every shade of the rainbow. It was her retreat to consult spirits, compose areítos, and hold private audiences, supreme to every man and woman before her save one, her husband. The sweet scent of myriad blossoms freshly dewed belied both husband and wife's shrewd intuition. Later that morning, Anacaona would dress with her finest gold earrings, armbands, feathers, and nagua, further belying that shrewdness.

"All invited are coming," Caonabó observed.

"Don't presume to dictate an alliance," Anacaona cautioned. "Let consensus give birth to it and then nurture it." She smiled. "Don't start by telling them you told them so."

"All will have their say," Caonabó acknowledged. "But I'm certain of the path."

During the day, husband and wife solemnly greeted Haiti's supreme caciques as they arrived in the great ballcourt, accompanied merely by a nitaíno or two, forgoing the bravado of a martial or ceremonial entrance owing to the council's gravity and secrecy. Guacanagarí hadn't been invited, and two subordinate caciques had been summoned—Guarionex's Guatiguaná, whose subjects were abused daily, and Manicoatex, Caonabó's eldest younger brother. When he arrived, Behecchio warmly hugged Anacaona and they stole away intimately to review family affairs. Caonabó enjoyed a brief reminiscence with Higüey's Cayacoa. Guarionex conferred with Guatiguaná but otherwise stood cordially silent, as did Mayobanex, as emergency rather than camaraderie had brought them there.

Anacaona's nitaínos served refreshments throughout the afternoon and, after all had arrived, delicacies for dinner at sunset, albeit in frugal amounts, in anticipation of a cohaba ceremony. In the morning, Caonabó invited the caciques and Anacaona to sit on duhos set in a circle in the ballcourt.

"It's been a year since many of us met," Caonabó reminded, turning slowly to peer into each cacique's eyes. "All now understand that the pale men are a brutish, dangerous people." Caonabó fixed on Guarionex. "They are our enemy. Their leader, the Guamiquina, intends to subjugate all of Haiti." He circled back to the others. "We must expel them from the island, and I've invited all of you here to band together to accomplish that."

"They're lawless, prurient, and savages, seizing land and defiling our spirits daily," Guarionex somberly acknowledged. "Caonabó was first to recognize their hostility," he admitted. "But I'm not as convinced as Caonabó that the Guamiquina has resolved to conquer the island."

Caonabó stole a glance at Anacaona and nodded graciously. "The Guamiquina possesses three territories, with soldiers. The coastal encampment is now a fortified village with a dozen large structures and gardens, manned by perhaps three hundred soldiers, builders, and artisans. It's meant to be permanent, whether they bring their womenfolk or not. While small, the same is true of the fort in the Cibao. The Guamiquina marches with soldiers as conqueror, not friend, warning those in his path to submit. While he was absent, his army initiated the third intrusion, where our crops best support them—along the Yaque. More reinforcements arrived in vessels this June. It's incontrovertible—the Guamiquina intends to rule all of us."

"I trade with the Yamayans and Cubans," Behecchio interjected. "Their caciques report the Guamiquina assured them peace if they bowed in submission—just as he's beguiled the weakling, Guacanagarí." Behecchio riveted upon Guarionex, beaming confidently as Haiti's most powerful cacique. "There's no doubt the Guamiquina covets ruling our entire world, not just Haiti."

"He harbored in my chiefdom, completing an inspection of the entire coastline," Cayacoa pushed. "The intent to conquer the entire island is transparent."

"I suspect you're all correct," Guarionex responded. "But I haven't spoken to the Guamiquina myself, and I don't believe any of you have, save Mayobanex. What I don't know is what he would do if I confronted him. How would he react if I warned him of the vastly larger army of warriors we together command and prompted him to limit his men's presence to merely the coastal settlement and the Cibao fort, to be used only for trading? My informants have always reported that he seeks gold before anything else."

"He didn't erect the fort and garrison soldiers in your chiefdom without your permission simply to trade gold with you," Caonabó replied sternly, hardly suppressing his scorn. "His men aren't pillaging Guatiguaná's people and burning cemís in order to trade gold, either."

"Perhaps he's angry that you massacred the men he left here, and he's built the Cibao fort as a base from where to bring you to justice," Guarionex replied curtly. "You may have the most to fear of us all."

Caonabó bristled with indignation. "I didn't invite you here to seek an alliance to protect myself. Your subjects—and Guatiguaná's—have borne the brunt of the Guamiquina's invasion." He raised his voice. "You're the ones who need immediate protection."

There was a nettled silence. Anacaona lowered her eyes, signaling for Caonabó to soften his tone.

Mayobanex broke it, speaking in Macorís, with translation into Taíno by an interpreter, addressing them all. "I met this Guamiquina when he first came. It's clear to me he wants both gold and conquest." He grimaced. "In hindsight, we would've been better off telling him we have no gold. I understand Lucayans less sophisticated and powerful told him just that—and he passed them by." He nodded to Guarionex. "But that's no longer an option, my friend. Words won't dislodge him, only arrows." He turned to Caonabó. "Before uniting, we must understand what you envision at each of the sites the Guamiquina occupies."

"Agreed." Caonabó opened his arms, inviting Guatiguaná to speak. "Your territory is terrorized daily. What would you request from us?"

Guatiguaná lowered his eyes deferentially and, through an interpreter, bared his torment. "The pale men's invasion is more terrible than you understand. You know they loot and rape. They also enslave the meek and youth to be servants. They scoff and denigrate everything we cherish, including our food, our ceremonies, and even our spirits. They burn our cemís and plant their own spirit's mark in our plazas and sacred places." He lifted his eyes to scan about the circle. "Their Christ-spirit has cast an evil spell upon hundreds of my subjects, striking them with an ugly pestilence, followed by pain, stupor, and death."

"Our own spirits must ward this spell away!" Anacaona urged.

"My behiques invoke them, day after day, with no success,"

Guatiguaná replied to her, shrugging his shoulders. He pivoted to Caonabó. "What I would ask is that your warriors invade my chiefdom and slay the pale men, every last one of them, including the Guamiquina. Many of my subjects will perish as the pale men fight back, but that's better than living as slaves to them."

Silence followed.

"Mayobanex, what would you have us do at the coastal settlement?" Caonabó probed.

"I'll never answer to another cacique, whether benign or malevolent, either of pale or olive skin," Mayobanex replied, emphasizing the last phrase and staring back. "We must assault it, and I'll contribute my warriors. It's not impregnable."

"I'll commit my warriors to both attacks," Behecchio assured all assembled. "Xaraguá is distant from the invasions, but the Guamiquina eventually will lust for it."

"Count me in," Cayacoa barked. "We must strike now, before the Guamiquina is further reinforced."

Caonabó looked to Guarionex, and all hushed.

"I certainly oppose conquest by the pale men, and I won't oppose whatever actions you collectively decide, including at the fort in my chiefdom," Guarionex responded. "But I'm not ready for war. Other than Guatiguaná's, my subjects won't join. I continue to believe that meeting the Guamiquina in person might avert both war and conquest—without bloodshed. Were I alone in this, that's what I'd do first." Guarionex frowned. "It goes without saying that none of us shall expand his own territory at the expense of another."

Caonabó nodded deferentially, concealing his disappointment. "I hear consensus that we drive the pale men from the island."

All but Guarionex murmured concurrence, and Anacaona bid her naborias to serve pineapple juice. After a few moments, Caonabó resumed.

"You'd desire their annihilation tomorrow, were it possible," he reflected, gazing to Mayobanex and Guatiguaná. "So do I. But direct assaults favor their weaponry, particularly their beasts." Caonabó studied the caciques' eyes startle, their brows wrinkle. "That's particularly true at the coastal settlement. When we attack, wherever we attack, it's essential that victory be total, denying reprisal. As a strategy, it'd be better to whittle their numbers first, starving them by withholding food and assassinating them in small bands." Caonabó avoided Guarionex's stare, grimacing prelude to confessing his intrusion. "That's what I've done to them in the Cibao."

"Mere assassinations will result in reprisals to my subjects," Guatiguaná protested, raising his voice. "It already has. When we ambush one of them, they torture and slay many in return. My subjects would suffer less if all the pale men were slaughtered at once."

"Your people must avoid retaliation by fleeing the villages the pale men occupy," Caonabó instructed. "I'll dispatch warriors to join in the assassinations."

"I'll care for your subjects who flee," Guarionex assured.

"I'll send warriors to ambush pale men traveling between the coast and the Cibao," Manicoatex promised.

Caonabó reassured all. "When their ranks are depleted inland, we'll attack there. When the interior's reclaimed, we'll storm the coastal settlement."

"What should we do with Guacanagarí?" Behecchio interrupted gruffly. "Informants warn he's such a coward that he'll do whatever the Guamiquina bids."

"He's a traitor, and we share no information with him. Ostracize him, and beware of his informants," Caonabó replied. "But we shouldn't waste our forces on him until the pale men are expelled."

"Understood, but you expressed your contempt by stealing a wife. Now it's my turn," Behecchio declared, curtly. "My scouts shall murder one."

The council deliberated long into the afternoon. Behecchio recounted what he'd learned of the Guamiquina's visit to Yamaye and Cuba, particularly the battle fought with the ferocious barking dog. Guatiguaná shared his observations of the Christ-spirit's pestilence, and Anacaona questioned him about the pale men's incantations and the Christ-spirit's potency. Guatiguaná also described the enormous beasts the pale men mounted to rush as if evil spirits, and Mayobanex and Cayacoa proposed how to slay them. Caonabó scrutinized Guarionex, suspecting he'd deal secretly with the Guamiquina for an advantage uncertain, and Guarionex mused whether Caonabó schemed more than the pale men's expulsion.

That evening, the caciques abstained from dinner and, before retiring, vomited their bellies dry of any food still digesting, commencing purification prelude to the intended cohaba ceremony. They rose the next day to maintain abstinence and, at sunset, Caonabó and his senior behique called the ceremony at the ballcourt's center, their exhortations to Yúcahu intensifying after the moon ascended.

Caonabó implored victory over the Guamiquina. Privately, Guarionex beseeched a path to undoing the dreadful prophecy of extinction. Not invited, Anacaona retired to her garden to invoke Yúcahu himself to vanquish the Christ-spirit. At the ceremony's frenzied conclusion, Caonabó proclaimed Yúcahu's blessings for alliance and war and all shrieked approval except Guarionex.

Ambush of Spaniard (in Puerto Rico, 1510), taken from Theodor de Bry, 1594. John Carter Brown Library, portion of rec. no. 09887-6.

Alexander and Fernando, *September 1494*

In early September, Pope Alexander seethed that King Charles had crossed the Alpine pass in Savoy with thirty thousand foot soldiers, supported by a fleet in the Ligurian Sea bearing ten thousand more, advancing to claim the Neapolitan throne. Alexander had denied Charles's request to pass through the Papal States to claim it, and Charles was bringing his army to Rome's doorstep to compel a reconsideration. Ominously, crowds in Savoy, Turin, and Asti welcomed the French invasion, roused by the prophecy of a fiery Dominican friar named Girolamo Savonarola (b. 1452) that a conqueror would punish the church for its decay and depravity, epitomized by Alexander himself, and then purify it.

Feverishly, Alexander had sought military and financial support from Italian states and foreign princes, but Charles largely had secured the formers' neutrality, and King Henry VII and Emperor Maximilian saw little at stake for them in the outcome. Desperate, Alexander even wrote to the infidel Bayezid II, emperor of the Ottoman Empire, requesting the annual payment due the papacy for continuing to confine Bayezid's rival brother Jem from returning to Istanbul to seize Bayezid's throne.

But King Fernando came through, honoring his prior assurances. He formally committed to contribute an army and navy and spearhead the establishment of a broad military alliance for the purpose of defending the church, expelling the French, and preserving his lineage on the Neapolitan throne. He and Isabel remained mute as to any other design. They selected a decorated veteran of the Reconquista as commander and ordered Archdeacon Fonseca to assist the preparations.* The initial army contributed by the sovereigns would include over two thousand foot soldiers and three hundred cavalry, and Fonseca would arrange a fleet of twenty-five ships to transport them.

The drain on the sovereigns' financial resources was considerable. They hoped their Indian conquest would contribute to those resources rather than compete for them.

*Gonzalo Fernández de Córdoba.

VI

RESISTANCE AND SLAVERY

Reunions at Isabela, *September 29–December 1494*

On September 29, five months gone, the tattered *Niña*, *San Juan*, and *Cardera* creaked past the northern reef sheltering Isabela's promontory, and the *Niña* berthed at the pier under construction at the town's beach. Most ashore were astonished, having suspected the expedition had perished or vanished, lost forever. Brothers Bartolomé and Diego rushed aboard to find Cristóbal prone and delirious. Cristóbal gaped through a haze of visions and nightmares to recognize them both, and his joy for reuniting with Bartolomé brought tears to his eyes.

"You survive! Embrace me!" Cristóbal rasped hoarsely in Ligurian.

"So do you!" Bartolomé replied in the same, sobbing, falling to his knees to kiss Cristóbal's cheek in a prolonged embrace.

"My sons?"

"Dressed and fed like princes, pages at the royal court. The queen received them herself."

"Father?"

"Still tottering in Genoa, boasting of your renown. Close your eyes, Cristoforo. Rest, and Giacomo [Diego] and I will inform you of everything."

All ashore were stunned—friend and foe alike—when Bartolomé, Diego, and the *Niña*'s officers lowered the Admiral overboard on a stretcher and brought him ashore like a corpse. Cristóbal was ported to his residence, now built, and laid in a bed with proper sheets, where Pedro Salcedo fed him raisins and honey, newly resupplied in June.

Isabela's residents reunited with the expedition's crews, astounded to learn of their exploits and trials and that the Admiral had brought them home without losing a man—or discovering gold or temples. The crews feasted on the fresh wine and Spanish meat and beheld that the village's construction was nearly complete, including the large storehouse, reinforced as a fort to withstand attack, and the earthen defensive wall, now lining the eastern perimeter. Thankfully, the hospital appeared less packed than before, the residents' health having stabilized.

Within days, Cristóbal regained his wits, and he wanly bid Bartolomé brief him alone at his bedside.

"How much gold has been collected?"

"Some, Cristoforo." Bartolomé responded, sighing. "Each Spaniard's pockets are lined with it, but there's little for the king." He spoke deliberately to ensure his brother's comprehension. "Fray Buil and Margarite have deserted to return to Spain, seizing the ships I brought here." Bartolomé winced as his brother's haggard face contorted in helpless anger. "I tried to stop them, but they'd enlisted many others in their treachery, who also abandoned you."

"Margarite discovered Española's gold and other riches?"

"No. He disobeyed your orders and did nothing but criticize you—and Giacomo and myself. He never marched anywhere."

"Buil opposed you and Giacomo?"

Bartolomé nodded. "I replaced Giacomo on the council when I arrived, and Buil opposed every effort I made to corral Margarite into obedience." Bartolomé paused, allowing Cristóbal a moment to regain composure before dashing it again. "Buil and Margarite conspire to discredit you before the king and queen."

Cristóbal gasped. "Who's been loyal to me?"

"There're many. Carvajal and Coronel, on the council. They expect to be your business partners as the settlement grows. But there're many opposed, slandering that you've lied about the gold.

On the council, the sovereigns' courtier Luján always sided with Buil and Margarite." Bartolomé wiped sweat from Cristóbal's brow with a damp handkerchief. "I've openly favored your supporters with better rations than your enemies, so those in between understand to support you."

"Most sailors have been loyal, the crown's men always traitors and jealous of my title, my superior ability. Satisfying the soldiers and artisans is key to my command." He gazed up into Bartolomé's eyes. "What instructions do you bear from the king and queen? How do they rank my achievements?"

"Torres made them well satisfied with you and the entire business. They've approved most of your recommendations. Torres will bring their full response when he returns this autumn with more supplies."

"They'll punish Soria and the Lanzas?"

"I trust so—they'll investigate them."

Cristóbal exhaled sharply, spry enough to appreciate Bartolomé's circumspection. "You met with Berardi? The sovereigns will use him to supply us, rather than Fonseca?"

"He's impressive. He understands this business, and the sovereigns trust his judgment, but they trust Fonseca's loyalty." Bartolomé shrugged.

Cristóbal grunted in disapproval. "Berardi can sell Caribes for us?"

"Not yet," Bartolomé responded. "We can send him those we want to train as interpreters. But the king and queen deferred approving more than that."

"When'll they decide?" Cristóbal barked.

"That's unclear."

Cristóbal swooned, envisioning a noose tightening about him. He asked Salcedo for a sip of water. "Berardi's still eager to finance me?"

"Definitely." Bartolomé pitied the anguish transparent in his brother's voice and, reluctantly, broached yet further dire news. "Margarite never kept his troops from roughing up the Indians, and he abandoned them in the Vega Real, where they now roam and pillage without restraint. It's no longer safe for small bands of men to pass between Isabela and Santo Tomás. Indians ambush and massacre them."

"Margarite failed to subdue the Indians?"

"Yes. Worse, he's inflamed seething discontent."

"You've punished the Indians who attack?"

"The soldiers dispense their own justice."

"Hostile Indians must be executed. Ten Indians for each Christian slain. I'll march through the island to make good what Margarite failed, when I'm well." Cristóbal gnawed on his vision that Indians would acquiescence in servitude. "Abusive soldiers must also be disciplined."

"But only without jeopardizing their loyalty," Bartolomé cautioned warily, doubting that vision. He tarried to let Cristóbal rest and then asked, "Did you locate Cathay and the Grand Khan?"

"We're too far south, approaching the Golden Chersonese," Cristóbal murmured. "When I recover, you'll sail north to find them, perhaps five hundred leagues." He shut his eyes, his whisper fading. "Indians speak of a great landmass to the south—I'll claim it for ourselves and the sovereigns."

Within days, Cristóbal appointed Bartolomé as *Adelantado* (frontier governor) to administer the Indies while he recovered, and they determined to establish forts on the route between Isabela and Santo Tomás to protect men traveling between the two. They would quash the ambushes and subdue the entire Vega Real's population. Interpreters would be necessary for the new outposts, and Cristóbal ordered Bakako and Yutowa to speed their training of the most promising guides from the Bajabonico villages, the teenagers Wasu and Ukuti.

◘ ◘ ◘

As Admiral and Bartolomé reunited, Bakako and Yutowa also bonded warmly, squatting in the shade of the watchtower of Admiral's residence, available to serve when summoned. Bakako recounted the Cuban and Yamayan reactions to the pale men and Admiral's now practiced bluster that he'd come to befriend the good and punish the bad. Yutowa deplored the atrocities the pale soldiers committed in the Yaque valley and that his escort of their deserting commander back to Isabela undoubtedly had unleashed worse.

"The Haitians' hatred swells," Yutowa observed. "They're no longer afraid to slay the pale men one by one—whether passing on trails between settlements, fetching water by a river, or even napping in full daylight."

"How do Admiral's men respond?"

"Like savages. They'll massacre an entire village—women, children, and infants included—to punish one villager's vengeance." Yutowa faltered, stupefied. "It's more horrific. Countless villagers are stricken with diseases, just as we were in Admiral's homeland. Many are dying, just as Xamabo and the others did. Some decry the disease strikes from the crosses planted, that the Christ-spirit spearheads the invasion."

Bakako searched for words but found none, and a remembrance of his baptism triggered a pang of shame.

"Bakako, we risk being slain by Haitians ourselves, for being traitors," Yutowa warned, touching Bakako's shoulder. "You can't venture alone outside the settlement, even to do Admiral's bidding, no less escape."

Bakako shuddered that his life's sole cheer would be denied, and he probed, "It wouldn't be safe to visit the villages close by—along the Bajabonico?"

Yutowa shrugged. "The pale men's savagery has been contained here. The locals still barter, too scared to refuse. Wasu and Ukuti are safe among their people. But that's not proof a Guanahanían would be." He touched Bakako's shoulder. "Your girl came by, last week, afraid you'd died and would never return. She's with child."

⊡ ⊡ ⊡

Guacanagarí sat imperious and forlorn in his greatest war canoe as warriors briskly coursed it east through pounding swells toward Isabela, brooding over the hatred Haiti's paramount caciques vehemently bore for him and his alliance with Admiral. Days earlier, he'd buried one of his younger wives, brazenly murdered when bathing in daylight at a crowded riverbank. Behecchio had dispatched a runner to vaunt contemptuously that the assassins were his and the days of Guacanagarí's rule were numbered.

The hostility, scorn, and intransigence pronounced by the abduction and now murder of wives was desolating, and Guacanagarí cursed that his conqueror remained his only friend. He'd promised Admiral subservience in return for his continued rule, his people's freedom, and vengeance on Caonabó. So far, Admiral had honored the first two, sparing Guacanagarí's subjects the pillage and rape suffered by the villagers along the Yaque. Guacanagarí grasped he'd been a fool to trust Admiral's virtue a year ago and that continuing to do so could compound his jeopardy. But he would rely on Admiral rather than risk alone the enmity and spite of those caciques his equal. So far, Admiral's settlement at the coast did reside peacefully beside its neighbors. It was time to remind Admiral of his last promise.

Upon arrival, Guacanagarí debarked with naborias bearing baskets of fruit and cazabi and was escorted ceremonially to greet Admiral at his bedside inside the fortified residence. He was shocked by Admiral's frail countenance and feeble greeting. As before, Bakako and Yutowa were summoned to translate, and the two leaders renewed their friendship.

"Enjoy my pineapple and papaya, and you'll be restored, my friend," Guacanagarí assured. "I've prayed for your health and that of Fernando and Isabel."

"Your visit delights me. Fernando and Isabel appreciate your loyalty and send their love."

"Their love is well deserved. While you were gone, I've aided men of yours who suffered, and I've stood ready to supply your settlement its needs. You'll remember that I fed the men you left behind and didn't harm a single one of them."

"I remain grateful." Cristóbal bid attendants to prop him to sit. "Do you come to trade gold or for another purpose?"

"I've come to wish you good health. I also want you to understand the price I've paid for my loyalty." Guacanagarí waited as Bakako translated. "Caciques throughout the island revile me for befriending you. As you know, Caonabó abducted one of my wives. Behecchio has murdered another. I have been ostracized, and some of my own nitaínos even question my wisdom."

"I promised that I'd defend you from your enemies," Cristóbal replied. Instinctively, a shrewdness parsed the haze of his feverous disorientation, and he inquired, "What are these caciques up to?"

"You promised you'd help me punish Caonabó, retrieve my wife, and steal his," Guacanagarí blurted, not to be diverted from a commitment.

"So I did—and I will, when I recover. But first, I need to learn what Caonabó intends for me and my settlements."

Guacanagarí's heart pounded in panic and shame. Revealing information about other Haitian caciques—not just Caonabó—betrayed his civilization, if not his subjects. But his awe and jealousy surged that misleading Admiral or feigning ignorance jeopardized Admiral's protection and frustrated Caonabó's punishment.

"My informants report that Caonabó has incited the island's caciques to an alliance to defeat you and drive you away," he divulged. "I don't know when or how. But the alliance includes my enemy Behecchio and likely Guarionex, whose territory you occupy in the Cibao and along the Yaque."

Bakako dutifully translated, glimpsing at Yutowa through the corner of his eye, both Guanahaníans incredulous. They'd promised Xamabo to warn Guacanagarí of Admiral's objectives, never conceiving Guacanagarí would volunteer to assist attaining them.

"You're the wisest among your people," Cristóbal replied. "I bring peace and friendship for the good who submit and punish those who oppose." He relished the seething enmity between Guacanagarí and Caonabó and recalled that Lugo had exploited similar discords to accomplish his Canarian conquests. "I plan to march inland to establish my rule, and I invite you and your warriors to join me. I don't know when I'll bring Caonabó to justice, but you may be at my side when I do."

"That would be my honor and pleasure."

Cristóbal steeled his voice. "You must keep me informed."

⊡ ⊡ ⊡

Bakako identified a party of soldiers departing Isabela to barter for food and enlisted to lead it, regardless that Wasu and Ukuti had been doing so for months. He studied the astonishment, apprehension, and joy in Niana's face when he greeted her father in their village plaza. As the soldiers bartered, he smiled warmly toward her, and he delighted when she smiled back and winked, as before. He beheld her belly's bulge and flushed proudly that his manhood was proven. Their eyes met for a long embrace, and each nodded toward the papaya grove. He passed her side as he departed with the pale men toward Isabela. She softly cautioned, "Be vigilant."

Bakako informed the troop's leader that he'd part to befriend another cacique, and he withdrew a silver bracelet from their sack of truck to bear as a gift. As the soldiers moved on, he sought the cover of the forest and lay hidden in a fern grove until the moon rose, when he emerged to hike stealthily to the site of their prior rendezvous. A thunderstorm rumbled in, and drenched and windblown, he shivered among the papaya trees as he waited Niana. But inside he burned warmly in anticipation.

When she arrived, Bakako and Niana kissed and embraced deeply, and she took his hand to her belly and whispered, "This is yours."

Bakako flushed radiant with love and defiance, awed to have carved an existence, purpose, and loyalty utterly his own and beyond Admiral's grasp. Enraptured, he drew her even closer. "When will it come?"

"Three moons, maybe less." Niana flushed radiant to receive the adoration, hopeful that Bakako's love would embrace their child. Oblivious to the tempest, their eyes met in union, shimmering in the storm clouds' moonlit glow. "I thought you'd died!"

"I almost did, many times!" Bakako replied, relaxing his hug. "We need shelter, quickly. Let's use a lean-to, and I'll set a fire."

"There's one in the field beyond, stoked with wood, used daily. Come! I brought cloth to dry us."

Within moments they huddled in the lean-to, tenderly shared the cloth to dry each other, and found the earth warm beside the firepit. Niana drew Bakako to lie there, on the cloth beside her.

"I will be gentle," he whispered.

The two teenagers made love side by side eagerly but softly, their heat and passion dispelling awareness of the wind curling in the darkness about them. When done, Bakako gave Niana the silver bracelet, and she was charmed to set it upon her wrist. He rose to rekindle a fire, recounting his journey as he searched for pine needles and dry leaves, which he found stashed beside a wood pile. Niana listened intently for some moments, marveling at the ordeal.

"What happened here while I was gone?" Bakako asked.

Niana curled her body more tightly to conserve heat, letting her hair fall over eyes and face. "Everything has gone badly. The pale men have savaged my people and our spirits. Not so much here, but in the valley over the mountains."

"Have you been harmed?"

"No. But there's more than abuse and sacrilege. There's disease, and its spreading. People in neighboring villages have been afflicted, repulsively disfigured, and many are dying." Niana sighed, resolved to do her duty. "Bakako, what does your master now intend? What will happen to my father and people? We have served him, as if a friend."

"Will you tell your father what I say?"

"Of course."

Bakako knelt low to exhale upon pine needles he'd placed atop embers, patiently waiting the lightest sniff of smoke and considering his loyalties. He trembled with the realization that he'd lost his youth. The pale men's conquest of Haitians didn't necessarily harm a Guanahanían, but his woman and child lay before him.

"My master will march throughout the island to establish more settlements. His men will punish any who resist, including the cacique Caonabó. He'll also subjugate Cuba and Yamaye." Bakako reflected. "If your father allies with Caonabó or resists in any way, my master may execute him. If your father allies with my master or the cacique Guacanagarí, he'll become my master's vassal but escape death."

A spark flickered amidst the pine needles, and Bakako blew softly where it vanished. He detected smoke and a tiny flame flickered, on which he laid a few dry twigs.

"Niana, now tell me what your father and the Haitian caciques intend."

"You'll tell your master?"

"I may, as his fate affects my own. He has other sources of information, some better than me."

"Why do you care about him? The pale men are evil."

"Am I safe on your island without him? I'm just a Guanahanían fisherman turned slave. You wouldn't even be with me if I weren't with him."

The fire took hold. Bakako stoked it with a pyramid of larger kindling and moved to sit at Niana's side, caressing her tenderly. He parted her hair from her face to find her tearing, silently.

Niana fought to retain composure. She also considered her loyalties and grasped her youth was gone. She loved her father and people, but she loved her child at least as much. The future loomed dark and indiscernible, and, for that moment, she clung to the hope that the child's father would protect the child.

"Caonabó has summoned caciques to starve and assassinate the pale men so they depart the island. Caciques beyond the Bajabonico have agreed, and my father's been urged to align." Niana skirted revelations about her father. "Father must decide what to do." She pained for her child's father's fate. "Bakako, if Father joins Caonabó, my people will assassinate pale men, and you're correct—you'd be in danger, too, and it'd be dangerous for us to meet." She peered into his eyes, stoic but heartbroken. "Then Father wouldn't approve that we marry."

The fire's flames shot high above the kindling, fanned by the gale, and Bakako and Niana were relieved by its heat. He lay down beside her and cuddled close, smothering her face with kisses until her tears ceased. "Whatever happens, I'll try to protect you and the baby."

They lay together until dawn, gazing forlornly into the night while the storm swirled about them, mostly speechless, as there were no answers to express.

◘ ◘ ◘

In late October, Antonio de Torres departed Cádiz for Isabela commanding a fleet of four resupply ships provisioned largely by Juanoto Berardi. He bore Isabela's letter to Cristóbal of August 16, a copy of the treaty agreed at Tordesillas, and Cristóbal's original memorandum to him of the prior February, now marked with the sovereigns' complete responses. The ships anchored at Isabela in late November, bearing wine, food, supplies, and a few Spanish women, and, for the Admiral and his staff, a more fulsome, nobler selection of delicacies and household furnishings. They also brought devotional wares, clothing, and household items for Fray Buil and his friars to assist their holy mission, unaware that Buil and many of them had sailed in the other direction.

Albeit weak, Cristóbal met with Bartolomé and Torres to review the sovereigns' correspondence. Vexed and bewildered, Cristóbal pondered the sovereigns' written response to his proposal for slave trading Caribes, which indicated merely that its consideration had been postponed until Cristóbal wrote again concerning the matter. Torres cautioned that the sovereigns remained uncomfortable with the idea, but Cristóbal appreciated the invitation to reargue it and a reluctance on the sovereigns' behalf to themselves deny it. Cristóbal dismissed the sovereigns' request that he or Bartolomé return to Spain to trace the world's division with João's mariners, a task that bore no prospect for his financial gain. He relished the vindication apparent in Isabel's approval of the justice he administered.

With Cristóbal's approval, Bartolomé soon commenced the imposition of a harsher regime of punishments on those guilty of crimes or disloyalty, including public executions. Two guards who had stolen food from the storehouse were hanged. The sovereigns' courtier Juan de Luján, who had been critical of Cristóbal's governance, was found guilty of aiding Pisa and sodomy and beheaded. Cristóbal's own brother-in-law, Miguel Muliarte, would be tortured for assisting the preparation of a letter criticizing Cristóbal. There were many lesser punishments, which Bartolomé applied more harshly to those he distrusted.

Cristóbal summoned Margarite's men back to Isabela, and many came. Many didn't, frightened or loathsome of Cristóbal's rigorous command and fierce justice, content with their fiefdom over Indian women and servants. Cristóbal also organized a troop of soldiers and artisans to construct a fort at the Yaque River crossing site where the Indians' recurring vengeance endangered travel to Santo Tomás, intent on crushing those attempting assassinations. While yet seeking peaceful conquest, he now mused that armed resistance to it would serve as a just basis for the slavery he'd otherwise been prohibited—so long as the resisters hadn't converted to Christianity.

Since the first voyage, Cristóbal repeatedly had sought the sovereigns' enlistment of more clergy, and their desertions, and the queen's failure to dispatch fresh contingents of them on the resupply ships, mystified and disappointed him. Just half a dozen remained. Buil's brittle efforts had yet failed to achieve conversions, and, with Buil's departure, Cristóbal assumed oversight of the remaining missionaries. In November, he directed the establishment of the first mission, summoning to his courtyard the young Hieronymite friar Ramón Pané. King Fernando had met Fray Pané while convalescing in the monastery where Pané served and recommended him for enlistment.

"I've ordered the construction of a fort along the River of Gold and appointed a gentleman, Luis de Arriaga, as its warden, responsible for maintaining a garrison there," Cristóbal advised. "It'll be named Fort La Magdalena, on account of the beautiful river valley. I want you to accompany Arriaga, live with the Indians, and bring them to the faith. They'll flock to become Christians on learning the accounts of Genesis and the Incarnation."

"My Lord Admiral, that's what I came to do," Ramón replied humbly, his happiness transparent. Ramón had chosen not to depart with Fray Buil, his resolve to baptize Indians undimmed by the last year's many trials. "I pray my efforts satisfy both you and the Lord."

Cristóbal was pleased with Ramón's earnest demeanor. He'd noticed enough of Pané to be satisfied with his piousness and enthusiasm, believing that piousness—rather than theological sophistication—was core to the missionary task. While simple and lacking formal education, Pané also had demonstrated a willingness to learn the Indians' language, understanding that integral to his work.

"You have two responsibilities, in addition to evangelizing. I charge that you write down what you learn about the Indians' beliefs, rites, and idolatries. They aren't ignorant, and they appear to believe in a supreme god or gods." Cristóbal recalled the encounters in Cuba and Yamaye. "They believe in the soul's immortality and judgment on death." He raised his forefinger to punctuate the second order. "If you learn that they intend us foul, you must keep Arriaga informed."

"I understand both, my Lord Admiral," Ramón promised. "I've already seen that the Indians are ready to receive the faith."

"Take the two Burgundians to assist," Cristóbal instructed, referring to the Franciscan friars Juan Leudelle and Juan de Tisín.*

*Leudelle was known also as el Bermejo or Juan de Borgoña.

"Teach the Indians the Pater Noster, Ave María, and Creed [the Lord's Prayer, Hail Mary, and Apostles' Creed]."

Cristóbal raised his forefinger again. "Conversion of heathens requires understanding, and, with the papal nuncio departed, baptisms are subject to my approval."

Cristóbal's punishment of Spaniards, taken from Theodor de Bry, 1594. John Carter Brown Library, portion of rec. no. 09887-9.

ISABEL AND FERNANDO'S COURT,
Madrid, November 1494–January 1495

Wintering in Madrid, Isabel and Fernando received daily reports of King Charles's advance toward Rome. Charles was hailed as liberator when his army entered Pisa on November 7 and Florence on November 17, and the Dominican preacher Savonarola declared that God was the invasion's leader and retribution was at hand. On

November 22, Charles issued a manifesto to Christian princes, proclaiming that he marched not for conquest but simply to recover the Neapolitan throne rightfully his so that he might use it as a base to mount the Turks' expulsion and liberate the Holy Land. He also threatened to depose Alexander for corruption. Cardinal Giuliano della Rovere rode at Charles's side, pining to call the necessary church council, along with other cardinals who could attest to Alexander's simony, having accepted the simonious payments themselves. By December 10, the French army and navy surrounded Rome and blockaded its port at Ostia, and Romans beheld their food stores dwindle.

With the French at Naples's doorstep, Fernando—for the first time—instructed his ambassadors to warn Charles that Naples was Aragonese, just as Granada was Castilian. Fernando would oppose Charles's invasion not merely to defend the pope, aid a kindred lineage, or preserve the unity of Christian princes—but because the Neapolitan throne was Fernando's. Charles could no longer trust or hope that their Treaty of Barcelona required Fernando's neutrality—Fernando's army and fleet, then assembling in Cartagena, would fight the French to assert Fernando's own entitlement, regardless of the pope's or his Neapolitan cousin's fates.

In Rome, Pope Alexander promptly rewarded Fernando's fortitude, granting him a tenth of Aragón's benefices otherwise due the papacy for use in funding the papacy's defense.

Amidst this furor, Isabel and Fernando were surprised to learn that Fray Buil and Margarite had debarked at Cádiz in late November and, in December, they summoned both to court. Each man was quite ill, and Isabel and Fernando graciously acknowledged that as a sufficient basis for excusing further duty in Española. But it came out that both had departed without their admiral's consent or even knowledge, and that disturbed the sovereigns and warned them to probe all the information they'd received regarding the Indies so far. Margarite's audience was the more critical to them, as they looked to his practical experience to evaluate the prospects of the entire enterprise.

"Your Highnesses, my judgment is that you'll never recover the considerable sums you're investing in this," Margarite pronounced.

"There are no gold mines—to say otherwise is simply a lie. I was stationed inland, where the Admiral reports *rivers* filled with gold, but my men found mostly mud."

"Admiral's requested miners, as the Indians have no capability," Fernando replied. "We've dispatched some, and we'll dispatch more. Perhaps they'll prove the Admiral correct."

"Your Highness, I don't share that optimism. We would've found barrels of gold already if it were as abundant as the Admiral boasts. I've returned with ships bearing the fruits of months of collection—not even a bucketful. I think you could scour the entire island without finding enough gold to make even that effort worthwhile."

Fernando stared at Margarite, challenging him. "There aren't spices and other treasures to profit by?"

"No, the entire business is a farce," Margarite pronounced, staring back. "This isn't civilized territory, Your Highness. There're no roads, ports, or even comestible food. The Indians are bestial and poor. The Grand Kahn's splendid court and wealth haven't been found. He's led you to remote islands populated by savages."

"The Indians do trade gold, regardless of their sophistication," Isabel interjected, surprised by the pessimism. "The Admiral has traded for it since the days of his first discovery." Isabel and Fernando shared a wary glance, startled by the intensity of Margarite's contempt and betrayal of Colón, bewildered that they'd awarded him special compensation upon Colón's praise and recommendation but months before.

"They do have gold jewelry and idolatries. That's the only gold I've brought." Margarite shook his head, signaling yet a direr revelation. "Your Highness, you should understand that the Indians aren't friendly, and the Genoese's assurance otherwise is a lie. They've attacked my men as we searched for gold and food. They massacred the men left at Navidad, as you know. I lived among them, and, when I departed, the risk of ambush was ever present. Some of my men had been slain."

There was silence.

"How's the men's morale?" Isabel probed.

"Terrible. Famine and sickness rule, and many have perished." Margarite paused, as if marshalling an indictment. "Our crops don't flourish, and Colón has awarded rations unfairly, exacerbating the hunger and misery. He favors his supporters with greater rations, withholding from those critical of him. It's criminal."

"That's why you've objected to his command?" Fernando asked, grimacing to underscore the gravity of a soldier's disobedience in the field.

"One of myriad justifications, Your Highness. He treats your settlement as if it's a Genoese family business. When he went exploring, he appointed his unqualified youngest brother to govern rather than your senior advisors. He inflicts corporal punishments on Christians whose only crime is that they hunger, and he's failed to punish Navidad's murderers. He's long lost the respect required of leadership—most of the settlement despises him."

"Fray Buil is similarly disheartened?" Isabel inquired.

"You should ask him, but I know so. He understands you aren't in the business of converting savages if their territory can't be made profitable."

While jarred, Isabel and Fernando weren't convinced of what they heard, continuing to favor Torres and Colón's reports over Margarite's. But they recognized Colón as a promoter and were dissatisfied enough to favor dispatching an investigator to Española to parse the stark inconsistencies and scrutinize Colón's boasts. When they interviewed Fray Buil, he caustically echoed and surpassed Margarite's criticisms of Colón, revealing the utter disunity among the leadership they had selected, and their apprehension over Cristóbal's leadership surged.

"Have Indians embraced the faith?" Isabel probed.

"Your Highness, they don't understand Spanish, so little progress has been made," Fray Buil admitted. "They're idolaters, worshipping totems. Our men often throw these in the fire, hoping to wean the Indians of their falsities. But interpreters are essential."

Isabel was surprised by the tactic's harshness but didn't criticize it. "How many friars returned home with you?"

"A few, Your Majesty. Some are sick. Some doubt the efforts will succeed."

"Has the Admiral observed my instruction to treat the Indians kindly and lovingly?"

Buil shrugged. "He's failed to punish heathens who've killed Christians."

⌑ ⌑ ⌑

On Christmas morning, as Romans hungered and disavowed him, Pope Alexander rose before daybreak, celebrated mass in the Sistine Chapel, and dispatched a cardinal to grant King Charles permission to enter the city. French troops occupied the Tiber's left bank. Charles himself entered the city on December 31, accompanied by Rovere and other cardinals allied, discourteously receiving a diffident reception by those cardinals opposed. Negotiations over the fate of the Neapolitan throne and Alexander's papacy then ensued and, initially, went nowhere. On January 5, Alexander fainted, distraught. Two days later, he and a handful of yet loyal cardinals fled the Vatican by a secret underground tunnel and cloisters to the Castle of Sant' Angelo nearby.

Yet none wished bloodshed at the steps of Saint Peter's Basilica. By mid-January, Alexander returned to the Vatican in a public procession to meet Charles in the Papal Palace, and a truce was struck. Alexander conceded Charles's passage through the Papal States to Naples without recognizing Charles's right to the Neapolitan throne, leaving that for a later resolution, and granted amnesty to cardinals who had favored Charles. In return, Charles conceded the legitimacy of Alexander's papacy and possession of the Vatican, kneeling to kiss Alexander's foot and dumping Rovere outraged and superseded, outmaneuvered by Alexander yet again.

Not to be outshined in piousness, Fernando labored to establish a broad alliance for the purpose of defending the church from its French invaders and Christendom from the Turks—without mentioning his own design for the Neapolitan throne. On January 20, as a cornerstone prelude to that alliance, he and Isabel concluded a pact, proposed for years, for the double marriage of their Prince Juan and Princess Juana to the Holy Roman emperor Maximilian's children, Princess Margaret and Archduke Philip.

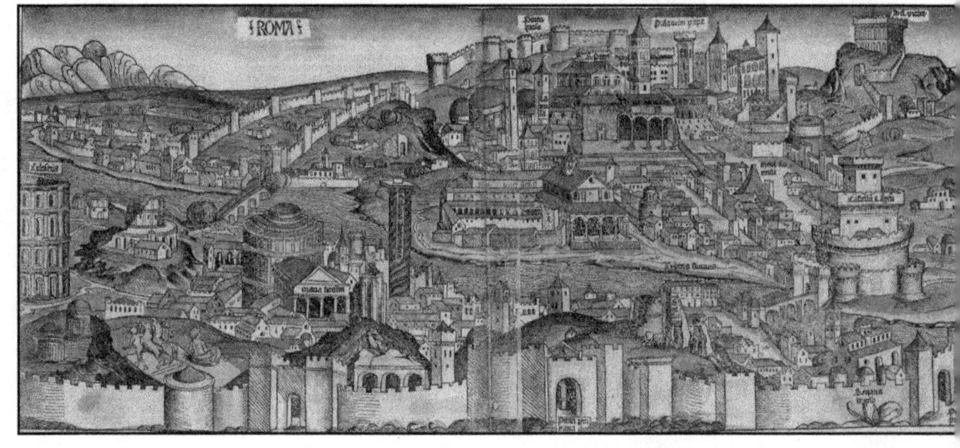

Roma, engraving from the Nuremberg Chronicle of 1493.

Fray Pané and Guatícabanu,
Fort Magdalena, December 1494–February 1495

In early December, Fray Ramón Pané and the Franciscan friars Leudelle and Tisín departed Isabela with commander Luis de Arriaga and a contingent of soldiers, artisans, and a few horsemen to cross the mountains to encamp on a small bluff overlooking the Yaque, downstream the fording site on the trail to Fort Santo Tomás. They promptly commenced the construction of a wood and earthen fort capable of supporting a garrison of three dozen soldiers and the missionaries.

Arriaga and the young interpreter Wasu introduced themselves to Guanáoboconel, the Macorix cacique of the nearest village, and Arriaga assured that his soldiers came in peace and, if necessary, to maintain peace by force. He warned that any further transgressions against Christians would be punished severely. Guanáoboconel, a subordinate of Guatiguaná, understood enough of Wasu's Taíno dialect, and he reciprocated with a perfunctory, diffident welcome—cowed by the injustices that the pale men had inflicted throughout the Yaque's floodplain, horrified by the pestilence radiating therefrom, and chilled by the rumor Guatiguaná and Caonabó were plotting war. He was powerless to reject the fort's establishment anyway.

Pané soon ventured alone from the encampment dressed in his simple monk's tunic, intent on offering his friendship, love, and faith to Guanáoboconel. Pané understood Indians had assassinated solitary Christians, and he was cautious to walk genially, greeting those met with an amicable grin and outstretched arms, displaying he was unarmed. He'd also discovered that the Indian words he learned while at Isabela weren't understood by every local and that communication would be most difficult. But he was content the Lord watched over him and that Guanáoboconel's people feared reprisals if they harmed him. In his pocket, he carried as a gift a small wooden cross strung on a leather strand, resembling the silver chain and crucifix about his neck.

The two men met in the small plaza outside Guanáoboconel's caney. The caciqual family clustered round, sons clutching spears and wives and daughters bearing infants on their hips or cuddling children. Pané spread his arms again to signal he came in peace, and Guanáoboconel grudgingly nodded he understood the gesture, while doubting its sincerity.

"Fray Pané," Pané announced, pointing to himself.

"Guanáoboconel," the cacique replied, touching his own chest.

Surprising all, Pané knelt to the ground to trace a rough outline of Española in the dirt. "Haiti," he exclaimed.

Guanáoboconel nodded, unsure what followed.

Pané poked his forefinger in the center of Haiti's sketch and then swept his other hand broadly about the village, shrugging his shoulders.

A slender teenage boy stepped forward cautiously and replied "Macorix." Turning to Guanáoboconel, his father, the youth exclaimed in Macorís, "The pale man wants to know our homeland's name."

Pané pointed to the teenager.

"I'm Guatícabanu," the youth responded.

Pané repeated "Guatícabanu" and then pivoted, halting to face each villager, young and old, inviting each to introduce himself or herself. All did, bemused, and the children giggled, dispelling the lingering apprehension. Pané surmised Guanáoboconel's household numbered at least sixteen relatives, including wives, Guatícabanu, and four brothers, as well as naborias. He returned his attention to Guanáoboconel and pronounced in Taíno, "Guanáoboconel chief Macorix."

There were murmurs and chuckles of appreciation, all present admiring that a pale man at last respected a tongue spoken on Haiti, albeit Taíno. Pané continued, grasping the silver cross at his chest and pointing to himself again. "Servant Christ."

Guanáoboconel was apprehensive. He'd observed the Christ-spirit's crosses erected throughout the valley and heard the rumor the spirit invaded bodies to conjure pestilence.

Pané resorted to Catalan, unable to explain the next thought in Taíno, no less Macorís. He knew he wouldn't be understood but trusted in the Lord's assistance. "I come to teach you of God and Christ." He presented Guanáoboconel with the necklace. After examining it, the cacique acknowledged the gift with a nod but refused to place it about his neck.

Pané drew a small satchel from beneath his robe and displayed its contents to the cacique and others crowded around.

"Crop," Pané explained in Taíno, adding in Catalan, "from King Fernando and Queen Isabel." He snatched a pinch of wheat seed from the satchel to display in the palm of his hand. "Sow. Garden. Tomorrow," he pronounced in Taíno, pointing to the village gardens. He knelt on the ground again, sifted his hand through the soil, and depicted how he'd spread the seed upon it, sprinkling the pinch where he'd silted.

"He'll plant his crop for us," Guatícabanu exclaimed.

Guanáoboconel warily nodded approval and bid his wives serve cazabi and papaya juice. Before partaking, Pané crossed himself, cupped his hands, marveled the sky, and recited the Ave María. All appreciated he invoked spirits, gleaning he was a behique. He then sat among the household contentedly, sharing their offering, permitting the children to touch his tunic's cloth. Soon he departed, the first day's work done.

On the second day, Pané returned to the village with Leudelle and Tisín, bearing a wood crate and a shovel and hoe with iron blades. Guanáoboconel offered them a garden patch, and the villagers studied as the behiques turned the earth with a method and tools strange to those they knew. But the villagers readily understood the behiques shared the same objective—preparing the earth to receive seed. Guatícabanu and his brothers delighted in taking a turn with the shovel and hoe.

After the wheat was sown, Pané set the crate at the garden's edge and placed on it a wooden altar cross bearing the image of Christ. "Christ, the son of God," he pronounced solemnly, pointing to the cross.

For all to behold, Pané, Leudelle, and Tisín knelt before the cross, stared to the heavens, and recited the Lord's Prayer. The entire village beheld the veneration, understanding the spirit or spirits different than those they honored but the veneration's objective as the same. The behiques appeared to believe the Christ-spirit would bring life and rain to the seed, just as would Yúcahu and Yúcahu's mother, Attabeira.

Guatícabanu sidled up to Pané, raised his arm to the sky, and then let it drop softly, twitching his fingers lightly as he placed them on the ground. "You've asked your spirit to bring life and rain to your seed?" he asked.

Pané nodded.

"We'll invoke Yúcahu and Attabeira that they do the same," Guanáoboconel exclaimed. He instructed Guatícabanu to bury a stone cemí of Yúcahu in the ground sown and, just as Pané had, stared to the sky. Leading his household, he sought Yúcahu and Attabeira's beneficence in bringing life to the pale man's seed and rain to nurture it. He knew Yúcahu and Attabeira would grace the crop's fertility, but he pondered whether the pale men's spirit would tend to their seed more effectively.

On the third day, and for weeks thereafter, Pané and the two Franciscans returned to tend their garden, recite their prayers, learn Macorís, and teach of Christ and his father and mother. Guanáoboconel participated in lessons courteously but trembled whether other caciques deplored the hospitalities he extended. By January, the pale men had erected their fort and commandeered a bohío in another village nearby to shelter over three dozen of their brothers who'd grown ill elsewhere along the Yaque. Guanáoboconel vexed that Guatiguaná didn't communicate at all—not a single advice, information, order, or forewarning.

But Guanáoboconel's sons, particularly Guatícabanu, grew evermore respectful of Pané, captivated by the material advancements of the pale men and the behique's spectral demeanor and willingness to learn and speak Macorís. Whether Yúcahu and Attabeira's blessing or the Christ-spirit's, the pale men's seed did sprout. In turn, Pané peppered the youth with questions regarding the spirits his people worshipped. Guatícabanu recounted that his peoples had emerged to populate the world from a Haitian cave named the Cacibajagua, led by their ancestral leader, Guahayona, while the rest of mankind had emerged from a cave without importance. He explained that a boy heroic for his perseverance, Deminán Caracaracol, had dropped the great spirit Yaya's gourd, releasing a flood on the earth that became the sea and its fish.

In early February, Fray Pané sought to advance Guatícabanu's understanding to the threshold of Christianity. They sat before the altar cross, gazing at women roasting fish and fowl before a bohío nearby.

"Heavens," Pané pronounced tentatively in Macorís, pointing to the sky, and then "earth," touching the ground. Guatícabanu nodded that he understood.

Pané rose and solemnly cast his arm in every direction, pointing to the heavens and the earth, the sun, the forest and river, the village and its plaza, the fish and fowl cooking close by, and finally himself, Guatícabanu, and all the villagers in sight. In Macorís, he pronounced, "Heavens, sun, moon, earth, sea, men, fish, birds," and then, with frustration in Catalan, twirling his forefinger in a circle, "everything. Absolutely everything."

Guatícabanu pondered the words and gestures, searching for the greater concept he sensed Pané sought to express. He hesitated, and then ventured, "The heavens, sun, and moon above. The sea and fish below. The peoples, birds, and animals in between."

"God," Pané proclaimed, opening the palm of his hand as if to bestow a gift and then loudly repeating as best he could the boy's last words. He thought to himself in Catalan, *God created heaven and earth and everything in them.*

Guatícabanu smiled knowingly, as if a riddle had been solved. The pale men understood their God-spirit had made the heavens, the earth, the sea, and all things in them. Other than the sea's origin, the thought might supplement his own understandings. He replied deliberately, "I understand. God made the heavens for our spirits and the earth for its creatures, including men, so all may live in harmony."

Pané understood enough to be pleased that Guatícabanu grasped an essence. Gratified, he reached into his robe, withdrew another leather string with a wooden cross, and lifted it over Guatícabanu's head to lay it on his shoulders.

Friars evangelizing, taken from Philoponus, 1621. John Carter Brown Library, portion of rec. no. 04056-3.

Hostilities and Slaves,
Forts Magdalena and Santo Tomás, January–February 1495

Caonabó, brother Manicoatex, and Uxmatex conferred in the shelter of a lean-to at the outskirts of Caonabó's village late into the night, seated before a bristling windblown fire. In the valley beyond, stretching far into the distance, an army lay to sleep, huddled for warmth before hundreds of fires swirling in the gale, beneath cloudy heavens and intermittent rain. Caonabó had summoned them from throughout Maguana, having concluded he could no longer wait on disease and hunger to weaken the pale men, given their establishment of a second inland fort.

"Has the time come to attack?" he posed prudently, as a general, yet weighed by the imperative of having received pleas to war from other Haitian caciques daily.

"Guatiguaná exhorts it," Manicoatex replied. "The pale men's new fort mocks his authority. He's assembled his own army, and all thirst for revenge."

"There remain but six or seven hundred pale men—at the coast, the two forts, the Yaque valley combined," Uxmatex reported. "Many hunger, many are sick. Informants relate that the Guamiquina is ill, too, perhaps dying." He waved to the encampment before them. "Over five thousand await your command."

"Destroying the forts and annihilating those strewn along the Yaque is a matter of head count," Caonabó reasoned. "But can we drive them from the coast?"

"I'm not sure," Uxmatex responded forthrightly. "But taking the forts and the Yaque valley further reduces their head count and halts their aggression inland." He raised his spear. "I fear nonengagement as much as war. We cannot permit further penetration inland."

Caonabó anguished the advice was honest and that a protracted war loomed at the coast. For an instant, he recalled his father's boyhood lessons to make friends rather than enemies and his uncle's admonition to temper his arrogance. But the Guamiquina's territorial avarice and brutality left no room for diplomacy.

"We'll overrun both forts at once, slaying the pale men living inside and nearby," Caonabó affirmed. To Uxmatex, he ordered, "Take a squadron to join Guatiguaná and his assault on the Yaque fort." To Manicoatex, he commanded, "We'll lead most of the army to strike the Cibao fort." Caonabó bid the two men rise and embraced each. "We depart at dawn."

In starlight, Caonabó strode through his village, hailed by those he encountered, returning to his caney to sleep in his inner sanctum, celibate, as was the warriors' tradition prior to battle. Before retiring, he summoned Onaney first.

"I march tomorrow, but not alone. The alliance you wished is strong," Caonabó confided. Touching Onaney's cheek tenderly, he promised, "As always, I'll return to you."

They held each other dearly for a moment, gazing at the flickering embers in the sanctum's fire circle, and Onaney held back tears. Caonabó dismissed her with a kiss and summoned Anacaona.

"No one can invoke the spirits as wisely as you," he said. "Do so now, with all your power." He grasped Anacaona's shoulders and stared steadfastly into her eyes. "If I don't return, rule as you would, not as I would."

Anacaona flushed and trembled with despair, alarm, gratitude, and pride, confused and graven beyond response, having sought to rule as a cacique her entire life—only now to pine that the instruction be unnecessary and her husband return victorious. She promised she would, and they held each other dearly, thankful as husband and wife they'd complimented each other to rise to yet unsurpassed power. Caonabó dismissed her, too, with a kiss.

In solitude, Caonabó steeled himself for battle, embracing a warrior's dauntless confidence in his own supremacy, dominance, and invincibility. He relished that overwhelming head count should crush horrific weaponry. He flushed that warriors defending their families and homeland should fight more courageously than conquerors. He exulted that the Taíno people's birthright was to populate the world and that other peoples should never displace them. He retrieved the pale men's cemí of the Christ-spirit from the reed basket and tossed it into the fire circle, inspired by the spirit's vulnerability as it burst into flame—just as villagers' cemís had over the past months. But a general's wariness held the warrior's exuberance in check.

◻ ◻ ◻

Days later, in the twilight before dawn, Guatiguaná led his Macorix army west along the Yaque toward the enemy's fort, accompanied by Uxmatex's squadron. They seized a dozen sleeping pale men en route, who were hauled back to Guatiguaná's village for torture and execution. Surging with confidence, they snuck upon the bohío where pale men were convalescing, shrieked a battle cry, and torched it. Pale men staggered out through billowing smoke, terrified, and the warriors hailed arrows and spears upon them, massacring over three dozen. The warriors then marched to surround the bluff of the pale men's fort, and, as Guatiguaná exhorted them to charge, victory seemed in their grasp.

But it wasn't. Fort Magdalena's commander, Arriaga, was prepared. As the Indians swarmed in, his soldiers discharged an array of firepower never seen before in battle on Haiti, decimating all attackers. Crossbows propelled arrows so far into the ranks of those charging that most fell before their own arrows could be hurled or shot. Harquebuses and falconets thundered and smoked, slaying warriors at even greater distance. The few who jumped the trenches to mount the fort's walls were mauled by barking dogs, attacking as viciously as barracuda, gnawing flesh to inflict incredible pain and mortal blood loss. Guatiguaná and Uxmatex ordered waves of assault, and the fort was set ablaze, but the pale men persevered within.

In the Cibao, Caonabó brought his army to surround Fort Santo Tomás at dusk, and he surveyed the surrounding terrain—the fort's plateau, the valleys below, and the facing ridges across the river ravine. The pale men were awaiting attack, precluding any hope of surprise, and he stationed himself on the highest ridge to spy into the fort and upon the battlefield. As the moon rose, he saw a wiry pale man walking the fort's perimeter to confer with his soldiers, and Caonabó surmised him to be the general to be outwitted.

From the fort, Alonso de Hojeda scanned the same terrain, spying outward to gauge the number of Indians that besieged and their vantages, pondering when and how they would attack and whether the notorious Caonabó was present. He quivered that the battle for raising his stature and fame was at hand, and he brimmed with confidence in his weaponry's dominance, convinced of the Christian superiority over heathens. More profoundly—beyond doubt—he trusted in the Lord and Virgin's favor and support. If death came, it would be in the glory of their honor. Alonso ordered his sentries to conserve their arrows and ammunition, firing only when targets were so close that killing was assured. He commanded his horsemen to feed and water their mounts for combat and his dog keepers to keep the hounds hungering ravenously.

Caonabó sprung his attack in the twilight before dawn, with a war cry of thousands that resounded from all about—valleys, ridges, and, ominously close, the plateau. Warriors hurtled toward the fort, charging with spears and macanas. Arrows hailed from all directions, including hundreds firelit to torch the fort. Caonabó beheld pale men stricken, shrieking, and bloody within the fort as his warriors clambered through the moats to assault the fort's walls.

But Caonabó was astonished as the pale men's enormous dogs hurtled wildly from the fort, barking an unknown cry so alien that his warriors halted in dread, many savaged by the beasts' vicious jaws and bloodied even worse. Pale men riding their enormous beasts then burst from the fort at incredible speed, with awesome brawn and vigor, to penetrate at will among his warriors, slaying them all about, immune to any blow or jab thrust back—as if evil spirits. Aghast, Caonabó beheld hundreds of his warriors fleeing in dread as but a few pale men atop beasts pursued, voraciously massacring countless with lengthy spears.

By sunrise, with the rout accomplished, Hojeda withdrew his forces into the fort, appreciating that the siege and battle had just begun. During the day, he bid his dog keepers feed the hounds on the Indian corpses strewn on the battlefield, horrifying the besiegers. When dusk came, he dispatched horsemen to charge the Indian encampments, routing the Indians before nightfall and permitting his men to secure water from the river. The Reconquista had known both tactics.

The sieges of Forts Magdalena and Santo Tomás continued for days at a standoff. Caonabó received Uxmatex's reports from the Yaque valley, and he was shocked that he'd failed to dislodge the enemy from even their most vulnerable settlements, regardless of overwhelming warrior head counts. Yet it was too soon to be daunted, and he ordered that the sieges persevere tenaciously to crush the Guamiquina's own resolve for conquest.

At daybreak and sunset, Caonabó reviewed the warriors stationed closest to the fort, fortifying their courage and morale, gauging the pale men's intent. Hojeda also reviewed them—from Santo Tomás's watchtower—scrutinizing their movements. The two men came to recognize each other and, as the siege wore on, to respect the other as a worthy opponent.

◘ ◘ ◘

Soldiers responsible for resupplying Forts Magdalena and Santo Tomás urgently brought the news to Isabela that Magdalena had been besieged, and likely Santo Tomás, too. The settlement at Isabela ignited with alarm, anger, righteous indignation, and bloodthirst for revenge. The refrain that ten Indians must die for each Christian slain burgeoned to one hundred to one.

Bakako and Yutowa squatted in Admiral's courtyard, overhearing as Admiral and brother Adelantado plotted their Christian response.

"Dispatch two hundred men to rout them, Magdalena first and then Santo Tomás," Adelantado urged.

"Routing them alone fails the sovereigns and the Lord," Admiral exclaimed, raising his voice. "The entire island must tremble that those who harm Christians will be punished!" His voice curdled. "We shall enslave the perpetrators—as does every Christian prince in war, the king and queen no exception." The ships Torres had brought in November were due for return to Spain, and Cristóbal shuddered they wouldn't bear even a chest of gold. "Berardi shall receive a considerable shipment at last."

"How many do we seize?"

"Far more than fill four ships. Justice and expediency demand that we furnish slaves for those here, as well."

Bakako and Yutowa slumped petrified, reviling their assignments and aghast at the enormous number of captives contemplated. Admiral shouted, "Diego, Yutowa," and they dutifully entered his chamber.

"You'll accompany soldiers to haul the guilty to justice at Magdalena," Admiral ordered Bakako. "Find the caciques who led it." To Yutowa, Admiral directed, "Caonabó's the root of this evil. When we relieve Santo Tomás, you'll assist Hojeda in his capture." Admiral bluntly rued, "I intended that long ago."

Within days, foot soldiers and horsemen crossed over the mountains to Fort Magdalena, and Guatiguaná's army retreated without engagement, cowed. Commander Arriaga reported that

Guatiguaná was the attack's ringleader, and Bakako assisted soldiers in hunting him down. Soldiers commenced a series of slave raids throughout the valley, and, although most villagers living close to the fort hadn't participated in the siege, they were among the first corralled and towed to Isabela, including their womenfolk. Guanáoboconel's village was spared on information that Pané had entreated its inhabitants to embrace the faith. Over the next weeks, the raids extended throughout the valley, occasionally capturing warriors who had participated in the attacks, but typically seizing those best suited for slavery's toil, men and women. Many were held at Fort Magdalena's ruins, pending transfer to Isabela.

Slave raiding, taken from Theodor de Bry, 1595. John Carter Brown Library, portion of rec. no. 34724-5.

Through interrogation, Bakako identified Guatiguaná upon his apprehension, and the cacique and two nitaínos were bound in rope and hauled to grovel at Cristóbal's feet in his residence's courtyard. Cristóbal and Guatiguaná glared hatefully at each other, Cristóbal enraged that the chieftain had disrupted the course of conquest, Guatiguaná defiant that his people would remain unconquered. Bakako was tortured by a vision of the remora releasing its prey upon being pulled from the sea.

"You're guilty of murdering Christians. You're guilty of rebellion to King Fernando and Queen Isabel," Cristóbal pronounced imperiously. "Christian justice is due these crimes."

Guatiguaná listened to Bakako's Taíno translation and understood enough to respond contemptuously. "Your pale men's justice is the crime. You punish the victims of crimes, not the perpetrators."

"Your punishment is execution, by arrow shot, at noon tomorrow, for all to behold," Cristóbal pronounced, staring mercilessly back. "Your two noblemen share your fate, as will the chieftains you led, when they're rounded up."

"My death matters nothing!" Guatiguaná scorned. "Countless of my warriors will avenge it, and you and your men shall receive true justice, far more terrible!"

Cristóbal shook his head vigorously and exhorted, "Countless of your warriors and their women shall now be enslaved. All will understand that slavery is the fate of those who resist me."

Bakako trembled as he translated, haunted whether Admiral had designed this very conclusion from the moment Admiral first stepped onto the beach at Guanahaní.

That evening, Cristóbal's sentries neglected their duty, and Guatiguaná and his nitaínos gnawed through their ropes and jumped to the sea, evading Cristóbal's fate for them. Cristóbal was enraged but worried little for Guatiguaná's revenge, comforted that the threat of enslavement would be communicated to Española's peoples.

◘ ◘ ◘

Better watch was kept over Guatiguaná's peoples destined for servitude. Bands upon bands of them were towed to Isabela within the month, to be restrained in densely packed pens near the storehouse. Soon, there were sixteen hundred of them, including women and children, alone constituting the greatest population ever present at the settlement. Their cries and wails drowned the wash of the sea, and the stench of sweat, urine, and excrement suffocated the promontory regardless of the breeze.

Cristóbal had beheld slave markets since youth and throughout his travels, including in Genoa, Scio (Chios), Lisbon, Seville, and Mina. As many of Isabela's settlers, he'd also witnessed the crude process of selecting the best slaves from a pool of captives. In late February, that process—examination of a captive's health, size, strength, and, if a woman, beauty—was conducted before the storehouse, whereby 550 of the most suited were selected for transport to Spain for delivery to Berardi for the sovereigns' account. No heed or mercy was given to family relationships, and selected husbands, wives, or children simply were yanked from their loved ones. The head count chosen contemplated teeming them aboard ship far more densely than in the pens, severely testing the ships' stowage limit.

Cristóbal didn't stop when that process concluded and announced a second round, delighting the settlers and incenting their loyalty. All of them—noblemen, gentlemen, artisans, and commoners—were entitled to choose their own slaves from the thousand remaining. They rushed to scour the pens to claim the strongest manservants and mountable chambermaids left, eager to alleviate the rigor of daily work, household chores, and lust. Boys and girls were seized as investments for the same satisfactions.

Finally, a blessed four hundred remained unchosen—the infirm, the sick, the dying, toddlers, and breastfeeding mothers—and they were released to freedom or death and told to decamp, which they did in panic, a few infants left behind in the pandemonium.

That evening, as he said his prayers before retiring, Cristóbal thanked the Lord for allowing justice to be done and the Indies' business finally to progress.

⌑ ⌑ ⌑

Torres's four ships sailed for Spain on February 24, bearing the 550 and Cristóbal's letter to Isabel and Fernando reporting on the discovery of the Golden Chersonese. Brother Diego accompanied Torres, dispatched to inform the sovereigns of the settlement's progress and counter criticisms undoubtedly levied by Buil and Margarite. Cuneo had seen enough and departed, too, as did Bernal de Pisa, in chains.

At Cristóbal's instruction, Fray Pané relocated from Magdalena to Isabela pending reassignment. With Cristóbal's permission, he brought along Guatícabanu and his brothers and a few relatives, whose interest in Christianity was blossoming and service as interpreters would assist Pané's mission. They were astonished by the chime of Isabela's church bell, heralding Christ's presence in their world, as well as the enslavements his followers practiced.

◘ ◘ ◘

In the Cibao, Caonabó had received runners dispatched by Uxmatex, apprising of Guatiguaná's rout, and he roiled his own siege would remain a draw. He raged when Uxmatex arrived at Santo Tomás to report of the mass enslavements.

Caonabó grasped territorial conquest, Caribe wife raiding, exemplary punishment, and torture, but the mass deportation and enslavement of noncombatants, including women and children, was beyond his tactical and strategic visions and Taíno practice. He and Uxmatex conferred gravely as they spied down on the pale men from the ridges above the fort.

"Does the Guamiquina intend that as exemplary punishment?" Caonabó rankled darkly. "Or is it prelude to mass enslavement of our peoples?"

Uxmatex shrugged.

"I'll dispatch a nitaíno to Guacanagarí, demanding that he ask the Guamiquina why this was done."

"Why not commence discussions with the Guamiquina directly?"

"An overture to meet best come from him, lest he perceive we'll accept less than the departure of all his men."

Guacanagarí received Caonabó's nitaíno and quivered with dread and shame. He, too, was horrified that Admiral had enslaved hundreds of noncombatants, including caciques, nitaínos, and their women. His informants at Isabela reported that the wives of Guatiguaná's vassal caciques and nitaínos now served as the pale men's cooks and concubines. The pale men recognized neither rank nor status among those they seized.

But Guacanagarí shied from both ignoring Caonabó's demand and fulfilling it himself, certain Caonabó would punish him if he could, uncertain of Admiral's continuing friendship. Instead, he dispatched two nitaínos to ask Admiral why he'd taken noncombatants as slaves. Guacanagarí would learn that Admiral brushed the nitaínos away and bid him come discuss it in person.

◘ ◘ ◘

Bakako and Yutowa also had beheld the slave markets of Lisbon and Seville, and they were horrified as Isabela fleetingly had its own and transformed to become home to as many slaves as masters. Pale noblemen now possessed staffs to wash their robes, artisans laborers to lug and hoist, and soldiers diggers for their trenches. Many had new women and girls to lie with.

As February waned, Bakako stole before dawn to meet Niana, craving her tenderness after brutal weeks at Admiral's call, pining to learn of their child's birth, whether boy or girl. He was confident to hike alone, certain the villagers along the Bajabonico were too intimidated by the pale men's fresh victories and atrocities to risk any reprisal, and he anguished whether Niana would still love and receive him, regardless of the same.

There was an eerie tranquility to the first hillside village he passed, and Bakako puzzled whether all had fled to avoid enslavement. But the trappings of death—flies and buzzards—were unmistakable, and he veered from the trail to survey the village plaza. It was empty, not a single woman cooking or child wandering about. He strode to scan inside the village caney and abruptly pulled back, repulsed by a powerful stench of decay. Corpses lay within, motionless.

Shaken, Bakako returned to the path and, more urgently than before, resumed his trek to Niana. The trail soon wove by another village, and he spied a young man and woman bleakly seated before the nearest bohío, staring vacuously back. Bakako waved and approached cautiously, as neither reciprocated any greeting. Again, he halted abruptly, recognizing their bodies were wrought with red hives and scabs from head to toe. Buzzards soared above and wandered among bohíos beyond. He retreated, shocked that the couple's only response to his arrival and departure was to droop their heads.

At the trail, Bakako swooned to his knees, abruptly tossed by the realization that his hope must be that Niana had fled rather than finding her. He rose to redouble his pace, shunning the inspection of other villages until he sighted hers, to which he ran, bursting into its plaza, panting with foreboding.

There were women and children huddled in the plaza before her father's caney, afflicted by the onset of the pestilence, and death's presence was apparent, as in the prior villages. Bakako hastened before them and pled, "Where's Niana?"

The women stared back forlornly, motionless. "We need water and cazabi," one murmured.

Bakako searched for a gourd, filled it at the village stream, and handed it to her. There was no cazabi in sight. Beyond the caney, corpses lay everywhere.

Bakako began his search in terror there, desperate to avoid finding a once pretty face, a sensuous body rotting, or a motionless newborn. Shuddering, he recognized her father, darkened, decaying, and swarmed by flies, his bloated chest yet adorned with a guanín medallion. Terrified, he found the bodies of women and girls nearby, undoubtedly mothers and sisters, but none that he recognized as Niana. As the sun rose to the horizon, he scoured the remainder of the village, relieved she appeared to have fled.

But a vision of the papaya grove and lean-to arrested him, and, with a dark premonition that she would wait him there, he ran to them in agony, invoking Yúcahu's blessing that it be not so. The breeze upon the hillside dissipated odor, but, as he came to the lean-to, he beheld a body within.

Crushed, Bakako fell to his knees beside it, wailing cries of love lost and bitter remorse, tears gushing, his frame convulsing uncontrollably. The silver bracelet remained on Niana's wrist, the corpse of a newborn girl lay cradled in her arms, and Niana's eyes stared hopelessly to her, forevermore.

As the sun rose high and bright, he sat with Niana and their daughter for the first and last time, ruing the utter darkness Admiral's new world had wrought upon the old.

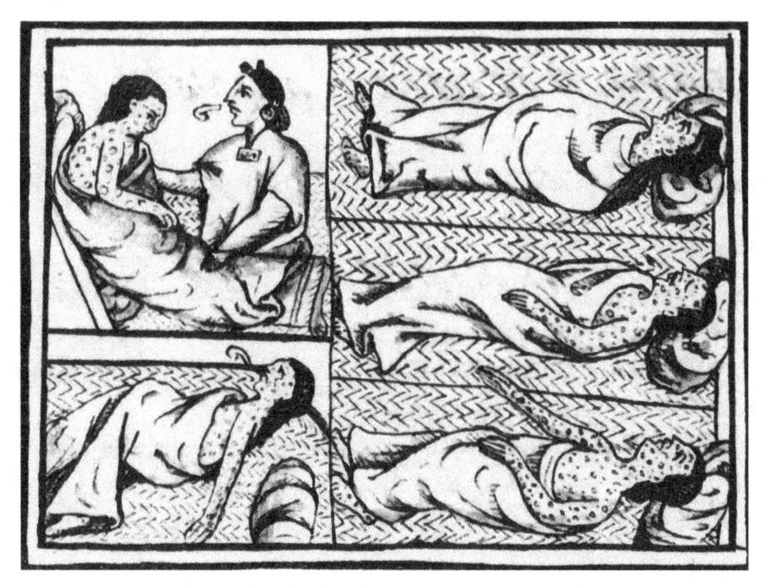

Epidemic death of Nahua, Mexico, sixteenth century.
Florentine Codex, bk. 12, fol. 53v.

Isabel and Fernando's Court,
Madrid, January–March 1495

The prior autumn, Isabel and Fernando had celebrated their twenty-fifth wedding anniversary. They'd long established a mutual understanding of their joint rule that obviated the frictions experienced in the marriage's early years over Isabel's supremacy in Castile, the might of their kingdoms. But a fleeting relapse of disagreement briefly resurfaced in January when Cardinal Mendoza died, leaving the archbishopric of Toledo vacant, Spain's highest church office.

"Alfonso's the right successor," Fernando advocated, referring to his illegitimate son, the archbishop of Zaragoza, born of a young Aragonese noblewoman at the time of Isabel and Fernando's marriage.* "He's trained in both politics and faith." Alfonso had assisted Fernando's governance of Aragón for over a decade, serving as archbishop since only a child, and Isabel had accepted him at court—but not his mother.

"Dear Alfonso is too young, and I'd prefer a true religious," Isabel responded. "Cisneros is perfect for the post. He's been stern

*Alfonso of Aragón.

and relentless in reforming the orders." Isabel's endeavor to Christianize her kingdoms, first devoted to the Reconquista and the Inquisition, had turned to the purification of the church's clergy, then infected by luxury, ostentation, and concubinage, and she'd appointed Cisneros to reform the Castilian Franciscan orders (1494). "He locked the Toledan monks and their *barraganas* [concubines] from the monastery," she added with a smile.

"He's zealous, and hated and feared by many," Fernando responded dryly. "While the latter is hardly a bar, you can't trust him to understand or implement temporal policies. He's no Mendoza or Talavera. He's fanatical, unworldly."

"The world must be reformed in God's image—and Ximénes is best suited to that task. He knows the scriptures. His faith is uncompromising." Isabel peered softly into Fernando's eyes, seeking to convince. "That hardly can be said of Alfonso, who's always lacked religious training."

"You err, grossly. Cisneros is unpredictable, raptured by harsh deprivations, whetted by animosity and defiance. You need someone in league with us, compliant."

"Alfonso is compliant to me?" Isabel's stare turned cold. "His blood is Aragonese—both mother and father. Or have you forgotten?" Her acrid tone condemned the rampant infidelity of her husband's youth.

"My wife, my loyalty has been proven for decades."

"In the court and on the battlefield," Isabel acknowledged, eliding reference to their bedroom, angered to be pressed to award Fernando's illegitimate with an archbishopric. "Remember the capitulations you vowed when we wed—this is my appointment to make, from among Castilians."

Isabel denied her husband's wishes and son. While angered, Fernando knew to follow rather than contest her word, supreme for Castile, and he dutifully supported her request to Pope Alexander for approval of Cisneros's appointment. Alexander would have preferred a candidate closely allied with his family and papacy and less openly committed to Saint Francis's vows of poverty, chastity, and obedience. But, on February 22, he quickly approved the appointment.

⧈ ⧈ ⧈

Upon Alexander's refusal to hand over the Neapolitan throne, King Charles had departed the Vatican to take it by force and marched his army into Naples on February 22. Resistance was meager and crowds cheered in adulation. Naples's King Alfonso already had fled to cousin Fernando's Sicily, abdicating the throne to his son Ferrante II, who then embarked for Sicily, too, without abdicating.*

Over the next weeks, adulation soured to contempt as Neapolitans witnessed the conquering French plunder their homes and lie with or rape their women and girls, including visiting their prostitutes. A year had passed since the twelve ships of Torres's first return voyage had arrived at Cádiz from Española. The unknown strains of venereal disease carried by the sailors and voyagers of that fleet by then had migrated to other European ports and cities, afflicting either or both the French soldiers and the Neapolitans lain with, raped, or visited. Naples suffered an outbreak of the disease, confounding doctors, who had never seen anything like it. The Italians called it the *French disease*, the French the *Italian disease*.

King Fernando declared that his kingdoms' peace with France established by the 1493 treaty was terminated, and he labored to convince Emperor Maximilian and powerful Italian princes to unite with the pope to drive the French from the Italian peninsula. The sovereigns' expeditionary force had barracked on Sicily, poised to engage, but Fernando would not fight alone. At the end of March, Venice, Milan, and Maximilian joined Spain and the pope in the Treaty of Venice, whereby all agreed to support armies to protect the Holy See from its French invaders, as well as each other against French aggression.

To allies, Fernando vowed to fight in King Ferrante's name and reestablish Ferrante upon the Neapolitan throne. But he and his queen now held their own design for that throne, if and when their soldiers achieved such control of Neapolitan territory that none could object.

⧈ ⧈ ⧈

Over the winter, Alonso de Lugo and a small force of troops and cavalry had recommenced the broken conquest of Tenerife. By February,

*Fernando had been king of Sicily since youth (1468).

Alonso successfully established two garrisons on the island, prelude to the invasion of a larger army that autumn. Alonso reaffirmed peace and vassalage treaties with the chieftains who had submitted before, and, when the garrisons suffered sporadic Guanche resistance, he captured and enslaved the attackers and their wives and children. Benitomo scorned vassalage. Both men prepared for battle.

As those on Haiti and in Naples, neither man nor their peoples understood that the invading troops, or their animals, rats, and lice, bore pestilences mortally contagious to the invaded. Soon, Guanches took ill with fevers, rashes, and stupors near Alonso's landing site and the garrisons. Ominously, the pestilence began to emanate throughout the island.* Alonso's troops proclaimed it the Lord's revenge for Benitomo's massacre of the prior year and the consequence of abandoning their comrades' corpses unburied.

◻ ◻ ◻

Cisneros had never sought the archbishopric of Toledo, and Isabel didn't offer it to him or even advise him of it until early March, when she showed him Alexander's letter of approval, which Cisneros couldn't bear to read. He rejected the appointment, as he'd rejected becoming her confessor initially, unwilling to sacrifice the intimate relationship with Christ attained through an aesthetic poverty and solitude for the office's worldly focus and high trappings. He immediately fled Isabel and Madrid for isolation in the countryside for months. Fernando glanced piercingly into Isabel's eyes, reminding that he'd warned her. But Isabel wouldn't be denied, and she was content to leave the office unoccupied until she discovered how to force Cisneros to assume it.

◻ ◻ ◻

As March waned, the sovereigns did make time to administrate the Indies regardless of the press of European matters, and Fernando received a memorial from Juanoto Berardi assessing how to bring the Indies to profitability, ever more important as expenditures escalated for the Italian war. The only fleet arriving from the Indies in the past year had borne but a cargo of deserters, hardly the barrels of the gold the Admiral had promised. Española obviously wasn't Mina.

*Typhus?

In the absence of matching revenue, the sovereigns had grown tardy in the payment of some obligations due—even the mothers, widows, and orphans of the men of the first voyage who'd perished at Navidad remained largely unpaid. Ongoing expenses loomed, including for a fleet of resupply ships Fonseca then was outfitting and accumulated wages of over ten million maravedís owed men then serving in Española.

Berardi proposed a plan designed to encourage the island's settlement and reduce future crown expenditures by introducing private enterprise, including as a central element a novel idea to cancel that ten million maravedís debt. Instead of paying the men on their return, the sovereigns would use the ten million to purchase a dozen ships to be stationed in Española that the men there could use to explore other islands—instead of returning to Spain—using goods provided cheaply by the sovereigns to trade for gold and other items in those islands and retaining the profits themselves, other than a royal duty of one-fifth. Española itself would remain a crown monopoly, but its settlers' trade in other islands discovered would flourish and grow, and eventually merchants in Spain would find provisioning a thriving settlement on Española profitable itself, without crown support. In time, hopefully the only ongoing crown commitment would be to provide—as an incentive for Española's settlement—two years of free victuals and wine while a settler established his own garden. Berardi promised no harm should come to the Indians.

Berardi sought a leading role in provisioning the Indies on an ongoing basis, whether pursuant to his memorial or otherwise, and Isabel and Fernando at least were convinced he deserved that. As they considered Berardi's proposal, their apprehension over Colón's leadership and inclination to investigate it boiled over, fueled by the stark absence of any communication from Colón for a year, no less gold shipments. They resolved to dispatch an investigator, considering a military commander who also could fill Margarite's vacant post.* The written orders would require him to review and remedy unfairness in the distribution of the settlement's food supply, but the brief would run far deeper—to probe Colón's fitness and wrongdoing.

*Diego Carrillo.

Cristóbal and Guarionex, Understanding and Brotherhood,

Guaricano, Late February–Early March 1495

As the four slave ships departed for Cádiz, Cristóbal ruminated that Española's Indians were so numerous they could chase his settlement back to Castile if they mustered the resolve. Only the Lord's will or a miracle now prevented that, since they had a leader with the fortitude, cunning, and boldness to so attempt. He judged critical achieving Caonabó's peaceful submission or harming him as greatly as possible, as well as securing Guarionex's alliance promptly, before Caonabó did.

Within days, Cristóbal led some hundred soldiers, horsemen, and artisans over the mountains into the Vega Real, marching east beyond the Yaque's watershed into the Camú's, intent on winning Guarionex's friendship and understanding that a new fort would be constructed close to Guaricano. Cristóbal's squadron included the gentleman Juan de Ayala, appointed to build and captain the fort, to be named La Concepción, with a permanent garrison of three dozen men. Frays Pané and Leudelle accompanied, shepherding Guatícabanu and brothers, directed to reestablish Pané's mission by Guaricano, if Guarionex so permitted. Cristóbal hoped then to march to Santo Tomás to relieve Caonabó's siege and strike peace with him. Bakako and Yutowa accompanied as interpreters, as did Wasu and Ukuti, now well trained. Bakako wondered if they'd be left with Ayala.

Guarionex's entreaties to meet Cristóbal had never been granted, yet he remained resolute that an audience could reshape a harmony acceptable to all. When Cristóbal arrived, a nitaíno escorted him and his men through the myriad of Guaricano's bohío-lined streets to Guarionex's ballcourt, brimming with warriors stationed at its perimeter. Cristóbal was astonished by the town's great size and population and captivated by the beauty of its gentle hillsides, which rose to a commanding hillside peak just three miles south, and the fertility of its farms, nurtured by a gushing tributary of the Camú.* Guarionex rose solemnly from his duho, and the two men came

*The peak is now known as Santo Cerro, the river as the Río Verde.

face-to-face and raised their hands as a gesture of peace, their peoples congregating round to listen. Cristóbal commanded that his soldiers place their weapons on the ground.

"I come to offer my friendship," Cristóbal pronounced first.

"Why should I believe that?" Guarionex stared directly into Cristóbal's eyes. "You've built two forts in my chiefdom, without my permission. Your men have enslaved my subjects and raped our women. You've defiled my villages with totems of your spirits and blasphemed my own." As Bakako translated, soldiers and warriors girded to brandish their weapons, and the crowd—both pale and olive skin—hushed as Cristóbal considered his response.

"Much has happened that I did not anticipate," Cristóbal replied courteously, denying an apology. "When I first came to your island, I left men who were murdered. When I went exploring west, some of my men disobeyed my commands."

"Your men's conduct is your own."

"We come to trade for gold and offer the favors, protection, and rule of my King Fernando and Queen Isabel," Cristóbal replied, ignoring the reproach. "The forts were built to those ends, and those who attacked them have been or will be punished." He studied Guarionex's visage for fright, outrage, or contempt, yet it remained impenetrable. "I intend to construct another here by you, and I present myself to offer a more peaceful path in the future, one where both peoples complement each other and prosper."

"What if I request that you and your people depart the island?" Guarionex thrust back. "We would trade thereafter for gold, at the coast, in peace."

"We've come to stay. Forever." Cristóbal shook his head resolutely. Soldiers knelt for their weapons, warriors gripped their spears, and he raised his arms, palms open, for calm. "But my men's conduct and society shouldn't affront you, and I've come to discuss that. Your people will benefit by the goods we trade and our customs and clothing. I offer to teach you and your people of Christ the Lord."

"Your intent is to conquer the entire island?" Guarionex demanded, sensing the gaze of his subjects, judging him wise or foolish, brave or cowardly.

"My intent is that your peoples allow my peoples to live here, throughout the island, all under the rule and protection of King Fernando and Queen Isabel. That is conquest, but through love."

"Your intent is novel, as my people have never desired nor permitted strangers to reside with us," Guarionex warned. Yet he envisioned that an opportunity short of war did remain for protecting, if not benefiting, Magua's peoples—so long as the Guamiquina would honor promises. "But stay some nights in my village, so we may talk further."

Cristóbal accepted, flush with the vigor of a predator entrapping prey, and Guarionex graciously arranged bohíos for him, Bartolomé, and senior officers. Cristóbal ordered his soldiers and other men to encamp outside the town, displaced from women.

That evening, Guarionex hosted a ceremonial dinner, and the two men scrutinized the other's mettle and sincerity. Cristóbal related the sovereign relationship he sought, conversing with the animation of a Genoese merchant seizing an opportunity. Guarionex inquired of Fernando and Isabel and the meaning of vassalage to them, deeply mistrustful, gauging Cristóbal's true self-interest in fulfilling promises baited. They talked long into the night, and Cristóbal had the patience to attempt to satisfy Guarionex's scrutiny.

When the sun rose, discussions commenced in earnest, the two men seated on duhos in the ballcourt, Bakako squatting in between. They discussed Cristóbal's settlement at the coast and its function as his main township and then turned to Guarionex's territory.

"How many men do you propose to reside here—if I consented?" Guarionex inquired. "What would they do?"

"Just a few men—perhaps three dozen. They'd trade for food and gold."

"You'd prohibit them from wandering from the fort, demanding my subjects' labor, demeaning our spirits, and lusting for our women?"

"The men would be so disciplined, ordered to live and remain close by the fort," Cristóbal replied, knowing that hardly achievable, if not a lie. "Men would travel between here and Isabela regularly, supplying food and porting out gold, prohibited from disturbing your people."

"You care that they obey you?" Guarionex challenged.

"Certainly, they are Christians," Cristóbal proclaimed. "I'll agree to that prohibition if we otherwise see eye to eye."

"The gold is in the streams of the Cibao, and the Cibao is mostly in my chiefdom." Guarionex frowned. "The gold is mine to trade, not Caonabó's."

"So my men would trade with you for it," Cristóbal replied, perceiving jealousy and contempt for Caonabó. "But it's Caonabó's warriors who besiege my men in the Cibao—isn't it?" he pressed, sternly.

"Yes, not mine. I've awaited these discussions, which I'd requested earlier, before participating in hostilities. I haven't yet sent warriors to assist Caonabó, although he'd welcome that."

"Might you request that Caonabó desist the siege, so all again are at peace—trading for gold?"

"You must deal with Caonabó yourself."

"But you can agree not to ally with him?"

"I can agree many things on behalf of my people. But my people must be protected from harm and the brutality and crudeness of your people." Guarionex rose curtly from his duho. "Your men have proven themselves uncivil and lawless. You must address that, credibly."

Guarionex retired to his caney for the remainder of the day, leaving Cristóbal to stew. In solitude, Guarionex consulted Yúcahu, invoking the spirit's approval that Cristóbal be educated in harmony and friendship so that his conduct be altered. *Lure him to the bohío*, Yúcahu entreated.

Abruptly alone, Cristóbal observed Sext, worshipping Christ and the Virgin, who prompted patience in hearing out the chieftain, although the visit likely would extend longer than anticipated. They urged promises rather than threats. *Enlighten him of eternal salvation*, they beckoned.

The two men resumed the next day under a blazing sun, and Guarionex led Cristóbal and Bakako to the shade cast by his ceremonial bohío on Guaricano's outskirts. Guarionex sensed Cacibaquel's presence and approval, and, together, they relished confronting the leader of the clothed people at the dreaded prophecy's very origin, the most suited ground for undoing it. Guarionex implored Yúcahu to reform the Guamiquina's conduct and recast a harmonious future.

"Guamiquina, here's where I worship my people's spirits. Since time immemorial, they've guided my subjects to live in harmony with each other, giving to and receiving from each other so that all prosper, without unnecessary confrontation. Do you respect that learning?"

"Those are noble aspirations," Cristóbal acknowledged. "My Lord teaches much the same—that all men should live in peace."

"Why do you wish that my people worship the Christ-spirit?" Guarionex probed.

"We know him to be true," Cristóbal replied. "If you follow Christ, your soul will live after death in paradise, forever."

"My soul will live in a good place, without Christ, because I've heeded my spirits' wisdom to live in harmony with others—and I know those spirits true," Guarionex countered plainly. "Will your Christ assist your soul to survive in paradise despite the failure of peace between our peoples? My spirits wouldn't be so forgiving."

Cristóbal had doubted the Lord's blessing countless times over the past decade, sensing the Lord's reproach for his vanity and self-importance. But he'd never perceived that his actions as conqueror jeopardized his afterlife, envisioning the Lord's approval and support instead. Yet he did appreciate the conquered's viewpoint, and the question didn't affront him.

"Christ directs the destinies of all men," Cristóbal replied steadfastly. "He approves what I've done because I serve him to bring you and your people to him."

Guarionex was speechless, startled by both the conviction apparent in Cristóbal's response and its hypocrisy, justifying evil to teach of a spirit that supposedly was good. He vexed whether the Guamiquina's conviction was sincere or deceitful.

"I've brought a friar with me, and I offer to leave him with you to teach you and your people about Christ," Cristóbal continued, eschewing the need for further self-justification. "I've also asked him to understand your spirits, if you wish to teach him."

"I'd be content to both learn and teach," Guarionex compromised. "But first, tell me why you plant the crossed sticks everywhere, including in our ballcourts and private places—sometimes even our sacred burial plots."

"Christ died on a cross to save all men, including you, my lord. These crosses honor him and mark his presence among us."

"My people suffer great sickness wherever you plant crosses, and many have died. Why?"

Bakako broke into tears, startling the two men, and they deferred for him to recover. "The deaths sadden me," he muttered in both languages, regaining composure, expunging Niana's embrace from his thoughts.

"Christ knows all, but rarely reveals all," Cristóbal observed. He stared to Heaven and threatened, "Undoubtedly, he punishes those who've refused trading food so Christians hunger."

Each unsatisfied, the two men sat silently for some moments and then ambled back to Guaricano's plaza, both aware there was little else to discuss and that the moment had come to strike their relationship or part. The next morning, alone, Guarionex led Cristóbal and Bakako into the hillside, out of his subjects' earshot.

"You've heard me—what is it that you propose for our relationship?" Guarionex asked.

"You must agree to the fort's establishment, welcome my men, and pledge to maintain peace and not assist those who resist me, including Caonabó. You'll remain ruler of your people, and my friar will live here to teach you Christianity."

"That fails the essence," Guarionex exclaimed, halting. "You must pledge that your men never harm or enslave my subjects, including our women, and that you'll punish severely any who do. This is my chiefdom, my laws, and my peoples' customs and traditions—and your men must respect them. They must cease blaspheming and burning our spirits. You may construct your new fort, but your men may reside only there and at the others now established, and the number of your men cannot increase." Guarionex raised an arm and forefinger. "You forget, while our weapons are not equal to yours, our number is far greater."

Cristóbal stood hush, and Guarionex puzzled whether he had stepped too far, but he stepped even further resolutely, determined to bind the Guamiquina's soul and peoples.

"Our agreement and relationship must be memorialized and

bonded, by spiritual union and marriage," he proclaimed. "You must become my brother in spirit, sharing my heritage and love for my people. I will bestow an areíto upon you, whereby my peoples' spirits will inform your conduct." He pointed to Bakako. "You shall give your Diego in marriage to one of my sisters."

Cristóbal recovered his voice and agreed to consider the requests. Bakako was stunned.

That evening, as he lay to sleep, Guarionex contemplated how the sacred Taíno brotherhood ceremony might alter the Guamiquina's conduct. It was rarely invoked, typically only to honor a foreign cacique's friendship long proven, whereby bequeathing an areíto upon him conferred the ancestry and homeland of the giving cacique, uniting the two in brotherhood. But it was more than an honor, representing the most sacred promise of friendship deliverable. The recipient was meant to be transformed before the spirits to respect the giver and his people as a brother would, as if born of them. Guarionex recognized that the Guamiquina might not understand or respect it as such, but the spirits would, and perhaps they'd guide or force the Guamiquina and his subjects to treat Guarionex's subjects as brothers rather than as targets for exploitation.

As the moon rose, Cristóbal shrewdly calculated it was expedient to recognize Guarionex's limitations on stationing his men and prohibiting enslavements. It didn't much matter what was agreed, so long as Guarionex refrained from aligning with Caonabó, as every promise might be ignored and discarded with impunity once Caonabó was subdued. The loss of Bakako's services was unfortunate, but he'd be well positioned to spy and report back on Guarionex, as would Pané. Cristóbal summoned Bakako in the moonlight.

"What's the areíto ceremony?" Cristóbal asked.

"You promise be friend. Like promise men took obey Fernando, Isabel, and you, hand on Bible. Christ punish men break promise. Yúcahu punish men break promise."

Cristóbal nodded, grasping Guarionex's intent—and immediately dismissing that a heathen brotherhood ceremony held the significance of an oath upon the scriptures.

"As I promised, you shall be husband to a Haitian princess, far above your station when you first swam aboard my launch. When I depart, you'll live henceforth with Guarionex. But remember, you'll always remain my Diego. You must advise Ayala continuously what Guarionex and the other caciques intend."

Cristóbal was moved by their long journey together and the recognition that no other person had shared so much of his triumphs and tragedies in the Indies as the boy before him. "Diego, we'll meet again, perhaps often, and I'll always protect you."

Bakako trembled, overwrought by the sudden changes in fortune that now came daily, mesmerized by the brief intimacy displayed by the man on earth he most honored and despised, who'd carved his destiny from the sands of Guanahaní to the shores of a new world and back. Instinctively, he dutifully stepped forward, head bowed, as if a son to a father, rather than a slave, and Admiral reciprocated with a brief embrace. Tears came again to Bakako's eyes, and Admiral smiled affectionately and kissed his forehead before dismissing him.

In the morning, Cristóbal and Guarionex agreed their truce, and the ceremonial preparations were set by the end of their week together. Before dusk, a chorus of Guarionex's nitaínos sang an areíto to Cristóbal, conferring his brotherhood to Guarionex, and Bakako was wed to one of Guarionex's youngest sisters and pronounced a cacique vassal to Guarionex. Bakako first met Ariana at the ceremony, and they were escorted to a secluded bohío for the night to consummate the union and alliance. She was pretty, but almost twice Bakako's age—old enough to be his mother—and Bakako felt strange to lie with her and command her about. But she obeyed, and, while he envisioned Niana, their intimacy was agreeable. When done, he lay astonished that he was a cacique of Haiti's peoples.

Bakako rose before dawn's twilight, whispered to Ariana that he'd return, and then stole from the bohío to reunite with Yutowa before Yutowa departed with Admiral's entourage for Santo Tomás. He found his friend lying by a fire circle in the ballcourt, and the two teenagers embraced.

"Take care of yourself," Bakako whispered, anxious Yutowa would swoon into the angst that Bakako often had helped him surmount. "We'll both survive, I here, and you wherever Admiral takes you." Bakako hesitated and, at last, sadly refrained from promising they'd return to Guanahaní.

"You watch out—your second master is too compromising to overcome the pale men's wickedness," Yutowa wanly replied. He lamented, "Our souls will survive, be it in a good place or bad, wherever we end."

Bakako gripped Yutowa's shoulders and shook hard. "It's too soon for death."

"You remain Bakako, my friend. You also still find reason to live. I hope that continues for you."

Yet again, Bakako burst into tears.

Caonabó and Hojeda,
Maguana, Early March 1495

Caonabó was asleep in a hammock strung between trees on the hillside overlooking the pale men's Santo Tomás when scouts woke him in the moonlight. They reported that the Guamiquina and soldiers had departed his lengthy council with Guarionex and were on the march south to liberate the fort. Caonabó summoned Uxmatex, and they sat before a fire stoked by naborias, interrogating the scouts.

"Is Guarionex friend or foe?"

"We don't have an informant, but he hosted the Guamiquina at length and they parted amicably," the elder scout replied. "You must assume he's struck some understanding with the Guamiquina."

Somber, Caonabó puzzled the potential scope of betrayal. He turned to Uxmatex, bidding that the general evaluate the situation.

"How many men and beasts approach?" Uxmatex inquired.

"More than a hundred men, half a dozen enormous beasts, half a dozen small."

"They intend to invade Maguana or simply break our siege?"

The scouts shrugged.

"Do Guacanagarí's or Guarionex's warriors accompany them?"

"No."

Caonabó turned to Uxmatex. "Guarionex was never with us. We

must assess whether his guile poisons our allies' resolve. We aren't going to fight the pale men alone."

Uxmatex grimaced bitterly.

"Lift the siege before dawn. We retreat home, avoiding any altercation," Caonabó ordered. "If the pale men are so imprudent to pursue through the mountains, we'll ambush them when vulnerable in the ravines and riverbeds we know. But we must reconfirm our alliances before resuming war."

Caonabó pondered some moments. "Perhaps communication and trickery are better than siege," he observed, shedding his prior reluctance to approach the Guamiquina, staring into Uxmatex's eyes to reassure that the war would resume nonetheless. "Dispatch a nitaíno to the pale men's coastal settlement bearing gifts and feigning friendship. While he fawns and flatters, he must reconnoiter a plan of attack."

◻ ◻ ◻

Alonso de Hojeda woke at dawn to inspect his troops and the Indian encampments about Santo Tomás, and he was startled that the Indians appeared to have departed, or at least hidden themselves well. Suspecting ambush, he nevertheless dispatched two horsemen north to race to Isabela to inform the Admiral about the siege. Hojeda was even more stunned to behold the two riders reappearing by noon to announce that the Admiral himself approached the fort, with a squadron a hundred strong.

By dusk, Cristóbal, Yutowa, and the squadron arrived, and Cristóbal and Hojeda reunited and reviewed what had transpired since they last met. The fort's garrison starved for Spanish food, and, that evening, the squadron shared the little it had toted in a small feast. Cristóbal, with Bartolomé and Yutowa at his side, instructed Hojeda on the mission that remained unfulfilled.

"We cannot conquer Caonabó in his homeland," Cristóbal warned, appreciating Hojeda's vigorous nod of agreement. "We must take him by deception. With Margarite's treason, it falls to you to brave confronting him there. Take but a few men so he recognizes you come to reason, not blows. Invite him to meet me in Isabela, promising a parley's safe conduct so we may discuss peace. But seize him when he's unaware."

"Should I kill him—if the opportunity presents?"

"No. It's critical I convince him to bow to the king and queen. That'll convince the island's other princes to submit. Fawn and flatter rather than harm. Promise riches. Assure the sovereigns will delight that he'll rule his people as their most valued lord." Cristóbal grittily envisioned the audience. "You may threaten that we'll destroy him otherwise. But do him no injury." Pointing to Yutowa, he added, "You'll need the boy to express these sentiments."

"How should I seize him?"

"Use your ingenuity. Perhaps gift him a shirt and, as he dons it, suddenly bind him."

⌑ ⌑ ⌑

The next morning, after Admiral and the squadron departed back to Isabela, Yutowa squatted forlornly outside Hojeda's hut, awaiting commands. He studied the few pale men standing lookout or working within the fort, astonished how a year there had wizened and steeled them. They were the surviving soldiers, the toughest of the original posting, and Yutowa recognized that his new master was the most resilient and envenomed of them all.

By noon, Hojeda selected a half dozen of the most audacious men and a horse for the mission, which he mounted, and they departed south well armed. The horse bore no provisions other than gifts for Caonabó and to trade en route, as the men had grown accustomed to Indian food. Hojeda instructed Yutowa to find the path to Caonabó's village and announce to villagers met that they journeyed to pay their respects to the great lord, peacefully. But villagers retreated on sight of the horse, rendering it difficult to obtain direction. On the first night out, the pale men commandeered bohíos in a village where everyone had fled.

Yet within a day, villagers stood their ground to identify the route, and Yutowa realized that they'd been ordered to draw the band to its destination. Village caciques fearfully, but obediently, offered bohíos and feasts the next two nights. Yutowa was impressed Hojeda did maintain his men's discipline and that there were no abuses, of women or otherwise. He grew mesmerized by the august beauty of Haiti's mountains, musing whether they presaged a peaceful, rather than violent, encounter. He accepted that it might be violent and that the pale men might be massacred, and likely himself, too—a possibility that no longer daunted him.

On the fourth day, Yutowa led Hojeda's band over a mountain pass, affording a spectacular view of an enormous valley, to which they descended. They forded a river at the valley's edge (a tributary to the San Juan), and soon countless villagers crowded a respectful distance from the pathway, astonished to behold the horse and its alien gait. They arrived at the outskirts of Caonabó's town in the afternoon, where an elderly nitaíno stepped forward to usher them to the great ballcourt. An army of warriors lined its perimeter, bearing spears and macanas. Naborias served cazabi and papaya juice, and the nitaíno pronounced that Caonabó would receive them.

After tarrying some moments, Caonabó strode from his caney to meet Hojeda at the ballcourt's center. The two men recognized each other immediately and scrutinized the other's intimate features, previously undiscernible at the distance of the siege. Caonabó was surprised by the pale man's small stature but captivated by the energy shimmering in his wide eyes. The cemí strung about his neck bore an image of a woman, perhaps the Christ-spirit's mother, a strange if not eerie choice for a bold warrior. Hojeda was startled by the chieftain's considerable age and omnipotent demeanor, impressed that he was both ruler and general, with the stature of a European prince. Hojeda sunk to his knees in obeisance and directed his men to do the same. He bid Yutowa translate.

"It's time—and an honor—that we finally meet," Alonso lauded, reminding of their standoff across the ravine. "I'm Alonso de Hojeda, the Admiral's lieutenant. I come in friendship on his behalf to talk."

"What about?" Caonabó scowled, folding his arms.

"Our peoples have been at blows, but that needn't be the case. The Admiral invites you to parley with him at Isabela, his village on the northern coast. You and he would discuss how our peoples might live in love and friendship."

"Why should I believe that is Admiral's purpose—rather than cowardly murder?" Caonabó glared into Hojeda's eyes. "If Admiral wants peace, tell him to come kneel before me, here."

Hojeda stood and stared back but spoke deferentially. "The Admiral offers you splendid gifts and a favored relationship with his caciques, Queen Isabel and King Fernando. Your safe conduct to Isabela and back would be assured. Just as you've afforded me safe conduct here."

"I have never stooped to another man, and I never will—particularly to an intruder." Caonabó stepped closer, his height commanding over Hojeda's, evoking the memory of spying down on him from above.

"The Admiral wasn't an intruder. He was given permission to establish a garrison on your island." Alonso stared upward and clenched his jaw, impenitent. "Someone massacred the men he was permitted to leave here."

Caonabó's heart thumped, but his visage remained impenetrable. "That was the fate their conduct merited."

"Their fate was the Admiral's judgment to make, no one else's." Hojeda caught his ire, recognizing there was no advantage to argument or accusations. "The Admiral understands you are the island's most renowned king and that it is with you he must talk." Hojeda reached into his jerkin, withdrew a gift, and extended his arm to bequeath it—a red cap adorned with Guinean ivory. "This is a small token of his esteem for you. If you meet him in Isabela, he will bestow much greater."

Caonabó studied the cap, momentarily scorning that anyone could contemplate such a gift might assuage his distrust or bend his will. The thought of slaying the pale man and his band crossed his mind, but—as a general—he quashed the temptation, as the opportunities to interrogate an enemy leader face-to-face were rare and invaluable. A vision of Anacaona accosted him. He curtly accepted the gift and stepped back.

Hojeda sighed heavily, relieved. "It's to be worn on your head, as if one of your feather crowns, a great honor among my people."

Caonabó scoffed the invitation to wear the cap and handed it to a nitaíno. He paused for a lengthy moment, as if reluctant to grant Hojeda's wish, but then apparently relented. "I'll consider Admiral's invitation, and we'll talk tomorrow."

That evening, Anacaona's naborias served a feast of fish and fowl, but there was no celebration. Caonabó and Hojeda would have delighted to slay the other but weeks before, and each had dreamed that during the siege. The two met tensely in the ballcourt the following morning, seated on duhos, with Yutowa kneeling between.

"You propose I visit your so-called Isabela," Caonabó postured. "How many of Admiral's soldiers would await me there?"

"It doesn't matter—you'd be given safe conduct," replied Hojeda shrewdly, suspecting calculation motivated the question, not timidity.

"Safety would be found in the absence of soldiers, not promises," Caonabó probed. "My scouts estimate less than five hundred at Isabela. They estimated you had almost sixty at your fort when we first besieged you, perhaps thirty surviving when we departed. Am I wrong?"

"King Fernando and Queen Isabel are constantly dispatching more soldiers. There's no limit to the number that'll arrive for the Admiral's use, all provisioned with the same weapons and horses you couldn't dislodge at the fort. They'll be able to crush you right here, someday." Alonso caught himself again, and he humbled his tone, reverting to fawn rather than intimidate. "You must understand that King Fernando and Queen Isabel are the most powerful princes in the world, and the most magnanimous. The Admiral has related great accounts of yourself, and they're eager to shower you with acclaim. If you visit the Admiral in Isabel, he'll show you the church bell which daily speaks to summon the village to worship Christ. It's one of Queen Isabel's gifts to the island."

Caonabó had learned from informants about the bell, which was made of a shiny metal (brass) unknown on Haiti and possessed a mystical voice and tenor never heard before, a unique invocation to spirits. But the pale men's head count stirred him far more. "How many men do your caciques plan to send to Haiti?" he inquired.

Hojeda hesitated to respond, uncertain whether to lie high or low, and he retreated from an answer. "The king will decide that." He withdrew a second gift from inside his jerkin. "I present another token expressing my sovereigns' desire for your friendship—a shirt of the finest silk. You may wear this on your arms and chest."

Caonabó inspected the gift carefully and slowly donned it, admiring the shimmer and softness of the strange fabric, intimating it was softening his resistance. "If I come to Isabela, I'll march as the supreme cacique of my people, accompanied by my nitaínos and warriors, commensurate to those Admiral commands or will then command, every bit as equal as Admiral in stature."

Hojeda drew breathless, certain he'd made progress, uncertain the attendant peril. There was silence, awkward at first but soon resolute. Caonabó then rose abruptly to terminate the audience. "Reflect on that and we'll meet to conclude our discussions tomorrow morning," he pronounced.

◘ ◘ ◘

That evening, Caonabó retired to the sanctum of his caney, summoning Anacaona, his brother Manicoatex, and Uxmatex to join him. He turned first to Anacaona and was struck by her anxiety and that her constancy matched her beauty.

"Our alliance remains strong, in your view?" he asked.

"It grows stronger every day, every hour, regardless of prior defeats and Guarionex's absence," she assured, without exaggeration, yet wary this truth would fuel her husband's audacity. "We've received countless messengers from caciques throughout the island, urging you to drive the pale men out. All cry that failure to do so will forsake independence for servitude."

Manicoatex nodded gravely. "If they're not expelled, we'll all be their slaves. We can't shirk the bloodshed of full-blown war."

"That time has come," Caonabó judged, cautious to maintain a soldier's discipline, yet resolute a plan was feasible. "We shall accept the Guamiquina's entreaty that I parley with him at his coastal settlement. But we will bring our warriors along and bid other caciques to dispatch theirs."

He glanced to Anacaona, who averted her eyes, and then turned to Manicoatex and Uxmatex. "I'll enter his compound with an elite troop, as if for my honor and guard, and you and a great army will surround the settlement. While I meet the Guamiquina, we'll stun them with our greatest assault, attacking from both within and without their walls, terrifying and confusing them. Their weapons will massacre many of us, perhaps thousands, but our numbers should prevail. When he returns, my nitaíno will advise the compound's layout."

"And what of you?" Uxmatex responded, grimacing.

"I'll slay the Guamiquina with my bare hands at the sound of your battle cry."

"And what of you, then?" pled Anacaona, raising her eyes to draw Caonabó's, her voice raised.

Caonabó shrugged. "I'll be surrounded by our finest warriors. Jumping to the sea would provide escape, but we must prevail."

Manicoatex and Uxmatex gaped to the floor, excusing themselves from a silent communication between husband and wife.

◘ ◘ ◘

In the morning, Caonabó and Hojeda met in the ballcourt, Yutowa assisting.

"I agree to parley with Admiral at his settlement, accompanied by my nitaínos and warriors. You may escort me there. If the parley fails, we part without bloodshed—at that time."

"My Lord, the Admiral will delight, and you won't be disappointed. There are few honors greater than recognition as King Fernando and Queen Isabel's loyal prince, and the Admiral will bestow you great riches." Hojeda reached into his jerkin and pulled yet a third gift. "Here's another token of the Admiral's love—two bracelets bound in friendship, forged of the same ores as the great bell." Hojeda handed Caonabó brass manacles. "It can be worn by two friends at once, or just one alone, and Christian princes sport them as a great jewel when they dance together."

Stunned, Yutowa studied Caonabó marvel at the strength and texture of the metal, opening and shutting the manacles on his wrists a few times. Caonabó mused whether the clever devise truly was worn in ceremony rather than to bind a prisoner. Hojeda scrutinized closely as Caonabó stuffed the manacle in the pouch strung from his caciqual belt.

Within hours, the two men commenced their journey north. Hojeda shared his mount with Caonabó, while Yutowa and the rest of Hojeda's band hiked vigorously behind, Caonabó's elite troop trailing some distance. When they disappeared, Manicoatex and Uxmatex sprang to assemble their greatest army to march the following dawn.

As they rode, Caonabó was astonished by Hojeda's mastery over the beast, directing it to the right or left, to speed forward or halt, just as if Hojeda had become one with it, capturing its enormous strength as if his own. Hojeda obliged his guest by bringing the horse to a gallop, and Caonabó grasped the military superiority of those possessing such a commanding mobility. Yutowa and the band trotted vigorously to stay close.

When they came to the river skirting the mountains, Hojeda halted for his men and Yutowa to arrive so they might ford together. He studied the distance separating his band from Caonabó's troop, which had grown long.

"Let's bathe while your warriors catch up," he cheerfully suggested. Yutowa translated, surprised at the suggestion, as the pale men bathed as rarely as Taínos bathed often.

As he and Caonabó dismounted, Hojeda warmly proposed, "You may don the bracelets, as if a Christian prince."

Yutowa continued to translate, quivering and swooning with guilt, aghast that yet again he was thrust to assist the pale men's deception. A voice within him cried that he warn of the trick, but another shouted that so doing would seal his death at the pale men's hands. He remembered stepping forward to save Admiral from murder by hostile Cubans, and he was tortured by a vision of countless trampled peoples shrieking to condemn his failure to step aside.

Hojeda amicably took the manacles as Caonabó reflexively pulled them from his pouch, still digesting the mount's strength and speed. Hojeda placed a cuff on his own wrist and the other on Caonabó's. "Let's go into the water."

Yutowa crumbled to the ground, unwilling and unable to translate. Through the corner of his eye, he spied Hojeda's band clamoring to surround the chieftain in the river, while one of them forded the mount. Hojeda abruptly bellowed a command, and the evil was consummated, as the pale men rushed Caonabó and tackled him underwater to subdue him, wrenching his arms behind his back to bind the manacle to both his wrists and locking it.

Caonabó fought to brace his feet upon the riverbed and defiantly heaved upward, thrusting to the surface, astonishing his attackers and hurling them aside. He gasped for air and howled desperately for his warriors, striding headlong through the water, homeward. But Hojeda's men pounced again and overcame him, dragging him across the river, half-drowned yet screaming. Rage wrought him as they fettered his ankles. Shame for his unwariness racked him as they stuffed cloth down his throat to muffle his shout. Hatred consumed him as they hoisted him back upon the mount and bound him by rope to Hojeda. Visions of his dozen wives, scores of children and grandchildren, and countless nitaínos and common subjects brought him to an unbearable misery that he'd failed them inexcusably.

Hojeda barked for Yutowa to ford the river, and Yutowa meekly rose. Yet the voices within him implored that he'd had enough, he should've been done with the pale men long before, and death would be preferable to continuing with them. He regained composure and stared directly at Hojeda across the river, firmly shaking his head.

With that, Hojeda galloped his mount northeast into the mountains, his men trotting behind, desperate to evade the chase of Caonabó's warriors.

When the warriors arrived at the riverbank, they panicked that their chieftain hadn't waited their crossing, and they urgently commenced that pursuit.

Terror had resuscitated Yutowa's will to survive, and, barely a moment before, he'd forded the river to hide in forest nearby, dreading what the Haitian warriors would do if they discovered him. An enemy Guanahanían slave certainly deserved worse than death.

⧈ ⧈ ⧈

Back in Guaricano, bewildered, anxious, and lonely for Yutowa, Bakako sought to adjust to yet another life and new roles—as Admiral's emissary to Guarionex and Guarionex's brother-in-law.

Commander Ayala commenced Fort Concepción's construction on a gentle rise overlooking the southern bank of Guaricano's river, which provided a defensive separation from most of the town. Guarionex's caney and ballcourt lay a fifteen-minute walk upstream on the northern bank. Guarionex awarded Bakako a bohío abutting the river directly opposite the fort, facilitating Bakako's straddle of both peoples, including his protection by the pale men and his maintenance by his wife's two dozen naborias, over whom he'd become master upon marriage.

Bakako's wife dutifully supervised the preparation of his meals and ongoing satisfactions. Ayala and Guarionex sought his daily participation in arranging the fort's construction and the pale men's food supply, and he assisted Guarionex and Fray Pané in their initial discussions regarding Guarionex's examination of Christianity. At night, he brooded whether Niana had wished this for them and what Yutowa would say if he survived to see it.

VII
WAR AND TRIBUTE

Cristóbal and Caonabó, Hojeda and Manicoatex, Battle in Magua,
March 1495

The sun was setting when Hojeda dismounted outside the Admiral's residence in Isabela, haggard, famished, and exhausted after three days of headlong flight north. He'd bivouacked for the first nights at streams to drink and water the horse and his captive, taken his only proper meal at Santo Tomás, and, with a fresh mount, arrived at Isabela in record time. His small band would straggle into Santo Tomás a day later.

Caonabó ached and hungered far more than his captor—his muscles pulverized by the horse's canter, wrists and ankles bloodied by the chafe of the manacles and fetters, and soul devastated by the liberty and sovereignty denied. But his wit and composure—as ruler and general—survived acute. Guards yanked him into the compound's courtyard, furnished a washbasin for cleansing, and thrust him upon a pale men's duho, still manacled and fettered. Two Haitian youths offered a gourd of water and the pale men's cazabi and then crouched at his side, as if to serve rather than spy on him. Without ado, and without need of introduction, the Guamiquina appeared from a doorway of the stone hut and strode to sit on a similar duho, directly facing him.

Each man sensed he knew much of the other, having vilified him for over a year, and each was stunned finally to behold the flesh and soul existing beyond reputation and rumor. Days earlier, Caonabó's nitaíno had delivered gold-inlaid masks and spindles as an overture of friendship.

"I intend you no harm," Cristóbal began forthrightly, allowing Wasu or Ukuti a moment to translate. "I received with happiness your gift and wish to be your friend." Cristóbal scrutinized Caonabó's features, a brow wrinkled with age seemingly more advanced than his own, a torso retaining the leanness of a youthful warrior yet similarly withered, and eyes as sharp and penetrating as King Fernando's. The murderer of the Navidad garrison indeed was a king rather than a rogue.

"From this seat, that's difficult to comprehend," Caonabó replied, contemptuously manifesting the sovereign demeanor he'd cultivated for decades. He examined the Guamiquina from head to toe, noting the commanding height and sturdy frame, an august visage well worn by the sea, and eyes as sharp and penetrating as he'd ever seen. The pale men's commander indeed had a presence worthy to lead an invasion.

"I've come to conquer this island, and you. But I seek to do so through friendship rather than force. If you submit to my king and queen's rule, you may continue to govern your people." Cristóbal stared into Caonabó's eyes. "Nothing would please me more than to unshackle you and return you to your kingdom, as friend and vassal to my king and queen."

"I don't care for your friendship, nor will Haitian caciques submit to rule from afar." Caonabó reflected that he did have something to compromise. "I would be content to forget what's transpired since our peoples first met and to trade gold with you, just as you've seen. But you must remove all your men from our shores."

"My Lord, I've come to conquer, and the lands of the island's princes are now the lands of King Fernando and Queen Isabel of Castile. Those princes who accept this will remain their people's rulers, prosper in trade, and receive protection from their enemies—just as the Lord Guacanagarí. Those who don't will die in chains or at the sword. You have no choice but to accept Fernando and Isabel's rule." Cristóbal stood. "I leave you to consider that, and we'll talk in the morning."

Caonabó was shunted to a dim second room within the residence, separated from the Guamiquina's living space by an internal wall and doorway, with a mat of straw to lie on, and chained to the ground to prevent movement, still manacled and fettered. As he lay to sleep, Caonabó confronted captivity's forlornness, which he'd never experienced, and accepted that disaster had sundered his strategy. But he remained alive, and Manicoatex and Uxmatex undoubtedly were marching their army north, as well as the armies of allies, hopefully to attack, perhaps to ransom his release. He burned that his capture would solidify, rather than cow, the alliance's resolve to fight. From the courtyard, he had eyed the settlement, judging the pale men ragged and weary, and he weighed whether the Guamiquina's brazen demeanor belied doubts in the conquest's fulfillment.

Cristóbal couldn't sleep, as he pondered what to do with the defiant lord lying, breathing, and chained but feet away. He would try first to break the defiance, coercing submission with both rigor and courtesy, offering the shackles' release only on unequivocal surrender. Execution would enrage the Indians, and, while within his authority, Cristóbal believed his sovereigns preferred such a decision reserved for themselves. He reflected that, failing timely submission, transporting Caonabó to Spain could accomplish both the sovereigns' review and soften the chieftain's heart for the better—or at least erode his fame and power on Española. Dispatching Caonabó with a shipload of defeated warriors would remind the sovereigns that enslavement was fair punishment for resistance to their rule.

Before dawn, Caonabó stirred first and, to their surprise, called for Wasu and Ukuti.

"Tell your master I summon him," he barked.

Wasu and Ukuti didn't translate it that way, and Cristóbal bid that Caonabó be hauled before him in the courtyard.

"If my land is now your rulers', you must protect it for me from my own enemies—at least until you release me."

"Who threatens it?" Cristóbal responded in disbelief.

"All my neighbors, my ancestral enemies. Undoubtedly, they've discovered my capture, and they'll invade my chiefdom to usurp it."

Caonabó.

Cristóbal eyed Caonabó warily. "What would you have me do?"

"Dispatch your soldiers to my chiefdom to defend it. Assist my brother Manicoatex in repelling those who invade."

"Your enemies are so quick to act?" Cristóbal smirked, distrusting. "That's the price of your submission?"

Caonabó nodded twice and surmised Cristóbal's disbelief. "The cacique Guacanagarí would relish deposing me."

Cristóbal saw a trap transparent and rejected the gambit, countering, "All will be subdued in due course, and your chiefdom preserved." He appreciated Caonabó's understanding of the vassalage relationship to be imposed and the decision thrust upon him.

Cristóbal. Ridolfo di Domenico Bigordi
(the Ghirlandaio), sixteenth century.

Vengeance by Caonabó's brother and subjects loomed inevitable, and Cristóbal directed Bartolomé and Hojeda to organize the largest squadron of healthy men they could muster. He also dispatched a messenger summoning Guacanagarí, desperate to augment Isabela's meager head count with the countless warriors Guacanagarí might provide, resolved to divide the enemy to conquer them.

◘ ◘ ◘

Days earlier, the urgent report of Caonabó's abduction had staggered Anacaona, Manicoatex, and Uxmatex, and they'd pined through day and night for word of his rescue. On the morning after, at first twilight, they met exasperated to consider how to proceed. Sleepless and frightened, Anacaona felt awkward receiving the two men in the caney's inner sanctum—a prerogative rightfully only her husband's. But all three understood that their desperation best remain concealed until a strategy were resolved, and, while unspoken, both men recognized her authority in Caonabó's absence.

"If they've taken him captive, we must storm the settlement—as he originally intended," Manicoatex urged. "When our nitaíno returns, he'll inform how."

"Your brother plotted assaulting from within and without," Uxmatex counseled somberly. "We don't have that advantage now. Nor would he have the protection of his guard. It's also just an assumption they're imprisoning him." Uxmatex averted his eyes from Anacaona, as if to afford her privacy, refraining from a premonition of her husband's execution.

Anacaona trembled, dreading that fate and overwhelmed that she'd never been responsible for military decisions. She trusted and respected the judgments of both men with her, each over a decade her senior, but she trusted her husband more, and the issue was clear to her. "What would my husband now do?"

"He'd devise the most prudent, bold action," Uxmatex responded. He considered his master's instincts and thought aloud. "He wouldn't leave a chieftain's abduction unavenged, but he wouldn't assault the settlement on the promontory at first, failing the advantage of warriors within. He'd storm their presence along the Bajabonico—destroying their gardens and denying them and their beasts access to water. He'd then besiege the promontory. He might wish that we capture them while porting water—to exchange for his ransom."

"There'll be outrage throughout Haiti when this crime is known," Anacaona exclaimed, ignoring execution's specter. "Our alliances will strengthen, not wither."

"If we fight," Manicoatex warned. "If we don't, both the enemy and our people will perceive us weak and cowards. We must revenge, promptly, viciously, relentlessly. The only issue is where to engage."

"Lead the army north and attack, prudently and relentlessly, as you both wish," Anacaona ordered gingerly, trembling to exercise such authority.

After the two departed, Anacaona remained too distraught to rest. She stole from the caney before dawn to sit alone in the cool serenity of her garden, listening to the village river's tranquil gurgle. She perceived the delicate fragility of the blossoms and stems surrounding her and mused how love and power were as frail and fleeting. Her meditation soon bore deeper, to contemplate the spirit and very survival of her people, and tears came to her eyes.

Anacaona despaired that the enemy had yet to be routed—regardless of her husband's cunning and valor—and countless people now suffered, many who'd never even met a pale man. The alien illnesses that first appeared closest to the pale men's settlements and crosses had spread to more distant villages, as if blown by the wind, whether according to the Christ-spirit's design or not. Caonabó had forced the enemy to hunger, but many villagers in the Cibao and the Yaque valley now hungered also, having ceased to sow fresh yuca—exhausted and decimated from the pestilence, keen on the enemy's starvation, or simply having fled for the mountains. Those who'd fled starved worse, as the mountains' roots and herbs failed in nourishment. Most feared abandonment by their spirits, and she herself had invoked the spirits to arrest these calamities, but to no avail.

Visions of Caonabó cascaded through her thoughts—his first kiss of their wedding night, his grasp as he carried her from the birthing tree with their newborn daughter, his insistence that the pale men were enemy. In anguish, she revisited her earlier question, *What would he now do?* Her heart pounded, and she grasped that it wasn't just a military question but encompassed all, and she shuddered that he'd already answered it for her. *Rule as you would, not as I would.* But what did that mean!

As the sun rose, Anacaona's thoughts were interrupted as the slender, supple body of a eleven-year old cuddled beside her. Anacaona gently rested Higueymota's head on her shoulders and scanned whether her daughter's pigtails were braided properly.

"Is Father in danger?" Higueymota asked.

"Yes. But he's our cacique, and he's accustomed to being in danger," Anacaona replied wanly. "He'll figure out what to do."

Higueymota sensed her mother's angst. "Don't worry. He'll protect us."

Soon, the nitaíno dispatched with gifts to the coastal settlement returned to reveal its inner layout. Days later, scouts reported that Caonabó sat chained as a common prisoner within. Word of the dishonor reverberated throughout Haiti as a lightning bolt cracking from the heavens, igniting an outrage and resolution more fervid than the previous discontent. Manicoatex and Uxmatex marched north for war, commanding an army of five thousand men, including warriors contributed by Behecchio and Cayacoa, all exhilarated by the conviction they fought for their liberty and civilization.

◘ ◘ ◘

Within a week of Caonabó's incarceration, riders dispatched from Fort Magdalena and the nascent Fort Concepción raced to Isabela to alarm that large Indian armies were amassing in the Yaque valley and near Guaricano. Magdalena's warden, Arriaga, cried that the escaped Guatiguaná had returned to amass a force not only of his own subjects but Indians from other corners of the island, some possessing bows rather than just arrow slings. Commander Ayala exhorted that Manicoatex had led Caonabó's army mere miles from Fort Concepción, likely intent both on destroying it and descending upon Isabela. Cristóbal didn't panic, but he was relieved when informed that Guacanagarí had honored the demand to come to Isabela, and he summoned the chieftain to his courtyard.

On entering, Guacanagarí gasped breathless and staggered on discovering Caonabó sitting outside a residence doorway, chained to the ground. Caonabó's bolted upright, his temples pulsing hotly, and he glowered contemptuously back and spat.

"Traitor!" Caonabó barked.

"Trespasser, thief, murderer!" Guacanagarí scowled vehemently, his astonishment subsiding to an abiding hatred.

"You'll perish in disgrace, despised by our people!" Caonabó rasped in return.

"*Our people?*" Guacanagarí cried. "You've never considered that you and I are of the same people! It's your arrogant disdain that's disgraceful and despicable." Guacanagarí's eyes glimmered, and he grinned maliciously. "How does it feel to be treated as the inferior rump?" He hesitated, grew solemn, and slowly approached Caonabó.

"People aren't defined by olive or pale skin, whether naked or clothed, or even the spirits worshipped—but by conduct, and you've been more enemy to me than this Guamiquina has ever proven," Guacanagarí reproached. "My people will honor my ascendancy as the Guamiquina's ally—especially over you and those you call your people."

"*My conduct!*" Caonabó cried back. "What of the Guamiquina's conduct, or his men's conduct!" Caonabó rose to his knees. "Rape. Massacre. Desecration. Enslavement. That's your ally's essence, and now yours, an infamy your people will never forgive!"

"Your own massacres have sealed your subjects' demise," Guacanagarí thrust. "My subjects honor me for saving them that fate."

"Your subjects despise you as a fool and coward!" Caonabó scorned. He returned a malicious smile. "As well as a weakling. I've enjoyed your pretty wife, for months on end."

Guacanagarí stooped to smirk and whisper. "As you grovel bound as a slave, think of me as I lay upon Anacaona and execute your Onaney."

While Cristóbal couldn't understand the conversation, he relished that his ally was well motivated, and he bid Guacanagarí join him at the seaside, out of Caonabó's earshot.

"What do you understand of the armies amassing to attack my people?" Cristóbal demanded, Wasu at his side to interpret.

"Admiral, they intend to drive you from the island, and I'm your sole friend. My warriors shall fight alongside yours, and I expect great favor for that loyalty." Guacanagarí quivered to conceal that he had little other choice, as the other supreme caciques despised him, and he now desired Admiral's alliance as much as Admiral desired his. "When we're victorious, I shall be entitled to Caonabó's chiefdom and wives."

"You'll receive the king and queen's enduring love and greatest honors," Cristóbal grandly assured, deeply relieved, yet struggling to appear sincere, since he no longer cared a whit for Guacanagarí's fate so long as he contributed warriors. "How many warriors will you field?"

"Over a thousand. My scouts will be invaluable, as they can spy among our enemies to forewarn their tactics."

On March 24, Cristóbal marched from Isabela with Bartolomé and Hojeda and two hundred of the healthiest settlers, twenty horsemen, twenty dogs, and Guacanagarí's warriors and scouts, intent on conquering the Indians' armies before they descended on Isabela. Two days later, on the flat Yaque floodplain, his men engaged a vastly larger army of Haiti's peoples, and routed them. Those toting harquebuses decimated spear bearers, and crossbowmen annihilated arrow slingers. The cavalry drove all to flight, and the hounds ripped their victims to shreds. Guacanagarí's warriors infiltrated their opponents' ranks and smote them in crossfire. The Christian refrain that for each Christian slain a hundred Indians should die was more than satisfied, and corpses lay everywhere.

As victory emerged, Cristóbal urgently dispatched Hojeda with seventy footmen, a few horsemen and dogs, and a portion of Guacanagarí's scouts and warriors to march east to attack the army amassed near Fort Concepción. It was too late to rescue the fort—a band of Manicoatex's lieutenants had already destroyed it, sneaking at night around Guaricano to torch it without triggering a confrontation with Guarionex's warriors. Uxmatex's scouts tracked Hojeda's advance from its inception, and, when Hojeda's army halted for the night nearby Guaricano, Uxmatex and Manicoatex resolved to entrap it. That night, they split their army into five squadrons and surrounded Hojeda's encampment, stationing themselves and the largest squadron atop a hillside with a strategic view.

The next day, March 27, the hostilities commenced with a bloodcurdling war cry, and the five squadrons rushed inward. Hojeda and his men retreated into a defensive circle, and in desperation they ripped apart the bohíos they'd commandeered for the night to make a rampart to hide behind. For much of the day, they were trapped, nearly vanquished. For the first time, Christian wounds and casualties abounded.

But most of the battlefield was flat, and Hojeda eventually ordered his horsemen to charge back, and Manicoatex's warriors were lanced attempting to overturn the horses. Yet again, harquebus, crossbow, cavalry, and dogs ultimately prevailed, and Hojeda's troops freed themselves. Most of Manicoatex's warriors then dispersed and fled, and pursuit followed.

As night fell, Manicoatex and Uxmatex forlornly recognized that—whether they'd won the battle or not—they'd lost the war. In the following days, Hojeda's soldiers captured both of them.

Seminal battle in Magua. Panel from cover page of Herrera's *Historia General*, vol. 2, 1601.

Isabel and Fernando, Decisions and Nondecision, *Madrid, March–April 1495*

As the battle raged, in late March, Antonio de Torres's four slave ships approached Madeira, five weeks after departing Isabela. The fleet had suffered two weeks skirting east along Española's coast, bucking headwinds, merely to attain Boriquén, where it had veered northeast, encountering increasingly colder weather and inclement seas. Most of the 550 slaves aboard then had grown severely ill, and Michele da Cuneo observed they were unaccustomed to the European winter. Whether it was the winter, or diseases transmitted by Torres' crews, the fleet's rats, or introduced on the layover at Madeira, some two hundred of the slaves perished—and their bodies were thrown overboard—before April 7, when the fleet anchored in Cádiz.

Fonseca, newly promoted to the bishopric of Badajoz, promptly dispatched a horseman to the sovereigns in Madrid, alerting that Torres had arrived—bearing letters from Colón, Bernal de Pisa as prisoner, more haggard voyagers deserting Española, and some 350 Indian slaves, half of whom were ill.

As the fleet approached Cádiz, Isabel and Fernando anxiously anticipated its return but knew not when, and they continued to press Fonseca to prepare another resupply fleet for prompt departure to Española. They also accepted Juanoto Berardi's recommendation that private enterprise be introduced in the Indies, although not as he proposed, and sought to better incent their subjects' gold collection, although retaining their right to all gold the Indians traded on Española.

On April 10, as Fonseca's horseman galloped, the sovereigns issued a pronouncement permitting Castilians both to emigrate to Española as unsalaried freemen and to explore and trade in the Indies. Emigrants would be provisioned by the sovereigns for one year and receive a hereditary land allotment on which they could farm their own crops and livestock. They also were entitled to a third of the gold they mined, remitting two-thirds to the sovereigns, as well as the entirety of whatever else they traded for, remitting a tax of one-tenth. The pronouncement shied from cancelling the salaries of those already on Española, which the sovereigns ordered Fonseca to pay relatives in Spain, and allowed them also to retain a small portion of the gold they mined. Castilian merchants could sell provisions and merchandise to settlers in the Indies and, other than on Española, trade with Indians, subject to taxes. The sovereigns finagled Colón's entitlement to underwrite one-eighth of each ship sailing to the Indies by allowing him to underwrite an eighth ship for every seven ships sailed by others.

The sovereigns awarded Berardi a boost, granting him a lucrative contract to provision the next three fleets resupplying the Indies, four ships each, including those Fonseca then was arranging. As for the courtier to be entrusted to probe Colón's fitness, Isabel and Fernando opted for one versed in politics and intrigue rather than a general, selecting Juan Aguado. Juan, the provisioner of their household who'd returned from Española with Margarite and Buil in 1494, already was familiar with the criticisms leveled.

On the morning of April 12, Isabel and Fernando then delighted to learn that Torres had arrived at Cádiz with four ships, apparently brimming with Indian captives. That afternoon, they dispatched a horseman back to Fonseca, summoning Torres and Pisa to Madrid and directing Fonseca to sell the Indians as slaves as best he could.

◻ ◻ ◻

That evening, Isabel and Fernando lingered alone at the royal palace's chapel, exhausted from a day of considering both their Italian war and alliances and the reordering of the Indies business, excited that soon they'd receive fresh word of the latter's progress. But both beheld the depiction of Christ on the altar and were reminded that his judgment extended to their conduct, and they realized that they'd erred, carelessly and without evil intent, but seriously nonetheless.

"We never told him he could enslave Indians!" Isabel whispered hoarsely. "We told him he couldn't even enslave the Caribes until he wrote again to convince us." She flushed with remorse. "The Indians were to be our subjects!"

Fernando nodded gravely and grew distrustful. "I trust he's sent an explanation."

"We must revoke Fonseca's authority to sell these people until we understand more," Isabel exclaimed, affronted and raising her voice, ashamed that a lust for revenue had gotten the better of her Christian decision making.

"Let's not be hasty twice. We must think this through."

Over the next three days, husband and wife met frequently to discuss the captives' enslavement and sale, sometimes with advisors and clerics but often alone, beyond the record of court chroniclers and history. Both recognized the pope had approved their conquest of Indian territory without also approving the Indians' enslavement, and both understood they held the temporal power to prohibit enslavement of Indians, if they wished. Isabel repined Cisneros's absence and the want of his advice.

"The Indians aren't hostile to Christ, as are Mohammedans and Jews," Isabel observed in a private moment. "Colón has advised so, repeatedly." She reflected on current church doctrines. "So those captives open to Christianity shouldn't be enslaved. Our duty is to convert them."

"But there are circumstances permitting enslavement," Fernando responded. "As in the Canaries, justification may be that the captives warred against our conquest."

"We might be comfortable with that," Isabel admitted. Yet her unease simmered. "But Colón has assured—time and again—that the Indians are timid and cowardly. What if he's simply corralled them like sheep, seizing the unwary and innocent?"

Fernando shrugged and thought out loud. "Perhaps the captives include flesh eaters. Many argue that flesh eating alone justifies enslavement, both to cure and punish the depravity."

"We have been told they are Indians, not Caribes." Isabel studied the altar cross. "What else would justify this sale?"

"Some returning from Española counsel the Indians are inferior, not human, and may be enslaved by those superior," Fernando observed, shaking his head.

"Naked and inferior, but we know them human." Isabel bristled. "We've already embraced and baptized six of them, serving as godparents. The argument is insincere."

"João and the Portuguese aren't concerned with sincerity," Fernando dryly observed, rolling his eyes. "Your uncle Henrique always said that enslavement benefits the heathen, who gives a life of servitude in return for a life with Christ."*

"The argument is profane," Isabel uttered in disgust. While a converso deserved to be burned at the stake for denying Christ, the Jews expelled from her kingdoms, and conquered Mohammedans

*Portugal's Prince Henrique (the "Navigator"), Isabel's great-uncle.

enslaved, she believed an obedient heathen entitled to receive Christ without submission to slavery. "We offer Christ freely. The pope demands missionaries, not slave traders."

Fernando nodded, and the two were silent, staring at the altar cross briefly.

"My Queen, most of our advisors are looking to us to permit slave trading, at least of the flesh eaters. Berardi and the financiers pine for it. Colón has conceived it from the beginning. The commoners sailing to the Indies dream of manservants and maids, if not slaves and concubines. If there were gold to compensate everyone, as at Mina, we could just say, 'No—bring us the gold, but no slaves, and you'll be paid in gold.'" Fernando grasped Isabel's hands. "But the gold hasn't been found—yet. There's no compensation to offset either the extraordinary expense or hardship—save slaves."

"Not all favor enslavement—some learned men and clerics believe it unlawful, as well as others." Isabel gazed into Fernando's eyes. "Including both of us, at least in our hearts." Her gaze turned to a stare. "My husband, our souls are at risk, too."

"We must leave our souls out of this. Doctrine supplies the answer. Our hands are tied. Prohibitions on our financiers must come from the church."

On April 16, Isabel and Fernando dispatched another horseman to speed to Fonseca, advising that they wanted learned men, theologians, and lawyers to advise if, in good conscience, they could sell the captives as slaves, which required reviewing the Admiral's letters to understand the basis for enslavement. Fonseca could conduct the crown's sale only on a contingent basis while the determination was made, withholding from Colón the 10 percent of sale proceeds due him under his entitlements. The Indians would be manumitted, and all sale proceeds returned, if enslavement was determined unlawful.

In Seville, the reversal stunned and disappointed the slave traders, who understood from Torres and others returning that the Indians were war captives, justly enslaved. Berardi and Vespucci selected a few Indians for training as interpreters, and they contingently sold most of those fit enough to attract the interest of buyers on the crown's behalf. Fonseca would deliver fifty to the navy for contingent enslavement in the royal galleys in payment of the navy commander's salary.

Isabel and Fernando let on that they'd appointed a commission to study the Indians' enslavement because some learned men and theologians doubted its legality—they themselves being undecided. The identities of the commissioners and the times of deliberation were undisclosed—just as if the commission never existed. Cristóbal's letter to them didn't address the justification for enslavements, but the view they were just war captives persisted.

When Torres arrived at court, the sovereigns learned that settlers in Española had taken their own slaves there, but the sovereigns took no action to prescribe those enslavements. The same war captive justification applied, and perhaps contingent manumission seemed harsh, considering the settlers' hardships, and impossible to enforce, given the enormous intervening ocean.

Disease soon took those Indians surviving the sale, whether they'd been sold or not, whether the sale would be determined lawful or not.

Queen Isabel.
Juan de Flandes, c. 1500-4.

King Fernando.
Michael Sittow, late 15th century.

Michele da Cuneo passed through Seville on his way home to Liguria, where he learned of the sovereigns' April 10 proclamation inviting emigrants and merchants to the Indies. Michele concluded King Fernando didn't expect much from the Indies anymore. He figured that Cristóbal would have to abandon everything if Bartolomé failed to find more on his contemplated voyage north than had been found in Cuba.

CRISTÓBAL AND GUARIONEX, "TREATY" IMPOSED,
Guaricano, Late March–May 1495

When Manicoatex's lieutenants torched Fort Concepción, Bakako had dreaded the peace between Admiral and Guarionex would disintegrate and his own murder, either by Haitians victorious or brothers of Haitians vanquished. But Guarionex's warriors didn't join the battles raging, and Guaricano was spared violence, other than the fort's destruction.

That quiescence abruptly ended in late March when Hojeda stormed into Guaricano, encamping his squadron and hundreds of captives at the fort's smoldering ruins, demanding that Guarionex provide the soldiers food and shelter. Bakako translated Hojeda's demands, frightened to find that Ukuti had replaced Yutowa, whose fate was unknown. That evening, Bakako spied Guarionex in council with his nitaínos and, over the next days, in audience with countless messengers arriving from throughout the island. Bakako couldn't overhear, but pain, despondency, and resignation were as palpable as the sun's noontime heat.

Admiral, Adelantado, and their soldiers then stomped into Guaricano. They'd already corralled hundreds of captives farther west to serve as settlers' slaves at Isabela. Bakako would have greeted Admiral promptly, but Admiral summoned him first.

"Has Guarionex been friend or foe?" Admiral pressed brusquely, foregoing any salutation.

"His warriors no fight."

"Does he plot resistance to us?"

Bakako shrugged, embittered by the word *us*. "I no know. But guess he talk peace with others."

That was Cristóbal's estimation, and, for an instant, he appreciated Bakako's observations and loyalty. Together, they strode to meet Hojeda and Ukuti at Guaricano's riverbank. Dozens of decapitated corpses and skulls lay in a heap.

"These are the chieftains who fought for Caonabó, brought to justice," Hojeda pronounced vindictively, pointing to the bodies. "Two remain for your decision," he added, nodding toward Manicoatex and Uxmatex, both hunched on their knees, rope bound. "The younger is the rebellion's leader, one of Caonabó's brothers, no less. The elder is Caonabó's general—who plotted Santo Tomás's siege."

Cristóbal recalled the trap Caonabó had schemed, and his eyes met Manicoatex's in a protracted glare. But Cristóbal perceived no purpose in executing the chieftain or even offering a choice of vassalage. He simply pronounced, "As your brother, you will serve me and King Fernando and Queen Isabel of Castile." He glanced at Uxmatex and was even briefer. "Behead him."

Breathless, Bakako beheld the general's shoulders shoved forward, a broadsword raised and violently thrust downward, and the general's head rolling to the side, blood streaming from the torso. Admiral's ruthless determination to destroy those that resisted petrified Bakako as much as the gore. Admiral's next command was to him.

"Inform Guarionex the rebellion has hardened my heart. I summon him to meet tomorrow to recast our relationship."

Guarionex foresaw Bakako's arrival and demand and dismissed him courteously. He retired to his ceremonial bohío, alone but for his elderly behique, who set the cemí of Yúcahu and father Cacibaquel's skull upon the ceremonial table yet again. Guarionex's councils and audiences had revealed few sought war with the pale men, and, while not unanimous, most saw submission preferable to further hostilities.

"Father, the pale men can overcome us and kill us, as Yúcahu warned," Guarionex acknowledged to Cacibaquel, whispering. "The invocation of the Guamiquina's brotherhood has failed, utterly," he admitted, wretched for his own naivete. "But we need not die, and the prophecy of extinction need not be borne out." Tears came to his eyes. "We could survive as a conquered people, suffering servitude on terms to be agreed. Perhaps forever, perhaps only until we find a way out. But I see no other course at this time."

There was silence, but for the din of crickets and tree frogs.

Guarionex wiped his eyes and invoked Yúcahu's mercy as forthrightly as he'd ever spoken to a spirit, communicating through thought alone. *Revoke your prophecy. Your people must survive, whatever hardship you place upon us.*

In the morning, Guarionex and Cristóbal met seated in the ballcourt, Bakako squatting between.

"I recognize that you haven't borne arms against me," Cristóbal allowed. "But many of the island's caciques have, and I've crushed their rebellion. My wish remains to obtain the island's gold, peacefully. But I'll no longer barter for it. Your island's peoples now must pay it to me in tribute, as subjects of King Fernando and Queen Isabel. Those who don't will be enslaved or die."

"What are the terms of this tribute?" Guarionex replied. A vision of trees bending to the hurícan flickered through his thoughts.

"Each of your subjects fourteen years or older—man and woman—must furnish a hawks' bell of gold every three months. Your vassal caciques shall collect and deliver the gold to you, which you then deliver to me. My men will conduct a census to determine each cacique's responsibility."

"That's impossible!" Guarionex cried, aghast. "There's no point in such an agreement. That quantity of gold simply can't be found in streambeds every three months."

"I don't believe you," Cristóbal retorted vehemently, affronted by the denial of the truth upon which he'd staked his enterprise. "You yourself sought to trade it, standing where you stand now, but weeks ago."

Guarionex shook his head vigorously. "Believe what you will, but that amount of gold can't be delivered. I also possess no authority to bind or cajole other supreme caciques to participate."

"I demand that you agree—and accept responsibility for payment—only where your authority extends," Cristóbal replied brusquely. "I'll impose the same terms directly upon caciques not vassal to you, and the terms I impose on Caonabó shall be steeper."

Guarionex was silent, and Cristóbal let him reflect some moments.

"What do you promise in return?" Guarionex appealed.

"What do you beg for?"

"As we agreed before—that you restrict your men to living only in their settlements. They must leave my subjects entirely alone, unmolested, free to live and worship as we always have, without denigration of our spirits. Your people may not use my people to dig for gold. We shall provide it in tribute, but not as slaves. It's an obligation, not enslavement."

Cristóbal mused again that it didn't much matter what Guarionex wanted or conceived, as he had no intent of observing any restriction that impeded conquest. Yet Guarionex's requests were similar to those of conquered peoples everywhere, including infidel and Christians subjugated by the other on terra firma, and they didn't impede his immediate objective. The use of the Indian chieftains to collect the gold from their subjects allowed him to minimize the number of his own salaried men necessary to garrison on the island and might even reduce the frictions between peoples. Cristóbal nodded his approval, summarily signaling their audience concluded.

That afternoon, Manicoatex was hauled before him, chained. Cristóbal related the agreement with Guarionex and imperiously folded his arms.

"Your brother incited the rebellion, and those terms aren't offered to you. You must supply a calabash of gold for your brother's kingdom every two months."

Manicoatex replied defiantly, "I'll take execution before agreeing to that."

"That wish may be granted. But before then, you'll be hauled to your brother's kingdom to behold my men as they pillage and enslave your brother's subjects—unless you so agree. Your brother's life also hangs in the balance. That'll be your choice."

⊡ ⊡ ⊡

Cristóbal soon returned to Isabela, dispatching Hojeda with Manicoatex to Maguana. In April and May, Hojeda plundered Caonabó's chiefdom as threatened and Manicoatex relented, assuming responsibility for Maguana's tribute as Cristóbal had dictated. Not all Maguanans agreed to participate, and Hojeda's men suffered frequent ambushes, to which they responded by slaughtering the Indians they found nearby, as well as pursuing the assailants.

Anacaona despaired the pale men's treatment of her husband, envisioning abominations for his comforts and diet, horrors and cruelties to coerce his submission, or worse. She despised beholding her brother-in-law in chains, as well his shame and ignominy on his release, but she was relieved to avoid the burden and stigma of his tribute obligation, allowing that men's arrogant dismissal of a woman's rule—apparently universal—for once proved a blessing.

The chaos into which her people and society had rapidly plummeted terrified her, and Anacaona gleaned at least one meaning to her husband's instruction. Warfare—his vision—was no longer an option, and something else had to be pursued. She wept that she would discover it.

VIII
OPPRESSION, DISEASE, FAMINE

TRIBUTE EXACTED,
April–October 1495

After recasting Guarionex's subjugation, Cristóbal and Bartolomé departed Guaricano to impose tribute in the other territories Cristóbal occupied on Española, massacring resistance where they found it. Countless more villagers fled for refuge in Haiti's mountains.

Cristóbal left commander Ayala with instructions to rebuild Fort Concepción a mile south of Guaricano atop a strategic bluff closer to the hillside peak dominating the great valley. The new fort would serve as the main settlement for collecting the Cibao's gold. Cristóbal had approved the fort's new site, enchanted by its gushing spring and temperate airs, conceiving that the outpost wouldn't have an equal anywhere in the world, including Mina. He would reminisce of this enchantment later in life.

Over the next week, Guarionex established Cristóbal's tribute among his vassal caciques and subjects. Villagers readily understood the concept, since caciques had always received food in tribute from their subjects for reapportionment among all, as well as a portion of gold from the annual gold homage, and the human chain for collecting tribute already existed. But searching for gold dramatically altered everyone's daily life, diverting countless hours and effort from producing food to that search. Men were accustomed to digging streambed gold during the gold homage, but that lasted only two or three weeks a year, and the remainder of the year they hunted and fished daily. Women were responsible for farming, and, while a husband might satisfy a wife's tribute, many women were forced to search for gold rather than plant the fresh yuca and other crops critical for future harvests. Villagers were robbed of the vigor necessary to provide for themselves, and their tribute payments were satisfied most readily by relinquishing gold jewelry and gold pieces torn from ancestral face masks, robbing their most cherished possessions.

Taínos gathering gold tribute. Oviedo's *Historia General*, 1535, lam. 2.

After two months, Guarionex knew he and his subjects would fail their tribute obligation by the end of the third month. He summoned

Bakako, who had relocated with his wife and naborias to a new bohío close by the new fort.

"The Guamiquina's tribute can't be satisfied—just as I warned him," Guarionex pronounced. "What will he do when I fail to make the first payment?"

Bakako shook his head. "The Guamiquina will demand the gold."

"His men hunger. What will he say if I propose to pay him in food instead?"

"I wouldn't propose food." Bakako hesitated, terrified of counseling about Admiral rather than for Admiral, but gratified that a supreme Haitian cacique sought that of him. He sensed their common heritage and replied, "The Guamiquina may excuse the shortfall, if you explain you did your best. He well understands when he has no choice."

⧈ ⧈ ⧈

Food shortages now extended through and beyond the Camú and Yaque valleys, and famine had grown desperate in the Bajabonico watershed, near Isabela. In many places, disease or flight had decimated entire villages, and farming, hunting, and fishing had simply ceased. The men at Isabela had to scavenge much farther from the settlement to locate villages capable of providing cazabi, and Cristóbal turned to Guacanagarí—even more distant—to meet the shortfall.

As he marched as conqueror, Cristóbal discovered his route increasingly constrained by the absence of Indian food to support his men and that the Indians' own hunger had grown acute. He observed that everywhere he went famine had killed some Christians and countless Indians. In places, Indians were dying at an incredible pace. When he visited the Cibao, he concluded it was the worst affected and that most of its Indians had starved to death. He attributed the famine to the Indians' own decision to halt growing crops to drive his settlement away. His abiding concern was that tribute payments would be diminished by the deaths and population decline, which appeared to be accelerating.

In July, Cristóbal returned to Guaricano to collect the first payment due, and he conducted his audience with Guarionex courteously but firmly, with Bakako and Wasu present, Wasu now squatting at Cristóbal's side. It was obvious the gold items proffered failed the hawks' bells required.

"You must fulfill the shortfall promptly," Cristóbal warned. "This can't become a precedent. You must do better for your king and queen."

"I can provide only so much," Guarionex replied. "You must understand that our food production suffers as my people hunt for gold—they have less time to attend to crops, and many are too tired to sow or hunt." He disregarded Bakako's counsel. "If I were to pay you tribute in food rather than gold, I could farm a garden stretching from the north coast to the south, and no one would hunger—neither your people nor mine."

Cristóbal frowned, considering the offer disingenuous. "Our understanding is for gold."

"I told you there isn't enough gold to satisfy your requirement," Guarionex responded. "All would be far better off if my people turned to producing what they can in abundance—yuca, mahisi, boniata." He spread his arms widely, ushering comprehension of the famine's exceptionality. "Haiti's peoples have never hungered before, ever."

Cristóbal shook his head, adamantly refusing that his assurances to king and queen be undone.

"You must understand there are many caciques—including vassals of mine right here in the valley—where gold simply can't be dug," Guarionex persisted. "Imposing your tribute on them will drive them to starvation without producing anything for the king and queen. You must accept leniency that reflects the capacity for tribute of each cacique."

Bakako studied Cristóbal ponder the request, recollecting Cristóbal's collapse at the end of the Cuban exploration. Admiral now appeared entirely merciless, utterly unmoved by the Haitians' famine and death, except to the extent those conditions affected the riches he could extract, pitiless and shameless for the Haitian society's demise.

Cristóbal recognized that he'd never contemplated mining the valley. "I'll consider receiving cotton or peppers from caciques whose territory holds no gold," he relented. "But not from you or Manicoatex."

That evening, Bakako invited Wasu to stay in his bohío, and they spoke late into the night.

"Where's Ukuti?" Bakako inquired.

"Near death," Wasu replied. "Admiral's men serve him food and water daily, but he worsens. His entire family perished."

"Have you been sick?"

"Yes, weeks ago. I thought I'd die, but it passed." Wasu stared at the ground. "I lost my family, as well."

Bakako embraced him and said he was sorry, momentarily tortured by visions of intimate moments with Niana and her cradling their newborn in death. The memories were unbearable, and he sought relief by resuming conversation.

"Where has Admiral taken you?"

"Mostly to meet caciques along the coast. I accompanied him to meet Guacanagarí."

"To obtain food?"

"Yes, and to impose tribute."

Astonished, Bakako recalled translating for Admiral and Guacanagarí aboard the *Niña* as Admiral promised everlasting friendship for the rescue from the *Santa María*'s demise. "What was Guacanagarí's reaction?"

"He thought he'd be treated differently than the others, but Admiral gave him no choice," Wasu responded. "His subjects now suffer, just as all of us. His warriors who fought with Admiral have grown ill, as have their wives and children." Wasu sighed uneasily. "What happened to Yutowa?"

"The pale man Hojeda would know, but I haven't asked him. Perhaps Yutowa's died." Bakako silently rued the possibility of suicide. "But I suspect he's wandering to escape the pale men."

"Which master do you now serve?" Wasu boldly asked.

Bakako was affronted, perceiving an insult intended, as the decision to relocate his bohío to obtain the pale men's protection was transparently his own. Wasu well knew Bakako would serve Admiral first. "Remember, I'm not Haitian, as you," Bakako replied coldly. "I haven't forsaken my people."

"I meant no insult, Bakako. We must each make our own choices. But you are now a Haitian cacique, not a Guanahanían fisherman. Perhaps you have more choices than you think."

◻ ◻ ◻

Cristóbal soon departed Guarionex to demand tribute from caciques in the Yaque valley, and Bartolomé marched south to Caonabó's Maguana, where attacks by hostile Indians persisted. They instituted a system whereby each Indian satisfying his or her three-month quota was issued a copper token to hang about the neck, so all knew who remained obligated or deserving of punishment. When accepting tribute in cotton, Cristóbal imposed a periodic requirement of twenty-five pounds per subject.

Bartolomé's thrashing of resisters typically was harsher than Cristóbal's. He apprehended Caonabó's youngest brother for inciting rebellion—apparently with Manicoatex's tacit approval—and dispatched the brother in chains to Isabela, together with Manicoatex's ten-year-old son, taken as hostage to quash the chieftain's ongoing disloyalty. They were chained in the slave pens by the storehouse, apart from Caonabó.

Cristóbal resolved to build new forts to facilitate tribute's collection in every region subjugated. Isolated ambushes of his men continued in most regions, and the forts would garrison soldiers to dispense exemplary punishment, including enslavements to serve settlers. His soldiers' corporal punishments now frequently exhibited a wanton cruelty or bestiality well beyond his and Bartolomé's wishes and that they failed to prevent.

For an interlude in June, both conqueror and conquered ceased attending to tribute, as a tremendous storm ravaged Haiti. The conquerors adopted the conquered's word for it—*huricán*—as the storm's might and fury so exceeded their experience that a new word was appropriate. The hurricane uprooted trees and shelters throughout the island, including shacks at Isabela, and three of the four ships anchored at Isabela sank, the *Niña* alone surviving. Some settlers believed Satan intended to confound the baptism of Indians. Some villagers warmed that their own spirits sought to blow the pale men away. Gardens were ruined or abandoned, and Haiti's famine worsened.

After the hurricane, Cristóbal and Bartolomé resumed invading about the island to compel tribute payments. Bartolomé's voyage north to locate Cathay, as well an exploration south for a great landmass, had been postponed in favor of crushing Indian resistance. The ships' loss now precluded those diversions, although Cristóbal ordered Isabela's artisans to construct two caravels, designed as the *Niña*.

Bartolomé optimistically estimated tribute was then owed by 1,100,000 subjects at least fourteen years old in the territories conquered—principally Magua, Maguana, and Marien—based in part on each cacique's acknowledgment of his own responsibility. Cristóbal perceived that in places only a quarter of the original population remained because the rest of those surviving had fled to the mountains, and he consented that tribute payments be reduced to three times a year.

Hurricane. Theodor de Bry, 1594. John Carter Brown Library, rec. no. 09887-10.

The physical suffering, loss of loved ones and homes, and extraordinary dislocation of daily life resulted in abject misery. Unburied corpses littered the landscape, and the stench of death was ever present.

Cristóbal completed his next letter to Isabel and Fernando on October 15, 1495, while collecting tribute from Manicoatex in Maguana. He advised that he had subjugated the entirety of Española and was continuing to discover vast gold deposits and collect gold paid in tribute to them. Massacres weren't mentioned, but Cristóbal admitted that a self-inflicted famine was ravaging the Indian population and threatened payments. He assured that he hoped to earn not a little profit if the Indians survived the famine, as gold payments then would surge and fewer salaried men could collect it. Taking aim at the sovereigns' reluctance on slavery, he wrote that the Indians he'd enslaved and dispatched to Spain had been loved by the Lord, having escaped starvation in favor of the opportunity of conversion.

Cristóbal and Aguado,
October–November 1495

Berardi failed timely to prepare the first four ships he'd contracted—stretched too thin supplying Lugo's Tenerife conquest—and Isabel and Fernando, exasperated, relied on Fonseca to procure them. The fleet finally sailed from Cádiz on August 5, with Juan Aguado as captain, bearing letters from them instructing Cristóbal to not withhold food from anyone but those worthy of the death penalty and permitting him to send persons home in order to limit Española's salaried payroll to five hundred. Their instructions to Aguado bid he inform Cristóbal they hadn't made up their minds on a slave trade since the theologians were still reviewing the matter. The ships arrived at Isabela while Cristóbal was in Maguana.

Aguado—a Sevillian, proud of years of household service for the queen—debarked with a marked display of royal prerogative, insulting Bartolomé at the pier and soon criticizing the town's minor officials loyal to Cristóbal. He arrested some sailors and let on that he'd returned to Española in an elevated capacity to judge everyone's fate, including the Admiral's. Bartolomé dispatched a horseman to warn Cristóbal of Aguado's apparent mission and critical outlook, undoubtedly warped by Buil and Margarite, and admonished return to Isabela.

But Aguado arranged his own entourage and interpreter and departed south on horseback, having previously traversed the route to the Cibao. He informed caciques in the Vega Real that the Admiral would be replaced by a successor instructed to treat them better. Manicoatex rejoiced when the word reached him, and he pined for Cristóbal's speedy demise and tribute's elimination. Cristóbal met Aguado in the valley and was courteous and deferential, extending the resources necessary to investigate the settlement. But Cristóbal was forthright that he ruled as viceroy and governor until the sovereigns decided otherwise, and he rued that it was essential to return to court to defend his enterprise before Aguado lambasted it.

Aguado passed weeks interrogating witnesses about the Admiral's conduct and was deluged with criticisms, particularly about the Genoese brothers' dispensing of scarce food unfairly to their supporters. Most—including those supporters—implored him to approve their return to Castile. Incontrovertibly, the settlement was famished, sick, and unruly, and those healthy were roaming the island largely to loot the Indians' food, commit other crimes, and enslave those they could.

But the hopes of settlers pining to return to Castile, and of Haitians for the Guamiquina's demise, soon were obliterated. The Lord, or Guabancex, hurled a second hurricane upon Isabela, destroying Aguado's entire fleet, sparing but the indomitable *Niña* again, rendering both return and demise impossible until at least one of the caravels under construction was fit.

Cristóbal grimly recognized that Isabela was no longer suited to be the seat of his enterprise—the territory around it held no gold, and the Indians at the Bajabonico had died or fled, so Indian food and labor was unavailable. An enclosed port was essential given the recurrence of hurricanes. He'd learned from Manicoatex and other caciques that gold deposits abounded along a river the Indians called the Jaina, which entered the sea on Española's southern coast, and Cristóbal dispatched two loyal men south to investigate.* He prayed the information wasn't merely a ruse to deflect tribute's collection.

Lugo, Benitomo, and Bentor, Tenerife's Conquest, *Late 1495*

On November 2, Alonso de Lugo led his small army to debark on Tenerife at Santa Cruz and united with the troops in the two garrisons established in February, amassing together fifteen hundred foot soldiers and a hundred cavalry—roughly the same troop count as the prior year, but more heavily armed. Fernando Guanarteme, the Gran Canarian chieftain previously baptized by the sovereigns, accompanied with two dozen Canarian warriors. Alonso quickly affirmed alliances with those chieftains who'd submitted to the sovereigns' rule. He brought his army onto a plain surrounding a lagoon north of Santa Cruz (now San Cristóbal de La Laguna), where the cavalry could maneuver, searching to engage Benitomo, chief of the Taoro.

Benitomo perceived the size of his own army—five thousand warriors, including those of allied chieftains—ample to vanquish the invaders, as he had before, but without the advantage of a ravine in which to entrap them. On November 14, he rejected Alonso's requirement that he submit to Isabel and Fernando's rule or die and engaged the battle. Spaniards, Canarians, and Guanches, including Alonso, Fernando Guanarteme, and Benitomo, fought hand to hand for hours, desperately, and the plain grew littered with the bodies and blood of all peoples. But as the afternoon waned, Benitomo was beheaded, and his army routed—spears, clubs, and stones no match for cavalry, harquebus, and crossbow. Those captured were enslaved and shipped to Spain for sale. Alonso dispatched Fernando Guanarteme to compel the Taoros' surrender by Benitomo's son and successor, Bentor. Bentor refused.

Alonso didn't rest, and over the next weeks his army pursued the Taoro and other hostile chiefdoms, including in a victorious Christmas Day battle in the ravine where he'd been routed the prior year. Victories and enslavements were accomplished far more easily than expected, as the pestilence arriving in February had permeated

*Francisco de Garay and Miguel Diaz.

the island, decimating not only potential warriors but everyone, including shepherds and fishermen, with hunger weakening most. Benitomo's death and the enslavements broke the islanders' fierce love of independence, and most of the last resisting chieftains chose vassalage over slavery. Bentor chose neither, but to hurl himself from a high precipice in ritual suicide.

As the new year dawned, Alonso gleaned the enslavement and sale of those yet resisting wouldn't cover the conquest's expenses and that the sale of some of the peoples with whom he'd made peace treaties would be necessary, as well.

Fray Pané and Guarionex, First Lessons in Christianity,

Guaricano, Late 1495

Bakako's boyhood aspirations hadn't even fantasized the minor chieftainship he owed Admiral. But Wasu's last question vexed him, and Bakako often lay sleepless brooding whether goodness, and his soul's fate, obliged that he abet Guarionex against Admiral, short of open rebellion. When he dozed, he dreamed of spurning his post as remora—whose servitude never wavered—by allowing Admiral's prey to escape the doom intended. When he awoke, he returned to the nightmare—Guarionex's people were fleeing and dying, for which Admiral was remorseless, and there wasn't any conceivable step he might take to alter that. Sharing their fate loomed as the only consequence of disobedience.

Fray Pané saw the Indians' suffering, and he prayed earnestly that their conversion to the faith would rejuvenate them to harmony within the Lord's fold and under the Spanish yoke and custom to be imposed. He also perceived as the Lord's wish that he and his followers live among their potential flock, rather than at Fort Concepción, and little risk that Guarionex would harm them. He resolved to learn more Taíno, understanding that as Guarionex's dialect.

Guarionex was as keen to study the pale men's spirits as Pané was to teach, although he sought not only to understand why and whether to worship them but how to defeat them if necessary. He awarded Pané a bohío for residence in Guaricano and plots for a garden and to worship, permitting the construction of a so-called "church" of wood and reed, its "altar" sanctified with a statue of the Christ-spirit. When the day came for Guarionex's first lesson, he summoned Bakako to translate, and the three men met at the church, together with Fray Leudelle. Within, Guatícabanu was reciting an invocation at the altar, addressing his brothers solemnly in the pale men's tongue.

"I hope to teach you that devotion in Spanish someday," Pané announced in Catalan, addressing Guarionex and pointing at Guatícabanu. "We call it the Apostles' Creed. It summarizes everything one must understand, and Diego knows it well." He nodded toward Bakako to translate.

"Then it's a good place to begin," Guarionex replied courteously but doubtfully, as he expected the learning lacked comprehension of the spirits he knew. "What's the meaning of Apostles' Creed?"

"The apostles were twelve disciples Christ dispatched to preach God's Word, and the creed is the Word's core truths."

Pané invited Guarionex inside the church, where they sat facing each other, Bakako at their side. Guatícabanu and his brothers were astonished by the preeminent cacique's presence and awkwardly rose to depart, but Pané instructed them to remain and heed the lesson. Guarionex surmised that the pale men's spirits were meant for rulers and commoners alike—just as Taíno spirits—and the inclusiveness comforted him.

"Today we'll discuss the first three truths, speaking in your language," Pané began. "God, the Father Almighty, created heaven and earth. Jesus Christ was his only son. Christ was conceived by God's spirit and born of the Virgin Mary." Pané evaluated Guarionex's reaction, perceiving him favorably moved and inclined to accept.

Guarionex was merely astonished, struck by the first belief's wisdom of the very beginning, venturing beyond an explanation for the peoples living and the sea to encompass the sky and earth's origin, which he'd understood existed forever—timeless, without beginning.

"Do you believe in a supreme spirit?" Pané asked, nodding to indicate he assumed Guarionex did.

"I do. My people believe that spirit is Yaya, who lives in the sky, as other spirits. Where does your God live?"

"In Heaven above," Pané replied, pointing to the sky. "Perhaps you already believe in God by a different name?" he encouraged, eager for Guarionex to so recognize.

"What does your God look like?" Guarionex responded, instead irritated to be led.

"God created man in his image, but he is invisible."

Guarionex was surprised by the parallel. Yaya also resembled man yet was invisible. "But your God's son appears just as a man. So, your Christ is both spirit and man?" He observed Pané's nod and was intrigued that a people so sophisticated believed such a combination occurred.

"That's the essence," Pané pronounced. "God is the almighty spirit in Heaven. His son, Christ the Lord, is also a man, and lived on earth. Men and women felt his touch."

"Christ has pale skin?" Guarionex probed.

"People saw him," Pané replied cautiously. "His mission on earth was for all people, including yours. Christ invites all peoples to his fold."

"What's God and Christ's relationship to the omnipotent Yúcahu?" Guarionex pushed. "Yúcahu blesses us with cazabi from the land and fish from the sea."

"Christ is the Lord who blesses all people with bread and fish."

"Are you saying Yúcahu doesn't?"

"You must decide that yourself when our teaching progresses," Pané replied, eschewing confrontation, conscious the chieftain's spirituality and intellect far exceeded that of Guatícabanu. Bringing him to the faith would be a greater challenge. Guatícabanu had embraced God simply on learning that he'd made heaven and earth, but Guarionex firmly possessed a religion to undo. "I assure you, all blessings and trials of men come from the Lord Christ."

"It is Yúcahu who has provided for and protected my people since they emerged to populate the earth," Guarionex replied softly, in dissent, yet signaling he also wished to avoid contention. He mused, taken by the confluence of similarities and contrasts. "Yúcahu is spirit, not man, and born of a woman spirit, but fatherless. Tell me of Christ's mother."

"The Virgin Mary is blessed, watchful for those in danger, generous to those in need, and revered among women for her womb's fruit. She forgives sinners who repent."

Guarionex was dumbfounded by the similarity of the Virgin's powers to those of Attabeira, Yúcahu's mother. "But you say the Virgin Mary is woman, not spirit. As woman, how does she award these blessings? Is she a chieftain?" He pondered whether the Virgin Mary might, in truth, be none other than Attabeira.

"The Virgin is unique, conceived free of sin," Pané replied.

Bakako dutifully translated but grasped that Guarionex wouldn't understand the last strange concept—that all men were sinners who needed forgiveness. He added for Guarionex's benefit that sin would be explained in another lesson.

Guarionex and Pané discussed the first truths for an hour, amicably but with growing tension, as Guarionex gathered that Pane's spirits ultimately would be taught as replacement to his own rather than supplementary. Pané wasn't dismayed but grew firm that the pale men's spirits were the true spirits, albeit flexible that parting with others wasn't essential—until Guarionex was so convinced. To close the lesson, he invited Guatícabanu and his brothers to recite the entire Apostles' Creed in Spanish, with Bakako translating into Taíno.

Guarionex chafed, skeptical the youths understood much of the foreign tongue they chanted, perceiving instead that they adored the pale behique's novel clothing and somber ritual and the pale men's superior know-how and possessions. He doubted the youths even realized they were dishonoring the spirits their people knew to be true.

◘ ◘ ◘

Within a week, Guarionex returned for the second lesson. With Bakako translating, Pané related the creed's second three truths.

"The ruler Pontius Pilate punished Christ," he began. "Christ was crucified on the cross, suffered, and died for all men's sake. He was buried and, on the third day, was resurrected to rise to Heaven." Pané pointed to the altar cross. "That's Christ dying on the cross.

The Admiral plants crosses everywhere we settle to remind us daily of Christ's presence."

"Why would a chieftain punish your supreme spirit?" Guarionex pressed.

"Pilate refused to believe that Christ is the Lord, and he heeded the Jews, who sought Christ's death." Pané realized too much begged explanation, and he sought to simplify. "Christ died on the cross according to God's design, to atone the sins of all men who believe in him. All men sin in their daily lives, but by repenting and accepting Christ, their sins are forgiven."

"Why would a father plan his son's death?" Guarionex puzzled, recalling Yaya's murder of his own son for disobedience and in self-defense. "Did Christ disobey God?"

"Christ didn't disobey God," Pané replied. "God sacrificed him so that you and I may be saved—so that our souls live with God in Heaven after death, in eternal bliss. The souls of all Christ's followers live there."

Guarionex was incredulous, recalling his prior conversation with the Guamiquina. "For my people, the souls of those who do good in life continue after death in a good place. For your people, that blessing depends on the Christ-spirit's death and belief in him?"

Pané sympathized with the chieftain's moral expectation that the soul warranted a blissful afterlife following a life's worth of good conduct, but was firm. "My friend, being good, alone, is not enough to ensure your soul has everlasting joy. Christ requires that you believe in him."

"What happens to the souls of pale men who don't?"

"Depending on their sins, their souls roast in eternal fire in a place we call Hell, suffering everlasting agony." Pané hesitated, uncertain whether to deliver a stronger warning. "Christ loves those who believe in him, but those who oppose may face Christ's wrath." Guarionex revealed no affront, and Pané stepped further. "Christ protects the Christians who seek to spread his Word against the evils wrought by those like Pilate, who deny the Word."

Guarionex suppressed his affront and relished that the behique had revealed critical information—the Christ-spirit was both beneficent and vengeful. He frowned and rejoined, "Does the Christ-spirit love those who loot, rape, murder, and conquer simply because they believe in him?"

⌑ ⌑ ⌑

Pané was stung by Guarionex's criticism of the conduct of Española's Spaniards—which he knew to be true—and he grasped that the threat of damnation was counterproductive, at least with the chieftain. He invited Guarionex and Bakako to the third lesson, keen to emphasize the everlasting glory of admittance to God's kingdom.

"Christ was resurrected from death to rise to sit in Heaven at God's right hand," he explained, relating the creed's final truths. "Soon, at a time unannounced, Christ will return to earth to make final judgment on the living and the dead. Those who have believed in God, Christ, the resurrection, the church, baptism, and the forgiveness of sins will be blessed with life everlasting in Heaven."

Bakako translated, fearful whether Christ detected his own insincerity in faith.

Proudly, Pané introduced a reward for faith. "When a person understands that the creed summarizes the sole truth and that Christ is the one Lord, he then is welcomed and reborn into Christ's fold—baptized, we say—in community with Christ and all other believers, with a new name." He pointed to Bakako and smiled proudly. "Diego was baptized and reborn with his Christian name, through the grace of none other than King Fernando and Queen Isabel."

Bakako drew breathless, mortified that Guarionex undoubtedly detected his insincerity, as well as betrayal of the spirits he and Guarionex knew true.

Guarionex reflected that Christ's return to earth was unexceptional. Yúcahu—as most spirits—passed freely and often from earth to the sea beneath and the heavens above and resided in the heavens. But the baptism and name mutation, and Christ's acute focus on the judgment affecting the soul's afterlife, perturbed him. He was angered by the allusion to Christ's dominance or exclusiveness.

"I've always understood worship of spirits as essential for their alliance and my soul's fate. But why does worshipping your Christ-spirit involve such rebirth and change?" Guarionex glowered, recalling the Guamiquina's promise that he'd remain his people's ruler. "My people honor me as Guarionex, as well by titles for territory I rule. Were I to consider your spirits, I wouldn't want a new name." Guarionex rankled that he'd never consent to be known by a pale man's name.

"Belief in Christ is the key to baptism, not the reborn name." Pané shied from confrontation again, appreciating Guarionex's affront and that baptism's rituals could be discussed later, after belief roosted. He expected the Admiral eagerly would seek the chieftain's baptism as a beacon for his subjects' conversion and permit deviations from Christian practice. He turned to Bakako. "I've heard Diego's intimates refer to him by a prior name—Bakako, I believe."

Bakako's mortification grew, and he saddened that few remained who called him that.

Guarionex nodded, satisfied with Pané's retreat, and probed further. "I understand Christ judges conduct for admittance to Heaven, but I have questions. What does he do for his worshippers besides judging them? How does he provide for them during their lives?"

"God gave men the earth to live on and seed, fowl, fish, and beasts to nurture, eat, and rule. Christ rewards his followers with these fruits of the earth."

Guarionex was pleased Christ functioned as Yúcahu and other spirits, but Christ's blessings gave humans an unusual ascendance in the natural order. "So, men are meant to rule fish and fowl? A shark can feed on a man, just as a man feeds on a shark. Men can eat fish, but if they take too many from the same place, the fish will be gone." Guarionex was surprised by Pané's misunderstanding. "Spirits rule the earth, not men, and they may cause a man to become a creature and the reverse. Men must live in harmony with the earth and its creatures."

Pané shrugged. The point didn't seem necessary to confront to win Guarionex's conversion.

"Does Christ forgive all sinners and admit them to Heaven?" Guarionex inquired.

"All baptized who confess their sins and repent may be forgiven and admitted."

"So a life of thievery doesn't preclude admittance if one confesses and repents before death?" Guarionex raised his voice gravely. "Christ forgives the rapist his rape, the murderer his murder?" He folded his arms across his chest. "What's the importance of proper conduct during life if one's soul enters Heaven with but a repentance?"

Bakako relished translating and eyeing the behique wax even paler, but he puzzled silently whether Guarionex misunderstood Christ and the pale men. *Was Christ so blindly forgiving? Or was the outrage that the pale men didn't consider raping or murdering those they called "Indians" as sins necessary to be forgiven?*

"Our spirits are not so forgiving," Guarionex exhorted, before Pané could respond. "If one steals, rapes, or murders, they offer no forgiveness for one's soul thereafter, nor should they." His visage steeled to scorn. "Do pale men worship Christ because he absolves them of all sins? If I were to honor Christ and then slay all the pale men on Haiti, would Christ admit my soul to Heaven upon a confession?"

Pané had heard enough. "If I teach you Christ's Word, you would never do that."

Guarionex perceived Pané's simple intellect and inability to transcend his own vantage to appreciate its duplicity. He calmed himself, resolved yet again to maintain civility, and posed the practical question whose answer he craved.

"Does the Christ-spirit seek my people's destruction?" Guarionex demanded, sensing father Cacibaquel's presence and vigor. "There is murder, pestilence, and death everywhere his cross rises—and nowhere else."

"No! You don't understand!" Pané exclaimed, raising his arms. "Christ welcomes your people. You must cast aside resistance and learn to obey him. King Fernando and Queen Isabel cherish your friendship. Their greatest wish is that you and your subjects join the community of all Christ's followers."

Guarionex appreciated the response as Pané's sincere understanding of the Christ-spirit, regardless of its truth or falsity. It was premature to hold Christ as an enemy, although his followers were.

"I understand the Apostles' Creed," Guarionex replied courteously. "I wish to learn more of Christ. Let's meet regularly."

Pané flushed with triumph. "The Lord is pleased, and we will."

Pané remembered the Admiral's instruction. "You must also tell me of the spirits your people worship."

"You wish to worship them as well?"

Pané shook his head. "We want to understand the extent you already perceive the truth by a different name."

◘ ◘ ◘

As year-end approached, Cristóbal visited Fort Concepción to collect the tribute due, meeting with Ayala and Bakako to review Guarionex's loyalty and, with Pané, the missionary effort and study of Indian idolatries.

"The Lord's work is progressing," Pané related. "More than a dozen men and boys are receiving lessons daily. Most can recite the Apostles' Creed by memory. Guarionex takes instruction often and appears on the verge of accepting God as the supreme being, and I'm learning of the Indians' crude incantations through him."

"Are any ready for baptism?" Cristóbal asked, observant of the church's requirement that adults converting must have achieved simple doctrinal understanding.

"None yet," Pané replied. "But there's a youth and his family that I expect soon will be."

Cristóbal grew somber, disappointed with both the small number of Indians receiving instruction, regardless of their enormous population, and the absence of a single conversion to report to the queen, after almost two years.

"I approve their baptisms, when you're satisfied," he responded. He doubted Guarionex's loyalty and reflected that—regardless of Christian readiness—the chieftain's conversion would compromise punishment and enslavement of him and his peoples if they resisted thereafter.

"But not Guarionex's," Cristóbal ordered. "You must revert for my express approval before baptizing him."

BAKAKO, IDENTITY,
Guaricano

As weeks passed, Bakako grew more fitful. His nightmares were tormented by his traitorous service as remora and his daily routine by the relentless obliteration of his prior existence. He was greeted as Cacique Diego by virtually all about—not only pale men, but also Guarionex and hundreds of his subjects. Bakako had bid his wife and naborias to call him Bakako when outside the presence of pale men, and, while his wife still obeyed, the naborias now constantly erred, recognizing his authority founded in being Diego. One night, he dreamed of being hailed as Bakako.

Bakako, a voice called from beyond his bohío. *Bakako, it's me, Yutowa.*

Visions of Guanahaní and groveling with Yutowa on the *Santa María*'s deck as Admiral abducted them flickered through the dream.

Bakako, come outside—I've returned.

Fleeting recollections of Yutowa's fellowship supplanted the abduction, ushering a glow of camaraderie obliterating the despair of exile from Guanahaní.

Bakako, I'm desperate for food!

A tremor of desperation overtook that glow, along with a looming specter of Yutowa's and his own starvation on Haiti.

Bakako then felt the touch of a naboria on his shoulder and woke abruptly.

"Cacique Diego, your friend is outside and calls you," the naboria whispered.

Bakako, stunned and disorientated, rose to step outside into the moonlight.

"Bakako!" Yutowa exclaimed hoarsely, tears in his eyes.

Bakako trembled with an elation and astonishment far surpassing that borne of dreams or nightmares and burst into tears, too. "You've survived!" he blurted, his voice cracking and breath heaving.

The two Guanahanians embraced tightly, weeping. Bakako was alarmed by the frailty of Yutowa's frame, the deathly revelation of his skeleton beneath his flesh, and the bruises and scabs tattering his skin, horrifically pocked. He shuddered that his friend barely remained human.

"Come inside," Bakako implored. "You must drink and eat!"

With his naboria and wife's help, Bakako laid Yutowa next to the bohío's firepit and sat down to prop Yutowa's head in his lap, tenderly offering pineapple juice from a gourd. The naboria stoked the fire to provide dim illumination and warmth.

"Where have you been?" Bakako asked softly.

"Wandering alone, in the mountains," Yutowa rasped. "I'll no longer serve Admiral or the pale men."

"You assisted Caonabó's capture?"

"My last betrayal of our world's peoples," Yutowa acknowledged, his shoulders contorting in remorse. "Almost as terrible as saving Admiral from the Cubans."

"Rest," Bakako begged, frightened that his friend's angst itself would bring death, then and there. "You've done that required to survive, nothing more." He asked his wife for cazabi and tore a small piece to place at Yutowa's lips. "Eat. Did Haitians feed you?"

"My pocks frighten all away. I scrounged cazabi in the villages of the dead and dying."

"You'll now live with me, here, and you'll recover," Bakako urged, horrified by the ostracism. "My household welcomes you, and we have food."

"I won't serve Admiral!"

"You won't have to." Bakako surmised neither Admiral nor any other pale man would care, given Yutowa's pitiful state. "You'll be my nitaíno, here at my bohío."

Feebly, Yutowa bent his arm to caress Bakako's thigh. "I cherish you as my own brother, regardless of the decisions you make for yourself. You're the only family I have left."

Bakako teared again.

"How's your wife?" Yutowa asked, gazing at her.

Bakako motioned for her sit with them and replied, "Ariana is with child."

"I'm happy for you," Yutowa whispered to them both. "How's ruling as Cacique Diego?"

Bakako sadly recalled their conversation in the church garden in Cádiz and his plea that Yutowa call him Bakako. He vacillated, weighing whether to reiterate it—Yutowa being the only person remaining to whom it meant anything. "I survive," he surrendered.

Berardi and Vespucci,
Seville, October 1495–February 1496

As winter approached, Isabel and Fernando were delighted to learn of Lugo's victory on Tenerife and other favorable news from throughout their kingdoms—with one exception.

King Charles had been enraged by Fernando's establishment of an alliance against him and sorely grasped that he risked his own capture by remaining in Italy. He'd crowned himself emperor of Naples in May but then promptly fled, returning to France in October with half his army, leaving the other half to battle for honor, if not victory.

Cisneros finally had returned to court to assume the archbishopric of Toledo and vigorously cleanse the Spanish church of opulence and concubinage. Hundreds of straying friars were departing their posts in trepidation or outrage. Pope Alexander soon dispatched him an instruction to dress splendidly like a bishop rather than haggardly as a hermit.

Isabel's nemesis, Portugal's King João, had died in late October after a rule of fourteen years of peaceful but strained relations, succeeded by his cousin Manoel, as the sovereigns had hoped. João's last testament had delivered his parting retort to Isabel, referring to his cousin Juana as the queen of Portugal and Castile. Regardless, the sovereigns eagerly redoubled their efforts to prod Princess Isabel to marry Manoel.

But arrangements relating to the Indies continued to flounder and disappoint. In October, still waiting the expert determination whether Indians could be enslaved, Isabel and Fernando nevertheless credited a large sum to Juanoto Berardi in compensation for the slaves provisionally sold that April, presuming they were resisters appropriately enslaved. They were keen to provide Juanoto enabling credit to assist his arranging—at long last—the first ships he'd contracted to provide.

Unexpectedly, before those ships sailed, Berardi died suddenly in mid-December, dictating his last testament as he expired in bed, leaving his principal business associate and the will's coexecutor—Amerigo Vespucci—to liquidate the business. Isabel and Fernando had no ready recollection or impression of Vespucci, although he'd accompanied Juanoto to court several times and was one of Colón's Italian acquaintances.

Vespucci, born of the sovereigns, Fonseca, and Colón's generation (b. 1454?), was the third surviving son of a well-connected Florentine notary of modest means and had assisted Berardi's slave trading and seaborn merchant business for three years. He'd received a classical education that hadn't inspired him. On adulthood, he'd carved a niche for himself managing the meager businesses of his extended family and, more profitably, some household affairs and incidental pursuits of patriarchs of the powerful Medici family. He traded gems as agent, collected debts, and arranged whatever the patriarchs wanted fixed in the alleys of Florence, including arranging their own dalliances with concubines and others.

By 1489, the Medicis had asked Vespucci to evaluate Berardi as a trading partner in Seville, and, impressed, he'd arranged Berardi's engagement. By 1492, he'd decided his prospects were better as merchant than fixer and enlisted to serve Berardi in Seville, departing Florence, his family, and his lover and daughter for good. Within a short time, Berardi had entrusted him with responsibility, impressed by his talents as a salesman and willingness to shrewdly execute unseemly tasks without qualm. Vespucci had little use for faith and perceived trading slaves no different than trading gems.

Vespucci was delighted when Berardi's testament was read. It placed on him the undesirable responsibility of working off the debts of Berardi's failed business, but it commended him and others to Colón's service. He remained responsible for the resupply fleet poised for dispatch, providing him a platform to rise in prominence before the sovereigns, Colón, and the Andalusian merchant community.

Vespucci's resupply fleet sailed for Española on February 3, 1496. But, unfortunately for his incipient career as merchant, as well as those in Española hungering for Spanish food, five days later the ships sank in a violent storm en route to the Canaries.

IX
SOUTHERN CROSSING

PREPARATIONS, ISABELA AND MAGUANA, *February–March 10, 1496*

After dusk, Caonabó and Cristóbal sat together gazing seaward to the darkening horizon from the promontory abutting Cristóbal's residence, alone but for Wasu and Ukuti. Caonabó's wrists and ankles remained shackled so he couldn't escape into the night or murder Cristóbal. The two men had lived just feet apart for months and grown habituated and, while eschewing friendship, respectful that their intellects were commensurate and exceeded those about them, both pale and olive. Regardless, Caonabó resolutely had denied Cristóbal a single gesture of respect, and, in return, Cristóbal had denied any pity or hope that the irons would be unlocked until Caonabó submitted to Fernando and Isabel. But they had warmed to the stimulation of conversation occasionally, awaiting the completion of a caravel companion to the *Niña* to make the voyage to Spain. Cristóbal had directed careful nursing of the chieftain's ongoing bouts with pestilence—convinced his death would incite the Indians yet again and that his submission to vassalage was key to Española's final subjugation.

"My people worship their ancestors, not just spirits," Caonabó mused, puzzling on Cristóbal's daily—and sometimes hourly—spirit worship. "When I die, my soul will reunite with my father's in a great valley, where we will enjoy pleasures and comforts together." He pointed north through the gloom, toward Aniyana. "He was a Lucayan cacique. While I live, I'll always venerate him and seek his wisdom."

"It's he that urges you to resist?" Cristóbal asked, reverting bluntly but softly to the topic of subjugation. "My people honor our ancestors, too, but ancestors aren't holy, like Christ." Belatedly, Cristóbal startled that Caonabó had foreign lineage. "You weren't born on Española?"

"I wasn't born on Haiti. I was born on Aniyana, but my mother was Maguanan, and I crossed the sea as a teenager to return to her family's chiefdom." He turned to Cristóbal, responding to the first question. "My father does implore resistance—to remain free, whatever the price."

"When did you last see him?"

"He died quite a few years ago," Caonabó replied. "But I last spoke to him this morning."

Cristóbal reflected silently on his own father, Domenico, who yet survived, although they hadn't reunited for over a dozen years. Cristóbal saddened, guilty for his failure to revisit Genoa occasionally and pitiful that Domenico had been a freeman but never enjoyed freedom, forever struggling to earn enough to support his family. "My father still lives, and I think of him often to admire his example—his determination and love of family."

"Does or did he serve your Fernando and Isabel, or their ancestors?"

Cristóbal shook his head.

"How then did you rise to become Guamiquina?"

Cristóbal was startled, as his family's lineage wasn't for anyone's meddling, no less a naked, conquered prisoner's. But he gleaned the thread of Caonabó's inquiry bent on leadership's attainment, not caste. "Like yourself, I departed my father's kingdom to seek opportunity. Fernando and Isabel knighted me as their kingdom's lord to discover the route here."

"I've suspected you're from a different chiefdom than your men. They treat you as a foreigner, with less respect. They speak courteously to your face and then meanly when your back is turned. I encountered that once, but I overcame it."

Cristóbal perceived the observation sharp-witted but forward, due a retort. "Regardless of their jealousies, I've led these men to subjugate most of the island's princes—not only yourself and your brother, but Guarionex and Guacanagarí. How come you never accomplished that?"

"Because I am Taíno. I married to extend my influence, but I never usurped another's land."

Cristóbal studied the chieftain and revisited an interrogation thrust many times over the last year, pondering whether Caonabó would yet refuse to answer. "You massacred the men I left with Guacanagarí, on his soil, without his consent—didn't you?" He paused and then twisted a reprieve. "The answer's now inconsequential. If you submit to Fernando and Isabel, you'll return as a king and your chiefdom will be restored, regardless of your crimes. If you refuse submission, you'll perish, regardless of innocence."

Caonabó ruminated for some moments, acknowledging the offer's rationality, if not sincerity, and pondering how to express his innocence truthfully. "Some of your men died of pestilence, others at their own hands. But I executed most of them, for crimes against my people and the liberty of my homeland."

Cristóbal's heart thumped, not from surprise or rage at Caonabó's guilt, but from vindication and hatred for Buil and Margarite. He sweetened the reprieve. "If you please Fernando and Isabel, they'll let you rule all the other chieftains. Both Guacanagarí and Guarionex would answer to you."

"The enjoyment of that wouldn't equal the dishonor of serving Fernando, Isabel, and yourself."

Both men had grown accustomed to their enmity, and they lingered in silence for some moments, listening to the sea speak into the night. Cristóbal considered sending Caonabó to his room, but curiosity of Caonabó's boyhood prevailed. "So, you were raised on a small island and understand the sea?"

Caonabó nodded. "I fished lagoons, reefs, and the open sea and canoed between islands. I've lived with its beauty and peril."

"You'll recognize both on the journey to Castile. It'll take weeks, perhaps six or more."

Caonabó concealed his astonishment and respect for the pale men's know-how to make such a lengthy, landless journey and shrugged his shoulders. "A futile waste of time. You already know I won't submit."

◘ ◘ ◘

One sunbaked morning, Anacaona welcomed Manicoatex in her garden, and he broke the news they'd dreaded for months. He'd received a pale messenger who'd informed that the Guamiquina would haul Caonabó across the ocean to grovel at Fernando and Isabel's feet. Manicoatex's son and Caonabó's youngest brother also would be taken and, were Caonabó executed, forced to submit in his stead. The Guamiquina hadn't been replaced and would return. Tribute remained due, and the Guamiquina's brother would see to its collection from Manicoatex, unabated.

Anacaona embraced Manicoatex, her eyes misting for her husband's and his ordeals and fate. After excusing him, she composed herself and summoned Onaney and Caonabó's other wives. They assembled in the heat, seated upon reed mats laid by naborias.

"We've all known that our husband would never yield to the enemy," she proclaimed, raising her fists. "Word has arrived that he yet survives, and undoubtedly he plots our people's revenge!" Yet she understood the wives hungered for information, not a speech, and she immediately sobered. "But there is terrible news—the Guamiquina will abduct him across the ocean to meet distant pale caciques."

Anacaona tarried briefly, as they gasped or cried out, and then clutched her heart. "Perhaps he may find a solution and return. But we should recognize—as we've known all along—that the pale men may take his life."

Wailing followed, and Anacaona waited longer for them to hush.

"What happens to us?" she posed. "We all come from esteemed caciqual families. We all could return easily to our ancestral villages, with honor. Many of them remain untouched by the enemy."

All assembled knew that to be most true for Anacaona herself, who could stand beside her brother to rule Haiti's greatest chiefdom, Xaraguá, never violated inland by the pale men.

"But that time hasn't come," Anacaona pronounced. "Our

husband will remain cunning and resolute through his last breath, whenever that may be, and we won't lose hope or cease praying for him unless we know he's lost. The spirits work in unknown ways, and, while he breathes, we remain his wives, here, supporting him in the chiefdom he refuses to relinquish."

The wives murmured approval, thankful that direction finally had emerged from the chaos swirling about them. Anacaona invited them to linger, and naborias served papaya juice as she spoke intimately with each of them before they left.

Onaney remained to the last, and the two women embraced bittersweetly, aware that they rarely had before.

"You have different circumstances," Anacaona consoled. "Should Caonabó perish, I can ask my brother to arrange a canoe to bear you to Aniyana."

Onaney hugged more tightly before departing, indicating she appreciated the gesture. "For now, we remain resolute, together, here."

Alone, Anacaona relished the solitude and serenity of her garden. But the question that had scorched her thoughts for weeks returned to engulf her, as its answer burned due—how should she rule if Caonabó perished? She begged Yúcahu's guidance and ambled aimlessly about the garden, mesmerized by the beauty of Haiti's blossoming trees, shrubs, and cacti, which glowed radiant in the sunlight, and desperate for their wisdom.

Anacaona minced beneath the shade of the magnolia trees, both sturdy and pretty, which reminded her of the wives just departed—straightforward, loyal, and dependable. They were the backbone of the garden, and the broad tapestry of their white petals and reddish fruits spoke of the ascendance of beauty and goodness over grotesqueness and evil. She was taken by the size and strength of the supporting limbs. But Yúcahu warned that a woman didn't rule by those qualities.

She came to the garden's pond abutting the riverbank, gazing sadly upon the lilies floating within. Their pink-and-white flowers shone with beauty, as the magnolias, but they lay apart, out of reach but for wading. Anacaona was taken by their separation and isolation. But Yúcahu observed that isolation alone was a fragile solution, as the pale men weren't shy to trespass, even across an ocean.

She strolled among the orchids, patient for revelation. They were far more alluring than the magnolias and lilies, yet far more delicate, bewitching greater desire and adoration, but, as young girls, easily destroyed in conflict. Her own beauty rivaled them. Prior to marriage, she'd well known how to bring men to pant before her, and she was taken by the orchids' power to smite. But Yúcahu warned that the power to smite wasn't enough without the power to destroy.

Tiring, Anacaona sat among the cacti, which were resolute, forbidding, and vicious, ascendant when the sun was most brutal, warning aggressors away, and piercing them if they trespassed too close. Without forethought, her eyes passed over the pretty pink blossoms cloaking the delicate limbs of a Bayahibe bush, which emanated gracefully from an inner torso, largely shrouded unseen behind the many blossoms.* It had been a wedding gift from Higüey's Cayacoa, her husband's friend, and its trunk was as cactus, covered with needles.

Roused, Anacaona fell to her knees upon her nagua to peek beneath the branches to the bristling trunk, sensing Yúcahu's design to have brought her before it. The bush was both alluring and vicious, perhaps not as enticing as the orchid or even the lily, or as sturdy as the magnolia or other cactuses, but neither delicate nor destructible. She grasped that it was sublimely endowed to draw the unsuspecting close and then stab. Yúcahu intimated that it flourished as a beautiful woman might rule, alluring enemy to friendship, warming if friendship were reciprocated, piercing if not, and never truly befriending, with barbs ever vigilant and poised to preserve her people's civilization. Olive men had once pined for her affections, and pale men certainly would.

Anacaona sat back on her heels, wary of accepting the revelation impetuously, resolved to ponder it as she waited on her husband's fate.

Soon, she felt a shadow creep over her, and she eyed upward to find her daughter staring down. Shifting to sit, she brought Higueymota to lie before her, cradling the girl in her arms. Higueymota had been crying.

"Will we ever see Father again?" she asked.

---

* *Leuenbergeria quisqueyana*, the Bayahibe rose, the Dominican Republic's national flower.

"I hope so. But if he never returns, we may speak to his soul whenever we wish, and he'll always watch over us."

"What will happen to us?"

"We must trust in Yúcahu to guide us," Anacaona replied. She recognized that she had taken her life's one husband, and she was resolute never to have another. But she bit her lip and hugged her daughter, unnerved what survival required.

⌑ ⌑ ⌑

The two caravels under construction at Isabela incorporated wood stripped from Aguado's sunken fleet and planking hewn from the surrounding forest. Over the winter, the hulls had been shoved from the beach to berth at the dock, where artisans labored to erect masts and rigging. Cristóbal had directed his men to seize healthy Indians in Maguana—subjects of Caonabó, purportedly war captives—for display to Isabel and Fernando when he presented the chieftain at court, envisioning that the most opportune moment for convincing the sovereigns of a slave trade's profitability. In the meantime, these captives had hauled the timbers of the ship that would haul them. Cristóbal named the caravel that would accompany the *Niña* to Spain the *Santa Cruz*. The artisans and sailors nicknamed it the *India*.

Isabela's hunger, food rationing, and disease persisted, and most prayed that God bless a berth to Castile. But not all was bleak, as the winter's exploration near the island's southern coast had discovered gold deposits. Cristóbal suspected he'd rediscovered ancient treasures known to King Solomon and ordered Bartolomé to build a blockhouse at the site, optimistically titled the San Cristóbal mines. Three new forts had been built to protect passage along the Yaque from Isabela to Fort Concepción and a fourth was planned to guard the route south to these mines.* Cristóbal also had awarded Bakako a small village on farmland north of Guaricano and Fort Concepción, on the now-worn route from Isabela, entrusting Bakako to feed and care for men stationed at the fort who grew ill.

As his departure approached, Cristóbal reconfirmed his delegation to Bartolomé of sole authority to govern Española as adelantado

*The forts Esperanza, Santa Catalina, and Santiago along the Yaque and, toward the "mines," at Bonao, Dominican Republic.

while Cristóbal was in Spain, avoiding—in his view—the prior debacle of a council and justified by the absence of other senior sovereign advisors. Brother Diego, who'd returned to Española with Aguado, stood by as second-in-command and successor. Cristóbal consented that Hojeda return to Spain, having suffered illness often, as well as deserving that release more than anyone else.

Cristóbal and Bartolomé frequently discussed what Bartolomé would accomplish during Cristóbal's absence, duration unknown. One afternoon, they angrily summoned Juan Aguado to join them in Cristóbal's courtyard.

"My liege, I decide who returns to Spain, not you," Cristóbal warned.

"Admiral, I disagree, and, regardless of that, almost everyone has asked my permission to sail home," Aguado responded. "They don't like it here." He stalled sarcastically on the extraordinary understatement, leaving pregnant the reality that many settlers reviled both brothers. "They'd expected more gold, less cruelty," he gibed.

"Desist awarding passage! You've no command here whatsoever!" Cristóbal retorted, glaring into Aguado's eyes. "Your brief is merely to report to the sovereigns. I assure you—they will hear my views, including of you." Cristóbal brusquely waved his hand, indicating the audience and pretense of ongoing civility were both concluded.

"Spanish swine," Bartolomé blurted, once Aguado vanished beyond the courtyard's gate. "His life's accomplishment is buttering the queen's biscuits." He turned to Cristóbal. "Take as many of the troublemakers to Spain as you can," he urged. "That'll make it easier for me here."

"That will fill the court with critics. There must be supporters going home, too." But most all sailing would be critics, however Cristóbal selected, and the brothers sat sullenly for some moments.

"Our men can no longer live here," Cristóbal admitted. "It's too far from the new mines, there's neither food nor labor nor harbor, and the crops fail."

"The Spanish sloth are too lazy to tend the crops."

"You must found a new town after I depart—call it New Isabela, indicating progress but continuity. Monte Plata [Puerto Plata] on the northern coast might work. But investigate sites near the mines, particularly along the river the Indians call the Ozama. When I returned from the Golden Chersonese, I saw the river flows strongly at the sea, with a good harbor."

"Finding and building a site with indolent Spaniards will take months," Bartolomé warned. "Who should be appointed to assist Diego here while I'm away?"

"Roldán," Cristóbal replied, referring to Francisco Roldán, a member of Cristóbal's personal staff appointed on the recommendation of Mendoza's office. "I'll promote him to be island's chief magistrate as the town winds down." Cristóbal had already charged him with supervising miners and serving as Isabela's magistrate.

"At least he's not traitor to his king and queen, like most of their subjects," Bartolomé scowled.

Taíno slave labor, taken from Theodor de Bry, 1598. John Carter Brown Library, portion of rec. no. 0683-8.

By early March, pleas, arguments, and altercations over who would sail home rose to a crescendo, and Cristóbal awarded the final berths. While each caravel typically would sail with a crew of two dozen, permitting jamming of fifty passengers each, Cristóbal relented to allow over twice as many passengers. As mariner, he regretted the decision as rashly begging the Lord to provide kind weather uninterrupted for months. Yet as governor and viceroy, he deemed essential the departure of the most dissatisfied, both for the morale of those remaining and to preclude rebellion by those denied. In total, 225 sailors and settlers would return home, reducing the salaried population to below the sovereigns' limit. Thirty Indians would also be taken, including Caonabó, his brother and nephew, and—following in Bakako's footsteps to be baptized—Wasu and Ukuti.

Cristóbal, Hojeda, and Caonabó would sail on the *Niña*, Aguado on the *India*, avoiding the most odious proximity. Other Indians corralled at Isabel couldn't be accommodated, and Cristóbal would leave them as a salve for the settlers remaining, to be slaved or released as they wished.

⊡ ⊡ ⊡

On March 10, Caonabó's ankle chains were unlocked and Wasu and Ukuti led him into Cristóbal's courtyard, where, to his surprise, he was received by Hojeda. Each had remained respectful of the other's boldness and cunning as a warrior.

"I brought you here in manacles to submit to the Admiral," Hojeda said, bowing slightly to offer his esteem. "They remain on you of your own choice. So, on the Admiral's behalf, I escort you to the ship to sail to Castile, where you shall submit directly to my king and queen."

Caonabó reciprocated the bow and stared into Hojeda's eyes. "It makes no difference which pale men you bring me to. I didn't submit to you or the Guamiquina, and I'll never submit to your caciques. As a warrior, do me the honor of executing me here, in my homeland, rather than in yours."

Wasu struggled to translate, but Hojeda stared piercingly back. "My Lord, a greater honor awaits you. When you bow before the power and majesty of the world's greatest rulers, Queen Isabel and King Fernando, your eyes and soul will recognize the glory of serving them."

Caonabó strode at his own pace behind Hojeda, departing Cristóbal's residence to board the *Niña*, Wasu and Ukuti skirting his heels. He felt the contempt of countless pale men as he passed, and he was stunned by their appearance—bodies unclean and wizened from hunger, faces downcast, clothing torn, countless debilitated by syphilis or unknown diseases. He swelled with contempt for his own botchery, grasping that, if he hadn't been seized, his plan to storm the site would have succeeded. His self-contempt burgeoned to rage when he beheld the countless burial plots surrounding the church and then to fury at the storehouse, where guards slept as no food remained within to hoard.

But when he arrived at the dock, Caonabó grew pensive again, astonished by the know-how of the ships. Hojeda escorted him across a plank onto the Guamiquina's vessel and led him to sit on its forecastle near the bow, nestled beside a rail overlooking the sea, to which he was chained. The ship was crammed with pale men, barely a place to sit, but they shied to sit close by, and he possessed his own space. His brother and nephew soon were chained beside him, as well most of the other captives, and he comforted the boy, remarking that father Manicoatex would be proud of his bravery.

Caonabó studied the Guamiquina stride aboard the same plank, which ushered a great commotion aboard, as sails were unfurled, ropes to the dock unbound, and an anchor pulled. For an instant, Caonabó was awestruck that he'd even contemplated defeating the pale men. The vessel's operation required the coordination of many workers with different tasks, far more complicated than a canoe. While not as swift, the vessel was fit to bear food and water to venture incredibly farther distances. But his fury quickly rekindled to ravage him as he confessed that—on land—he could have driven the pale men from Haiti. Unbearably, that was the sole victory that had mattered.

Cristóbal veered his fleet of two northwest to curl around Isabela's barrier reef and then came about to tack east into strong winds. Each pale man aboard adored the Lord and Virgin for deliverance from

Española, many collapsing in relief and tears, and each olive man dreaded the fate the Lord and Virgin would impose.

Caonabó scanned north across the landless sea toward Aniyana, recalling his boyhood voyage from there to Haiti, beaching just a day's canoe west. He'd come as an unknown to compete to become the supreme cacique of a chiefdom, recognizing that failure was a possibility. But he'd triumphed.

Caonabó wept. He'd never imagined that he'd lose that chiefdom to a people unknown. He felt the terrified stare of his nephew, dreaded the younger generations' fate, and hid his face in his hands.

Return to Guadalupe, *March 11–April 20, 1496*

The *Niña*—seventy feet long, twenty-one at its widest—had never borne over a hundred passengers, and their cramping on and below deck hampered the crew's work. Cristóbal imposed tight rations from the outset and set his course toward the islands he'd discovered on the outward voyage, as they were shortest landless distance from Spain known, contemplating restocking provisions there before veering northeast to cross the ocean. He resolved to care for the Indians aboard at least as attentively as the Spaniards—Caonabó's survival was key to conquest and healthy Maguanans were critical to demonstrating the slave trade's potential.

Caonabó grasped Cristóbal's intentions, and, while praying for his relatives' and subjects' survival, he austerely concluded that his own life's singular remaining purpose—likely futile—was to discover some unknown compromise to preserve his people's freedom and independence. Failing that, death was preferable to participating in the spectacle Hojeda envisioned.

The ships labored two weeks against headwinds simply to attain Española's eastern tip. Bartolomé accompanied the voyage as far as the inlet at Monte Plata, where he debarked to reconnoiter its potential to serve as Isabela's successor. He and Cristóbal quickly concluded that equally good sites could be found on the southern coast along the Ozama River, and Cristóbal ordered Bartolomé to found New Isabela there.

On March 22, the ships left Española behind, beating east toward Boriquén rather than veering north toward the Azores or Spain. While standing at the rail, Cristóbal greeted Caonabó, and they resumed their ongoing polemic, Wasu and Ukuti translating.

"Your vessels don't brave the wind well," Caonabó criticized. "My canoes would've sped here in four days, not two weeks."

Cristóbal simply nodded, dispensing with a rejoinder. "We sail east now, to the islands of the flesh eaters." He examined the chieftain's health and was content it hadn't deteriorated at sea or from diseases stalking those huddled nearby. "Do you fear your people's enemies?"

"I fought them often in my youth, vanquishing them many times."

"Fernando and Isabel will protect your subjects from these people."

"My subjects have always relied on me for that. We've always repelled Caribes from settling on Haiti, just as we'll repel you."

"You're not protecting anyone while in chains," Cristóbal retorted coldly. "When you submit, we'll tell your subjects you've been restored."

On April 10, with the provisions diminished from three more weeks beating eastward, Cristóbal brought his two ships to anchor in rough seas off Guadalupe's black-sand beach, where his fleet of seventeen had harbored two years before (Grande Anse, Basse-Terre). To his dismay, its inhabitants had ugly memories of his prior visit and abductions, and a band of Caribe women gathered, brandishing bows and arrows.

Caonabó esteemed the grit and determination of his ancestral enemy, womenfolk no less. *Lure the Guamiquina closer ashore*, he beseeched Yúcahu silently.

Cristóbal dispatched Wasu and Ukuti to the beach, just as Bakako before. "The Christians come in peace," they implored in Taíno. "For cazabi, not gold. Not slaves."

"Visit our husbands at the village on the western shore," the Caribe women replied in broken Taíno, lowering their bows. "They will trade with you."

Caonabó grinned on overhearing the youths' report to Cristóbal, admiring that the women baited a trap. *Guide the Guamiquina into ambush*, he implored Yúcahu.

Cristóbal brought the ships off a small cove and village on the western shore (Anse à la Barque?), where the greeting was yet more hostile—a large crowd, including a few Caribe warriors, dispatched a hail of arrows.

Caonabó grimaced when the arrows fell short and invoked Yúcahu a third time. *Entreat the pale men into the village.*

Cristóbal dispatched armed men ashore, as replenishing provisions was essential. The Caribes feigned flight but then swarmed from the forest to attack, only truly to flee on the boom of the ships' lombards, leaving the village unoccupied.

Caonabó writhed as the Christians looted, rampaged, and commandeered bohíos. He was astonished when his own subjects were ferried from the *Niña* and set to work in the village baking cazabi with the villagers' yuca supply and utensils. He begged Yúcahu to reverse the onslaught. *Spring the warriors' assault at night, when the pale men sleep*, he urged.

But Cristóbal sent a raiding party inland to seize a dozen women and boys, including a chieftain's wife and daughter, to hold hostage aboard the *Niña*, admonishing that the consequence of counterattack would be severe.

For nine days, Cristóbal's men and the Indians he was hauling to Spain sat together in the Caribe village baking cazabi with the Caribes' yuca, stocking for the ocean crossing. Cazabi was the singular focus, not whether one was Christian or heathen, nor whether the Caribe hostages ate human flesh. Three weeks' supply was baked.

Caonabó perceived that, unlike Haiti, the Guamiquina appeared to hold no ambition to seize Caribe territory for a permanent settlement, satisfied merely with food, believing there was no gold.

On April 20, immediately prior to departure, Cristóbal conferred rewards on the Caribe hostages and released all but the chieftain's wife and daughter. The wife would serve well to present to the sovereigns, and Cristóbal chained her and the daughter at the rail among Caonabó's subjects. Caonabó shuddered to behold their gloom and contemplated his own wives and daughters bearing such outrage.

At Sea,
April 20–Early June 1496

From Guadalupe, Cristóbal coursed the ships toward Madeira and Spain, taking the wind as close off the starboard bow as possible. His own voyage home in 1493 had traversed the ocean from Samaná to the Azores in about twenty-five days. Torres had sailed much the same route all the way to Cádiz in but twenty-five days in 1494, and Torres's 1495 crossing from Boriquén to Madeira had been accomplished in twenty-three days. But the winds north of Guadalupe were weaker than previously experienced, occasionally becalming the ships.* Cristóbal was want for an explanation, as his route from the Canaries to Guadalupe in 1493 had been blessed with consistent winds, often gales, and he was vexed by the ships' slow progress.

On May 20, a month gone from Guadalupe, Cristóbal concluded that they'd reached a latitude just south of the Azores, yet more than a hundred leagues west, and he veered the ships east to Portugal, with tailwinds. He also announced the reduction of each person's daily ration to six ounces of cazabi and a pint and a half of water. The overcrowding of passengers had reduced the foodstuffs far more rapidly than on prior crossings, and worse, while fish could be caught to eat, the remaining fresh water was dangerously depleted. The settlers' gratitude for the cazabi baked on Guadalupe by the Indians aboard waned as hunger and thirst waxed. Within days, parched murmurs of desperation and discontent burst into pleas and demands.

"Admiral, throw the Indians overboard to preserve the water."

"That wouldn't be Christian," Cristóbal replied.

"Admiral, these beasts eat men—so let's eat them."

"We'll live or die as Christians," Cristóbal warned. "There's no shorter route to Hell than such blasphemy."

The admonitions quashed the complaints. Cristóbal believed his responses, although he did pine to present the sovereigns with healthy slaves. Deep within, beyond conscious faith, he was a mariner, and, outside hostilities, he'd never thrown a person to the merciless sea, and he'd never test the Lord with such cruelty.

---

*The "horse latitudes," between the easterly trade winds to the south and the westerlies to the north.

Caonabó perceived the unrest and the base desires of the pale men, which confirmed all that he thought of them. Their hearts and instincts were brutish beyond reform. They viewed his people simply as exploitable and expendable providers of food and labor through death, nothing more. He ached whether Anacaona could sort some solution, providing food but not territory, similar to what he'd just witnessed on the Caribe homeland.

After reducing the daily ration, Cristóbal came to ascertain Caonabó's health.

"We'll arrive in Spain in but weeks. Rest—your audience with Fernando and Isabel approaches. Their embrace will transform your outlook."

"I'd prefer death," Caonabó replied coldly, relieved to learn the voyage's remaining duration.

"Then your soul will go to Hell," Cristóbal responded, inured to the chieftain's intransigence. "If you must die, wait until the sovereigns teach you of Christ and baptize you so your soul achieves Heaven—if you repent your murders. We'll tell your subjects of your glorious example."

"I'm already in Hell—with you, your caciques, and your people. On death, my soul will escape to live forever in a good place, without pale men."

Cristóbal strode away.

Caonabó drew no satisfaction in the idle pique delivered. He gazed to the ocean and was overwrought that the time had come to decide his own course of action and invoke Yúcahu's guidance. He despised the shame of kneeling before a conqueror, preferring death. *Should I survive to meet the pale caciques?* He vexed whether there was any hope or reason to suffer that disgrace.

Caonabó's thoughts raced angrily through the Guamiquina's relentless trail of encroachments—a tiny coastal outpost, then a settlement, followed by inland forts, culminating in battles, tributes, and enslavements—all heralded, step-by-step, with the lie of peace and friendship. Bitterly, he acknowledged his own defeat and that the Guamiquina's undaunted perseverance had prevailed. He cursed that the Guamiquina would shrewdly concoct lies about the audience with the pale caciques if it transpired—fabricating peaceful submission, acceptance of tribute, or even worship of the Christ-spirit. Anacaona had now to fashion her own response, and he was racked by a vision of the Guamiquina beguiling her with falsities.

With Yúcahu's concurrence, Caonabó at last accepted there was nothing more he could do for Anacaona and their people but die, relishing that death would deny the Guamiquina an opportunity for deception and a victor's gloat. Caonabó would steal the final victory in their contemptuous rivalry by never submitting.

That afternoon, when a sailor came to dispense the daily ration, Caonabó took both the water and the cazabi, but he passed the latter to his nephew.

"You must grow strong," Caonabó counseled softly. "When you return to Haiti, you'll assist your aunt and father in keeping these beasts apart from our people."

"But what of you?" the boy responded, startled. "You must lead us."

"I have. But that has brought us here." Caonabó looked sternly into the boy's eyes. "It is now your aunt and father's turn, and you must survive to return to assist them." Caonabó waited for the boy to grasp his intent, then kissed his forehead. "It'll be your honor to defeat the pale men."

As the ships bore northeast, while everyone's thirst and hunger raged, Caonabó weakened, as if prelude to a cohaba ceremony, and he welcomed a dialogue with the spirits. He implored Yúcahu to guide Anacaona and Manicoatex to a path for their people's survival. He beseeched—if useful—the sacrifice of Guacanagarí to the pale men's enslavement, as his ignorance and traitorous conduct had assisted their ascendancy. He begged Yúcahu's forgiveness for his own gullibility in permitting his capture and that Yúcahu acquiesce in his crossing from life to death to reunite with his forefathers in Maguana's great valley.

As June dawned, Cristóbal again visited to review Caonabó's health and, unaware of his fast, grew concerned he was wan. "Rest," Cristóbal implored, again. "We'll arrive in Spain in a week."

When the day's ration came, Caonabó passed both the water cup and cazabi to his nephew. His mouth and throat already were desiccated, and he fought his instincts to gulp down the water, invoking

Yúcahu to fortify his resolve. His nephew refrained from drinking and offered the cup back, but Caonabó refused.

That evening, Caonabó gazed to the stars, transfixed by their timeless permanence, saddened that his Haiti didn't share that immutability, but content that he soon would return into the natural order with the souls of his father, mother, and their ancestors. He recalled both humble origins and great triumphs. A remembrance of his father's lectures on boyhood conduct faded into a vision of Maguana's caciqual medallion being hung about his neck. A memory of his first boyhood kiss with an equally nameless Onaney conjured that of leading the remarkable Anacaona to a secluded bohío to consummate their marriage. A flush of exhilaration evoking his first ocean journey from Aniyana to Haiti burst into the piercing exuberance of leading warriors into battle against Caribes.

The next morning, his brother and nephew propped him against the rail when the daily ration arrived and retained his water in a bowl for him to partake as he wished at any time, although they expected he'd soon fail the consciousness to do so. Those olive skinned about him now understood what transpired, and they grew hush, astounded and humbled by the willpower necessary to thirst to death, frightened by the desperate agony that their chieftain suffered, and proud that the Guamiquina would be denied submission.

As evening fell again, Caonabó drifted in and out of consciousness, cognizant only of the endless roll of waves falling behind beneath him as the *Niña* surged over them. Visions of his mother, Onaney, Anacaona, and Higueymota soothed him, and memories of his father, Manicoatex, and Uxmatex ennobled him. As the moon reached its zenith, his last dream was of learning to duck hunt on Aniyana as a boy, gazing along the water's surface to an unsuspecting prey and discovering that he was destined to be a hunter, not the hunted.

X
HOMELAND JOURNEYS

Cristóbal, Cádiz to Burgos, Castile,
Early June–September 1496

At sea, Cristóbal never slept continuously through the night, rising often to review the weather, his ships' trim and trajectory, and the stars' progression. As the moon crested, he peered the short distance from the *Niña*'s stern across masses prone on deck to his key cargo, apparently slumbering against the forward rail. An hour later, when Cristóbal returned, he realized Caonabó hadn't stirred, and a recollection of discerning Navidad utterly silent haunted him, admonishing that the Lord constantly posed obstacles to his success. At twilight, Cristóbal surmised Caonabó had departed, and, with Wasu, he wended quietly through the sleeping to the huddle of Indians near the bow. Some roused, aware why he came, panicked what he might do. All hushed as he knelt to confirm Caonabó's death.

Cristóbal pivoted east to the horizon's glow, thanking the Lord for the wind that smacked his back and brought him home but incredulous that the Lord so punished him, frustrating the chieftain's display before the sovereigns—after a year of patient care and grisly cohabitation! He stared to Heaven and begged forgiveness of his vanities for acclaim and nobility and his swollen self-pride. Yet he didn't perceive other sins to confess and felt only wronged by, and no sorrow for, the deceased. Fleetingly, he pondered whether the

Lord held Caonabó's massacre of Navidad's men as sin, and he was relieved the brother and nephew survived to haul before the court.

Cristóbal summoned Hojeda to unlock the chieftain's chains, seeking the body's disposition before sunrise to avoid a spectacle of the Indians' grief or the settlers' clamor to eat it. He bid Wasu comfort the Indians that they had moments to grieve and pray as they wished. When the sun pricked the horizon, he ordered the body of the great chieftain thrown overboard. As it vanished into the deep, Cristóbal appreciated that death at least quashed the Indians' hope for the chieftain's return and dimmed his renown. The Indians aboard wailed their last parting, forlorn their liberty had been lost forever.

⊡ ⊡ ⊡

The court had settled in Almazán that spring, and, while Cristóbal's ships approached Spain, Isabel and Fernando received Alonso de Lugo as a hero. He towed along a parade of Tenerife's submitting chieftains to be baptized. The slave markets in Seville were busy selling the subjects of the chieftains who'd resisted.

Berardi's death and the loss of his first four ships in February had been a rude disappointment, and the sovereigns had implored Fonseca, rather than Vespucci, rapidly to equip another resupply fleet. By early June, three ships lay anchored in Cádiz, to be provisioned and sail under the command of Pero Alonso Niño, Cristóbal's trusted pilot on his first voyage. Pero Alonso bore the sovereigns' letters to Cristóbal. While the experts had yet to decide whether Indians could be enslaved generally, the sovereigns had conceded that Indians attacking Christians could be, as war captives.

⊡ ⊡ ⊡

On June 8, Cristóbal sighted the coast of Portugal three dozen miles north of Cape Saint Vincent, nearly spot-on where he'd dead reckoned landfall after crossing the entire ocean. The pilots aboard were dazzled, expecting to be much farther north, and Cristóbal's preeminence as a mariner again was hailed.

Yet he appreciated that such stature mattered nothing in the absence of gold or Cathay. En route to Cádiz, he retired to his cabin to plot his homecoming and the defense of his realm. He'd brought

Indian gold pieces and jewelry to impress the sovereigns—lustered by a gold-inlaid crown and necklace for Caonabó's brother—but his critics would assault the failure of full barrels, and the enterprise cried for justification and impetus otherwise. Failing their enslavement, the Indians' evangelization remained an unassailable glory, dear to Isabel's heart and already wrapped in the enterprise's conception. Cristóbal did envision himself as the Lord's instrument for bringing the Indians to Christianity, regardless that a single Indian had yet to be baptized on Española. As disembarkation approached, he fixed to jettison both his admiral's finery and practical sailors' clothing and to dress thereafter in faith's image, robing in the plain brown habit of a Franciscan friar. He also would go unshaven.

On June 11, so garbed, with a sash at the waist, Cristóbal strode onto the quay at Cádiz proclaiming humble penitence rather than noble rank or professional preeminence, astonishing the townsfolk. They hadn't expected his return, and his dressing beneath his station and beyond his profession confounded them. Their amazement turned to horror when the settlers straggled ashore—thin, sick, and bedraggled—as if dead men walking, and the refrain resounded throughout the town and into Andalusia that the Indies were a dead loss. When the Indians followed, the townsfolk weren't captivated by their nakedness, as in prior years, peremptorily dismissing that they lived in valuable lands. Aguado debarked determined to debunk and demote Cristóbal.

Pero Alonso was stunned by Cristóbal's dress and demeanor, perceiving him half-crazed, and rushed to meet him. Cristóbal was astonished and grateful to embrace him and learn that the resupply fleet would sail in days.

"How are my sons?" Cristóbal gasped.

"King, queen, and prince treat them kindly, but they suffer the scorn of most everyone else," Pero Alonso replied honestly.

"Tell me what I must know," Cristóbal urged. "What do the king and queen think?"

"There's doubt you've found a shortcut to Cathay," Pero Alonso replied gingerly, studying Cristóbal's face contort with pain and outrage.

"I've sailed *beyond* Cathay, to the Golden Chersonese!" Cristóbal stammered, consumed with indignation. "I'll prove it to them. To the critics!"

Pero Alonso waited for Cristóbal to catch his breath and pushed softly on. "The king and queen are willing to license other expeditions. They've authorized Vicente Pinzón to sail with two ships, destination unknown."

Cristóbal's eyes bulged, his mouth gaped, and he flushed with rage that an old adversary would be permitted to usurp his territory. "I'll put an end to that!" he cried.

Pero Alonso gently touched Cristóbal's arm. "Berardi died this winter, and Vespucci is running the business. It's not clear he can make a go of it. He provisioned the first four ships, but they sank before reaching Gomera. Fonseca has provisioned mine."

Cristóbal buried his face in his hands. "What of the slave trade?" he lamented. "Who will sell them, if the sovereigns approve?"

"Vespucci can. I'm sure Fonseca would, too. But the sovereigns haven't approved it. They've said only that you can take war captives. I carry their letters to you."

Cristóbal's fortitude and perseverance were never punctured for long. By evening, after reviewing the sovereigns' correspondence, he recovered smartly and strove on, composing his own instruction to Bartolomé directing the enslavement and transport to Spain of Indians captured in hostilities. Lugo's mass enslavements whetted his expectations.

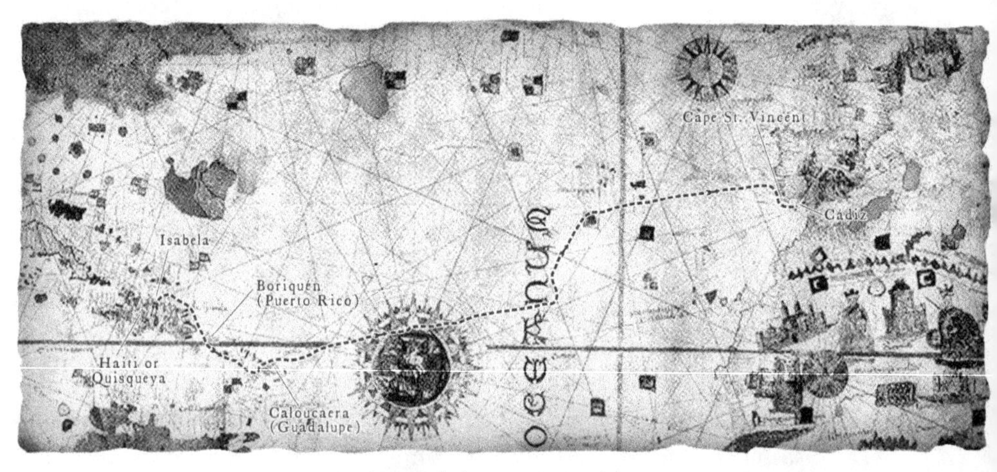

Portion of Juan de la Cosa's World Map, 1500, marked for route of return voyage to Spain.

Pero Alonso's three ships sailed from Cádiz on June 15, and, within a week, Cristóbal departed for Seville by mule, where he'd await the sovereigns' invitation to court. Emulating his return from the first voyage, he arrayed his naked Indians and trophies to publicize the triumph of the Indies. Wasu, Ukuti, and the others were bedecked with the gold jewelry, face masks, belts, and necklaces collected in tribute. Cristóbal now introduced Caonabó's brother as Don Diego, falsely imparting the impression of prior baptism, and Don Diego donned the crown and necklace in audiences with local nobility.

⊡ ⊡ ⊡

In late June, Cristóbal arrived to reside in the home of Andrés Bernáldez, the curate of Los Palacios (near Seville), together with Don Diego. The other Indians slept in the gardens of Bernáldez's church across the street. Bernáldez was compiling information to write a glowing history of Isabel and Fernando's reign, and Cristóbal lent him copies of various correspondence to help with chapters on the Indies.* Bishop Fonseca also visited, and Bernáldez did his best to buffer the animosity between the two men.

"I'll propose my prompt return to Española and request a fleet," Cristóbal pronounced, advising his intention for the sovereign audience.

"They'll want to consider Aguado's report first," Fonseca pricked dryly. "Perhaps they'll requisition a fleet without you."

Cristóbal revealed no affront, having long concluded disputes with Fonseca were best handled behind his back, directly with the sovereigns.

"Perhaps they won't approve a fleet at all," Fonseca brusquely belittled. "You must understand they have important matters to deal with. The French war lingers, and that requires scores of ships alert on the frontiers. Princess Juana is to be transported to Flanders for marriage, with a princess brought in return for the prince—that requires over a hundred vessels more." Fonseca paused for emphasis. "If only you had found gold or the Grand Khan. I'm skeptical they'll throw more money into your pit."

"Profitability would be attained through a slave trade, as permitted for Lugo," Cristóbal argued. "Until the gold mines are producing."

**Historia de los Reyes Católicos D. Fernando y Doña Isabel.*

"The *theologians* haven't blessed it," Fonseca retorted, smirking, disdainful for the sovereigns' indecision. "But once you're done trotting your Indians before the king and queen, I'll sell them contingent on that blessing. Unless they turn sick and die on us first."

⌑ ⌑ ⌑

The sovereigns did invite Cristóbal to court, but with none of the urgency preceding his departure three years before. In Seville, waiting their instructions, he encountered such mockery on the street that he remained mostly indoors. In late July, at last summoned, he and his Indian entourage commenced their mule ride north through Extremadura to Burgos.

En route, they rested for three days at the monastery in Guadalupe while Cristóbal rejuvenated and worshipped. On July 29, he led Wasu and Ukuti to be baptized at the monastery's high altar, whereupon they were christened Cristóbal and Pedro. That evening, he brought them before the renowned Virgin, just as Bakako before, and they whispered in Taíno as they knelt before her.*

"She's just as Bakako described," Wasu gaped, spellbound by the size of the large cemí.

"We must honor her," Ukuti urged. "Unequivocally, without Bakako's reservations and hostility. We are now Christ's followers, in community with all his followers."

"There's no other choice," Wasu assented. "We have no other community to belong to."

The youths glimpsed forlornly at each other. Everyone at home along the Bajabonico had died, and most of the thirty Indians with them were now sick and infirm.

⌑ ⌑ ⌑

In mid-September, Cristóbal and his Indians arrived in Burgos before the court had settled there. Isabel was traveling south from Laredo on the Bay of Biscay, where she'd dispatched Juana in a fleet of 130 ships, some heavily armed, that would escort the princess and a guard of ten thousand soldiers around enemy France to marry Maximilian's son, Archduke

*Our Lady of Santa María of Guadalupe, held to have been entombed with Saint Luke, buried by Hispanic clergy when fleeing the infidel in the eighth century, and revealed centuries later by the Virgin to a local herdsman.

Philip. The fleet would then return bearing Maximilian's daughter, Princess Margarite, to wed Prince Juan. Fernando was in Gerona reviewing his troops' readiness along the Pyrenean border, where he and Charles each had threatened to invade the other's kingdom.

Cristóbal waited patiently. Yet to his chagrin, when both sovereigns at last reunited in Burgos, the audience was delayed indefinitely. He simmered jealously that the sovereigns failed to perceive the Indies as their greatest endeavor. Other affairs took precedence and their attention, as well as countless more ships, apparently not so precious as the far fewer he'd ever sought or been awarded.

Charles's principal surviving garrisons in Italy had surrendered to the sovereigns or their allies in July, and Isabel and Fernando had worked vigorously that summer to tighten the noose of alliances strung about France, imploring Henry VII to invade. Henry had shied from that, but, on October 1, the perennial negotiations to wed Catalina to Henry's son Arthur were concluded, with marriage delayed until the two reached maturity. Fernando hadn't withdrawn his troops from the Italian peninsula, and when the Neapolitan throne passed yet again to another cousin on October 7, Fernando perceived himself ungratefully snubbed.* He'd now earned that throne, and he and Isabel plotted whether carving up Italy with Charles was now opportune and preferable to continuing to fight him.

In limbo, Cristóbal sullenly prepared his defense, the Indies second fiddle to England, France, and Naples. He rankled to learn that the sovereigns had assisted Fray Buil in arranging a religious posting in Rome on behalf of his hermetic order. He despised to discover they had awarded Margarite a tenancy in Castile. He dreaded Aguado would be granted prior access.

Bartolomé and Bakako, Santo Domingo and Slave Raiding,
July–September 1496

Pero Alonso's ships anchored at Isabela in July, hailed by the frenzied applause and cravings of those unlucky to remain there, who hadn't

*Ferrante II died, passing the throne to his uncle Federico.

received fresh supplies for nine months. Bartolomé appreciated Pero Alonso's devotion to Cristóbal, and they conferred alone in the residence's courtyard.

"He survived the voyage healthy, his wit keen?" Bartolomé inquired.

"He's not bedridden," Pero Alonso affirmed, hesitating. "He's aged a lot since I last saw him, fraught that all will be lost. His officers said he rarely sleeps." His eyes darted to the ground. "You must know that already. When did he don the Franciscan habit?"

"He worships often, and his faith grows ever stronger," Bartolomé replied casually, concealing his shock. *Gambit or craze?* he despaired to himself, vexed Cristóbal's vision of destiny now confounded his stature.

"He seems as sharp as ever, but the swagger and boast are gone, leaving gravity and insistence," Pero Alonso observed, gazing back for confirmation.

Bartolomé nodded gravely, signaling an end to intimate questions. "Did he break the Indian chieftain's will?"

"The chieftain died at sea. I never saw him."

Bartolomé faltered, brooding what that meant for the island's subjugation. "What orders do you bear me?"

"To establish New Isabela on the southern coast. A command that Indians resisting should be enslaved."

Bartolomé's eyes glimmered. "When must you return?"

"Within weeks, so bring me as much gold as you can. Or resisters."

Within days, Bartolomé left brother Diego in command of Isabela and departed south with a troop of soldiers and artisans to establish New Isabela. He chose a bluff overlooking the Ozama River nearby the sea and left the artisans to construct a fort and wooden church, prelude to migrating the men at Isabela there. But he disregarded Cristóbal's instruction and named the settlement Santo Domingo, in honor of their father Domenico, which he sanctified that August by celebrating the town's founding on the feast of Saint Dominic on a Sunday (*domingo* in Spanish).

Bartolomé and soldiers then marched back north, slave raiding on the return to Isabela, seizing over three hundred Indians destitute near previous skirmish sites in Maguana and the Vega Real, regardless of whether they'd participated in hostilities or assassinations. En route, he halted briefly to remind Manicoatex of the pending tribute obligation and to inform that Caonabó had perished. He briefly encamped his troop and slaves at Fort Concepción, visiting Guaricano to advise Guarionex the same, deriding the chieftain's outrage that slaves be hauled to the threshold of his home. Finally, he slept a night with Bakako, in the bohío and village awarded the teenager north of Guaricano, where the fort's ill were parked. The two conferred in Spanish and some Taíno, which Bartolomé had sought to learn.

"The Admiral sends his love," Bartolomé pronounced.

"I pray he's well," Bakako mustered, frightened at hosting a master slave master.

"Identify Indians that rebel so I may enslave them," Bartolomé instructed. "Just like those I've brought with me."

Bakako nodded wanly, disgraced that duty as remora continued to include slave raiding, breaching Guarionex's understanding when submitting to tribute.

"Guarionex remains loyal to our king and queen?"

"So far," Bakako affirmed gingerly, concealing his revulsion for Bartolomé's arrogant violation. "But your enslavements test that loyalty."

"Resisters may be enslaved, the submissive not!" Bartolomé barked, forbidding any challenge. "Feed and care for the men relocating from Isabela when they pass through."

Cowed, Bakako nodded again, incredulous at the demand. His naborias had sown fresh yuca, but its harvest remained months away, and there was scant to eat at his village, the fort, or Guaricano. He and Yutowa scrounged and scavenged daily in less populated areas just to procure barely enough cazabi for those then in his charge, olive and pale.

By mid-September, Bartolomé returned to Isabela and directed that its settlers depart in bands for Santo Domingo over the following year, leaving only the shipbuilders and a small garrison behind under brother Diego's command.

Desolate, Manicoatex departed his chiefdom in the Cibao's foothills to trek to Caonabó's hometown to inform the wives of their husband's death.

On September 29, Pero Alonso sailed for Spain with the three hundred slaves and a few gold pieces. Guarionex agonized for the fate of his subjects.

Bakako remained in his village, pondering with Yutowa whether his villagers and Haiti's peoples would survive the famine. The only respite was that there were countless fewer mouths left to feed each day.

Anacaona, Maguana to Xaraguá, *(Autumn 1496)*

Anacaona knew the moment her brother-in-law arrived that Caonabó had perished—grief flagged Manicoatex's gait, dimmed his gaze, and hushed his greeting. Her eyes misted.

"He's died, at sea," Manicoatex whispered, grasping her shoulders firmly.

Anacaona's tears streamed, but she withheld any cry. They embraced, and she led him to her garden, beyond earshot and view.

"The others?" she inquired, anxious for Manicoatex's son.

"The Guamiquina's brother spoke only of your husband," Manicoatex replied, steeling his composure. His voice drew strength. "I do understand this—Caonabó never surrendered to serve the pale men. I asked whether he remained chained to the last, and the Guamiquina's brother merely shrugged—not the response if they sought to proclaim Caonabó's submission."

Anacaona flushed with pride and wiped her tears. Both appreciated the time had come to discuss Maguana's succession, and she guided him to the noontime shade of the magnolia trees, allowing him to speak first.

"I'd be honored to take you as wife," Manicoatex vouched. "But that isn't the answer—either for you, me, or our peoples." He grasped her hands, and she held tightly in return, nodding that she appreciated the gesture and concurred that marriage made no sense.

"The pale men's truces with Guarionex, myself, and others are lies," Manicoatex decried. "They enslave our peoples regardless. Renewed resistance is the only recourse, in Maguana and throughout the other chiefdoms they've possessed." He grimaced. "It is for me to lead my brother's subjects in that."

Anacaona bit her lip, distraught what that meant for Manicoatex's future yet esteeming him as a worthy brother-in-law. But her heart pounded and she trembled, speechless, overcome with both remorse and ambition that she remain to fulfill her husband's wish.

"There's no peaceful solution here," Manicoatex counseled grittily. "There also is little and few left to rule. Gardens and farms lay ruined, and most of my brother's vassal caciques have died, fled, or been enslaved."

"I must have a role!" Anacaona blurted. *I promised him*, she cried to herself. *It's my right and due.*

"You will, but better elsewhere," Manicoatex recommended. "Xaraguá remains untouched. Your brother is free to design his own solution with the pale men. I don't know whether he can keep them from entering Xaraguá, or on what terms."

Anacaona peered into Manicoatex's eyes, having pondered that approach for Xaraguá for months, as well as her role in it.

"You should return to Xaraguá to advise Behecchio how," Manicoatex prompted. "No one would consider that desertion at this point—including Caonabó. He envisioned that you might discern a harmonious resolution, not command warrior bands desperately revolting."

Anacaona embraced her brother-in-law again, tormented by her conflicting emotions, gratified that he offered release from a Maguana now destitute—should she desire that. They listened to the crickets, Anacaona vacillating some moments.

"Caonabó fought not just for Maguana," she observed, "but for all the island's peoples. Our civilization must endure."

"That responsibility may fall to Behecchio—and you."

⊡ ⊡ ⊡

That afternoon, after reconciling herself, Anacaona summoned Caonabó's other wives to the garden and Manicoatex broke the news, met with tears, sobbing, and grief.

"There's a place in my household for each of you," he offered.

"Our husband's caney remains yours until you depart, either

for your ancestral village or to live with Manicoatex," Anacaona assured. "For myself, I'll leave for Xaraguá within the moon." All grew hush, forlorn their own lives had been uprooted.

"Caonabó's death shall be honored, befitting our traditions," Manicoatex pronounced. "All his subjects shall be summoned."

Days later, at dawn, half a dozen drummers congregated in Caonabó's great ballcourt. They pounded a resonant deep beat drawing villagers within earshot and triggering drummers distant to join in, rumbling the invitation throughout the great valley. All came—nitaíno and naboria, half-starved and starved, young and old—until the ballcourt overflowed. At the center, a smooth carved boulder was set on end to serve as a shoulder-height pillar around which senior behiques gathered to invoke the spirits. For years, Anacaona had sung areítos to audiences congregated about it.

As Manicoatex addressed the mourners, Anacaona anguished that the funeral was embittering rather than ennobling. Caonabó's subjects were decimated, having lost loved ones or entire families to disease or conquest, and rather than being uplifted by their chieftain's legacy, his death brusquely reminded of the deaths about them and that the spirits had forsaken them. Manicoatex's exaltation of Caonabó's bravery left them disconsolate, as all doubted their own bravery thereafter could revenge the harms Caonabó had failed to repel.

Anacaona despaired most grievers had lost a purpose or will to live and that Manicoatex's eulogy failed to boost them to find meaning in their ongoing lives or comfort from their spirits. Over the past year, countless villagers in the territories invaded had chosen suicide before degradation, enslavement, lingering illness, or starvation. They'd gulped the yuca root's poisonous juice or hurled themselves from precipices. Pregnant woman had aborted babies, distraught they couldn't be fed or would be enslaved or shattered by rape that had conceived them. Anacaona rose to conclude the ceremony.

"Our chieftain never faltered in his resolve to defend our civilization, because it is superior to the pale men's, and to all others of the world. We must go forward, bearing descendants, uplifting and honoring our spirits, and preserving our heritage. We shall survive this assault and hardship, until our spirits reward our perseverance with our renewed ascendancy."

Anacaona.

⊡ ⊡ ⊡

Weeks later, on the eve of departure for Xaraguá, Anacaona invoked Yúcahu's guidance for her homecoming, seated alone in her garden by the Bayahibe bush, its bristles glistening in fulsome moonlight. She would stand loyally at her older brother's side, as she had her entire youth. But she prayed Behecchio would heed her advice. While not a renowned warrior as Caonabó, he was brave in battle and a craftier statesman, and he brimmed with a Xaraguán confidence in his ascendency over other chieftains—be it social, military, or aesthetic. He'd studied the pale men's victories over Caonabó and the others, and she cringed he'd conclude he could do better.

Close by, Onaney ambled alone about the empty ballcourt, reminiscing woefully that Caonabó's caney had been home all her adult life and their children's birthplace. She would have chosen to be buried with him, and she had mused often whether life's purpose now included her death so their souls remained together in afterlife. But their eldest son had returned to Aniyana years ago, to compete to be its chieftain, and she had acknowledged Anacaona's offer of transporting her there so she could nurture him to mature as his father. She believed Caonabó would approve of that, and she would accompany Anacaona to Xaraguá to perserve that option.

Both women retired to sleep in their husband's caney for the last time and rose early to review Anacaona's escort as it assembled in the ballcourt. Scores of naborias would port Anacaona's possessions and bear Anacaona, Onaney, and a few elder nitaínos on litters of wood and reed mat hoisted on their shoulders, journeying over 130 miles southwest. A band of warriors would accompany as the mark of caciqual authority. Anacaona gracefully minced among the tearful villagers assembled, thanking them for years of homage, wishing them better health, and exhorting their confidence that life could improve. After the last goodbye, she sat upon her litter with Higueymota, now approaching womanhood, and, when lifted above the crowd, desperately fought back her own tears.

As Caonabó's funeral, the scene devastated her. Just three years before, such an escort would have included thousands of naborias and hundreds of warriors. All would have been healthy, well fed, bursting with energy, brimming with pride and confidence in themselves and their chiefdom, and bearing innumerable baskets of fruit, fowl, and fish to dispense to local caciques and villagers en route. Those before her were but the wizened survivors of that past, ravaged in body and spirit, aimlessly mimicking prior pageants. The few baskets of cazabi and fruit ported were meant for her and the caciqual party alone, hopefully enough to feed them until they arrived in Xaraguá's fertile farmland.

Anacaona smiled and waved bravely a last time, reciprocating the villagers' love and adoration as best she could, and the entourage departed the ballcourt to pass south through Maguana's great river valley. The sights there were yet more shocking. Anacaona was aghast to discover entire villages obliterated by pillage or pestilence, their plazas scattered with survivors crumpled motionless and helpless, apparently but awaiting death. Countless corpses lay strewn near riverbanks, where those collapsing had congregated for water, with hordes of vultures crowing to scavenge, and emanating a horrific stench. Gardens and crops, once fertile and abundant, lay wasted and overgrown.

That evening, Anacaona's escort rested at a village on the valley's southern rim, vacant but for corpses, as those surviving had fled to the mountains for roots or to escape the pale men's slave raiding. They then climbed for two days south over the mountains (the Sierra de Neiba), traversing a parched desert highland, eventually encountering local caciques in tiny villages who paid tribute to Behecchio. All soon gathered who passed, and Anacaona frequently halted to accept homage. She was heartened to discover the villages swelled with Maguanans who'd wandered across the mountains to seek the villagers' kindness and cazabi.

The entourage progressed into the fertile valley of the Neiba river, and Anacaona was astonished by the transformation of existence, which kindled piercing recollections of how life once had been.* Yuca, maize, sweet potato, and pepper crops lined the riverbanks and a web of irrigation channels fed by mountain streams. Villagers thronged to Anacaona's litter to praise her and overwhelmed her naborias and warriors with cazabi and fruit, which they ravenously accepted. Anacaona released her escort to feed and rest, and, in the evening, she strolled with local caciques along the river. She related the evil the pale men brought and Caonabó's death, promising that Behecchio and she would evade that fate. They begged how, and she flourished the spirits' rescue, unable to offer practical explanation.

The retinue's pace and swagger gained momentum as they veered west into Xaraguá proper, passing through verdant valleys south of

*The modern Río Yaque del Sur in the Neiba Valley, Dominican Republic.

the lakes Hagueygabon, Yainagua, and Guacca.* Anacaona remembered it vividly—field after field where women tended crops, forests and streams where men hunted and fished, all blessed by the spirits without hunger or other want. Within days, they arrived at the village a few miles west of Lake Guacca where Behecchio resided. When she dismounted in its plaza, he emerged from his massive caney to embrace her and welcome her home, to the thunderous applause of those gathered.†

⧈ ⧈ ⧈

Brother and sister sat alone in the shade of a secluded oasis of trees and shrub, gazing at the village stream placidly meandering before them.

"My husband failed to drive the pale men from the island, despite being a great warrior," Anacaona observed.

"Guarionex failed to strike a side-by-side coexistence with them, miserably, despite being a great statesman," Behecchio retorted. "They covet gold and our crops and relish enslaving us, nothing more." He shrugged his shoulders. "If the choices were war or coexistence, which would you choose, and what would you do differently than Caonabó or Guarionex?"

"Behecchio, they seek gold—first and foremost—and that's the objective of their settlements and truces," Anacaona explained. "That's to our advantage, because we have little—and we must tell them we have none. They must grasp that. Then maybe they'll leave Xaraguá alone."

Behecchio pondered before replying. "So, you favor a separate coexistence, not war?"

"A separate coexistence on the island. War isn't winnable, as they're now entrenched, with multiple forts," she answered, turning away, anxious that he wouldn't infer an insult. "Side-by-side coexistence doesn't work. They're brutish and wickedly abuse the superiority of their weapons when living among us. Their Christ-spirit is powerful, and he thrusts pestilence upon us wherever they erect his crosses." She

*Lake Enriquillo (Dominican Republic) and Lakes Étang Saumâtre and Trou Caïman (Haiti), respectively.

†In Haiti's Cul-de-Sac Plain, east of Port-au-Prince.

pointed east. "But our homeland is buffered from the rest of Haiti by mountain and desert. Perhaps we can convince them an invasion wouldn't yield gold and secure their promise to stay away."

"Caonabó was correct—they'll honor only agreements cast by arrow and spear," Behecchio lectured knowingly. "It's pointless simply to confess that Xaraguá hasn't any gold."

Anacaona frowned, angered by the machismo and disdain. "Behecchio, we'd be offering to acknowledge their presence elsewhere on the island and to trade peacefully with them, including food, for which they desperately hunger."

"They must dread that I can bring countless warriors to the battlefield, far more than they've already beheld." Behecchio clenched his teeth. "We'll burn any crosses they erect in Xaraguá."

"I suggest outstretching your hand as friend rather than foe," Anacaona reproved crossly. "We can't wait for their trespass. We must plot the first encounter with the Guamiquina or his brother and seduce them to an arrangement we can live with, before they impose one we can't."

"What if you're wrong? What if trade and food isn't enough for them? Suppose they want my subjects—and you and I—as slaves."

"That's not acceptable. But we can consider other traditional arrangements, as well." Anacaona rose from her duho to kneel directly before her brother, rasping her voice. "Years ago, our uncle gave my hand to Caonabó to protect our border, and we've always used marriage to cement alliances and truces between caciques. Those types of arrangements, uniquely reliant on women, are often more successful than arrows and spears."

XI

BATTLES OF SPIRITS AND MEN

Haiti's First Baptism,
Guaricano, September 21, 1496

Guarionex received Pané's invitation to witness Guatícabanu's baptism with remorse and contempt. The chieftain and his wives and children had devoted over a year to studying Christianity, training to pray daily and mastering the Apostles' Creed, the Ave María, and the Pater Noster. But he hadn't warmed to it spiritually or intellectually, and he'd abandoned his pursuit of the Christ-spirit's favor after the summer's slave raiding violated his understanding with the Guamiquina. As a practical matter, his invocation of the spirit increasingly jeopardized his vassal caciques' and subjects' loyalty, as Manicoatex and others now exhorted retaliation for the slave raiding, decrying continued submission. Guarionex agreed to attend the ritual merely as culmination of his education and because he'd yet to decide his own participation in resistance.

On September 21, in the morning cool, Frays Pané and Leudelle presided outside their church in Guaricano, delighted that the trials of the last three years at last would bear fruit with the baptism of Indians. The friars heartily welcomed Guatícabanu's family—four brothers, their mother, and almost a dozen others—who eagerly anticipated Guatícabanu's ceremony and that their own would follow in days. Pané hailed Guarionex with a grand salutation, although both knew their relationship had soured. Pané also warmly received Bakako as the chieftain's translator, commending that there'd now be another baptized Indian with whom to worship.

"Let's enter the Lord's house," Pané invited all in Catalan. "Today, we honor Saint Matthew, one of the apostles sent forth to teach all nations his Word. Matthew watches over us, together with all Christ's followers, as we welcome Guatícabanu into Christ's fold."

Pané beckoned Guatícabanu to kneel at the altar. The youth's brothers followed to wait at his side, bearing gourds of water.

"Are you ready and willing to accept Christ freely, of your own will?" Pané inquired.

"Yes. Soul ready," replied Gautícabanu, nodding thoughtfully.

Outwardly impassive, inwardly saddened, Guarionex considered the response honest but the trust in Christ astray. Bakako recognized the sincerity but despised that he'd never desired his own baptism.

"You *are* ready, and we proceed," Pané pronounced. "Your sponsor is none other than Admiral Cristóbal Colón, our governor for their most blessed Highnesses, King Fernando and Queen Isabel." He crossed Guatícabanu's forehead, recited verses from Matthew's gospel, and, to the congregation, firmly thrust, "Do all present renounce Satan and sin?"

All affirmed solemnly, save Guarionex and Bakako. Guarionex seethed that the enemy's Christ and Satan were but the head and tail of the same snake. Bakako coldly ignored the question, exhausted from living with the pale men's hypocrisy for nearly four years.

Pané dabbed sacramental oil on Guatícabanu's forehead and entreated him to vouch the same.

"I do," Guatícabanu vowed, dedicating himself to a peaceful life—just as his Taíno life of past, but with Christ.

Pané bid the brothers to raise their gourds and blessed the water within. "Douse your brother, a first time, to cleanse his body and soul from sin."

The brothers poured upon Guatícabanu's head, and the water cascaded down over his forehead to rinse his naked shoulders and body. Acknowledging the Holy Trinity, Pané reiterated the instruction twice more, and Guatícabanu glowed with a sense of purification and rebirth.

Guarionex trenchantly conceded the ritual's potent symbolism, impressed that the youth believed he was transforming. The pale men's religion offered not only the spirits' alliance during life but a bettered, transformed life. Guarionex admitted that many of his subjects would have found solace in Christ but for the pale men who brought him. Bakako scorned that his baptism's greatest fruit was protection from the pale men themselves.

"The Holy Spirit shall dwell in you hereafter, and you shall be united forever with Christ and with Christ's followers," Pané proclaimed resoundingly, gazing upon Gautícabanu. "I baptize you Juan Mateo in the name of the Father, the Son, and the Holy Ghost."

Gasps of astonishment passed through the congregation. Pané placed a white linen sash around Juan Mateo's neck and taught, "This represents the purity of your soul, dressing you as Christ."

Pané summoned the family forward to congratulate Juan Mateo, and Bakako courteously did so. Guarionex was circumspect, briefly wishing Guatícabanu the best and quickly departing, pondering whether the youth perceived the ritual as also embracing the Guamiquina's rule.

Guarionex, Rejection of Christianity,

Guaricano and Fort Concepción, Autumn 1496

Out of Pané's sight, Guarionex's pace slowed, and he trod darkly to his ceremonial bohío, devastated that his submission to the Guamiquina's tribute had failed to curb even the most horrific abuses. The trusted elderly behique posted at the bohío had sickened and died, and Guarionex instructed a youthful replacement to set Cacibaquel on the cohaba table.

"Father, no compromise protects us, even the most degrading," Guarionex confessed silently. "The pale men betray their promises. They enslave rather than spare us." He stared into the sockets of Cacibaquel's skull. "Caonabó's judgments were correct and mine have erred repeatedly."

Guarionex shut his eyes and sought his father's forgiveness. A vision of Cacibaquel soon dominated his consciousness and granted it, admonishing resistance rather than reproach.

"Manicoatex implores that we take up spears again, and we must!" Guarionex exhorted, overwrought by the memory of Adelantado demanding tribute while parading slaves in Guaricano.

Yet a warrior's hubris had eluded him his entire life—a disdain of hostility, rather than lack of bravery—and he desperately cried, "But am I fit to be the general? Can I plot and lead the enemy's annihilation?"

The vision of Cacibaquel lingered solemnly and indefinitely through the afternoon as storm clouds drifted by, birds flew in and out, and the sun passed its zenith. Unflinching, Guarionex came to appreciate that Cacibaquel counseled he had no choice but to try.

As the sun dipped west, Guarionex at last opened his eyes and reflected that he'd been a fool to permit Pané to reside within Guaricano. The pale behique undoubtedly served as spy, and Guatícabanu and his family likely would also. They all had to be rid from Guaricano before plotting the uprising—and the plot had to be hidden from Bakako.

⌑ ⌑ ⌑

A moon later, at dusk, Guarionex called Pané and Bakako to his ballcourt.

"I'll no longer study Christ," Guarionex bluntly announced. "I find him brother to Satan. How else can you explain the sins of his followers?"

Bakako looked to the ground as he translated, avoiding Pané's gaze.

"My Lord, you haven't prayed with me for weeks," Pané observed patiently, neither surprised by the notice nor cowed by the inflammatory heresy. "I understand you've been reproached by others for worshipping Christ when Christians have taken your lands." Pané spread his arms. "But we've come to teach the faith so you may attain eternal salvation. All of Juan Mateo's family have now been baptized."

Guarionex scowled.

"My Lord, remember the apostles' fate. Just as yourself, they were the first to see Christ's light and obey, and they suffered gruesome persecutions for that. The animosity you suffer from others will wash away when they understand what you understand of Christ, and they will praise you."

Guarionex studied Bakako's demeanor, concluding that he, too, was appalled by Pané's incomprehension of the devastation the pale men had wrought in Christ's name.

"Fray Pané, I'll no longer serve as apostle to lead my subjects to follow your spirit. I'll admonish them not to."

"Then I must depart," Pané threatened, shrugging his shoulders.

Guarionex shrugged back. "Good."

⊡ ⊡ ⊡

A week later, Bakako passed by Pané's church to say goodbye, catching Pané at the moment of departure. The congregation was erecting a small bohío nearby.

"Where are you going?" Bakako inquired.

"South, on the route to the new settlement, Santo Domingo," Pané replied. "The Adelantado's men say there's a cacique along the way named Mabiatué who wishes to follow Christ."

"Those here?"

"We'll all go, eventually. Fray Leudelle and Juan Mateo will accompany me to arrange our new home and chapel, and I'll summon the full congregation when Mabiatué agrees." Pané smiled contentedly. "Until then, they'll reside in the bohío to watch over the church's crucifix and relics. You should watch over them."

Bakako nodded, having no intention to do so.

"The Lord has a design for each of us," Pané observed, preaching to Bakako a last time. "The fruits of my labor aren't spoiled, as they will follow me and sow Mabiatué's subjects. You, in turn, can serve as the Christian cacique here instead of Guarionex."

Bakako nodded again, in courtesy alone, and waved as Pané, Leudelle, and Juan Mateo departed by foot.

⊡ ⊡ ⊡

At dawn two days later, Guarionex ordered six of his naborias to confront the olive Christians at the church and command that they destroy their crucifix and other cemís and, failing obedience, to seize the objects and destroy and bury them. He believed that justified retaliation—albeit woefully insufficient—for the countless times pale men had denigrated, burned, or looted his subjects' cemís, as well as defiant proof that he hadn't adopted Christianity. The crucifix would dwell in the earth, just as cemís of Yúcahu, forcing Christ to nurture cazabi and sweet potato for Guarionex's subjects rather than the Guamiquina's. Guarionex prohibited the naborias from harming the congregation beyond that necessary to fulfill his order, as his subjects weren't punishable for spiritual choices.

Several boys were tending the church when the naborias arrived, and they bravely denied the command and refused admission inside. But the naborias brusquely punched them aside to barge within and seize every cemí, including the crucifix and images of Christ, the Virgin, and revered saints, chortling mockery as they looted. Some boys were beaten as they sought to arrest the crime, others ran wailing to alert the congregation's elders, and a few trailed the naborias outside to ascertain the cemís' fate.

The naborias halted in a sweet potato field nearby to stomp on cemís and bury the crucifix in the earth, just as Guarionex had ordered, and they urinated upon the crucifix's grave, shouting to the Christ-spirit, "Now you will yield good and abundant fruit."

⊡ ⊡ ⊡

Fort Concepción's then commander, Miguel Ballester, an elderly Catalan from Tarragona, quickly dispatched alarm of the heathen atrocities to Bartolomé in the Yaque valley, where he was extracting tribute, and Bartolomé promptly marched with soldiers to the fort to punish the guilty. On arrival, he summoned Guarionex for interrogation.

Guarionex hadn't visited the multibuilding compound in weeks, since the last tribute payment, and he approached regally, attended by a ceremonial warrior and borne on a litter, determined to remind that he remained the direct sovereign of his chiefdom and subjects. On arrival, he sat down face-to-face with Bartolomé across a table set outside Ballester's hut, with Ballester and the warrior standing at their sides and Bakako squatting at their feet to interpret.

"Who did this heinous crime?" Bartolomé brusquely demanded.

"My subjects, of course," Guarionex retorted. "For over a year, your men have looted and destroyed my people's possessions daily, including countless cemís we venerate. Your brother promised to prevent such crimes. Perhaps the example of his betrayal corrupted a few of my subjects, and they destroyed a handful of your people's cemís." He glared into Bartolomé's eyes. "Perhaps a few viewed the retaliation as justice, given the promise."

Bartolomé slammed his fist to the table, outraged to be addressed as an equal, inflamed that the chieftain rudely dismissed the abomination of Christianity's denigration. "The Admiral never promised to tolerate pagan mockery!" he shouted, searching for stronger words. "Those who did this are the devil's agents and shall burn in Hell, forever. My king and queen would have them executed immediately, at the stake!"

Bakako nodded gravely as he translated the last sentence, confirming to Guarionex that such would be the perpetrators' fate in Spain.

"In my chiefdom, we don't punish so severely," Guarionex scorned. "You, of course, don't punish your own men at all, regardless that they mock our spirits daily."

Bartolomé shuddered with contempt but sat back in his chair to compose himself. Guarionex couldn't be punished, whether he'd orchestrated the crime or not. With Caonabó gone, Guarionex's friendship—or at least its appearance—remained the foundation for Española's peaceful subjugation.

"I demand again—who did this?" Bartolomé inquired, lowering his voice, refraining from probing Guarionex's involvement.

Guarionex shrugged, continuing to glare into Bartolomé's eyes.

"Who?" Bartolomé blurted to Bakako.

"I don't know," Bakako stammered, apprehensive that Guarionex's naborias would monitor every contact he made with Bartolomé thereafter.

Bartolomé blinked, distrustful of Bakako's response. "It's easy to determine, regardless of your intransigence," he retorted icily to Guarionex. "The friar's congregation cried out to us." He rose, indicating the audience concluded. "Don't permit such heresies ever again," he threatened. "When I return for the next tribute, be certain to possess every last bell of gold due. There'll be no accommodations." He and Ballester withdrew to the hut.

As they departed, Guarionex's warrior—his commanding general—scrutinized the defenses for weakness, and Guarionex sidled beside Bakako. "My brother-in-law, be mindful of what you say and do hereafter," he whispered.

Bakako was left to linger anxiously at the table, neither master trusting him to follow.

⊡ ⊡ ⊡

Within days, Bartolomé and Ballester hunted down the six naborias with the assistance of Juan Mateo's brothers. The defilers were bound, hauled before the church, summarily tried, and publicly executed in a manner never witnessed before on Haiti, scorching the onlookers with an abiding dread and terror for the pale men's brutality.

Soldiers set stakes, piled wood beneath, bound the six thereto, and lit the pyres. Flames kindled and rose. The six shrieked as their legs burned, writhed as their torsos roasted, gasped as smoke stole their breath, and heaved and convulsed as the flames towered to their eyes, their pain bursting inconceivable. The onlookers were petrified by the drawn pace of the agony and the victims' torture to implore death far sooner than it came.

Word of the unknown savagery passed from village to village through Haiti—more slowly than in prior years, as far fewer villages existed with villagers able to speak. In territory subjugated, the news revolted but didn't surprise, and, together with the most recent enslavements, it kindled a renewed thirst for revenge and war in lieu of submission.

Guarionex consoled the naborias' widows, and he harnessed the burgeoning anger, summoning his vassal caciques to a war council and cohaba ceremony many had beseeched.

⊡ ⊡ ⊡

Caciques from throughout Magua journeyed alone or with an inconspicuous escort to congregate surreptitiously one afternoon at Guarionex's ballcourt in Guaricano, where he greeted them gravely. Bakako wasn't invited. Many were so hungry that the vomiting purification ritual prior to a cohaba ceremony was unnecessary. They met at the ceremonial bohío that evening.

Burning at the stake in Mexico, taken from Theodor de Bry, 1598.
John Carter Brown Library, portion of rec. no. 0683-5.

"You must choose whether to unite with me in war," Guarionex entreated. "I'm resolute to exterminate the pale men, and to die for that. Those who participate must amass warriors so steeled."

"What's your plan?" a cacique demanded.

"I have one, but I'll reveal it only when I summon you for battle. It cannot be betrayed by a weakling. You must trust me."

"When must we be prepared?" a second cacique asked.

"Within three moons, but I'll advise merely a week in advance."

"I will fight, respecting Guarionex's wisdom and bravery," a third affirmed. "Caonabó's memory and soul urge us on."

"Those committed must join me in cohaba to invoke our union and victory," Guarionex concluded. "Those unsure should depart."

The cohaba ceremony commenced, dozens of caciques participating.

Cristóbal, Isabel and Fernando, Audience,
Burgos, October–December 1496

By October's end, Isabel and Fernando had interrogated Juan Aguado. His report echoed Fray Buil and Margarite's criticisms of Colón and dire predictions of the discoveries' economic failure, utterly at odds with Colón's repeated written assurances. Both sovereigns judged the time long passed for locating Cathay's temples and emperors, the receipt of gold shipments, and the settlement's self-sufficiency. But the criticisms and prognostications had been borne by imperfect messengers, and they resolutely looked forward to probing Cristóbal's own views in person, themselves, for the first time in over three years.

They anticipated he would puff and boast—as he always had—and they wouldn't trust or rely on his word alone. But choosing to replace or supplement him with another leader loomed impractical, as his knowledge and ability were indispensable and the risk of alienating his participation too great. Abandoning the enterprise would be foolishly premature, given he'd established an outpost in abundant islands *somewhere* in or nearby the Indies. The other heathen territories conquerable to expand their realms were limited. Informants now warned that Portugal's King Manoel I was eager to renew the race to Cathay by circumnavigating Guinea.

They summoned Cristóbal to meet in the great hall of the Casa de Cordón palace. Courtiers had forewarned that he'd appear in a friar's habit—some sniping it a ruse of humility, others a symptom of lunacy. Cristóbal did enter the hall so dressed, and Isabel was stunned instantly by the blister and wear of his skin, his unkept beard, and the slowness of his gait compared to years prior.

As he approached, she realized that he'd suffered greatly, and she was struck that the habit might be neither ruse nor lunatic but just as it appeared, a statement that his trials had brought him closer to the Lord, just as her own had brought her. Fernando was equally astonished by the apparent exhaustion, and he quickly surmised that

Cristóbal had endured just as much agony as the men he led, as a true commander should. Both grasped that his critics had pained for the crown's account far less.

As he reached their dais, Cristóbal was heartened by Isabel's smile—just as he remembered—and Fernando's gracious wave to forgo a prolonged genuflection. Yet his gut wrenched for his demise, his haunt since discovering Navidad's fate. His sons, with whom he'd reunited earlier, had cautioned that the sovereigns would be skeptical of him at best, perhaps entirely dismissive, disenchanted by courtiers bent on his ruin. Scores of them swarmed about the great hall, gaping like vultures eyeing a carcass. But the sovereigns had been unrelenting skeptics for seven years, and he'd surmounted the same critics to convince them he'd find the quickest route to the Indies and its gold. Cristóbal steeled himself to present confidently. He'd come to show those promises satisfied. He knelt to kiss their feet humbly and then rose to address them.

"Your Highnesses, I bring you news of great triumphs in your name," Cristóbal heralded, emulating the bravado of past as best he could. "Your Española has been subjugated, countless other islands possessed, and terra firma's eastern extremities explored. Since my last letters, we've discovered Española's greatest gold mines. All is as I promised."

"My Admiral, that heartens us," Isabel responded cordially. "Tell us of each island and the mainland, starting with Española. How goes the settlement and my subjects' welfare?"

"Your Highnesses, I'll show you first, for I've brought you gifts," Cristóbal replied, bidding his naked Indians to enter the hall. The assembled hushed and gawked as the surviving band paraded forth, adorned with gold jewelry and gold-inlaid belts, bearing face masks, plants, and squawking, brightly colored parrots.

"I present Don Diego, brother of the late king Caonabó, ruler of Española's interior," Cristóbal proclaimed, bidding the Indian kneel. "He humbles himself to acknowledge submission to your rule." Cristóbal tarried as Fernando scrutinized Don Diego's gold crown and necklace, more elegant in design and fulsome in gold than those worn by the Canarian rulers he'd embraced over the past decades.

"Most of Española's kings have submitted," Cristóbal declared, directing Wasu and Ukuti to place a small chest at the sovereigns' feet. "They have agreed to pay you tribute every three months, typically in gold." Cristóbal pointed to the jewelry and the few gold nuggets. "This is but a sample of that paid in tribute, alone. This winter, rich mines were found near the island's southern coast and a blockhouse built for the miners, who've just begun to dig."

Cristóbal gazed to Isabel, and he waved toward Wasu and Ukuti. "These boys are my servants, born on Española near the township established in your name. Just weeks ago, they received the baptismal waters in Guadalupe before the great Virgin and were reborn—as Cristóbal and Pedro."

Cristóbal pivoted toward Fernando. "There're now seven forts, stretching from the township of Isabela south to the mines." He puckered his lips, as if somber. "Conquest hasn't been as easy as I'd hoped." Cristóbal bid Wasu and Ukuti to lay a few bows and arrows at the king's feet. "As I warned in my letters, there's been resistance to your rule and the need for defensive protections, and war captives have been taken. But the route to the mines is now well protected."

Cristóbal folded his arms across his chest, daring any critic to challenge his showmanship, pausing while Isabel and Fernando evaluated the gold. He then dismissed the Indians and commenced his fuller explanation, relating a chronology of what had transpired over the three years, including the trials and his solutions. He barely disguised his enmity toward Pisa, Margarite, Aguado, and Buil and loathsomely recounted the failings and disobedience of the first two. He was forthright about the precarious condition of the settlement and the need to resupply it immediately.

The sovereigns interrupted often, seeking detailed information on the mines, the island's timber, cotton, and other treasures. They queried the settlement's progress toward farming its own food and the settlers' health. They understood and approved the proposed relocation of Isabela to the southern coast, closer to the mines.

"When will they commence production?" Fernando inquired of the mines. "When will we receive the gold tendered in tribute?"

"We need more trained miners," Cristóbal advised. "But I expect production this year," he crowed, sensing the critics hovering. "Tribute payments also shall increase, as we institute the process for its collection and more territory is subjugated," he lied.

"Do settlers remain loyal to you and your brother?" Fernando pushed.

"Those prepared to work and suffer the hardships typical of new settlements have always been loyal," Cristóbal assured, gazing at the king. Turning to the audience, he warned, "Those who've shirked their duty to you and the queen have been more difficult to command."

"Are you distributing food to the hungry?" Isabel pried. "Do the settlers view your punishments as too harsh?"

"All hunger, including myself and my brothers, and all receive their rations." Cristóbal pondered the second question. "I take a firm hand to disobedience to your rule."

"What of the Indians? Do you treat them kindly, as I instructed?"

"Other than resisters," he lied again, nodding. "The Lord punishes those hostile with starvation and pestilence."

Isabel and Fernando probed little further on the last questions, as they'd heard Aguado. Nearly all settlers hungered and decried the Colóns' justice. Looting, rape, and abuse of Indians abounded, including their enslavement as manservants, maids, and concubines and wanton cruelties. The latter revelation hadn't really surprised either sovereign. Both well understood the excesses of men hungry and lonely in military campaigns and the expectation that looting, rape, and enslavements were rewards for hardship. Both recognized their vassals' contempt for naked heathens and presumption that servitude was due. Neither even mentioned nor invited Cristóbal to challenge Aguado's report, seeing little benefit in inflaming false denials.

Cristóbal concluded by recounting the arduous explorations of Cuba and Yamaye and his identification that Cuba was the Golden Chersonese, captivating everyone and forcing even the critics to recognize his extraordinary ability as mariner and explorer. With those credentials reaffirmed, he stepped forward to promote his third voyage.

"Your Highnesses, the Indians say there's a great landmass to the south, apart and distinct from terra firma," Cristóbal explained.

"King João always expected as much and fought to preserve his claim to it in the treaty negotiated. It behooves us to find it, claim what is yours, and possess its treasures."

Cristóbal opened his arms in supplication and glanced into Isabel's eyes and then Fernando's. "I must return to Española promptly, to ensure the mines' production and plant your banners on this prize."

The audience cringed, hushed and quivering, flabbergasted to foresee dethronement wither, reauthorization blossom, and the carcass reborn.

"What do you request of us?" Fernando asked.

"Eight ships, two to sail immediately, with meat, wine, and other provisions to resupply the settlement. Six to sail soon thereafter under my command, bearing more supplies and to discover the southern landmass."

"You've done us signal service," Isabel commended grandly. "You must continue exploring, and we view your request favorably."

"Draw up the particulars of what you need," Fernando instructed definitively. "Understand that crises abound at home that demand funding."

Cristóbal felt his limbs sag and bones tremble, and he fought to maintain his balance as he bowed deeply. "I will, and I praise and adore Your Highnesses for your understanding and support."

Isabel raised her hand solemnly and gravely addressed her admiral. "You must treat our Spanish vassals and the Indians well," she cautioned. "In the future, be more moderate and less severe with them both."

⊡ ⊡ ⊡

That evening, Isabel and Fernando conferred alone, beyond earshot of courtiers and court chroniclers.

"How much more shall we expend on the Indies?" Isabel mused, shrugging her shoulders.

"Not a maravedí more, until Colón delivers the gold promised," Fernando rasped. "We tell Fonseca to sit on his heels until then, regardless of Colón's request."

"What of the two ships—and the immediate resupply of those hungry?"

Burgos in the sixteenth century. Civitates Orbis Terrarum.

"They volunteered for Española, and they haven't produced the gold yet."

On October 29, Pero Alonso Niño's slave ships anchored in Cádiz with the paltry gold shipment and almost three hundred slaves yet surviving in the summer heat, who were transferred to Fonseca's agents for sale. Pero Alonso estimated his slave cargo worth millions of maravedís, and, without mentioning the slaves, he wrote the sovereigns that he'd arrived with gold worth that amount and then tarried at home in Moguer as the slaves were sold, rather than rushing to court.

The sovereigns delighted upon learning gold had arrived! They congratulated themselves that the Indies now could self-fund! Fernando committed sums previously earmarked for the third voyage to troop deployments along the Pyrenees, advising Cristóbal to finance the voyage with the gold shipped.

The sovereigns raged upon learning gold hadn't arrived! They stormed on discovering the enslavements! Furious, they summoned Cristóbal to answer for Pero Alonso's conduct, and the Indies' critics circled round, clamoring again that the gold was a fraud, the Admiral a liar. Isabel and Fernando reprimanded Cristóbal, admonishing that the permissibility of a slave trade remained in doubt. The funds previously earmarked no longer were available to him.

But they didn't revoke their approval for the third voyage or their permission that Pero Alonso's "gold" be used for its funding, including permitting that the slaves be bartered to satisfy debts outright.

◘ ◘ ◘

On November 30, Isabel, Fernando, and Portugal's Manoel I had cause to celebrate—after years of coaxing, Princess Isabel at last had consented to marry Manoel, and marriage terms were finalized. The widowed princess was loath to forsake the memory of her departed spouse, João's son, Afonso, and she insisted that the marriage contract require Manoel to expel the Jews from Portugal, just as her parents had expelled them from Spain. Since Afonso's death, her retreats into solitary worship had grown more mystical and intense and Cisneros's bearing and outlook more influential. She believed the Jews had cast an evil spell on Afonso causing his fall, meriting the severest justice.

Isabel and Fernando's own expulsion edict had offered their Jewish subjects the choice of conversion to Christianity or emigration, and the largest portion of those emigrating from Spain had crossed the border to Portugal, the easiest path (1492). At the time, João permitted those wealthy or craftsmen to purchase the right to remain in his kingdom and required all others to emigrate in eight months. That subsequent emigration largely had failed to occur, as ships weren't provided and the intended emigrants lacked resources, and they remained in Portugal to be subjected to repressions, property confiscations, and enslavements under João's rule.

Young Manoel, then twenty-seven, viewed the presence of the Jews more benignly, and he had freed those enslaved after assuming the crown. Nevertheless, as promised, on December 5, he issued a similar edict of expulsion, affording all Jews ten months to convert or depart Portugal, vanquishing an entire people yet a second time.

◘ ◘ ◘

Back in Española, settlers continued to disparage the Indians' superstitions and loot and burn their false idolatries. More crosses rose at Santo Domingo to mark Christianity and ward off Satan and the Indians' evil spirits.

⧈ ⧈ ⧈

The sovereigns soon celebrated a signature achievement.

Decades past, the papacy had bestowed Charles's father, Louis XI, with the honorific the Most Christian King, which Charles blithely had assumed. For two years, Pope Alexander had pondered awarding Fernando and Isabel a title to commemorate their defending the papacy against the French, as well as the Reconquista's fulfillment, the Jews' expulsion, and other Christian triumphs. In December, he relished formally awarding it and mocking Charles.

By bull dated December 19, Alexander acclaimed Isabel and Fernando the Catholic Monarchs, heralding that the French throne had been surpassed and demoted.

Anacaona, Behecchio, and Bartolomé,
Xaraguá, Early 1497

Anacaona sat secluded with Behecchio in his tree-bound oasis. The village stream coursed before them, twinkling sublimely as sunlight flickered through leaves and limbs canopied above.

"Scouts report the slave master approaches," Behecchio acridly related. "He's done wresting cazabi from those starving along the Yaque and burning Guarionex's naborias to death. He's usurped land at the Ozama's mouth, trampled its residents, and destroyed their cemís." He pivoted to his sister, seated beside him. "Now he turns on us."

"Undoubtedly, for gold and food," Anacaona replied. "Meet him before he arrives, peacefully. Lie that we haven't any gold. Show him our farmlands. Offer to pay him crops every three moons upon his promise the pale men won't intrude into Xaraguá. Seize the opportunity to spare us from the others' fate."

"My sister, the pale men don't honor promises," Behecchio rebuked haughtily. "Guarionex has learned that twice now. So has the fool Guacanagarí." He sighed, regretful for revisiting their prior argument, and softened his tone. "The scouts say the Guamiquina's brother marches with barely a hundred soldiers. My warriors could destroy them all."

"Then what?" Anacaona exclaimed, as dismissively. "The Guamiquina will return, craving vengeance! Don't be the fool yourself, Behecchio. You sent warriors to fight with Guatiguaná and Manicoatex, and their battles ended in defeat." She searched for the counter to Behecchio's criticism. "You must convince them of three things—you can render them food, you have no gold, and—if necessary—you can annihilate any trespassers. Then they'll have no incentive to invade, promise or not."

Behecchio pondered some moments, grittily accepting Anacaona's observations on the futility of open warfare, yet doubtful the pale men could be frightened away or take his word Xaraguá hadn't gold. "I'll bring the Guamiquina's brother here, and together we'll judge if such a truce should be struck. If not, I'll slay them in their sleep." Forlorn, he cast a pebble into the water, beholding the ripples subside and vanish, the pebble's impact fleeting and inconsequential to the stream's inexorable flow.

⌑ ⌑ ⌑

Bartolomé brought his band of a hundred men to ford a fulsome river in a fertile floodplain, four days' march west from Santo Domingo through unexplored territory. He'd just spent weeks supervising the ongoing construction of Cristóbal's new fortified residence and a storehouse overlooking the Ozama. His experienced guides and interpreters, Indians from the Bajabonico once tutored by Bakako, informed him the river was the Neiba and that local caciques farther west would be vassal to Xaraguá's Behecchio. Bartolomé dispatched half his men south along the coast to examine the timber of forests Cristóbal had sighted from the sea. He and the remainder bivouacked at the river for the night.

The next morning, before dawn, Bartolomé's lookouts roused all to warn that a large Indian army was approaching, and they quickly grouped in a defensive circle. But the Indians halted beyond shouting distance, and, when the sun rose, a small delegation approached, apparently led by a cacique. Bartolomé stepped from his circle and, with his interpreters and two armed soldiers, cautiously advanced to meet the cacique, raising his arms weaponless.

"I am the Adelantado, Bartolomé Colón, ruler of this island in my brother's absence," he pronounced, lowering his arms to fold them across his chest.

"I am Behecchio, the sole and supreme ruler of Xaraguá," Behecchio countered, observing Bartolomé gauge the size of his army. "You approach my dominion. Those behind me are my warriors, who defend it. Why do you come?"

"I arrive to demand that you pay gold tribute to my brother, just as other caciques do," Bartolomé rejoined, ignoring the challenge. "We mean you and your people no harm."

Behecchio was astonished by the pale man's arrogant confidence and brazen courage. "We possess no gold to give you, even if we desired to. You should depart."

"If you have no gold, you may pay us timber, cotton, and cazabi," Bartolomé retorted calmly, confidently, and firmly.

"What do you offer to trade in return?"

"Peace, vassalage to the earth's greatest Christian princes, and Christ, the Lord."

"Peace is insufficient, vassalage unacceptable, and Christ unwanted," Behecchio responded, matching Bartolomé's demeanor in every respect. "But I'm willing to discuss a peaceful relationship of our peoples, based on mutual respect." He studied Bartolomé's visage, perceiving comprehension and calculation, if not flexibility. "The spirits I honor favor respectful arrangements, even among those who aren't friends."

"What do you envision?"

"We must trust each other, before we decide," Behecchio warned. "Come visit my village. I promise you and your men no harm, and we will parley."

Bartolomé consented, and Behecchio escorted him and his band back to the residence near Lake Guacca, a journey of three days. Bartolomé was stunned by the irrigation of the valleys traversed, the production of yuca, maize, fruit, and cotton, and the health of the Indians compared to those in territory conquered. Xaraguá's food supply could alleviate every settler's hunger.

Behecchio relished that Adelantado was so impressed. But he loathed Adelantado's pitiless apathy that the territories conquered, and peoples subjugated, also had been fertile and healthy before the pale men's arrival. Adelantado was kin to a shark, relentless in motion from prey to prey to sustain himself.

Anacaona had arranged a tremendous reception. Behecchio's thirty wives and scores of daughters and nieces met the pale men as they entered the village, dancing and singing, the wives naked but for naguas and jewelry, the girls but for headbands—delighting Bartolomé's band and lulling them to feel safe. Cazabi, fruits, and chicha satisfied their hunger and thirst. At dusk, the celebration continued with a great feast of fish, fowl, and more chicha and dancing, all snug inside Behecchio's grand caney.

Anacaona then made her entrance, to sit with Behecchio and Bartolomé as they enjoyed the performances.

"This is my sister, Anacaona," Behecchio announced, spellbinding Bartolomé's interpreters that they sat in the presence of Haiti's most renowned woman.

"Your Highness, a pleasure," Bartolomé replied courteously, struck by the Indian woman's uncommon elegance and beauty. The slender nagua strung from her naval swayed between her legs to advise she was married.

"Adelantado, how long have you lived on Haiti?" Anacaona asked, smiling.

"Over two years."

"So, you have met many of our caciques?" she inquired, as if inviting a chat.

"Most of them."

"What is your opinion of them?" she puzzled, as if intrigued. "Are they as brave and intrepid as rulers in your homeland?" She shot a glance into his eyes and arched her back, protruding her breasts. "You yourself must be very courageous to come here with so few men."

"Those who befriend us are very wise, my lady." Bartolomé shot an eye back, attracted but resolutely and visibly unmoved. "Those who oppose are not."

"I've known many of them—Guacanagarí, Guarionex, Caonabó," Anacaona responded, undeterred. "Brave men all—but you've treated them differently?"

"Much differently, Your Highness, and it serves as good warning to your brother," Bartolomé cautioned, peering into Anacaona's eyes, as if to force the pluck of his manhood before her. "Those who accept King Fernando and Queen Isabel's rule survive, those who reject it perish."

Anacaona's eyes widened, as if impressed by that pith. "How did Caonabó die?"

Bartolomé's interpreters squirmed to translate the question, alarmed by their master's ignorance of whom he addressed. "Aboard ship, too foolish to submit, forgotten by his people," Bartolomé pronounced, his eyes smitten to wander over her body.

Anacaona smiled again, leading the fool's eyes back to her face, concealing her pride in her husband's indomitability, exalting inwardly. "You don't take no for an answer, do you," she lured.

As the evening waned, Behecchio offered Bartolomé's men a dozen different bohíos for the night, isolating them apart, and welcomed Bartolomé and six others into his caney. Before retiring, he conferred with Anacaona, admitting that it'd be premature to assassinate them.

⊡ ⊡ ⊡

The next morning, Behecchio led Bartolomé on a tour of nearby cazabi and cotton gardens, expounding how his people irrigated the land to harvest crops year-round, producing far more food than needed. At midday, he invited Bartolomé to another banquet set under a great reed canopy erected beside his caney, and Anacaona sang an areíto to explain that spirituality, civility, and beauty were Xaraguá's greatest treasures, although it possessed no gold. By then, Bartolomé's interpreters had alerted him that Anacaona had been Caonabó's wife, for which he felt no remorse, although her slyness and absence of a husband intrigued him. At the feast's conclusion, Behecchio and Anacaona led Bartolomé to sit between them at the canopy's edge, overlooking Behecchio's ballcourt, and Behecchio announced that his warriors would demonstrate their bravery and ferocity.

At that instant, horrific war cries resounded from the ends of the ballcourt, spears and arrows arched in flight in both directions across it, and two squadrons of warriors oiled in red and black war paint charged across to assault each other in mortal combat. Stone axes pierced limbs, macanas crushed bones, and the stingray's venom—borne by arrow and spear tips—burned flesh from within. Shrieks terrorizing turned to howls of pain, blood gushed over the war paint, and many fell wounded, two dead.

"Our warriors exalt sacrifice in defense of our homeland and traditions," Behecchio pronounced, gazing as if proudly upon the battle raging. "They will obey any command I give, instantly, regardless of certain death."

"My men are the same, selfless," Bartolomé lied, cognizant that his band was then vulnerable but steeled to retain a conqueror's composure. "Their weapons are fierce," he reminded.

"They must be very brave, as well," Behecchio complimented. "Because they are so few."

"They're assisted by our horses and dogs, and the chieftains now allied with us," Bartolomé blustered.

Two more perished in agony on the ballcourt.

"My warriors would die to the last man defending myself and my rule," Behecchio proclaimed.

"They should die no more today," Bartolomé replied, subdued by the spectacle. "I come in peace so that no one dies."

"I also want peace." Behecchio thrust his arm to the sky, shouted for the battle to end, and turned to Bartolomé. "But I'm prepared for war unless you leave my chiefdom alone."

⌑ ⌑ ⌑

On the third day, Behecchio and Anacaona greeted Bartolomé and interpreters in the ballcourt, cleansed of the bloodshed, yet pregnant with it.

"King Fernando and Queen Isabel are now the island's supreme rulers," Bartolomé brusquely noted. "What is the tribute you consent to pay them?"

"Adelantado, your caciques are not sovereign over Xaraguá," Behecchio replied. "I am that, alone." He stared into Bartolomé's eyes. "But I will pay you ransom in return for your promise that your people will not settle in my chiefdom and never enter it. I also won't oppose your subjugation of the remainder of the island."

Bartolomé hesitated, angered by the refusal to submit but cognizant that European princes often made similar arrangements.

He reasoned the concept sufficient for the moment and nodded. "What will you pay?"

"Cazabi, other crops, cotton. As you know, we have no gold."

Bartolomé scrutinized Behecchio and Anacaona's gold jewelry, disbelieving but resigned to relent. "The produce must be in quantity sufficient to feed my men on an ongoing basis. You must sow and provide more cotton in lieu of gold."

"You agree to not settle here and prohibit your men's trespass?"

"We must enter your chiefdom to collect that due, every three months," Bartolomé coldly observed. "Otherwise, we will comply," he promised, doubting he could ensure all Spaniards did so.

"Your food supply depends on that compliance," Behecchio concluded, rising to leave for his caney, marking he cared nothing for Adelantado's friendship. "I bid you depart, promptly."

But Anacaona lingered in the ballcourt. "When you return, I'll show you how we live in Xaraguá, as a civilized people." She grinned amicably. "Perhaps we can achieve a peace and separateness based on love rather than fear."

Uprising,
Fort Concepción, Early 1497

Although the village awarded him was but twenty minutes' walk to Guaricano and then twenty more to the fort, Bakako's existence there had now escaped the daily oversight of both his brother-in-law and Admiral's officers for months. He remained charged to care for pale men too sick to commingle at the fort, lodging them in a bohío nearby his own, but Commander Ballester hadn't the resources or time to supervise or visit. Bakako and his wife, Ariana, expanded his bohío to become a chieftain's caney, and while existence remained precarious, his naborias' harvest of fresh yuca plantings averted the perish of both his villagers and pale men.

Bakako also renewed frequent conversation with Yutowa, whom he treated as if a nitaíno, although Yutowa grew increasingly frail and unsound. To keep him occupied, as well as residing apart, Bakako built him a lean-to at the far end of the yuca field, entrusting him to supervise naborias grinding and baking the yuca and affording shelter at night.

Ariana soon went into labor, and naborias attended as she grasped the limb of a nearby tree to hang for hours squatting below, groaning softly at first and then wailing before the baby came. Bakako was graven by the pain suffered on his behalf and then delighted to behold and cradle the infant, a boy. As customary, Ariana wrapped the babe's head in cotton and a wood piece to flatten the forehead, and she and Bakako and Yutowa conferred names. Bakako's chose his father's, commemorating Guanahaní, and Ariana chose Diego, so the child might have a safe future.

Bakako's sabbatical from chaos expired when Bartolomé arrived one morning in March, trudging south from Isabela with almost two hundred settlers, intending to press two dozen more invalids into Bakako's custody. Resupply ships hadn't arrived for eight months, and on returning from Xaraguá, Bartolomé had found Isabela once again decimated by pestilence and hunger. Over half of the three hundred remaining residents lay infirm, incapacitated, or dying. Most of the ill were to be relocated in the forts between Isabela and Santo Domingo where food still was procurable, each fort to bear a portion. The healthy would march on to Santo Domingo. Bakako pleaded to be saddled with fewer charges, as his crops wouldn't support so many.

Bartolomé denied the request stridently, ruling that Bakako muster food elsewhere in the valley, and summarily departed—his entourage shambling behind—within the hour to remind Guarionex and Ballester that tribute fell due shortly. Despondent, Bakako ordered his naborias to erect an additional bohío and ushered the newcomers to live in the shade of trees in the interim.

After dusk, Bakako ambled from the morbid gloom and disarray of his compound to while away the evening with Yutowa, secluded in the lean-to, surrounded by bountiful green yuca bobbing sublimely in a soft breeze as the stars revealed themselves in the darkening sky.

"Why have the spirits set this course, for both peoples?" Yutowa lamented. "We hate the pale men's presence. They hate being here."

"These men suffer to deliver conquest and gold to Admiral, Isabel, and Fernando," Bakako replied, doubting Yutowa would provide cheer. "Admiral and his caciques care nothing of suffering—either our peoples' or theirs."

"Why should you heal them?" Yutowa challenged. "Why should I bake their yuca? I could leave it uncured, so they die in agony."

"We eat the cazabi, too, my friend," Bakako answered firmly. "You, my family, and my naborias. So, keep pressing the poison out." He stared across the yuca field. "Our lot remains a nightmare, but it's better than before—and preferable to death." Bakako shrugged. "I have no explanation for the spirits' design."

"Why shouldn't I die?" Yutowa blurted, burying his face in his hands. "The Cubans were going to murder Admiral—and I protected him! I saved the evilest man ever born!"

"You didn't know that then," Bakako comforted, despairing for his friend. "You did what any Taíno would do, knowing what you did. You're a good person, Yutowa, not bad."

"Where's Admiral now?" Yutowa whined. "Has he left everyone to die—both slaves and soldiers?"

Bakako shrugged and placed his hands over his own ears tightly.

◘ ◘ ◘

Earlier that afternoon, Guarionex curtly had assured Bartolomé and Ballester that he'd deliver the gold due in two weeks. Gruffly accepting, Bartolomé had departed for Santo Domingo.

Guarionex relished that Bartolomé's entourage appeared desperately hungry and withered, plainly including slave masters scabbing at the penis. Scouts reported that the Guamiquina had yet failed to return and reinforcements for his settlement hadn't arrived. The pale men were languishing and dying everywhere they'd trespassed. The graveyards at Isabela were the only plots growing there, and the forts now served largely as infirmaries, housing—together with the new settlement at the Ozama—most of the invasion. Astonishingly, scouts estimated Isabela had dwindled to but a hundred men after the current relocations, and Guarionex puzzled whether the pale men's chieftains had lost interest or resolve in their conquest. Whatever the cause, the pale men's presence had waned to the weakest since its inception, and he steeled himself to overthrow it.

Guarionex and his general also cringed at their own people's decimation, that their warriors numbered far fewer than before, with those surviving lean skeletons of prior selves. But they were confident in mustering an army of fifteen thousand. As Bartolomé's backside vanished south, they resumed urgent plotting. Surprise, speed, and secrecy were essential.

"When you deliver the tribute, armed warriors must port it rather than naborias," the general proposed. "The pale guardsmen will divert to observe them, leaving the perimeter unwatched. When you hand over the gold and cazabi, do so with a flourish and a speech, so I have time to encircle the army about the fort."

"How long will you need?" Guarionex inquired, confident he could feign homage to the Guamiquina and pale caciques at great length.

"Five minutes, at most," the general responded. "I won't bring the entire army close. Only the fittest. They must storm the compound before the guardsmen arm their weapons or mount or release their beasts." He contemplated Guarionex's resolve, proud of his chieftain's audacity and courage. "I won't wait for you to give a signal. The warriors porting the tribute must protect you."

Guarionex nodded, unperturbed by death, jealous instead to witness Ballester wilt in terror on perceiving ruin and Christ's desertion. For an instant, Guarionex's vigor surged, overcome by a vision of demolishing the fort and marching north and south to crush the other settlements.

"The pale men have their own scouts and spies," he cautioned. "When do I summon our armies to assemble and trek here?"

"No more than a few days prior," the general replied. "The pale men's eyes and ears are focused most keenly on you. Go about your daily activities, calmly, as you always would, avoiding suspicion."

Guarionex understood and judged that no change in his routine or demeanor was required. He would seclude often to worship the spirits in his ceremonial bohío. None would suspect he invoked Yúcahu's alliance and victory.

◘ ◘ ◘

After a week, consistent with habit, Guarionex did summon Bakako to assist in reporting to Ballester.

"How many pale men do you feed now?" he inquired, as his naborias hoisted him on a litter.

"Almost forty," Bakako replied, doubting the question was idle conversation. "Two died this month. They refused our remedies." Bakako treaded close below the chieftain as the walk south commenced.

"Are any healthy?" Guarionex probed, without concealing satisfaction at the deaths.

"No. All healthy go to the fort."

"We shall arrange for tribute's delivery next week." He gazed down to scrutinize Bakako's face, alert for the slightest reaction to that suggestion—but there was none. "How are my sister and youngest nephew?"

"Both are well," Bakako replied, glancing upward, cautious that the question seemed more than courtesy.

"May you and they remain in good health," Guarionex remarked. "A man's highest duty is to care for his family and people."

When they arrived at the fort, pale sentries led them inside the compound to meet Ballester.

"We will come with tribute—this day, next week," Guarionex advised.

"We need cazabi, maize, and sweet potato, in addition to the gold," Ballester directed.

"I offered to plant a garden coast to coast to furnish you that," Guarionex retorted coldly, as Ballester had come to expect. "But your master required gold instead." Guarionex studied Ballester's reaction to the rebuke, relishing that the pale commander would die by the spear rather than hunger or a burning crotch. "Nevertheless, we'll bring as much food as we can. I trust the Guamiquina will appreciate that—and my loyalty and obedience to your king and queen. Will Adelantado attend to acknowledge my service?"

"He's in Santo Domingo," Ballester replied. "But he'll appreciate it."

Business done, enmity radiating, Guarionex and Bakako departed back to Guaricano.

"I'll summon you when I'm prepared to return here," Guarionex instructed, gazing down from atop his litter. "Until then, rest at home—caring for my sister and nephew. Alert me to anything Ballester requests of you."

Bakako nodded, and the two waved goodbyes when Guarionex diverted to his caney.

⊡ ⊡ ⊡

Bakako shied from returning directly to his village, disgusted by the idle of its pale men as they barked for naborias to fetch water and cazabi. He poked through Guaricano instead, brooding on Guarionex's instructions to inform—never before expressed so bluntly. He wandered past Pané's church, still standing and, to Bakako's surprise, still functioning.

Guatícabanu's brothers were tending the fields beside it, one standing close by the church. Bakako approached.

"How goes it, Diego?" the brother amiably hailed. "I hear you have a son."

Bakako grinned and related the infant's birth. "How goes it with Juan Mateo?"

"He's assisted Fray Pané in building a new church, to the south. Soon he'll return to lead us there." The brother clasped his hands and smiled to show contentedness. "We'll help the pale men bring our people to the faith."

Bakako nodded and then wandered on, shying from confiding that duty as a remora was perilous.

⊡ ⊡ ⊡

Bartolomé had spent but days in Santo Domingo when he received Ballester's urgent message that Indians were planning to attack Fort Concepción. Indefatigable, as his brother, Bartolomé gathered his healthy men and trekked north, day and night, entering the fort's compound within two days, before dawn.

"What do we know?" he demanded, panting.

"Indians living near the fort have fled, fearing violence," Ballester replied. "An attack's certain."

"Diego reports what?" Bartolomé stammered.

"Nothing. He claims he's heard no rumors of plotting or alliances," Ballester deplored, shrugging. "Only that the slave raiding alienates Guarionex."

Bartolomé groaned derisively, distrustful.

"But I had the Christian Indians interrogated," Ballester reported. "One had heard that Guarionex dispatched runners throughout the valley days ago. Another suspected that warriors have arrived to lodge in villages nearby."

"Have you confronted Guarionex?"

"I saw risk, as he's likely involved, possibly orchestrating," Ballester explained. "He came to visit a week ago, confirming that he'd come tomorrow morning to submit the tribute." Ballester sucked in heavily and exhaled, his voice cracking. "My Adelantado, that delivery appears deceit! It's the attack itself!"

Bartolomé winced and concurred. "We don't have enough men! Guarionex can summon thousands." He mused further but was decisive. "We must seize him as hostage tonight, together with his vassal caciques."

Ballester's eyes widened, stunned by the violent man-to-man assaults proposed, awed by the audacity and courage called to pull them off—in darkness, no less.

"That'll leave the heathens without commanders, and we shall ransom the caciques' lives for the treason's cessation," Bartolomé exhorted.

Terrified, Ballester grasped the gambit essential to their safety and agreed. "We know the huts where Guarionex's vassals reside," he assured, having collected cazabi from them many times. "Some are miles away."

"I will seize Guarionex myself," Bartolomé pronounced. "When the moon rises, dispatch your captains to capture as many caciques as they can."

◘ ◘ ◘

Guarionex couldn't sleep, and, as the moon rose, he sat alone inside his caney before its firepit, fortifying himself to command and fight and suffer the bloodshed of wounds inevitable. His meditative trance waxed and waned past the moon's zenith, then abruptly shattered as he heard footsteps charging rapidly and glimpsed silhouettes darting at the caney's threshold. His confidence and vision collapsed as soldiers slammed him to the ground. His plot's discovery crushed and drained his soul, even so far as numbing the brutish jabs of being bound, gagged, and hauled from his home. The villainy of Adelantado's voice and the degradation of groveling at his feet at the fort were the most horrific of all.

"You've plotted against the Admiral!" Bartolomé shouted in the moonlight. "You've committed treason to your king and queen! Tell me who's going to attack, immediately!" He raised his fist and lied. "Or you'll die, here and now."

Guarionex vacillated, drawn to the release of death. But he remained responsible for his people and struggled to respond.

"All my people thirst to attack, without exception!" he scorned. "It's you, your brother, and your caciques who've broken promises, and you'll never undo our hatred." He glared into Bartolomé's eyes, calling his bluff. "Kill me, kill us all, and then enjoy starvation! Your race is too lazy to grow its own food, your caciques too derelict to feed your men themselves!"

"Take him to the dungeon!" Bartolomé screamed, furious to be wasting time, resolved that abducting every cacique possible was the urgent imperative.

By twilight, Ballester's captains had succeeded in capturing thirteen, including miles distant from the fort. All were dragged, bound and gagged, to be arrayed in a line before the compound's entrance, mangled and bleeding from the brutal transport. At dawn, Bartolomé summoned all the fort's men—healthy and ill, all sleepless—to stand guard over the compound and the prisoners, outwardly displaying the few horses and dogs they possessed, warning of severe justice to any who attacked. As the sun rose, villagers and warriors began to congregate at a distance to behold the fate of their rulers, and Bartolomé dispatched a runner to summon Bakako, who arrived obediently to stand at his side. As the crowd thickened, soldiers erected stakes and gathered wood, and Guarionex was brought from the dungeon and thrown again at Bartolomé's feet, beside the vassal caciques.

"Who are the ringleaders?" Bartolomé shouted for all to hear, as if requesting Guarionex to respond, bidding Bakako cry out the translation.

The burgeoning crowd grew hush.

Bartolomé pointed menacingly to two of the bound caciques and bellowed, "Let them understand the fate of those who challenge King Fernando and Queen Isabel!" He stared sharply at Bakako, demanding an equally resounding translation.

"Their punishment is death!" he exhorted, commanding soldiers to set the chosen on the stakes and the pyres aflame.

Shrieks of horror and cries for mercy thundered as the two caciques writhed within rising flames and billowing smoke. Caciques in the crowd, now five thousand strong, stepped forward to beg that Bartolomé at least spare Guarionex the same savagery, if not the remaining eleven.

Bartolomé glared imperiously at the crowd, shunning the requests, glancing occasionally at the stakes as if to monitor whether the two caciques' agony was sufficient justice. He staggered with relief that warriors weren't raising their spears to charge. Guarionex anguished that he might shout for them to attack, irrespective of his own fate, but he writhed that surprise had been lost. The pale men's weapons and beasts were already hoisted, mounted, and barking, his warriors leaderless. Bakako trembled whether both men held him a traitor.

Bartolomé retreated from setting additional caciques ablaze and directed that Guarionex be unbound for all to behold. The two men retired inside the compound to sit at the table by Ballester's command hut, accompanied by Bakako, leaving Ballester to preside over the crowd.

"You'll receive mercy only if you heed my commands," Bartolomé threatened, albeit in a calculated tone curbed from before. "Order your people never again to revolt! Direct them to obey and serve Christians humbly! Warn them that transgressors will be punished harshly. Today's mercy won't be repeated."

"Your brother promised you'd leave my people alone, that you'd not enslave them!" Guarionex exhorted.

"I'll enslave any who resist my brother's rule, including yourself," Bartolomé thrust back. But he repressed the urge to discipline further. "You must continue your tribute payments, including cazabi and cotton. If you address your subjects as I've commanded, you'll remain their ruler and the king and queen's honored vassal."

Guarionex nodded wretchedly, resigned there were then no alternatives.

"Diego and I will listen carefully," Bartolomé threatened, rising to return to the crowd. "Obey!"

The five thousand quieted as Bartolomé and Guarionex emerged from the compound.

"The rulers of your island, King Fernando, Queen Isabel, and my brother, are merciful to those who accept their rule," Bartolomé pronounced. Bakako trembled as he translated the lie.

Undone and heartbroken, Guarionex rose to address his people, commanding his subjects to lay down their arms and obey the pale men because they remained the island's conquerors.

Skirting the truth, shy of a lie, Bakako confirmed to Bartolomé that Guarionex spoke roughly as commanded. Triumphant but worn, Bartolomé bid his soldiers release the eleven surviving caciques.

Vanquished, Guarionex strode to his subjects, to be borne home on a litter.

Anacaona and Bartolomé, Anacaona's Garden, *Xaraguá, April 1497*

"He refused to fight with my husband and then fought too late," Anacaona critiqued sadly upon learning of Guarionex's humiliating defeat. Years prior he'd been one of her many marriage suitors. "His heart is good, too good, and it failed him." She faced her brother, both seated in his ballcourt. "I grieve for him."

"Guarionex's fate is no longer our concern," Behecchio responded. "The cotton has been gathered. I'll invite Adelantado to collect it, and I'll remind him to stay out of my chiefdom otherwise—just as I've stayed out of his."

"My brother, you must afford him the same dignities you would another supreme cacique. Demonstrate a willingness to live in harmony, separately, without contempt. Be friendly, not menacing."

⌑ ⌑ ⌑

Within days, Bartolomé received Behecchio's nitaíno in Santo Domingo and, with the nitaíno's escort, promptly trekked with soldiers and an interpreter to meet Behecchio in the chieftain's village.

Settlers traveling in Magua, the Cibao, and the Yaque valley now risked Indian ambush daily, as hatred for Guarionex's surrender boiled. Yet Bartolomé felt secure in his journey, trusting in Behecchio's sincerity and the absence of Indian resistance around Santo Domingo. His loyal officers and brother Diego had warned that the settlers' own discontent boiled. Most decried that the king and queen judged the Admiral a failure and liar and had abandoned his folly—and them.

Behecchio and Anacaona hailed Bartolomé nobly in the ballcourt, along with thirty-two of Behecchio's vassal caciques, all splendidly adorned, with singing and dancing wives. With a flourish, Behecchio led Bartolomé to a bohío brimming with spindles of cotton and proclaimed that each cacique's subjects were baking cazabi for him, so much so that hauling it and the cotton to Santo Domingo would require scores of naborias. Bartolomé expressed satisfaction and proposed instead that a ship sail from Isabela to retrieve the tribute at the seaside nearest, and Behecchio dispatched a runner to Isabela bearing Bartolomé's instructions to that end.

The harmony extended into the evening, when the three sat under the great canopy, together with Bartolomé's interpreter, dining on a feast of *hutia* (a cat-size rodent), fish, and—although settlers had been too disgusted to sample it—iguana.

"You must try this, my Adelantado," Anacaona coaxed graciously as a naboria passed a platter bearing the skinned carcass of the roasted lizard, snout and eyes intact. "It's a delicacy, traditional in banquets honoring distinguished caciques to our chiefdom."

"Your Highness, if you insist," Bartolomé replied, puckering his lips, qualmishly sampling a morsel. He savored it conspicuously and pronounced, "It's good, and I'll eat more," which he did.

Behecchio appreciated that Bartolomé could affect a ruler's courtesy—as well as cruelty. "The cazabi's preparation will take some days," he observed. "I extend you the honor of visiting with us until then."

"That'd be my pleasure," Bartolomé replied.

"You must be exhausted from your exertions in Magua," Behecchio observed, introducing a graven tone, gazing across the ballcourt.

Bartolomé lingered, as if on the translation, and then replied, "Disobedience with my sovereigns' rule won't be tolerated."

"My friend Guarionex would've welcomed my warriors, but I wouldn't trespass upon your sovereigns' territory. Just as your men must never trespass in mine."

Iguana. Oviedo's *Historia General*, 1535, lam. 4.

Cordial festivities and banquets continued while the cazabi baked. As dinner concluded one evening, Anacaona invited Bartolomé to stroll, alone but for the interpreter, beneath an ascending moon.

"You may call me Anacaona," she charmed. "May I call you Bartolomé?" When he nodded, she proposed, "Let me show you my garden, Bartolomé. I think its beauty will stir you."

They ambled past the ballcourt to a glade near the village stream, and Anacaona led Bartolomé inside. It wasn't as grand as the garden she'd cultivated in Maguana, but the alluring scents of magnolias and orchids enveloped them, inviting sensuous delight.

"Do you have flower gardens in your homeland?" she inquired. When he nodded, she probed. "Do you have poetry? Do you pleasure in them?"

"My lady Anacaona, we have both," Bartolomé answered. He struggled on the final question, as the only proper flower gardens he'd visited were in the sovereigns' court and churches, the only poetry psalms, the latter perhaps less aesthetic than she contemplated, neither to his fancy. "I revel in them," he lied.

"This is a magnolia tree," Anacaona observed, studying the petals dim shimmer in the moonlight. She plucked a flower and sniffed it, inviting his gaze to her lips. "I sit here when I compose areítos."

"What are they about?" Bartolomé wondered.

Anacaona minced by the orchids and cactuses, grasping Bartolomé's hand to draw him along. "Some are about man's tenderness, others man's harshness. But mostly, I portray the spirits' wisdom and generosity, as they reveal such to me."

"Come, let's sit here," she enticed, pointing to two duhos. "This is the most enchanting corner, before the bush with the most alluring flowers," she intrigued, hushing her voice, pointing to a Bayahibe. She seated the pale man with his back close against its flowers and herself even closer before him.

"This is Attabeira," she whispered, grasping the small amulet that hung from her neck, beckoning his eyes to her breasts.

Bartolomé was drawn yet resisted leaning too close. As his older brother, he'd abstained from the Indian women, wishing to set an example for their men, but his lust for women remained strong rather than eviscerated by thirst for the Indies' conquest. "Do you compose of her?" he mustered.

"Yes, often. She brings rain for crops and fertility to the womb," Anacaona replied, peeking through the Bayahibe's flowers to discern its needles. "That is Christ that hangs before your chest?"

Bartolomé nodded, peeking toward Anacaona's womb.

"Did Christ design what's occurred on Haiti?" she whispered, catching the pale man's eyes dart, his back arch backward, pressing the Bayahibe's petals. "Is he happy now?" Anacaona cooed softly. "Are you?" She watched him withdraw farther, nigh to being pricked, and she relished she would feign surprise if he pained.

"We came in peace," Bartolomé excused, loath to be duped or misled yet lusting conciliation. He leaned forward to Anacaona and stared into her eyes. "Neither my king, queen, nor brother intended that your husband die or that your people starve or fall ill."

They sat a moment, the silence broken only by their breathing and heartbeats.

"Are you married in your homeland?" Anacaona whispered.

Bartolomé shook his head. "Do you plan to marry again?" he mused, gazing at her nagua.

"I'll marry only an equal. Other than my brother, there's no Taíno my equal left on Haiti," she responded, shifting her legs so the nagua fell to one side. "Most are vassals to you and your brother." She spied him glance to her crotch. "Do you consider yourself my equal?" she challenged and tempted.

Bartolomé's heart pounded, yet he wouldn't let a naked heathen woman play him, even fleetingly to satisfy desire. He drew yet closer but raised his eyebrows to excuse that his thoughts raced. Marriages and alliances were the sovereigns' and Cristóbal's prerogatives, unthinkable without concession of sovereignty. Marriage to an unbaptized heathen was unimaginable, no matter how powerful, beautiful, and articulate. But he pined to temper his response again. "My lady Anacaona, you're the most beautiful woman I've ever beheld. Perhaps companionship without marriage would suit you."

Anacaona affected a giggle, as if she'd consider it, pleased to have smitten one of her husband's murderers, convinced that he'd never accept her people's equal station, and content that his affection might serve as protection in the future. She relished his lust unquenched. "You must be tired," she soothed. "I'll escort you back to Behecchio's caney."

⊡ ⊡ ⊡

The cazabi was baked, and, upon word of the ship's arrival, Anacaona told Bartolomé that she and Behecchio would enjoy inspecting the vessel. Behecchio led naborias and the pale men from his residence toward the coast, where he maintained another massive caney and often resided. The entourage halted midway for a night, in a village where Anacaona maintained the caciqual family's possessions, including ornate duhos and decorated pottery. She displayed them to Bartolomé that evening, alone in the storage bohío, and bestowed him gifts of both.

"These are for you, tokens of my affection for you, not ransom for your brother or your caciques," Anacaona confided intimately. "Your courage and kindness warm me." She riveted his eyes into hers. "I hope you reciprocate friendship, for me and my people."

Bartolomé nodded, bewildered what she expected or desired, cowed that her command, presence, and wit rivaled that of any woman he'd ever met, no less even Queen Isabel. He roused to have her and reached to embrace and kiss.

Anacaona resisted and gently pushed him away, whispering, "Love follows friendship, when proven."

◘ ◘ ◘

In the morning, the party continued west to Behecchio's seaside caney overlooking Haiti's enormous western gulf, and Behecchio and Anacaona were astonished to behold Bartolomé's vessel anchored offshore (the Bay of Port-au-Prince and the Gulf of Gonâve). The ship was the second constructed by Isabela's artisans, and its crew had raced it to the rendezvous, hungering for the cazabi.

Bartolomé offered Behecchio and Anacaona a sail and summoned the ship's launch to ferry them from the beach. Behecchio favored the regal entrance traditional for Haiti's greatest sovereign and rode instead in his most decorated war canoe. Anacaona chose to sit close beside Bartolomé in the launch rather than in her own canoe. The ship's crew discharged cannons in royal salute, frightening the Taíno paddlers. Flutes, fifes, and drums heralded the Xaraguáns' arrival aboard.

"You crossed the ocean from your homeland in this?" Anacaona inquired, growing withdrawn.

"Not this ship, but in others just like it," Bartolomé replied. He perceived her awed by the height of the ship's masts and the know-how involved.

Bartolomé toured his guests about the deck, shrewdly noting the cannons, and he ordered the sails unfurled and anchors weighed. "She harnesses the wind," he explained to Behecchio, who also grew somber. Bartolomé surmised him cowed by the ship's rapid acceleration and potential might in warfare.

As for Anacaona, her thoughts were with Caonabó. As the vessel pounded growing swells, she parted from Bartolomé to amble alone, apparently inspecting the vessel's operation but oblivious to that and the pale men gawking at her naked beauty. There was no skull to address, but she spoke silently to her husband nonetheless.

Where did they bind you, my husband? she lamented, studying the deck rails and masts.

Where did you perish? she cried, peering into the hold, tears welling in her eyes.

Did the Christ-spirit torture you? she barked, observing the sails billowing in the wind. *I invoked our spirits daily in your defense*, she assured.

She gazed bitterly to the sea and shrieked, *Where did they cast you away?*

Contemptuously, Anacaona studied Bartolomé conferring with her brother. Muffled by the wind's hiss about the rigging, she whispered scornfully, "You have yet to be cast upon the Bayahibe!"

Rebellion and Rape, Collapse and Desolation, Justice,
Española, May 1497

In Isabela, with Cristóbal departed and Bartolomé engaged elsewhere, the relationship between brother Diego and Francisco Roldán, whom Cristóbal had appointed Española's chief magistrate, frayed openly as settlers departed for Santo Domingo and the town wound down. Born a commoner just as the Colóns, Roldán openly protested that the Admiral had died or deserted and the sovereigns had abandoned everyone. He publicly demanded that Diego dispatch the caravel sent to Xaraguá to Spain on its return, bearing the sovereigns an urgent plea for fresh supplies. When Diego refused, Roldán harangued the remaining settlers that the Admiral's command could no longer be tolerated.

"The Genoese are our enemies, foreigners spilling Spanish blood rather than their own to build this colony," he ranted to those who detested the Colóns' Genoese origin. "We're free Spaniards, but they work us as slaves."

"They plot ruling the island as tyrants, usurping the king and queen, whom they've duped of our hunger and their injustices," he accused to those rankled by the Admiral's unsympathetic rigor and crude favoritism. "They'll hoard the mines' gold for themselves."

"Their justice is cruel—torturing, decapitating, and butchering us on the most trifling pretexts," he cried to all those punished for scheming to obtain excess rations. "As the king and queen's magistrate, I know it unlawful."

Isabela erupted in celebration when the caravel bearing the Xaraguán cazabi arrived, although the joy was fleeting. Diego promptly had the ship beached to prevent Roldán from commandeering it to Spain, and Roldán and those drawn to him were enraged. Worse, Guarionex's subjects now ambushed settlers at Fort Concepción and assaulted the fort continuously. Diego and Roldán's inevitable reckoning loomed but was postponed, as Diego dispatched Roldán to lead forty men to quash the resistance.

Roldán's task was gritty and dangerous. When he arrived at the fort, four soldiers had been killed that day defending it. The next day, Indians pillaged and burned bohíos where the men resided outside the fort, and he pursued to slay seventeen. On the third day, he vanquished another assault on the fort and surrounding bohíos and dispensed frontier vengeance, including in Guaricano, massacring warriors as they fled and raping women, including one of apparent caciqual stature.

There wasn't enough food at the fort to share with Roldán's men, and he soon departed on the trail back toward Isabela to hunt for it. He halted at Bakako's village, pleading for cazabi, but Bakako also had none to spare. He marched on, eventually encamping his men some miles northwest from the fort in the chiefdom of a Guarionex vassal, who did relinquish cazabi.* Indians besieged his encampment there for three days and, though his ammunition was nearly spent, his band repelled them.

Roldán rankled that he hadn't ventured to Española to risk his life to remain an undistinguished, unempowered commoner, enduring

*The cacique was named Marque.

unrewarded, ignominious servitude to either Genoese weavers or Spanish noblemen who presumed his obeisance. He had fomented his men's fury to rebel, and, as they rested exhausted, he exhorted them to do so.

"Follow me, as the sovereigns' magistrate!" he shouted. "We rise against the Admiral and his brothers' tyranny—in the sovereigns' name and as their loyal subjects!"

"Española's wealth is rightfully ours!" he bellowed. "You've earned it in sweat and blood." He raised his fists. "The Indians' food and labor, and their women's love, is for our taking! Just as we've always understood since we first arrived!"

Most of the men clamored approval.

"The Admiral's battles and oppressions have failed us miserably," he charged. "There's blood on our shirts, not bread in our bellies!" he wailed to rousing cheers.

"If we were better Christians, the Indians would delight to be our manservants and maids and lay beneath us," he argued, asserting a vision for a more harmonious, peaceful Española.

The clamor crested, and those thoughtful were confused.

"I bear the king's staff of justice, and you who obey me will never be punished!" he assured, drawing the exuberance back. "Follow me to the town you've built! We'll claim the arms, the supplies, the cattle, and the horses that rightfully are ours!"

Most of Roldán's men applauded, righteously or vindictively, the pent angst and suffering of three years igniting a burning resolve—not only to overthrow the Admiral, but to raise their station on Española. They pined to sunder the shackles of their old-world status as laborers and assume a fresh entitlement in the new one they were building.

A few were aghast, reviling Roldán's scheme as treason to the king and queen, not just the Admiral. Roldán berated them, seized their arms, and dispatched them without harm to lodge under Ballester's command in Fort Concepción.

Within days, Roldán began his march on Isabela. He delayed only to visit Bakako's village, brusquely depositing for care his loyalists ill or wounded and enticing a few of Bakako's charges to join the mutiny.

Bakako cursed consenting to care for additional men—of whatever loyalty. Far worse, he dreaded that Admiral or Adelantado would judge him a traitor for serving as a hospital or recruiting ground for Roldán's rebellion.

⌑ ⌑ ⌑

Guarionex raged uncontrollably on learning of the rape of one of his younger wives, irrevocably antagonized by the flouting of his submission with the gravest humiliation. The disgrace before his subjects rivaled his surrenders, baring his impotency and the futility of surrender. Countless of his subjects no longer respected his command to cease resistance, and he couldn't fault them for that. Those who yet obeyed him lamented that he would continue to fail them, accepting degradation and humiliation as their lot. An alarming number now chose suicide to either resistance or degradation, and their number tragically grew daily.

Guarionex vexed again that death at the fort would have been grace, but he beseeched Yúcahu for the strength to continue, for his life did have a remaining, desperate purpose—the prophecy's undoing and the preservation of his civilization. He summoned the wife violated and consoled her. He summoned Bakako and interrogated him.

"Which pale man did this crime?"

"Miguel de Barahona is his name," Bakako responded forthrightly, scrutinizing Guarionex's reaction to the loyalty inherent in the prompt revelation. "I informed Ballester, who'll inform Adelantado, who'll punish him."

"Will he burn at the stake—as my vassal caciques and naborias?"

"I doubt that," Bakako replied. "But you should demand that of Adelantado, as the crime was a violation of his promises to you."

Guarionex chafed forlornly that prior understandings were meaningless—observed by neither people—and the pale men never punished their own. Neither parleys, promises, homages, or pleas to Adelantado would result in justice, restore dignity, or preserve his chiefdom or people. Arrows and spears were the sole recourse.

"Vassal caciques report that the pale men hate their Guamiquina and threaten disobedience. Is that true?"

"Pale men are deceitful and disloyal by nature, conspiring and conniving against each other, constantly," Bakako assessed. "Admiral was disobeyed when he first came here," he added, alluding to the desertion of the *Pinta*'s captain. "Plots have been hatched against him and his brothers ever since, always discovered and the guilty punished. The rapist's commander now has declared a rebellion."

Guarionex nodded and frowned. "To whom are you loyal, Admiral or this commander?"

"Admiral," Bakako responded instantly, terrified even to contemplate otherwise.

Taíno suicide. Benzoni's *History of the New World*, 1565.

"Is that loyalty in our people's interest?" Guarionex huffed, satisfied that Bakako flinched with anxiety. "Shouldn't I invoke the spirits to drive the pale men to destroy themselves? Shouldn't I assist this commander's treason?"

Bakako trembled and shrugged, and silence followed, which Guarionex concluded with a sigh.

"All peoples suffer traitors," Guarionex lashed, glaring into Bakako's eyes. "How did the pale men know of my plan to attack their fort?"

"It wasn't me!" Bakako replied sharply, glaring back. "You kept me in the dark."

"Then who was it?" Guarionex barked back, satisfied with his brother-in-law's sincerity. Bakako quivered, and Guarionex again excused a reply. "I believe we both know."

⌑ ⌑ ⌑

Roldán's band stormed Isabela with a vengeance, shouting, "Long live the king!" They raided the storehouse of munitions and other supplies, and his adherents who'd remained in Isabela reunited at his side, including minor noblemen who shared his hatreds or ambitions. Brother Diego was forced to retreat into Cristóbal's fortified residence with those mere thirty still loyal. Roldán's seventy then descended upon the cattle and horse corrals to slaughter or seize the beasts that remained fit. The entire plunder was accomplished without human bloodshed, albeit threatened.

Once equipped and provisioned, Roldán and rebels stomped back through the Vega Real, halting briefly at the forts built along the Yaque to cajole recruits. Within days, he encamped again some miles northwest of Fort Concepción, envisioning ruling Española from it, and he prepared to take it, preferably by persuasion. He first entreated the men lodging outside the fort's compound, but their captain would have none of treason, declaring that he and his men served the king, not Roldán.* Roldán promised to burn them all up one day, but he turned to the fort instead, seeking to sway Ballester.

Ballester refused even to talk and clamped the fort's gates shut. He'd already sent messengers to warn Bartolomé.

⌑ ⌑ ⌑

After dispatching the caravel to Isabela, Bartolomé had departed Behecchio and Anacaona by trekking with his band north through

*Garcia de Barrantes.

territory settlers had never explored, arriving at one of the Yaque forts after Roldán passed through.* There, he learned of the next peril threatening Cristóbal's life's work and resolved to crush it. The rebellion's obliteration was critical to retaining the sovereigns' confidence in Cristóbal's leadership.

Bartolomé hastened first to Isabela to obtain Diego's report and assemble a larger squadron of men, assuring rich rewards to those serving, including two Indian slaves apiece. Diego's report and Ballester's warning devastated him—the rebel force far exceeded their own—and Bartolomé surmised he had no choice but to seek a reconciliation rather than surrenders and executions. He returned to the Yaque forts to gather more men and arms but found that one of the wardens had since deserted to join the rebellion, stealing more recruits, including a minor nobleman.† Furious and desperate, Bartolomé and his squadron hiked to reunite with Ballester at Fort Concepción, stealing by moonlight from the established path to slink around the village where Roldán's men slept.

Roldán woke to learn that Bartolomé commanded the fort, and Bartolomé summoned him to parley, promising safe conduct.

"What do you and your traitors want?" Bartolomé probed icily, staring at Roldán through a window in the fort's main gate.

"First, that you dispatch the ship to the king and queen, begging provisions," Roldán demanded. "If you wish, authorize me to dispatch it, as their magistrate."

"The ship isn't fit for an ocean voyage yet. Any seaman could tell you that," Bartolomé snapped. "Even if it were, we'd then have no ship for escape if the Indians amassed an assault." Bartolomé softened. "What else could satisfy you?" Without waiting a response, he declared, "You must resign your office, compel your men to relinquish their arms, and return to work, in the Admiral's service. But otherwise, we can settle our differences."

"Unacceptable!" Roldán retorted. "All will die of hunger obeying you. Your brother appointed me to govern as well as you, and I won't resign or follow you any longer."

---

*Fort Esperanza.

†Diego de Escobar, the warden of Fort Esperanza, and Adrian de Mojica, the minor nobleman.

"You injure us all!" Bartolomé admonished. "Our infighting encourages the Indians to attack. Our disarray saps everyone's energy. The settlement will decay rather than flourish."

"Flourish?" Roldán stammered. "Decay triumphs under your watch. I now represent the king and queen, for everyone's well-being."

Bartolomé ignored the assertion. "If you resign and disarm your men, I'll grant you and them amnesty," he offered. " But you must hand over Barahona for punishment. I owe that to Guarionex."

"All warn you'll cut off my head if we disarm, and none of my men wish to share that fate," Roldán disdained. "I won't turn over a single supporter. Your word has proven worthless."

The two men sparred for hours and failed to find agreement. But neither saw hostilities as a solution, and Roldán grasped that his ascendant position wasn't powerful enough to break down the fort's door or seize all those loyal to the Admiral.

"Where should I take my men to live, under my authority?" Roldán finally asked.

"Go live in the village of the Indian Diego Colón, under the Admiral's authority," Bartolomé responded, resigned to a stalemate.

"He already cares for a few of my men, as well as yours, but he has no food," Roldán observed. "We'll stay where we are, farther from the fort."

In the months thereafter, Bartolomé would shunt between Santo Domingo and Fort Concepción, supervising Santo Domingo's construction and the final relocations of men from Isabela. He would renew attempts to conclude Roldán's rebellion and fail.

Roldán proclaimed his new vision for the harmony of all Española's peoples to caciques throughout Magua and the Yaque valley. Those who befriended him were released from tribute and vassalage to the Guamiquina and Adelantado. In return, Roldán and his seventy men expected receipt of food, the restoration of peaceful relations among both peoples, and the attentive service and love of their womenfolk. In lieu of tribute, he did continue to receive Manicoatex's payments of gold and cotton in trade for beads and other truck, and he corralled one of the chieftain's sons and some nephews as hostages to secure those payments.

⊡ ⊡ ⊡

Guarionex sat secluded in his ceremonial bohío, his only untouched haven from the violence that swirled about him and his subjects' misery. He'd received word that Fray Pané's Christian youth, Guatícabanu, had returned to collect his brothers and lead them south to Pané's new church.

Guarionex honored his cemí of Yúcahu, set upon the cohaba table, and sought confirmation that execution of the youth and the brothers was the appropriate punishment. He was certain the brothers had divulged clues about the fort's attack to the pale men.

He felt sorry for Guatícabanu and the brothers. He himself had been woefully guilty of dismissing the peril of accommodating the pale men, an ignorance of immeasurably more tragic consequence. The youths' guilt was borne of a similar ignorance, an attraction to the pale men's spirits, and they bore no guilt whatsoever for Adelantado's savage immolation of the six naborias who raided their church.

But the boys' betrayal of Guarionex's preparations initiating the fort's attack stepped beyond ignorance to imperil, if not forsake, his people's very survival. Guarionex's justice saw no cause for mercy. He couldn't countenance punishing persons for the spirits they worshipped, however false, but treason against his rule—and the very rebellion meant to restore it—merited death.

Yúcahu concurred, and Guarionex summoned a nitaíno to render the punishment with warriors, and it was done, swiftly. Each youth perished uttering, "I am a servant of God."

Other than Frays Pané and Leudelle, Española's pale men didn't even notice these Indians' executions. Indians lay dead and dying everywhere. Fray Pané was certain the boys had been martyred for being Christian, as did Christians who learned of them thereafter. Among Maguans, word spread that sweet potatoes in the field of the crucifix's burial had grown tangled in the shape of a cross, confirming the Christ-spirit's power.

Guarionex's satisfaction in bringing traitors to justice was short-lived. Ballester soon summoned him to remind that tribute was due and express the urgency of providing cazabi.

ANACAONA AND ONANEY,
Xaraguá

After Adelantado's departure, Anacaona had returned to Behecchio's inland residence, content with their effort to protect their chiefdom. Scouts posted along Xaraguá's eastern perimeter stood vigil for pale men trespassing, and informants and caciques throughout Haiti—including brother-in-law Manicoatex—were alert to report on the pale men's scheming.

At sunset one evening, she summoned Onaney to chat in her garden. Both women yet suffered their husband's absence and appreciated that as their remaining bond, and Anacaona anticipated an intimate unburdening of that longing and the void left by his death. When the older woman arrived, Anacaona was startled by her worn appearance, unusually unkempt for the wife of a supreme cacique. Her hair was uncombed and nagua unwashed, as if the void had overcome her. They sat by the Bayahibes.

"I've arranged a war canoe to bear you to Aniyana," Anacaona advised pleasantly. "You'll have to wait some months, until after the hurricane season."

"It doesn't need to be large," Onaney replied. "I have few possessions to return with—just personal items, so my son may remember his father."

"If you wish, tell me," Anacaona indulged, intrigued. "What are they?"

"There's a spear Caonabó carried decades ago, before his anointment, with which he fought Caribes," Onaney wanly responded, pensive. "There's the belt he wore when anointed, a few years before your marriage." She saddened. "He wore it at my marriage."

"You must be fond of these, heartened by their memories," Anacaona encouraged. "You must show me them before you depart!" she exclaimed, injecting a cheer apparently forsaken.

"There's three heirlooms, from Aniyana," Onaney responded, shepherded by the invitation, groping for the contentedness lost. "A stone amulet passed on from Caonabó's father. A cemí of Yúcahu that was his mother's." Onaney smiled, signaling a singular affection. "There's a withered mask carved from a calabash gourd, with two eyelets—Caonabó wore it when he first learned to hunt duck, as a boy. I watched him don it, perhaps the only time I ever saw him frightened."

Anacaona harkened, both to the memory and Onaney's arousal, and she mused whether Caonabó was present and pleased, as well. "He always recognized danger, even when others didn't," Anacaona observed. "But his bravery always surmounted."

There was a momentary silence, pregnant with intimacy, and Onaney broke it, softly. "Did you learn how he died?"

"The pale men told me nothing!" Anacaona blurted. "But I walked upon one of their vessels and could imagine it. Before death, he would have been bound like a captive Caribe, likely to posts on the vessel somewhere."

"Did they torture him?"

"They wouldn't admit that. I didn't ask."

"Where did he die?" Onaney probed intently. "Was he close to Haiti, or far at sea?"

Anacaona shrugged.

Onaney stared away, shy of stepping too far, but compelled nonetheless. "You brought Adelantado here, alone?"

Anacaona nodded. "I sought to ensure his friendship to my brother and people."

"What was he like?"

"Brutish, arrogant, calculating—wicked." Anacaona hesitated, and then added, without affront, "I didn't lie with him, either here or elsewhere."

"I would have relished enticing him—and then stabbing him to death!" Onaney blurted vehemently.

"That's what Caonabó would have wished for you to do," she responded, nodding graciously, eschewing a debate. "But that wasn't our husband's wish for me." She gazed to the Bayahibes. "He wanted me to lead his subjects to survive, as a free people. I can't do that anymore, but I must seek that here in Xaraguá, for our civilization." She clenched a fist gently. "I pray they'll bend before me, not I to them."

The women sat gravely a few moments, beholding hummingbirds hover and dart.

"I'm pleased not to share your responsibility," Onaney admitted, affirming her respect for her husband's premier wife. "My fortitude wanes."

"Before you depart, we'll discuss what you must tell your son about the pale men," Anacaona assured, returning to the chat's origin.

"I return as wife and mother, to pass Caonabó's memory to his son," Onaney excused uneasily. "It'd be best that one of your nitaínos accompany to deliver your wisdom for the future."

XII
AGONIES AND FATES

Cristóbal, Adrift and Renewed,
Castile, January–July 1497

Cristóbal passed the winter in Burgos at the fringe of court, smarting from the rebuke for Niño's slave shipment dealt by the Catholic Monarchs, as they now were heralded. He was heartened by his sons' companionship, although they related that the sovereigns labored on Italian intrigues, French hostilities, and Prince Juan's marriage—not the Indies. The sovereigns' counselors occasionally consulted him about interpretations of the Tordesillas treaty and how King Manoel might be excluded from the Indies altogether. He related stories of the Indians and their idol worship to the sovereigns' humanist, Pedro Mártir, who marveled at the superstitions, which he found ridiculous and childlike, perhaps in comparison to Christian doctrine, its inquisitions and expulsions, and the spells cast by Satan, Jews, and others.

But Cristóbal's days largely were solitary, absent access to the sovereigns, and he languished waiting for them to issue the writs and proclamations requisitioning the vessels, recruitment, and provisions necessary to dispatch even just the immediate resupply ships, no less the subsequent fleet. Garbed in his monk's habit, he secluded himself daily in the chapels of the town's cavernous grand cathedral or in local monasteries, beseeching the Lord to aid his brothers and loyalists to survive Española's neglect during his absence.* He avoided lingering in public, as unknown passersby often would scorn the Indies to his face. A decade had lapsed since he'd studied the earth's geography in learned texts—Marco Polo, Cardinal Pierre d'Ailly, John Mandeville, Seneca, and Esdras—and he now resumed examinations, not to reconfirm his geographical theory, which he held proven, but to divine his own role in the Lord's design.†

Cristóbal mulled the scriptures, Saint Augustine, and again Cardinal d'Ailly, delving beyond the gospels written after Christ's resurrection to consider the wisdom of the heroes and prophets written centuries before his first coming, including Daniel, Jeremiah, and Ezekiel. Isaiah captivated him. While he understood Isaiah as foretelling that resurrection, Cristóbal gleaned that Isaiah also had prophesized his discoveries and his destiny to proclaim the Lord's word in the islands of the Ocean Sea.

"*The Lord will reach out his hand to reclaim his people, including from the islands of the sea*," Isaiah pronounced, heralding an evangelization of the world's peoples. "*You that go down to the sea, sing his praise from the ends of the earth*," Isaiah instructed mariners. Cristóbal grasped his voyage as that outreach and himself as that mariner.

"*In his law the islands will put their hope*," Isaiah foretold. "*His sons will come from afar.*" Cristóbal knew of scant Indians who so hoped or came—his enslaved guides and interpreters, Pané's flock—and multitudes those words obviously couldn't describe, even remotely. Yet he imagined that inspiration unfolding under his leadership.

"*I have chosen you my servant from among the earth's chief men*," Isaiah assured. "*Fear not. I will uphold you, and those incensed against you shall be ashamed, confounded, and perish.*" Cristóbal glowed to perceive that holy designation and victory over his enemies and misfortunes.

"*The islands' sons will come, bearing their silver and gold*," Isaiah proclaimed. "*The Lord's glorious temple will be adorned.*"

Cristóbal delighted. The gold would be found and spent to reclaim Jerusalem.

---

*The grand cathedral being the Cathedral of Santa María de Burgos.

†See *Encounters Unforeseen*, chapter V, for discussion of the learned texts.

◻ ◻ ◻

As spring approached, Fernando and Isabel agreed a cease-fire and truce with France, and the lovely Margarite of Austria arrived in Burgos. In early April, at the sovereigns' invitation, Cristóbal attended Prince Juan and Margarite's wedding, culminating weeks of ceremonial pomp. Cisneros presided, Cristóbal's sons Diego and Fernando participated as Juan's pages, and, as the groom united in one person the kingdoms of Castile and Aragón and the bride affixed the Holy Roman emperor's kinship, the wedding was attended—in young Fernando's view—by the most illustrious concourse of people ever assembled in Spain.

When the celebrations concluded, Isabel and Fernando did turn to the Admiral's third voyage. They'd received warnings their claim to the Indies would be challenged. Further procrastination jeopardized it.

Most alarmingly, informants in Lisbon had alerted that five ships guarded by crown sentries were being refit for a lengthy voyage and would sail by the summer, flying King Manoel's colors. While the captains were unknown, the destination undoubtedly was either the Indies or the southern continent predicted by King João. Less interpretable, over a year earlier, the sovereigns' ambassador to England had reported that an Italian like Colón was proposing an undertaking like that of the Indies to King Henry VII. Fernando had instructed the ambassador to admonish Henry of the pope's award of the Indies to Spain and Portugal, but Henry's ongoing silence boded ill.

◻ ◻ ◻

Following his coronation, King Manoel had been eager to resume the circumvention of Guinea, proven possible by Bartolomeu Dias (1488) but ignored by João as he focused on succession and contesting the rights to Colón's discoveries. Manoel's appetite was whetted by the failure of the Spanish yet to locate a single golden temple or even literate peoples. He still could be the first to trade by sea with wealthy Indian civilizations and perhaps seize heathen lands en route. Gloriously, he even might achieve the hallowed vision of his great-uncle

Prince Henrique—locating the reputed Christian kings of Ethiopia and uniting with them to drive the infidel from Jerusalem!* In 1496, Manoel's court had dismissed the idea of a follow-up voyage, judging the Indies too distant for their small kingdom to possess and control effectively, preferring instead a more realistic focus on Guinea, which had been famously profitable, and possessions in the Ocean Sea. But Manoel prevailed, believing Jerusalem's reconquest to be his destiny and that the Indies' gold and spice yet could be won by the eastward route. A crown-sponsored voyage was approved.

Manoel had selected a minor nobleman of João's court as the expedition leader, reputed to be brave, bold, and quick-tempered. In his midtwenties, Vasco da Gama hailed from the port of Sines and had rendered occasional maritime services to the crown, including seizing French warships that raided a cargo of gold returning from Mina. Vasco would command four ships, sailing on his flagship the *São Gabriel*, with two other ships accompanying to the Indies. The fourth vessel would attend as a supply ship until its stores were depleted, and Bartolomeu Dias would sail a fifth ship as far as the Cape Verde islands, from where he'd divert to Mina to assume its captaincy. The Indies-bound and supply ships were considerably larger than the *Niña*, fitted—under Bartolomeu's supervision—with stowage for three years of provisions. Their crews included sailors who had accompanied Bartolomeu to the Cape of Good Hope, and their maps and instruments had been furnished by one of the mathematicians who'd recommended that João reject Colón's voyage.†

To the north, in Bristol, England's largest western port, carpenters were refitting a single ship, the *Matthew*, roughly the capacity of the *Niña*, to sail under the command of a Venetian citizen born in Genoa known to King Henry as John Caboto, who was about the same age as Cristóbal. Henry keenly regretted dismissing Bartolomé Colón years earlier and was delighted for a second chance. He'd carefully considered Pope Alexander's bulls and already commissioned John—before receiving Fernando's admonishment. The voyage authorized was to sail east, west, or north—but not south—to find a northern

*The legendary kings titled the Prester John.

†*Encounters Unforeseen*, chapter IV, depicts the rejection.

route to the Indies and conquer heathen or infidel territory not then possessed by a Christian prince.

Henry and John knew Española was an island, not the mainland, and they surmised that once John had found the Indies up north, he might then course the Indian coast south, possessing the land Colón had yet to debark upon. Under John's patent letter, territory conquered would be the English crown's, with John granted hereditary title to govern as the king's vassal, and John would bear all expenses, remitting one-fifth the profits to the crown, retaining the remainder. Evangelization was neither contemplated, ballyhooed, or even mentioned.

John had proposed a fleet of five but succeeded in financing one. Yet finding sailors had been easy, as Bristol's seamen had traded in Thule (Iceland) and fished its waters and those of islands or a landmass farther west for centuries—including a typical voyage to Thule two decades earlier on which a young Genoese seaman, Cristoforo Columbo, had enlisted.*

⌑ ⌑ ⌑

Isabel, Fernando, and Cristóbal met frequently, earnestly, and frankly over the spring to reorder the Indies' operation and Cristóbal's entitlements. Their audiences commenced in Burgos's Casa de Cordón and, when the court moved to Medina del Campo in June, resumed in its royal palace or, occasionally, at retreats to the Monastery of the Mejorada nearby.

"What will it take to make this business succeed?" Isabel demanded. "It's an embarrassment rather than a triumph, a joke when compared to João's Mina."

"What's the leanest operation we must commit to—the fewest men necessary to extract the gold and treasures?" Fernando pried. "What will motivate your men to build a self-funding, enduring operation? It must be self-sufficient—immediately. Our patience is worn."

"Cristóbal, the settlers must be able to produce their own food!" Isabel exclaimed. "We can't continue to fund that or supply it all the way across the Ocean Sea!"

---

*See *Encounters Unforeseen*, chapter III.

"What are our Indian subjects doing for us?" Fernando pushed. "You must collect the tribute payments uniformly, as our taxes are collected here."

"How goes their baptism and integration into my kingdom?" Isabel pressed.

Cristóbal hemmed and hawed, puffed and retreated, and unstintingly cast the disloyalty of sovereign-designated officers as the root of all previous failure. He then held to what he thought workable. The sovereigns never accepted defeat easily and, when the thrash of their interrogation was done and Cristóbal's agreement secured, they thought the plan addressed prior travails and was worthy of a next effort.

From April through July, Isabel and Fernando issued writs and instructions to maintain the ongoing settlement of the Indies—islands and continent—with 330 salaried residents composed of 140 officers, soldiers, and laborers, 60 seamen and midshipmen, 20 gold miners, 60 farmers and vegetable gardeners, 20 tradesmen, and 30 women, with salaries payable from the Indies' revenues. To motivate food production and the settlement's construction, they delegated Cristóbal the authority to award settlers hereditary and alienable land plots on which to build their own homes, farms, and vineyards—so long as they occupied them for four years—and sell what they produced. Cristóbal could adjust the foregoing composition and increase the settlement population to 500, provided any additional salaries and supplies necessary were funded by the settlement alone. Settlers could return home, but new recruits were nigh impossible to find, and, to ensure the population could be maintained at no expense, a pardon was granted criminals—other than heretics, sodomizers, ax murderers, and the like—who agreed to become residents, without salary. Courts and sheriffs were instructed that thenceforth those sentenced to banishment be sent to Española.

Plowing and animal husbandry were to be introduced so residents could sustain themselves, and the farmers would be furnished grain and livestock. Solvent merchants were to be identified to trade clothing and merchandise at their own expense with the settlement, although the sovereigns would bear the risk of loss at sea. While not specified, the women would be available for Christian marriages and home keeping or for other services. Gold on land awarded was reserved for the crown.

Isabel and Fernando appreciated the tribute system Cristóbal had established and instructed him to lead the Indians to serve and remain benignly under their sovereignty and subjugation in peace and order. They reaffirmed that tribute payments were to be evidenced by a brass token worn about the neck so that those delinquent could be identified, arrested, and given a light penalty. The Indians' conversion remained a priority, and monks and priests of good character had to be recruited. The sovereigns rejected yet again Cristóbal's plea for an ongoing slave trade.

The discussions regarding Cristóbal's governance and entitlements also were plainspoken and, for Cristóbal, more embittered.

"I've suffered four years bickering with your appointments in Seville to make this enterprise work," Cristóbal bemoaned. "Your bishop cares nothing for it."

"You dispatched an investigator who discredited my authority, and you criticize me for the chaos?" he lamented. "Your own papal appointment and general deserted the field!"

"You anger at the absence of the crown's profit, but what of my own share? My expenses and ordeals on your behalf haven't been compensated, either!" he stammered. "My award is that you license other mariners, in violation of our understanding?"

"Accusations and jealousies abound that you no longer stand by me or our agreements!" he rasped.

Isabel and Fernando retreated, although firm in their criticisms of the settlement and his governance. His original entitlement had been to receive a tenth of all profits, plus an eighth more if he underwrote an eighth of expenses. As there hadn't been profits, they consented to let him keep whatever he'd taken to date and, for the next three years, to pay him the tenth of profits plus an eighth of revenues, excusing him from underwriting, whereupon the original deal would resume. Cristóbal declined receiving a substantial land grant on Española as compensation, outwardly professing that he'd be accused of favoring its development—inwardly eschewing reliance on its uncertain prospects and a narrowing focus to his own enrichment. The sovereigns signaled that their prior invitation to license Indies voyages to other mariners was revoked, without conceding their power to do so.

Capping all, Isabel and Fernando pronounced that the honorific *Admiral* and the authorities they had awarded him at Santa Fe and Granada in 1492 were reconfirmed, heralding to critics that Cristóbal remained their admiral for the Indies and was to be obeyed. Similarly, while noting it their prerogative, they proclaimed Bartolomé titled and empowered as the Indies' adelantado in Cristóbal's absence, confirming the appointment first made two years earlier. Privately, they consented to appoint Torres to replace Fonseca and authorized Cristóbal to record his hereditary entitlements in a trust binding regardless of contrary law.

The discussions and writs were almost concluded when warning arrived that Manoel's ships had departed Lisbon on July 8, seen coursing toward Guinea. On July 19 and 20, while in retreat with the sovereigns at the Monastery of the Mejorada, Cristóbal urgently assisted courtiers to compose a memorandum amassing arguments allocating the entirety of the Indies to Spain under the Tordesillas treaty—regardless of who arrived from east or west to possess first, ignoring the treaty's affirmation of Portugal's prior rights to circumvent Guinea eastward to the Indies. Among bluff and carp, the memorandum declared that João had always understood and since respected an eastern boundary to Portugal's right to newly discovered territory, corollary to the already well-understood western boundary in the Ocean Sea. That line, the memorandum baldly concocted, was the Cape of Good Hope—beyond which João had never ventured and Manoel had no right to plant his crown's flag.

As the memorandum's ink dried, Cristóbal departed the sovereigns on July 22, accompanied by the few Indians brought to court who had survived Spain's winter—including his two baptized interpreters, now Cristóbal and Pedro, but neither Don Diego nor Caonabó's nephew. Cristóbal would pass through Guadalupe, honoring its Virgin briefly, and then continue to Seville, where he intended promptly to provision and dispatch the two resupply ships Española's settlers desperately awaited.

◻ ◻ ◻

In the Ocean Sea, Vasco da Gama's fleet then approached the Cape Verde islands, eager to pass the Cape of Good Hope, possess new discoveries in the Arabian and Indian Seas, and debark in fabled cities roofed with gold.

Unknown to Vasco, Cristóbal, Isabel, and Fernando, John Caboto had already sailed from Bristol on May 20 and, after a speedy ocean voyage west, sighted an enormous land mass on June 24 (the northern tip of Newfoundland). Unknown to all of them, including John, shrouded by the veil of five centuries, Norsemen led by Leifur Eiríksson had once established a colony but miles from the site of John's landfall (commencing AD 1001 at L'Anse aux Meadows).*

John had planted a cross and Henry's flag to take possession and—for good measure, should a dispute arise—Pope Alexander's banner. He'd explored south for three weeks, and, while not finding the Grand Khan's residence, he surmised he'd arrived terra firma and offshore islands.

Isabel and Fernando, the Lord Taketh,
Castile, Autumn–Winter 1497

With Juan's wedding, the marital alliances struck against the French were complete but for consummation of eleven-year-old Catalina's wedding to King Henry VII's ten-year-old Arthur. On September 14, the Catholic Monarchs departed Medina del Campo to escort Princess Isabel to marry King Manoel in Valencia de Alcántara, a small farming village close to the Portuguese frontier, reestablishing the bond that fostered peace on the Hispanic peninsula.

Begrudgingly, the sovereigns were satisfied that Manoel had honored the letter, if not the spirit, of his commitment to eliminate the Jews from his kingdom. He had brandished reprisals on his Jews instead of providing sufficient transport, including absconding with children to force Christian educations, and then mass-baptized thousands who remained, assuring their Christian sincerity wouldn't be challenged for twenty years—and thereby avoiding the exodus of their mercantile community. Regardless of sincerity—either Manoel's or the Jews'—the sovereigns considered the crude baptisms an acceptable step toward the Christianization of the entire peninsula.

*See *Encounters Unforeseen*, chapter III.

As they rode toward the Portuguese border, Isabel and Fernando—now in their midforties—swelled with confidence that their kingdoms' defensive alliances were strong and opportunities for aggrandizement could be seized or harvested. Italy, the Canaries, the Indies—if Colón at last made it work—and even Africa beckoned. But the linchpin to their dynasty was the succession established in their son, which ensured that Castile and Aragón would be ruled by their child, not a foreign spouse. They ached that nineteen-year-old Prince Juan's frailty was advancing—his body emasculating, his strength, vigor, and appetite ebbing.* More than anyone, Isabel understood the trials of a ruling queen, and she prayed that her dynasty wouldn't rely on a daughter following in her footsteps.

Isabel and Fernando hadn't yet risked delegating their son important crown assignments—as Fernando had received at a much earlier age—cautious for Juan's health and limited intellect. But they'd awarded him his own estates, including the city of Salamanca, where he would live on his own for the first time, with his bride. They delighted to watch him smitten by her, energized to take her to bed at all hours. Courtiers had warned that Juan was debilitating himself toward the grave and jeopardizing succession with the frequent sex. Isabel had dismissed the advice as both irreverent to the Lord's design for marriage and inimical to the procreation of their dynasty. At the end of September, the young couple entered Salamanca on their own to rousing acclaim and ceremonies the sovereigns had arranged.

Isabel and Fernando gave daughter Isabel's hand to Manoel on September 30, and nuptial celebrations were set for a week. But a rider arrived before dawn on October 2, his steed exhausted from the hundred-mile journey, to warn that Juan lay desperately ill in Salamanca. A pall enveloped the festivities, and Isabel and Fernando conferred alone, stunned that Juan's health had deteriorated so precipitously, and they prayed the bout would pass. Another horseman galloped in on October 3 to report that Juan's fevers grew worse and couldn't be contained.

Leaving Isabel to conclude the ceremonies, Fernando mounted his horse and, with a small retinue, struck northeast into the night, cantering dusty roads and paths across the Tajo River's floodplain

*Consumption (pulmonary tuberculosis)?

and through Castile's central mountain range, under starlight. He anguished that the Lord had destined Juan with a weak constitution. But the horse's gait revived memories that heartened resilience and optimism. Fernando recalled a similar nighttime ride three decades earlier, when he'd boldly stolen from Aragón into Castile to claim Isabel as his bride, against her older brother's wishes and evading sentries bent on thwarting that—the very inception of the dynasty, then unknown. His pride welled on recalling his journey to Aragón with Juan, just a toddler, to take its court's vow to obey the child as his successor and, triumphantly, successor to Castile. He was ennobled by a vision of riding side by side with Juan, at the cusp of manhood, uphill toward Granada's imposing Alhambra fortress to receive it from the vanquished infidel—the greatest victory of the dynasty, then renowned.

But when Fernando arrived at Juan's bedside in Salamanca the next morning, the memories and visions were crushed by the pallid limpness of Juan's face and corpse, and Fernando's visions of dynasty collapsed, leaving the grief of losing a son.

"Have strength, do not give up!" Fernando whispered hoarsely, eyes misting, as he exhorted the imperative by which he'd led his entire life. "Hope often cures the gravest illness."

"Father, I'm reconciled to death," Juan responded wanly, taken by his father's outburst.

"You are young, your resilience will prevail!" Fernando urged, balking at resignation.

"It is God's will," Juan replied. "Father, you must accept it, too."

Father and son held hands throughout the day. Juan confided that Margarite believed she was pregnant, and Fernando shed tears, vexed bittersweet that Juan's seed might rule what the Lord denied him. Fernando churned how and what to tell Isabel, and he chose to dispatch a series of riders, advising that Juan grew better and then worse, but concealing death. He would reveal that only at her side, so he might cushion her stagger with an embrace. By evening, Juan was given last rites.

"Accept God's kingdom," Fernando counseled when the end was imminent. "It's far greater than that which would have been yours." He brooded that God had spared his own fate in conquest and intrigue countless times but now took an innocent—perhaps punishment for his own sins.

Word of Juan's passing emanated from the bedside, and Salamancans donned sackcloth in mourning, aghast what it meant for their kingdom and children's futures. Harrowed, Fernando soon departed for Valencia de Alcántara.

Isabel had received Fernando's dispatches stoically, and she'd stolen frequently from banquets and toasts to pray for their son's survival. As Fernando, she'd pained on the Lord's design, and she drew fortitude from memories of his beneficence during motherhood. She thankfully recalled beseeching Guadalupe's Virgin for a son—after eight years of marriage, barren but for daughter Isabel—and the pregnancy that wondrously followed. She glowed to reminisce of cuddling Juan to her breast upon his birth in Seville and the eruption of tumultuous celebrations throughout Castile, Aragón, and even Catalonia that the prince of them all had arrived. She savored the spring wedding in Burgos, proud to have sheltered, nurtured, and tutored him to manhood to take his own queen.

But that optimism shattered when she saw the pain written in Fernando's face as he arrived, and they retired alone again, shielding their agony and Isabel's tears and collapse, crushed by the abrupt change in their fortunes. Not a week before, they'd stood perhaps invincible, destined always to surmount the struggles the Lord dealt and attain that they desired. But the Lord had cruelly reminded they weren't, that some defeats were everlasting. There were other means to ensure their dynasty, but the one they'd nurtured for two decades was forever denied. Neither love nor faith had prevented that.

When composed, the sovereigns emerged, and, without tears, Isabel simply mustered a few words for their subjects.

"The Lord has given, the Lord has taken away, blessed be his name," she pronounced from the scriptures, austerely. Her dynasty would continue, within his design. More darkly, she also recognized that that design included sins' punishment, but acknowledgment of that was for her and Fernando's consciences alone, not for their subjects.

News of the prince's death resounded throughout Spain and the Christian world. Dressed in mourning black, Spaniards from all walks of life paraded gravely throughout the kingdoms' cities and villages, and shops closed for forty days. A funeral procession carried Juan's body from Salamanca to Ávila, where he was entombed in the Monastery of Saint Tomás, where an aging Inquisitor General Tomás de Torquemada resided. After the service, the sovereigns led their court west for an extended, somber residence at Acalá de Henares, arriving November 8.

Margarite's belly swelled, and all of Spain prayed for a grandson.

◘ ◘ ◘

Cristóbal's press to dispatch the resupply ships promptly was dashed even before the tragedy, as the sovereigns had been dissatisfied with Torres on his replacement of Fonseca, and the bishop had resumed responsibility for provisioning by July. But Juan's death, the sovereigns' grief, and the mourning observances brought the preparations to an utter standstill.

Cristóbal languished the autumn in Seville, residing in Violante's home, worshipping daily in the city's great cathedrals and monasteries. He whiled the time compiling in one document all the writings that embodied his titular and financial entitlements.* He commenced drafting the testamentary disposition authorized by the sovereigns, welling with a pride long suppressed in his Genoese birthright and a resentment toward the sovereigns theretofore concealed.† His sons joined him after Prince Juan's death, but Isabel offered to retake them as her own pages, and, in early November, the boys departed for Alcalá de Henares.

The specter of dethronement aggravated the woe of oblivion. Cristóbal corresponded with a Bristol wine merchant residing in Andalusia, who related John Caboto's triumphant possession for King Henry of a northern mainland and that Henry hoped to explore it the next year with ten or twelve ships.‡ Absent reports, Cristóbal acridly sulked that Vasco da Gama's fleet would succeed in rounding Guinea's cape.

Vasco did. After watering on the Cape Verde islands in July, he had encountered the contrary Guinean coastal winds and currents experienced by Bartolomeu Dias, and, to skirt them, he'd veered his fleet on

*The document is known as the *Book of Privileges*.

†The *majorat*.

‡John Day.

an audacious, untested maneuver far into the Ocean Sea. The ships coursed southwest, harnessing the easterly winds blowing offshore, as Cristóbal had done twice, and then, weeks deep into the ocean, circled south beating against the wind until they found the southwesterly gales that had driven Bartolomeu past the Cape of Good Hope. The gambit—a landless circuit spanning forty-five hundred miles and three months, far longer than Cristóbal's voyages—paid off, and, by November 22, Vasco's fleet had rounded the cape.

⊡ ⊡ ⊡

The sovereigns' yearning for a grandson was short-lived, and the Lord took a second time. On December 14, Margarite miscarried a girl, and the sovereigns and Spain suffered a second trial of grief.

The thrones of Castile and—were it to permit a queen's ascension—Aragón then devolved to the sovereign's oldest daughter, Isabel. Graven by the successive tragedies, the sovereigns dispatched messengers to her and Manoel, summoning them to return to Castile for investiture as Castile and Aragón's next rulers. Manoel confirmed they would come, but only after approval of his court, which required assurance his kingdom wouldn't be absorbed into the sovereigns'.

As 1498 dawned, Isabel and Fernando maintained their daily routine of audiences and administration, assuring their subjects that their rule would continue to flourish. But they grew gloomily introspective, and court pageantry and entertainments withered. Isabel resolved to dress in mourning black till death. As always, she resorted to the Lord often and, increasingly, to her confessor Cisneros, finding solace in his stark adherence to Christian piety, rejection of earthly enjoyments, and hatred of heretical beliefs.

Soon, Ximénez would sear his own mark upon Spain.

Guacanagarí, Judgments,
Marien

Guacanagarí sat in a small bohío in a tiny village, secluded deep within his chiefdom's remotest mountains, where he, brother Matuma, and the few wives, nitaínos, and naborias yet loyal to him had fled. He was feverous, undoubtedly from a disease inflicted by the Christ-spirit that had claimed thousands of his subjects' lives. He was gaunt, having subsisted on roots, herbs, spiders, and an occasional snake for months—although the illness dulled his hunger. He'd long since thrown Admiral's necklace of the Christ-spirit's mother upon a fire.

Guacanagarí's bitterness toward Admiral and five years of deception tortured him more than his affliction. Kindness and charity had been betrayed by an invasion, the promise of a preeminent alliance double-crossed by tribute's imposition and the same atrocities inflicted on others. Haitians throughout the island despised him for fighting beside Admiral and facilitating Admiral's enslavements, and his surviving subjects had deserted him.

He summoned Matuma for their last embrace.

"It's my time," Guacanagarí advised softly, bidding Matuma kneel before him. "This is now yours," he pronounced, removing the caciqual medallion that hung about his neck and placing it on Matuma's. "I will retire to the lean-to by the peak."

"You've lived as a Taíno," Matuma responded, having anticipated this moment for days, as his brother weakened. "You offered friendship..."

"Stop." Guacanagarí raised his hand. Both knew he had failed his people.

"Mistakes in judgment aren't the same as evil, no matter how grave," Matuma persisted.

Guacanagarí shut his eyes, and Matuma quieted. Both knew his heart guilty of more than mistakes in judgment. "I'm honored by your enduring loyalty—and may you find a route to survival." Wanly, he grasped for Matuma, and Matuma reached forward to pull them together, each resting his head on the other's shoulders, recollecting their long journey from the same womb.

At dusk, Guacanagarí staggered on a path from the bohío across a high ridge to a sentries' lean-to with a commanding view, supported by two older wives and an elderly naboria, who carried a water gourd and a pouch of cohaba. The stark absence of a grateful crowd or even token ceremony brusquely reminded him of his subjects' demise and that his own death already was forgotten. He hugged his wives and thanked his naboria a last time, grateful for years of marriage and service, and consoled them that, on their deaths, their souls would travel to a good place. They sat him on a duho and departed as the sun vanished, and Guacanagarí gazed upon his chiefdom's mountains and valleys as they majestically embraced darkness—just as he embraced Yúcahu's presence and death.

His thoughts drifted uneasily to his antagonist, musing where Caonabó's soul had journeyed after death. Caonabó's massacre of Admiral's garrison, torching of Guarico, and abduction of the young wife had been evil. Yet Caonabó's accusations that Guacanagarí was a fool, coward, and traitor were now the judgments of Guacanagarí's own people. Guacanagarí winced, accepting guilt only for being a fool, protesting that he had always sought and fought for his own subjects' well-being.

As the moon rose, Guacanagarí's contempt and malevolence for Caonabó's soul drifted to a deeper, and more abiding, hatred for Admiral and his monumental betrayal. Visions of seventeen ships, hundreds of soldiers, and enormous and vicious beasts hurtled through Guacanagarí's thoughts, and he cursed that he had assisted them and trembled for what he might have done differently. He should have just told Admiral to move on when the vessel sank, regardless that the remaining vessel hadn't sufficient capacity. A year later, he should have swallowed his pride to unite with Caonabó to drive Admiral from the island.

Guacanagarí gazed into the night and beseeched Yúcahu to reveal whether friendship with pale men from a new world could work. *Had the last five years been misdeeds singular to Admiral and his soldiers—or was the tragedy destined to be perpetual?* Yúcahu was mute, refusing an answer.

An owl's silhouette soared across the moon. Guacanagarí reached for the cohaba and invited Yúcahu's direction, resolved not to inquire or plead where his soul was destined.

Guarionex, Bakako, and Yutowa, Final Conversations, *Magua*

Guarionex refused Ballester's invitation to participate in the fort's celebration of the High Mass honoring Christ's birth, reviling that reverence and Ballester's inevitable prompting that tribute next fell due in the spring. He'd compelled his subjects to fulfill the payments previously required—including the cazabi desperately sought—but resolved never to do so again. He was uncertain how and when to divulge that disobedience to his nitaínos.

Guarionex summoned Bakako to confer alone, in the inner sanctum of his caney. Bakako entered the dim recess in trepidation, having never been invited before, certain a secret from all—both olive and pale—was afoot.

"How did your masters react to my execution of the traitors?" Guarionex pried, referring to Guatícabanu and his brothers. "I thought the pale men massacred a hundred of us for each Christian slain."

"Other than Pané, I'm not sure they noticed it," Bakako replied circumspectly. "It's passed, and I've heard nothing about punishing you."

"You're baptized," Guarionex poked. "So, a baptized olive skin matters less than a baptized pale skin?" He glared into Bakako's eyes, evincing the abiding hatred he held for the pale men, and Bakako puckered his lips, acknowledging he recognized the bigotry.

"What will happen if I don't deliver the next tribute payment?" Guarionex probed. "They'll certainly notice that."

"Then you'd be punished," Bakako observed. "But you're too important to them, as you provide most of their tribute. You wouldn't be executed."

"I understand that. But how will it affect the pale men?" Guarionex raised a finger. "Will they finally starve to death?"

Bakako pondered, reluctant to be sucked in league with resistance, yet comfortable he wasn't revealing confidences. "All hunger, including the men I harbor, and some weaken toward death. Disease contributes. If you fail to deliver cazabi, I expect many might succumb."

"The Guamiquina's been absent almost two years, and he hasn't resupplied his men for over a year," Guarionex reminded. "Has he left them to die?"

"Many of the pale men fear that."

Guarionex requested a naboria to fetch pineapple juice and then inquired of Ariana and little Diego, indicating he'd obtained the information he sought. Bakako was startled, as little had been communicated that Guarionex didn't know or couldn't reason. They simply chatted about family and acquaintances who'd died of pestilence, and, when the day grew hot, Guarionex concluded the audience.

"Take care of yourself, and my sister and little nephew," Guarionex cautioned, satisfied he'd forewarned. "I alone will communicate my intentions to Ballester," he admonished, lying.

⌑ ⌑ ⌑

Confounded, Bakako returned to his village. But as days passed, his apprehension that Guarionex would refuse to deliver tribute receded to an afterthought, as the chieftain's daily routine remained typical and Maguans continued to scavenge gold pieces and cazabi to submit. Ballester remained uninformed to the contrary.

Bakako's disquiet returned inward, to his own responsibilities—satisfying the hunger of his family and villagers and the dozens of pale men in his custody. Yutowa's misery deepened, and Bakako offered an open invitation to join his family for dinner.

When Yutowa failed to show for a few days, Bakako ambled to chat with him under starlight at his lean-to, where the yuca's poison was drained.

"I've missed you," Bakako chided softly, distressed that his friend lay curled on the ground, remiss in bathing for weeks.

Yutowa raised himself, and the two Guanahanians sat side by side on a log.

"Guarionex has lost the will to fight," Yutowa observed. "He will fail his people, just as the other caciques."

"He's tried to maintain peace so his subjects aren't slaughtered," Bakako responded plainly, seeking to curtail a rant's inception. "When's the last time you ate?" he inquired, appalled that even night's shade didn't conceal the protrusion of ribs from Yutowa's chest.

"This morning," Yutowa lied, his tone firm. He hesitated, staring into Bakako's eyes, intimating he pined for a reasoned discussion—just as countless times before. "Do you respect him?"

"Guarionex has retained his dignity, regardless of defeat," Bakako responded. "He's not a coward, but I suspect he wishes he had fought with Caonabó."

"Caonabó was the bravest," Yutowa judged, reflecting on the brief moments he'd sat between Caonabó and Hojeda. "But none of the island's caciques have been cowards, save perhaps Guacanagarí. Even he released the Boriquén women from Admiral's enslavement." He spread his arms, heralding the question that had mesmerized them both for four years. "So—why have they all failed to defeat Admiral's conquest?"

"Admiral's weapons and beasts," Bakako answered. "They're too fearsome, too vicious."

Yutowa shook his head vigorously. "The Haitians have so vastly outnumbered the pale men that their weapons don't explain it. The weapons and beasts are part of it, but not the key."

"The diseases and famine have brought everyone to their knees," Bakako responded. "The Christ-spirit devastates every village where a cross is planted."

"There remain today far more Haitians than necessary to massacre all Admiral's men, even after the staggering decimation," Yutowa pronounced, shaking his head a second time. "Disease and famine aren't the critical reason, either."

Bakako grew pensive, surmising where Yutowa led. Failing cowardice, weapons, disease, and famine, there remained one grave explanation. As obvious as night following day, it had always haunted them.

"The pale men are far more ruthless and belligerent than our people, and our people too compromising, too conciliatory," Bakako concluded. "They have no moral rules, and their Christ-spirit provides an excuse for all evil done in his name. Our respect for harmony and our spirits' sincerity have left us vulnerable."

Tears welled in Yutowa's eyes, and he shuddered. "That's the essence."

Bakako put his arm around his friend's shoulders to comfort him, but to no avail.

"I'm the very proof of that—the most guilty!" Yutowa wailed. "The very first compromiser, conciliator, harmonizer, betrayer. The Cubans would've killed Admiral five years ago—but for me!" He shoved Bakako away and stood, head bowed. "I convinced them to spare the conqueror!" he cried. "My soul deserves darkness, not joy."

Bakako stood to yank Yutowa back to the log, chafing that they'd discussed this before, petrified by Yutowa's intensity. But Yutowa resisted, more strength in his feeble frame than apparent, and wiped his tears with the back of his hand.

"Bakako, you survive to live in both peoples' worlds. I don't condemn that choice, and I will always love you. We are Guanahanían." Yutowa stared directly into Bakako's eyes. "Support your wife, raise your son, and don't follow me. The pale men's conquest won't be reversed, and, as Admiral's olive-son, they won't harm you."

Bakako clutched his comrade in a strong embrace, intent that intimacy and brotherhood anchor him in life and to rest. Yutowa gradually relented, and Bakako laid him to sleep on the lean-to's mat. "That's enough talk for tonight," Bakako whispered hoarsely. "Rest. I'll bring you fruit in the morning." He scanned the lean-to to detect a gourd that might contain the yuca's poison but saw none, and then departed.

As he trod to his caney, Bakako strained for the hoot of an owl but was heartened to recognize only the chirping of tree frogs and grasshoppers. In the distance, he spied some villagers seated before a firepit, smoking *tabako* (tobacco), which dispelled their hunger—but not their despair. He passed the bohíos where the pale men resided, and he scorned that they were fit to rule anyone. Upon entering his caney, he stood beside Ariana's hammock, where she lay cradled with their son. She stirred, smiled, and told him to sleep, whereupon he lay beside her.

Yet he couldn't. Bakako remained vigil for an owl's hoot, and his thoughts whirled with visions of Yutowa and their long journey together. He mourned that Yutowa was the final link to his prior life, to an existence that he would never relive or revisit, to an identity that could no longer survive. Admiral, or Admiral's men, would conquer those they chose to conquer. Contemplating a world without them was just a dream. Resistance meant execution for himself and starvation for his wife and son.

Bakako emerged from the caney at twilight, after slumbering but brief interludes, to sight buzzards circling low in the sky above the lean-to. He sat and watched, weeping until the sun tipped the horizon. He then awoke Ariana to advise he was leaving to prepare Yutowa's burial.

"From now on, call me Diego," he instructed her. "For all others, it's Cacique Diego. Cacique Diego Colón."

Cristóbal, Testament,
Seville, Winter 1498

At dawn in early February 1498, Cristóbal stood with Bishop Fonseca on a wharf overlooking the Guadalquivir, observing the *Niña* and *India* weigh anchor to commence the float downstream from Seville to enter the sea at Sanlúcar de Barrameda, at last bound to resupply Española's settlement. The ocean crossing would be the *Niña*'s fifth and the *India*'s first homeward bound. Their destination was the new settlement brother Bartolomé had established on the island's southern coast. With Fonseca's approval, Cristóbal had selected as the caravels' captain general Pedro Fernández Coronel, the gentleman who'd served as the second voyage's chief constable and on Isabela's governing council during the Cuban exploration, now one of Cristóbal's trusted subordinates.

The caravels were heavy with meat, wine, weapons, and ammunition. When fully loaded at Sanlúcar, they would berth over a hundred passengers, a majority being soldiers to subdue Indian rebellion and oversee their labor. There were almost two dozen unskilled workmen, ten pardoned murderers, a few women, and a substantial contingent of those proven loyal to Cristóbal, including his black manservant, Juan Portugués.

Cristóbal and the bishop studied the caravels' launches tug to aim the bows downstream, conferring professionally but coldly, resigned they would chafe often while requisitioning the additional ships for Cristóbal's third voyage. They hadn't received news from Española since December 1496, and both feared the settlement's state to be far direr than Cristóbal had depicted to the sovereigns. The bishop galled that the sovereigns were wasting their time and money. Cristóbal's letter to Bartolomé, then borne by Coronel, exulted vindication—that the sovereigns had reconfirmed Cristóbal's authorities and redoubled their commitment. Yet it also bemoaned that Cristóbal had come to abominate life itself, suffering endless setbacks in financing the third fleet while anguishing for Bartolomé's struggles during the hiatus of resupply.

As the caravels drifted away, Cristóbal scanned upstream beyond the river bridge toward the Carthusian monastery where he'd resided after his first voyage. He now worshipped there often and had befriended a friar, and the monastery's quiet solitude beckoned.* But he felt obligated to accompany the bishop back to the city's enormous Cathedral.

"Six more to arrange," Cristóbal remarked as the two passed through a gate in the city's wall. "Three for exploration, three for resupply."

"Provided the financing is mustered and the prisons boot enough felons to fill the ships," the bishop replied. "Assuming the king and queen aren't distracted by important matters."

"They won't be. They have a lofty spirit," Cristóbal rejoined. "They perceive the spiritual and temporal greatness of this business, not just the expense." He acridly disdained that the bishop's annual benefices likely exceeded the voyage's entire cost.

"No one's patience lasts forever," Fonseca retorted. "Theirs expires if your settlement can't stand on its own feet."

"It will. Remember, Spain's princes have yet to win foreign lands," Cristóbal cautioned. "I bring the king and queen the opportunity of another world."

"But they seek marvelous possessions, filled with gold," the bishop observed. "Not treasure-less hinterlands."

The two men parted at the Cathedral, where the bishop retired to the administrative offices, his passion mercantile ledgers rather than scriptures. Cristóbal searched to find a solitary pew in an unoccupied chapel in which to contemplate his life and legacy rather than pray. He'd worshipped in the Cathedral before, as in other renowned churches of the city, and its chapels and tombs exceeded those of all others, proudly memorializing Andalusia's nobility, high clergy, and even kings. But Cristóbal had found the edifice too imperial, and the bishop's and his aides' faith insufficiently sincere, to attract his devotion.

---

*The Monasterio de la Cartuja de Santa María de las Cuevas and Fray Gaspar Gorricio.

Cristóbal jealously ruminated that his title, authority, and accomplishments did merit his own entombment there, and he chafed that the sovereigns or their successors might never admit that. He bristled that the bishop and countless other Spaniards felt a license to demean him and threaten his abandonment, ceaselessly, and that—for too long—he'd forsaken his Genoese heritage to appease their envies.*

⊡ ⊡ ⊡

Later that month, Cristóbal completed the testamentary disposition he intended to serve as the root and foundation of his lineage in perpetuity, sometimes with learned assistance, often without, relying on the Lord's guidance and his own self-learning. It commenced with a brief summation of his life's work—the Holy Trinity had inspired his voyage west to the Indies, the sovereigns being pleased to sponsor, and the discovery of the Indies mainland and many islands. One of the islands the Indians called Haiti and others Cipangu, now conquered for the sovereigns as Española, its peoples paying them tribute.

On his death, his title *Admiral* and his authorities and financial entitlements would pass to his elder son Diego and then Diego's son or sons or, failing that line, his younger son Fernando and his line, and so forth to brothers Bartolomé and Diego's lines, and, if the only successor were a woman, that woman until a next male kin were identified. Diego and successors were bound to provide maintenance to the others, so long as they remained loyal, and to adopt, as his own, the cryptic signature Cristóbal had conceived for himself after the first voyage. All descendants were to bear Cristóbal's coat of arms. Impudently, Cristóbal summarized the financial entitlements as aggregating 25 percent of the Indies revenues, aggrandizing the 10 percent and one-eighth interests in profits and a salary he believed owed Castile's admiral.

Proudly, defiantly, the testament roundly pronounced that long sublimated—Cristóbal had come from and was born in Genoa. He would no longer hush that heritage, and the testament instructed Diego and successors to support one of their lineage with a house and income to live with a wife in Genoa forever, benefitting as a citizen in its aid

*Since 1898, the Cathedral has housed a crypt commemorated as containing Cristóbal's final remains. The Faro a Colón (Columbus Lighthouse) in Santo Domingo does as well.

and protection and working for its honor and growth, albeit without conflicting with the church or Fernando and Isabel. The inheritance's savings were to be invested in Genoa's powerful Bank of Saint George.

The testament was gracious and loyal to the sovereigns and their lineage, yet it expressed no love or concern for their kingdoms or countrymen and couched indications that Cristóbal could have other means and potential support. It acclaimed Genoa as a noble and powerful city. It recounted that Cristóbal's intent in serving the sovereigns had been that they use the Indies' profits to reclaim Jerusalem, and it authorized son Diego to use the monies held in the bank to do so if Isabel and Fernando failed. As customary, it entreated Isabel and Fernando to deny consent to the testament's disfigurement, as well as the pope to provide any mandate necessary for the testament to be fulfilled, under penalty of excommunication.

For the Indies, Cristóbal directed that Diego or heirs build a church on Española dedicated to Santa María de Concepción, with a hospital and a chapel, where mass would be said for Cristóbal's and his ancestors' and successors' souls—just as Cristóbal had seen worshippers do for Prince Henrique at Mina's church. He directed that four missionaries be maintained and supported on the island, responsible for converting the Indians, and that a monument be erected in the church reminding of his final wishes. Other than their conversion, the testament expressed no hopes or visions—nor gracious sentiments, acclamations, or bequests—for Española's Indians. The one Indian Cristóbal briefly had favored as if a son, now Cacique Diego Colón, was neither provided for nor mentioned.

Hell in Haiti,
March–April 1498

Five years had passed since the pale men's first arrival. The surviving Haitian caciques and peoples now grieved their homeland as horrifically wounded by a broad swath of Christian crosses, occasional forts, and a multitude of corpses stretching northwest to southeast across the island's entire central territory. Therein, civility had fallen to hatred, tranquility to hostility, and liberty to enslavement. Dread of death by famine or plague racked every woken hour, and it was difficult to conceive that the hell the pale men warned of could be worse. Yet the pale men suffered also, nursing the caciques' forlorn hope the conquerors might yet depart or defeat themselves. Guarionex and Behecchio's scouts and informants spied intently upon the hostilities between the pale men's opposing factions and to discern the Guamiquina's return or intentions.

In late March, scouts on the southern coast reported that two vessels were approaching the new settlement at the Ozama. Informants there soon admonished that the vessels had borne fresh soldiers, weapons, and now pale-faced women, as well as the pale men's foodstuffs, and that the settlers there rejoiced, although the Guamiquina hadn't returned. Scouts inland then relayed that Adelantado and his men were dashing urgently from Fort Concepción to the new settlement, with the rebel leader and his band bustling close behind, their respective food supplies having dwindled precariously.

Portion of Andrés de Morales's map of Española showing forts, published by Peter Martyr d'Anghera in his *de Orbe Novo*, 1516. Reprinted with permission of the University Library of Bologna.

◘ ◘ ◘

Bartolomé denied Francisco Roldán's rebels access to the Santo Domingo compound and refused to share food, weapons, or ammunition with them. He admonished Roldán that the Admiral was returning with six ships and the Colóns' authority reaffirmed by king and queen, and again he offered the rebels a pardon for resumed obedience. Roldán again refused, loathing his men were denied even letters from their loved ones, surmising he'd be prosecuted for treason on abandoning arms.

Both men seethed—Bartolomé that he couldn't cure the rebellion before Cristóbal's return, Roldán that the sovereigns yet trusted the Genoese brothers. Roldán agreed only to depart without hostilities, retiring angrily back to his encampment in the Vega Real, and Bartolomé commenced criminal proceedings.

◘ ◘ ◘

Roldán and his famished band soon found the yuca harvestable at their encampment entirely depleted, and he desperately turned to Cacique Diego Colón for cazabi.

"I can't give you any," Diego replied, trembling that Bartolomé would punish him for dispensing food when Bartolomé had denied it. "My villagers and I, and the men I harbor, don't have enough for ourselves," he excused.

"I order you to give me what you have!"

Diego faltered, tortured that even his adopted identity might fail to shield him from punishment by pale men. "Is that Adelantado's wish?"

"Fear not. I grant you a pardon," Roldán responded, conceding that Bartolomé would consider it treason. "In the name of the king and queen."

Confounded, Diego reflected upon Admiral's vindictiveness, Adelantado's cruelties, and Roldán's craven pretenses and uncertain prospects. His chest pounded, welling with an abiding allegiance to Admiral over all other pale men, and his breath froze, unnerved Roldán yet might prevail over Admiral and punish refusal. For an instant, he writhed that the remora never faced such choices. He recalled Yutowa's exhorting survival and Guarionex's reminder to care for loved ones. He spied Ariana in his caney's doorway gazing anxiously back, little Diego at her hip. The present moment held only one choice—as Roldán's band likely would seize what they needed anyway.

"Take what you need, but then depart," Cacique Diego Colón responded. *I will not harbor you*, he cried to himself, haunted by a vision of his own mother coddling him and whispering *Bakako*.

⊡ ⊡ ⊡

The rebels devoured Cacique Diego's last cazabi within days, and Roldán soon concluded that the Vega Real's population loss and crop failures precluded encamping there any longer.

"There's nothing more to eat in this hellhole, nor healthy servants to farm it! The womenfolk are blighted from disease," Roldán scorned to his men. "We must move on."

Moans of hunger registered desperate agreement.

"So, we depart for Xaraguá," he commanded. "I'll release its rulers from tribute, and we'll delight as the Genoese tyrant takes his own turn starving! We'll feast on Xaraguá's gardens and prevail on its people's service."

⊡ ⊡ ⊡

In Guaricano, after learning of the resupply ships' arrival, Guarionex saddened that the pale men's hunger would subside temporarily. The time had come for all to understand he would no longer participate in tribute. Before dawn one morning, he and his nitaínos and wives stole from Guaricano north, seeking to harbor with the Ciguayan chieftain Mayobanex, a friend for decades.

Bartolomé soon received Ballester's dispatch that Guarionex had fled, tribute would fail, and Fort Concepción risked attack from Guarionex and allied chieftains to the north. Bartolomé's anger toward Roldán paled, supplanted by desperation that Guarionex flouted his obligations, cornerstone to Española's conquest. Bartolomé commanded lieutenants promptly to muster a well-armed force to root Guarionex from hiding and haul him back to perform his duties for the king and queen.

□ □ □

Behecchio received scouts at his inland residence, informing that the rebel band—some seventy strong—now were tramping, lawlessly and lewdly, toward Xaraguá. He was outraged that the pale men would violate their agreement, cornerstone to denying Xaraguá's conquest. He dispatched a runner to Anacaona at the coast, bidding her prompt return to discuss the band's annihilation.

Anacaona,
Xaraguá

Anacaona and Onaney gazed to the ocean, warmed by the faint glow of sunrise on their backs, observing Anacaona's nitaíno direct a crew of two dozen to provision the war canoe that would bear Onaney back to Aniyana. This would be their last goodbye.

"I pray the pale men never find Aniyana," Anacaona implored. "But those there and on the neighboring islands must understand what we've learned. Above all, your son must know to deny possessing gold."

"It's your nitaíno's duty to so instruct my son," Onaney responded. "I simply pass Caonabó's legacy and love and a few cherished possessions." Pointing to the nitaíno, she assured, "I've spoken to him, and he understands."

"Are you sad to leave Haiti?" Anacaona asked, sensing despondency.

"This has been our husband's island—where he ruled—more important to him than Aniyana, although he loved his birthplace," Onaney averred. "I often reflect whether I should've joined him in death while in Maguana, to honor him."

"I appreciate that," Anacaona commended, aware that Onaney's gloom always had revealed that angst. She set her arm about the older woman's shoulders, drawing her close. "But I'm glad you didn't. There's nothing to honor left there." She searched to impart optimism. "You shall honor Caonabó by reuniting with his son, passing his spear to a successor. Your son needs you."

"I'd cherish embracing my son once more," Onaney rasped passionately. She hesitated and softened her tone, gravely. "But it's no longer necessary. He's older than you, and he doesn't need guidance." She pivoted to face Anacaona directly. "You are Caonabó's successor."

Each peered intently into the other's eyes, both trembling, Anacaona as the revelation crept through her, Onaney for imparting it.

"None of us has joined our husband's soul on its journey," Onaney whispered hoarsely. "I am his first wife, and it is time I do so." She waited as the startle apparent in Anacaona's visage settled to comprehension. "Maguana could have been more appropriate, but I will join him in the sea—whose fierceness he honored since childhood and into which he last departed."

They held each other silently for some moments, and Anacaona fought an impulse to convince Onaney otherwise. The decision was appropriately each wife's own, and no Taíno spirit would object. She asked simply, "Where?"

"The pale men didn't inform you where they cast him, and it doesn't matter," Onaney judged. "But those traveling to and from Aniyana navigate by the great mountain on the northern coast.* When Caonabó first brought me here, we coursed toward it for hours and came ashore nearby. Your warriors will veer the canoe north at the mountain, and that's where my soul will depart to join his."

Anacaona hugged Onaney closer, pierced by the poetry of the choice.

Shortly, the canoe was provisioned and set, including with a sack of the cherished heirlooms. The two released each other with a parting kiss. Onaney boarded, the warriors hunkered beside the hull to shove it into the surf, jumping inside as momentum built, and, with an austere grimace and wave, she commenced her final journey.

Anacaona respectfully observed the canoe as it shrank into the horizon. But she had received Behecchio's dire summons, and she then departed forthwith, bound for their inland residence, borne on a litter.

◘ ◘ ◘

At dusk, she found her brother secluded in the oasis by the village stream.

*Cabo del Morro, Dominican Republic.

"Scouts report seventy pale men are approaching, led by the rebel leader, enemy to Adelantado," Behecchio related. "They'll soon trespass, in violation of Adelantado's promise."

"Is their trespass his wish?" Anacaona inquired, roused to discern betrayal.

"I care not. He assured that pale men wouldn't enter Xaraguá," Behecchio retorted impatiently. "We've suffered ransom to be spared. Adelantado answers for every pale man on Haiti."

"But does he control these rebels?"

"No. They've confronted each other for months. Wherever he intrudes, the rebel leader excuses the Guamiquina's payments in return for demanding his own." Behecchio curdled his voice. "Perhaps he assumes we'll so agree."

Anacaona vacillated, waiting Behecchio's plotting.

"We're entitled to massacre these pale men when they enter Xaraguá," he pronounced. "That's the justice due Adelantado's breaching his word." He grasped Anacaona's shoulders. "But I don't know whether Adelantado would approve or disapprove of that."

Anacaona frowned, also unsure.

"Or we could welcome these rebels—and then accept their release from Adelantado's payments," Behecchio pondered. "But that would forsake our effort to curry his favor, the isolation he promised, and the spell you've cast upon him."

Recollections of Adelantado's lustful clutch and the bulwarks of his vessel tormented Anacaona's thoughts, darkly ushering a vision of Caonabó lashed aboard and dying. She would relish defying Adelantado's ransom and scorning his lust face-to-face! But she shrugged, resisting impulse. "Who will prevail between the pale men—Adelantado or this rebel?"

"Scouts inform that the Guamiquina has resupplied Adelantado, so his men won't hunger soon," Behecchio reported, shrugging in return. "But Guarionex has abandoned them."

Brother and sister debated how best to divide and arrest the pale men, just as the Guamiquina had sought to splinter the Haitian caciques.

"One band may eliminate the other," Behecchio calculated. "Leaving us to eliminate it alone."

"It's premature to assassinate these rebels," Anacaona agreed. "Let's meet them to weigh which relationship augurs best." She was certain she could smite the rebel leader, just as Adelantado or any other man.

◻ ◻ ◻

That evening, in moonlight, Anacaona strolled alone in her garden. Blossoms of magnolias, orchids, cacti, and Bayahibes beckoned, offering respite from the cascade of devastations and looming threats. Instead, she sought the spirits' alliance and her husband's blessing.

She exhorted Yúcahu to vanquish the two forces she'd never met or worshipped—her husband's killer, the Guamiquina, and the pale men's herald and warrior, the Christ-spirit. Their evil savagery had to be undone prelude to any resolution. She brooded incredulous that the Guamiquina, his rulers, and the Christ-spirit let misery befall even their own subjects, and she implored Yúcahu to exploit the vulnerability of that betrayal.

An owl hooted, perched in the magnolias, and Anacaona brusquely waved her arms and scowled, "Begone!" *Hover over the pale men, not my people.*

She beseeched Caonabó for the wisdom to scheme wisely and vindicate his death, as she emerged from his shadow to lead their civilization. Tenderly, she honored his primacy, ferocity, bravery, and guile, and assured her resilience. But she pleaded that persuasion and manipulation now be tested.

At last, when exhausted and the moon high, Anacaona found herself standing before the Bayahibes. She received a revelation to proceed as she always had prior to the pale men's arrival—by conquering life's obstacles without ever grasping a spear.

PARTICIPANTS AND TAÍNO SPIRITS

TAÍNOS

Supreme Taíno caciques and family members (all historic persons and, except as indicated, with historic names):

Anacaona, Caonabó's premier wife, of Xaraguá's caciqual family, younger sister to Behecchio

Higueymota, Anacaona's daughter

Ariana, younger sister of Guarionex, historic person with fictitious name

Behecchio, supreme cacique of Xaraguá

Cacibaquel, deceased supreme cacique of Magua, Guarionex's father

Caonabó, supreme cacique of Maguana

Cayacoa, supreme cacique of Higüey

"Don Diego," younger brother of Caonabó, historic person, with name conferred by Cristóbal Colón, Taíno name unknown

Guacanagarí, supreme cacique of Marien

Guarionex, supreme cacique of Magua

Manicoatex, cacique in northern Cibao, younger brother of Caonabó

Matuma, Guacanagarí's brother, historic person with fictitious name

Mayobanex, supreme cacique of Ciguayo

Onaney, Caonabó's first wife, likely historic person with name accorded in various traditions

Taínos taken by Cristóbal Colón to Castile on his first voyage (all historic persons with fictitious birth names):

Abasu, Cuban, enslaved November 11, 1492, baptized Juan

Bakako, Guanahanían, enslaved October 14, 1492, baptized Diego

Xamabo, Haitian, nitaíno related to Guacanagarí, baptized Fernando

Yutowa, Guanahanían, enslaved October 14, 1492

Other Taínos:

Guanáoboconel, Macorix cacique residing along the Yaque, vassal to Guatiguaná, historic person with historic name

Guatiguaná, cacique of Macorix along the Yaque, vassal to Guarionex, historic person with historic name

Guatícabanu, Macorix youth, son of Guanáoboconel, the first Indian baptized in the Americas, as Juan Mateo, historic person with historic names

Mabiatué, cacique residing on route between Fort Concepción and Santo Domingo, historic person with historic name

Marque, cacique in Magua, vassal to Guarionex, historic person with historic name

Mayreni, cacique in Marien, vassal to Guacanagarí, historic person with historic name

Niana, born in a village along the Bajabonico River, Bakako's girlfriend, fictitious person

Ukuti, born in a village along the Bajabonico River, enslaved in 1494, historic person with fictitious name

Uxmatex, Maguanan, Caonabó's general, historic person with historic name

Wasu, born in a village along the Bajabonico River, enslaved in 1494, historic person with fictitious name

EUROPEANS

Spanish royal family:

King Fernando II of Aragón, king of Castile

Queen Isabel I of Castile, queen of Aragón

Isabel, daughter

Prince Juan, first in line to his parents' thrones

Juana, daughter

María, daughter

Catalina, daughter

Alfonso of Aragón, archbishop of Zaragoza, Fernando's illegitimate son

Portuguese royal family:

King João II

Queen Leonor, João's wife and cousin

Afonso, son (d. 1491)

Jorge, João's illegitimate son

King Manoel I, Leonor's brother and João's brother-in-law and cousin

Papacy:

Pope Alexander VI, the Aragonese Rodrigo Borja

Cardinal Giuliano della Rovere, Alexander's rival

Cristóbal Colón and family:

Admiral Cristóbal Colón (Cristoforo Colombo in Ligurian), often referred to by Taínos as the Guamiquina (the "leader" of his people)

Diego, Cristóbal's first son, born of his deceased Portuguese wife, Filipa Moniz Perestrelo

Fernando, Cristóbal's second son, born of his Andalusian mistress, Beatriz Enríquez de Arana

Bartolomé Colón, Cristóbal's oldest surviving younger brother

Diego Colón, Cristóbal's youngest brother

Violante Moniz, Cristóbal's sister-in-law and Filipa's sister

Miguel Muliarte, Violante's husband

Noblemen, churchmen, courtiers, and voyage suppliers to Queen Isabel and King Fernando, in Spain:

Pedro Mártir de Anglería, Italian humanist in Isabel's court

Juanoto Berardi, leading slave trader/financier in Seville

Andrés Bernáldez, curate of Los Palacios (near Seville)

Ximénez de Cisneros, confessor to Isabel, later archbishop of Toledo

Juan Rodríguez de Fonseca, archdeacon of Seville, later bishop of Badajoz

Alonso de Lugo, Canarian conquistador

Pedro González de Mendoza, Cardinal of Spain, archbishop of Toledo

Juan de Soria, chief accountant for Indies matters

Amerigo Vespucci, business associate of Juanoto Berardi

Crown courtiers, staff, or appointees voyaging to Española on the second voyage:

Juan Aguado, supply provisioner in Isabel's household

Bernardo Buil, papal nuncio to the Indies

Alonso Sánchez de Carvajal, on Isabel's staff during Reconquista, city councilman, voyage provisioner

Ginés de Gorvalán, gentleman veteran of Reconquista

Juan de Luján, a sovereign courtier

Melchior Maldonado, Castilian diplomat

Pedro Margarite, Catalan nobleman

Diego Marquez, gentleman overseer associated with treasury and accounting functions

Bernal de Pisa, chief accountant in Indies

Gaspar de Salinas, assistant to Bernal de Pisa

Antonio de Torres, brother to Prince Juan's governess

Fermín Zedo, goldsmith

Crew and other voyagers and settlers traveling to Española on the second voyage, unless otherwise indicated:

Diego de Arana, quartermaster of first voyage fleet, second cousin to Cristóbal's mistress, Beatriz Enríquez de Arana

Luis de Arriaga, gentleman appointed warden of Fort La Magdalena

Juan de Ayala, gentleman appointed captain of Fort La Concepción

Miguel Ballester, Catalan appointed to succeed as Fort La Concepción's commander

Chachu, *Santa María*'s boatswain on first voyage

Diego Alvarez Chanca, physician

Guillermo Coma, surgeon

Pedro Fernández Coronel, fleet's chief constable

Juan de la Cosa, *Santa María*'s master on first voyage and participant on second (mapmaker of 1500 world map)

Michele da Cuneo, from Savona (near Genoa), Cristóbal's childhood friend

Rodrigo de Escobedo, royal secretary on first voyage

María Fernández, Cristóbal's chambermaid

Pedro Gutiérrez, royal observer on first voyage

Alonso de Hojeda, Castilian formerly an associate of the Duke of Medinaceli in Puerto de Santa María

Juan Leudelle (also known as el Bermejo or Juna de Borgoña), Burgundian Franciscan friar

Pero Alonso Niño, *Santa María*'s pilot on first voyage and participant on second

Ramón Pané, Catalan Hieronymite friar

Juan Portugués, Cristóbal's Guinean manservant on first voyage

Francisco Roldán, on Cristóbal's personal staff, appointed Española's magistrate

Pedro de Salcedo, Cristóbal's page on first and second voyages

Pedro de Terreros, Cristóbal's steward on first and second voyages

Juan de Tisín, Burgundian Franciscan friar

Other European royalty:

King Charles VIII of France

King Henry VII of England

Arthur, son

Emperor Maximilian I, Holy Roman emperor

Archduke Philip, son

Princess Margarite, daughter

Neapolitan Throne:

King Ferrante I of Naples, Fernando's cousin

Juana of Aragón, King Ferrante I's wife and Fernando's sister

King Alfonso, Ferrante I's son

King Ferrante II, Alfonso's son

Other:

John Caboto, Italian explorer for King Henry VII

Bartolomeu Dias, Portuguese explorer for King João II

Vasco da Gama, Portuguese explorer for King Manoel I

CANARIANS

Benitomo, Guanche ruler of the Taoro peoples on Tenerife

Bentor, son

Fernando Guanarteme, Gran Canarian ruler vassal to Fernando and Isabel, formerly Tensor Semidan (prior to conquest and baptism)

TAÍNO SPIRITS AND ANCESTRAL PERSONS

Yúcahu, the spirit of yuca and male fertility, also being master of the sea, fatherless, and the most important spirit in daily life

Attabeira, Yúcahu's mother and the provider of water for crops and other nourishment

Deminán Caracaracol, born into adversity but learns proper Taíno conduct to prosper

Guabancex, the female spirit of hurricanes and destruction

Yaya, the supreme spirit

GLOSSARY

TAÍNO WORDS

Taíno words typically are presented with their Spanish spelling except for some islands, where the likely Taíno phonetic form is retained. Based upon Julian Granberry and Gary Vescelius's *Languages of the Pre-Columbian Antilles*, William F. Keegan and Lisabeth A. Carlson's *Talking Taíno: Caribbean Natural History from a Native Perspective,* and other sources.

aji	hot pepper
areíto	song, dance
batey	ball game, ballcourt, or ceremonial plaza
behique	shaman (i.e., a priest and doctor)
bohío	house, home
boniata	sweet potato
cacique	chief
caney	a chieftain's home
Caniba	a Caribe person
cazabi	cassava, a toasted bread made from yucca
cemí	spirit or object that represents spirit, typically of stone, wood, or cotton
chicha	corn beer

cocuyo	large firefly
cohaba	narcotic powder used in communication with spirits, or the communication ceremony itself
duho	ceremonial or chief's seat
guaicán	remora or shark sucker
guanín	a composition of gold, copper, and silver, with reddish hue
hicotea	turtle
huricán	hurricane
hutia	cat-sized rodent
iguana	iguana
macana	wooden club
mahisi	corn
naboria	servant, the servant class
nagua	married woman's loincloth
nitaíno	nobleman, lord
taíno	noble or good person
yuca	yucca, manioc

ISLANDS AND PLACES

Taíno names:

Amina	Amina River, Dominican Republic
Aniyana	Middle Caicos, Turks and Caicos
Ayay	St. Croix
Bajabonico	Bajabonico River, northern Dominican Republic
Bohío	A name for the island of the Dominican Republic and Haiti, typically used by Lucayans (including Bakako and Yutowa) and used by Cristóbal in his journal of the first voyage (in reliance on Bakako and Yutowa) until he renamed it La Isla Española
Boriquén	Puerto Rico
Camú	Camú River, Dominican Republic

Cibao	rocky, mountainous region in central Dominican Republic
Ciguayo	Mayobanex's chiefdom, northern Dominican Republic
Cuba	Cuba
Guacca	Lake Trou Caïman, Haiti
Guanahaní	San Salvador?
Guaricano	Guarionex's hometown, near La Vega Vieja, Dominican Republic
Guarico	Guacanagarí's hometown, near Bord de Mer de Limonade, Haiti
Hagueygabon	Lake Enriquillo, Dominican Republic
Haiti	*Ayiti* phonetically, a name for the island of the Dominican Republic and Haiti
Higüey	Cayacoa's chiefdom, eastern Dominican Republic
Jaina	Jaina River, Dominican Republic
Lucayans	island people, from the Bahamas or Turks and Caicos
Magua	Guarionex's chiefdom, central Dominican Republic
Maguana	Caonabó's chiefdom, southwestern Dominican Republic
Marien	Guacanagarí's chiefdom, northern Haiti and Dominican Republic
Neiba	Yaque del Sur River, Dominican Republic
Niti	Location of gold deposits, somewhere in Caonabó's Maguana
Ozama	Ozama River, Dominican Republic
Quisqueya	A name for the island of the Dominican Republic and Haiti
Samaná	Samaná Peninsula, Dominican Republic
Unijíca	Unijica River, Dominican Republic
Xaraguá	Behecchio's chiefdom, southwestern Haiti and Dominican Republic

Yainagua	Lake Étang Saumâtre, Haiti
Yamaye	Jamaica
Yaque	Yaque del Norte River, Dominican Republic
Yaramaqui	Antigua
Yasica	Yásica River, Dominican Republic

Caribe (Kalinago) names:

Caloucaera	Basse-Terre, Guadalupe
Ouitoucoubouli	Dominica

Spanish names:

La Isla Española	The Spanish Island, a name for the island of the Dominican Republic and Haiti
La Vega Real	The Royal Plain, Dominican Republic, largely Guarionex's Magua
Puerto de los Hidalgos	Pass of the Gentlemen, Dominican Republic

SOURCES

The principal primary (P) and secondary (S) sources considered in writing each story are set forth below (whether supportive or at variance with the story), including, for primary sources, the chapter, section, paragraph, or date considered. Stories occasionally quote or paraphrase words from the primary sources so identified (or, infrequently, secondary sources), without quotation marks to preserve the novel style, and the acknowledgment of those who have graciously permitted such usage is set forth at the end of the immediately following note.

PRINCIPAL PRIMARY AND SECONDARY SOURCES AND PERMISSION

Ferdinand Columbus stated in his father's biography (cited below, chap. 16) that Columbus kept journals of all four voyages, and Andrés Bernáldez indicated in his history (cited below, chap. 123) that in 1496 Columbus left him with various of Columbus's writings, including relating to the second voyage. But a Columbus journal or diary for the second voyage has not been known for centuries. This has made it more difficult for historians to reconstruct the Caribbean events from 1493 to 1498 than Columbus's Journal (cited below) permits for the period of the first voyage.

The principal contemporaneous documentary evidence—all European—regarding the events portrayed herein are: (1) Columbus's letters and memorials to Queen Isabella and King Ferdinand, including the "Libro Copiador" and the "Torres Memorandum" noted below; (2) Columbus's orders and communications to his lieutenants and others; (3) Isabella and Ferdinand's orders and communications to Columbus and others, as well as royal proclamations and edicts; (4) letters or reports of voyage participants or voyage administrators or suppliers, particularly Ramón Pané (who studied the Taínos' religion), Dr. Chanca (a fleet doctor), Michele da Cuneo (Columbus's childhood friend), Nicolò Scillacio's letter translating letters from Guillermo Coma (a fleet surgeon), Juanoto Berardi (Columbus's principal financier), and Francisco Roldán (one of Columbus's officers); and (5) observations of travelers to the Americas in the sixteenth century, including Girolamo Benzoni.

The principal primary accounts chronicling events relating to the Indies—also all European—are the works of the following contemporaries: Andrés Bernáldez, Bartolomé de Las Casas, Ferdinand Columbus, Peter Martyr d'Anghera, and Gonzalo Fernández de Oviedo. As to solely European events, primary chronicles also include works by Jerónimo Zurita.

In 1985, copies of lost letters purportedly of Columbus were discovered, now known as the "Libro Copiador" (cited below). While some question the authenticity of these letters, I believe they reflect a knowledge, outlook, and writing style that Columbus did have; do not reflect a typical forger's error of inadvertently including knowledge or outlook that could only have been understood subsequently; and constitute the sole written reports by Columbus to Isabella and Ferdinand known today of certain important events (i.e., of events not reported in the Columbus written communications to them known prior to 1985). The letters of the "Libro Copiador" do not provide a daily account, as would a journal, but they do provide an outline of the main order of events—which, with limited exception, I have favored over other sources.

Over centuries, historians and others have searched for, collected, complied in editions, and sometimes translated into English (from the original Spanish, Latin, or other languages) the various primary sources, although the selections translated into English often have a Columbus or European focus and omit portions of works relating solely to the Taínos. I have used the following editions for the principal primary sources:

P: d'Anghera, Peter Martyr. *De Orbe Novo: The Eight Decades of Peter Martyr d'Anghera*. Translated by Francis Augustus MacNutt. New York: Burt Franklin, 1912 (together with the "Raccolta De Orbe Novo" noted below, "Martyr").

P: de Anglería, Pedro Mártir. *Epistolario*. Translated (into Spanish) by José López de Toro. Vol. 9, *Documentos inéditos para la historia de España*. Madrid: Imprenta Góngora, 1953 (together with the "Raccolta Epistolario" noted below, "Martyr Epistolario").

P: Anghiera, Peter Martyr of. *The Discovery of the New World in the Writings of Peter Martyr of Anghiera.* Edited by Ernesto Lunardi, Elisa Magioncalda, and Rosanna Mazzacane. Translated by Feliz Azzola, revised Luciano F. Farina. Vol. 2, *Nuova Raccolta Colombiana.* Rome: Istituto Poligrafico e Zecca Dello Stato, 1992. The *Nuova Raccolta Colombiana* is a collection of contemporary sources—Spanish texts and Italian and English translations—and analyses sponsored by the Italian Ministry of Cultural and Environmental Assets, National Commission for the Celebration of the Quincentennial of the Discovery of America, with English translations provided by The Ohio State University (the editions I used). This contains English translations of portions of Martyr's *Epistolario* ("Raccolta Epistolario") and *De Orbe Novo* ("Raccolta De Orbe Novo").

P: Benzoni, Girolamo. *History of the New World; Shewing His Travels in America, from AD 1541 to 1556: with some Particulars of the Island Canary.* Translated and edited by W. H. Smyth, 1857. Reprint, Cambridge: Cambridge University Press, 2009 ("Benzoni").

P: Bernáldez, Andrés. *Historia de los Reyes Católicos D. Fernando y Doña Isabel.* Seville: D. José María Geofrin, 1870. 2 vols. (together with "Jane Bernáldez" and "Raccolta Bernáldez" noted below, "Bernáldez").

P: *The Diario of Christopher Columbus's First Voyage to America, 1492–1493.* Translated by Oliver Dunn and James E. Kelley, Jr. Norman: University of Oklahoma Press, 1989 (the "D&K Journal").

P: *The Journal of Christopher Columbus (During His First Voyage, 1492–93) and Documents Relating the Voyages of John Cabot and Gaspar Corte Real.* Translated by Clements R. Markham, 1893. Reprint, Cambridge: Cambridge University Press, 2010 (together with the D&K Journal, "Journal").

P: *Christopher Columbus: Accounts and Letters of the Second, Third and Fourth Voyages, Part 1.* Edited by Paolo Emilio Taviani, Consuelo Varela, Juan Gil, and María Conti, translated by Marc A. Beckwith and Luciano F. Farina. Vol. 6, *Nuova Raccolta Colombiana.* Rome: Istituto Poligrafico e Zecca Dello Stato, 1994. Section 2 of this *Part 1* includes the "Libro Copiador" in Spanish and English (together with the Spanish versions in the "CDDD" noted below, the "Libro Copiador"). *Part 2* of this *Nuova Raccolta Colombiana* volume, identically titled, presents explanatory analysis of the letters (a secondary source, the "Raccolta Letters Notes").

P: Columbus, Ferdinand. *The Life of the Admiral Christopher Columbus.* Translated and annotated by Benjamin Keen. New Brunswick, NJ: Rutgers University Press, 1959 ("Ferdinand Columbus").

P: Cristóbal Colón. *Textos y documentos completos*, edición de Consuelo Varela. *Nuevas cartas*, edición de Juan Gil. 2nd ed. Madrid: Alianza Universidad, 2003 ("Varela Gil Textos").

P: Dotson, John, ed. and trans. *Christopher Columbus and His Family: The Genoese and Ligurian Documents.* Vol. 4, *Repertorium Columbianum.* Turnhout, Belgium: Brepols Publishers, 1998 ("Dotson"). The *Repertorium Columbianum* is a comprehensive collection of contemporary sources—Spanish or Italian texts and English translations—and analyses relating to Columbus's four voyages published under the auspices of the UCLA Center for Medieval and Renaissance Studies, undertaken at the time of the quincentenary anniversary of 1492.

P: Gil, Juan and Consuelo Varela, ed. *Cartas de particulares a Colón y relaciones coetáneas.* Madrid: Alianza Editorial, 1984 ("Gil Varela Cartas").

P: Jane, Cecil, trans. and ed. *The Four Voyages of Columbus: A History in Eight Documents, Including Five by Christopher Columbus, in the Original Spanish, with English Translations.* 2 vols. New York: Dover, 1988 ("Jane"). Contains, inter alia, Columbus's "Letter to Santángel," dated February 15, 1493, postscript dated March 4, 1493 ("Letter to Santángel"), Dr. Diego Alvarez Chanca's letter to Seville's mayor of January 1494 ("Chanca"), Columbus's memorandum of January 30, 1494 sent by Antonio de Torres to Ferdinand and Isabella ("Torres Memorandum"), a translation of Bernáldez, chaps. 123–131 ("Jane Bernáldez"), and Columbus's letter of October, 18, 1498 to Ferdinand and Isabella regarding the third voyage ("Third Voyage Letter").

P: Las Casas, Bartolomé de. *A Short Account of the Destruction of the Indies.* Edited and translated by Nigel Griffin. London: Penguin, 1992 ("Las Casas Short Account").

P: Las Casas, Bartolomé de. *Apologetica historia de las Indias.* 3 vols. Edition by Vidal Abril Castelló, Jesús A. Barreda, Berta Ares Quieja, and Miguel J. Abril Stoffels. Vols. 6, 7, 8, *Fray Bartolomé de Las Casas: Obras Completas.* Madrid: Alianza Editorial, 1992 ("Las Casas Apologetica").

P: Las Casas, Bartolomé de. *Historia de las Indias.* 3 vols. With prologue, notes, and chronology by André Saint-Lu. Caracas, Venezuela: Biblioteca

Ayacucho, 1986 ("Las Casas Historia"). This is the work in Spanish and remains untranslated in its entirety.

P: *Las Casas on Columbus: Background and the Second and Fourth Voyages*. Edited and translated by Nigel Griffin. Vol. 7, *Repertorium Columbianum*. Turnhout, Belgium: Brepols Publishers, 1999 ("Las Casas Repertorium"). This work of the *Repertorium Columbianum* translates into English portions of *Historia de las Indias* relating to Columbus other than the *Journal*, as well as some portions of other works of Las Casas.

P: *Las Casas on Columbus: The Third Voyage*. Edited by Geoffrey Symcox, textual edit by Jesús Carrillo, translated by Michael Hammer and Blair Sullivan. Vol. 11, *Repertorium Columbianum*. Turnhout, Belgium: Brepols Publishers, 2001 ("Las Casas Repertorium—Third Voyage").

P: Morison, Samuel Eliot, ed. and trans. *Journals and Other Documents on the Life and Voyages of Christopher Columbus*. New York: Heritage, 1963 ("Morison Documents"). Contains, inter alia, Columbus's Memorial to the Sovereigns on Colonial Policy, April 9, 1493 ("Columbus's 1493 Memorial"), the Sovereigns' Instructions to Columbus for His Second Voyage of May 29, 1493 ("Sovereigns' 1493 Instructions"), Michele da Cuneo's letter of October 28, 1495, to a fellow citizen of Savona ("Cuneo"), and Nicolò Scillacio's letter of December 13, 1494, to the Duke of Milan translating letters of Guillermo Coma ("Coma").

P: Nader, Helen, ed. and trans. *The Book of Privileges Issued to Christopher Columbus by King Fernando and Queen Isabel 1492–1502*. Philologist Luciano Formisano. Vol. 2, *Repertorium Columbianum*. Eugene, OR: Wipf & Stock, 1996 ("Nader"). This work, as well as Parry & Keith below, contains translations of key documents relating to the evolution of Isabella and Ferdinand's colonial policy for the Indies, including the sovereigns' license for Castilian subjects to settle or trade in the Indies of April 10, 1495 ("Sovereigns' 1495 License to Trade").

P: Navarrete, Martín Fernández de. *Colección de los Viages y Descubrimientos que Hicieron por Mar Los Españoles Desde Fines del Siglo XV*. Vols. 1–5. Buenos Aires: Editorial Guarania, 1945 ("Navarrete").

P: Oviedo, Gonzalo Fernández de. *Historia General y Natural de Las Indias*. Edition by Juan Pérez de Tudela Bueso. Madrid: Biblioteca de Autores Espanoles, 1959 ("Oviedo").

P: *Oviedo on Columbus*. Edited by Jesús Carrillo, translated by Diane Avalle-Arce. Vol. 9, *Repertorium Columbianum*. Turnhout, Belgium: Brepols Publishers, 2000 ("Oviedo Repertorium").

P: Pané, Ramón. *An Account of the Antiquities of the Indians*. New edition by José Juan Arrom, translated by Susan C. Griswold. Durham, NC: Duke University Press, 1999 ("Pané" and, as to Arrom's introduction and footnotes, "Arrom *Pané*").

P: Parry, John H. and Robert G. Keith. *New Iberian World: A Documentary History of the Discovery and Settlement of Latin America to the Early 17th Century*. Vol. 2. New York: Times Books, 1984 ("Parry & Keith"). Contains, inter alia, Columbus's instructions of April 9, 1494, to Pedro Margarite ("Margarite Instructions"), a list of products received by Columbus in tribute from March 10, 1495, to February 19, 1496 ("Tribute Items List"), the sovereigns' instructions to Juan Aguado of April 1495 ("Aguado Instructions"), Juanoto Berardi's memorial to Ferdinand, c. end 1494–March 1495 ("Berardi Memorial"), and Francisco Roldán's letter of October 10, 1499 to Cardinal Cisneros ("Roldán Letter").

P: Pérez de Tudela, Juan (director), Carlos Seco Serrano, Ramón Ezquerra Abadía and Emilio López Oto. *Colección documental del descubrimiento (1470–1506)*. 3 vols. Spain: Real Academia de la Historia, Conejo Superior de Investigaciones Cientificas, Fundación MAPFRE América, 1994 ("CDDD"). This is a very comprehensive, modern compilation of the documentary sources and includes letters of the Libro Copiador as published by Antonio Rumeu de Armas (docs. 183, 190, 256, and 315).

P: Phillips, Jr., William D., ed. and trans. *Testimonies from the Columbian Lawsuits*. Philologist Mark D. Johnston, translated by Anne Marie Wolf. Vol. 8, *Repertorium Columbianum*. Turnhout, Belgium: Brepols Publishers, 2000 (the "Pleitos," i.e., the "lawsuits"). Following Columbus's death in 1506, his heirs and the Spanish crown contested Columbus's hereditary entitlements in lawsuits spanning decades, and the witnesses included men enlisted on Columbus's second and other voyages.

P: Rumeu de Armas, Antonio. *Libro Copiador de Cristóbal Colón Correspondencia Inedita con Los Reyes Católicos Sobre Los Viajes a America*. Vol. 1. Madrid: Testimonio Compania Editorial, 1989. This is Rumeu de Armas's analysis of the Libro Copiador. Vol. 2 contains his transcription of the letters.

P: Symcox, Geoffrey ed. *Italian Reports on America 1453–1522: Letters, Dispatches and Papal Bulls.* Vol. 10, *Repertorium Columbainum.* Additional editing and translation by Giovanna Rabitti and Peter D. Diehl. Turnhout, Belgium: Brepols Publishers, 2001 ("Symcox *Italian Texts*").

P: Symcox, Geoffrey, ed., Luciano Formisano, Theodore J. Cachey, Jr., and John C. McLucas, eds. and trans. *Italian Reports on America 1493–1522: Accounts by Contemporary Observers.* Vol. 12, *Repertorium Columbianum.* Turnhout, Belgium: Brepols Publishers, 2002 ("Italian Reports Repertorium").

P: Triolo, Gioacchino and Luciano F. Farina, trans. *Christopher Columbus's Discoveries in the Testimonials of Diego Alvarez Chanca and Andrés Bernáldez.* Vol. 5, *Nuova Raccolta Colombiana.* Rome: Istituto Poligrafico e Zecca Dello Stato, 1992 ("Raccolta Bernáldez"). This contains an English translation of Bernáldez chapters 118–131.

P: Zurita, Jerónimo. *Historia del Rey Don Hernando el Católico: de las Empresas y Ligas de Italia.* 6 vols. Edition by Angel Canellas Lopez. Zaragoza, Spain: Diputación General de Aragón, 1989 ("Zurita *Hernando*").

The principal works of anthropologists, archaeologists, linguists, historians, and others regarding the Taínos and Caribes and disease transmission that I consulted are:

S: Arrom, José Juan. *Estudio de Lexicología Antillana.* 2nd ed. San Juan, Puerto Rico: Editorial de la Universidad de Puerto Rico, 2000 ("Arrom *Lexicología*").

S: Arrom, José Juan. *Mitología y artes prehispánicos de las Antillas.* 2nd ed. Coyoacán, Mexico: Siglo Veintiuno Editores, 1989 ("Arrom *Mitología*").

S: Barreiro, José, "A Note on Tainos: Wither Progress?" In "View from the Shore: American Indian Perspectives on the Quincentenary," edited by José Barriero, Columbus Quincentenary Edition, *Northeast Indian Quarterly.* Vol. 7, no. 3, Fall 1990, pp. 4–22.

S: Boucher, Philip P. *Cannibal Encounters: Europeans and Island Caribs, 1492–1763.* Baltimore: John Hopkins University Press, 1992 ("Boucher").

S: Cook, Noble David. *Born to Die: Disease and New World Conquest, 1492–1650.* Cambridge: Cambridge University Press, 1998 ("Cook *Disease*").

S: Cook, Noble David and W. George Lovell. *"Secret Judgments of God": Old World Disease in Colonial Spanish America*. Norman, OK: University of Oklahoma Press, 1992 ("Cook *Judgments*").

S: Crosby Jr., Alfred W. *Ecological Imperialism: The Biological Expansion of Europe, 900–1900*. 2nd ed. Cambridge: Cambridge University Press, 2015 ("Crosby *Ecological*").

S: Crosby Jr., Alfred W. *The Columbian Exchange: Biological and Cultural Consequences of 1492*. 30th anniv. ed. Westport, CT: Praeger Publishers, 2003 ("Crosby *Exchange*").

S: Curet, L. Antonio, and Mark W. Hauser. *Islands at the Crossroads: Migration, Seafaring, and Interaction in the Caribbean*. Tuscaloosa: University of Alabama Press, 2011.

S: Deagan, Kathleen, and José María Cruxent. *Columbus's Outpost among the Taínos: Spain and America at La Isabela, 1493–1498*. New Haven, CT: Yale University Press, 2002 ("Deagan *Isabela*").

S: Forbes, Jack D. *The American Discovery of Europe*. Urbana: University of Illinois Press, 2007.

S: Forbes, Jack D. *Africans and Native Americans: The Language of Race and the Evolution of Red-Black Peoples*. 2nd ed. Urbana & Chicago: University of Illinois Press, 1993 ("Forbes *Native Americans*").

S: Granberry, Julian and Gary Vescelius. *Languages of the Pre-Columbian Antilles*. Tuscaloosa: University of Alabama Press, 2004 ("Granberry *Languages*").

S: Granberry, Julian. *The Americas That Might Have Been: Native American Social Systems Through Time*. Tuscaloosa: University of Alabama Press, 2005 ("Granberry *Americas*").

S: Guitar, Lynne. "Cultural Genesis: Relationships among Indians, Africans, and Spaniards in rural Hispaniola, first half of the sixteenth century. PhD diss., Vanderbilt University, Nashville, TN. UMI Microform no. 9915091.

S: Hulme, Peter. *Colonial Encounters Europe and the Native Caribbean, 1492–1797*. London: Methuen, 1986 ("Hulme").

S: Keegan, William F. *Taíno Indian Myth and Practice: The Arrival of the Stranger King*. Gainesville: University of Florida Press, 2007 ("Keegan *Myth*").

S: Keegan, William F., and Lisabeth A. Carlson. *Talking Taíno: Caribbean Natural History from a Native Perspective*. Tuscaloosa: University of Alabama Press, 2008.

S: Keegan, William F. and Corinne L. Hofman. *The Caribbean before Columbus*. New York: Oxford University Press, 2017 ("Keegan *Caribbean*").

S: Lovén, Sven. 1935. *Origins of the Tainan Culture, West Indies*. Preface by L. Antonio Curet. Tuscaloosa: University of Alabama Press, 2010.

S: Milanich, Jerald T. and Susan Milbrath, eds. *First Encounters: Spanish Explorations in the Caribbean and the United States, 1492–1570*. Gainesville, FL: LibraryPress@UF, 2017. Includes Deagan, Kathleen A., "The Search for la Navidad, Columbus's 1492 Settlement" ("Deagan *Navidad*").

S: Montas, Onorio, Pedro José-Borrell, and Frank Moya Pons. *Arte Taíno*. Santo Domingo: Banco Central de la República Dominicana, 1983 ("Montas *Arte*").

S: Oliver, José R. *Caciques and Cemí Idols: The Web Spun by Taíno Rulers Between Hispaniola and Puerto Rico*. Tuscaloosa: University of Alabama Press, 2009 ("Oliver").

S: Oliver, José R., Colin McEwan, and Anna Casas Gilberga, eds. *El Caribe precolombino: Fray Ramón Pané y el universo taíno*. Spain: Ministerio de Cultura, Museu Barbier-Mueller d'Art Precolombí, Fundación Caixa Galicia, 2008. Includes Consuelo Varela and Juan Gil, chap. "La Española a la llegada de Ramón Pané" ("Varela Gil *Pané*"); and José R. Oliver, chap. "Tiempos difíciles: Fray Ramón Pané en la Española, 1494–1498" ("Oliver *Pané*").

S: Raudzens, George, ed. *Technology, Disease, and Colonial Conquests: Sixteenth to Eighteenth Centuries*. Boston: Brill Academic, 2003. Chap. 2, George Raudzens, "Outfighting or Outpopulating? Main Reasons for Early Colonial Conquests, 1493–1788" ("Raudzens").

S: Reid, Basil A. *Myths and Realities of Caribbean History*. Tuscaloosa: University of Alabama Press, 2009 ("Reid").

S: Restall, Matthew. *Seven Myths of the Spanish Conquest.* Oxford: Oxford University Press, 2003 ("Restall").

S: Robiou Lamarche, Sebastián. Trans. by Grace M. Robiou Ramírez de Arellano. *Tainos and Caribes: The Aboriginal Cultures of the Antilles.* San Juan: Editorial Punto y Coma, 2019 ("Lamarche").

S: Rouse, Irving. *The Tainos: Rise and Decline of the People Who Greeted Columbus.* New Haven: Yale University Press, 1992 ("Rouse").

S: Sauer, Carl Ortwin. *The Early Spanish Main.* London: Cambridge University Press, 1966 ("Sauer").

S: Settipane, Guy A., MD, ed. *Columbus and the New World: Medical Implications.* Providence, RI: OceanSide Publications, 1995 ("Settipane").

S: Stevens-Arroyo, Antonio M. *Cave of the Jagua: The Mythological World of the Taínos.* Scranton, PA: University of Scranton Press, 2006 ("Stevens-Arroyo").

S: Sued-Badillo, Jalil. *La mujer indígena y su sociedad.* 6th ed. Río Piedras, Puerto Rico: Editorial Cultural, 2010 ("Sued-Badillo *Mujer*").

S: Sued-Badillo, Jalil. *Los Caribes: Realidad o Fabula.* Río Piedras, Puerto Rico: Editorial Antillana, 1978 ("Sued-Badillo *Caribes*").

S: Vega, Bernardo. *Los Cacicazgos de la Hispaniola.* Santo Domingo, Dominican Republic: Museo del Hombre Dominican, 1987.

S: Watson, Kelley L. *Insatiable Appetites: Imperial Encounters with Cannibals in the North Atlantic World.* New York: New York University Press, 2015 ("Watson").

S: Wilson, Samuel M., ed. *The Indigenous People of the Caribbean.* Gainesville: University Press of Florida, 1997 ("Wilson *Indigenous People*").

S: Wilson, Samuel M. *Hispaniola: Caribbean Chiefdoms in the Age of Columbus.* Tuscaloosa: University of Alabama Press, 1990 ("Wilson *Hispaniola*").

The principal historical studies of Columbus and Isabella and Ferdinand that I consulted are:

S: Ballesteros Beretta, Antonio. *Cristóbal Colón y el Descubrimiento de América.* 1st ed. Vols. 4, 5. *Historia de América y de los Pueblos Americanos.* Barcelona: Salvat Editores, 1945 ("Ballesteros").

S: Carroll, Warren H. *Isabel of Spain: The Catholic Queen.* Front Royal, VA.: Christendom Press, 1991 ("Carroll").

S: Fernández-Armesto, Felipe. *Columbus.* London: Gerald Duckworth, 1996 ("Fernández-Armesto *Columbus*").

S: Fernández-Armesto, Felipe. *Columbus and the Conquest of the Impossible.* London: Phoenix, 2000 ("Fernández-Armesto *Conquest*").

S: Fernández-Armesto, Felipe. *Ferdinand and Isabella.* New York: Dorsett, 1975 ("Fernández-Armesto *Ferdinand Isabella*").

S: Liss, Peggy K. *Isabel the Queen: Life and Times.* Rev. ed. Philadelphia: University of Pennsylvania Press, 2004 ("Liss").

S: Morison, Samuel Eliot. *Admiral of the Ocean Sea: A Life of Christopher Columbus.* Boston: Little, Brown, 1942 ("Morison *Admiral*").

S: Phillips, Jr., William D., and Carla Rahn Phillips. *The Worlds of Christopher Columbus.* Cambridge: Cambridge University Press, 1992 ("Phillips").

S: Prescott, William H. *History of the Reign of Ferdinand and Isabella.* Vols. 1, 2. New York: J. B. Millar, 1985 ("Prescott").

S: Rubin, Nancy. *Isabella of Castile: The First Renaissance Queen.* Lincoln, NE: ASJA Press, 2004 ("Rubin").

S: Rumeu de Armas, Antonio. *La Politica Indigenista de Isabel La Católica.* Valladolid, Spain: Instituto "Isabel La Católica" de Historia Eclesiastica, 1969 ("Rumeu de Armas *Indigenista*").

S: Varela, Consuelo. *La caída de Cristóbal Colón.* Madrid: Marcial Pons Historia, 2006 ("Varela *caída*").

Many other works provide insight into what occurred, some related to subsequent history, including:

S: Cervantes, Fernando. *The Devil in the New World: The Impact of Diabolism in New Spain.* New Haven: Yale University Press, 1994 ("Cervantes *Devil*").

S: Danticat, Edwidge. *Anacaona: Golden Flower*. New York: Scholastic, 2005.

S: Greenblatt, Stephen. *Marvelous Possessions: The Wonder of the New World*. Chicago: University of Chicago Press, 1991.

S: Mann, Charles C. *1493: Uncovering the New World Columbus Created*. New York: Alfred A. Knopf, 2011.

S: Reséndez, Andrés. *The Other Slavery: The Uncovered Story of Indian Enslavement in America*. Boston: Houghton Mifflin Harcourt, 2016.

S: Townsend, Camilla. *Malintzin's Choices: An Indian Woman in the Conquest of Mexico*. Albuquerque, NM: University of New Mexico Press, 2006.

Throughout the novel, Isabella and Ferdinand's whereabouts track the study done by Antonio Rumeu de Armas, and Columbus's whereabouts in Spain generally track the study done by Jesús Varela Marcos and M. Montserrat León Guerrero:

Marcos, Jesús Varela and M. Montserrat León Guerrero. *El Itinerario de Cristóbal Colón (1451–1506)*. Valladolid: Diputación de Valladolid, et al., 2003.

Rumeu de Armas, Antonio. *itinerario de los reyes católicos: 1474–1516*. Madrid: Biblioteca Reyes Católicos, 1974.

I thank the UCLA Center for Medieval and Renaissance Studies for permission to quote or paraphrase words, phrases, and sentence portions from volume 2 of the Repertorium Columbianum noted above. The volumes of the Repertorium Columbianum include English translations of Las Casas's works that provide information relating to Taíno as well as European participants in the events; accordingly, I am especially grateful to both the UCLA Center for Medieval and Renaissance Studies and Brepols Publishers n.v. for undertaking the endeavor to make and publish the English translations in the first place.

This book is a novel for which I bear full responsibility, and no person, institution, or publisher has participated in or bear any responsibility for how I have used their work herein.

CHAPTER I: AUTUMN 1493

Caonabó, Maguana, Haiti (September 1493)

P, prev. cit.: Benzoni, bk. 1. Bernáldez, chap. 120. Chanca. Coma. Cuneo. Ferdinand Columbus, chaps. 49, 50. Las Casas Repertorium, secs. 5.1, 5.2, 5.4. Libro Copiador, letters 2 (c. February 1, 1494), 3 (c. mid-April 1494). Martyr, decade 1, bk. 2. Oviedo Repertorium, secs. 3.9, 3.11.

S, prev. cit.: Arrom *Mitología*; Ballesteros; Deagan *Isabela*; Keegan *Myth*; Morison *Admiral*; Oliver; Phillips; Raccolta Letters Notes; Sauer; Wilson *Hispaniola*.

S: Gould, Alicia B. *Nueva Lista Documentada de los Tripulantes de Colón en 1492*. Madrid: Real Academia de la Historia, 1984 ("Gould").

There is no account written by the crew members left at Navidad of what transpired on Haiti after Columbus departed in January 1493. The foregoing primary sources contain almost all the limited information known. No primary or secondary source relates that the caciqual council occurred.

As discussed in *Encounters Unforeseen*'s Sources section, I have speculated that Caonabó was a Lucayan Taíno born on Middle Caicos (as opposed to a Caribe or Haitian Taíno) and that the Onaney of tradition also was born there. Caonabó's birthplace and the reason for his arrival in Maguana decades earlier are unknown. Onaney's thoughts and actions herein are fictitious.

Isabel and Fernando, Gerona, Catalonia, September 8, 1493

European:

P, prev. cit.: Bernáldez, chaps. 107, 109, 115–117. Martyr Epistolario, docs. 105, 108 (letters describing Cisneros, April 5 and May 29, 1492). Zurita *Hernando*, bk. 1, chaps. 1, 3, 4, 7–9, 14, 15, 18, 20–22, 24.

S, prev. cit.: Carroll; Fernández-Armesto *Ferdinand Isabella*; Liss; Prescott; Rubin.

S: Batlle y Prats, Luis. "El viaje de los Reyes Católicos a Gerona, ultima etapa de la recuperación de la Cerdaña y Rosellón." In Hispania, vol. 13, Oct. 1, 1943, pp. 631–645.

S: Bergenroth, G.A., ed. *Calendar of Letters, Despatches, and State Papers relating to the Negotiations between England and Spain*. Vol. 1. London: Longman Green, 1862.

S: Bridge, John S. C. *A History of France from the Death of Louis XI. Vol. 1, Reign of Charles VIII, Regency of Anne of Beaujeu, 1483–1493. Vol. 2, Reign of Charles VIII, 1493–1498*. Oxford: Clarendon Press, 1921 ("Bridge").

S: Edwards, John. *Ferdinand and Isabella: Profiles in Power*. Harlow, UK: Pearson Education, 2005 ("Edwards").

S: Hibbert, Christopher. *The Borgias and Their Enemies, 1431–1519*. Boston: First Mariber Books, 2009 ("Hibbert").

S: Hillgarth, J. N. *The Spanish Kingdoms, 1250–1516*. Vol. 2. Oxford: Clarendon Press, 1978 ("Hillgarth").

S: Mallet, Michael. *The Borgias: The rise and fall of the most infamous family in history*. London: Granada Publishing, 1969 ("Mallet").

S: Menéndez Pidal, Ramón. *Historia de España. Vol. 17, La España de los Reyes Católicos, vol. 2*. 4th ed., by Suárez Fernández, Luis and Manuel Fernández Alvarez. Madrid: Espasa-Calpe, 1990 ("Menéndez Pidal").

S: Pastor, Ludwig. *The History of the Popes: From the Close of the Middle Ages*. 2nd ed. Vols. 5, 6. Edited by Frederick Ignatius Antrobus. St. Louis: B. Herder, 1901 ("Pastor").

S: Pérez, Joseph. *Cisneros, el cardenal de España*. 3rd ed. Barcelona: Penguin Random House Grupo Editorial, 2015 ("Pérez *Cisneros*").

S: Thomas, Hugh. *Rivers of Gold: The Rise of the Spanish Empire, from Columbus to Magellan*. New York: Random House, 2003 ("Thomas *Rivers*").

S: Vicens Vives, Jaime. *Approaches to the History of Spain*. Translated and edited by Joan Connelly Ullman. Berkeley: University of California Press, 1970.

Columbian:

P, prev. cit.: Bernáldez, chap. 104. CDDD, docs. 52 (sovereigns' letter re:

Portuguese fleet, May 2, 1493), 63 (funding from Hermandad, May 23, 1493), 90 (sovereigns' instructions to Berardi to purchase Columbus's flagship, May 23, 1493), 122 (sovereigns' instructions to Berardi to provision biscuits, June 1, 1493), 133 (sovereigns' order recommending Juan Aguado, June 30, 1493), 149 (sovereigns' letter insisting Maldonado enlist, August 3, 1493), 155 (sovereigns' note to Columbus re: Soria, August 4, 1493), 156 (funding from Duke of Medina Sidonia, August 4, 1493), 157 (sovereigns' thank-you note to Berardi, August 4, 1493), 159 (sovereigns' note to Buil re: Soria, August 4, 1493), 161 (sovereigns' first reprimand to Soria, August 5, 1493), 166 (sovereigns' second reprimand to Soria, August 18, 1493), 170 (sovereigns' instructions to Fonseca, September 5, 1493). Jane, Letter to Santángel. Journal, December 16 and 26, 1492. Las Casas Repertorium, sec. 3.3 (sovereigns' objective to rule as emperors). Morison Documents, Articles of Agreement, April 17, 1492; Conditional Grant of Titles and Honor, April 30, 1492; the Sovereigns' 1493 Instructions. Nader, Santa Fe Capitulations, April 17, 1492; Granada Capitulations, April 30, 1492; Preface to 1493 Confirmation of the Granada Capitulations, May 23, 1493; Warrant to the Admiral and Juan Rodríguez de Fonseca to Outfit the Second Voyage, May 24, 1493; Appendix to 1493 Confirmation of the Capitulations, May 28, 1493; Writ giving Admiral Sole Right of Appointing his Officers, May 28, 1493; letter from Isabel to Columbus, September 5, 1493. Parry & Keith, docs. 15:2 (royal instructions to Columbus for second voyage, May 29, 1493), 15:4 (royal letter to Fonseca on respect to be shown by officials to Columbus, August 18, 1493). Symcox *Italian Texts*, Piis Fidelium (June 25, 1493). Zurita *Hernando*, bk. 1, chap. 25.

P: Barros, João de. *Da Asia*. Lisbon: Na Regia Officina Typografica, 1778 ("Barros"). Decade 1, bk. 3, chap. 11.

P: Davenport, Frances Gardiner. *European Treaties Bearing on the History of the United States and its Dependencies to 1468*. Translated by William Bollan. Washington, DC: Carnegie Institution of Washington, 1917 ("Davenport"). Romanus Pontifex (January 8, 1455), Inter Caetera (March 13, 1456), Treaty between Spain and Portugal, concluded at Alcáçovas, September 4, 1479, Aeterni Regis, June 21, 1481, Inter Caetera (May 3, 1493), Eximiae Devotionis (May 3, 1493), and Inter Caetera (May 4, 1493).

S, prev. cit.: Ballesteros; Deagan *Isabela*; Gould; Morison *Admiral*; Rumeu de Armas *Indigenista*.

S: Catz, Rebecca. *Christopher Columbus and the Portuguese, 1476–1478*. Westport, CT: Greenwood Press, 1993 ("Catz"). The appendix includes a translation of Barros, Decade 1, bk. 3, chap. 11.

S: Fernández-Armesto, Felipe. *Before Columbus: Exploration and Colonization from the Mediterranean to the Atlantic, 1229–1492.* Philadelphia: University of Pennsylvania Press, 1987 ("Fernández-Armesto *Before Columbus*").

S: Fonseca, Luís Adão da. *D. João II.* Lisbon: Círculo de Leitores e Centro de Estudios dos Poves e Culturas de Expressão Portuguesa, 2011 ("Fonseca").

S: Pagden, Anthony. *The fall of natural man: The American Indian and the origins of comparative ethnology.* Paperback ed. Cambridge: Cambridge University Press, 1986 ("Pagden").

S: Varela, Consuelo. *Colón y los florentinos.* Madrid: Alianza Editorial, 1988 ("Varela *florentinos*").

S: Vilar Sánchez, Juan Antonio. *1492–1502: Una Década Fraudulenta; Historia del Reino Cristiano de Granada desde su fundación hasta la muerte de la Reina Isabel la Católica.* Granada: Editorial Alhulia, 2004 ("Vilar Sánchez").

Canarian:

P, prev. cit.: Bernáldez, chaps. 132, 133.

S: Castellano Gil, José M., and Fransisco J. Macías Martín. *History of the Canary Islands.* Translated by M. del Pino Minguez Espino. Tenerife, Spain: Centro de la Cultura Popular Canaria, 1993 ("Gil/Martín").

S: Fernández-Armesto, Felipe. *The Canary Islands after the Conquest: The Making of a Colonial Society in the Early Sixteenth Century.* Oxford: Clarendon Press, 1982 ("Fernández-Armesto *Canary*").

S: Gambia García, Mariano. *De Colón a Alonso de Lugo. Las Capitulaciones de Descubrimiento y Conquista a Finales Del Siglo XV: America, Canarias y Africa.* XVIII Coloquio de Historia Canario-Americana, October 2006. Las Palmas de Gran Canaria, Spain: Casa de Colón ("Gambia García").

S: Morales Padrón, Francisco. *Canarias: Crónicas de su Conquista.* 3rd ed. Madrid: Cabildo de Gran Canaria, 2008. Introducción ("Padrón").

S: Rumeu de Armas, Antonio. *Alonso de Lugo en la Corte de los Reyes Catolicos 1496–1497* ("Rumeu de Armas *Lugo*").

S: Thomas, Hugh. *The Slave Trade: The Story of the Atlantic Slave Trade, 1440–1870*. New York: Simon & Schuster Paperbacks, 1997 ("Thomas *Slave Trade*").

S: Viera y Clavijo, Joseph de. *Noticias de la Historia General de las islas de Canaria*. Vol. 2. Madrid: Imprenta de Blas Romàn, 1773 ("Viera y Calvijo").

Cristóbal, Cádiz, Castile, Mid-September 1493

P, prev. cit.: Bernáldez, chaps. 118, 119. Coma. CDDD, docs. 82, 85, 158 (sovereigns' orders re: weaponry, May 23 and August 4, 1493), 84 (sovereigns' letter to royal secretary to find twenty lanzas ginetas, May 23, 1493), 90 (sovereigns' instructions to Berardi to purchase Columbus's flagship, May 23, 1493), 120 (sovereigns' order to Inquisition re: furnishing Violante Moniz), 152, 170 (sovereigns' orders re: preparation of Artieta's ships, August 4 and September 5, 1493). Davenport, Inter Caetera (May 4, 1493). Ferdinand Columbus, chap. 45. Jane, Letter to Santángel. Las Casas Repertorium, secs. 4 (Hojeda's youth), 5.2. Martyr, decade 1, bk. 1. Las Casas Repertorium—Third Voyage, chap. 162 (Columbus's advice to enlistees). Morison Documents, Columbus's 1493 Memorial, Sovereigns' 1493 Instructions. Nader, Writ ordering captains and mariners to obey the Admiral as Captain General, May 28, 1493. Oviedo Repertorium, sec. 3.9. Parry & Keith, doc. 18:1 (sovereigns' instructions for Bernal de Pisa, June 7, 1493). Pleitos doc. 13.3, testimony of Alonso de Ojeda. Symcox *Italian Texts*, Piis Fidelium (June 25, 1493).

S, prev. cit.: Ballesteros; Deagan *Isabela*; Fernández-Armesto *Columbus*, *Conquest*; Gould; Liss; Morison *Admiral*; Phillips; Raccolta Letters Notes; Sauer; Thomas *Rivers*; Varela *caída*, *florentinos*; Vilar Sánchez. Navarrete, vol. 3, ilustracion 1, biography of Hojeda.

S: Fernández-Armesto, Felipe. *Amerigo: The Man Who Gave His Name to America*. New York: Random House, 2008 ("Fernández-Armesto *Amerigo*").

S: Fierro Cubiella, Juan Antonio. *El Cádiz del Siglo XV y Cristóbal Colón*. Cádiz: Jimenez Mena Artes Gráficas, 2006 ("Fierro Cubiella").

S: Gil, Juan. *Columbiana: Estudios sobre Cristóbal Colón 1984–2006*. Santo Domingo: Academia Dominicana de la Historia, 2007 ("Gil").

S: Manzano Manzano, Juan. *Cristóbal Colón: Siete años decisivos de su vida, 1485–1492*. Madrid: Ediciones Cultura Hispánica, 1964 ("Manzano *Siete*").

S: Martínez-Hidalgo, José María. *Las naves de Colón*. Barcelona: Editorial Cadi, 1969.

S: Morison, Samuel Eliot. *The European Discovery of America: The Southern Voyages, AD 1492–1616*. Oxford: Oxford University Press, 1974 ("Morison *Southern*").

S: Parry, J.H. *The Spanish Seaborne Empire*. Berkeley: University of California Press, 1990.

S: Ramos Perez, Demetrio. *El conflict de las Lanzas Jinetas: el primer alzamiento en tierra Americana, durante el segundo viaje colombino*. Santo Domingo: Fundación Garcia-Arévalo, 1982 ("Ramos").

The ship and enrollment registers for Columbus's second voyage have been lost to history. Primary and secondary sources differ as to the ships and their specifications, the captains, and the number and identities of those sailing. In particular, while there is agreement that the fleet consisted of seventeen ships, the estimate of the number of persons aboard ranges from twelve hundred to fifteen hundred. I have relied on Bernáldez, Martyr, Morison (whose view considered the ships' capacity), and Varela in using the smaller number.

Primary or secondary sources identify the persons named as sailing on September 25, 1493, although there is no consensus that Pero Alonso Niño did, whom I have included following Gould's analysis.

Bakako and Yutowa, Cádiz (Mid-September 1493)

P, prev. cit.: Bernáldez, chap. 118. CDDD, docs. 66, 69 (sovereigns' letter requesting Dr. Chanca enlist, May 3, 1493, and acceptance, May 23, 1493), 138 (sovereigns' order re: purchase of religious articles, July 12, 1493). Chanca. Davenport, Inter Caetera (May 4, 1493). Ferdinand Columbus, chap. 62. Jane, Letter to Santángel. Journal, November 12, 1492. Las Casas Repertorium, secs. 3.3, 4. Libro Copiador, letter 2 (c. February 1, 1494). Martyr, decade 1, bk. 1. Oviedo Repertorium, secs. 3.7, 3.8. Pané, chaps. 9, 10, 26 (spirit who made all things). Symcox *Italian Texts*, Letter of Giovanni de' Strozzi (undated).

S, prev. cit.: Arrom *Pané*; Ballesteros; Cook *Disease*, *Judgments*; Ballesteros; Forbes *Native Americans*; Morison *Admiral*; Stevens-Arroyo; Thomas *Rivers*; Varela *caída*.

S: Angel Ortega, P. *La Rábida: Historia Documental Crítica*. Vol. 2. Seville:

Impr y Editorial de San Antonio, 1880 ("Ortega").

S: Puig Ortiz, José Augusto. *Por la valorización de las ruinas de La Isabela: Primera ciudad del nuevo mundo.* Santo Domingo: Editorial Nacional, 2011.

I have followed Ballesteros, Morison, and Varela in placing Pané on the fleet departing September 1493, rather than on a resupply fleet in 1494, as Strozzi states and some historians believe.

Guacanagarí, Guarico, Marien

The same primary sources listed under "Caonabó, Maguana, Haiti (September 1493)" above.

S, prev. cit.: Morison *Admiral.*

Pope Alexander VI, Dudum Siquidem (Bull of Extension), Vatican, Rome (September 25, 1493)

P, prev. cit.: Davenport, Dudum Siquidem (September 26, 1493). Zurita *Hernando*, bk. 1, chaps. 11, 22, 24.

S, prev. cit.: Hibbert; Mallet; Pastor.

CHAPTER II: SECOND CROSSING

Cristóbal, Cádiz to San Sebastian, Gomera (Canary Islands), September 25–October 13, 1493

P, prev. cit.: Bernáldez, chap. 119. Coma. Chanca. Ferdinand Columbus, chaps. 45, 46. Las Casas Repertorium, secs. 3.3, 5.1. Libro Copiador, letter 2 (c. February 1, 1494). Jane, Letter to Santángel, Torres Memorandum. Martyr, decade 1, bks. 1, 2. Oviedo Repertorium, sec. 3.9.

S, prev. cit.: Arrom *Pané*; Ballesteros; Boucher; Cook *Disease*; Crosby *Ecological*, *Exchange*; Fernández-Armesto *Amerigo*, *Columbus*, *Conquest*; Fierro Cubiella; Forbes *Native Americans*; Gil; Gould; Morison *Admiral*; Phillips; Rouse; Rumeu de Armas *Indigenista*; Settipane; Thomas *Rivers*.

S: Taviani, Paolo Emilio. *The Voyages of Columbus: The Great Discovery.* Translated by Marc A. Beckwith and Luciano F. Farina. Novara: Istituto Geografica de Agostini, 1991 ("Taviani").

In the absence of records, I have speculated persons sailing on the *María Galante* by deduction based on (1) their presence at subsequent events on the ship or its launch, e.g., Libro Copiador, letter 2, indicates Buil had a cabin on the ship, and Cuneo describes Cuneo riding in the launch, which Martyr and Libro Copiador indicate Columbus dispatched ashore; (2) Columbus's likely desire for their services or friendship on the flagship, e.g., the Taínos so identified, Dr. Chanca, and Diego Columbus; and/or (3) their participation in the same events ashore in which Columbus participated.

As Gil explains, there is no evidence that the third personal servant who accompanied Columbus on the first voyage—the Guinean Juan Portugués—sailed on the second, and I have speculated he remained in Spain.

Chanca, Morison, and others relate that Columbus discussed the Caribe islands east of Española with the captives for the purpose of determining the route to the closest landfall across the ocean, as reflected in the text. Some historians and anthropologists believe Columbus planned the voyage's southeastern route for the additional purpose of enslaving, or confirming the feasibility of enslaving, Caribes. I do not read the primary sources as so convincing but speculate that, when the fleet departed, Columbus was uncertain that Española's gold would match his promises (many historians see this uncertainty arising later in 1494, some earlier) and hopeful the shortest ocean crossing would also discover a potential source of slaves to compensate gold's absence. Columbus's writings unambiguously evidence a desire to enslave at least some category of Indians—be it idolaters, Caribes, or resisters—commencing from the first moments he arrived in the Caribbean in 1492 (Journal 10/14/92, 12/16/92, 12/26/92; Jane, Letter to Santángel), and his first writing back to the sovereigns on the second voyage (Libro Copiador, letter 2) focuses at least as much on the cannibal islands offering an infinite number of captives as their closeness to the Canaries. I know of no primary source indicating that Columbus told the sovereigns in advance of the voyage that he had decided to take a more southeasterly route, for either purpose.

Caonabó and Guacanagarí, Marien (Late October 1493)

The same primary sources listed under chap. I, "Caonabó, Maguana, Haiti (September 1493)" above.

S, prev. cit.: Ballesteros; Gould; Keegan *Myth*; Deagan *Navidad*; Morison *Admiral*; Oliver; Sued-Badillo *Caribes*.

The primary sources disagree which Taíno chieftain was responsible for executing the three separate bands of Europeans constituting the Navidad garrison, and historians and anthropologists often avoid attributing responsibility. Most primary sources expressly discussing an independent fate for the Gutiérrez-Escobedo band visiting Maguana do attribute that band's execution to Caonabó, as depicted in chap. I, "Caonabó, Maguana, Haiti (September 1493)." Ferdinand Columbus attributes the executions of almost all men to Caonabó (chaps. 50, 61), Benzoni attributes the executions to Guacanagarí (bk. 1), and Columbus later appears to doubt that all deaths should be attributed to Caonabó (Libro Copiador, letter 3).

Doubting Guacanagarí torched his own village, I have attributed the Arana band's death to Caonabó in this story, as viewed by Bernáldez, Chanca, Columbus, Ferdinand Columbus, Las Casas, and Morison. For discussion of sources doubting Caonabó's involvement, see chap. III, "Guarico and Navidad, November 26–December 2, 1493" below. Morison atributes the Chachu band's death to local caciques; I have followed that viewpoint in chap. I, "Guacanagarí, Guarico, Marien," but portray Guacanagarí as knowingly acquiescing in these executions because they occurred in his territory and to his knowledge.

Secondary sources typically agree that Caonabó stole one of Guacanagarí's wives (as reported in Ferdinand Columbus, chap. 61) but question or disagree whether the motivation was related to the European presence or an unrelated grudge, as well as when the abduction occurred. I speculate as portrayed in the story in part because of Columbus's assertion in Libro Copiador, letter 2, that Guacanagarí begged him to help destroy Caonabó and capture his wives.

Hierro (Canary Islands) to Caloucaera (Guadalupe, Caribbean Islands), October 13–November 9, 1493

P, prev. cit.: Bernáldez, chap. 119. Chanca. Coma (judgment Caribes be reduced to bondage). Cuneo. Ferdinand Columbus, chaps. 46, 47. Journal, 11/27/1492. Las Casas Repertorium, sec. 5.1. Libro Copiador, letter 2 (c. February 1, 1494). Jane, Letter to Santángel. Martyr, decade 1, bk. 2. Martyr Epistolario, letters to Cardinal Ascanio Sforza and Count of Tendilla/Archbishop of Granada, September 13, 1493, letter to Archbishop of Braga, October 1, 1493, letter to Cardinal Ascanio Sforza, November 1, 1493. Oviedo Repertorium, sec. 3.9.

P: Acosta, Joseph de. *The Natural and Moral History of the Indies.* Vol. 1. *The Natural History.* Edited by Clements R. Markham. 1880. Reprint, Cambridge: Cambridge University Press, 2009 ("Acosta"). Bk. 1, chaps. 2, 3.

S, prev. cit.: Boucher; Granberry *Languages*; Hulme; Keegan *Caribbean, Myth*; Lamarche; Morison *Admiral*; Oliver; Reid; Restall; Rouse;

Sued-Badillo *Caribes*; Watson; Wilson *Indigenous People*.

S: Gibson, Carrie. *Empire's Crossroads: A History of the Caribbean from Columbus to the Present Day*. New York: Atlantic Monthly Press, 2014 ("Gibson").

S: Hulme, Peter. "Making Sense of the Native Caribbean." *New West Indian Guide*. Vol. 67, no. 3 & 4 (1993) pp. 189–220.

Throughout the text, I have relied on Granberry and Vescelius's analysis of the languages of Española, the Bahamas, Cuba, Jamaica, and Puerto Rico in depicting the ability of the Guanahanían captives—Bakako and Yutowa—to communicate with other Caribbean peoples. As Lucayans (Bahamians), they likely spoke a Taíno language dialect similar to those in eastern Cuba and could converse with those speaking Taíno dialects in those places and in most of Española, Puerto Rico, and islands east until Guadalupe. Macorís was the language spoken on Española's central and eastern northern coast south to the Yaque River and on the Samaná Peninsula, including by Columbus's Samanán captives and the Ciguayan chieftain Mayobanex. But the Samanán captives and others speaking Macorís would also have been conversant to varying degrees in the Taíno language, which served as lingua franca throughout the Taíno Caribbean.

Some believe it was the indigenous ashore in Guadalupe who said "Taíno," others Spanish sailors in the launch, but I believe it was Bakako in the launch, consistent with the interpretation/translation of Chanca in Jane.

Anthropologists and historians still debate whether and the extent the Kalinago (Caribe) practiced cannibalism, including prominent experts who deny that they did, as well as a former chieftain I spoke to in the Kalinago Territory on Dominica. I have found Lamarche most persuasive, although the text incorporates other views, as well.

Commencing with encounters in Guadalupe and St. Croix, the European primary sources continue to identify Caribbean inhabitants as "Indians," the term Columbus coined on the first voyage, but "Indians" now excludes "Caribes."

Hostilities and Violations, Ayay (Saint Croix) and Boriquén (Puerto Rico), November 10–19, 1493

P, prev. cit.: Bernáldez, chap. 119. Chanca. Coma. Cuneo. Ferdinand Columbus, chap. 48. Italian Reports Repertorium, letter of Simone dal Verde (March 20–May 10, 1494). Las Casas Repertorium, sec. 5.1. Libro Copiador, letter 2 (c. February 1, 1494). Martyr, decade 1, bk. 2. Oviedo Repertorium, sec. 3.9. Symcox *Italian Texts*, letter of Giovanni de' Bardi (April 19, 1494).

S, prev. cit.: Ballesteros; Forbes *Native Americans*; Morison *Admiral*; Lamarche; Rouse; Sauer; Taviani; Wilson *Indigenous People*.

S: Paiewonsky, Michael. *Conquest of Eden: 1493–1515*. St. Thomas: MAPes MONDe, 1990.

S: Paquette, Robert L. and Stanley L. Engerman, eds. *The Lesser Antilles in the Age of Exploration*. Gainesville, FL: University Press of Florida, 1996.

Rouse concludes that the archaeological evidence indicates that the St. Croix inhabitants seized likely were Taínos practicing bride capture, not Caribes as the European primary sources assert. I have followed Chanca and Lamarche instead, as well as the US National Park Service's analysis presented at the Salt River Bay National Park, St. Croix, that the site was a significant Taíno village seized by Caribes in the early fifteenth century, and the story depicts those who fled or fought as Caribe and the women and dismembered boys as Taíno slaves. See also, Arnold R. Highfield. *The Cultural History of the American Virgin Islands and the Danish West Indies: A Companion Guide*, St. Croix: Antilles Press, 2018.

The primary sources differ why Columbus stopped at St. Croix; how the St. Croix skirmish enfolded; the total number of inhabitants taken aboard in Guadalupe and St. Croix; the number that escaped; and the non-Caribe versus Caribe proportions. I have followed the primary sources that indicate one of Columbus's purposes was to capture inhabitants to determine his position and route to Española, and I've speculated in the text that he never intended to release any taken aboard. I estimate about twenty-five inhabitants remained on board when the fleet departed Puerto Rico for Española, and I believe Columbus understood the predominance of inhabitants aboard were captives of Caribes (i.e., "Indians," or "Taínos"), not Caribes.

While most historians writing before the Libro Copiador's discovery believe Columbus sailed along Puerto Rico's southern coast, letter 2 and Taviani indicate it was the northern coast.

Guarionex, Magua

P, prev. cit.: Ferdinand Columbus, chap. 62, and Pané, chap. 25 (the prophecy).

No primary or secondary source relates the afternoon depicted.

CHAPTER III: BETRAYAL

Samaná and Monte Christi, November 22–26, 1493

P, prev. cit.: Bernáldez, chap. 120. Chanca. Cuneo. Ferdinand Columbus, chap. 49. Las Casas Repertorium, sec. 5.1 (Columbus's instruction to Samanán). Libro Copiador, letter 2 (c. February 1, 1494). Martyr, decade 1, bk. 2. Oviedo Repertorium, sec. 3.9.

S, prev. cit.: Morison *Admiral.*

I speculate Mayobanex previously met Columbus on January 14, 1493, as explained in the Sources to *Encounters Unforeseen.*

Guarico and Navidad, November 26–December 3, 1493

P, prev. cit.: Benzoni, bk. 1. Bernáldez, chap. 120. Chanca. Coma. Cuneo. Ferdinand Columbus, chaps. 49, 50. Italian Reports Repertorium, letter of Simone dal Verde (March 20–May 10, 1494). Las Casas Repertorium, sec. 5.2 (Columbus's opposition to punishing Guacanagarí). Libro Copiador, letter 2 (c. February 1, 1494). Martyr, decade 1, bk. 2. Oviedo Repertorium, secs. 3.9, 3.11.

S, prev. cit.: Ballesteros; Gould; Deagan *Navidad*; Fernández-Armesto *Conquest*; Morison *Admiral*; Oliver; Phillips; Sauer; Wilson *Hispaniola.*

Some historians and anthropologists argue that Guacanagarí participated in Caonabó's massacre of the Arana band in Navidad, finding that most consistent with Guacanagarí's fabrication of the wound and instigation of the women captives' flight, and some primary sources attributing that attack to Caonabó do acknowledge that possibility. Nevertheless, I have followed Morison and the primary sources noted under chap. II, "Caonabó and Guacanagarí, Marien (Late October 1493)" above to the contrary.

The primary sources do not recount the terms of the political relationship Columbus and Guacanagarí established in their discussions, and I have speculated as written largely based on their conversations at year-end 1492 (see the Sources to *Encounters Unforeseen*) and Guacanagarí's actions subsequent to December 1493.

CHAPTER IV: SETTLEMENT AT ISABELA, CONQUEST PROCLAIMED

Voyage East and Establishment of Isabela, December 4, 1493–January 6, 1494

P, prev. cit.: Bernáldez, chap. 120. CDDD, doc. 138 (sovereign order re: sacraments, July 12, 1493). Chanca. Coma. Cuneo. Ferdinand Columbus, chap. 51. Journal, January 10, 1493. Las Casas Repertorium, sec. 5.2. Libro Copiador, letter 2 (c. February 1, 1494). Martyr, decade 1, bks. 2, 3. Oviedo Repertorium, secs. 3.9, 3.11.

S, prev. cit.: Cook *Disease*; Deagan *Isabela*; Morison *Admiral*; Phillips; Raccolta Letters Notes; Sauer; Settipane; Wilson *Hispaniola*.

Ferdinand Columbus reported that his father was too busy and ill to record his journal from December 11, 1493, until March 12, 1494 (chap. 51), which some historians find suspicious, since this period included mostly events that wouldn't have pleased the sovereigns. The primary sources provide scant information regarding the eastward passage from December 3, 1493, through January 2, 1492, and my depiction is based largely on Columbus's brief account in the Libro Copiador and Morison's navigational analysis, which predates the Libro Copiador's discovery.

Macorís was spoken west and south of Isabela. While some experts believe Macorís was spoken at Isabela, archeological examinations of two indigenous villages close to Isabela reveal Taíno rather than Macorix culture, and I have speculated that Taíno was the indigenous language spoken about Isabela.

Niana is fictitious.

Cristóbal, His Officers, and Slaves, January 7–March 11, 1494

P, prev. cit.: Bernáldez, chap. 120. Chanca. Coma. Cuneo. Ferdinand Columbus, chap. 51. Jane, Torres Memorandum. Las Casas Repertorium, sec. 5.2. Libro Copiador, letters 2 (c. February 1, 1494), 3 (April 1494). Martyr, decade 1, bks. 2, 3. Oviedo Repertorium, secs. 3.11, 3.12, 3.13. Symcox *Italian Texts*, Letters of Giambattista Strozzi March 19, 1494), Giovanni de' Bardi (April 19, 1494).

S, prev. cit.: Ballesteros; Cook *Disease*, *Judgments*; Deagan *Isabela*; Gil; Fernández-Armesto *Conquest*; Lamarche; Morison *Admiral*; Nader; Sauer; Settipane; Thomas *Rivers*; Varela *caída*; Wilson *Hispaniola*.

Columbus and his officers typically used interpreters for important or first-time encounters with Taíno caciques during the period of this novel, but the primary sources do not identify the interpreters other than, infrequently, "Diego" (Bakako). Both Bakako and Yutowa's presence were requested by Guacanagarí when he met Columbus in November 1493, but Yutowa's specific identification in events that involve an interpreter after January 6, 1494 is speculative, in part because other interpreters were being trained and became available for use. I have speculated that it was Yutowa who accompanied the Hojeda expedition depicted, as well as events over the following year involving Hojeda and Margarite, because the guides local to the Bajabonico then had no or lesser Spanish language skills and Columbus preferred Bakako at his side.

Historians agree Columbus's punishments included execution, although there is little consensus who was executed or when. I have followed Varela's analysis of primary sources that Gaspar de Salinas was executed for assisting Pisa in writing the charges and surmised that the execution(s) Buil reported to the sovereigns later in 1494 included Salinas's.

There is no record of the absolute numbers of European voyagers who either died before Torres returned to Spain or departed with him, but Martyr reports nine hundred men then remained on Española, indicating the combined total of men then dead or departing was roughly three hundred. Some historians assert that Torres transported hundreds of voyagers returning simply because they were ill or discontent, but the three hundred must have included sailors competent to man twelve ships, and I have speculated that the number of passengers discontent or ill was not great.

Experts debate the extent to which venereal diseases known to Europeans in 1492 included Caribbean syphilis strains.

I am not aware of any primary or secondary source asserting that Isabela's fire was set by Taínos, whether ordered by Caonabó or another. I speculate it was: Columbus contemporaneously expressed fear of just such an attack in the Torres Memorandum; while he didn't attribute the fire to an attack in subsequent writings, he would have shied from admitting Indian hostility arising so soon; and indigenous Caribbean peoples used fire as a weapon, such as the attack on Guacanagarí's village previously depicted.

Conquest Proclaimed, Fort Santo Tomás, March 12–29, 1494

P, prev. cit.: Bernáldez, chaps. 121, 122. Cuneo. Ferdinand Columbus, chaps. 51, 52, 53. Las Casas Repertorium, sec. 5.2 (Columbus's resolve to instill fear). Libro Copiador, letters 3 (April 1494), 4 (February 26, 1495), 5 (October 15, 1495). Martyr, decade 1, bk. 3. Oviedo Repertorium, sec. 3.12.

S, prev. cit.: Ballesteros; Deagan *Isabela*; Keegan *Myth*; Morison *Admiral*; Sauer; Varela *caída*; Wilson *Hispaniola*.

Primary sources do not report Caonabó besieging or attacking Fort Santo Tomás at this time, and I have speculated Caonabó's rationale.

Isabel and Fernando's First Impressions, February–April 1494

P, prev. cit.: Bernáldez, chap. 120. CDDD, docs. 185 (sovereigns' letter to

Torres, March 19, 1494, 191 (sovereigns' order to Fonseca, April 30, 1494). Ferdinand Columbus, chap. 61. Jane, Torres Memorandum. Las Casas Repertorium, sec. 5.4. Libro Copiador, letters 2 (c. February 1, 1494), 3 (April 1494). Martyr, decade 1, bk. 1. Martyr Epistolario, letter of October 20, 1494, to Juan Borromeo. Nader, letter from Fernando and Isabel to Admiral (April 13, 1494). Symcox *Italian Texts*, letters of Giambattista Strozzi (March 19, 1494), Giovanni de' Bardi (April 19, 1494), Morelletto Ponzone (June 11, 1494). Zurita *Hernando*, bk. 1, chaps. 24, 27, 28.

S, prev. cit.: Ballesteros; Bridge; Carroll; Cook *Disease*, *Judgments*; Fernández-Armesto *Amerigo*, *Conquest*, *Ferdinand Isabella*; Gil; Gould; Mallet; Morison *Admiral*; Pastor; Rubin; Sauer; Stevens-Arroyo; Thomas *Rivers*, *Slave Trade*; Varela *caída*, *florentinos*; Wilson *Hispaniola*.

Many historians believe Fonseca simply sold the twenty-six captives as slaves, but, following Thomas *Slave Trade*, I speculate they were given to Berardi, as depicted, and traveled from Seville to Medina del Campo and back, my deduction from primary sources. I suspect they died of European diseases while training for enslavement as interpreters. I have deduced the chronological order of sovereign audiences—Bartolomé, Torres, Berardi—from primary and secondary sources, which neither express that order, describe Berardi as the one parading the captives before the sovereigns, or their transport back to Vespucci. Vespucci was a Berardi associate in Seville at the time.

There is no record that Cisneros communicated the thoughts indicated to Isabella—merely one of her guilty conscience.

Punishments, March 29–Mid-April 1494

P, prev. cit.: Benzoni, bk. 1. Bernáldez, chap. 122. Ferdinand Columbus, chaps. 53, 54. Jane, Torres Memorandum. Las Casas Repertorium, sec. 5.2. Libro Copiador, letter 3 (April 1494) (Columbus's punishment warnings). Martyr, decade 1, bk. 3. Oviedo Repertorium, secs. 3.11, 3.12, 3.15. Parry & Keith, Margarite Instructions (reflected in Columbus's instructions to Hojeda).

S, prev. cit.: Ballesteros; Cook *Disease*; Deagan *Isabela*; Fernández-Armesto *Conquest*; Keegan *Myth*; Morison *Admiral*; Raccolta Letters Notes; Sauer; Settipane; Varela *caída*; Wilson *Hispaniola*.

The reductions of Isabela's population to roughly 300 is calculated by the following numbers presented in the text: 1,200 voyagers initially, declining to 900 upon Torres departure, less 60 men posted initially to Santo Tomás, less 470 sent to the interior subsequently, less 60 for the Cuba exploration.

CHAPTER V: EXPLORATIONS, PILLAGES, AND ALLIANCES

Terra Firma, Cuba, and Yamaye (Jamaica), Mid-April–July 7, 1494

P, prev. cit.: Bernáldez, chaps. 123–130. Cuneo. Ferdinand Columbus, chaps. 54–58. Gil Varela Cartas, Informe y Juramento de como Cuba Era Tierra Firme (June 12, 1494). Las Casas Repertorium, sec. 5.3. Libro Copiador, letters 3 (April 1494), 4 (February 26, 1495). Martyr, decade 1, bk. 3 (conversation on July 7, 1494). Martyr Epistolario, letter to Juan Borromeo, October 20, 1494. Oviedo Repertorium, sec. 3.11. Pleitos 5.8, testimony of Miguel de Toro.

S, prev. cit.: Ballesteros; Deagan *Isabela*; Fernández-Armesto *Conquest*; Gould; Keegan *Myth*; Morison *Admiral*; Raccolta Letters Notes; Rouse; Sauer; Thomas *Rivers*.

While the primary sources are silent, I have speculated that the elderly man who spoke with Columbus on July 7, 1494, was a behique. None of the primary sources relating the conversation attribute anti-European remarks to Bakako or any remarks to the cacique.

Rape of the Vega Real, Mid-April–August 1494

P, prev. cit.: Benzoni, bk. 1. Ferdinand Columbus, chap. 61. Las Casas Apologetica, chap. 120 (transl. in Pané, app. C). Las Casas Repertorium, sec. 5.4. Las Casas Short Account, chap. "Hispaniola." Libro Copiador, letters 4 (February 26, 1495), 5 (October 15, 1495). Martyr, decade 1, bk. 4. Oviedo Repertorium, secs. 3.12, 3.13, 3.16, 3.18.

S, prev. cit.: Cervantes *Devil*; Cook *Disease*, *Judgments*; Crosby *Ecological*, *Exchange*; Deagan *Isabela*; Fernández-Armesto *Conquest*; Keegan *Myth*; Montas *Arte*; Morison *Admiral*; Oliver; Oliver *Pané;* Ortega; Raccolta Letters Notes; Sauer; Settipane; Stevens Arroyo; Rouse; Thomas *Rivers*; Varela *caída*; Wilson *Hispaniola*.

Oviedo admired Margarite, and some historians assert Margarite wanted a policy more kind to the Indians than did Columbus. I have followed Las Casas and others to the contrary.

Benzoni recounts that missionaries routinely destroyed cemís, and many historians and anthropologists conclude that Española's settlers systematically destroyed Taíno cemís and suppressed worship rites. Las Casas asserts that the devil spoke through cemís and that Española's Indians desperately hid them from Spaniards, Oviedo that Indians angered because Spaniards disapproved of their rites, Bernáldez (chap. 120) that Spaniards tried to take cemís from Indians as appropriate to burn, and Martyr (decade 1, bk. 9) that all cemís were taken to Spain to teach the foolishness of the images and deceits of the devil. I have speculated the burning of cemís commenced during the period presented.

Lugo and Benitomo, Tenerife (Canary Islands), May 1494

P, prev. cit.: Bernáldez, chap. 133.

S, prev. cit.: Fernández-Armesto *Canary*; Gambia García; Gil/Martín; Padrón; Viera y Calvijo.

S: Rumeu de Armas, Antonio. *La Conquista de Tenerife: 1494–1496*. Madrid: Aula de Cultura de Tenerife, 1975 ("Rumeu de Armas *Tenerife*").

Treaty at Tordesillas and Isabel's Gentle Instructions, May–August 1494

P, prev. cit.: Barros, Decade 1, bk. 3, chap. 11. CDDD, docs. 213 (sovereigns' letter to Fonseca regarding Berardi, July 15, 1494), 215 (sovereigns' letter re: cosmographers, July 30, 1494), 224, 225 (sovereigns' orders to obey Admiral, August 16, 1494). Davenport, Inter Caetera (May 4, 1493), Dudum Siquidem (September 26, 1493), Treaty between Spain and Portugal concluded at Tordesillas (June 7, 1494). Nader, docs. 11 (sovereigns' order to obey Admiral, August 16, 1494), 15 (sovereigns' letter to Admiral, August 16, 1494). Las Casas Repertorium, sec. 5.2. Zurita *Hernando*, bk. 1, chap. 29.

S, prev. cit.: Catz; Fernández-Armesto *Ferdinand Isabella*, *Conquest*; Fonseca; Morison *Admiral*; Ortega; Parry & Keith; Prescott; Raccolta Letters Notes; Rubin; Thomas *Rivers*; Varela *florentinos*.

S: Azcona, Tarsicio de. *Juana de Castilla, Mal Llamada La Beltraneja: Vida de la hija de Enrique IV de Castilla y su exilio en Portugal (1462–1530)*. Madrid: La Esfera de los Libros, 2007.

S: Rumeu de Armas, Antonio. *El Tratado de Tordesillas*. Madrid: Editorial MAPFRE, 1992 ("Rumeu de Armas *Tordesillas*").

S: Sanceau, Elaine. *The Perfect Prince; A Biography of the King Dom João II*. Porto: Livraria Civilização–Editora, 1959.

Return to Haiti, Desertions, Delirium, July 8–September 28, 1494

P, prev. cit.: Bernáldez, chap. 131. Cuneo. Ferdinand Columbus, chap. 60. Las Casas Repertorium, sec. 5.3. Las Casas Short Account, chap. "Hispaniola." Libro Copiador, letter 4 (February 26, 1495). Martyr, decade 1, bks. 3, 4.

S, prev. cit.: Deagan *Isabela*; Morison *Admiral*; Ortega; Raccolta Letters Notes; Ramos; Rouse; Sauer; Thomas *Rivers*; Varela *caída*; Wilson *Hispaniola*.

In my view, primary sources do not support complete understanding of Margarite and Fray Buil's motivations for deserting their posts, and I have speculated motivations that for me are most likely and, following Las Casas and Martyr, are selfish rather than policy driven. No primary source records a conversation between Bartolomé and these two men, and the day they seized the ships prior to September 29, 1494, is unknown.

Caonabó's Council and the Alliance against Pale Men, Maguana, (Autumn 1494)

P, prev. cit.: Ferdinand Columbus, chap. 61. Las Casas Repertorium, sec. 5.4. Libro Copiador, letter 5 (October 15, 1495). Martyr, decade 1, bk. 4. Oviedo Repertorium, sec. 3.12.

S, prev. cit.: Deagan *Isabela*; Keegan *Myth*; Raccolta Letters Notes; Rouse; Sauer; Wilson *Hispaniola*.

S: Irving, Washington. *The Life and Voyages of Christopher Columbus*. Hertfordshire, UK: Wordsworth Editions, 2008 ("Irving").

Primary sources report the caciqual alliance established, describe Caonabó as the most militant of the supreme Taíno caciques, and relate that Caonabó was the cacique other caciques urged to expel Columbus's invasion. I have speculated the caciqual council and that Caonabó hosted it.

Some historians and anthropologists doubt Caonabó took a leading role in opposing Columbus's invasion from April 1494 to March 1495, believing Columbus and chroniclers had an exaggerated perception of Caonabó's importance and that Caonabó posed no menace. Others believe that Caonabó did substantially more than lead the alliance's establishment, including—as reported by Ferdinand Columbus—physically reconnoitering

Isabela to plan an attack. I believe Columbus had ample indigenous sources of information to make a sound judgment of the resistance he faced, and Libro Copiador letter 5 shows he sought to capture Caonabó ultimately because of Caonabó's centrality to indigenous resistance, not merely in vengeance for Navidad.

Primary sources indicate Caonabó had several brothers but do not indicate their Taíno birth names. As the Raccolta Letters Notes and some others, I believe the cacique Manicoatex was one of the brothers, about ten years Caonabó's junior, since primary source reports of Manicoatex's activities closely match those reported for Caonabó's brothers. Some historians understand Manicoatex as unrelated to Caonabó and/or vassal to Guarionex.

Alexander and Fernando, September 1494

P, prev. cit.: Zurita *Hernando*, bk. 1, chaps. 27, 28, 31–37.

S, prev. cit.: Ballesteros; Bridge; Carroll; Fernández-Armesto *Ferdinand Isabella*; Hillgarth; Menéndez Pidal; Pastor; Vilar Sánchez.

S: Cook, M. A., ed. *A History of the Ottoman Empire to 1730*. Cambridge: Cambridge University Press, 1976.

CHAPTER VI: RESISTANCE AND SLAVERY

Reunions at Isabela, September 29–December 1494

P, prev. cit.: Bernáldez, chap. 131. CDDD, docs. 204 (list of goods to be supplied settlement, July 1, 1494), 209 (list of goods to be supplied Admiral's household, July 4, 1494), 221 (list of items to be supplied Fray Buil, August 1494). Cuneo. Ferdinand Columbus, chaps. 61, 62. Jane, Torres Memorandum. Las Casas Apologetica, chap. 120 (transl. in Pané, app. C). Las Casas Repertorium, sec. 5.4. Las Casas Short Account, chap. "Hispaniola." Libro Copiador, letters 4 (February 26, 1495), 5 (October 15, 1495). Pané, introduction, chap. 25 (Columbus's instruction to Pané). Martyr, decade 1, bk. 4. Nader, doc. 15 (sovereigns' letter to Admiral, August 16, 1494).

S, prev. cit.: Deagan *Isabela*; Fernández-Armesto *Conquest*; Keegan *Myth*; Morison *Admiral*; Oliver; Ortega; Raccolta Letters Notes; Ramos; Rouse; Sauer; Varela *caída*; Varela Gil *Pané*; Wilson *Hispaniola*.

I have followed Varela's analysis of primary sources regarding the punishments of Isabela's settlers, although the timing of the executions is uncertain.

Some historians relate that Bartolomé's designation as Adelantado occurred when Columbus departed for Spain in March 1496, but I believe primary sources, including Cuneo, establish it occurred earlier. Bartolomé's voyage north to find Cathay (reported by Cuneo) never occurred.

Wasu and Ukuti are fictional names of historic persons whose first named identification in the historic record is in 1496, when Columbus takes them to Spain (see chap. X, "Cristóbal, Cádiz to Burgos, Castile, Early June–September 1496"). I speculate—without sources—that these two youths were from villages along the Bajabonico near Isabela.

Isabel and Fernando's Court, Madrid, November 1494–January 1495

P, prev. cit.: Bernáldez, chap. 131. CDDD, doc. 244 (sovereigns' letter calling Fray Buil to court, December 3, 1494). Ferdinand Columbus, chap. 61. Jane, Torres Memorandum. Las Casas Repertorium, sec. 5.4 (Margarite's report to sovereigns). Martyr, decade 1, bk. 4. Oviedo Repertorium, secs. 3.12, 3.13 (syphilis in Naples). Parry & Keith, Aguado Instructions. Zurita *Hernando*, bk. 1, chaps. 36–38, 40–42.

P: Burchard, Johann. Edited and translated by Geoffrey Parker. *At the Court of the Borgia, being an Account of the Reign of Pope Alexander VI written by his Master of Ceremonies*. The Folio Society Edition. London: The Bath Press, 2004. Chap. 6.

S, prev. cit.: Ballesteros; Bridge; Carroll; Fernández-Armesto *Conquest*, *Ferdinand Isabella*; Mallet; Menéndez Pidal; Morison *Admiral*; Ortega; Pastor; Rouse; Rubin; Thomas *Rivers*.

S: Vicens Vives, Jaime. *Historia Critica de la Vida y Reinado de Fernando II de Aragón*. Zaragoza, Spain: Institución "Fernando el Católico," 2007.

Historians debate when Isabella and Ferdinand first understood their men's mistreatment of Indians. While some historians believe that the sovereigns understood it by the end of 1494, and some believe Margarite and/or Fray Buil imparted the information critically, I believe otherwise on both accounts, finding little in the primary sources or Margarite's or Buil's conduct to support the view that either cared about the Indians' treatment. The sovereigns' orders to the investigator they dispatched to the Indies resulting from their conversations with Margarite and Buil (the Aguado Instructions) lacked instructions regarding mistreatment of Indians. See chap. VIII, "Cristóbal and Aguado, October–November 1495" below.

No primary source relates the substance of the conversation depicted between Isabella and Buil.

Fray Pané and Guatícabanu, Fort Magdalena, December 1494–January 1495

P, prev. cit.: Ferdinand Columbus, chaps. 61, 62. Las Casas Apologetica, chap. 120 (transl. in Pané, app. C). Las Casas Repertorium, sec. 5.4. Martyr, decade 1, bk.9. Pané, chaps. 1–4, 9, 10, 25, 25 bis.

S, prev. cit.: Deagan *Isabela*; Keegan *Myth*; Oliver; Oliver *Pané*; Rouse; Sauer; Stevens-Arroyo; Varela *caída*; Wilson *Hispaniola*.

S: Aymar i Ragolta, Jaume. *Fra Ramon Pané l'Univers Simbòlic Taí.* Barcelona: Facultat de Teologia de Catalunya, 2009.

S: Deloria, Jr., Vine. *God Is Red: A Native View of Religion.* 30th anniv. ed. Golden, CO: Fulcrum, 2003 ("Deloria").

S: Dussel, Enrique. Translated and revised by Alan Neely. *History of the Church in Latin America: Colonialism to Liberation (1492–1979).* Grand Rapids, MI: William S. Eerdman, 1981 ("Dussel").

Pané's account does not indicate Guatícabanu's age or relationship to Guanáoboconel, but I have surmised that he was a son with four brothers and younger than Pané.

Hostilities and Slaves, Forts Magdalena and Santo Tomás, January–February 1495

P, prev. cit.: Ferdinand Columbus, chap. 61. Cuneo. Las Casas Repertorium, sec. 5.4. Martyr, decade 1, bk. 4. Oviedo Repertorium, 3.15. Pané, chaps. 25, 25 bis.

S, prev. cit.: Cook *Judgments*; Crosby *Exchange*; Deagan *Isabela*; Fernández-Armesto *Conquest*; Keegan *Myth*; Morison *Admiral*; Oliver; Raccolta Letters Notes; Raudzens; Rouse; Sauer; Varela *caída*, *florentino*; Wilson *Hispaniola*.

The foregoing primary and secondary sources differ on the dates, sequence, and relationship of and participants in: Guatiguaná's attacks on the bohío serving as a hospital; the construction and siege of Fort Magdalena; the siege of Fort Santo Tomás; and Columbus's slave raids. Las Casas and

Ferdinand Columbus do not discuss either siege; Martyr and Oviedo discuss Caonabó's siege of Hojeda at Santo Tomás; Pané discusses only "Caonabó's subjects'" siege of Fort Magdalena, which he witnessed; and various secondary sources interpret that Guatiguaná besieged Fort Magdalena soon after its construction. I've speculated Caonabó's approval of and involvement in both sieges, believing that best reconciles Pané's perception and the other primary sources.

Primary sources do not indicate that Caonabó wished for Anacaona to succeed him in Maguana, and his brother Manicoatex would have been a traditional choice; in the absence of evidence, however, I have speculated Caonabó chose Anacaona before his capture and subsequent events described herein because of her greater stature with his subjects and all Haiti's peoples and the alliance with her brother Behecchio, the island's most powerful ruler.

Cuneo reports that a cacique was captured and chewed his ropes to escape, and I've speculated that it was Guatiguaná, although not all secondary sources concur.

Isabel and Fernando's Court, Madrid, January–March 1495

P, prev. cit.: Bernáldez, chap. 133. CDDD, docs. 254 (sovereigns' letter to Fonseca of February 17, 495 re: resupply fleet), 262 (sovereigns' letter to Fonseca of April 9, 1495 re: Carillo/Aguado mission). Oviedo Repertorium, sec. 3.13. Parry & Keith, Berardi Memorial. Zurita *Hernando*, bk. 1, chap. 43; bk. 2, chaps. 1-4.

S, prev. cit.: Ballesteros; Bridge; Carroll; Crosby *Exchange*; Fernández-Armesto *Amerigo*, *Canary*, *Columbus*, *Ferdinand Isabella*; Gambia García; Gil/Martín; Liss; Mallet; Morison, *Admiral*; Padrón; Pastor; Pérez *Cisneros*; Phillips; Rumeu de Armas *Tenerife*; Rubin; Thomas *Rivers*; Varela, *caída*, *florentinos*; Viera y Calvijo.

S: Pérez de Tudela, Juan. *Las armadas de Indias, y los orígenes de la politica de la colonización*. Madrid 1956 ("Tudela").

Historians disagree when Aguado returned to Spain; I speculate it was with Buil and Margarite, as Aguado appeared later to have knowledge of Española's inland settlements (precluding departure earlier).

Cristóbal and Guarionex, Understanding and Brotherhood, Guaricano, Late February–Early March 1495

P, prev. cit.: Ferdinand Columbus, chap. 61. Las Casas Repertorium, sec.

5.4. Libro Copiador, letter 5 (October 15, 1495) (Columbus's thoughts on Española's Indians and Caonabó). Martyr, decade 1, bk. 4. Oviedo Repertorium, 3.15. Pané, chap. 25.

S, prev. cit.: Deagan *Isabela*; Oliver *Pané*; Sauer; Wilson *Hispaniola*.

S: Kulstad-González, Pauline M. *Hispaniola–Hell or Home? Decolonizing Grand Narratives about Intercultural Interactions at Concepción de la Vega (1494 –1564)*. Leiden, Netherlands: Sidestone Press, 2020 ("Kulstad").

S: Perez Montas, Eugenio. *Republica Dominicana: Monumentos Historicos y Arqueologicos*. Mexico: Instituto Panamericano de Geografia e Historia, 1984 ("Perez Montas").

Historians disagree on the sequence of events from February through April 1495 and the date Fort Concepción was established. In this and subsequent stories, I have followed a chronology partly reconciling the Libro Copiador, Pané, and Martyr.

Based on Pané, Kulstad and the Dominican Academy of History believe Fort Concepción was established in December 1494, possibly by an advance party prelude to Columbus's arrival.

Caonabó and Hojeda, Maguana, Early March 1495

P, prev. cit.: Bernáldez, chap. 131. Ferdinand Columbus, chap. 61. Las Casas Repertorium, sec. 5.4. Libro Copiador, letter 5 (October 15, 1495). Martyr, decade 1, bk. 4. Oviedo Repertorium, 3.15. Pané, chap. 25. Parry & Keith, Margarite Instructions.

S, prev. cit.: Deagan *Isabela*; Keegan *Myth*; Morison *Admiral*; Perez Montas; Raccolta Letters Notes; Raudzens; Sauer; Wilson *Hispaniola*.

Columbus's instructions to Margarite ordered that Caonabó be seized by a false reassurance of friendship and a trick permitting physical seizure of his body. The other primary sources confirm false reassurance as the essential method, with the exception of Ferdinand Columbus (who wrote the seizure occurred more honorably, during battle). While following the chronology of Martyr, the text dramatizes a portion of the European lore of the trick embellished by Las Casas, sometimes paraphrasing both sources.

CHAPTER VII: WAR AND TRIBUTE

Cristóbal and Caonabó, Hojeda and Manicoatex, Battle in Magua, March 1495

P, prev. cit.: Ferdinand Columbus, chap. 61. Las Casas Repertorium, sec. 5.4. Libro Copiador, letter 5 (October 15, 1495). Martyr, decade 1, bk. 4 (conversation between Columbus and Caonabó). Oviedo Repertorium, 3.15. Pané, chap. 25. Parry & Keith, Tribute Items List (see also CDDD doc. 258).

S, prev. cit.: Deagan *Isabela*; Kulstad; Morison *Admiral*; Perez Montas; Raccolta Letter Notes; Raudzens; Sauer; Wilson *Hispaniola*.

S: Guitar, Lynne. "What Really Happened at Santo Cerro? Origin of the Legend of the Virgin de las Mercedes." *Issues in Caribbean Amerindian Studies*, Vol. 3, Feb. 2001–Feb. 2002 ("Guitar").

S: Nouel, Carlos. *Historia Eclesiástica de la Arquidiócesis de Santo Domingo: Primada de América.* Vol. 1. Santo Domingo: Editora de Santo Domingo, 1979.

The first item on the Tribute Items List is a gold tribute payment received from a "brother" of Caonabó on March 10, 1495; some believe this was offered as a ransom payment delivered after Caonabó was captured, but my analysis of the sequence of events is otherwise, and, as presented in the text, my speculation is that it was a ruse.

Christian tradition recounts that the battle took place on a steep hill of commanding height, now named Santo Cerro, and that Columbus's men were saved and then prevailed through divine intervention (see Nouel). The primary sources do not agree when, how, or where the battle(s) occurred, and secondary sources have even more divergent opinions. I have mostly followed Martyr and the Libro Copiador.

Isabel and Fernando, Decisions and Nondecision, Madrid, March–April 1495

P, prev. cit.: Bernáldez, chap. 120. CDDD, docs. 261 (sovereigns' letter to Fonseca of April 7, 1495), 262 (sovereigns' letter to Fonseca of April 9, 1495), 265 (sovereigns' instruction to Fonseca to pay salaries of April 9, 1495), 268, 270, 272 (sovereigns' credentialing of Juan Aguado of April 9, 1495), 277 (sovereigns' contract with Berardi of April 9, 1495), 280 (sovereigns' instructions to Fonseca to sell slaves of April 12, 1495), 285 (sovereigns' instruction to Fonseca to hold proceeds of sale of slaves while legality determined of April 16, 1495), 295 (sovereigns' instructions to Fonseca of June 1, 1495), 302 (sovereigns' letter to Berardi of June 2, 1495), 326 (sovereigns' letter to Fonseca of January 13, 1496). Cuneo. Las Casas Repertorium, sec. 5.4. Nader, Santa Fe Capitulations, April 17, 1492, Sovereigns' 1495 License to Trade. Parry & Keith, Aguado Instructions, Berardi Memorial.

S, prev. cit.: Fernández-Armesto *Amerigo*, *Columbus*, *Conquest*, *Ferdinand Isabella*; Gibson; Gould; Liss; Pagden; Rumeu de Armas *Indigenista*; Thomas *Rivers*, *Slavery*; Tudela; Varela, *florentinos*.

S: Deive, Carlos Esteban. *La Española y la Esclavitud del Indio*. Santo Domingo: Fundación García Arévalo, 1995 ("Deive").

S: Mira Caballos, Esteban. *La Española, epicentro del Caribe en el siglos XVI*. Santo Domingo: Academia Dominicana de la Historia, 2010 ("Mira Caballos").

No primary source relates the conversation fictionalized between Isabella and Ferdinand. Historians speculate which crown advisors counseled against selling the Taínos as slaves between April 12–16, some asserting Margarite, Buil, and/or Cisneros. I believe that Margarite and Buil were unlikely to do so and that Cisneros was not available.

Historians debate when and the extent Isabella and Ferdinand obtained knowledge of Española's substantial population decline and atrocities committed by their subjects. On April 16, 1495, the sovereigns' latest information was that provided by Margarite and Buil, who had left Española in 1494, and I speculate that the sovereigns had been provided little information on the atrocities and none on the population decline at that date. That would soon change.

Cristóbal and Guarionex, "Treaty" Imposed, Guaricano, April–May 1495

P, prev. cit.: Ferdinand Columbus, chap. 61. Las Casas Repertorium, sec. 5.4. Libro Copiador, letter 5 (October 15, 1495). Martyr, decade 1, bk. 4. Oviedo Repertorium, 3.15. Pané, chap. 25. Parry & Keith, Tribute Items List (see also CDDD doc. 258).

S, prev. cit.: Deagan *Isabela*; Guitar; Kulstad; Morison *Admiral*; Perez Montas; Raccolta Letters Notes; Sauer; Wilson *Hispaniola*.

CHAPTER VIII: OPPRESSION, DISEASE, FAMINE

Tribute Exacted, April–October 1495

P, prev. cit.: Benzoni, bk. 1; Bernáldez, chap. 131. Ferdinand Columbus, chap. 61. Las Casas Repertorium, sec. 5.4 (Columbus's discussions with Guarionex). Las Casas Short Account, chaps. "Hispaniola," "The Kingdoms of Hispaniola." Libro Copiador, letter 5 (October 15, 1495) (Columbus's enchantment with Fort Concepción, observations on famine). Martyr, decade 1, bk. 4. Oviedo Repertorium, 3.15. Tribute Items List (see also CDDD doc. 258). Varela Gil Textos, Columbus's Testament and Codicil, May 19, 1506.

S, prev. cit.: Cook; Deagan *Isabela*; Irving; Morison *Admiral*, *Documents*; Raccolta Letters Notes; Sauer; Wilson *Hispaniola*.

S: Cook, Sherburne F. and Woodrow Borah. *Essays in Population History: Mexico and the Caribbean*. Vol. 1. Berkeley: University of California Press, 1971. Chap. 6, "The Aboriginal Population of Hispaniola."

S: Denevan, William M. Denevan, ed. *The Native Population of the Americas in 1492*. 2nd ed. Madison: University of Wisconsin Press, 1992. Chap. 2, Ángel Rosenblat, "The Population of Hispaniola at the Time of Columbus."

S: Henige, David. *Numbers from Nowhere: The American Indian Contact Population Debate*. Norman, OK: University of Oklahoma Press, 1998.

S: Mann, Charles C. *1491: New Revelations of the Americas Before Columbus*. New York: Alfred A. Knopf, 2005.

Experts debate Española's precontact population in 1492, based in part on primary sources, with estimates ranging from 100,000 to 8 million. See Cook and Borah, Rosenblatt, Sauer, and Henige above. Libro Copiador letter 5 suggests that Bartolomé had completed a census of those owing tribute in subjugated territory by the date of the letter but refrains from expressing the number concluded; although Columbus had the motive for stating a high number (to inflate the gold payments due the sovereigns), the letter cautions that famine and flight already jeopardized tribute payments. Cook and Borah analyze that primary sources suggest that Columbus and/or Bartolomé concluded that the number owing tribute in subjugated territory was 1.1 million, which underlies an estimate of 3 to 4 million for Española's total pre-contact population. Whatever the actual precontact population of Española, I find a belief in that 1.1 million number consistent with

Columbus's writings from 1493–1495 and speculate that was the pre-famine and flight number he optimistically had in mind for subjugated areas in October 1495.

While the primary sources fall short of definitive information, I have speculated that: Caonabó's tribute obligation was imposed on his brothers, principally Manicoatex; another brother was the cause of ongoing resistance in Maguana in 1495 and was seized subsequent to the battle of March 27, although he could have been seized contemporaneously; and that the Caonabó nephew seized (according to primary sources) was a son of Manicoatex.

Cristóbal and Aguado, October–November 1495

P, prev. cit.: CDDD, docs. 296, 297 (sovereigns' orders to Colón of June 1, 1495). Las Casas Repertorium, sec. 5.4 (settlers roaming the island). Oviedo Repertorium, 3.12.

S, prev. cit.: Deagan *Isabela*; Fernández-Armesto *Columbus*; Morison *Admiral*; Thomas *Rivers*.

Lugo, Benitomo, and Bentor, Tenerife's Conquest, Late 1495

P, prev. cit.: Bernáldez, chap. 133. Zurita *Hernando*, bk. 2, chap. 15.

S, prev. cit.: Crosby *Exchange*; Gil/Martín; Fernández-Armesto *Canary*; Gambia García; Padrón; Rumeu de Armas *Tenerife*; Viera y Calvijo.

Fray Pané and Guarionex, First Lessons in Christianity, Guaricano, Late 1495

P, prev. cit.: Benzoni, bk. 1. Gil Varela Cartas, Fray Leduelle's letter to Cisneros, October 1500. Las Casas Apologetica, chap. 120 (transl. in Pané, app. C). Las Casas Repertorium—Third Voyage, chaps. 150, 179. Martyr Epistolario, letter to Pomponius, June 13, 1497 (discussing Pané's findings), letter to Bernardino de Carvajal, July 27, 1497 (relating Taíno belief in sea's origin). Pané, chaps. Intro, 2, 4, 25, 25 bis, 26.

S, prev. cit.: Arrom *Pané*; Deloria; Dussel; Gil; Oliver; Oliver *Pané*; Stevens-Arroyo; Varela *caída*; Varela Gil *Pané*.

I have followed Arrom's analysis that Columbus and Pané met during this period. Neither Pané nor other primary sources recount the text's conversations between Pané and Guarionex or Pané and Columbus.

Pané's account—his report to Columbus—credits Guatícabanu's baptism as Columbus's work, and from that I have reasoned that Columbus approved Guatícabanu's baptism. In 1500, one of the principal charges brought against Columbus in the crown's investigation of his conduct—designed to remove him from office—was that he deliberately withheld approval of Indians' baptisms so he could enslave them, and Varela presents various investigation testimony to that end or incidental, including from Pané. Many don't agree with or shy from the conclusion, given Columbus's devoutness: in particular, in *Historia de Las Indias*, Las Casas unambiguously asserts that Columbus hoped Indians would fail to pay tribute and/or rebel so that he would be justified in enslaving them (chap. 150) but withholds judgment on the baptism charge when discussing the investigation, noting it sacrilege to baptize the uninstructed (chap. 179). Pané's account is silent whether Columbus reserved the prerogative to approve Guarionex's baptism, and I have speculated Columbus did, Guarionex's baptism representing the most important instance when he would have wanted to reserve flexibility to punish/enslave.

More importantly for me, much discussion about the failure of early baptisms in Española seems premised on assumptions that Taínos would have been baptized in fulsome numbers but for Columbus's nonapproval, the sovereigns' meager missionary effort, and/or the language barrier. I speculate instead—as sometimes reflected in the text—that Taínos were satisfied with their own religion and didn't want to be baptized by their conquerors, and that this social/religious rejection of Christianity, rather any impediment imposed by Columbus or other failures, almost fully explains the small number of baptisms.

Bakako, Identity, Guaricano

No primary or secondary sources.

Yutowa's activities after Hojeda's capture of Caonabó can't be speculated from primary sources, and his story thereafter is entirely fictitious.

Berardi and Vespucci, Seville, October 1495–February 1496

P, prev. cit.: CDDD, docs. 320 (Juanoto Berardi's testament, December 15, 1495), 323 (accounts for payment of Berardi's contract, October 1495 through January 1496). Zurita *Hernando*, bk. 2, chap. 15.

S, prev. cit.: Carroll; Fernández-Armesto *Amerigo*, *Columbus*; Gould; Liss; Mallett; Ortega; Pastor; Rubin; Rumeu de Armas *Indigenista*; Tudela; Varela, *florentinos*.

CHAPTER IX: SOUTHERN CROSSING

Preparations, Isabela and Maguana, February–March 10, 1496

P, prev. cit.: Bernáldez, chap. 131. Ferdinand Columbus, chaps. 61-63, 75. Las Casas Historia, chaps. 111, 113, 117. Las Casas Repertorium, sec. 5.4. Libro Copiador, letter 5 (October 15, 1495). Martyr, decade 1, bks. 4, 5. Oviedo Repertorium, 3.15. Parry & Keith, Roldán Letter.

S, prev. cit.: Deagan *Isabela*; Fernández-Armesto *Conquest*; Gould; Morison *Admiral, Southern*; Navarrete; Ortega; Raccolta Letters Notes; Varela *caída*.

S: Floyd, Troy S. *The Columbus Dynasty in the Caribbean 1492–1526*. Albuquerque, NM: University of New Mexico Press ("Floyd").

S: Watts, David. *The West Indies: Patterns of Development, Culture, and Environmental Change since 1492*. Cambridge: Cambridge University Press, 1987.

Primary sources reveal little of the conversations between Columbus and Caonabó or how Anacaona learned of Caonabó's death or her reaction thereto.

Historians disagree when Hojeda returned to Spain; while Navarrete believed 1498, I have followed Ortega, depicting Hojeda in the text, although it could have been another officer. Primary sources do not indicate the fate of the Taíno captives who were not transported to Spain.

Primary sources are unclear whether, when, and where Columbus formally granted Bakako a village and/or larger estate, but that has been the perception, then and since, and I reason that he did prior to departure for Spain in 1496, nearby Guarionex.

Return to Guadalupe, March 11–April 20, 1496

P, prev. cit.: Bernáldez, chap. 131. Ferdinand Columbus, chaps. 63, 64. Las Casas Repertorium, sec. 5.5. Martyr, decade 1, bk. 4. Oviedo Repertorium, 3.15.

S, prev. cit.: Morison *Admiral*.

Ferdinand Columbus reports that the Caribe chieftain's wife voluntarily decided to go to Spain.

No primary source recounts Caonabó's thoughts. No primary source identifies the route sailed from Española to the Guadalupe archipelago.

At Sea, April 20–Early June 1496

Same as "Return to Guadalupe, March 11–April 20, 1496" above.

Martyr recounts that Caonabó "died of grief," from which I have speculated the suicide depicted. Bernáldez says death was due to disease or the dangerous living conditions, but the primary sources describing the voyage do not indicate that European or Taíno passengers died (other than Caonabó or relatives).

CHAPTER X: HOMELAND JOURNEYS

Cristóbal, Cádiz to Burgos, Castile, Early June–September 1496

P, prev. cit.: Bernáldez, chap. 131. CDDD, docs. 317, 318 (sovereigns' recommendations of Buil to pope and papal ambassador, October 21, 1495), 321, 372 (sovereigns' approval for Vicente Yáñez Pinzón's voyage, December 1495, and payment, January 1496 thru July 1497), 328 (sovereigns' letter to Fonseca, February 28, 1496), 338 (monastery's notice for baptism of Cristóbal and Pedro, July 20, 1496). Ferdinand Columbus, chaps. 64, 65. Las Casas Historia, chap. 113. Las Casas Repertorium, secs. 5.5, 6.0. Las Casas Repertorium—Third Voyage, chap. 150. Martyr, decade 1, bk. 5. Oviedo Repertorium, secs. 3.15, 3.18 (appearance of settlers returning and disillusionment with Indies). Zurita *Hernando*, bk. 2, chaps. 8, 23–29, 32, 33.

S, prev. cit.: Ballesteros; Bridge; Deagan *Isabela*; Fernández-Armesto *Amerigo*, *Conquest*, *Ferdinand Isabella*; Floyd; Gibson; Hillgarth; Morison *Admiral*, *Southern*; Phillips; Raccolta Letters Notes; Rubin; Rumeu de Armas *Indigenista*, *Tenerife*; Thomas *Rivers*, *Slave Trade*; Varela *florentinos*.

S: Manzano Manzano, Juan, and Ana María Manzano Fernández-Heredia. *Los Pinzones y el Descubrimiento de America*. Vol. I. Madrid: Ediciones de Cultura Hispanica, 1988.

S: Ortiz, Luis Scheker, ed. *Santo Domingo and its Colonial Monuments*. 2nd ed. Santo Domingo: Ediciones Pasado, 2000.

To my knowledge, history has not preserved either the letters Isabella and Ferdinand would have dispatched to Columbus with Pero Alonso's resupply fleet, particularly any written instrument reflecting their approval of enslavement of Indian "war captives," or Columbus's letter to his brother confirming that. Martyr confirms the sovereigns so approved and that this approval was the basis for the slave shipment depicted in the next story, and Las Casas and many historians conclude or infer the sovereigns so approved.

While some assert Caonabó's brother "Don Diego" was so baptized by Bernáldez or otherwise, Bernáldez merely writes that Columbus called him that. The primary sources do not hail the brother's baptism, as one might expect if it had occurred, and I have speculated that, as Caonabó, he never was baptized.

Historians disagree why Columbus dressed in a friar's habit, and a minority assert he did not—that the habit was merely common sailors' clothing. As many, I suspect it was a deliberate attempt to portray humility. But I speculate it went deeper, both attempting to evoke the voyage's religious justification and revealing a conviction that he was the Lord's chosen instrument.

Manzano's analysis is that the sovereigns engaged Vicente Yáñez Pinzón's two ships to serve in the Italian campaign, but, as the ship's destination and mission was unspecified, I suspect Niño and Columbus would have been suspicious.

Bartolomé and Bakako, Santo Domingo and Slave Raiding, July–September 1496

P, prev. cit.: Ferdinand Columbus, chap. 73. Las Casas Historia, chap. 113. Las Casas Repertorium, secs. 5.4. Martyr, decade 1, bk. 5. Oviedo Repertorium, sec. 3.12.

S, prev. cit.: Deagan *Isabela*; Floyd; Phillips; Raccolta Letters Notes; Thomas *Slave Trade*.

Primary sources do not indicate how the three hundred slaves Bartolomé dispatched on Columbus's instruction were captured or Bartolomé's itinerary in these months, and the text is my speculation that he, rather than officers, directed it with the itinerary depicted, as the most trusted officers commanded the forts.

Anacaona, Maguana to Xaraguá, (Autumn 1496)

P, prev. cit.: Benzoni, Bk. 1. Las Casas Historia chap. 114. Martyr, decade 1, bk. 5; decade 3, bk. 8. Oviedo Repertorium, 3.15.

S, prev. cit.: Rouse; Wilson *Hispaniola*.

Historians disagree when Anacaona returned to Xaraguá, and I simply have assumed it was shortly after the earliest she could have learned of Caonabó's death (i.e., after the arrival of Pero Alonso's fleet). To my knowledge, no primary source identifies who succeeded Caonabó to rule Maguana or the other events depicted.

CHAPTER XI: BATTLES OF SPIRITS AND MEN

Haiti's First Baptism, Guaricano, September 21, 1496

P, prev. cit.: Ferdinand Columbus, chap. 62. Las Casas Apologetica, chap. 120 (transl. in Pané, app. C). Matthew, 28:18–20. Pané, chaps. 25, 25 bis, 26.

S, prev. cit.: Oliver; Oliver *Pané*.

Pané's account does not describe the ceremony or attendees.

Guarionex, Rejection of Christianity, Guaricano and Fort Concepción, Autumn 1496

P, prev. cit.: Ferdinand Columbus, chaps. 62, 76. Las Casas Apologetica, chap. 167 (transl. in Pané, app. C). Las Casas Repertorium, sec. 5.4. Pané, chaps. 25, 25 bis, 26.

S, prev. cit.: Oliver; Wilson *Hispaniola*.

No primary source relates the various conversations depicted, but the text incorporates parts of Pané's description of Guarionex's isolation and the urination. For discussion of related events, see "Rebellion and Rape, Collapse and Desolation, Justice, Española, May 1497" below.

Cristóbal, Isabel and Fernando, Audience, Burgos, October–December 1496

P, prev. cit.: Bernáldez, chap. 131. Ferdinand Columbus, chap. 65. Jane, Third Voyage Letter. Las Casas Repertorium, secs. 6.1 (Isabella's commendation and instruction to explore), 6.2. Las Casas Repertorium—Third Voyage, chap. 176. Oviedo Repertorium, 3.12 (Isabella's instruction to treat Spanish and Indians well). Zurita *Hernando*, bk. 2, chap. 40; bk. 3, chap 6.

P: Rodriguez Valencia, Vicente. *Isabel La Catolica en la Opinion de Españoles y Extranjeros. Vol 1.* Valladolid: Instituto "Isabel La Catolica" de Historia Eclesiastica, 1970. Pope Alexander VI's bull of December 19, 1496.

S, prev. cit.: Carroll; Gould; Liss; Morison *Admiral*; Phillips; Menéndez Pidal.

S: Beinart, Haim. *The Expulsion of the Jews from Spain.* Translated by Jeffrey M. Green. Oxford: Littman Library of Jewish Civilization, 2002.

S: Benbassa, Esther, and Aron Rodrigue. *Sephardi Jewry: A History of the Judeo-Spanish Community, 14th–20th Centuries.* Berkeley: University of California Press, 2000 ("Benbassa/Rodrigue").

To my knowledge, Juan Aguado's report to the sovereigns, if written, has not been preserved, and primary sources do not recount his meeting with the sovereigns.

Primary sources—both court chroniclers and others—rarely criticized Isabella and Ferdinand about anything, no less the population declines, atrocities, and enslavements on Española at this time, and many modern historians refrain from attributing the sovereigns with, or absolve them from, knowledge thereof. As related in the text previously, Columbus's letter informed of substantial population loss; Cuneo's letter (which the sovereigns didn't receive) informed of enslavements by settlers, indicating (in my view) that such would have been common knowledge among the crown officials and suppliers who met settlers returning, i.e., Fonseca, Berardi, Vespucci; and Las Casas circumspectly observed that the sovereigns must have assumed that the slave shipments prior to 1499 were of war captives alone. I reason Columbus also communicated something of the dramatic declines in person, and I speculate Aguado communicated something of the enslavements and atrocities to criticize Columbus.

There is no written order from the sovereigns to Fonseca telling him to delay satisfying Columbus's eventual provisioning request. Many primary and secondary sources cast Fonseca as acting independently from the sovereigns and his tardiness (rather than the sovereigns' tardiness) in responding to Columbus's requests to animosity between himself and Columbus. I speculate he complied with his sovereigns' wishes at least in this instance, irrespective of the animosity.

Some historians write that Columbus didn't reveal his intention to use a portion of the third voyage fleet for exploration, but I have followed Las Casas and others that that intent was express and built into the fleet preparation. See chap. XII, "Cristóbal, Testament, Seville, Winter 1498" below.

Anacaona, Behecchio, and Bartolomé, Xaraguá, Early 1497

P, prev. cit.: Las Casas Historia, chaps. 113, 114. Martyr, decade 1, bk. 5.

S, prev. cit.: Deagan *Isabela*; Sauer; Rouse; Wilson *Hispaniola*.

The site of Behecchio's village is unknown.

Uprising, Fort Concepción, Early 1497

P, prev. cit.: Ferdinand Columbus, chaps. 74, 76. Las Casas Apologetica, chap. 167 (transl. in Pané, app. C). Las Casas Historia, chap. 115. Martyr, decade 1, bk. 5. Oviedo Repertorium, 3.16. Pané, chap. 26. Parry & Keith, Roldán Letter.

S, prev. cit.: Deagan *Isabela*; Mira Caballos; Oliver *Pané*; Rouse; Sauer; Wilson *Hispaniola*.

S: Varela, Consuelo. *Cristóbal Colón y la Construcción de un Mundo Nuevo, Estudios, 1983–2008*. Santo Domingo: Archivo General de la Nación, 2010 ("Varela *Estudios*").

The primary sources do not recount Guarionex's tactics for the attack. They do indicate that fourteen "guilty" caciques, including Guarionex and two ringleaders, were identified and captured; but I have speculated that Bartolomé had neither the time, information, nor inclination to parse "guilt" among caciques and simply rounded up Guarionex and thirteen others.

Anacaona and Bartolomé, Anacaona's Garden, Xaraguá, April 1497

P, prev. cit.: Las Casas Historia, chaps. 116. Martyr, decade 1, bk. 5.

S, prev. cit.: Deagan *Isabela*; Gil; Rouse; Sauer; Varela *Estudios*; Wilson *Hispaniola*.

Some speculate that Bartolomé and Anacaona had an intimate relationship.

Rebellion and Rape, Collapse and Desolation, Justice, Española, May 1497

P, prev. cit.: Benzoni, bk. 1. Ferdinand Columbus, chaps. 62, 74–77. Las Casas Apologetica, chap. 167 (transl. in Pané, app. C). Las Casas Historia, chaps. 117–119 (also, transl. in Parry & Keith). Las Casas Short Account, chaps. "Hispaniola," "The Kingdoms of Hispaniola." Martyr, decade 1, bks. 5, 7. Oviedo Repertorium, 3.16. Pané, chaps. 25, 25 bis, 26. Parry & Keith, Roldán Letter.

S, prev. cit.: Ballesteros; Deagan *Isabela*; Fernández-Armesto *Columbus*;

Floyd; Morison *Admiral*; Oliver; Oliver *Pané*; Rouse; Sauer; Thomas *Rivers*; Varela *caída*; Wilson *Hispaniola*.

Primary and secondary sources diverge widely on what events occurred in the spring of 1497 and their sequence. Ferdinand Columbus recounts that Roldán supported Guarionex's attack on Fort Concepción previously presented. Secondary sources often place Juan Mateo's execution proximate to the executions of the naborias who looted Pané's church previously presented. My depiction follows mostly Las Casas, believing he is the most comprehensively informed and least partisan primary source regarding these events, and incorporates information and sometimes words from Martyr, Ferdinand Columbus, Pané, and Roldán within Las Casas's framework.

Pané wrote that Juan Mateo and his brothers died as martyrs, i.e., for being Christians, and Las Casas wrote they died for assisting the Spanish rather than for being Christian. I again have found Las Casas more convincing and speculated in the text that Juan Mateo's family gave forewarning of the attack, although Las Casas stops short of that attribution. Ferdinand Columbus wrote that the forewarning came from one of the caciques attacking prematurely.

Anacaona and Onaney, Xaraguá

No primary or secondary sources.

CHAPTER XII: AGONIES AND FATES

Cristóbal, Adrift and Renewed, Castile, January–July 1497

P, prev. cit.: Barros, decade 1, bk. 4, chaps. 1, 2. Bernáldez, chap. 131. CDDD, docs. 312 (Jaime Ferrer's letter re: Tordesillas treaty, 1495), 361 (list of settlers' salaries, June 1497), 371 (the sovereigns' designation of Bartolomé as Adelantado, July 22, 1497). Dotson, doc. 149 (partial draft of Columbus's testament [majorat], 1497). Ferdinand Columbus, chap. 65. Jane, Third Voyage Letter. Las Casas Repertorium, secs. 6.1, 6.2. Martyr Epistolario, letter to Pomponius, June 13, 1497, letter to Bernardino de Carvajal, July 27, 1497. Nader, sovereigns' writ for payment of wages, April 23, 1497; sovereigns' instructions re: Indies colonization, April 23, 1497; sovereigns' permission to establish hereditary trust, April 23, 1497; sovereigns' confirmation of privileges, dated April 23, 1497; sovereigns' remission of taxes, May 6, 1497; sovereigns' orders re: Columbus's financial share, dated May 30 and June 12, 1497; sovereigns' revocation of prior permits, dated June 2, 1497; sovereigns' instructions re: colonists and supplies, June 15, 1497; sovereigns' prospective pardon of criminals, dated June 22, 1497;

sovereigns' order for banishments, dated June 22, 1497; sovereigns' grant of authority to apportion land, July 22, 1497; appointment of Bartolomé as Indies' interim governor, dated July 22, 1497; sovereigns' instruction to Fonseca, December 23, 1497. Oviedo Repertorium, 3.18. Zurita *Hernando*, bk.3, chap. 2.

P: Isaiah, 11: 11; 41: 9, 11; 42: 4, 10; 61: 4, 7, 9.

P: *Christopher Columbus's Book of Prophecies: Reproduction of the Original Manuscript With English Translation.* Kay Brigham, translator. Barcelona: Editorial CLIE, 1991.

P: D'Ailly, Pierre. *Ymago Mundi y otras opúsculos.* Prepared by Antonio Ramírez de Verger, revised by Juan Fernández Valverde y Francisco Socas. *Biblioteca de Colón, Vol. 2.* Madrid: Alianza Editorial, 1992 ("D'Ailly").

P: Rumeu de Armas, Antonio. *Un Escrito Desconocido de Cristóbal Colón: el Memorial de la Mejorada.* Madrid: Ediciones Cultura Hispanica, 1972. El Memorial de la Mejorada.

P: Rusconi, Roberto, hist. and text. ed. *The Book of Prophecies Edited by Christopher Columbus.* Blair Sullivan, trans. Vol. 3, *Repertorium Columbianum.* Eugene, OR: Wipf & Stock, 1997.

P: Williamson, J. A. *The Cabot Voyages and Bristol Discovery under Henry VII.* Published for the Hakluyt Society. Cambridge: Cambridge University Press, 1962 ("Williamson"). Letters patent granted John Caboto, March 5, 1496; Spanish sovereigns' letter to their ambassador, March 28, 1496; John Day's letter to Columbus, 1497.

S, prev. cit.: Ballesteros; Bridge; Carroll; Fernández-Armesto *Columbus*, *Conquest*; Hillgarth; Morison *Admiral*, *Southern*; Menéndez Pidal; Pérez *Cisneros*; Rumeu de Armas *Tordesillas*; Symcox *Enterprise*; Williamson. Nader, General Introduction.

S: Cervantes, Fernando. *Conquistadores: A New History.* Great Britain: Penguin Random House UK, 2020.

S: Davidson, Miles H. *Columbus Then and Now: A Life Reexamined.* Norman, OK: University of Oklahoma Press, 1997.

S: Fernández-Armesto, Felipe. *Pathfinders: A Global History of Exploration.* New York: W. W. Norton, 2006.

S: Morison, Samuel Eliot. *The European Discovery of America: The Northern Voyages, AD 500–1600*. Oxford: Oxford University Press, 1971.

S: Parry, J. H. *The Age of Reconnaissance: Discovery, Exploration and Settlement 1450 to 1650*. Berkeley: University of California Press, 1981.

S: Ravenstein, Ernst Georg, William Brooks Greenlee, and Pero Vaz de Caminha. *Bartolomeu Dias*. Edited by Keith Bridgeman and Tahira Arsham. England: Viartis, 2010 ("Ravenstein").

S: Subrahmanyam, Sanjay. *The Career and Legend of Vasco da Gama*. Cambridge: Cambridge University Press, 1997.

Primary sources provide scant information regarding Columbus's activities in 1497 prior to April. His *Book of Prophecies*, which compiles authorities and scriptural passages that he believed prophesized the Indies discovery and his destiny as the Lord's instrument therein, was completed, with substantial contributions by others, in 1502, and Columbus worked on that book between his third and fourth voyages. I suspect some scriptural review that eventually led to the *Book of Prophecies* occurred between the second and third voyages. Columbus's first letter reporting on the third voyage (October 18, 1498) proclaims Isaiah's prophecy of the Indies' discovery, and the text speculates that Columbus discovered his own destiny proclaimed in Isaiah during this period of limbo.

Historians disagree whether Columbus wrote the Mejorada memorandum, and I suspect not, as it has the style of an educated courtier or bureaucrat. Historians disagree when the issue of the Tordesillas antimeridian was considered, and I suspect only after the Tordesillas treaty, the parties to the treaty conceiving a race to possession by contrary routes rather than an understanding dividing the globe's other side.

I have assumed Don Diego and Caonabó's nephew died in Spain, having found no primary sources indicating their fates or that Columbus used them for any purpose on the third voyage.

Isabel and Fernando, the Lord Taketh, Castile, Autumn–Winter 1497

P, prev. cit.: Bernáldez, chaps. 153, 154. Ferdinand Columbus, chap. 65. Las Casas Repertorium, sec. 6.2. Martyr Epistolario, docs. 176 (letter re: Juan's health, June 13, 1497), 179 (letter re: doubt in Juan's succession, July 15, 1497), 182 (letter re: Juan's death, October 10, 1497), 187 (letter re: awaiting Margarite's child, December 1, 1497). Williamson, John Day's letter to Columbus, 1497. Zurita *Hernando*, bk. 3, chaps. 9, 18.

S, prev. cit.: Benbassa/Rodrigue; Carroll; Fernández-Armesto *Ferdinand Isabella*; Menéndez Pidal; Prescott; Rubin.

S: Livermore, H. V. *A New History of Portugal*. Cambridge: Cambridge University Press, 1969.

S: Miller, Townsend. *The Castles and the Crown: Spain 1451–1555*. New York: Coward-McCann, 1963.

Guacanagarí, Judgments, Marien

P, prev. cit.: Las Casas Repertorium, sec. 5.4. Las Casas Short Account, chap. "The Kingdoms of Hispaniola."

Guarionex, Bakako, and Yutowa, Final Conversations, Magua

P, prev. cit.: Benzoni, bk. 1. Las Casas Historia, chaps. 120–121. Las Casas Short Account, chap. "The Kingdoms of Hispaniola." Martyr, decade 1, bks. 5, 7. Oviedo Repertorium, 3.16.

S, prev. cit.: Deagan *Isabela*; Floyd; Granberry *Americas*; Morison *Admiral*; Rouse; Sauer; Thomas *Rivers*; Wilson *Hispaniola*.

No primary source relates the conversations dramatized.

My next book will depict Guarionex's departure from Magua, which Martyr explains as a decision to enlist another cacique to commence raids against the Spanish and Las Casas explains as a flight for refuge when Guarionex's subjects no longer respected him. I have speculated an alternative or additional motive, as presented in the text, that I believe best explains the European reaction to the departure.

Cristóbal, Testament, Seville, Winter 1498

P, prev. cit.: CDDD, docs. 394 (Columbus's letter to his brother Bartolomé, February 1498), 396 (Columbus's majorat, February 22, 1498). Ferdinand Columbus, chap. 77. Jane, Third Voyage Letter. Las Casas Repertorium, sec. 6.2 (translation of Columbus's letter to Bartolomé). Las Casas Historia, chaps. 119 (also, transl. in Parry & Keith).

P: Thacher, John Boyd. *Christopher Columbus: His Life, His Works, His Remains*. 3 vols. New York: G. P. Putnam's Sons, 1903–4. English translation of Majorat or Entail of His Estates and Titles by Christopher Columbus, February 22, 1498.

S, prev. cit.: Ballesteros; Fernández-Armesto *Columbus*; Gil; Las Casas Repertorium—Third Voyage, Introduction; Morison *Admiral*; Nader, Introduction; Raccolta Letters Notes; Thomas *Rivers*; Varela *caída*.

No primary or secondary source recounts the meeting or conversation depicted or Columbus's thoughts in the Cathedral, which now commemorates his remains, as does the Columbus Lighthouse in Santo Domingo. Historians disagree on the dates the ships departed from Sanlúcar, and, although some say January 23, I follow those believing February 6 and have reasoned that Seville was a few days earlier.

Hell in Haiti, March–April 1498

P, prev. cit.: Ferdinand Columbus, chap. 77. Las Casas Historia, chaps. 119–121. Las Casas Short Account, chap. "The Kingdoms of Hispaniola." Las Casas Repertorium—Third Voyage, chap. 147. Martyr, decade 1, bks. 5, 7. Parry & Keith, Roldán Letter (Roldán's pardon of Bakako).

S, prev. cit.: Deagan *Isabela*; Floyd; Morison *Admiral*; Rouse; Sauer; Wilson *Hispaniola*.

Anacaona, Xaraguá

No primary or secondary sources.

ACKNOWLEDGMENTS

The story line largely has been derived from primary sources, adjusted in consideration of the written analyses of historians, anthropologists, and other experts—some modern, some centuries departed—and then tested by on-site investigation. The protagonists' thoughts and feelings, particularly of those Taíno, also have been informed by discussions with some of these modern experts, and I am grateful for the access and time they afforded me.

First and foremost, I'm indebted to the esteemed L. Antonio Curet, curator of the Smithsonian Institution's National Museum of the American Indian, for entertaining speculative discussions of how fifteenth-century aboriginal Caribbean peoples would have thought about the events depicted herein, and to Pauline M. Kulstad-González, one of the eminent archaeologists resident in the Dominican Republic, for leading me to historic sites on my last trip to that country and commenting on the manuscript. Pauline introduced me to Santiago Duval, the director of the Department of Archaeology of the Dominican Republic's National Directorate of Monumental Heritage, and Francisco V. Coste, the chief archaeologist at La Vega Vieja, who both kindly accompanied me on a portion of that trip, including in Santo Domingo and to Santiago, La Vega Vieja, and La Isabela. Pauline and Francisco also led me exploring into field and bush to speculate the sites for Columbus's forts along the Yaque River and its tributaries, now lost to history.

I thank the numerous guides who accompanied me on my investigations and the museum staffs I met. They all provided insights into the events transpiring in their locale or the site visited, and I mention a few whose thoughts made a mark herein:

In the Dominican Republic, Carlos Mercedes resumed as my constant guide and companion throughout the country—his appetite for history and dirt-track driving whetted by the travels we shared researching *Encounters Unforeseen*. Richard Weber, the founder of Tours, Trips, Treks & Travel, also resumed to expertly plan and oversee the logistics of the "expedition," and Domingo Abreu, the Dominican archaeologist and speleologist (who previously took me to the remains of Fort Santo Tomás), shared his thoughts on the establishment of gold mines in the country's southern provinces. A youthful Cecilia Montás of Santo Domingo's Jardin Botanico National displayed "Española's" endemic flowering plants and trees.

In Cuba, Orelvis Jacomino Rodríguez, a law professor and lawyer, guided me from the Bahía de Cortés to Cabo Cruz, including into the forest along the southern coast to explore for encounter sites, cheerfully navigating gas shortages as well as potholes. The writer Tim Weed deftly oversaw the considerable logistics. Sonia López Castellanos of the Museo Arqueología Guamuhaya in Trinidad and Jorge L. Gálvez Soler of the Museo Antropológico Montané in Havana explained the Ciboney; and Mirtha Demetria Raballero of the Museo Indocubano Baní in Banes related the Taíno spirits worshipped.

In the Lesser Antilles, Faustulus Frederick, who served a term as chief of the Kalinago Territory in Dominica, and Samanta Francis, guided me about their cultural village on Dominica's eastern coast and explained Caribe culture and history. In Guadeloupe, Taïna Tharsis, founder of Guadeloupe Explor, took me to the likely encounter sites on Basse-Terre and the Museum Edgar Clerc on Grande-Terre. On St. Croix, Bryan Updyke, owner of Virgin Kayak & Canoe Outfitters, led me around the indigenous site at Salt River Bay and paddled with me to the beachhead where hostilities occurred.

In Spain, Marta Velasco assisted me at the Archivo General de Indias, and Señora Cisneros at the Biblioteca Colombina, both in Seville; Aarón Fernández Valdeolivas assisted in the Casa Museo Colón in Valladolid, as did staff in the nearby Archivo General de Simancas; and Álvaro Bernardo, director of La Mejorada, gave me a tour of the historic remains.

For literary editing, I thank Jon Ford, David Mandelkern, Monique Peterson, Heather Rodino, Sarah Vostok, and the spirited Hannah Rowen.

Last (but not least), I thank the team assembled for *Encounters Unforeseen* for returning to work on this sequel—Glen Edelstein, book and cover design; Robert Hunt, cover illustration; David Atkinson, newly drawn maps; Jerome McLain, webmaster; and Angelle Barbazon, publicity—as well as Boris De Los Santos, who kindly enlisted to draw internal sketches. As always, my friend Jonathan Mann provided practical advice throughout.

CPSIA information can be obtained
at www.ICGtesting.com
Printed in the USA
BVHW071913311021
620416BV00011B/168/J